Kiss Kiss
Switch Bitch
My Uncle Oswald

Kiss Kiss
Switch Bitch
My Uncle Oswald

ROALD DAHL

Kiss Kiss copyright © 1959 by Roald Dahl; copyright © 1958 Roald Dahl; Renewed

Switch Bitch copyright © 1974 by Roald Dahl

My Uncle Oswald copyright © 1979 by Roald Dahl

Published together specially in 2003 for Quality paperback Book Club by arrangement with Penguin Group (USA) and the estate of Roald Dahl.

This edition copyright © 2003 by Bookspan. All rights reserved.

Printed in the United States.

QUALITY PAPERBACK BOOK CLUB
NEW YORK

Kiss Kiss

CONTENTS

THE LANDLADY

BILLY WEAVER HAD TRAVELLED down from London on the slow afternoon train, with a change at Swindon on the way, and by the time he got to Bath it was about nine o'clock in the evening and the moon was coming up out of a clear starry sky over the houses opposite the station entrance. But the air was deadly cold and the wind was like a flat blade of ice on his cheeks.

'Excuse me,' he said, 'but is there a fairly cheap hotel not too far away from here?'

'Try The Bell and Dragon,' the porter answered, pointing down the road. 'They might take you in. It's about a quarter of a mile along on the other side.'

Billy thanked him and picked up his suitcase and set out to walk the quarter-mile to The Bell and Dragon. He had never been to Bath before. He didn't know anyone who lived there. But Mr Greenslade at the Head Office in London had told him it was a splendid city. 'Find your own lodgings,' he had said, 'and then go along and report to the Branch Manager as soon as you've got yourself settled.'

Billy was seventeen years old. He was wearing a new navy-blue overcoat, a new brown trilby hat, and a new brown suit, and he was feeling fine. He walked briskly down the street. He was trying to do everything briskly these days. Briskness, he had decided, was *the* one common characteristic of all successful businessmen. The big shots up at Head Office were absolutely fantastically brisk all the time. They were amazing.

There were no shops in this wide street that he was walking along, only a line of tall houses on each side, all of them identical. They had porches and pillars and four or five steps going up to their front doors, and it was obvious that once upon a time they had been very swanky residences. But now, even in the darkness, he could see that the paint was peeling from the woodwork on their doors and windows, and that the handsome white facades were cracked and blotchy from neglect.

Suddenly, in a downstairs window that was brilliantly illuminated by a street-lamp not six yards away, Billy caught sight of a printed notice propped up against the glass in one of the upper panes. It said BED AND BREAKFAST. There was a vase of pussy-willows, tall and beautiful, standing just underneath the notice.

He stopped walking. He moved a bit closer. Green curtains (some sort of velvety material) were hanging down on either side of the window. The pussy-willows looked wonderful beside them. He went right up and peered through the glass into the room, and the first thing he saw was a bright fire burning in the hearth. On the carpet in front of the fire, a pretty little dachshund was curled up asleep with its nose tucked into its belly. The room itself, so far as he could see in the half-darkness, was filled with pleasant furniture. There was a baby-grand piano and a big sofa and several plump armchairs; and in one corner he spotted a large parrot in a cage. Animals were usually a good sign in a place like this, Billy told himself; and all in all, it looked to him as though it would be a pretty decent house to stay in. Certainly it would be more comfortable than The Bell and Dragon.

On the other hand, a pub would be more congenial than a boarding-house. There would be beer and darts in the evenings, and lots of people to talk to, and it would probably be a good bit cheaper, too. He had stayed a couple of nights in a pub once before and he had liked it. He had never stayed in any boarding-houses, and, to be perfectly honest, he was a tiny bit frightened of them. The name itself conjured up images of watery cabbage, rapacious landladies, and a powerful smell of kippers in the living-room.

After dithering about like this in the cold for two or three minutes, Billy decided that he would walk on and take a look at The Bell and Dragon before making up his mind. He turned to go.

And now a queer thing happened to him. He was in the act of stepping back and turning away from the window when all at once his eye was caught and held in the most peculiar manner by the small notice that was there. BED AND BREAKFAST, it said. BED AND BREAKFAST, BED AND BREAKFAST, BED AND BREAKFAST. Each word was like a large black eye staring at him through the glass, holding him, compelling him, forcing him to stay where he was and not to walk away from that house, and the next thing he knew, he was actually moving across from the window to the front door of the house, climbing the steps that led up to it, and reaching for the bell.

He pressed the bell. Far away in a back room he heard it ringing, and then *at once* — it must have been at once because he hadn't even had time to take his finger from the bell-button — the door swung open and a woman was standing there.

Normally you ring the bell and you have at least a half-minute's wait before the door opens. But this dame was like a jack-in-the-box. He pressed the bell – and out she popped! It made him jump.

She was about forty-five or fifty years old, and the moment she saw him, she gave him a warm welcoming smile.

'*Please* come in,' she said pleasantly. She stepped aside, holding the door wide open, and Billy found himself automatically starting forward into the house. The compulsion or, more accurately, the desire to follow after her into that house was extraordinarily strong.

'I saw the notice in the window,' he said, holding himself back.

'Yes, I know.'

'I was wondering about a room.'

'It's *all* ready for you, my dear,' she said. She had a round pink face and very gentle blue eyes.

'I was on my way to The Bell and Dragon,' Billy told her. 'But the notice in your window just happened to catch my eye.'

'My dear boy,' she said, 'why don't you come in out of the cold?'

'How much do you charge?'

'Five and sixpence a night, including breakfast.'

It was fantastically cheap. It was less than half of what he had been willing to pay.

'If that is too much,' she added, 'then perhaps I can reduce it just a tiny bit. Do you desire an egg for breakfast? Eggs are expensive at the moment. It would be sixpence less without the egg.'

'Five and sixpence is fine,' he answered. 'I should like very much to stay here.'

'I knew you would. Do come in.'

She seemed terribly nice. She looked exactly like the mother of one's best school-friend welcoming one into the house to stay for the Christmas holidays. Billy took off his hat, and stepped over the threshold.

'Just hang it there,' she said, 'and let me help you with your coat.'

There were no other hats or coats in the hall. There were no umbrellas, no walking-sticks – nothing.

'We have it *all* to ourselves,' she said, smiling at him over her shoulder as she led the way upstairs. 'You see, it isn't very often I have the pleasure of taking a visitor into my little nest.'

The old girl is slightly dotty, Billy told himself. But at five and sixpence a night, who gives a damn about that? 'I should've thought you'd be simply swamped with applicants,' he said politely.

'Oh, I am, my dear, I am, of course I am. But the trouble is that I'm inclined to be just a teeny weeny bit choosey and particular – if you see what I mean.'

'Ah, yes.'

'But I'm always ready. Everything is always ready day and night in this house just on the off-chance that an acceptable young gentleman will come along. And it is such a pleasure, my dear, such a very great pleasure when now and again I open the door and I see someone standing there who is just *exactly* right.' She was half-way up the stairs, and she paused with one hand on the stair-rail, turning her head and smiling down at him with pale lips. 'Like you,' she added, and her blue eyes travelled slowly all the way down the length of Billy's body, to his feet, and then up again.

On the first-floor landing she said to him, 'This floor is mine.'

They climbed up a second flight. 'And this one is *all* yours,' she said. 'Here's your room. I do hope you'll like it.' She took him into a small but charming front bedroom, switching on the light as she went in.

'The morning sun comes right in the window, Mr Perkins. It *is* Mr Perkins, isn't it?'

'No,' he said. 'It's Weaver.'

'Mr Weaver. How nice. I've put a water-bottle between the sheets to air them out, Mr Weaver. It's such a comfort to have a hot water-bottle in a strange bed with clean sheets, don't you agree? And you may light the gas fire at any time if you feel chilly.'

'Thank you,' Billy said. 'Thank you ever so much.' He noticed that the bedspread had been taken off the bed, and that the bedclothes had been neatly turned back on one side, all ready for someone to get in.

'I'm so glad you appeared,' she said, looking earnestly into his face. 'I was beginning to get worried.'

'That's all right,' Billy answered brightly. 'You mustn't worry about me.' He put his suitcase on the chair and started to open it.

'And what about supper, my dear? Did you manage to get anything to eat before you came here?'

'I'm not a bit hungry, thank you,' he said. 'I think I'll just go to bed as soon as possible because tomorrow I've got to get up rather early and report to the office.'

'Very well, then. I'll leave you now so that you can unpack. But before you go to bed, would you be kind enough to pop into the sitting-room on the ground floor and sign the book? Everyone has to do that because it's the law of the land, and we don't want to go breaking any laws at *this* stage in the proceedings, do we?' She gave him a little wave of the hand and went quickly out of the room and closed the door.

Now, the fact that his landlady appeared to be slightly off her rocker didn't worry Billy in the least. After all, she was not only harmless — there was no question about that — but she was also quite obviously a kind and generous soul. He guessed that she had probably lost a son in the war, or something like that, and had never got over it.

So a few minutes later, after unpacking his suitcase and washing his hands, he trotted downstairs to the ground floor and entered the living-room. His landlady wasn't there, but the fire was glowing in the hearth, and the little dachshund was still sleeping in front of it. The room was wonderfully warm and cosy. I'm a lucky fellow, he thought, rubbing his hands. This is a bit of all right.

He found the guest-book lying open on the piano, so he took out his pen and wrote down his name and address. There were only two other entries above his on the page, and, as one always does with guest-books, he started to read them. One was a Christopher Mulholland from Cardiff. The other was Gregory W. Temple from Bristol.

That's funny, he thought suddenly. Christopher Mulholland. It rings a bell.

Now where on earth had he heard that rather unusual name before?

Was he a boy at school? No. Was it one of his sister's numerous young men, perhaps, or a friend of his father's? No, no, it wasn't any of those. He glanced down again at the book.

> *Christopher Mulholland*   *231 Cathedral Road, Cardiff*
> *Gregory W. Temple*   *27 Sycamore Drive, Bristol*

As a matter of fact, now he came to think of it, he wasn't at all sure that the second name didn't have almost as much of a familiar ring about it as the first.

'Gregory Temple?' he said aloud, searching his memory. 'Christopher Mulholland? . . .'

'Such charming boys,' a voice behind him answered, and he turned and saw his landlady sailing into the room with a large silver tea-tray in her hands. She was holding it well out in front of her, and rather high up, as though the tray were a pair of reins on a frisky horse.

'They sound somehow familiar,' he said.

'They do? How interesting.'

'I'm almost positive I've heard those names before somewhere. Isn't that queer? Maybe it was in the newspapers. They weren't famous in any way, were they? I mean famous cricketers or footballers or something like that?'

'Famous,' she said, setting the tea-tray down on the low table in front of the sofa. 'Oh no, I don't think they were famous. But they were extraordinarily handsome, both of them, I can promise you that. They were tall and young and handsome, my dear, just exactly like you.'

Once more, Billy glanced down at the book. 'Look here,' he said, noticing the dates. 'This last entry is over two years old.'

'It is?'

'Yes, indeed. And Christopher Mulholland's is nearly a year before that – more than *three years* ago.'

'Dear me,' she said, shaking her head and heaving a dainty little sigh. 'I would never have thought it. How time does fly away from us all, doesn't it, Mr Wilkins?'

'It's Weaver,' Billy said. 'W-e-a-v-e-r.'

'Oh, of course it is!' she cried, sitting down on the sofa. 'How silly of me. I do apologize. In one ear and out the other, that's me, Mr Weaver.'

'You know something?' Billy said. 'Something that's really quite extraordinary about all this?'

'No, dear, I don't.'

'Well, you see – both of these names, Mulholland and Temple, I not only seem to remember each of them separately, so to speak, but somehow or other, in some peculiar way, they both appear to be sort of connected together as well. As though they were both famous for the same sort of thing, if you see what I mean – like . . . like Dempsey and Tunney, for example, or Churchill and Roosevelt.'

'How amusing,' she said. 'But come over here now, dear, and sit down beside me on the sofa and I'll give you a nice cup of tea and a ginger biscuit before you go to bed.'

'You really shouldn't bother,' Billy said. 'I didn't mean you to do anything like that.' He stood by the piano, watching her as she fussed about with the cups and saucers. He noticed that she had small, white, quickly moving hands, and red finger-nails.

'I'm almost positive it was in the newspapers I saw them,' Billy said. 'I'll think of it in a second. I'm sure I will.'

There is nothing more tantalizing than a thing like this which lingers just outside the borders of one's memory. He hated to give up.

'Now wait a minute,' he said. 'Wait just a minute. Mulholland . . . Christopher Mulholland . . . wasn't *that* the name of the Eton schoolboy who was on a walking-tour through the West Country, and then all of a sudden . . .'

'Milk?' she said. 'And sugar?'

'Yes, please. And then all of a sudden . . .'

'Eton schoolboy?' she said. 'Oh no, my dear, that can't possibly be right because *my* Mr Mulholland was certainly not an Eton schoolboy when he came to me. He was a Cambridge undergraduate. Come over here now and sit next to me and warm yourself in front of this lovely fire. Come on. Your tea's all ready for you.' She patted the empty place beside her on the sofa, and she sat there smiling at Billy and waiting for him to come over.

He crossed the room slowly, and sat down on the edge of the sofa. She placed his teacup on the table in front of him.

'*There* we are,' she said. 'How nice and cosy this is, isn't it?'

Billy started sipping his tea. She did the same. For half a minute or so, neither of them spoke. But Billy knew that she was looking at him. Her body was half-turned towards him, and he could feel her eyes resting on his face, watching him over the rim of her teacup. Now and again, he caught a whiff of a peculiar smell that seemed to emanate directly from her person. It was not in the least unpleasant, and it reminded him – well, he wasn't quite sure what it reminded him of. Pickled walnuts? New leather? Or was it the corridors of a hospital?

'Mr Mulholland was a great one for his tea,' she said at length. 'Never in my life have I seen anyone drink as much tea as dear, sweet Mr Mulholland.'

'I suppose he left fairly recently,' Billy said. He was still puzzling his head about the two names. He was positive now that he had seen them in the newspapers – in the headlines.

'Left?' she said, arching her brows. 'But my dear boy, he never left. He's still here. Mr Temple is also here. They're on the third floor, both of them together.'

Billy set down his cup slowly on the table, and stared at his landlady. She smiled back at him, and then she put out one of her white hands and patted him comfortingly on the knee. 'How old are you, my dear?' she asked.

'Seventeen.'

'Seventeen!' she cried. 'Oh, it's the perfect age! Mr Mulholland was also seventeen. But I think he was a trifle shorter than you are, in fact I'm sure he was, and his teeth weren't *quite* so white. You have the most beautiful teeth, Mr Weaver, did you know that?'

'They're not as good as they look,' Billy said. 'They've got simply masses of fillings in them at the back.'

'Mr Temple, of course, was a little older,' she said, ignoring his remark. 'He was actually twenty-eight. And yet I never would have guessed it if he hadn't told me, never in my whole life. There wasn't a *blemish* on his body.'

'A what?' Billy said.

'His skin was *just* like a baby's.'

There was a pause. Billy picked up his teacup and took another sip of his tea, then he set it down again gently in its saucer. He waited for her to say something else, but she seemed to have lapsed into another of her silences. He sat there staring straight ahead of him into the far corner of the room, biting his lower lip.

'That parrot,' he said at last. 'You know something? It had me completely fooled when I first saw it through the window from the street. I could have sworn it was alive.'

'Alas, no longer.'

'It's most terribly clever the way it's been done,' he said. 'It doesn't look in the least bit dead. Who did it?'

'I did.'

'*You* did?'

'Of course,' she said. 'And have you met my little Basil as well?' She nodded towards the dachshund curled up so comfortably in front of the fire. Billy looked at it. And suddenly, he realized that this animal had all the time been just as silent and motionless as the parrot. He put out a hand and touched it gently on the top of its back. The back was hard and cold, and when he pushed the hair to one side with his fingers, he could see the skin underneath, greyish-black and dry and perfectly preserved.

'Good gracious me,' he said. 'How absolutely fascinating.' He turned away from the dog and stared with deep admiration at the little woman beside him on the sofa. 'It must be most awfully difficult to do a thing like that.'

'Not in the least,' she said. 'I stuff *all* my little pets myself when they pass away. Will you have another cup of tea?'

'No, thank you,' Billy said. The tea tasted faintly of bitter almonds, and he didn't much care for it.

'You did sign the book, didn't you?'

'Oh, yes.'

'That's good. Because later on, if I happen to forget what you were called, then I can always come down here and look it up. I still do that almost every day with Mr Mulholland and Mr . . . Mr . . .'

'Temple,' Billy said. 'Gregory Temple. Excuse my asking, but haven't there been *any* other guests here except them in the last two or three years?'

Holding her teacup high in one hand, inclining her head slightly to the left, she looked up at him out of the corners of her eyes and gave him another gentle little smile.

'No, my dear,' she said. 'Only you.'

WILLIAM AND MARY

WILLIAM PEARL DID NOT leave a great deal of money when he died, and his will was a simple one. With the exception of a few small bequests to relatives, he left all his property to his wife.

The solicitor and Mrs Pearl went over it together in the solicitor's office, and when the business was completed, the widow got up to leave. At that point, the solicitor took a sealed envelope from the folder on his desk and held it out to his client.

'I have been instructed to give you this,' he said. 'Your husband sent it to us shortly before he passed away.' The solicitor was pale and prim, and out of respect for a widow he kept his head on one side as he spoke, looking downward. 'It appears that it might be something personal, Mrs Pearl. No doubt you'd like to take it home with you and read it in privacy.'

Mrs Pearl accepted the envelope and went out into the street. She paused on the pavement, feeling the thing with her fingers. A letter of farewell from William? Probably, yes. A formal letter. It was bound to be formal – stiff and formal. The man was incapable of acting otherwise. He had never done anything informal in his life.

My dear Mary, I trust that you will not permit my departure from this world to upset you too much, but that you will continue to observe those precepts which have guided you so well during our partnership together. Be diligent and dignified in all things. Be thrifty with your money. Be very careful that you do not . . . et cetera, et cetera.

A typical William letter.

Or was it possible that he might have broken down at the last moment and written her something beautiful? Maybe this was a beautiful tender message, a sort of love letter, a lovely warm note of thanks to her for giving him thirty years of her life and for ironing a million shirts and cooking a million meals and making a million beds, something that she could read over and over again, once a day at least, and she would keep it for ever in the box on the dressing-table together with her brooches.

There is no knowing what people will do when they are about to die, Mrs Pearl told herself, and she tucked the envelope under her arm and hurried home.

She let herself in the front door and went straight to the living-room and sat down on the sofa without removing her hat or coat. Then she opened the envelope and drew out the contents. These consisted, she saw, of some fifteen or twenty sheets of lined white paper, folded over once and held together at the top left-hand corner by a clip. Each sheet was covered with the small, neat, forward-sloping writing that she knew so well, but when she noticed how much of it there was, and in what a neat businesslike manner it was written, and how the first page didn't even begin in the nice way a letter should, she began to get suspicious.

She looked away. She lit herself a cigarette. She took one puff and laid the cigarette in the ash-tray.

If this is about what I am beginning to suspect it is about, she told herself, then I don't want to read it.

Can one refuse to read a letter from the dead?

Yes.

Well . . .

She glanced over at William's empty chair on the other side of the fireplace. It was a big brown leather armchair, and there was a depression on the seat of it, made by his buttocks over the years. Higher up, on the backrest, there was a dark oval stain on the leather where his head had rested. He used to sit reading in that chair and she would be opposite him on the sofa, sewing on buttons or mending socks or putting a patch on the elbow of one of his jackets, and every now and then a pair of eyes would glance up from the book and settle on her, watchful, but strangely impersonal, as if calculating something. She had never liked those eyes. They were ice blue, cold, small, and rather close together, with two deep vertical lines of disapproval dividing them. All her life they had been watching her. And even now, after a week alone in the house, she sometimes had an uneasy feeling that they were still there, following her around, staring at her from doorways, from empty chairs, through a window at night.

Slowly she reached into her handbag and took out her spectacles and put them on. Then, holding the pages up high in front of her so that they caught the late afternoon light from the window behind, she started to read:

This note, my dear Mary, is entirely for you, and will be given you shortly after I am gone.

Do not be alarmed by the sight of all this writing. It is nothing but an attempt on my part to explain to you precisely what Landy is going to do to me, and why I have agreed that he should do it, and what are his theories and his hopes. You are my wife and you have a right to know these things. In fact you *must* know them. During the past few days, I have tried very hard to speak with you about Landy, but you have steadfastly refused to give me a hearing. This, as I have already told you, is a very foolish attitude to take, and I find it not entirely an unselfish one either. It stems mostly from ignorance, and I am absolutely convinced that if only you were made aware of all the facts, you would immediately change your view. That is why I am hoping that when I am no longer with you, and your mind is less distracted, you will consent to listen to me more carefully through these pages. I swear to you that when you have read my story, your sense of antipathy will vanish, and enthusiasm will take its place. I even dare to hope that you will become a little proud of what I have done.

As you read on, you must forgive me, if you will, for the coolness of my style, but this is the only way I know of getting my message over to you clearly. You see, as my time draws near, it is natural that I begin to brim with every kind of sentimentality under the sun. Each day I grow more extravagantly wistful, especially in the evenings, and unless I watch myself closely my emotions will be overflowing on to these pages.

I have a wish, for example, to write something about you and what a satisfactory wife you have been to me through the years and am promising myself that if there is time, and I still have the strength, I shall do that next.

I have a yearning also to speak about this Oxford of mine where I have been living and teaching for the past seventeen years, to tell something about the glory of the place and to explain, if I can, a little of what it has meant to have been allowed to work in its midst. All the things and places that I loved so well keep crowding in on me now in this gloomy bedroom. They are bright and beautiful as they always were, and today, for some reason, I can see them more clearly than ever. The path around the lake in the gardens of Worcester College, where Lovelace used to walk. The gateway at Pembroke. The view westward over the town from Magdalen Tower. The great hall at Christchurch. The little rockery at St John's where I have counted more than a dozen varieties of campanula, including the rare and dainty C. Waldsteiniana. But there, you see! I haven't even begun and already I'm falling into the trap. So let me get started now; and let you read it slowly, my dear, without any of that sense of sorrow or disapproval that might otherwise embarrass your understanding. Promise me now that you will read it slowly, and that you will put yourself in a cool and patient frame of mind before you begin.

The details of the illness that struck me down so suddenly in my middle life are known to you. I need not waste time upon them — except to admit at once how foolish I was not to have gone earlier to my doctor. Cancer is one of the few remaining diseases that these modern drugs cannot cure. A surgeon can operate if it has not spread too far; but with me, not only did I leave it too late, but the thing had the effrontery to attack me in the pancreas, making both surgery and survival equally impossible.

So here I was with somewhere between one and six months left to live, growing more melancholy every hour — and then, all of a sudden, in comes Landy.

That was six weeks ago, on a Tuesday morning, very early, long before your visiting time, and the moment he entered I knew there was some sort of madness in the wind. He didn't creep in on his toes, sheepish and embarrassed, not knowing what to say, like all my other visitors. He came in strong and smiling, and he strode up to the bed and stood there looking down at me with a wild bright glimmer in his eyes, and he said, 'William, my boy, this is perfect. You're just the one I want!'

Perhaps I should explain to you here that although John Landy has never been to our house, and you have seldom if ever met him, I myself have been friendly with him for at least nine years. I am, of course, primarily a teacher of philosophy, but as you know I've lately been dabbling a good deal in psychology as well. Landy's interests and mine have therefore slightly overlapped. He is a magnificent neuro-surgeon, one of the finest, and recently he has been kind enough to let me study the results of some of his work, especially the varying effects of prefrontal lobotomies upon different types of psychopath. So you can see

that when he suddenly burst in on me that Tuesday morning, we
were by no means strangers to one another.

'Look,' he said, pulling up a chair beside the bed. 'In a few
weeks you're going to be dead. Correct?'

Coming from Landy, the question didn't seem especially
unkind. In a way it was refreshing to have a visitor brave enough
to touch upon the forbidden subject.

'You're going to expire right here in this room, and then
they'll take you out and cremate you.'

'Bury me,' I said.

'That's even worse. And then what? Do you believe you'll go
to heaven?'

'I doubt it,' I said, 'though it would be comforting to think so.'

'Or hell, perhaps?'

'I don't really see why they should send me there.'

'You never know, my dear William.'

'What's all this about?' I asked.

'Well,' he said, and I could see him watching me carefully,
'personally, I don't believe that after you're dead you'll ever hear
of yourself again – unless . . .' and here he paused and smiled and
leaned closer '. . . unless, of course, you have the sense to put
yourself into my hands. Would you care to consider a proposition?'

The way he was staring at me, and studying me, and appraising
me with a queer kind of hungriness, I might have been a piece of
prime beef on the counter and he had bought it and was waiting
for them to wrap it up.

'I'm really serious about it, William. Would you care to consider
a proposition?'

'I don't know what you're talking about.'

'Then listen and I'll tell you. Will you listen to me?'

'Go on then, if you like. I doubt I've got very much to lose by
hearing it.'

'On the contrary, you have a great deal to gain – especially
after you're dead.'

I am sure he was expecting me to jump when he said this, but
for some reason I was ready for it. I lay quite still, watching his
face and that slow white smile of his that always revealed the
gold clasp on an upper denture curled around the canine on the
left side of his mouth.

'This is a thing, William, that I've been working on quietly for some years. One or two others here at the hospital have been helping me, especially Morrison, and we've completed a number of fairly successful trials with laboratory animals. I'm at the stage now where I'm ready to have a go with a man. It's a big idea, and it may sound a bit far-fetched at first, but from a surgical point of view there doesn't seem to be any reason why it shouldn't be more or less practicable.'

Landy leaned forward and placed both hands on the edge of my bed. He has a good face, handsome in a bony sort of way, with none of the usual doctor's look about it. You know that look, most of them have it. It glimmers at you out of their eyeballs like a dull electric sign and it reads *Only I can save you.* But John Landy's eyes were wide and bright and little sparks of excitement were dancing in the centres of them.

'Quite a long time ago,' he said, 'I saw a short medical film that had been brought over from Russia. It was a rather gruesome thing, but interesting. It showed a dog's head completely severed from the body, but with the normal blood supply being maintained through the arteries and veins by means of an artificial heart. Now the thing is this: that dog's head, sitting there all alone on a sort of tray, was *alive.* The brain was functioning. They proved it by several tests. For example, when food was smeared on the dog's lips, the tongue would come out and lick it away: and the eyes would follow a person moving across the room.

'It seemed reasonable to conclude from this that the head and the brain did not need to be attached to the rest of the body in order to remain alive — provided, of course, that a supply of properly oxygenated blood could be maintained.

'Now then. My own thought, which grew out of seeing this film, was to remove the brain from the skull of a human and keep it alive and functioning as an independent unit for an unlimited period after he is dead. *Your* brain, for example, after *you* are dead.'

'I don't like that,' I said.

'Don't interrupt, William. Let me finish. So far as I can tell from subsequent experiments, the brain is a peculiarly self-supporting object. It manufactures its own cerebrospinal fluid. The magic processes of thought and memory which go on inside it are manifestly not impaired by the absence of limbs or trunk or even of skull, provided, as I say, that you keep pumping in the right kind of oxygenated blood under the proper conditions.

'My dear William, just think for a moment of your own brain. It is in perfect shape. It is crammed full of a lifetime of learning. It has taken you years of work to make it what it is. It is just beginning to give out some first-rate original ideas. Yet soon it is going to have to die along with the rest of your body simply because your silly little pancreas is riddled with cancer.'

'No thank you,' I said to him. 'You can stop there. It's a repulsive idea, and even if you could do it, which I doubt, it would be quite pointless. What possible use is there in keeping my brain alive if I couldn't talk or see or hear or feel? Personally, I can think of nothing more unpleasant.'

'I believe that you *would* be able to communicate with us,' Landy said. 'And we might even succeed in giving you a certain amount of vision. But let's take this slowly. I'll come to all that later on. The fact remains that you're going to die fairly soon whatever happens; and my plans would not involve touching you at all until *after* you are dead. Come now, William. No true philosopher could object to lending his dead body to the cause of science.'

'That's not putting it quite straight,' I answered. 'It seems to me there'd be some doubts as to whether I were dead or alive by the time you'd finished with me.'

'Well,' he said, smiling a little, 'I suppose you're right about that. But I don't think you ought to turn me down quite so quickly, before you know a bit more about it.'

'I said I don't want to hear it.'

'Have a cigarette,' he said, holding out his case.

'I don't smoke, you know that.'

He took one himself and lit it with a tiny silver lighter that was no bigger than a shilling piece. 'A present from the people who make my instruments,' he said. 'Ingenious, isn't it?'

I examined the lighter, then handed it back.

'May I go on?' he asked.

'I'd rather you didn't.'

'Just lie still and listen. I think you'll find it quite interesting.'

There were some blue grapes on a plate beside my bed. I put the plate on my chest and began eating the grapes.

'At the very moment of death,' Landy said, 'I should have to be standing by so that I could step in immediately and try to keep your brain alive.'

'You mean leaving it in the head?'

'To start with, yes. I'd have to.'

'And where would you put it after that?'

'If you want to know, in a sort of basin.'

'Are you really serious about this?'

'Certainly I'm serious.'

'All right. Go on.'

'I suppose you know that when the heart stops and the brain is deprived of fresh blood and oxygen, its tissues die very rapidly. Anything from four to six minutes and the whole thing's dead. Even after three minutes you may get a certain amount of damage. So I should have to work rapidly to prevent this from happening. But with the help of the machine, it should all be quite simple.'

'What machine?'

'The artificial heart. We've got a nice adaptation here of the one originally devised by Alexis Carrel and Lindbergh. It oxygenates the blood, keeps it at the right temperature, pumps it in at the right pressure, and does a number of other little necessary things. It's really not at all complicated.'

'Tell me what you would do at the moment of death,' I said. 'What is the first thing you would do?'

'Do you know anything about the vascular and venous arrangement of the brain?'

'No.'

'Then listen. It's not difficult. The blood supply to the brain is derived from two main sources, the internal carotid arteries and the vertebral arteries. There are two of each, making four arteries in all. Got that?'

'Yes.'

'And the return system is even simpler. The blood is drained away by only two large veins, the internal jugulars. So you have four arteries going up – they go up the neck of course – and two veins coming down. Around the brain itself they naturally branch out into other channels, but those don't concern us. We never touch them.'

'All right,' I said. 'Imagine that I've just died. Now what would you do?'

'I should immediately open your neck and locate the four arteries, the carotids and the vertebrals. I should then perfuse them, which means that I'd stick a large hollow needle into each.

These four needles would be connected by tubes to the artificial heart.

'Then, working quickly, I would dissect out both the left and right jugular veins and hitch these also to the heart machine to complete the circuit. Now switch on the machine, which is already primed with the right type of blood and there you are. The circulation through your brain would be restored.'

'I'd be like that Russian dog.'

'I don't think you would. For one thing, you'd certainly lose consciousness when you died, and I very much doubt whether you would come to again for quite a long time – if indeed you came to at all. But, conscious or not, you'd be in a rather interesting position, wouldn't you? You'd have a cold dead body and a living brain.'

Landy paused to savour this delightful prospect. The man was so entranced and bemused by the whole idea that he evidently found it impossible to believe I might not be feeling the same way.

'We could now afford to take our time,' he said. 'And believe me, we'd need it. The first thing we'd do would be to wheel you to the operating-room, accompanied of course by the machine, which must never stop pumping. The next problem . . .'

'All right,' I said. 'That's enough. I don't have to hear the details.'

'Oh but you must,' he said. 'It is important that you should know precisely what is going to happen to you all the way through. You see, afterwards, when you regain consciousness, it will be much more satisfactory from your point of view if you are able to remember exactly *where* you are and *how* you came to be there. If only for your own peace of mind you should know that. You agree?'

I lay still on the bed, watching him.

'So the next problem would be to remove your brain, intact and undamaged, from your dead body. The body is useless. In fact it has already started to decay. The skull and the face are also useless. They are both encumbrances and I don't want them around. All I want is the brain, the clean beautiful brain, alive and perfect. So when I get you on the table I will take a saw, a small oscillating saw, and with this I shall proceed to remove the whole vault of your skull. You'd still be unconscious at that point so I wouldn't have to bother with anaesthetic.'

'Like hell, you wouldn't,' I said.

'You'd be out cold, I promise you that, William. Don't forget you *died* just a few minutes before.'

'Nobody's sawing off the top of my skull without an anaesthetic,' I said.

Landy shrugged his shoulders. 'It makes no difference to me,' he said. 'I'll be glad to give you a little procaine if you want it. If it will make you any happier I'll infiltrate the whole scalp with procaine, the whole head, from the neck up.'

'Thanks very much,' I said.

'You know,' he went on, 'it's extraordinary what sometimes happens. Only last week a man was brought in unconscious, and I opened his head without any anaesthetic at all and removed a small blood clot. I was still working inside the skull when he woke up and began talking.

'"Where am I?" he asked.

'"You're in hospital."

'"Well," he said. 'Fancy that."

'"Tell me," I asked him, "is this bothering you, what I'm doing?"

'"No," he answered. "Not at all. What *are* you doing?"

'"I'm just removing a blood clot from your brain."

'"You *are?*"

'"Just lie still. Don't move, I'm nearly finished."

'"So that's the bastard who's been giving me all those headaches," the man said.'

Landy paused and smiled, remembering the occasion. 'That's word for word what the man said,' he went on, 'although the next day he couldn't even recollect the incident. It's a funny thing, the brain.'

'I'll have the procaine,' I said.

'As you wish, William. And now, as I say, I'd take a small oscillating saw and carefully remove your complete calvarium — the whole vault of the skull. This would expose the top half of the brain, or rather the outer covering in which it is wrapped. You may or may not know that there are three separate coverings around the brain itself — the outer one called the dura mater or dura, the middle one called the arachnoid, and the inner one called the pia mater or pia. Most laymen seem to have the idea that the brain is a naked thing floating around in fluid in your head. But it isn't. It's wrapped up neatly in these three strong coverings, and the cerebrospinal fluid actually flows within the little gap between the two coverings, known as the subarachnoid space. As I told you before, this fluid is manufactured by the brain and it drains off into the venous system by osmosis.

'I myself would leave all three coverings — don't they have lovely names, the dura, the arachnoid, and the pia? — I'd leave them all intact. There are many reasons for this, not least among them being the fact that within the dura run the venous channels that drain the blood from the brain into the jugular.

'Now,' he went on, 'we've got the upper half of your skull off so that the top of the brain, wrapped in its outer covering, is exposed. The next step is the really tricky one: to release the whole package so that it can be lifted cleanly away, leaving the stubs of the four supply arteries and the two veins hanging underneath ready to be re-connected to the machine. This is an immensely lengthy and complicated business involving the delicate chipping away of much bone, the severing of many nerves, and the cutting and tying of numerous blood vessels. The only way I could do it with any hope of success would be by taking a rongeur and slowly biting off the rest of your skull, peeling it off downward like an orange until the sides and underneath of the brain covering are fully exposed. The problems involved are highly technical and I won't go into them but I feel fairly sure that the work can be done. It's simply a question of surgical skill and patience. And don't forget that I'd have plenty of time, as much as I wanted, because the artificial heart would be continually pumping away alongside the operating-table, keeping the brain alive.

'Now, let's assume that I've succeeded in peeling off your skull and removing everything else that surrounds the sides of the brain. That leaves it connected to the body only at the base, mainly by the spinal column and by the two large veins and the four arteries that are supplying it with blood. So what next?

'I would sever the spinal column just above the first cervical vertebra, taking great care not to harm the two vertebral arteries which are in that area. But you must remember that the dura or outer covering is open at this place to receive the spinal column, so I'd have to close this opening by sewing the edges of the dura together. There'd be no problem there.

'At this point, I would be ready for the final move. To one side, on a table, I'd have a basin of a special shape, and this would be filled with what we call Ringer's Solution. That is a special kind of fluid we use for irrigation in neurosurgery. I would now cut the brain completely loose by severing the supply arteries and the veins. Then I would simply pick it up in my hands and transfer it to the basin. This would be the only other time during the whole proceeding when the blood flow would be cut off; but once it was in the basin, it wouldn't take a moment to re-connect the stubs of the arteries and veins to the artificial heart.

'So there you are,' Landy said. 'Your brain is now in the basin, and still alive, and there isn't any reason why it shouldn't stay alive for a very long time, years and years perhaps, provided we looked after the blood and the machine.'

'But would it *function*?'

'My dear William, how should I know? I can't even tell you whether it would regain consciousness.'

'And if it did?'

'There now! That would be fascinating!'

'Would it?' I said, and I must admit I had my doubts.

'Of course it would! Lying there with all your thinking processes working beautifully, and your memory as well . . .'

'And not being able to see or feel or smell or hear or talk,' I said.

'Ah!' he cried. 'I knew I'd forgotten something! I never told you about the eye. Listen. I am going to try to leave one of your optic nerves intact, as well as the eye itself. The optic nerve is a little thing about the thickness of a clinical thermometer and about two inches in length as it stretches between the brain and the eye. The beauty of it is that it's not really a nerve at all. It's an outpouching of the brain itself, and the dura or brain covering extends along it and is attached to the eyeball. The back of the eye is therefore in very close contact with the brain, and cerebro-spinal fluid flows right up to it.

'All this suits my purpose very well, and makes it reasonable to suppose that I could succeed in preserving one of your eyes. I've already constructed a small plastic case to contain the eyeball, instead of your own socket, and when the brain is in the basin, submerged in Ringer's Solution, the eyeball in its case will float on the surface of the liquid.'

'Staring at the ceiling,' I said.

'I suppose so, yes. I'm afraid there wouldn't be any muscles there to move it around. But it might be sort of fun to lie there so quietly and comfortably peering out at the world from your basin.'

'Hilarious,' I said. 'How about leaving me an ear as well?'

'I'd rather not try an ear this time.'

'I want an ear,' I said. 'I insist upon an ear.'

'No.'

'I want to listen to Bach.'

'You don't understand how difficult it would be,' Landy said gently. 'The hearing apparatus — the cochlea, as it's called — is a far more delicate mechanism than the eye. What's more, it is encased in bone. So is a part of the auditory nerve that connects it with the brain. I couldn't possibly chisel the whole thing out intact.'

'Couldn't you leave it encased in the bone and bring the bone to the basin?'

'No,' he said firmly. 'This thing is complicated enough already. And anyway, if the eye works, it doesn't matter all that much about your hearing. We can always hold up messages for you to read. You really must leave me to decide what is possible and what isn't.'

'I haven't yet said that I'm going to do it.'

'I know, William, I know.'

'I'm not sure I fancy the idea very much.'

'Would you rather be dead altogether?'

'Perhaps I would. I don't know yet. I wouldn't be able to talk, would I?'

'Of course not.'

'Then how would I communicate with you? How would you know that I'm conscious?'

'It would be easy for us to know whether or not you regain consciousness,' Landy said. 'The ordinary electro-encephalograph could tell us that. We'd attach the electrodes directly to the frontal lobes of your brain, there in the basin.'

'And you could actually tell?'

'Oh, definitely. Any hospital could do that part of it.'

'But I couldn't communicate with you.'

'As a matter of fact,' Landy said, 'I believe you could. There's a man up in London called Wertheimer who's doing some interesting work on the subject of thought communication, and I've been in touch with him. You know, don't you, that the thinking brain throws off electrical and chemical discharges? And that these discharges go out in the form of waves, rather like radio waves?'

'I know a bit about it,' I said.

'Well, Wertheimer has constructed an apparatus somewhat similar to the encephalograph, though far more sensitive, and he maintains that within certain narrow limits it can help him to interpret the actual things that a brain is thinking. It produces a kind of graph which is apparently decipherable into words or thoughts. Would you like me to ask Wertheimer to come and see you?'

'No,' I said. Landy was already taking it for granted that I was going to go through with this business, and I resented his attitude. 'Go away now and leave me alone,' I told him. 'You won't get anywhere by trying to rush me.'

He stood up at once and crossed to the door.

'One question,' I said.

He paused with a hand on the doorknob. 'Yes, William?'

'Simply this. Do you yourself honestly believe that when my brain is in that basin, my mind will be able to function exactly as it is doing at present? Do you believe that I will be able to think and reason as I can now? And will the power of memory remain?'

'I don't see why not,' he answered. 'It's the same brain. It's alive. It's undamaged. In fact, it's completely untouched. We haven't even opened the dura. The big difference, of course, would be that we've severed every single nerve that leads into it – except for the one optic nerve – and this means that your thinking would no longer be influenced by your senses. You'd be living in an extraordinary pure and detached world. Nothing to bother you at all, not even pain. You couldn't possibly feel pain because there wouldn't be any nerves to feel it with. In a way, it would be an almost perfect situation. No worries or fears or pains or hunger or thirst. Not even any desires. Just your memories and your thoughts and if the remaining eye happened to function, then you could read books as well. It all sounds rather pleasant to me.'

'It does, does it?'

'Yes, William, it does. And particularly for a Doctor of Philosophy. It would be a tremendous experience. You'd be able to reflect upon the ways of the world with a detachment and a serenity that no man had ever attained before. And who knows what might not happen then! Great thoughts and solutions might come to you, great ideas that could revolutionize our way of life! Try to imagine, if you can, the degree of concentration that you'd be able to achieve!'

'And the frustration,' I said.

'Nonsense. There couldn't be any frustration. You can't have frustration without desire, and you couldn't possibly have any desire. Not physical desire, anyway.'

'I should certainly be capable of remembering my previous life in the world, and I might desire to return to it.'

'What, to this mess! Out of your comfortable basin and back into this madhouse!'

'Answer one more question,' I said. 'How long do you believe you could keep it alive?'

'The brain? Who knows? Possibly for years and years. The conditions would be ideal. Most of the factors that cause deterioration would be absent, thanks to the artificial heart. The blood-pressure would remain constant at all times, an impossible condition in real life. The temperature would also be constant. The chemical composition of the blood would be near perfect. There would be no impurities in it, or virus, no bacteria, nothing. Of course it's foolish to guess, but I believe that a brain might live for two or three hundred years in circumstances like these. Goodbye for now,' he said. 'I'll drop in and see you tomorrow.' He went out quickly, leaving me, as you might guess, in a fairly disturbed state of mind.

My immediate reaction after he had gone was one of revulsion towards the whole business. Somehow, it wasn't at all nice. There was something basically repulsive about the idea that I myself, with all my mental faculties intact, should be reduced to a small slimy blob lying in a pool of water. It was monstrous, obscene, unholy. Another thing that bothered me was the feeling of helplessness that I was bound to experience once Landy had got me into the basin. There could be no going back after that, no way of protesting or explaining. I would be committed for as long as they could keep me alive.

And what, for example, if I could not stand it? What if it turned out to be terribly painful? What if I became hysterical?

No legs to run away on. No voice to scream with. Nothing. I'd just have to grin and bear it for the next two centuries.

No mouth to grin with either.

At this point, a curious thought struck me, and it was this: Does not a man who has had a leg amputated often suffer from the delusion that the leg is still there? Does he not tell the nurse that the toes he doesn't have any more are itching like mad, and so on and so forth? I seemed to have heard something to that effect quite recently.

Very well. On the same premise, was it not possible that my brain, lying there alone in that basin, might not suffer from a similar delusion in regard to my body? In which case, all my usual aches and pains could come flooding over me and I wouldn't even be able to take an aspirin to relieve them. One moment I might be imagining that I had the most excruciating cramp in my leg, or a violent indigestion, and a few minutes later, I might easily get the feeling that my poor bladder — you know me — was so full that if I didn't get to emptying it soon it would burst.

Heaven forbid.

I lay there for a long time thinking these horrid thoughts. Then quite suddenly, round about midday, my mood began to change. I became less concerned with the unpleasant aspect of the affair and found myself able to examine Landy's proposals in a more reasonable light. Was there not, after all, I asked myself, something a bit comforting in the thought that my brain might not necessarily have to die and disappear in a few weeks' time? There was indeed. I am rather proud of my brain. It is a sensitive, lucid, and uberous organ. It contains a prodigious store of information, and it is still capable of producing imaginative and original theories. As brains go, it is a damn good one, though I say it myself. Whereas my body, my poor old body, the thing that Landy wants to throw away — well, even you, my dear Mary, will have to agree with me that there is really nothing about *that* which is worth preserving any more.

I was lying on my back eating a grape. Delicious it was, and there were three little seeds in it which I took out of my mouth and placed on the edge of the plate.

'I'm going to do it,' I said quietly. 'Yes, by God, I'm going to do it. When Landy comes back to see me tomorrow I shall tell him straight out that I'm going to do it.'

It was as quick as that. And from then on, I began to feel very much better. I surprised everyone by gobbling an enormous lunch, and shortly after that you came in to visit me as usual.

But how well I looked, you told me. How bright and well and chirpy. Had anything happened? Was there some good news?

Yes, I said there was. And then, if you remember, I bade you sit down and make yourself comfortable and I began immediately to explain to you as gently as I could what was in the wind.

Alas, you would have none of it. I had hardly begun telling you the barest details when you flew into a fury and said that the thing was revolting, disgusting, horrible, unthinkable, and when I tried to go on, you marched out of the room.

Well, Mary, as you know, I have tried to discuss this subject with you many times since then, but you have consistently refused to give me a hearing. Hence this note, and I can only hope that you will have the good sense to permit yourself to read it. It has taken me a long time to write. Two weeks have gone since I started to scribble the first sentence, and I'm now a good deal weaker than I was then. I doubt whether I have the strength to say much more. Certainly I won't say good-bye, because there's a chance, just a tiny chance, that if Landy succeeds in his work I may actually *see* you again later, that is if you bring yourself to come and visit me.

I am giving orders that these pages shall not be delivered to you until a week after I am gone. By now, therefore, as you sit reading them, seven days have already elapsed since Landy did the deed. You yourself may even know what the outcome has been. If you don't, if you have purposely kept yourself apart and have refused to have anything to do with it – which I suspect may be the case – please change your mind now and give Landy a call to see how things went with me. That is the least you can do. I have told him that he may expect to hear from you on the seventh day.

Your faithful husband,
William

PS. Be good when I am gone, and always remember that it is harder to be a widow than a wife. Do not drink cocktails. Do not waste money. Do not smoke cigarettes. Do not eat pastry. Do not use lipstick. Do not buy a television apparatus. Keep my rose beds and my rockery well weeded in the summers. And incidentally I suggest that you have the telephone disconnected now that I shall have no further use for it.

W.

Mrs Pearl laid the last page of the manuscript slowly down on the sofa beside her. Her little mouth was pursed up tight and there was a whiteness around her nostrils.

But really! You would think a widow was entitled to a bit of peace after all these years.

The whole thing was just too awful to think about. Beastly and awful. It gave her the shudders.

She reached for her bag and found herself another cigarette. She lit it, inhaling the smoke deeply and blowing it out in clouds all over the room. Through the smoke she could see her lovely television set, brand new, lustrous, huge, crouching defiantly but also a little self-consciously on top of what used to be William's worktable.

What would he say, she wondered, if he could see that now?

She paused, to remember the last time he had caught her smoking a cigarette. That was about a year ago, and she was sitting in the kitchen by the open window having a quick one before he came home from work. She'd had the radio on loud playing dance music and she had turned round to pour herself another cup of coffee and there he was standing in the doorway, huge and grim, staring down at her with those awful eyes, a little black dot of fury blazing in the centre of each.

For four weeks after that, he had paid the housekeeping bills himself and given her no money at all, but of course he wasn't to know that she had over six pounds salted away in a soap-flake carton in the cupboard under the sink.

'What is it?' she had said to him once during supper. 'Are you worried about me getting lung cancer?'

'I am not,' he had answered.

'Then why can't I smoke?'

'Because I disapprove, that's why.'

He had also disapproved of children, and as a result they had never had any of them either.

Where was he now, this William of hers, the great disapprover?

Landy would be expecting her to call up. Did she *have* to call Landy?

Well, not really, no.

She finished her cigarette, then lit another one immediately from the old stub. She looked at the telephone that was sitting on the worktable beside the television set. William had asked her to call. He had specifically requested that she telephone Landy as soon as she had read the letter. She hesitated, fighting hard now against that old ingrained sense of duty that she didn't quite yet dare to shake off. Then, slowly, she got to her feet and crossed over to the phone on the worktable. She found a number in the book, dialled it, and waited.

'I want to speak to Mr Landy, please.'

'Who is calling?'

'Mrs Pearl. Mrs William Pearl.'

'One moment, please.'

Almost at once, Landy was on the other end of the wire.

'Mrs Pearl?'

'This is Mrs Pearl.'

There was a slight pause.

'I am so glad you called at last, Mrs Pearl. You are quite well, I hope?' The voice was quiet, unemotional, courteous. 'I wonder if you would care to come over to the hospital? Then we can have a little chat. I expect you are very eager to know how it all came out.'

She didn't answer.

'I can tell you now that everything went pretty smoothly, one way and another. Far better, in fact, than I was entitled to hope. It is not only alive, Mrs Pearl, it is conscious. It recovered consciousness on the second day. Isn't that interesting?'

She waited for him to go on.

'And the eye is seeing. We are sure of that because we get an immediate change in the deflections on the encephalograph when we hold something up in front of it. And now we're giving it the news-paper to read every day.'

'Which newspaper?' Mrs Pearl asked sharply.

'The *Daily Mirror*. The headlines are larger.'

'He hates the *Mirror*. Give him *The Times*.'

There was a pause, then the doctor said, 'Very well, Mrs Pearl. We'll give it *The Times*. We naturally want to do all we can to keep it happy.'

'*Him*,' she said. 'Not it. *Him!*'

'Him,' the doctor said. 'Yes, I beg your pardon. To keep him happy. That's one reason why I suggested you should come along here as soon as possible. I think it would be good for him to see you. You could indicate how delighted you were to be with him again – smile at him and blow him a kiss and all that sort of thing. It's bound to be a comfort to him to know that you are standing by.'

There was a long pause.

'Well,' Mrs Pearl said at last, her voice suddenly very meek and tired. 'I suppose I had better come on over and see how he is.'

'Good. I knew you would. I'll wait here for you. Come straight up to my office on the second floor. Good-bye.'

Half an hour later, Mrs Pearl was at the hospital.

'You mustn't be surprised by what he looks like,' Landy said as he walked beside her down a corridor.

'No, I won't.'

'It's bound to be a bit of a shock to you at first. He's not very prepossessing in his present state, I'm afraid.'

'I didn't marry him for his looks, Doctor.'

Landy turned and stared at her. What a queer little woman this was, he thought with her large eyes and her sullen, resentful air. Her features, which must have been quite pleasant once, had now gone completely. The mouth was slack, the cheeks loose and flabby, and the whole face gave the impression of having slowly but surely sagged to pieces through years and years of joyless married life. They walked on for a while in silence.

'Take your time when you get inside,' Landy said. 'He won't know you're in there until you place your face directly above his eye. The eye is always open, but he can't move it at all, so the field of vision is very narrow. At present we have it looking up at the ceiling. And of course he can't hear anything. We can talk together as much as we like. It's in here.'

Landy opened a door and ushered her into a small square room.

'I wouldn't go too close yet,' he said, putting a hand on her arm. 'Stay back here a moment with me until you get used to it all.'

There was a biggish white enamel bowl about the size of a wash-basin standing on a high white table in the centre of the room, and there were half a dozen thin plastic tubes coming out of it. These tubes were connected with a whole lot of glass piping in which you could see the blood flowing to and from the heart machine. The machine itself made a soft rhythmic pulsing sound.

'He's in there,' Landy said, pointing to the basin, which was too high for her to see into. 'Come just a little closer. Not too near.'

He led her two paces forward.

By stretching her neck, Mrs Pearl could now see the surface of the liquid inside the basin. It was clear and still, and on it there floated a small oval capsule, about the size of a pigeon's egg.

'That's the eye in there,' Landy said. 'Can you see it?'

'Yes.'

'So far as we can tell, it is still in perfect condition. It's his right eye, and the plastic container has a lens on it similar to the one he used in his own spectacles. At this moment he's probably seeing quite as well as he did before.'

'The ceiling isn't much to look at,' Mrs Pearl said.

'Don't worry about that. We're in the process of working out a whole programme to keep him amused, but we don't want to go too quickly at first.'

'Give him a good book.'

'We will, we will. Are you feeling all right, Mrs Pearl?'

'Yes.'

'Then we'll go forward a little more, shall we, and you'll be able to see the whole thing.'

He led her forward until they were standing only a couple of yards from the table and now she could see right down into the basin.

'There you are,' Landy said. 'That's William.'

He was far larger than she had imagined he would be, and darker in colour. With all the ridges and creases running over his surface, he reminded her of nothing so much as an enormous pickled walnut. She could see the stubs of the four big arteries and the two veins coming out from the base of him and the neat way in which they were joined to the plastic tubes; and with each throb of the heart machine, all the tubes gave a little jerk in unison as the blood was pushed through them.

'You'll have to lean over,' Landy said, 'and put your pretty face right above the eye. He'll see you then, and you can smile at him and blow him a kiss. If I were you I'd say a few nice things as well. He won't actually hear them, but I'm sure he'll get the general idea.'

'He hates people blowing kisses at him,' Mrs Pearl said. 'I'll do it my own way if you don't mind.' She stepped up to the edge of the table, leaned forward until her face was directly over the basin, and looked straight down in William's eye.

'Hallo, dear,' she whispered. 'It's me — Mary.'

The eye, bright as ever, stared back at her with a peculiar, fixed intensity.

'How are you, dear?' she said.

The plastic capsule was transparent all the way round so that the whole of the eyeball was visible. The optic nerve connecting the underside of it to the brain looked a short length of grey spaghetti.

'Are you feeling all right, William?'

It was a queer sensation peering into her husband's eye when there was no face to go with it. All she had to look at was the eye, and she kept staring at it, and gradually it grew bigger and bigger, and in the end it was the only thing that she could see — a sort of face in itself. There was a network of tiny red veins running over the white surface of the eyeball, and in the ice-blue of the iris there were three or four rather pretty darkish streaks radiating from the pupil in the centre. The pupil was large and black, with a little spark of light reflecting from one side of it.

'I got your letter, dear, and came over at once to see how you were. Dr Landy says you are doing wonderfully well. Perhaps if I talk slowly you can understand a little of what I am saying by reading my lips.'

There was no doubt that the eye was watching her.

'They are doing everything possible to take care of you, dear. This marvellous machine thing here is pumping away all the time and I'm sure it's a lot better than those silly old hearts all the rest of us have. Ours are liable to break down at any moment, but yours will go on for ever.'

She was studying the eye closely, trying to discover what there was about it that gave it such an unusual appearance.

'You seem fine, dear, simply fine. Really you do.'

It looked ever so much nicer, this eye, than either of his eyes used to look, she told herself. There was a softness about it somewhere, a calm, kindly quality that she had never seen before. Maybe it had to do with the dot in the very centre, the pupil. William's pupils used always to be tiny black pinheads. They used to glint at you, stabbing into your brain, seeing right through you, and they always knew at once what you were up to and even what you were thinking. But this one she was looking at now was large and soft and gentle, almost cow-like.

'Are you quite sure he's conscious?' she asked, not looking up.

'Oh yes, completely,' Landy said.

'And he *can* see me?'

'Perfectly.'

'Isn't that marvellous? I expect he's wondering what happened.'

'Not at all. He knows perfectly well where he is and why he's there. He can't possibly have forgotten that.'

'You mean he *knows* he's in this basin?'

'Of course. And if only he had the power of speech, he would probably be able to carry on a perfectly normal conversation with you this very minute. So far as I can see, there should be absolutely no difference mentally between this William here and the one you used to know back home.'

'Good *gracious* me,' Mrs Pearl said, and she paused to consider this intriguing aspect.

You know what, she told herself, looking behind the eye now and staring hard at the great grey pulpy walnut that lay so placidly under the water, I'm not at all sure that I don't prefer him as he is at present. In fact, I believe that I could live very comfortably with this kind of a William. I could cope with this one.

'Quiet, isn't he?' she said.

'Naturally he's quiet.'

No arguments and criticisms, she thought, no constant admonitions, no rules to obey, no ban on smoking cigarettes, no pair of cold disapproving eyes watching me over the top of a book in the evenings, no shirts to wash and iron, no meals to cook — nothing but the throb of the heart machine, which was rather a soothing sound anyway and certainly not loud enough to interfere with television.

'Doctor,' she said. 'I do believe I'm suddenly getting to feel the most enormous affection for him. Does that sound queer?'

'I think it's quite understandable.'

'He looks so helpless and silent lying there under the water in his little basin.'

'Yes, I know.'

'He's like a baby, that's what he's like. He's exactly like a little baby.'

Landy stood still behind her, watching.

'There,' she said softly, peering into the basin. 'From now on Mary's going to look after you *all* by herself and you've nothing to worry about in the world. When can I have him back home, Doctor?'

'I beg your pardon?'

'I said when can I have him back — back in my own house?'

'You're joking,' Landy said.

She turned her head slowly around and looked directly at him. 'Why should I joke?' she asked. Her face was bright, her eyes round and bright as two diamonds.

'He couldn't possibly be moved.'

'I don't see why not.'

'This is an experiment, Mrs Pearl.'

'It's my husband, Dr Landy.'

A funny little nervous half-smile appeared on Landy's mouth. 'Well . . .' he said.

'It *is* my husband, you know.' There was no anger in her voice. She spoke quietly, as though merely reminding him of a simple fact.

'That's rather a tricky point,' Landy said, wetting his lips. 'You're a widow now, Mrs Pearl. I think you must resign yourself to that fact.'

She turned away suddenly from the table and crossed over to the window. 'I mean it,' she said, fishing in her bag for a cigarette. 'I want him back.'

Landy watched her as she put the cigarette between her lips and lit it. Unless he were very much mistaken, there was something a bit odd about this woman, he thought. She seemed almost pleased to have her husband over there in the basin.

He tried to imagine what his own feelings would be if it were *his* wife's brain lying there and *her* eye staring at him out of that capsule.

He wouldn't like it.

'Shall we go back to my room now?' he said.

She was standing by the window, apparently quite calm and relaxed, puffing her cigarette.

'Yes, all right.'

On her way past the table she stopped and leaned over the basin once more. 'Mary's leaving now, sweetheart,' she said. 'And don't you worry about a single thing, you understand? We're going to get you right back home where we can look after you properly just as soon as we possibly can. And listen dear . . .' At this point she paused and carried the cigarette to her lips, intending to take a puff.

Instantly the eye flashed.

She was looking straight into it at the time and right in the centre of it she saw a tiny but brilliant flash of light, and the pupil contracted into a minute black pinpoint of absolute fury.

At first she didn't move. She stood bending over the basin, holding the cigarette up to her mouth, watching the eye.

Then very slowly, deliberately, she put the cigarette between her lips and took a long suck. She inhaled deeply, and she held the smoke inside her lungs for three or four seconds; then suddenly, *whoosh*, out it came through her nostrils in two thin jets which struck the water in the basin, and billowed out over the surface in a thick blue cloud, enveloping the eye.

Landy was over by the door, with his back to her, waiting. 'Come on, Mrs Pearl,' he called.

'Don't look so cross, William,' she said softly. 'It isn't any good looking cross.'

Landy tuned his head to see what she was doing.

'Not any more it isn't,' she whispered. 'Because from now on, my pet, you're going to do just exactly what Mary tells you. Do you understand that?'

'Mrs Pearl,' Landy said, moving towards her.

'So don't be a naughty boy again, will you, my precious,' she said, taking another pull at the cigarette. 'Naughty boys are liable to get punished most severely nowadays, you ought to know that.

Landy was beside her now, and he took her by the arm and began drawing her firmly but gently away from the table.

'Good-bye, darling,' she called. 'I'll be back soon.'

'That's enough, Mrs Pearl.'

'Isn't he sweet?' she cried, looking up at Landy with big bright eyes. 'Isn't he heaven? I just can't wait to get him home.'

THE WAY UP TO HEAVEN

ALL HER LIFE, Mrs Foster had had an almost pathological fear of missing a train, a plane, a boat, or even a theatre curtain. In other respects, she was not a particularly nervous woman, but the mere thought of being late on occasions like these would throw her into such a state of nerves that she would begin to twitch. It was nothing much – just a tiny vellicating muscle in the corner of the left eye, like a secret wink – but the annoying thing was that it refused to disappear until an hour or so after the train or plane or whatever it was had been safely caught.

It was really extraordinary how in certain people a simple apprehension about a thing like catching a train can grow into a serious obsession. At least half an hour before it was time to leave the house for the station, Mrs Foster would step out of the elevator all ready to go, with hat and coat and gloves, and then, being quite unable to sit down, she would flutter and fidget about from room to room until her husband, who must have been well aware of her state, finally emerged from his privacy and suggested in a cool dry voice that perhaps they had better get going now, had they not?

Mr Foster may possibly have had a right to be irritated by this foolishness of his wife's, but he could have had no excuse for increasing her misery by keeping her waiting unnecessarily. Mind you, it is by no means certain that this is what he did, yet whenever they were to go somewhere, his timing was so accurate – just a minute or two late, you understand – and his manner so bland that it was hard to believe he wasn't purposely inflicting a nasty private little torture of his own on the unhappy lady. And one thing he must have known – that she would never dare to call out and tell him to hurry. He had disciplined her too well for that. He must also have known that if he was prepared to wait even beyond the last moment of safety, he could drive her nearly into hysterics. On one or two special occasions in the later years of their married life, it seemed almost as though he had *wanted* to miss the train simply in order to intensify the poor woman's suffering.

Assuming (though one cannot be sure) that the husband was guilty, what made his attitude doubly unreasonable was the fact that, with the exception of this one small irrepressible foible, Mrs Foster was and always had been a good and loving wife. For over thirty years, she had served him loyally and well. There was no doubt about this. Even she, a very modest woman, was aware of it, and although she had for years refused to let herself believe that Mr Foster would ever consciously torment her, there had been times recently when she had caught herself beginning to wonder.

Mr Eugene Foster, who was nearly seventy years old, lived with his wife in a large six-storey house in New York City, on East Sixty-second Street, and they had four servants. It was a gloomy place, and few people came to visit them. But on this particular morning in January, the house had come alive and there was a great deal of bustling about. One maid was distributing bundles of dust sheets to every room, while another was draping them over the furniture. The butler was bringing down suitcases and putting them in the hall. The cook kept popping up from the kitchen to have a word with the butler, and Mrs Foster herself, in an old-fashioned fur coat and with a black hat on the top of her head, was flying from room to room and pretending to supervise these operations. Actually, she was thinking of nothing at all except that she was going to miss her plane if her husband didn't come out of his study soon and get ready.

'What time is it, Walker?' she said to the butler as she passed him.

'It's ten minutes past nine, Madam.'

'And has the car come?'

'Yes, Madam, it's waiting. I'm just going to put the luggage in now.'

'It takes an hour to get to Idlewild,' she said. 'My plane leaves at eleven. I have to be there half an hour beforehand for the formalities. I shall be late. I just *know* I'm going to be late.'

'I think you have plenty of time, Madam,' the butler said kindly. 'I warned Mr Foster that you must leave at nine-fifteen. There's still another five minutes.'

'Yes, Walker, I know, I know. But get the luggage in quickly, will you please?'

She began walking up and down the hall, and whenever the butler came by, she asked him the time. This, she kept telling herself, was the *one* plane she must not miss. It had taken months to persuade her husband to allow her to go. If she missed it, he might easily decide that she should cancel the whole thing. And the trouble was that he insisted on coming to the airport to see her off.

'Dear God,' she said aloud, 'I'm going to miss it. I know, I know, I *know* I'm going to miss it.' The little muscle beside the left eye was twitching madly now. The eyes themselves were very close to tears.

'What time is it, Walker?'

'It's eighteen minutes past, Madam.'

'Now I really *will* miss it!' she cried. 'Oh, I wish he would come!'

This was an important journey for Mrs Foster. She was going all alone to Paris to visit her daughter, her only child, who was married to a Frenchman. Mrs Foster didn't care much for the Frenchman, but she was fond of her daughter, and, more than that, she had developed a great yearning to set eyes on her three grandchildren. She knew them only from the many photographs that she had received and that she kept putting up all over the house. They were beautiful, these children. She doted on them, and each time a new picture arrived she would carry it away and sit with it for a long time, staring at it lovingly and searching the small faces for signs of that old satisfying blood likeness that meant so much. And now, lately, she had come more and more to feel that she did not really wish to live out her days in a place where she could not be near these children, and have them visit her, and take them for walks, and buy them presents, and watch them grow. She knew, of course, that it was wrong and in a way disloyal to have thoughts like these while her husband was still alive. She knew also that although he was no longer active in his many enterprises, he would never consent to leave New York and live in Paris. It was a miracle that he had ever agreed to let her fly over there alone for six weeks to visit them. But, oh, how she wished she could live there always, and be close to them!

'Walker, what time is it?'

'Twenty-two minutes past, Madam.'

As he spoke, a door opened and Mr Foster came into the hall. He stood for a moment, looking intently at his wife, and she looked back at him — at this diminutive but still quite dapper old man with the huge bearded face that bore such an astonishing resemblance to those old photographs of Andrew Carnegie.

'Well,' he said, 'I suppose perhaps we'd better get going fairly soon if you want to catch that plane.'

'*Yes*, dear — *yes!* Everything's ready. The car's waiting.'

'That's good,' he said. With his head over to one side, he was watching her closely. He had a peculiar way of cocking the head and then moving it in a series of small, rapid jerks. Because of this and because he was clasping his hands up high in front of him, near the chest, he was somehow like a squirrel standing there – a quick clever old squirrel from the Park.

'Here's Walker with your coat, dear. Put it on.'

'I'll be with you in a moment,' he said. 'I'm just going to wash my hands.'

She waited for him, and the tall butler stood beside her, holding the coat and the hat.

'Walker, will I miss it?'

'No, Madam,' the butler said. 'I think you'll make it all right.'

Then Mr Foster appeared again, and the butler helped him on with his coat. Mrs Foster hurried outside and got into the hired Cadillac. Her husband came after her, but he walked down the steps of the house slowly, pausing halfway to observe the sky and to sniff the cold morning air.

'It looks a bit foggy,' he said as he sat down beside her in the car. 'And it's always worse out there at the airport. I shouldn't be surprised if the flight's cancelled already.'

'Don't say that, dear – *please.*'

They didn't speak again until the car had crossed over the river to Long Island.

'I arranged everything with the servants,' Mr Foster said. 'They're all going off today. I gave them half-pay for six weeks and told Walker I'd send him a telegram when we wanted them back.'

'Yes,' she said. 'He told me.'

'I'll move into the club tonight. It'll be a nice change staying at the club.'

'Yes, dear. I'll write to you.'

'I'll call in at the house occasionally to see that everything's all right and to pick up the mail.'

'But don't you really think Walker should stay there all the time to look after things?' she asked meekly.

'Nonsense. It's quite unnecessary. And anyway, I'd have to pay him full wages.'

'Oh yes,' she said. 'Of course.'

'What's more, you never know what people get up to when they're left alone in a house,' Mr Foster announced, and with that he took out a cigar and, after snipping off the end with a silver cutter, lit it with a gold lighter.

She sat still in the car with her hands clasped together tight under the rug.

'Will you write to me?' she asked.

'I'll see,' he said. 'But I doubt it. You know I don't hold with letter-writing unless there's something specific to say.'

'Yes, dear, I know. So don't you bother.'

They drove on, along Queen's Boulevard, and as they approached the flat marshland on which Idlewild is built, the fog began to thicken and the car had to slow down.

'Oh dear!' cried Mrs Foster. 'I'm *sure* I'm going to miss it now! What time is it?'

'Stop fussing,' the old man said. 'It doesn't matter anyway. It's bound to be cancelled now. They never fly in this sort of weather. I don't know why you bothered to come out.'

She couldn't be sure, but it seemed to her that there was suddenly a new note in his voice, and she turned to look at him. It was difficult to observe any change in his expression under all that hair. The mouth was what counted. She wished, as she had so often before, that she could see the mouth clearly. The eyes never showed anything except when he was in a rage.

'Of course,' he went on, 'if by any chance it *does* go, then I agree with you — you'll be certain to miss it now. Why don't you resign yourself to that?'

She turned away and peered through the window at the fog. It seemed to be getting thicker as they went along, and now she could only just make out the edge of the road and the margin of grassland beyond it. She knew that her husband was still looking at her. She glanced at him again, and this time she noticed with a kind of horror that he was staring intently at the little place in the corner of her left eye where she could feel the muscle twitching.

'Won't you?' he said.

'Won't I what?'

'Be sure to miss it now if it goes. We can't drive fast in this muck.'

He didn't speak to her any more after that. The car crawled on and on. The driver had a yellow lamp directed on to the edge of the road, and this helped him to keep going. Other lights, some white and some yellow, kept coming out of the fog towards them, and there was an especially bright one that followed close behind them all the time.

Suddenly, the driver stopped the car.

'There!' Mr Foster cried. 'We're stuck. I knew it.'

'No, sir,' the driver said, turning round. 'We made it. This is the airport.'

Without a word, Mrs Foster jumped out and hurried through the main entrance into the building. There was a mass of people inside, mostly disconsolate passengers standing around the ticket counters. She pushed her way through and spoke to the clerk.

'Yes,' he said. 'Your flight is temporarily postponed. But please don't go away. We're expecting this weather to clear any moment.'

She went back to her husband who was still sitting in the car and told him the news. 'But don't you wait, dear,' she said. 'There's no sense in that.'

'I won't,' he answered. 'So long as the driver can get me back. Can you get me back, driver?'

'I think so,' the man said.

'Is the luggage out?'

'Yes, sir.'

'Good-bye, dear,' Mrs Foster said, leaning into the car and giving her husband a small kiss on the coarse grey fur of his cheek.

'Good-bye,' he answered. 'Have a good trip.'

The car drove off, and Mrs Foster was left alone.

The rest of the day was a sort of nightmare for her. She sat for hour after hour on a bench, as close to the airline counter as possible, and every thirty minutes or so she would get up and ask the clerk if the situation had changed. She always received the same reply — that she must continue to wait, because the fog might blow away at any moment. It wasn't until after six in the evening that the loudspeakers finally announced that the flight had been postponed until eleven o'clock the next morning.

Mrs Foster didn't quite know what to do when she heard this news. She stayed sitting on her bench for at least another half-hour, wondering, in a tired, hazy sort of way, where she might go to spend the night. She hated to leave the airport. She didn't wish to see her husband. She was terrified that in one way or another he would eventually manage to prevent her from getting to France. She would have liked to remain just where she was, sitting on the bench the whole night through. That would be the safest. But she was already exhausted, and it didn't take her long to realize that this was a ridiculous thing for a elderly lady to do. So in the end she went to a phone and called the house.

Her husband, who was on the point of leaving for the club, answered it himself. She told him the news, and asked whether the servants were still there.

'They've all gone,' he said.

'In that case, dear, I'll just get myself a room somewhere for the night. And don't you bother yourself about it at all.'

'That would be foolish,' he said. 'You've got a large house here at your disposal. Use it.'

'But, dear, it's *empty*.'

'Then I'll stay with you myself.'

'There's no food in the house. There's nothing.'

'Then eat before you come in. Don't be so stupid, woman. Everything you do, you seem to want to make a fuss about it.'

'Yes,' she said. 'I'm sorry. I'll get myself a sandwich here, and then I'll come on in.'

Outside, the fog had cleared a little, but it was still a long, slow drive in the taxi, and she didn't arrive back at the house on Sixty-second Street until fairly late.

Her husband emerged from his study when he heard her coming in. 'Well,' he said, standing by the study door, 'how was Paris?'

'We leave at eleven in the morning,' she answered. 'It's definite '

'You mean if the fog clears.'

'It's clearing now. There's a wind coming up.'

'You look tired,' he said. 'You must have had an anxious day.'

'It wasn't very comfortable. I think I'll go straight to bed.'

'I've ordered a car for the morning,' he said. 'Nine o'clock.'

'Oh, thank you, dear. And I certainly hope you're not going to bother to come all the way out again to see me off.'

'No,' he said slowly. 'I don't think I will. But there's no reason why you shouldn't drop me at the club on your way.'

She looked at him, and at that moment he seemed to be standing a long way off from her, beyond some borderline. He was suddenly so small and far away that she couldn't be sure what he was doing, or what he was thinking, or even what he was.

'The club is downtown,' she said. 'It isn't on the way to the airport.'

'But you'll have plenty of time, my dear. Don't you want to drop me at the club?'

'Oh, yes – of course.'

'That's good. Then I'll see you in the morning at nine.'

She went up to her bedroom on the second floor, and she was so exhausted from her day that she fell asleep soon after she lay down.

Next morning, Mrs Foster was up early, and by eight-thirty she was downstairs and ready to leave.

Shortly after nine, her husband appeared. 'Did you make any coffee?' he asked.

'No, dear. I thought you'd get a nice breakfast at the club. The car is here. It's been waiting. I'm all ready to go.'

They were standing in the hall – they always seemed to be meeting in the hall nowadays – she with her hat and coat and purse, he in a curiously cut Edwardian jacket with high lapels.

'Your luggage?'

'It's at the airport.'

'Ah yes,' he said. 'Of course. And if you're going to take me to the club first, I suppose we'd better get going fairly soon, hadn't we?'

'Yes!' she cried. 'Oh, yes – please!'

'I'm just going to get a few cigars. I'll be right with you. You get in the car.'

She turned and went out to where the chauffeur was standing, and he opened the car door for her as she approached.

'What time is it?' she asked him.

'About nine-fifteen.'

Mr Foster came out five minutes later, and watching him as he walked slowly down the steps, she noticed that his legs were like goat's legs in those narrow stovepipe trousers that he wore. As on the day before, he paused halfway down to sniff the air and to examine the sky. The weather was still not quite clear, but there was a wisp of sun coming through the mist.

'Perhaps you'll be lucky this time,' he said as he settled himself beside her in the car.

'Hurry, please,' she said to the chauffeur. 'Don't bother about the rug. I'll arrange the rug. Please get going. I'm late.'

The man went back to his seat behind the wheel and started the engine.

'*Just* a moment!' Mr Foster said suddenly. 'Hold it a moment, chauffeur, will you?'

'What is it, dear?' She saw him searching the pockets of his overcoat.

'I had a little present I wanted you to take to Ellen,' he said. 'Now, where on earth is it? I'm sure I had it in my hand as I came down.'

'I never saw you carrying anything. What sort of present?'

'A little box wrapped up in white paper. I forgot to give it to you yesterday. I don't want to forget it today.'

'A little box!' Mrs Foster cried. 'I never saw any little box!' She began hunting frantically in the back of the car.

Her husband continued searching through the pockets of his coat. Then he unbuttoned the coat and felt around in his jacket. 'Confound it,' he said, 'I must've left it in my bedroom. I won't be a moment.'

'Oh, *please*!' she cried. 'We haven't got time! *Please* leave it! You can mail it. It's only one of those silly combs anyway. You're always giving her combs.'

'And what's wrong with combs, may I ask?' he said, furious that she should have forgotten herself for once.

'Nothing, dear, I'm sure. But . . .'

'Stay here!' he commanded. 'I'm going to get it.'

'Be quick, dear! Oh, *please* be quick!'

She sat still, waiting and waiting.

'Chauffeur, what time is it?'

The man had a wristwatch, which he consulted. 'I make it nearly nine-thirty.'

'Can we get to the airport in an hour?'

'Just about.'

At this point, Mrs Foster suddenly spotted a corner of something white wedged down in the crack of the seat on the side where her husband had been sitting. She reached over and pulled out a small paper-wrapped box, and at the same time she couldn't help noticing that it was wedged down firm and deep, as though with the help of a pushing hand.

'Here it is!' she cried. 'I've found it! Oh dear, and now he'll be up there for ever searching for it! Chauffeur, quickly — run in and call him down, will you please?'

The chauffeur, a man with a small rebellious Irish mouth, didn't care very much for any of this, but he climbed out of the car and went up the steps to the front door of the house. Then he turned and came back. 'Door's locked,' he announced. 'You got a key?'

'Yes — wait a minute.' She began hunting madly in her purse. The little face was screwed up tight with anxiety, the lips pushed outward like a spout.

'Here it is! No — I'll go myself. It'll be quicker. I know where he'll be.'

She hurried out of the car and up the steps to the front door, holding the key in one hand. She slid the key into the keyhole and was about to turn it — and then she stopped. Her head came up, and she stood there absolutely motionless, her whole body arrested right in the middle of all this hurry to turn the key and get into the house, and she waited — five, six, seven, eight, nine, ten seconds, she waited.

The way she was standing there, with her head in the air and the body so tense, it seemed as though she were listening for the repetition of some sound that she had heard a moment before from a place far away inside the house.

Yes – quite obviously she was listening. Her whole attitude was a *listening* one. She appeared actually to be moving one of her ears closer and closer to the door. Now it was right up against the door, and for still another few seconds she remained in that position, head up, ear to door, hand on key, about to enter but not entering, trying instead, or so it seemed, to hear and to analyse these sounds that were coming faintly from this place deep within the house.

Then, all at once, she sprang to life again. She withdrew the key from the door and came running back down the steps.

'It's too late!' she cried to the chauffeur. 'I can't wait for him, I simply can't. I'll miss the plane. Hurry now, driver, hurry! To the airport!'

The chauffeur, had he been watching her closely, might have noticed that her face had turned absolutely white and that the whole expression had suddenly altered. There was no longer that rather soft and silly look. A peculiar hardness had settled itself upon the features. The little mouth, usually so flabby, was now tight and thin, the eyes were bright, and the voice, when she spoke, carried a new note of authority.

'Hurry, driver, hurry!'

'Isn't your husband travelling with you?' the man asked, astonished.

'Certainly not! I was only going to drop him at the club. It won't matter. He'll understand. He'll get a cab. Don't sit there talking, man. *Get going!* I've got a plane to catch for Paris!'

With Mrs Foster urging him from the back seat, the man drove fast all the way, and she caught her plane with a few minutes to spare. Soon she was high up over the Atlantic, reclining comfortably in her aeroplane chair, listening to the hum of the motors, heading for Paris at last. The new mood was still with her. She felt remarkably strong and, in a queer sort of way, wonderful. She was a trifle breathless with it all, but this was more from pure astonishment at what she had done than anything else, and as the plane flew farther and farther away from New York and East Sixty-second Street, a great sense of calmness began to settle upon her. By the time she reached Paris, she was just as strong and cool and calm as she could wish.

She met her grandchildren, and they were even more beautiful in the flesh than in their photographs. They were like angels, she told herself, so beautiful they were. And every day she took them for walks, and fed them cakes, and bought them presents, and told them charming stories.

Once a week, on Tuesdays, she wrote a letter to her husband – a nice, chatty letter – full of news and gossip, which always ended with the words 'Now be sure to take your meals regularly, dear, although this is something I'm afraid you may not be doing when I'm not with you.'

When the six weeks were up, everybody was sad that she had to return to America, to her husband. Everybody, that is, except her. Surprisingly, she didn't seem to mind as much as one might have expected, and when she kissed them all good-bye, there was something in her manner and in the things she said that appeared to hint at the possibility of a return in the not too distant future.

However, like the faithful wife she was, she did not overstay her time. Exactly six weeks after she had arrived, she sent a cable to her husband and caught the plane back to New York.

Arriving at Idlewild, Mrs Foster was interested to observe that there was no car to meet her. It is possible that she might even have been a little amused. But she was extremely calm and did not overtip the porter who helped her into a taxi with her baggage.

New York was colder than Paris, and there were lumps of dirty snow lying in the gutters of the streets. The taxi drew up before the house on Sixty-second Street, and Mrs Foster persuaded the driver to carry her two large cases to the top of the steps. Then she paid him off and rang the bell. She waited, but there was no answer. Just to make sure, she rang again, and she could hear it tinkling shrilly far away in the pantry, at the back of the house. But still no one came.

So she took out her own key and opened the door herself.

The first thing she saw as she entered was a great pile of mail lying on the floor where it had fallen after being slipped through the letter box. The place was dark and cold. A dust sheet was still draped over the grandfather clock. In spite of the cold, the atmosphere was peculiarly oppressive, and there was a faint and curious odour in the air that she had never smelled before.

She walked quickly across the hall and disappeared for a moment around the corner to the left, at the back. There was something deliberate and purposeful about this action; she had the air of a woman who is off to investigate a rumour or to confirm a suspicion. And when she returned a few seconds later, there was a little glimmer of satisfaction on her face.

She paused in the centre of the hall, as though wondering what to do next. Then, suddenly, she turned and went across into her husband's study. On the desk she found his address book, and after hunting through it for a while she picked up the phone and dialled a number.

'Hello,' she said. 'Listen — this is Nine East Sixty-second Street ... Yes, that's right. Could you send someone round as soon as possible, do you think? Yes, it seems to be stuck between the second and third floors. At least, that's where the indicator's pointing ... Right away? Oh, that's very kind of you. You see, my legs aren't any too good for walking up a lot of stairs. Thank you so much. Good-bye.'

She replaced the receiver and sat there at her husband's desk, patiently waiting for the man who would be coming soon to repair the lift.

PARSON'S PLEASURE

Mr BOGGIS WAS DRIVING the car slowly, leaning back comfortably in the seat with one elbow resting on the sill of the open window. How beautiful the countryside, he thought; how pleasant to see a sign or two of summer once again. The primroses especially. And the hawthorn. The hawthorn was exploding white and pink and red along the hedges and the primroses were growing underneath in little clumps, and it was beautiful.

He took one hand off the wheel and lit himself a cigarette. The best thing now, he told himself, would be to make for the top of Brill Hill. He could see it about half a mile ahead. And that must be the village of Brill, that cluster of cottages among the trees right on the very summit. Excellent. Not many of his Sunday sections had a nice elevation like that to work from.

He drove up the hill and stopped the car just short of the summit on the outskirts of the village. Then he got out and looked around. Down below, the countryside was spread out before him like a huge green carpet. He could see for miles. It was perfect. He took a pad and pencil from his pocket, leaned against the back of the car, and allowed his practised eye to travel slowly over the landscape.

He could see one medium farmhouse over on the right, back in the fields, with a track leading to it from the road. There was another larger one beyond it. There was a house surrounded by tall elms that looked as though it might be a Queen Anne, and there were two likely farms away over on the left. Five places in all. That was about the lot in this direction.

Mr Boggis drew a rough sketch on his pad showing the position of each so that he'd be able to find them easily when he was down below, then he got back into the car and drove up through the village to the other side of the hill. From there he spotted six more possibles – five farms and one big white Georgian house. He studied the Georgian house through his binoculars. It had a clean prosperous look, and the garden was well ordered. That was a pity. He ruled it out immediately. There was no point in calling on the prosperous.

In this square then, in this section, there were ten possibles in all.
Ten was a nice number, Mr Boggis told himself. Just the right amount
for a leisurely afternoon's work. What time was it now? Twelve
o'clock. He would have liked a pint of beer in the pub before he
started, but on Sundays they didn't open until one. Very well, he
would have it later. He glanced at the notes on his pad. He decided to
take the Queen Anne first, the house with the elms. It had looked
nicely dilapidated through the binoculars. The people there could
probably do with some money. He was always lucky with Queen
Annes, anyway. Mr Boggis climbed back into the car, released the
handbrake, and began cruising slowly down the hill without the
engine.

Apart from the fact that he was at this moment disguised in the
uniform of a clergyman, there was nothing very sinister about Mr
Cyril Boggis. By trade he was a dealer in antique furniture, with his
own shop and showroom in the King's Road, Chelsea. His premises
were not large, and generally he didn't do a great deal of business, but
because he always bought cheap, very very cheap, and sold very very
dear, he managed to make quite a tidy little income every year. He
was a talented salesman, and when buying or selling a piece he could
slide smoothly into whichever mood suited the client best. He could
become grave and charming for the aged, obsequious for the rich,
sober for the godly, masterful for the weak, mischievous for the
widow, arch and saucy for the spinster. He was well aware of his gift,
using it shamelessly on every possible occasion; and often, at the end
of an unusually good performance, it was as much as he could do to
prevent himself from turning aside and taking a bow or two as the
thundering applause of the audience went rolling through the theatre.

In spite of this rather clownish quality of his, Mr Boggis was not a
fool. In fact, it was said of him by some that he probably knew as
much about French, English, and Italian furniture as anyone else in
London. He also had surprisingly good taste, and he was quick to
recognize and reject an ungraceful design, however genuine the article
might be. His real love, naturally, was for the work of the great
eighteenth-century English designers, Ince, Mayhew, Chippendale,
Robert Adam, Manwaring, Inigo Jones, Hepplewhite, Kent, Johnson,
George Smith, Lock, Sheraton, and the rest of them, but even with
these he occasionally drew the line. He refused, for example, to allow
a single piece from Chippendale's Chinese or Gothic period to come
into his showroom, and the same was true of some of the heavier
Italian designs of Robert Adam.

During the past few years, Mr Boggis had achieved considerable fame among his friends in the trade by his ability to produce unusual and often quite rare items with astonishing regularity. Apparently the man had a source of supply that was almost inexhaustible, a sort of private warehouse, and it seemed that all he had to do was to drive out to it once a week and help himself. Whenever they asked him where he got the stuff, he would smile knowingly and wink and murmur something about a little secret.

The idea behind Mr Boggis's little secret was a simple one, and it had come to him as a result of something that had happened on a certain Sunday afternoon nearly nine years before, while he was driving in the country.

He had gone out in the morning to visit his old mother, who lived in Sevenoaks, and on the way back the fanbelt on his car had broken, causing the engine to overheat and the water to boil away. He had got out of the car and walked to the nearest house, a smallish farm building about fifty yards off the road, and had asked the woman who answered the door if he could please have a jug of water.

While he was waiting for her to fetch it, he happened to glance in through the door to the living-room, and there, not five yards from where he was standing, he spotted something that made him so excited the sweat began to come out all over the top of his head. It was a large oak armchair of a type that he had only seen once before in his life. Each arm, as well as the panel at the back, was supported by a row of eight beautifully turned spindles. The back panel itself was decorated by an inlay of the most delicate floral design, and the head of a duck was carved to lie along half the length of either arm. Good God, he thought. This thing is late fifteenth century!

He poked his head in further through the door, and there, by heavens, was another of them on the other side of the fireplace!

He couldn't be sure, but two chairs like that must be worth at least a thousand pounds up in London. And oh, what beauties they were!

When the woman returned, Mr Boggis introduced himself and straight away asked if she would like to sell her chairs.

Dear me, she said. But why on earth should she want to sell her chairs?

No reason at all, except that he might be willing to give her a pretty nice price.

And how much would he give? They were definitely not for sale, but just out of curiosity, just for fun, you know, how much would he give?

Thirty-five pounds.

How much?

Thirty-five pounds.

Dear me, thirty-five pounds. Well, well, that was very interesting. She'd always thought they were valuable. They were very old. They were very comfortable too. She couldn't possibly do without them, not possibly. No, they were not for sale but thank you very much all the same.

They weren't really so very old, Mr Boggis told her, and they wouldn't be at all easy to sell, but it just happened that he had a client who rather liked that sort of thing. Maybe he could go up another two pounds – call it thirty-seven. How about that?

They bargained for half an hour, and of course in the end Mr Boggis got the chairs and agreed to pay her something less than a twentieth of their value.

That evening, driving back to London in his old station-wagon with the two fabulous chairs tucked away snugly in the back, Mr Boggis had suddenly been struck by what seemed to him to be a most remarkable idea.

Look here, he said. If there is good stuff in one farmhouse, then why not in others? Why shouldn't he search for it? Why shouldn't he comb the countryside? He could do it on Sundays. In that way, it wouldn't interfere with his work at all. He never knew what to do with his Sundays.

So Mr Boggis bought maps, large scale maps of all the counties around London, and with a fine pen he divided each of them up into a series of squares. Each of these squares covered an actual area of five miles by five, which was about as much territory, he estimated, as he could cope with on a single Sunday, were he to comb it thoroughly. He didn't want the towns and the villages. It was the comparatively isolated places, the large farmhouses and the rather dilapidated country mansions, that he was looking for; and in this way, if he did one square each Sunday, fifty-two squares a year, he would gradually cover every farm and every country house in the home counties.

But obviously there was a bit more to it than that. Country folk are a suspicious lot. So are the impoverished rich. You can't go about ringing their bells and expecting them to show you around their houses just for the asking, because they won't do it. That way you would never get beyond the front door. How then was he to gain admittance? Perhaps it would be best if he didn't let them know he was a dealer at all. He could be the telephone man, the plumber, the gas inspector. He could even be a clergyman. . . .

From this point on, the whole scheme began to take on a more practical aspect. Mr Boggis ordered a large quantity of superior cards on which the following legend was engraved:

THE REVEREND
CYRIL WINNINGTON BOGGIS

President of the Society   *In association with*
for the Preservation of   *The Victoria and*
Rare Furniture   *Albert Museum*

From now on, every Sunday, he was going to be a nice old parson spending his holiday travelling around on a labour of love for the 'Society', compiling an inventory of the treasures that lay hidden in the country homes of England. And who in the world was going to kick him out when they heard that one?

Nobody.

And then, once he was inside, if he happened to spot something he really wanted, well -- he knew a hundred different ways of dealing with that.

Rather to Mr Boggis's surprise, the scheme worked. In fact, the friendliness with which he was received in one house after another through the countryside was, in the beginning, quite embarrassing, even to him. A slice of cold pie, a glass of port, a cup of tea, a basket of plums, even a full sit-down Sunday dinner with the family, such things were constantly being pressed upon him. Sooner or later, of course, there had been some bad moments and a number of unpleasant incidents, but then nine years is more than four hundred Sundays, and that adds up to a great quantity of houses visited. All in all, it had been an interesting, exciting, and lucrative business.

And now it was another Sunday and Mr Boggis was operating in the country of Buckinghamshire, in one of the most northerly squares on his map, about ten miles from Oxford, and as he drove down the hill and headed for his first house, the dilapidated Queen Anne, he began to get the feeling that this was going to be one of his lucky days.

He parked the car about a hundred yards from the gates and got out to walk the rest of the way. He never liked people to see his car until after a deal was completed. A dear old clergyman and a large station-wagon somehow never seemed quite right together. Also the short walk gave him time to examine the property closely from the outside and to assume the mood most likely to be suitable for the occasion.

Mr Boggis strode briskly up the drive. He was a small fat-legged man with a belly. The face was round and rosy, quite perfect for the part, and the two large brown eyes that bulged out at you from this rosy face gave an impression of gentle imbecility. He was dressed in a black suit with the usual parson's dog-collar round his neck, and on his head a soft black hat. He carried an old oak walking-stick which lent him, in his opinion, a rather rustic easy-going air.

He approached the front door and rang the bell. He heard the sound of footsteps in the hall and the door opened and suddenly there stood before him, or rather above him, a gigantic woman dressed in riding-breeches. Even through the smoke of her cigarette he could smell the powerful odour of stables and horse manure that clung about her.

'Yes?' she asked, looking at him suspiciously. 'What is it you want?'

Mr Boggis, who half expected her to whinny any moment, raised his hat, made a little bow, and handed her his card. 'I do apologize for bothering you,' he said, and then he waited, watching her face as she read the message.

'I don't understand,' she said, handing back the card. 'What is it you want?'

Mr Boggis explained about the Society for the Preservation of Rare Furniture.

'This wouldn't by any chance be something to do with the Socialist Party?' she asked, staring at him fiercely from under a pair of pale bushy brows.

From then on, it was easy. A Tory in riding-breeches, male or female, was always a sitting duck for Mr Boggis. He spent two minutes delivering an impassioned eulogy on the extreme Right Wing of the Conservative Party, then two more denouncing the Socialists. As a clincher, he made particular reference to the Bill that the Socialists had once introduced for the abolition of bloodsports in the country, and went on to inform his listener that his idea of heaven – 'though you better not tell the bishop, my dear' – was a place where one could hunt the fox, the stag, and the hare with large packs of tireless hounds from morn till night every day of the week, including Sundays.

Watching her as he spoke, he could see the magic beginning to do its work. The woman was grinning now, showing Mr Boggis a set of enormous, slightly yellow teeth. 'Madam,' he cried, 'I beg of you, *please* don't get me started on Socialism.' At that point, she let out a great guffaw of laughter, raised an enormous red hand, and slapped him so hard on the shoulder that he nearly went over.

'Come in!' she shouted. 'I don't know what the hell you want, but come on in!'

Unfortunately, and rather surprisingly, there was nothing of any value in the whole house, and Mr Boggis, who never wasted time on barren territory, soon made his excuses and took his leave. The whole visit had taken less than fifteen minutes, and that, he told himself as he climbed back into his car and started off for the next place, was exactly as it should be.

From now on, it was all farmhouses, and the nearest was about half a mile up the road. It was a large half-timbered brick building of considerable age, and there was a magnificent pear tree still in blossom covering almost the whole of the south wall.

Mr Boggis knocked on the door. He waited, but no one came. He knocked again, but still there was no answer, so he wandered around the back to look for the farmer among the cowsheds. There was no one there either. He guessed that they must all still be in church, so he began peering in the windows to see if he could spot anything interesting. There was nothing in the dining-room. Nothing in the library either. He tried the next window, the living-room, and there, right under his nose, in the little alcove that the window made, he saw a beautiful thing, a semicircular card-table in mahogany, richly veneered, and in the style of Hepplewhite, built around 1780.

'Ah-ha,' he said aloud, pressing his face hard against the glass. 'Well done, Boggis.'

But that was not all. There was a chair there as well, a single chair, and if he were not mistaken it was of an even finer quality than the table. Another Hepplewhite, wasn't it? And oh, what a beauty! The lattices on the back were finely carved with the honeysuckle, the husk, and the paterae, the caning on the seat was original, the legs were very gracefully turned and the two back ones had that peculiar outward splay that meant so much. It was an exquisite chair. 'Before this day is done,' Mr Boggis said softly, 'I shall have the pleasure of sitting down upon that lovely seat.' He never bought a chair without doing this. It was a favourite test of his, and it was always an intriguing sight to see him lowering himself delicately into the seat, waiting for the 'give', expertly gauging the precise but infinitesimal degree of shrinkage that the years had caused in the mortice and dovetail joints.

But there was no hurry, he told himself. He would return here later. He had the whole afternoon before him.

The next farm was situated some way back in the fields, and in order to keep his car out of sight, Mr Boggis had to leave it on the road and walk about six hundred yards along a straight track that led directly into the back yard of the farmhouse. This place, he noticed as he approached, was a good deal smaller than the last, and he didn't hold out much hope for it. It looked rambling and dirty, and some of the sheds were clearly in bad repair.

There were three men standing in a close group in a corner of the yard, and one of them had two large black greyhounds with him, on leashes. When the men caught sight of Mr Boggis walking forward in his black suit and parson's collar, they stopped talking and seemed suddenly to stiffen and freeze, becoming absolutely still, motionless, three faces turned towards him, watching him suspiciously as he approached.

The oldest of the three was a stumpy man with a wide frog-mouth and small shifty eyes, and although Mr Boggis didn't know it, his name was Rummins and he was the owner of the farm.

The tall youth beside him, who appeared to have something wrong with one eye, was Bert, the son of Rummins.

The shortish flat-faced man with a narrow corrugated brow and immensely broad shoulders was Claud. Claud had dropped in on Rummins in the hope of getting a piece of pork or ham out of him from the pig that had been killed the day before. Claud knew about the killing -- the noise of it had carried far across the fields -- and he also knew that a man should have a government permit to do that sort of thing, and that Rummins didn't have one.

'Good afternoon,' Mr Boggis said. 'Isn't it a lovely day?'

None of the three men moved. At that moment they were all thinking precisely the same thing -- that somehow or other this clergyman, who was certainly not the local fellow, had been sent to poke his nose into their business and to report what he found to the government.

'What beautiful dogs,' Mr Boggis said. 'I must say I've never been greyhound-racing myself, but they tell me it's a fascinating sport.'

Again the silence, and Mr Boggis glanced quickly from Rummins to Bert, then to Claud, then back again to Rummins, and he noticed that each of them had the same peculiar expression on his face, something between a jeer and a challenge, with a contemptuous curl to the mouth and a sneer around the nose.

'Might I inquire if you are the owner?' Mr Boggis asked, undaunted, addressing himself to Rummins.

'What is it you want?'

'I do apologize for troubling you, especially on a Sunday.'

Mr Boggis offered his card and Rummins took it and held it up close to his face. The other two didn't move, but their eyes swivelled over to one side, trying to see.

'And what exactly might you be wanting?' Rummins asked.

For the second time that morning, Mr Boggis explained at some length the aims and ideals of the Society for the Preservation of Rare Furniture.

'We don't have any,' Rummins told him when it was over. 'You're wasting your time.'

'Now, just a minute, sir,' Mr Boggis said, raising a finger. 'The last man who said that to me was an old farmer down in Sussex, and when he finally let me into his house, d'you know what I found? A dirty-looking old chair in the corner of the kitchen, and it turned out to be worth *four hundred pounds*! I showed him how to sell it, and he bought himself a new tractor with the money.'

'What on earth are you talking about?' Claud said. 'There ain't no chair in the world worth four hundred pound.'

'Excuse me,' Mr Boggis answered primly, 'but there are plenty of chairs in England worth more than twice that figure. And you know where they are? They're tucked away in the farms and cottages all over the country, with the owners using them as steps and ladders and standing on them with hobnailed boots to reach a pot of jam out of the top cupboard or to hang a picture. This is the truth I'm telling you, my friends.'

Rummins shifted uneasily on his feet. 'You mean to say all you want to do is go inside and stand there in the middle of the room and look around?'

'Exactly,' Mr Boggis said. He was at last beginning to sense what the trouble might be. 'I don't want to pry into your cupboards or into your larder. I just want to look at the furniture to see if you happen to have any treasures here, and then I can write about them in our Society magazine.'

'You know what I think?' Rummins said, fixing him with his small wicked eyes. 'I think you're after buying the stuff yourself. Why else would you be going to all this trouble?'

'Oh, dear me. I only wish I had the money. Of course, if I saw something that I took a great fancy to, and it wasn't beyond my means, I might be tempted to make an offer. But alas, that rarely happens.'

'Well,' Rummins said, 'I don't suppose there's any harm in your taking a look around if that's all you want.' He led the way across the yard to the back door of the farmhouse, and Mr Boggis followed him; so did the son Bert, and Claud with his two dogs. They went through the kitchen, where the only furniture was a cheap deal table with a dead chicken lying on it, and they emerged into a fairly large, exceedingly filthy living-room.

And there it was! Mr Boggis saw it at once, and he stopped dead in his tracks and gave a little shrill gasp of shock. Then he stood there for five, ten, fifteen seconds at least, staring like an idiot, unable to believe, not daring to believe what he saw before him. It *couldn't* be true, not possibly! But the longer he stared, the more true it began to seem. After all, there it was standing against the wall right in front of him, as real and as solid as the house itself. And who in the world could possibly make a mistake about a thing like that? Admittedly it was painted white, but that made not the slightest difference. Some idiot had done that. The paint could easily be stripped off. But good God! Just look at it! And in a place like this!

At this point, Mr Boggis became aware of the three men, Rummins, Bert, and Claud, standing together in a group over by the fireplace, watching him intently. They had seen him stop and gasp and stare, and they must have seen his face turning red, or maybe it was white, but in any event they had seen enough to spoil the whole goddamn business if he didn't do something about it quick. In a flash, Mr Boggis clapped one hand over his heart, staggered to the nearest chair, and collapsed into it, breathing heavily.

'What's the matter with you?' Claud asked.

'It's nothing,' he gasped. 'I'll be all right in a minute. Please – a glass of water. It's my heart.'

Bert fetched him the water, handed it to him, and stayed close beside him, staring down at him with a fatuous leer on his face.

'I thought maybe you were looking at something,' Rummins said. The wide frog-mouth widened a fraction further into a crafty grin, showing the stubs of several broken teeth.

'No, no,' Mr Boggis said. 'Oh dear me, no. It's just my heart. I'm so sorry. It happens every now and then. But it goes away quite quickly. I'll be all right in a couple of minutes.'

He *must* have time to think, he told himself. More important still, he must have time to compose himself thoroughly before he said another word. Take it gently, Boggis. And whatever you do, keep calm. These people may be ignorant, but they are not stupid. They are suspicious and wary and sly. And if it is really true — no it *can't* be, it *can't* be true . . .

He was holding one hand up over his eyes in a gesture of pain, and now, very carefully, secretly, he made a little crack between two of the fingers and peeked through.

Sure enough, the thing was still there, and on this occasion he took a good long look at it. Yes — he had been right the first time! There wasn't the slightest doubt about it! It was really unbelievable!

What he saw was a piece of furniture that any expert would have given almost anything to acquire. To a layman, it might not have appeared particularly impressive, especially when covered over as it was with dirty white paint, but to Mr Boggis it was a dealer's dream. He knew, as does every other dealer in Europe and America, that among the most celebrated and coveted examples of eighteenth-century English furniture in existence are the three famous pieces known as 'The Chippendale Commodes'. He knew their history backwards — that the first was 'discovered' in 1920, in a house at Moreton-in-Marsh, and was sold at Sotheby's the same year; that the other two turned up in the same auction rooms a year later, both coming out of Raynham Hall, Norfolk. They all fetched enormous prices. He couldn't quite remember the exact figure for the first one, or even the second, but he knew for certain that the last one to be sold had fetched thirty-nine hundred guineas. And that was in 1921! Today the same piece would surely be worth ten thousand pounds. Some man, Mr Boggis couldn't remember his name, had made a study of these commodes fairly recently and had proved that all three must have come from the same workshop, for the veneers were all from the same log, and the same set of templates had been used in the construction of each. No invoices had been found for any of them, but all the experts were agreed that these three commodes could have been executed only by Thomas Chippendale himself, with his own hands, at the most exalted period in his career.

And here, Mr Boggis kept telling himself as he peered cautiously through the crack in his fingers, here was the fourth Chippendale Commode! And *he* had found it! He would be rich! He would also be famous! Each of the other three was known throughout the furniture world by a special name — The Chastleton Commode, The First Raynham Commode, The Second Raynham Commode. This one would go down in history as The Boggis Commode! Just imagine the faces of the boys up there in London when they got a look at it tomorrow morning! And the luscious offers coming in from the big fellows over in the West End – Frank Partridge, Mallet, Jetley, and the rest of them! There would be a picture of it in *The Times*, and it would say, 'The very fine Chippendale Commode which was recently discovered by Mr Cyril Boggis, a London dealer. . . .' Dear God, what a stir he was going to make!

This one here, Mr Boggis thought, was almost exactly similar to the Second Raynham Commode. (All three, the Chastleton and the two Raynhams, differed from one another in a number of small ways.) It was a most impressive handsome affair, built in the French rococo style of Chippendale's Directoire period, a kind of large fat chest-of-drawers set upon four carved and fluted legs that raised it about a foot from the ground. There were six drawers in all, two long ones in the middle and two shorter ones on either side. The serpentine front was magnificently ornamented along the top and sides and bottom, and also vertically between each set of drawers, with intricate carvings of festoons and scrolls and clusters. The brass handles, although partly obscured by white paint, appeared to be superb. It was, of course, a rather 'heavy' piece, but the design had been executed with such elegance and grace that the heaviness was in no way offensive.

'How're you feeling now?' Mr Boggis heard someone saying.

'Thank you, thank you, I'm much better already. It passes quickly. My doctor says it's nothing to worry about really so long as I rest for a few minutes whenever it happens. Ah yes,' he said, raising himself slowly to his feet. 'That's better. I'm all right now.'

A trifle unsteadily, he began to move around the room examining the furniture, one piece at a time, commenting upon it briefly. He could see at once that apart from the commode it was a very poor lot.

'Nice oak table,' he said. 'But I'm afraid it's not old enough to be of any interest. Good comfortable chairs, but quite modern, yes, quite modern. Now this cupboard, well, it's rather attractive, but again, not valuable. This chest-of-drawers' – he walked casually past the Chippendale Commode and gave it a little contemptuous flip with his fingers – 'worth a few pounds, I dare say, but no more. A rather crude reproduction, I'm afraid. Probably made in Victorian times. Did you paint it white?'

'Yes,' Rummins said, 'Bert did it.'

'A very wise move. It's considerably less offensive in white.'

'That's a strong piece of furniture,' Rummins said. 'Some nice carving on it too.'

'Machine-carved,' Mr Boggis answered superbly, bending down to examine the exquisite craftsmanship. 'You can tell it a mile off. But still, I suppose it's quite pretty in its way. It has its points.'

He began to saunter off, then he checked himself and turned slowly back again. He placed the tip of one finger against the point of his chin, laid his head over to one side, and frowned as though deep in thought.

'You know what?' he said, looking at the commode, speaking so casually that his voice kept trailing off. 'I've just remembered . . . I've been wanting a set of legs something like that for a long time. I've got a rather curious table in my own little home, one of those low things that people put in front of the sofa, sort of a coffee-table, and last Michaelmas, when I moved house, the foolish movers damaged the legs in the most shocking way. I'm very fond of that table. I always keep my big Bible on it, and all my sermon notes.'

He paused, stroking his chin with the finger. 'Now I was just thinking. These legs on your chest-of-drawers might be very suitable. Yes, they might indeed. They could easily be cut off and fixed on to my table.'

He looked around and saw the three men standing absolutely still, watching him suspiciously, three pairs of eyes, all different but equally mistrusting, small pig-eyes for Rummins, large slow eyes for Claud, and two odd eyes for Bert, one of them very queer and boiled and misty pale, with a little black dot in the centre, like a fish eye on a plate.

Mr Boggis smiled and shook his head. 'Come, come, what on earth am I saying? I'm talking as though I owned the piece myself. I do apologize.'

'What you mean to say is you'd like to buy it,' Rummins said.

'Well . . .' Mr Boggis glanced back at the commode, frowning. 'I'm not sure. I might . . . and then again . . . on second thoughts . . . no . . . I think it might be a bit too much trouble. It's not worth it. I'd better leave it.'

'How much were you thinking of offering?' Rummins asked.

'Not much, I'm afraid. You see, this is not a genuine antique. It's merely a reproduction.'

'I'm not so sure about that,' Rummins told him. 'It's been in *here* over twenty years, and before that it was up at the Manor House. I bought it there myself at auction when the old Squire died. You can't tell me that thing's new.'

'It's not exactly new, but it's certainly not more than about sixty years old.'

'It's more than that,' Rummins said. 'Bert, where's that bit of paper you once found at the back of one of them drawers? That old bill.'

The boy looked vacantly at his father.

Mr Boggis opened his mouth, then quickly shut it again without uttering a sound. He was beginning literally to shake with excitement, and to calm himself he walked over to the window and stared out at a plump brown hen pecking around for stray grains of corn in the yard.

'It was in the back of that drawer underneath all them rabbit-snares,' Rummins was saying. 'Go on and fetch it out and show it to the parson.'

When Bert went forward to the commode, Mr Boggis turned round again. He couldn't stand not watching him. He saw him pull out one of the big middle drawers, and he noticed the beautiful way in which the drawer slid open. He saw Bert's hand dipping inside and rummaging around among a lot of wires and strings.

'You mean this?' Bert lifted out a piece of folded yellowing paper and carried it over to the father, who unfolded it and held it up close to his face.

'You can't tell me this writing ain't bloody old,' Rummins said, and he held the paper out to Mr Boggis, whose whole arm was shaking as he took it. It was brittle and it cracked slightly between his fingers. The writing was in a long sloping copperplate hand:

Edward Montagu, Esq.   Dr
                                    To Thos. Chippendale
A large mahogany Commode Table of exceeding fine wood, very rich carvd, set upon fluted legs, two very neat shapd long drawers in the middle part and two ditto on each side, with rich chasd Brass Handles and Ornaments, the whole completely finished in the most exquisite taste...£87

Mr Boggis was holding on to himself tight and fighting to suppress the excitement that was spinning round inside him and making him dizzy. Oh God, it was wonderful! With the invoice, the value had climbed even higher. What in heaven's name would it fetch now? Twelve thousand pounds? Fourteen? Maybe fifteen or even twenty? Who knows?

Oh, boy!

He tossed the paper contemptuously on to the table and said quietly, 'It's exactly what I told you, a Victorian reproduction. This is simply the invoice that the seller – the man who made it and passed it off as an antique – gave to his client. I've seen lots of them. You'll notice that he doesn't say he made it himself. That would give the game away.'

'Say what you like,' Rummins announced, 'but that's an old piece of paper.'

'Of course it is, my dear friend. It's Victorian, late Victorian. About eighteen ninety. Sixty or seventy years old. I've seen hundreds of them. That was a time when masses of cabinet-makers did nothing else but apply themselves to faking the fine furniture of the century before.'

'Listen, Parson,' Rummins said, pointing at him with a thick dirty finger, 'I'm not saying as how you may not know a fair bit about this furniture business, but what I *am* saying is this: How on earth can you be so mighty sure it's a fake when you haven't even seen what it looks like underneath all that paint?'

'Come here,' Mr Boggis said. 'Come over here and I'll show you.' He stood beside the commode and waited for them to gather round. 'Now, anyone got a knife?'

Claud produced a horn-handled pocket knife, and Mr Boggis took it and opened the smallest blade. Then, working with apparent casualness but actually with extreme care, he began chipping off the white paint from a small area on the top of the commode. The paint flaked away cleanly from the old hard varnish underneath, and when he had cleared away about three square inches, he stepped back and said, 'Now, take a look at that!'

It was beautiful – a warm little patch of mahogany, glowing like a topaz, rich and dark with the true colour of its two hundred years.

'What's wrong with it?' Rummins asked.

'It's processed! Anyone can see that!'

'How can you see it, Mister? You tell us.'

'Well, I must say that's a trifle difficult to explain. It's chiefly a matter of experience. My experience tells me that without the slightest doubt this wood has been processed with lime. That's what they use for mahogany, to give it that dark aged colour. For oak, they use potash salts, and for walnut it's nitric acid, but for mahogany it's always lime.'

The three men moved a little closer to peer at the wood. There was a slight stirring of interest among them now. It was always intriguing to hear about some new form of crookery or deception.

'Look closely at the grain. You see that touch of orange in among the dark red-brown. That's the sign of lime.'

They leaned forward, their noses close to the wood, first Rummins, then Claud, then Bert.

'And then there's the patina,' Mr Boggis continued.

'The what?'

He explained to them the meaning of this word as applied to furniture.

'My dear friends, you've no idea the trouble these rascals will go to to imitate the hard beautiful bronze-like appearance of genuine patina. It's terrible, really terrible, and it makes me quite sick to speak of it!' He was spitting each word sharply off the tip of the tongue and making a sour mouth to show his extreme distaste. The men waited, hoping for more secrets.

'The time and trouble that some mortals will go to in order to deceive the innocent!' Mr Boggis cried. 'It's perfectly disgusting! D'you know what they did here, my friends? I can recognize it clearly. I can almost *see* them doing it, the long, complicated ritual of rubbing the wood with linseed oil, coating it over with french polish that has been cunningly coloured, brushing it down with pumice-stone and oil, bees-waxing it with a wax that contains dirt and dust, and finally giving it the heat treatment to crack the polish so that it looks like two-hundred-year-old varnish! It really upsets me to contemplate such knavery!'

The three men continued to gaze at the little patch of dark wood.

'Feel it!' Mr Boggis ordered. 'Put your fingers on it! There, how does it feel, warm or cold?'

'Feels cold,' Rummins said.

'Exactly, my friend! It happens to be a fact that faked patina is always cold to the touch. Real patina has a curiously warm feel to it.'

'This feels normal,' Rummins said, ready to argue.

'No, sir, it's cold. But of course it takes an experienced and sensitive finger-tip to pass a positive judgement. You couldn't really be expected to judge this any more than I could be expected to judge the quality of your barley. Everything in life, my dear sir, is experience.'

The men were staring at this queer moon-faced clergyman with the bulging eyes, not quite so suspiciously now because he did seem to know a bit about his subject. But they were still a long way from trusting him.

Mr Boggis bent down and pointed to one of the metal drawer-handles on the commode. 'This is another place where the fakers go to work,' he said. 'Old brass normally has a colour and character all of its own. Did you know that?'

They stared at him, hoping for still more secrets.

'But the trouble is that they've become exceedingly skilled at matching it. In fact it's almost impossible to tell the difference between "genuine old" and "faked old". I don't mind admitting that it has me guessing. So there's not really any point in our scraping the paint off these handles. We wouldn't be any the wiser.'

'How can you possibly make new brass look like old?' Claud said. 'Brass doesn't rust, you know.'

'You are quite right, my friend. But these scoundrels have their own secret methods.'

'Such as what?' Claud asked. Any information of this nature was valuable, in his opinion. One never knew when it might come in handy.

'All they have to do,' Mr Boggis said, 'is to place these handles overnight in a box of mahogany shavings saturated in sal ammoniac. The sal ammoniac turns the metal green, but if you rub off the green, you will find underneath it a fine soft silvery-warm lustre, a lustre identical to that which comes with very old brass. Oh, it is so bestial, the things they do! With iron they have another trick.'

'What do they do with iron?' Claud asked, fascinated.

'Iron's easy,' Mr Boggis said. 'Iron locks and plates and hinges are simply buried in common salt and they come out all rusted and pitted in no time.'

'All right,' Rummins said. 'So you admit you can't tell about the handles. For all you know, they may be hundreds and hundreds of years old. Correct?'

'Ah,' Mr Boggis whispered, fixing Rummins with two big bulging brown eyes. 'That's where you're wrong. Watch this.'

From his jacket pocket, he took out a small screwdriver. At the same time, although none of them saw him do it, he also took out a little brass screw which he kept well hidden in the palm of his hand. Then he selected one of the screws in the commode — there were four to each handle — and began carefully scraping all traces of white paint from its head. When he had done this, he started slowly to unscrew it.

'If this is a genuine old brass screw from the eighteenth century,' he was saying, 'the spiral will be slightly uneven and you'll be able to see quite easily that it has been hand-cut with a file. But if this brasswork is faked from more recent times, Victorian or later, then obviously the screw will be of the same period. It will be a mass-produced, machine-made article. Anyone can recognize a machine-made screw. Well, we shall see.'

It was not difficult, as he put his hands over the old screw and drew it out, for Mr Boggis to substitute the new one hidden in his palm. This was another little trick of his, and through the years it had proved a most rewarding one. The pockets of his clergyman's jacket were always stocked with a quantity of cheap brass screws of various sizes.

'There you are,' he said, handing the modern screw to Rummins. 'Take a look at that. Notice the exact evenness of the spiral? See it? Of course you do. It's just a cheap common little screw you yourself could buy today in any ironmonger's in the country.'

The screw was handed round from the one to the other, each examining it carefully. Even Rummins was impressed now.

Mr Boggis put the screwdriver back in his pocket together with the fine hand-cut screw that he'd taken from the commode, and then he turned and walked slowly past the three men towards the door.

'My dear friends,' he said, pausing at the entrance to the kitchen, 'it was so good of you to let me peep inside your little home — so kind. I do hope I haven't been a terrible old bore.'

Rummins glanced up from examining the screw. 'You didn't tell us what you were going to offer,' he said.

'Ah,' Mr Boggis said. 'That's quite right. I didn't, did I? Well, to tell you the honest truth, I think it's all a bit too much trouble. I think I'll leave it.'

'How much would you give?'

'You mean that you really wish to part with it?'

'I didn't say I wished to part with it. I asked you how much.'

Mr Boggis looked across at the commode, and he laid his head first to one side, then to the other, and he frowned, and pushed out his lips, and shrugged his shoulders, and gave a little scornful wave of the hand as though to say the thing was hardly worth thinking about really, was it?

'Shall we say . . . ten pounds. I think that would be fair.'

'Ten pounds!' Rummins cried. 'Don't be so ridiculous, Parson, *please!*'

'It's worth more'n that for firewood!' Claud said, disgusted.

'Look here at the bill!' Rummins went on, stabbing that precious document so fiercely with his dirty fore-finger that Mr Boggis became alarmed. 'It tells you exactly what it cost! Eighty-seven pounds! And that's when it was new. Now it's antique it's worth double!'

'If you'll pardon me, no, sir, it's not. It's a second-hand reproduction. But I'll tell you what, my friend — I'm being rather reckless, I can't help it — I'll go up as high as fifteen pounds. How's that?'

'Make it fifty,' Rummins said.

A delicious little quiver like needles ran all the way down the back of Mr Boggis's legs and then under the soles of his feet. He had it now. It was his. No question about that. But the habit of buying cheap, as cheap as it was humanly possible to buy, acquired by years of necessity and practice, was too strong in him now to permit him to give in so easily.

'My dear man,' he whispered softly, 'I only *want* the legs. Possibly I could find some use for the drawers later on, but the rest of it, the carcass itself, as your friend so rightly said, it's firewood, that's all.'

'Make it thirty-five,' Rummins said.

'I *couldn't* sir, I *couldn't!* It's not worth it. And I simply mustn't allow myself to haggle like this about a price. It's all wrong. I'll make you one final offer, and then I must go. Twenty pounds.'

'I'll take it,' Rummins snapped. 'It's yours.'

'Oh dear,' Mr Boggis said, clasping his hands. 'There I go again I should never have started this in the first place.'

'You can't back out now, Parson. A deal's a deal.'

'Yes, yes, I know.'

'How're you going to take it?'

'Well, let me see. Perhaps if I were to drive my car up into the yard, you gentlemen would be kind enough to help me load it?'

'In a car? This thing'll never go in a car! You'll need a truck for this!'

'I don't think so. Anyway, we'll see. My car's on the road. I'll be back in a jiffy. We'll manage it somehow, I'm sure.'

Mr Boggis walked out into the yard and through the gate and then down the long track that led across the field towards the road. He found himself giggling quite uncontrollably, and there was a feeling inside him as though hundreds and hundreds of tiny bubbles were rising up from his stomach and bursting merrily in the top of his head, like sparkling-water. All the buttercups in the field were suddenly turning into golden sovereigns, glistening in the sunlight. The ground was littered with them, and he swung off the track on to the grass so that he could walk among them and tread on them and hear the little metallic tinkle they made as he kicked them around with his toes. He was finding it difficult to stop himself from breaking into a run. But clergymen never run; they walk slowly. Walk slowly, Boggis. Keep calm, Boggis. There's no hurry now. The commode is yours! Yours for twenty pounds, and it's worth fifteen or twenty thousand! The Boggis Commode! In ten minutes it'll be loaded into your car — it'll go in easily — and you'll be driving back to London and singing all the way!

Mr Boggis driving the Boggis Commode home in the Boggis car. Historic occasion. What *wouldn't* a newspaperman give to get a picture of that! Should he arrange it? Perhaps he should. Wait and see. Oh, glorious day! Oh, lovely sunny summer day! Oh, glory be!

Back in the farmhouse, Rummins was saying, 'Fancy that old bastard giving twenty pound for a load of junk like this.'

'You did very nicely, Mr Rummins,' Claud told him. 'You think he'll pay you?'

'We don't put it in the car till he do.'

'And what if it won't go in the car?' Claud asked. 'You know what I think, Mr Rummins? You want my honest opinion? I think the bloody thing's too big to go in the car. And then what happens? Then he's going to say to hell with it and just drive off without it and you'll never see him again. Nor the money either. He didn't seem all that keen on having it, you know.'

Rummins paused to consider this new and rather alarming prospect.

'How can a thing like that possibly go in a car?' Claud went on relentlessly. 'A parson never has a big car anyway. You ever seen a parson with a big car, Mr Rummins?'

'Can't say I have.'

'Exactly! And now listen to me. I've got an idea. He told us, didn't he, that it was only the legs he was wanting. Right? So all we've got to do is to cut 'em off quick right here on the spot before he comes back, then it'll be sure to go in the car. All we're doing is saving him the trouble of cutting them off himself when he gets home. How about it, Mr Rummins?' Claud's flat bovine face glimmered with a mawkish pride.

'It's not such a bad idea at that,' Rummins said, looking at the commode. 'In fact it's a bloody good idea. Come on then, we'll have to hurry. You and Bert carry it out into the yard. I'll get the saw. Take the drawers out first.'

Within a couple of minutes, Claud and Bert had carried the commode outside and had laid it upside down in the yard amidst the chicken droppings and cow dung and mud. In the distance, half-way across the field, they could see a small black figure striding along the path towards the road. They paused to watch. There was something rather comical about the way in which this figure was conducting itself. Every now and again it would break into a trot, then it did a kind of hop, skip, and jump, and once it seemed as though the sound of a cheerful song came rippling faintly to them from across the meadow.

'I reckon he's balmy,' Claud said, and Bert grinned darkly, rolling his misty eye slowly round in its socket.

Rummins came waddling over from the shed, squat and froglike, carrying a long saw. Claud took the saw away from him and went to work.

'Cut 'em close,' Rummins said. 'Don't forget he's going to use 'em on another table.'

The mahogany was hard and very dry, and as Claud worked, a fine red dust sprayed out from the edge of the saw and fell softly to the ground. One by one, the legs came off, and when they were all severed, Bert stooped down and arranged them carefully in a row.

Claud stepped back to survey the results of his labour. There was a longish pause.

'Just let me ask you one question, Mr Rummins,' he said slowly. 'Even now, could *you* put that enormous thing into the back of a car?'

'Not unless it was a van.'

'Correct!' Claud cried. 'And parsons don't have vans, you know. All they've got usually is piddling little Morris Eights or Austin Sevens.'

'The legs is all he wants,' Rummins said. 'If the rest of it won't go in, then he can leave it. He can't complain. He's got the legs.'

'Now you know better'n that, Mr Rummins,' Claud said patiently. 'You know damn well he's going to start knocking the price if he don't get every single bit of this into the car. A parson's just as cunning as the rest of 'em when it comes to money, don't you make any mistake about that. Especially this old boy. So why don't we give him his firewood now and be done with it. Where d'you keep the axe?'

'I reckon that's fair enough,' Rummins said. 'Bert, go fetch the axe.'

Bert went into the shed and fetched a tall woodcutter's axe and gave it to Claud. Claud spat on the palms of his hands and rubbed them together. Then, with a long-armed high-swinging action, he began fiercely attacking the legless carcass of the commode.

It was hard work, and it took several minutes before he had the whole thing more or less smashed to pieces.

'I'll tell you one thing,' he said, straightening up, wiping his brow. 'That was a bloody good carpenter put this job together and I don't care what the parson says.'

'We're just in time!' Rummins called out. 'Here he comes!'

MRS BIXBY AND THE COLONEL'S COAT

AMERICA IS THE LAND of opportunities for women. Already they own about eighty-five per cent of the wealth of the nation. Soon they will have it all. Divorce has become a lucrative process, simple to arrange and easy to forget; and ambitious females can repeat it as often as they please and parlay their winnings to astronomical figures. The husband's death also brings satisfactory rewards and some ladies prefer to rely upon this method. They know that the waiting period will not be unduly protracted, for overwork and hypertension are bound to get the poor devil before long, and he will die at his desk with a bottle of benzedrines in one hand and a packet of tranquillizers in the other.

Succeeding generations of youthful American males are not deterred in the slightest by this terrifying pattern of divorce and death. The higher the divorce rate climbs, the more eager they become. Young men marry like mice, almost before they have reached the age of puberty, and a large proportion of them have at least two ex-wives on the payroll by the time they are thirty-six years old. To support these ladies in the manner to which they are accustomed, the men must work like slaves, which is of course precisely what they are. But now at last, as they approach their premature middle age, a sense of disillusionment and fear begins to creep slowly into their hearts, and in the evenings they take to huddling together in little groups, in clubs and bars, drinking their whiskies and swallowing their pills, and trying to comfort one another with stories.

The basic theme of these stories never varies. There are always three main characters – the husband, the wife, and the dirty dog. The husband is a decent clean-living man, working hard at his job. The wife is cunning, deceitful, and lecherous, and she is invariably up to some sort of jiggery-pokery with the dirty dog. The husband is too good a man even to suspect her. Things look black for the husband. Will the poor man ever find out? Must he be a cuckold for the rest of his life? Yes, he must. But wait! Suddenly, by a brilliant manoeuvre, the husband completely turns the tables on his monstrous spouse. The woman is flabbergasted, stupefied, humiliated, defeated. The audience of men around the bar smiles quietly to itself and takes a little comfort from the fantasy.

There are many of these stories going around, these wonderful wishful thinking dreamworld inventions of the unhappy male, but most of them are too fatuous to be worth repeating, and far too fruity to be put down on paper. There is one, however, that seems to be superior to the rest, particularly as it has the merit of being true. It is extremely popular with twice- or thrice-bitten males in search of solace, and if you are one of them, and if you haven't heard it before, you may enjoy the way it comes out. The story is called 'Mrs Bixby and the Colonel's Coat', and it goes something like this:

Mr and Mrs Bixby lived in a smallish apartment somewhere in New York City. Mr Bixby was a dentist who made an average income. Mrs Bixby was a big vigorous woman with a wet mouth. Once a month, always on Friday afternoons, Mrs Bixby would board the train at Pennsylvania Station and travel to Baltimore to visit her old aunt. She would spend the night with the aunt and return to New York on the following day in time to cook supper for her husband. Mr Bixby accepted this arrangement good-naturedly. He knew that Aunt Maude lived in Baltimore, and that his wife was very fond of the old lady, and certainly it would be unreasonable to deny either of them the pleasure of a monthly meeting.

'Just so long as you don't ever expect me to accompany you,' Mr Bixby had said in the beginning.

'Of course not, darling,' Mrs Bixby had answered. 'After all, she is not *your* aunt. She's mine.'

So far so good.

As it turned out, however, the aunt was little more than a convenient alibi for Mrs Bixby. The dirty dog, in the shape of a gentleman known as the Colonel, was lurking slyly in the background, and our heroine spent the greater part of her Baltimore time in this scoundrel's company. The Colonel was exceedingly wealthy. He lived in a charming house on the outskirts of town. No wife or family encumbered him, only a few discreet and loyal servants, and in Mrs Bixby's absence he consoled himself by riding his horses and hunting the fox.

Year after year, this pleasant alliance between Mrs Bixby and the Colonel continued without a hitch. They met so seldom – twelve times a year is not much when you come to think of it – that there was little or no chance of their growing bored with one another.

On the contrary, the long wait between meetings only made the heart grow fonder, and each separate occasion became an exciting re-union.

'Tally-ho!' the Colonel would cry each time he met her at the station in the big car. 'My dear, I'd almost forgotten how ravishing you looked. Let's go to earth.'

Eight years went by.

It was just before Christmas, and Mrs Bixby was standing on the station in Baltimore waiting for the train to take her back to New York. This particular visit which had just ended had been more than usually agreeable, and she was in a cheerful mood. But then the Colonel's company always did that to her these days. The man had a way of making her feel that she was altogether a rather remarkable woman, a person of subtle and exotic talents, fascinating beyond measure; and what a very different thing that was from the dentist husband at home who never succeeded in making her feel that she was anything but a sort of eternal patient, someone who dwelt in the waiting-room, silent among the magazines, seldom if ever nowadays to be called in to suffer the finicky precise ministrations of those clean pink hands.

'The Colonel asked me to give you this,' a voice beside her said. She turned and saw Wilkins, the Colonel's groom, a small wizened dwarf with grey skin, and he was pushing a large flattish cardboard box into her arms.

'Good gracious me!' she cried, all of a flutter. 'My heavens, what an enormous box! What is it, Wilkins? Was there a message? Did he send me a message?'

'No message,' the groom said, and he walked away.

As soon as she was on the train, Mrs Bixby carried the box into the privacy of the Ladies' Room and locked the door. How exciting this was! A Christmas present from the Colonel. She started to undo the string. 'I'll bet it's a dress,' she said aloud. 'It might even be two dresses. Or it might be a whole lot of beautiful underclothes. I won't look. I'll just feel around and try to guess what it is. I'll try to guess the colour as well, and exactly what it looks like. Also how much it cost.'

She shut her eyes tight and slowly lifted off the lid. Then she put one hand down into the box. There was some tissue paper on top; she could feel it and hear it rustling. There was also an envelope or a card of some sort. She ignored this and began burrowing underneath the tissue paper, the fingers reaching out delicately, like tendrils.

'My God,' she cried suddenly. 'It can't be true!'

She opened her eyes wide and stared at the coat. Then she pounced on it and lifted it out of the box. Thick layers of fur made a lovely noise against the tissue paper as they unfolded, and when she held it up and saw it hanging to its full length, it was so beautiful it took her breath away.

Never had she seen mink like this before. It *was* mink, wasn't it? Yes, of course it was. But what a glorious colour! The fur was almost pure black. At first she thought it *was* black; but when she held it closer to the window she saw that there was a touch of blue in it as well, a deep rich blue, like cobalt. Quickly she looked at the label. It said simply, WILD LABRADOR MINK. There was nothing else, no sign of where it had been bought or anything. But that, she told herself, was probably the Colonel's doing. The wily old fox was making darn sure he didn't leave any tracks. Good for him. But what in the world could it have cost? She hardly dared to think. Four, five, six thousand dollars? Possibly more.

She just couldn't take her eyes off it. Nor, for that matter, could she wait to try it on. Quickly she slipped off her own plain red coat. She was panting a little now, she couldn't help it, and her eyes were stretched very wide. But oh God, the feel of that fur! And those huge wide sleeves with their thick turned-up cuffs! Who was it had once told her that they always used female skins for the arms and male skins for the rest of the coat? Someone had told her that. Joan Rutfield, probably; though how *Joan* would know anything about *mink* she couldn't imagine.

The great black coat seemed to slide on to her almost of its own accord, like a second skin. Oh boy! It was the queerest feeling! She glanced into the mirror. It was fantastic. Her whole personality had suddenly changed completely. She looked dazzling, radiant, rich, brilliant, voluptuous, all at the same time. And the sense of power that it gave her! In this coat she could walk into any place she wanted and people would come scurrying around her like rabbits. The whole thing was just too wonderful for words!

Mrs Bixby picked up the envelope that was still lying in the box. She opened it and pulled out the Colonel's letter:

I once heard you saying you were fond of mink so I got you this. I'm told it's a good one. Please accept it with my sincere good wishes as a parting gift. For my own personal reasons I shall not be able to see you any more. Good-bye and good luck.

Well!

Imagine that!

Right out of the blue, just when she was feeling so happy.

No more Colonel.

What a dreadful shock.

She would miss him enormously.

Slowly, Mrs Bixby began stroking the lovely soft black fur of the coat.

What you lose on the swings you get back on the roundabouts.

She smiled and folded the letter, meaning to tear it up and throw it out of the window, but in folding it she noticed that there was something written on the other side:

ps. Just tell them that nice generous aunt of yours gave it to you for Christmas.

Mrs Bixby's mouth, at that moment stretched wide in a silky smile, snapped back like a piece of elastic.

'The man must be mad!' she cried. 'Aunt Maude doesn't have that sort of money. She couldn't possibly give me this.'

But if Aunt Maude didn't give it to her, then who did?

Oh God! In the excitement of finding the coat and trying it on, she had completely overlooked this vital aspect.

In a couple of hours she would be in New York. Ten minutes after that she would be home, and the husband would be there to greet her; and even a man like Cyril, dwelling as he did in a dark phlegmy world of root canals, bicuspids, and caries, would start asking a few questions if his wife suddenly waltzed in from a week-end wearing a six-thousand-dollar mink coat.

You know what I think, she told herself. I think that goddamn Colonel has done this on purpose just to torture me. He knew perfectly well Aunt Maude didn't have enough money to buy this. He knew I wouldn't be able to keep it.

But the thought of parting with it now was more than Mrs Bixby could bear.

'I've *got* to have this coat!' she said aloud. 'I've got to have this coat! I've got to have this coat!'

Very well, my dear. You shall have the coat. But don't panic. Sit still and keep calm and start thinking. You're a clever girl, aren't you? You've fooled him before. The man never has been able to see much further than the end of his own probe, you know that. So just sit absolutely still and *think*. There's lots of time.

Two and a half hours later, Mrs Bixby stepped off the train at Pennsylvania Station and walked quietly to the exit. She was wearing her old red coat again now and carrying the cardboard box in her arms. She signalled for a taxi.

'Driver,' she said, 'would you know of a pawnbroker that's still open around here?'

The man behind the wheel raised his brows and looked back at her, amused.

'Plenty along Sixth Avenue,' he answered.

'Stop at the first one you see, then, will you please?' She got in and was driven away.

Soon the taxi pulled up outside a shop that had three brass balls hanging over the entrance.

'Wait for me, please,' Mrs Bixby said to the driver, and she got out of the taxi and entered the shop.

There was an enormous cat crouching on the counter eating fishheads out of a white saucer. The animal looked up at Mrs Bixby with bright yellow eyes, then looked away again and went on eating. Mrs Bixby stood by the counter, as far away from the cat as possible, waiting for someone to come, staring at the watches, the shoe buckles, the enamel brooches, the old binoculars, the broken spectacles, the false teeth. Why did they always pawn their teeth, she wondered.

'Yes?' the proprietor said, emerging from a dark place in the back of the shop.

'Oh, good evening,' Mrs Bixby said. She began to untie the string around the box. The man went up to the cat and started stroking it along the top of its back, and the cat went on eating the fishheads.

'Isn't it silly of me?' Mrs Bixby said. 'I've gone and lost my pocketbook, and this being Saturday, the banks are all closed until Monday and I've simply got to have some money for the week-end. This is quite a valuable coat, but I'm not asking much. I only want to borrow enough on it to tide me over till Monday. Then I'll come back and redeem it.'

The man waited, and said nothing. But when she pulled out the mink and allowed the beautiful thick fur to fall over the counter, his eyebrows went up and he drew his hand away from the cat and came over to look at it. He picked it up and held it out in front of him.

'If only I had a watch on me or a ring,' Mrs Bixby said, 'I'd give you that instead. But the fact is I don't have a thing with me other than this coat.' She spread out her fingers for him to see.

'It looks new,' the man said, fondling the soft fur.

'Oh yes, it is. But, as I said, I only want to borrow enough to tide me over till Monday. How about fifty dollars?'

'I'll loan you fifty dollars.'

'It's worth a hundred times more than that, but I know you'll take good care of it until I return.'

The man went over to a drawer and fetched a ticket and placed it on the counter. The ticket looked like one of those labels you tie on to the handle of your suitcase, the same shape and size exactly, and the same stiff brownish paper. But it was perforated across the middle so that you could tear it in two, and both halves were identical.

'Name?' he asked.

'Leave that out. And the address.'

She saw the man pause, and she saw the nib of the pen hovering over the dotted line, waiting.

'You don't *have* to put the name and address, do you?'

The man shrugged and shook his head and the pen-nib moved on down to the next line.

'It's just that I'd rather not,' Mrs Bixby said. 'It's purely personal.'

'You'd better not lose this ticket, then.'

'I won't lose it.'

'You realize that anyone who gets hold of it can come in and claim the article?'

'Yes, I know that.'

'Simply on the number.'

'Yes, I know.'

'What do you want me to put for a description?'

'No description either, thank you. It's not necessary. Just put the amount I'm borrowing.'

The pen-nib hesitated again, hovering over the dotted line beside the word ARTICLE.

'I think you ought to put a description. A description is always a help if you want to sell the ticket. You never know, you might want to sell it sometime.'

'I don't want to sell it.'

'You might have to. Lots of people do.'

'Look,' Mrs Bixby said. 'I'm not broke, if that's what you mean. I simply lost my purse. Don't you understand?'

'You have it your own way then,' the man said. 'It's your coat.'

At this point an unpleasant thought struck Mrs Bixby. 'Tell me something,' she said. 'If I don't have a description on my ticket, how can I be sure you'll give me back the coat and not something else when I return?'

'It goes in the books.'

'But all I've got is a number. So actually you could hand me any old thing you wanted, isn't that so?'

'Do you want a description or don't you?' the man asked.

'No,' she said. 'I trust you.'

The man wrote 'fifty dollars' opposite the word VALUE on both sections of the ticket, then he tore it in half along the perforations and slid the lower portion across the counter. He took a wallet from the inside pocket of his jacket and extracted five ten-dollar bills. 'The interest is three per cent a month,' he said.

'Yes, all right. And thank you. You'll take good care of it, won't you?'

The man nodded but said nothing.

'Shall I put it back in the box for you?'

'No,' the man said.

Mrs Bixby turned and went out of the shop on to the street where the taxi was waiting. Ten minutes later, she was home.

'Darling,' she said as she bent over and kissed her husband. 'Did you miss me?'

Cyril Bixby laid down the evening paper and glanced at the watch on his wrist. 'It's twelve and a half minutes past six,' he said. 'You're a bit late, aren't you?'

'I know. It's those dreadful trains. Aunt Maude sent you her love as usual. I'm dying for a drink, aren't you?'

The husband folded his newspaper into a neat rectangle and placed it on the arm of his chair. Then he stood up and crossed over to the sideboard. His wife remained in the centre of the room pulling off her gloves, watching him carefully, wondering how long she ought to wait. He had his back to her now, bending forward to measure the gin, putting his face right up close to the measurer and peering into it as though it were a patient's mouth.

It was funny how small he always looked after the Colonel. The Colonel was huge and bristly, and when you were near to him he smelled faintly of horseradish. This one was small and neat and bony and he didn't really smell of anything at all, except peppermint drops, which he sucked to keep his breath nice for the patients.

'See what I've bought for measuring the vermouth,' he said, holding up a calibrated glass beaker. 'I can get it to the nearest milligram with this.'

'Darling, how clever.'

I really must try to make him change the way he dresses, she told herself. His suits are just too ridiculous for words. There had been a time when she thought they were wonderful, those Edwardian jackets with high lapels and six buttons down the front, but now they merely seemed absurd. So did the narrow stovepipe trousers. You had to have a special sort of face to wear things like that, and Cyril just didn't have it. His was a long bony countenance with a narrow nose and a slightly prognathous jaw, and when you saw it coming up out of the top of one of those tightly fitting old-fashioned suits it looked like a caricature of Sam Weller. He probably thought it looked like Beau Brummel. It was a fact that in the office he invariably greeted female patients with his white coat unbuttoned so that they would catch a glimpse of the trappings underneath; and in some obscure way this was obviously meant to convey the impression that he was a bit of a dog. But Mrs Bixby knew better. The plumage was a bluff. It meant nothing. It reminded her of an ageing peacock strutting on the lawn with only half its feathers left. Or one of those fatuous self-fertilizing flowers — like the dandelion. A dandelion never has to get fertilized for the setting of its seed, and all those brilliant yellow petals are just a waste of time, a boast, a masquerade. What's the word the biologists use? Subsexual. A dandelion is subsexual. So, for that matter, are the summer broods of water fleas. It sounds a bit like Lewis Carroll, she thought — water fleas and dandelions and dentists.

'Thank you, darling,' she said, taking the Martini and seating herself on the sofa with her handbag on her lap. 'And what did *you* do last night?'

'I stayed on in the office and cast a few inlays. I also got my accounts up to date.'

'Now really, Cyril, I think it's high time you let other people do your donkey work for you. You're much too important for that sort of thing. Why don't you give the inlays to the mechanic?'

'I prefer to do them myself. I'm extremely proud of my inlays.'

'I know you are, darling, and I think they're absolutely wonderful. They're the best inlays in the whole world. But I don't want you to burn yourself out. And why doesn't that Pulteney woman do the accounts? That's part of her job, isn't it?'

'She does do them. But I have to price everything up first. She doesn't know who's rich and who isn't.'

'This Martini is perfect,' Mrs Bixby said, setting down her glass on the side table. 'Quite perfect.' She opened her bag and took out a handkerchief as if to blow her nose. 'Oh look!' she cried, seeing the ticket. 'I forgot to show you this! I found it just now on the seat of my taxi. It's got a number on it, and I thought it might be a lottery ticket or something, so I kept it.'

She handed the small piece of stiff brown paper to her husband who took it in his fingers and began examining it minutely from all angles, as though it were a suspect tooth.

'You know what this is?' he said slowly.

'No dear, I don't.'

'It's a pawn ticket.'

'A what?'

'A ticket from a pawnbroker. Here's the name and address of the shop – somewhere on Sixth Avenue.'

'Oh dear, I *am* disappointed. I was hoping it might be a ticket for the Irish Sweep.'

'There's no reason to be disappointed,' Cyril Bixby said. 'As a matter of fact this could be rather amusing.'

'Why could it be amusing, darling?'

He began explaining to her exactly how a pawn ticket worked, with particular reference to the fact that anyone possessing the ticket was entitled to claim the article. She listened patiently until he had finished his lecture.

'You think it's worth claiming?' she asked.

'I think it's worth finding out what it is. You see this figure of fifty dollars that's written here? You know what that means?'

'No, dear, what does it mean?'

'It means that the item in question is almost certain to be something quite valuable.'

'You mean it'll be worth fifty dollars?'

'More like five hundred.'

'Five hundred!'

'Don't you understand?' he said. 'A pawnbroker never gives you more than about a tenth of the real value.'

'Good gracious! I never knew that.'

'There's a lot of things you don't know, my dear. Now you listen to me. Seeing that there's no name and address of the owner . . .'

'But surely there's something to say who it belongs to?'

'Not a thing. People often do that. They don't want anyone to know they've been to a pawnbroker. They're ashamed of it.'

'Then you think we can keep it?'

'Of course we can keep it' This is now *our* ticket.'

'You mean *my* ticket,' Mrs Bixby said firmly. 'I found it.'

'My dear girl, what *does* it matter? The important thing is that we are now in a position to go and redeem it any time we like for only fifty dollars. How about that?'

'Oh, what fun!' she cried. 'I think it's terribly exciting, especially when we don't even know what it is. It could be *anything*, isn't that right, Cyril? Absolutely anything!'

'It could indeed, although it's most likely to be either a ring or a watch.'

'But wouldn't it be marvellous if it was a *real* treasure? I mean something *really* old, like a wonderful old vase or a Roman statue.'

'There's no knowing what it might be, my dear. We shall just have to wait and see.'

'I think it's absolutely fascinating! Give me the ticket and I'll rush over first thing Monday morning and find out!'

'I think I'd better do that.'

'Oh no!' she cried. 'Let *me* do it!'

'I think not. I'll pick it up on my way to work.'

'But it's *my* ticket! *Please* let me do it, Cyril! Why should *you* have all the fun?'

'You don't know these pawnbrokers, my dear. You're liable to get cheated.'

'I wouldn't get cheated, honestly I wouldn't. Give the ticket to me, please.'

'Also you have to have fifty dollars,' he said, smiling. 'You have to pay out fifty dollars in cash before they'll give it to you.'

'I've got that,' she said. 'I think.'

'I'd rather you didn't handle it, if you don't mind.'

'But Cyril, *I found* it. It's mine. Whatever it is, it's mine, isn't that right?'

'Of course it's yours, my dear. There's no need to get so worked up about it.'

'I'm not. I'm just excited, that's all.'

'I suppose it hasn't occurred to you that this might be something entirely masculine – a pocket-watch, for example, or a set of shirt-studs. It isn't only women that go to pawnbrokers, you know.'

'In that case I'll give it to you for Christmas,' Mrs Bixby said magnanimously. 'I'll be delighted. But if it's a woman's thing, I want it myself. Is that agreed?'

'That sounds very fair. Why don't you come with me when I collect it?'

Mrs Bixby was about to say yes to this, but caught herself just in time. She had no wish to be greeted like an old customer by the pawnbroker in her husband's presence.

'No,' she said slowly. 'I don't think I will. You see, it'll be even more thrilling if I stay behind and wait. Oh, I do hope it isn't going to be something that neither of us wants.'

'You've got a point there,' he said. 'If I don't think it's worth fifty dollars, I won't even take it.'

'But you said it would be worth five hundred.'

'I'm quite sure it will. Don't worry.'

'Oh, Cyril. I can hardly wait! Isn't it exciting?'

'It's amusing,' he said, slipping the ticket into his waistcoat pocket. 'There's no doubt about that.'

Monday morning came at last, and after breakfast Mrs Bixby followed her husband to the door and helped him on with his coat.

'Don't work too hard, darling,' she said.

'No, all right.'

'Home at six?'

'I hope so.'

'Are you going to have time to go to that pawnbroker?' she asked.

'My God, I forgot all about it. I'll take a cab and go there now. It's on my way.'

'You haven't lost the ticket, have you?'

'I hope not,' he said, feeling in his waistcoat pocket. 'No, here it is.'

'And you have enough money?'

'Just about.'

'Darling,' she said, standing close to him and straightening his tie, which was perfectly straight. 'If it happens to be something nice, something you think I might like, will you telephone me as soon as you get to the office?'

'If you want me to, yes.'

'You know, I'm sort of hoping it'll be something for you, Cyril. I'd much rather it was for you than for me.'

'That's very generous of you, my dear. Now I must run.'

About an hour later, when the telephone rang, Mrs Bixby was across the room so fast she had the receiver off the hook before the first ring had finished.

'I got it!' he said.

'You did! Oh, Cyril, what was it? Was it something good?'

'Good!' he cried. 'It's fantastic! You wait till you get your eyes on this! You'll swoon!'

'Darling, what is it? Tell me quick!'

'You're a lucky girl, that's what you are.'

'It's for me, then?'

'Of course it's for you. Though how in the world it ever got to be pawned for only fifty dollars I'll be damned if I know. Someone's crazy.'

'Cyril! Stop keeping me in suspense! I can't bear it!'

'You'll go mad when you see it.'

'What is it?'

'Try to guess.'

Mrs Bixby paused. Be careful, she told herself. Be very careful now.

'A necklace,' she said.

'Wrong.'

'A diamond ring.'

'You're not even warm. I'll give you a hint. It's something you can wear.'

'Something I can wear? You mean like a hat?'

'No, it's not a hat,' he said, laughing.

'For goodness sake, Cyril! Why don't you tell me?'

'Because I want it to be a surprise. I'll bring it home with me this evening.'

'You'll do nothing of the sort!' she cried. 'I'm coming right down there to get it now!'

'I'd rather you didn't do that.'

'Don't be silly, darling. Why shouldn't I come?'

'Because I'm too busy. You'll disorganize my whole morning schedule. I'm half an hour behind already.'

'Then I'll come in the lunch hour. All right?'

'I'm not having a lunch hour. Oh well, come at one-thirty then, while I'm having a sandwich. Good-bye.'

At half past one precisely, Mrs Bixby arrived at Mr Bixby's place of business and rang the bell. Her husband, in his white dentist's coat, opened the door himself.

'Oh, Cyril, I'm so excited!'

'So you should be. You're a lucky girl, did you know that?' He led her down the passage and into the surgery.

'Go and have your lunch, Miss Pulteney,' he said to the assistant, who was busy putting instruments into the sterilizer. 'You can finish that when you come back.' He waited until the girl had gone, then he walked over to a closet that he used for hanging up his clothes and stood in front of it, pointing with his finger. 'It's in there,' he said. 'Now – shut your eyes.'

Mrs Bixby did as she was told. Then she took a deep breath and held it, and in the silence that followed she could hear him opening the cupboard door and there was a soft swishing sound as he pulled out a garment from among the other things hanging there.

'All right! You can look!'

'I don't dare to,' she said, laughing.

'Go on. Take a peek.'

Coyly, beginning to giggle, she raised one eyelid a fraction of an inch, just enough to give her a dark blurry view of the man standing there in his white overalls holding something up in the air.

'Mink!' he cried. 'Real mink!'

At the sound of the magic word she opened her eyes quick, and at the same time she actually started forward in order to clasp the coat in her arms.

But there was no coat. There was only a ridiculous fur neckpiece dangling from her husband's hand.

'Feast your eyes on that!' he said, waving it in front of her face.

Mrs Bixby put a hand up to her mouth and started backing away. I'm going to scream, she told herself. I just know it. I'm going to scream.

'What's the matter, my dear? Don't you like it?' He stopped waving the fur and stood staring at her, waiting for her to say something.

'Why yes,' she stammered. 'I ... I ... think it's ... it's lovely ... really lovely.'

'Quite took your breath away for a moment there, didn't it?'

'Yes, it did.'

'Magnificent quality,' he said. 'Fine colour, too. You know something my dear? I reckon a piece like this would cost you two or three hundred dollars at least if you had to buy it in a shop.'

'I don't doubt it.'

There were two skins, two narrow mangy-looking skins with their heads still on them and glass beads in their eye sockets and little paws hanging down. One of them had the rear end of the other in its mouth, biting it.

'Here,' he said. 'Try it on.' He leaned forward and draped the thing around her neck, then stepped back to admire. 'It's perfect. It really suits you. It isn't everyone who has mink, my dear.'

'No, it isn't.'

'Better leave it behind when you go shopping or they'll all think we're millionaires and start charging us double.'

'I'll try to remember that, Cyril.'

'I'm afraid you mustn't expect anything else for Christmas. Fifty dollars was rather more than I was going to spend anyway.'

He turned away and went over to the basin and began washing his hands. 'Run along now, my dear, and buy yourself a nice lunch. I'd take you out myself but I've got old man Gorman in the waiting-room with a broken clasp on his denture.'

Mrs Bixby moved towards the door.

I'm going to kill that pawnbroker, she told herself. I'm going right back there to the shop this very minute and I'm going to throw this filthy neckpiece right in his face and if he refuses to give me back my coat I'm going to kill him.

'Did I tell you I was going to be late home tonight?' Cyril Bixby said, still washing his hands.

'No.'

'It'll probably be at least eight-thirty the way things look at the moment. It may even be nine.'

'Yes, all right. Good-bye.' Mrs Bixby went out, slamming the door behind her.

At that precise moment, Miss Pulteney, the secretary-assistant, came sailing past her down the corridor on her way to lunch.

'Isn't it a gorgeous day?' Miss Pulteney said as she went by, flashing a smile. There was a lilt in her walk, a little whiff of perfume attending her, and she looked like a queen, just exactly like a queen in the beautiful black mink coat that the Colonel had given to Mrs Bixby.

ROYAL JELLY

'IT WORRIES ME to death, Albert, it really does,' Mrs Taylor said.

She kept her eyes fixed on the baby who was now lying absolutely motionless in the crook of her left arm.

'I just know there's something wrong.'

The skin on the baby's face had a pearly translucent quality and was stretched very tightly over the bones.

'Try again,' Albert Taylor said.

'It won't do any good.'

'You have to keep trying, Mabel,' he said.

She lifted the bottle out of the saucepan of hot water and shook a few drops of milk on to the inside of her wrist, testing for temperature.

'Come on,' she whispered. 'Come on, my baby. Wake up and take a bit more of this.'

There was a small lamp on the table close by that made a soft yellow glow all around her.

'Please,' she said. 'Take just a weeny bit more.'

The husband watched her over the top of his magazine. She was half dead with exhaustion, he could see that, and the pale oval face, usually so grave and serene, had taken on a kind of pinched and desperate look. But even so, the drop of her head as she gazed down at the child was curiously beautiful.

'You see,' she murmured. 'It's no good. She won't have it.'

She held the bottle up to the light, squinting at the calibrations.

'One ounce again. That's all she's taken. No — it isn't even that. It's only three-quarters. It's not enough to keep body and soul together, Albert, it really isn't. It worries me to death.'

'I know,' he said.

'If only they could *find out* what was wrong.'

'There's nothing wrong, Mabel. It's just a matter of time.'

'Of course there's something wrong.'

'Dr Robinson says no.'

'Look,' she said, standing up. 'You can't tell me it's natural for a six-week-old child to weigh less, less by more than *two whole pounds* than she did when she was born! Just look at those legs! They're nothing but skin and bone!'

The tiny baby lay limply on her arm, not moving.

'Dr Robinson said you was to stop worrying, Mabel. So did that other one.'

'Ha!' she said. 'Isn't that wonderful! I'm to stop worrying!'

'Now, Mabel.'

'What does he want me to do? Treat it as some sort of a joke?'

'He didn't say that.'

'I hate doctors! I hate them all!' she cried, and she swung away from him and walked quickly out of the room towards the stairs, carrying the baby with her.

Albert Taylor stayed where he was and let her go.

In a little while he heard her moving about in the bedroom directly over his head, quick nervous footsteps going tap tap tap on the linoleum above. Soon the footsteps would stop, and then he would have to get up and follow her, and when he went into the bedroom he would find her sitting beside the cot as usual, staring at the child and crying softly to herself and refusing to move.

'She's starving, Albert,' she would say.

'Of course she's not starving.'

'She *is* starving. I know she is. And Albert?'

'Yes?'

'I believe you know it too, but you won't admit it. Isn't that right?'

Every night now it was like this.

Last week they had taken the child back to the hospital, and the doctor had examined it carefully and told them that there was nothing the matter.

'It took us nine years to get this baby, Doctor,' Mabel had said. 'I think it would kill me if anything should happen to her.'

That was six days ago and since then it had lost another five ounces.

But worrying about it wasn't going to help anybody, Albert Taylor told himself. One simply had to trust the doctor on a thing like this. He picked up the magazine that was still lying on his lap and glanced idly down the list of contents to see what it had to offer this week:

> *Among the Bees in May*
> *Honey Cookery*
> *The Bee Farmer and the B. Pharm.*
> *Experiences in the Control of Nosema*

The Latest on Royal Jelly
This Week in the Apiary
The Healing Power of Propolis
Regurgitations
British Beekeepers Annual Dinner
Association News

All his life Albert Taylor had been fascinated by anything that had to do with bees. As a small boy he often used to catch them in his bare hands and go running with them into the house to show to his mother, and sometimes he would put them on his face and let them crawl about over his cheeks and neck, and the astonishing thing about it all was that he never got stung. On the contrary, the bees seemed to enjoy being with him. They never tried to fly away, and to get rid of them he would have to brush them off gently with his fingers. Even then they would frequently return and settle again on his arm or hand or knee, any place where the skin was bare.

His father, who was a bricklayer, said there must be some witch's stench about the boy, something noxious that came oozing out through the pores of the skin, and that no good would ever come of it, hypnotizing insects like that. But the mother said it was a gift given him by God, and even went so far as to compare him with St Francis and the birds.

As he grew older, Albert Taylor's fascination with bees developed into an obsession, and by the time he was twelve he had built his first hive. The following summer he had captured his first swarm. Two years later, at the age of fourteen, he had no less than five hives standing neatly in a row against the fence in his father's small back yard, and already – apart from the normal task of producing honey – he was practising the delicate and complicated business of rearing his own queens, grafting larvae into artificial cell cups, and all the rest of it.

He never had to use smoke when there was work to do inside a hive, and he never wore gloves on his hands or a net over his head. Clearly there was some strange sympathy between this boy and the bees, and down in the village, in the shops and pubs, they began to speak about him with a certain kind of respect, and people started coming up to the house to buy his honey.

When he was eighteen, he had rented one acre of rough pasture alongside a cherry orchard down the valley about a mile from the village, and there he had set out to establish his own business. Now, eleven years later, he was still in the same spot, but he had six acres of ground instead of one, two hundred and forty well-stocked hives, and a small house he'd built mainly with his own hands. He had married at the age of twenty and that, apart from the fact that it had taken them over nine years to get a child, had also been a success. In fact, everything had gone pretty well for Albert until this strange little baby girl came along and started frightening them out of their wits by refusing to eat properly and losing weight every day.

He looked up from the magazine and began thinking about his daughter.

That evening, for instance, when she had opened her eyes at the beginning of the feed, he had gazed into them and seen something that frightened him to death — a kind of misty vacant stare, as though the eyes themselves were not connected to the brain at all but were just lying loose in their sockets like a couple of small grey marbles.

Did those doctors really know what they were talking about?

He reached for an ash-tray and started slowly picking the ashes out from the bowl of his pipe with a matchstick.

One could always take her along to another hospital, somewhere in Oxford perhaps. He might suggest that to Mabel when he went up-stairs.

He could still hear her moving around in the bedroom, but she must have taken off her shoes now and put on slippers because the noise was very faint.

He switched his attention back to the magazine and went on with his reading. He finished the article called 'Experiences in the Control of Nosema', then turned over the page and began reading the next one, 'The Latest on Royal Jelly'. He doubted very much whether there would be anything in this that he didn't know already:

What is this wonderful substance called royal jelly?

He reached for the tin of tobacco on the table beside him and began filling his pipe, still reading.

Royal jelly is a glandular secretion produced by the nurse bees to feed the larvae immediately they have hatched from the egg. The pharyngeal glands of bees produce this substance in much the same way as the mammary glands of vertebrates produce milk. The fact is of great biological interest because no other insects in the world are known to have evolved such a process.

All old stuff, he told himself, but for want of anything better to do, he continued to read.

Royal jelly is fed in concentrated form to all bee larvae for the first three days after hatching from the egg; but beyond that point, for all those who are destined to become drones or workers, this precious food is greatly diluted with honey and pollen. On the other hand, the larvae which are destined to become queens are fed throughout the whole of their larval period on a concentrated diet of pure royal jelly. Hence the name.

Above him, up in the bedroom, the noise of the footsteps had stopped altogether. The house was quiet. He struck a match and put it to his pipe.

Royal jelly must be a substance of tremendous nourishing power, for on this diet alone, the honey-bee larva increases in weight fifteen hundred times in five days.

That was probably about right, he thought, although for some reason it had never occurred to him to consider larval growth in terms of weight before.

This is as if a seven-and-a-half-pound baby should increase in that time to five tons.

Albert Taylor stopped and read that sentence again. He read it a third time.

This is as if a seven-and-a-half-pound baby . . .

'Mabel!' he cried, jumping up from his chair. 'Mabel! Come here!'
He went out into the hall and stood at the foot of the stairs calling for her to come down.
There was no answer.
He ran up the stairs and switched on the light on the landing. The bedroom door was closed. He crossed the landing and opened it and stood in the doorway looking into the dark room. 'Mabel,' he said. 'Come downstairs a moment, will you please? I've just had a bit of an idea. It's about the baby.'
The light from the landing behind him cast a faint glow over the

bed and he could see her dimly now, lying on her stomach with her face buried in the pillow and her arms up over her head. She was crying again.

'Mabel,' he said, going over to her, touching her shoulder. 'Please come down a moment. This may be important.'

'Go away,' she said. 'Leave me alone.'

'Don't you want to hear about my idea?'

'Oh, Albert, I'm *tired*,' she sobbed. 'I'm so tired I don't know what I'm doing any more. I don't think I can go on. I don't think I can stand it.'

There was a pause. Albert Taylor turned away from her and walked slowly over to the cradle where the baby was lying, and peered in. It was too dark for him to see the child's face, but when he bent down close he could hear the sound of breathing, very faint and quick. 'What time is the next feed?' he asked.

'Two o'clock, I suppose.'

'And the one after that?'

'Six in the morning.'

'I'll do them both,' he said. 'You go to sleep.'

She didn't answer.

'You get properly into bed, Mabel, and go straight to sleep, you understand? And stop worrying. I'm taking over completely for the next twelve hours. You'll give yourself a nervous breakdown going on like this.'

'Yes,' she said. 'I know.'

'I'm taking the nipper and myself *and* the alarm clock into the spare room this very moment, so you just lie down and relax and forget all about us. Right?' Already he was pushing the cradle out through the door.

'Oh, Albert,' she sobbed.

'Don't you worry about a thing. Leave it to me.'

'Albert . . .'

'Yes?'

'I love you, Albert.'

'I love you too, Mabel. Now go to sleep.'

Albert Taylor didn't see his wife again until nearly eleven o'clock the next morning.

'Good *gracious* me!' she cried, rushing down the stairs in dressing-gown and slippers. 'Albert! Just look at the time! I must have slept twelve hours at least! Is everything all right? What happened?'

He was sitting quietly in his armchair, smoking a pipe and reading the morning paper. The baby was in a sort of carry-cot on the floor at his feet, sleeping.

'Hullo, dear,' he said, smiling.

She ran over to the cot and looked in. 'Did she take anything, Albert? How many times have you fed her? She was due for another one at ten o'clock, did you know that?'

Albert Taylor folded the newspaper neatly into a square and put it away on the side table. 'I fed her at two in the morning,' he said, 'and she took about half an ounce, no more. I fed her again at six and she did a bit better that time, two ounces . . .'

'*Two ounces!* Oh, Albert, that's marvellous!'

'And we just finished the last feed ten minutes ago. There's the bottle on the mantelpiece. Only one ounce left. She drank three. How's that?' He was grinning proudly, delighted with his achievement.

The woman quickly got down on her knees and peered at the baby.

'Don't she look better?' he asked eagerly. 'Don't she look fatter in the face?'

'It may sound silly,' the wife said, 'but I actually think she does. Oh, Albert, you're a marvel! How did you do it?'

'She's turning the corner,' he said. 'That's all it is. Just like the doctor prophesied, she's turning the corner.'

'I pray to God you're right, Albert.'

'Of course I'm right. From now on, you watch her go.'

The woman was gazing lovingly at the baby.

'You look a lot better yourself too, Mabel.'

'I feel wonderful. I'm sorry about last night.'

'Let's keep it this way,' he said. 'I'll do all the night feeds in future. You do the day ones.'

She looked up at him across the cot, frowning. 'No,' she said. 'Oh no, I wouldn't allow you to do that.'

'I don't want you to have a breakdown, Mabel.'

'I won't, not now I've had some sleep.'

'Much better we share it.'

'No, Albert. This is my job and I intend to do it. Last night won't happen again.'

There was a pause. Albert Taylor took the pipe out of his mouth and examined the grain on the bowl. 'All right,' he said. 'In that case I'll just relieve you of the donkey work, I'll do all the sterilizing and the mixing of the food and getting everything ready. That'll help you a bit, anyway.'

She looked at him carefully, wondering what could have come over him all of a sudden.

'You see, Mabel, I've been thinking . . .

'Yes, dear.'

'I've been thinking that up until last night I've never even raised a finger to help you with this baby.'

'That isn't true.'

'Oh yes it is. So I've decided that from now on I'm going to do *my* share of the work. I'm going to be the feed-mixer and the bottle-sterilizer. Right?'

'It's very sweet of you, dear, but I really don't think it's necessary . . .'

'Come on!' he cried. 'Don't change the luck! I done it the last three times and just *look* what happened! When's the next one? Two o'clock, isn't it?'

'Yes.'

'It's all mixed,' he said. 'Everything's all mixed and ready and all you've got to do when the time comes is to go out there to the larder and take it off the shelf and warm it up. That's *some* help, isn't it?'

The woman got up off her knees and went over to him and kissed him on the cheek. 'You're such a nice man,' she said. 'I love you more and more every day I know you.'

Later, in the middle of the afternoon, when Albert was outside in the sunshine working among the hives, he heard her calling to him from the house.

'Albert!' she shouted. 'Albert, come here!' She was running through the buttercups towards him.

He started forward to meet her, wondering what was wrong.

'Oh, Albert! Guess what!'

'What?'

'I've just finished giving her the two-o'clock feed and she's taken the whole lot!'

'No!'

'Every drop of it! Oh, Albert, I'm so happy! She's going to be all right! She's turned the corner just like you said!' She came up to him and threw her arms around his neck and hugged him, and he clapped her on the back and laughed and said what a marvellous little mother she was.

'Will you come in and watch the next one and see if she does it again, Albert?'

He told her he wouldn't miss it for anything, and she hugged him again, then turned and ran back to the house, skipping over the grass and singing all the way.

Naturally, there was a certain amount of suspense in the air as the time approached for the six-o'clock feed. By five thirty both parents were already seated in the living-room waiting for the moment to arrive. The bottle with the milk formula in it was standing in a saucepan of warm water on the mantelpiece. The baby was asleep in its carry-cot on the sofa.

At twenty minutes to six it woke up and started screaming its head off.

'There you are!' Mrs Taylor cried. 'She's asking for the bottle. Pick her up quick, Albert, and hand her to me here. Give me the bottle first.'

He gave her the bottle, then placed the baby on the woman's lap. Cautiously, she touched the baby's lips with the end of the nipple. The baby seized the nipple between its gums and began to suck ravenously with a rapid powerful action.

'Oh, Albert, isn't it wonderful?' she said, laughing.

'It's terrific, Mabel.'

In seven or eight minutes, the entire contents of the bottle had disappeared down the baby's throat.

'You clever girl,' Mrs Taylor said. 'Four ounces again.'

Albert Taylor was leaning forward in his chair, peering intently into the baby's face. 'You know what?' he said. 'She even seems as though she's put on a touch of weight already. What do you think?'

The mother looked down at the child.

'Don't she seem bigger and fatter to you, Mabel, than she was yesterday?'

'Maybe she does, Albert. I'm not sure. Although actually there couldn't be any *real* gain in such a short time as this. The important thing is that she's eating normally.'

'She's turned the corner,' Albert said. 'I don't think you need worry about her any more.'

'I certainly won't.'

'You want me to go up and fetch the cradle back into our own bedroom, Mabel?'

'Yes, please,' she said.

Albert went upstairs and moved the cradle. The woman followed with the baby, and after changing its nappy, she laid it gently down on its bed. Then she covered it with sheet and blanket.

'Doesn't she look lovely, Albert?' she whispered. 'Isn't that the most beautiful baby you've ever seen in your *entire* life?'

'Leave her be now, Mabel,' he said. 'Come on downstairs and cook us a bit of supper. We both deserve it.'

After they had finished eating, the parents settled themselves in armchairs in the living-room, Albert with his magazine and his pipe, Mrs Taylor with her knitting. But this was a very different scene from the one of the night before. Suddenly, all tensions had vanished. Mrs Taylor's handsome oval face was glowing with pleasure, her cheeks were pink, her eyes were sparkling bright, and her mouth was fixed in a little dreamy smile of pure content. Every now and again she would glance up from her knitting and gaze affectionately at her husband. Occasionally, she would stop the clicking of her needles altogether for a few seconds and sit quite still, looking at the ceiling, listening for a cry or a whimper from upstairs. But all was quiet.

'Albert,' she said after a while.

'Yes, dear?'

'What was it you were going to tell me last night when you came rushing up to the bedroom? You said you had an idea for the baby.'

Albert Taylor lowered the magazine on to his lap and gave her a long sly look.

'Did I?' he said.

'Yes.' She waited for him to go on, but he didn't.

'What's the big joke?' she asked. 'Why are you grinning like that?'

'It's a joke all right,' he said.

'Tell it to me, dear.'

'I'm not sure I ought to,' he said. 'You might call me a liar.'

She had seldom seen him looking so pleased with himself as he was now, and she smiled back at him, egging him on.

'I'd just like to see your face when you hear it, Mabel, that's all.'

'Albert, what *is* all this?'

He paused, refusing to be hurried.

'You do think the baby's better, don't you?' he asked.

'Of course I do.'

'You agree with me that all of a sudden she's feeding marvellously and looking one-hundred-per-cent different?'

'I do, Albert, yes.'

'That's good,' he said, the grin widening. 'You see, it's me that did it.'

'Did what?'

'I cured the baby.'

'Yes, dear, I'm sure you did.' Mrs Taylor went right on with her knitting.

'You don't believe me, do you?'

'Of course I believe you, Albert. I give you all the credit, every bit of it.'

'Then how did I do it?'

'Well,' she said, pausing a moment to think. 'I suppose it's simply that you're a brilliant feed-mixer. Ever since you started mixing the feeds she's got better and better.'

'You mean there's some sort of an art in mixing the feeds?'

'Apparently there is.' She was knitting away and smiling quietly to herself, thinking how funny men were.

'I'll tell you a secret,' he said. 'You're absolutely right. Although, mind you, it isn't so much *how* you mix it that counts. It's what you put in. You realize that, don't you, Mabel?'

Mrs Taylor stopped knitting and looked up sharply at her husband. 'Albert,' she said, 'don't tell me you've been putting things into that child's milk?'

He sat there grinning.

'Well, have you or haven't you?'

'It's possible,' he said.

'I don't believe it.'

He had a strange fierce way of grinning that showed his teeth.

'Albert,' she said. 'Stop playing with me like this.'

'Yes, dear, all right.'

'You haven't *really* put anything into her milk, have you? Answer me properly, Albert. This could be serious with such a tiny baby.'

'The answer is yes, Mabel.'

'*Albert Taylor!* How could you?'

'Now don't get excited,' he said. 'I'll tell you all about it if you really want me to, but for heaven's sake keep your hair on.'

'It was beer!' she cried. 'I just know it was beer!'

'Don't be so daft, Mabel, please.'

'Then what was it?'

Albert laid his pipe down carefully on the table beside him and leaned back in his chair. 'Tell me,' he said, 'did you ever by any chance happen to hear me mentioning something called royal jelly?'

'I did not.'

'It's magic,' he said. 'Pure magic. And last night I suddenly got the idea that if I was to put some of this into the baby's milk . . .

'How *dare* you!'

'Now, Mabel, you don't even know what it is yet.'

'I don't care what it is,' she said. 'You can't go putting foreign bodies like that into a tiny baby's milk. You must be mad.'

'It's perfectly harmless, Mabel, otherwise I wouldn't have done it. It comes from bees.'

'I might have guessed that.'

'And it's so precious that practically no one can afford to take it. When they do, it's only one little drop at a time.'

'And how much did you give to our baby, might I ask?'

'Ah,' he said, 'that's the whole point. That's where the difference lies. I reckon that our baby, just in the last four feeds, has already swallowed about fifty times as much royal jelly as anyone else in the world has ever swallowed before. How about that?'

'Albert, stop pulling my leg.'

'I swear it,' he said proudly.

She sat there staring at him, her brow wrinkled, her mouth slightly open.

'You know what this stuff actually costs, Mabel, if you want to buy it? There's a place in America advertising it for sale at this very moment for something like five hundred dollars a pound jar! *Five hundred dollars!* That's more than gold, you know!'

She hadn't the faintest idea what he was talking about.

'I'll prove it,' he said, and he jumped up and went across to the large bookcase where he kept all his literature about bees. On the top shelf, the back numbers of the *American Bee Journal* were neatly stacked alongside those of the *British Bee Journal*, *Beecraft*, and other magazines. He took down the last issue of the *American Bee Journal* and turned to a page of small classified advertisements at the back.

'Here you are,' he said. 'Exactly as I told you. "We sell royal jelly — $480 per lb. jar wholesale."'

He handed her the magazine so she could read it herself.

'Now do you believe me? This is an actual shop in New York, Mabel. It says so.'

'It doesn't say you can go stirring it into the milk of a practically new-born baby,' she said. 'I don't know what's come over you, Albert, I really don't.'

'It's curing her, isn't it?'

'I'm not so sure about that, now.'

'Don't be so damn silly, Mabel. You know it is.'

'Then why haven't other people done it with *their* babies?'

'I keep telling you,' he said. 'It's too expensive. Practically nobody in the world can afford to buy royal jelly just for *eating* except maybe one or two multimillionaires. The people who buy it are the big companies that make women's face creams and things like that. They're using it as a stunt. They mix a tiny pinch of it into a big jar of face cream and it's selling like hot cakes for absolutely enormous prices. They claim it takes out the wrinkles.'

'And does it?'

'Now how on earth would I know that, Mabel? Anyway,' he said, returning to his chair, 'that's not the point. The point is this. It's done so much good to our little baby just in the last few hours that I think we ought to go right on giving it to her. Now don't interrupt, Mabel. Let me finish. I've got two hundred and forty hives out there and if I turn over maybe a hundred of them to making royal jelly, we ought to be able to supply her with all she wants.'

'Albert Taylor,' the woman said, stretching her eyes wide and staring at him. 'Have you gone out of your mind?'

'Just hear me through, will you please?'

'I forbid it,' she said, 'absolutely. You're not to give my baby another drop of that horrid jelly, you understand?'

'Now, Mabel . . .'

'And quite apart from that, we had a shocking honey crop last year, and if you go fooling around with those hives now, there's no telling what might not happen.'

'There's nothing wrong with my hives, Mabel.'

'You know very well we had only half the normal crop last year.'

'Do me a favour, will you?' he said. 'Let me explain some of the marvellous things this stuff does.'

'You haven't even told me what it is yet.'

'All right, Mabel. I'll do that too. Will you listen? Will you give me a chance to explain it?'

She sighed and picked up her knitting once more. 'I suppose you might as well get it off your chest, Albert. Go on and tell me.'

He paused, a bit uncertain now how to begin. It wasn't going to be easy to explain something like this to a person with no detailed knowledge of apiculture at all.

'You know, don't you,' he said, 'that each colony has only one queen?'

'Yes.'

'And that this queen lays all the eggs?'

'Yes, dear. That much I know.'

'All right. Now the queen can actually lay two different kinds of eggs. You didn't know that, but she can. It's what we call one of the miracles of the hive. She can lay eggs that produce drones, and she can lay eggs that produce workers. Now if that isn't a miracle, Mabel, I don't know what is.'

'Yes, Albert, all right.'

'The drones are the males. We don't have to worry about them. The workers are all females. So is the queen, of course. But the workers are unsexed females, if you see what I mean. Their organs are completely undeveloped, whereas the queen is tremendously sexy. She can actually lay her own weight in eggs in a single day.'

He hesitated, marshalling his thoughts.

'Now what happens is this. The queen crawls around on the comb and lays her eggs in what we call cells. You know all those hundreds of little holes you see in a honeycomb? Well, a brood comb is just about the same except the cells don't have honey in them, they have eggs. She lays one egg to each cell, and in three days each of these eggs hatches out into a tiny grub. We call it a larva.

'Now, as soon as this larva appears, the nurse bees — they're young workers — all crowd round and start feeding it like mad. And you know what they feed it on?'

'Royal jelly,' Mabel answered patiently.

'Right!' he cried. 'That's exactly what they do feed it on. They get this stuff out of a gland in their heads and they start pumping it into the cell to feed the larva. And what happens then?'

He paused dramatically, blinking at her with his small watery-grey eyes. Then he turned slowly in his chair and reached for the magazine that he had been reading the night before.

'You want to know what happens then?' he asked, wetting his lips.

'I can hardly wait.'

'"Royal jelly,"' he read aloud, '"must be a substance of tremendous nourishing power, for on this diet alone, the honeybee larva increases in weight *fifteen hundred times* in five days!'

'How much?'

'*Fifteen hundred times*, Mabel. And you know what that means if you put it in terms of a human being?' It means,' he said, lowering his voice, leaning forward, fixing her with those small pale eyes, 'it means that in five days a baby weighing seven and a half pounds to start off with would increase in weight to *five tons!*'

For the second time, Mrs Taylor stopped knitting.

'Now you mustn't take that too literally, Mabel.'

'Who says I mustn't?'

'It's just a scientific way of putting it, that's all.'

'Very well, Albert. Go on.'

'But that's only half the story,' he said. 'There's more to come. The really amazing thing about royal jelly, I haven't told you yet. I'm going to show you now how it can transform a plain dull-looking little worker bee with practically no sex organs at all into a great big beautiful fertile queen.'

'Are you saying our baby is dull-looking and plain?' she asked sharply.

'Now don't go putting words into my mouth, Mabel, please. Just listen to this. Did you know that the queen bee and the worker bee, athough they are completely different when they grow up, are both hatched out of exactly the same kind of egg?'

'I don't believe that,' she said.

'It's as true as I'm sitting here, Mabel, honest it is. Any time the bees want a queen to hatch out of the egg instead of a worker, they can do it.'

'How?'

'Ah,' he said, shaking a thick forefinger in her direction. 'That's just what I'm coming to. That's the secret of the whole thing. Now – what do *you* think it is, Mabel, that makes this miracle happen?'

'Royal jelly,' she answered. 'You already told me.'

'Royal jelly it is!' he cried, clapping his hands and bouncing up on his seat. His big round face was glowing with excitement now, and two vivid patches of scarlet had appeared high up on each cheek.

'Here's how it works. I'll put it very simply for you. The bees want a new queen. So they build an extra-large cell, a queen cell we call it, and they get the old queen to lay one of her eggs in there. The other one thousand nine hundred and ninety-nine eggs she lays in ordinary worker cells. Now. As soon as these eggs hatch into larvae, the nurse bees rally round and start pumping in the royal jelly. All of them get it, workers as well as queen. But here's the vital thing, Mabel, so listen carefully. Here's where the difference comes. The worker larvae only receive this special marvellous food for the *first three days* of their larval life. After that they have a complete change of diet. What really happens is they get weaned, except that it's not like an ordinary weaning because it's so sudden. After the third day they're put straight away on to more or less routine bees' food – a mixture of honey and pollen – and then about two weeks later they emerge from the cells as workers.

'But not so the larva in the queen cell! This one gets royal jelly *all the way through its larval life*. The nurse bees simply pour it into the cell, so much so in fact that the little larva is literally floating in it. And that's what makes it into a queen!'

'You can't prove it,' she said.

'Don't talk so damn silly, Mabel, please. Thousands of people have proved it time and time again, famous scientists in every country in the world. All you have to do is take a larva out of a worker cell and put it in a queen cell — that's what we call grafting — and just so long as the nurse bees keep it well supplied with royal jelly, then presto! — it'll grow up into a queen! And what makes it more marvellous still is the absolutely enormous difference between a queen and a worker when they grow up. The abdomen is a different shape. The sting is different. The legs are different. The . . .'

'In what way are the legs different?' she asked, testing him.

'The legs? Well, the workers have little pollen baskets on their legs for carrying the pollen. The queen has none. Now here's another thing. The queen has fully developed sex organs. The workers don't. And most amazing of all, Mabel, the queen lives for an average of four to six years. The worker hardly lives that many months. And all this difference simply because one of them got royal jelly and the other didn't!'

'It's pretty hard to believe,' she said, 'that a food can do all that.'

'Of course it's hard to believe. It's another of the miracles of the hive. In fact it's the biggest ruddy miracle of them all. It's such a hell of a big miracle that it's baffled the greatest men of science for hundreds of years. Wait a moment. Stay here. Don't move.'

Again he jumped up and went over to the bookcase and started rummaging among the books and magazines.

'I'm going to find you a few of the reports. Here we are. Here's one of them. Listen to this.' He started reading aloud from a copy of the *American Bee Journal*:

'"Living in Toronto at the head of a fine research laboratory given to him by the people of Canada in recognition of his truly great contribution to humanity in the discovery of insulin, Dr Frederick A. Banting became curious about royal jelly. He requested his staff to do a basic fractional analysis . . ."'

He paused.

'Well, there's no need to read it all, but here's what happened. Dr Banting and his people took some royal jelly from queen cells that contained two-day-old larvae, and then they started analysing it. And what d'you think they found?

'They found,' he said, 'that royal jelly contained phenols, sterols, glycerils, dextrose, *and* — now here it comes — and eighty to eighty-five per cent *unidentified* acids!'

He stood beside the bookcase with the magazine in his hand, smiling a funny little furtive smile of triumph, and his wife watched him, bewildered.

He was not a tall man; he had a thick plump pulpy-looking body that was built close to the ground on abbreviated legs. The legs were slightly bowed. The head was huge and round, covered with bristly short-cut hair, and the greater part of the face — now that he had given up shaving altogether — was hidden by a brownish yellow fuzz about an inch long. In one way and another, he was rather grotesque to look at, there was no denying that.

'Eighty to eighty-five per cent,' he said, 'unidentified acids. Isn't that fantastic?' He turned back to the bookshelf and began hunting through the other magazines.

'What does it mean, unidentified acids?'

'That's the whole point! No one knows! Not even Banting could find out. You've heard of Banting?'

'No.'

'He just happens to be about the most famous living doctor in the world today, that's all.'

Looking at him now as he buzzed around in front of the bookcase with his bristly head and his hairy face and his plump pulpy body, she couldn't help thinking that somehow, in some curious way, there was a touch of the bee about this man. She had often seen women grow to look like the horses that they rode, and she had noticed that people who bred birds or bull terriers or pomeranians frequently resembled in some small but startling manner the creature of their choice. But up until now it had never occured to her that her husband might look like a bee. It shocked her a bit.

'And did Banting ever try to eat it,' she asked, 'this royal jelly?'

'Of course he didn't eat it, Mabel. He didn't have enough for that. It's too precious.'

'You know something?' she said, staring at him but smiling a little all the same. 'You're getting to look just a teeny bit like a bee yourself, did you know that?'

He turned and looked at her.

'I suppose it's the beard mostly,' she said. 'I do wish you'd stop wearing it. Even the colour is sort of bee-ish, don't you think?'

'What the hell are you talking about, Mabel?'

'Albert,' she said. 'Your language.'

'Do you want to hear any more of this or don't you?'

'Yes, dear, I'm sorry. I was only joking. Do go on.'

He turned away again and pulled another magazine out of the bookcase and began leafing through the pages. 'Now just listen to this, Mabel. "In 1939, Heyl experimented with twenty-one-day-old rats, injecting them with royal jelly in varying amounts. As a result, he found a precocious follicular development of the ovaries directly in proportion to the quantity of royal jelly injected."'

'There!' she cried. 'I knew it!'

'Knew what?'

'I knew something terrible would happen.'

'Nonsense. There's nothing wrong with that. Now here's another, Mabel. "Still and Burdett found that a male rat which hitherto had been unable to breed, upon receiving a minute daily dose of royal jelly, became a father many times over."'

'Albert,' she cried, 'this stuff is *much* too strong to give to a baby! I don't like it at all.'

'Nonsense, Mabel.'

'Then why do they only try it out on rats, tell me that? Why don't some of these famous scientists take it themselves? They're too clever, that's why. Do you think Dr Banting is going to risk finishing up with precious ovaries? Not him.'

'But they *have* given it to people, Mabel. Here's a whole article about it. Listen.' He turned the page and again began reading from the magazine. '"In Mexico, in 1953, a group of enlightened physicians began prescribing minute doses of royal jelly for such things as cerebral neuritis, arthritis, diabetes, autointoxication from tobacco, impotence in men, asthma, croup, and gout ... There are stacks of signed testimonials ... A celebrated stockbroker in Mexico City contracted a particularly stubborn case of psoriasis. He became physically unattractive. His clients began to forsake him. His business began to suffer. In desperation he turned to royal jelly – one drop with every meal – and presto! he was cured in a fortnight. A waiter in the Café Jena, also in Mexico City, reported that his father, after taking minute doses of this wonder substance in capsule form, sired a healthy boy child at the age of ninety. A bullfight promoter in Acapulco, finding himself landed with a rather lethargic-looking bull, injected it with one gramme of royal jelly (an excessive dose) just before it entered the arena. Thereupon, the beast became so swift and savage that it promptly dispatched two picadors, three horses, and a matador, and finally ..."'

'Listen!' Mrs Taylor said, interrupting him. 'I think the baby's crying.'

Albert glanced up from his reading. Sure enough, a lusty yelling noise was coming from the bedroom above.

'She must be hungry,' he said.

His wife looked at the clock. 'Good gracious me!' she cried, jumping up. 'It's past her time again already! You mix the feed, Albert, quickly, while I bring her down! But hurry! I don't want to keep her waiting.'

In half a minute, Mrs Taylor was back, carrying the screaming infant in her arms. She was flustered now, still quite unaccustomed to the ghastly nonstop racket that a healthy baby makes when it wants its food. 'Do be quick, Albert!' she called, settling herself in the armchair and arranging the child on her lap. 'Please hurry!'

Albert entered from the kitchen and handed her the bottle of warm milk. 'It's just right,' he said. 'You don't have to test it.'

She hitched the baby's head a little higher in the crook of her arm, then pushed the rubber teat straight into the wide-open yelling mouth. The baby grabbed the teat and began to suck. The yelling stopped. Mrs Taylor relaxed.

'Oh, Albert, isn't she lovely?'

'She's terrific, Mabel – thanks to royal jelly.'

'Now, dear, I don't want to hear another word about that nasty stuff. It frightens me to death.'

'You're making a big mistake,' he said.

'We'll see about that.'

The baby went on sucking the bottle.

'I do believe she's going to finish the whole lot again, Albert.'

'I'm sure she is,' he said.

And a few minutes later, the milk was all gone.

'Oh, what a good girl you are!' Mrs Taylor cried, as very gently she started to withdraw the nipple. The baby sensed what she was doing and sucked harder, trying to hold on. The woman gave a quick little tug, and *plop*, out it came.

'Waa! Waa! Waa! Waa! Waa!' the baby yelled.

'Nasty old wind,' Mrs Taylor said, hoisting the child on to her shoulder and patting its back.

It belched twice in quick succession.

'There you are, my darling, you'll be all right now.'

For a few seconds, the yelling stopped. Then it started again.

'Keep belching her,' Albert said. 'She's drunk it too quick.'

His wife lifted the baby back on to her shoulder. She rubbed its spine. She changed it from one shoulder to the other. She laid it on its stomach on her lap. She sat it up on her knee. But it didn't belch again, and the yelling became louder and more insistent every minute.

'Good for the lungs,' Albert Taylor said, grinning. 'That's the way they exercise their lungs, Mabel, did you know that?'

'There, there, there,' the wife said, kissing it all over the face. 'There, there, there.'

They waited another five minutes, but not for one moment did the screaming stop.

'Change the nappy,' Albert said. 'It's got a wet nappy, that's all it is.' He fetched a clean one from the kitchen, and Mrs Taylor took the old one off and put the new one on.

This made no difference at all.

'Waa! Waa! Waa! Waa! Waa!' the baby yelled.

'You didn't stick the safety pin through the skin, did you, Mabel?'

'Of course I didn't,' she said, feeling under the nappy with her fingers to make sure.

The parents sat opposite one another in their armchairs, smiling nervously, watching the baby on the mother's lap, waiting for it to tire and stop screaming.

'You know what?' Albert Taylor said at last.

'What?'

'I'll bet she's still hungry. I'll bet all she wants is another swig at that bottle. How about me fetching her an extra lot?'

'I don't think we ought to do that, Albert.'

'It'll do her good,' he said, getting up from his chair. 'I'm going to warm her up a second helping.'

He went into the kitchen, and was away several minutes. When he returned he was holding a bottle brimful of milk.

'I made her a double,' he announced. 'Eight ounces. Just in case.'

'Albert! Are you mad? Don't you know it's just as bad to overfeed as it is to underfeed?'

'You don't have to give her the lot, Mabel. You can stop any time you like. Go on,' he said, standing over her. 'Give her a drink.'

Mrs Taylor began to tease the baby's upper lip with the end of the nipple. The tiny mouth closed like a trap over the rubber teat and suddenly there was silence in the room. The baby's whole body relaxed and a look of absolute bliss came over its face as it started to drink.

'There you are, Mabel! What did I tell you?'

The woman didn't answer.

'She's ravenous, that's what she is. Just look at her suck.'

Mrs Taylor was watching the level of the milk in the bottle. It was dropping fast, and before long three or four ounces out of the eight had disappeared.

'There,' she said. 'That'll do.'

'You can't pull it away now, Mabel.'

'Yes, dear. I must.'

'Go on, woman. Give her the rest and stop fussing.'

'But *Albert* . . .'

'She's famished, can't you see that? Go on, my beauty,' he said. 'You finish that bottle.'

'I don't like it, Albert,' the wife said, but she didn't pull the bottle away.

'She's making up for lost time, Mabel, that's all she's doing.'

Five minutes later the bottle was empty. Slowly, Mrs Taylor withdrew the nipple, and this time there was no protest from the baby, no sound at all. It lay peacefully on the mother's lap, the eyes glazed with contentment, the mouth half-open, the lips smeared with milk.

'Twelve whole ounces, Mabel!' Albert Taylor said. 'Three times the normal amount! Isn't that amazing!'

The woman was staring down at the baby. And now the old anxious tight-lipped look of the frightened mother was slowly returning to her face.

'What's the matter with *you*?' Albert asked. 'You're not worried by that, are you? You can't expect her to get back to normal on a lousy four ounces, don't be ridiculous.'

'Come here, Albert,' she said.

'What?'

'I said come here.'

He went over and stood beside her.

'Take a good look and tell me if you see anything different.'

He peered closely at the baby. 'She seems bigger, Mabel, if that's what you mean. Bigger and fatter.'

'Hold her,' she ordered. 'Go on, pick her up.'

He reached out and lifted the baby up off the mother's lap. 'Good God!' he cried. 'She weighs a ton!'

'Exactly.'

'Now isn't that marvellous!' he cried, beaming. 'I'll bet she must be back to normal already!'

'It frightens me, Albert. It's too quick.'

'Nonsense, woman.'

'It's that disgusting jelly that's done it,' she said. 'I hate the stuff.'

'There's nothing disgusting about royal jelly,' he answered, indignant.

'Don't be a fool, Albert! You think it's *normal* for a child to start putting on weight at this speed?'

'You're never satisfied!' he cried. 'You're scared stiff when she's losing and now you're absolutely terrified because she's gaining! What's the matter with you, Mabel?'

The woman got up from her chair with the baby in her arms and started towards the door. 'All I can say is,' she said, 'it's lucky I'm here to see you don't give her any more of it, that's all I can say.' She went out, and Albert watched her through the open door as she crossed the hall to the foot of the stairs and started to ascend, and when she reached the third or fourth step she suddenly stopped and stood quite still for several seconds as though remembering something. Then she turned and came down again rather quickly and re-entered the room.

'Albert,' she said.

'Yes?'

'I assume there wasn't any royal jelly in this last feed we've just given her?'

'I don't see why you should assume that, Mabel.' ·

'Albert!'

'What's wrong?' he asked, soft and innocent.

'How *dare* you!' she cried.

Albert Taylor's great bearded face took on a pained and puzzled look. 'I think you ought to be very glad she's got another big dose of it inside her,' he said. 'Honest I do. And this *is* a very big dose, Mabel, believe you me.'

The woman was standing just inside the doorway clasping the sleeping baby in her arms and staring at her husband with huge eyes. She stood very erect, her body absolutely still with fury, her face paler, more tight-lipped than ever.

'You mark my words,' Albert was saying, 'you're going to have a nipper there soon that'll win first prize in any baby show in the *entire* country. Hey, why don't you weigh her now and see what she is? You want me to get the scales, Mabel, so you can weigh her?'

The woman walked straight over to the large table in the centre of the room and laid the baby down and quickly started taking off its clothes. 'Yes!' she snapped. 'Get the scales!' Off came the little nightgown, then the undervest.

Then she unpinned the nappy and she drew it away and the baby lay naked on the table.

'But Mabel!' Albert cried. 'It's a miracle! She's fat as a puppy!'

Indeed, the amount of flesh the child had put on since the day before was astounding. The small sunken chest with the rib bones showing all over it was now plump and round as a barrel, and the belly was bulging high in the air. Curiously, though, the arms and legs did not seem to have grown in proportion. Still short and skinny, they looked like little sticks protruding from a ball of fat.

'Look!' Albert said. 'She's even beginning to get a bit of fuzz on the tummy to keep her warm!' He put out a hand and was about to run the tips of his fingers over the powdering of silky yellowy-brown hairs that had suddenly appeared on the baby's stomach.

'Don't you touch her!' the woman cried. She turned and faced him, her eyes blazing, and she looked suddenly like some kind of little fighting bird with her neck arched over towards him as though she were about to fly at his face and peck his eyes out.

'Now wait a minute,' he said, retreating.

'You must be mad!' she cried.

'Now wait just one minute, Mabel, will you please, because if you're still thinking this stuff is dangerous . . . That *is* what you're thinking, isn't it? All right, then. Listen carefully. I shall now proceed to *prove* to you once and for all, Mabel, that royal jelly is absolutely harmless to human beings, even in enormous doses. For example – why do you think we had only half the usual honey crop last summer? Tell me that.'

His retreat, walking backwards, had taken him three or four yards away from her, where he seemed to feel more comfortable.

'The reason we had only half the usual crop last summer,' he said slowly, lowering his voice, 'was because I turned one hundred of my hives over to the production of royal jelly.'

'You *what?*'

'Ah,' he whispered. 'I thought that might surprise you a bit. And I've been making it ever since right under your very nose.' His small eyes were glinting at her, and a slow sly smile was creeping around the corners of his mouth.

'You'll never guess the reason, either,' he said. 'I've been afraid to mention it up to now because I thought it might . . . well . . . sort of embarrass you.'

There was a slight pause. He had his hands clasped high in front of him, level with his chest, and he was rubbing one palm against the other, making a soft scraping noise.

'You remember that bit I read you out of the magazine? That bit about the rat? Let me see now, how does it go? "Still and Burdett found that a male rat which hitherto had been unable to breed . . ." ' He hesitated, the grin widening, showing his teeth.

'You get the message, Mabel?'

She stood quite still, facing him.

'The very first time I ever read that sentence, Mabel, I jumped straight out of my chair and I said to myself if it'll work with a lousy rat, I said, then there's no reason on earth why it shouldn't work with Albert Taylor.'

He paused again, craning his head forward and turning one ear slightly in his wife's direction, waiting for her to say something. But she didn't.

'And here's another thing,' he went on. 'It made me feel so absolutely marvellous, Mabel, and so sort of completely different to what I was before that I went right on taking it even after you'd announced the joyful tidings. *Buckets* of it I must have swallowed during the last twelve months.'

The big heavy haunted-looking eyes of the woman were moving intently over the man's face and neck. There was no skin showing at all on the neck, not even at the sides below the ears. The whole of it, to a point where it disappeared into the collar of the shirt, was covered all the way around with those shortish silky hairs, yellowy black.

'Mind you,' he said, turning away from her, gazing lovingly now at the baby, 'it's going to work far better on a tiny infant than on a fully developed man like me. You've only got to look at her to see that, don't you agree?'

The woman's eyes travelled slowly downward and settled on the baby. The baby was lying naked on the table, fat and white and comatose, like some gigantic grub that was approaching the end of its larval life and would soon emerge into the world complete with mandibles and wings.

'Why don't you cover her up, Mabel?' he said. 'We don't want our little queen to catch a cold.'

GEORGY PORGY

WITHOUT IN ANY WAY wishing to blow my own trumpet, I think that I can claim to being in most respects a moderately well-matured and rounded individual. I have travelled a good deal. I am adequately read. I speak Greek and Latin. I dabble in science. I can tolerate a mildly liberal attitude in the politics of others. I have compiled a volume of notes upon the evolution of the madrigal in the fifteenth century. I have witnessed the death of a large number of persons in their beds; and in addition, I have influenced, at least I hope I have, the lives of quite a few others by the spoken word delivered from the pulpit.

Yet in spite of all this, I must confess that I have never in my life — well, how shall I put it? — I have never really had anything much to do with women.

To be perfectly honest, up until three weeks ago I had never so much as laid a finger on one of them except perhaps to help her over a stile or something like that when the occasion demanded. And even then I always tried to ensure that I touched only the shoulder or the waist or some other place where the skin was covered, because the one thing I never could stand was actual contact between my skin and theirs. Skin touching skin, my skin, that is, touching the skin of a female, whether it were leg, neck, face, hand, or merely finger, was so repugnant to me that I invariably greeted a lady with my hands clasped firmly behind my back to avoid the inevitable hand-shake.

I could go further than that and say that any sort of physical contact with them, even when the skin wasn't bare, would disturb me considerably. If a woman stood close to me in a queue so that our bodies touched, or if she squeezed in beside me on a bus seat, hip to hip and thigh to thigh, my cheeks would begin burning like mad and little prickles of sweat would start coming out all over the crown of my head.

This condition is all very well in a schoolboy who has just reached the age of puberty. With him it is simply Dame Nature's way of

putting on the brakes and holding the lad back until he is old enough
to behave himself like a gentleman. I approve of that.

But there was no reason on God's earth why I, at the ripe old age
of thirty-one, should continue to suffer a similar embarrassment. I was
well trained to resist temptation, and I was certainly not given to
vulgar passions.

Had I been even the slightest bit ashamed of my own personal
appearance, then that might possibly have explained the whole thing.
But I was not. On the contrary, and though I say it myself, the fates
had been rather kind to me in that regard. I stood exactly five and a
half feet tall in my stockinged feet, and my shoulders, though they
sloped downward a little from the neck, were nicely in balance with
my small neat frame. (Personally, I've always thought that a little slope
on the shoulder lends a subtle and faintly aesthetic air to a man who is
not overly tall, don't you agree?) My features were regular, my teeth
were in excellent condition (protruding only a smallish amount from
the upper jaw), and my hair, which was an unusually brilliant ginger-
red, grew thickly all over my scalp. Good heavens above, I had seen
men who were perfect shrimps in comparison with me displaying an
astonishing aplomb in their dealings with the fairer sex. And oh, how I
envied them! How I longed to do likewise – to be able to share in a
few of those pleasant little rituals of contact that I observed continually
taking place between men and women – the touching of hands, the
peck on the cheek, the linking of arms, the pressure of knee against
knee or foot against foot under the dining-table, and most of all, the
full-blown violent embrace that comes when two of them join together
on the floor – for a dance.

But such things were not for me. Alas, I had to spend my time
avoiding them instead. And this, my friends, was easier said than
done, even for a humble curate in a small country region far from the
fleshpots of the metropolis.

My flock, you understand, contained an inordinate number of ladies.
There were scores of them in the parish and the unfortunate thing
about it was that at least sixty per cent of them were spinsters,
completely untamed by the benevolent influence of holy matrimony.

I tell you I was jumpy as a squirrel.

One would have thought that with all the careful training my
mother had given me as a child, I should have been capable of taking
this sort of thing well in my stride; and no doubt I would have done if
only she had lived long enough to complete my education. But alas,
she was killed when I was still quite young.

She was a wonderful woman, my mother. She used to wear huge bracelets on her wrists, five or six of them at a time, with all sorts of things hanging from them and tinkling against each other as she moved. It didn't matter where she was, you could always find her by listening for the noise of those bracelets. It was better than a cowbell. And in the evenings she used to sit on the sofa in her black trousers with her feet tucked up underneath her, smoking endless cigarettes from a long black holder. And I'd be crouching on the floor, watching her.

'You want to taste my martini, George?' she used to ask.

'Now stop it, Clare,' my father would say. 'If you're not careful you'll stunt the boy's growth.'

'Go on,' she said. 'Don't be frightened of it. Drink it.'

I always did everything my mother told me.

'That's enough,' my father said. 'He only has to know what it tastes like.'

'Please don't interfere, Boris. This is *very* important.'

My mother had a theory that nothing in the world should be kept secret from a child. Show him everything. Make him *experience* it.

'I'm not going to have any boy of mine going around whispering dirty secrets with other children and having to guess about this thing and that simply because no one will tell him.'

Tell him everything. Make him listen.

'Come over here, George, and I'll tell you what there is to know about God.'

She never read stories to me at night before I went to bed; she just 'told' me things instead. And every evening it was something different.

'Come over here, George, because now I'm going to tell you about Mohammed.'

She would be sitting on the sofa in her black trousers with her legs crossed and her feet tucked up underneath her, and she'd beckon to me in a queer languorous manner with the hand that held the long black cigarette-holder, and the bangles would start jingling all the way up her arm.

'If you must have a religion I suppose Mohammedanism is as good as any of them. It's all based on keeping healthy. You have lots of wives, and you mustn't ever smoke or drink.'

'Why mustn't you smoke or drink, Mummy?'.

'Because if you've got lots of wives you have to keep healthy and virile.'

'What is virile?'

'I'll go into that tomorrow, my pet. Let's deal with one subject at a time. Another thing about the Mohammedan is that he never never gets constipated.'

'Now, Clare,' my father would say, looking up from his book. 'Stick to the facts.'

'My dear Boris, you don't know anything about it. Now if only *you* would try bending forward and touching the ground with your forehead morning, noon, and night every day, facing Mecca, you might have a bit less trouble in that direction yourself.'

I used to love listening to her, even though I could only understand about half of what she was saying. She really was telling me secrets, and there wasn't anything more exciting than that.

'Come over here, George, and I'll tell you precisely how your father makes his money.'

'Now, Clare, that's quite enough.'

'Nonsense, darling. Why make a *secret* out of it with the child? He'll only imagine something much much worse.'

I was exactly ten years old when she started giving me detailed lectures on the subject of sex. This was the biggest secret of them all, and therefore the most enthralling.

'Come over here, George, because now I'm going to tell you how you came into this world, right from the very beginning.'

I saw my father glance up quietly, and open his mouth wide the way he did when he was going to say something vital, but my mother was already fixing him with those brilliant shining eyes of hers, and he went slowly back to his book without uttering a sound.

'Your poor father is embarrassed,' she said, and she gave me her private smile, the one that she gave nobody else, only to me — the one-sided smile where just one corner of her mouth lifted slowly upward until it made a lovely long wrinkle that stretched right up to the eye itself, and became a sort of wink-smile instead.

'Embarrassment, my pet, is the one thing that I want you never to feel. And don't think for a moment that your father is embarrassed only because of *you*.'

My father started wriggling about in his chair.

'My God, he's even embarrassed about things like that when he's alone with me, his own wife.'

'About things like what?' I asked.

At that point my father got up and quietly left the room.

I think it must have been about a week after this that my mother was killed. It may possibly have been a little later, ten days or a fortnight, I can't be sure. All I know is that we were getting near the end of this particular series of 'talks' when it happened; and because I myself was personally involved in the brief chain of events that led up to her death, I can still remember every single detail of that curious night just as clearly as if it were yesterday. I can switch it on in my memory any time I like and run it through in front of my eyes exactly as though it were the reel of a cinema film; and it never varies. It always ends at precisely the same place, no more and no less, and it always begins in the same peculiarly sudden way, with the screen in darkness, and my mother's voice somewhere above me, calling my name:

'George! Wake up, George, wake up!'

And then there is a bright electric light dazzling in my eyes, and right from the very centre of it, but far away, the voice is still calling me:

'George, wake up and get out of bed and put your dressing-gown on! Quickly! You're coming downstairs. There's something I want you to see. Come on, child, come on! Hurry up! And put your slippers on. We're going outside.'

'Outside?'

'Don't argue with me, George. Just do as you're told.' I am so sleepy I can hardly see to walk, but my mother takes me firmly by the hand and leads me downstairs and out through the front door into the night where the cold air is like a sponge of water in my face, and I open my eyes wide and see the lawn all sparkling with frost and the cedar tree with its tremendous arms standing black against a thin small moon. And overhead a great mass of stars is wheeling up into the sky.

We hurry across the lawn, my mother and I, her bracelets all jingling like mad and me having to trot to keep up with her. Each step I take I can feel the crisp frosty grass crunching softly underfoot.

'Josephine has just started having her babies,' my mother says. 'It's a perfect opportunity. You shall watch the whole process.'

There is a light burning in the garage when we get there, and we go inside. My father isn't there, nor is the car, and the place seems huge and bare, and the concrete floor is freezing cold through the soles of my bedroom slippers. Josephine is reclining on a heap of straw inside the low wire cage in one corner of the room — large blue rabbit with small pink eyes that watch us suspiciously as we go towards her. The husband, whose name is Napoleon, is now in a separate cage in

the opposite corner, and I notice that he is standing up on his hind
legs scratching impatiently at the netting.

'Look!' my mother cries. 'She's having the first one! It's almost out!'

We both creep closer to Josephine, and I squat down beside the
cage with my face right up against the wire. I am fascinated. Here is
one rabbit coming out of another. It is magical and rather splendid. It
is also very quick.

'Look how it comes out all neatly wrapped up in its own little
cellophane bag!' my mother is saying.

'And just look how she's taking care of it now! The poor darling
doesn't have a face-flannel, and even if she did she couldn't hold it in
her paws, so she's washing it with her tongue instead.'

The mother rabbit rolls her small pink eyes anxiously in our direction, and then I see her shifting position in the straw so that her body
is between us and the young one.

'Come round the other side,' my mother says. 'The silly thing has
moved. I do believe she's trying to hide her baby from us.'

We go round the other side of the cage. The rabbit follows us with
her eyes. A couple of yards away the buck is prancing madly up and
down, clawing at the wire.

'Why is Napoleon so excited?' I ask.

'I don't know, dear. Don't you bother about him. Watch Josephine. I
expect she'll be having another one soon. Look how carefully she's
washing that little baby! She's treating it just like a human mother
treats hers! Isn't it funny to think that I did almost exactly the same
sort of thing to you once?' The big blue doe is still watching us, and
now, again, she pushes the baby away with her nose and rolls slowly
over to face the other way. Then she goes on with her licking and clean-
ing.

'Isn't it wonderful how a mother knows instinctively just what she
has to do?' my mother says. 'Now you just imagine, my pet, that the
baby is *you*, and Josephine is *me* — wait a minute, come back over here
again so you can get a better look.'

We creep back around the cage to keep the baby in view.

'See how she's fondling it and kissing it all over! There! She's *really*
kissing it now, isn't she! Exactly like me and you!'

I peer closer. It seems a queer way of kissing to me.

'Look!' I scream. 'She's eating it!'

And sure enough, the head of the baby rabbit is now disappearing
swiftly into the mother's mouth.

'Mummy! Quick!'

But almost before the sound of my scream has died away, the whole of that tiny pink body has vanished down the mother's throat.

I swing quickly around, and the next thing I know I'm looking straight into my own mother's face, not six inches above me, and no doubt she is trying to say something or it may be that she is too astonished to say anything, but all I see is the mouth, the huge red mouth opening wider and wider until it is just a great big round gaping hole with a black centre, and I scream again, and this time I can't stop. Then suddenly out come her hands, and I can feel her skin touching mine, the long cold fingers closing tightly over my fists, and I jump back and jerk myself free and rush blindly out into the night. I run down the drive and through the front gates, screaming all the way, and then, above the noise of my own voice I can hear the jingle of bracelets coming up behind me in the dark, getting louder and louder as she keeps gaining on me all the way down the long hill to the bottom of the lane and over the bridge on to the main road where the cars are streaming by at sixty miles an hour with headlights blazing.

Then somewhere behind me I hear a screech of tyres skidding on the road surface, and then there is silence, and I notice suddenly that the bracelets aren't jingling behind me any more.

Poor Mother.

If only she could have lived a little longer.

I admit that she gave me a nasty fright with those rabbits, but it wasn't her fault, and anyway queer things like that were always happening between her and me. I had come to regard them as a sort of toughening process that did me more good than harm. But if only she could have lived long enough to complete my education, I'm sure I should never have had all that trouble I was telling you about a few minutes ago.

I want to get on with that now. I didn't mean to begin talking about my mother. She doesn't have anything to do with what I originally started out to say. I won't mention her again.

I was telling you about the spinsters in my parish. It's an ugly word, isn't it — spinster? It conjures up the vision either of a stringy old hen with a puckered mouth or of a huge ribald monster shouting around the house in riding-breeches. But these were not like that at all. They were a clean, healthy, well-built group of females, the majority of them highly bred and surprisingly wealthy, and I feel sure that the average unmarried man would have been gratified to have them around.

In the beginning, when I first came to the vicarage, I didn't have too bad a time. I enjoyed a measure of protection, of course, by reason of my calling and my cloth. In addition, I myself adopted a cool dignified attitude that was calculated to discourage familiarity. For a few months, therefore, I was able to move freely among my parishioners, and no one took the liberty of linking her arm in mine at a charity bazaar, or of touching my fingers with hers as she passed me the cruet at suppertime. I was very happy. I was feeling better than I had in years. Even that little nervous habit I had of flicking my earlobe with my forefinger when I talked began to disappear.

This was what I call my first period, and it extended over approximately six months. Then came trouble.

I suppose I should have known that a healthy male like myself couldn't hope to evade embroilment indefinitely simply by keeping a fair distance between himself and the ladies. It just doesn't work. If anything it has the opposite effect.

I would see them eyeing me covertly across the room at a whist drive, whispering to one another, nodding, running their tongues over their lips, sucking at their cigarettes, plotting the best approach, but always whispering, and sometimes I overheard snatches of their talk — 'What a shy person . . . he's just a trifle nervous, isn't he . . . he's much too tense . . . he needs companionship . . . he wants loosening up . . . we must teach him how to relax.' And then slowly as the weeks went by, they began to stalk me. I knew they were doing it. I could feel it happening although at first they did nothing definite to give themselves away.

That was my second period. It lasted for the best part of a year and was very trying indeed. But it was paradise compared with the third and final phase.

For now, instead of sniping at me sporadically from far away, the attackers suddenly came charging out of the wood with bayonets fixed. It was terrible, frightening. Nothing is more calculated to unnerve a man than the swift unexpected assault. Yet I am not a coward. I will stand my ground against any single individual of my own size under any circumstances. But this onslaught, I am now convinced, was conducted by vast numbers operating as one skilfully coordinated unit.

The first offender was Miss Elphinstone, a large woman with moles. I had dropped in on her during the afternoon to solicit a contribution towards a new set of bellows for the organ, and after some pleasant conversation in the library she had graciously handed me a cheque for two guineas. I told her not to bother to see me to the door and I went out into the hall to get my hat. I was about to reach for it when all at once – she must have come tip-toeing up behind me – all at once I felt a bare arm sliding through mine, and one second later her fingers were entwined in my own, and she was squeezing my hand hard, in out, in out, as though it were the bulb of a throat-spray.

'Are you really so Very Reverend as you're always pretending to be?' she whispered.

Well!

All I can tell you is that when that arm of hers came sliding in under mine, it felt exactly as though a cobra was coiling itself around my wrist. I leaped away, pulled open the front door, and fled down the drive without looking back.

The very next day we held a jumble sale in the village hall (again to raise money for the new bellows), and towards the end of it I was standing in a corner quietly drinking a cup of tea and keeping an eye on the villagers crowding round the stalls when all of a sudden I heard a voice beside me saying, 'Dear me, what a hungry look you have in those eyes of yours.' The next instant a long curvaceous body was leaning up against mine and a hand with red fingernails was trying to push a thick slice of coconut cake into my mouth.

'Miss Prattley,' I cried. 'Please!'

But she'd got me up against the wall, and with a teacup in one hand and a saucer in the other I was powerless to resist. I felt the sweat breaking out all over me and if my mouth hadn't quickly become full of the cake she was pushing into it, I honestly believe I would have started to scream.

A nasty incident, that one; but there was worse to come.

The next day it was Miss Unwin. Now Miss Unwin happened to be a close friend of Miss Elphinstone's *and* of Miss Prattley's, and this of course should have been enough to make me very cautious. Yet who would have thought that she of all people. Miss Unwin, that quiet gentle little mouse who only a few weeks before had presented me with a new hassock exquisitely worked in needlepoint with her own hands, who would have thought that *she* would ever have taken a liberty with anyone? So when she asked me to accompany her down to the crypt to show her the Saxon murals, it never entered my head that there was devilry afoot. But there was.

I don't propose to describe that encounter; it was too painful. And the ones which followed were no less savage. Nearly every day from then on, some new outrageous incident would take place. I became a nervous wreck. At times I hardly knew what I was doing. I started reading the burial service at young Gladys Pitcher's wedding. I dropped

Mrs Harris's new baby into the font during the christening and gave it
a nasty ducking. An uncomfortable rash that I hadn't had in over two
years reappeared on the side of my neck, and that annoying business
with my earlobe came back worse than ever before. Even my hair
began coming out in my comb. The faster I retreated, the faster they
came after me. Women are like that. Nothing stimulates them quite so
much as a display of modesty or shyness in a man. And they become
doubly persistent if underneath it all they happen to detect – and here
I have a most difficult confession to make – if they happen to detect,
as they did in me, a little secret gleam of longing shining in the backs
of the eyes.

You see, actually I was mad about women.

Yes, I know. You will find this hard to believe after all that I have
said, but it was perfectly true. You must understand that it was only
when they touched me with their fingers or pushed up against me
with their bodies that I became alarmed. Providing they remained at a
safe distance, I could watch them for hours on end with the same
peculiar fascination that you yourself might experience in watching a
creature you couldn't bear to touch – an octopus, for example, or a
long poisonous snake. I loved the smooth white look of a bare arm
emerging from a sleeve, curiously naked like a peeled banana. I could
get enormously excited just from watching a girl walk across the room
in a tight dress; and I particularly enjoyed the back view of a pair of
legs when the feet were in rather high heels – the wonderful braced-up
look behind the knees, with the legs themselves very taut as though
they were made of strong elastic stretched out almost to breaking-
point, but not quite. Sometimes, in Lady Birdwell's drawing-room,
sitting near the window on a summer's afternoon, I would glance over
the rim of my teacup towards the swimming pool and become agitated
beyond measure by the sight of a little patch of sunburned stomach
bulging between the top and bottom of a two-piece bathing-suit.

There is nothing wrong in having thoughts like these. All men
harbour them from time to time. But they did give me a terrible sense
of guilt. Is it me, I kept asking myself, who is unwittingly responsible
for the shameless way in which these ladies are now behaving? Is it
the gleam in my eye (which I cannot control) that is constantly
rousing their passions and egging them on? Am I unconsciously giving
them what is sometimes known as the come-hither signal every time I
glance their way? Am I?

Or is this brutal conduct of theirs inherent in the very nature of the
female?

I had a pretty fair idea of the answer to this question, but that was not good enough for me. I happen to possess a conscience that can never be consoled by guesswork; it has to have proof. I simply had to find out who was really the guilty party in this case – me or them, and with this object in view, I now decided to perform a simple experiment of my own invention, using Snelling's rats.

A year or so previously I had had some trouble with an objectionable choirboy named Billy Snelling. On three consecutive Sundays this youth had brought a pair of white rats into church and had let them loose on the floor during my sermon. In the end I had confiscated the animals and carried them home and placed them in a box in the shed at the bottom of the vicarage garden. Purely for humane reasons I had then proceeded to feed them, and as a result, but without any further encouragement from me, the creatures began to multiply very rapidly. The two became five, and five became twelve.

It was at this point that I decided to use them for research purposes. There were exactly equal numbers of males and females, six of each, so that conditions were ideal.

I first isolated the sexes, putting them into two separate cages, and I left them like that for three whole weeks. Now a rat is a very lascivious animal, and any zoologist will tell you that for them this is an inordinately long period of separation. At a guess I would say that one week of enforced celibacy for a rat is equal to approximately one year of the same treatment for someone like Miss Elphinstone or Miss Prattley; so you can see that I was doing a pretty fair job in reproducing actual conditions.

When the three weeks were up, I took a large box that was divided across the centre by a little fence, and I placed the females on one side and the males on the other. The fence consisted of nothing more than three single strands of naked wire, one inch apart, but there was a powerful electric current running through the wires.

To add a touch of reality to the proceedings, I gave each female a name. The largest one, who also had the longest whiskers, was Miss Elphinstone. The one with a short thick tail was Miss Prattley. The smallest of them all was Miss Unwin, and so on. The males, all six of them, were ME.

I now pulled up a chair and sat back to watch the result.

All rats are suspicious by nature, and when I first put the two sexes together in the box with only the wire between them, neither side made a move. The males stared hard at the females through the fence. The females stared back, waiting for the males to come forward. I could see that both sides were tense with yearning. Whiskers quivered and noses twitched and occasionally a long tail would flick sharply against the wall of the box.

After a while, the first male detached himself from his group and advanced gingerly towards the fence, his belly close to the ground. He touched a wire and was immediately electrocuted. The remaining eleven rats froze, motionless.

There followed a period of nine and a half minutes during which neither side moved; but I noticed that while all the males were now staring at the dead body of their colleague, the females had eyes only for the males.

Then suddenly Miss Prattley with the short tail could stand it no longer. She came bounding forward, hit the wire, and dropped dead.

The males pressed their bodies closer to the ground and gazed thoughtfully at the two corpses by the fence. The females also seemed to be quite shaken, and there was another wait, with neither side moving.

Now it was Miss Unwin who began to show signs of impatience. She snorted audibly and twitched a pink mobile nose-end from side to side, then suddenly she started jerking her body quickly up and down as though she were doing pushups. She glanced round at her remaining four companions, raised her tail high in the air as much as to say, 'Here I go. girls,' and with that she advanced briskly to the wire, pushed her head through it, and was killed.

Sixteen minutes later, Miss Foster made her first move. Miss Foster was a woman in the village who bred cats, and recently she had had the effrontery to put up a large sign outside her house in the High Street, saying FOSTER'S CATTERY. Through long association with the creatures she herself seemed to have acquired all their most noxious characteristics, and whenever she came near me in a room I could detect, even through the smoke of her Russian cigarette, a faint but pungent aroma of cat. She had never struck me as having much control over her baser instincts, and it was with some satisfaction, therefore, that I watched her now as she foolishly took her own life in a last desperate plunge towards the masculine sex.

A Miss Montgomery-Smith came next, a small determined woman who had once tried to make me believe that she had been engaged to a bishop. She died trying to creep on her belly under the lowest wire, and I must say I thought this a very fair reflection upon the way in which she lived her life.

And still the five remaining males stayed motionless, waiting.

The fifth female to go was Miss Plumley. She was a devious one who was continually slipping little messages addressed to me into the collection bag. Only the Sunday before, I had been in the vestry counting the money after morning service and had come across one of them tucked inside a folded ten-shilling note. *Your poor throat sounded hoarse today during the sermon*, it said. *Let me bring you a bottle of my own cherry pectoral to soothe it down. Most affectionately, Eunice Plumley.*

Miss Plumley ambled slowly up to the wire, sniffed the centre strand with the tip of her nose, came a fraction too close, and received two hundred and forty volts of alternating current through her body.

The five males stayed where they were, watching the slaughter.

And now only Miss Elphinstone remained on the feminine side.

For a full half-hour neither she nor any of the others made a move. Finally one of the males stirred himself slightly, took a step forward, hesitated, thought better of it, and slowly sank back into a crouch on the floor.

This must have frustrated Miss Elphinstone beyond measure, for suddenly, with eyes blazing, she rushed forward and took a flying leap at the wire. It was a spectacular jump and she nearly cleared it; but one of her hind legs grazed the top strand, and thus she also perished with the rest of her sex.

I cannot tell you how much good it did me to watch this simple and, though I say it myself, this rather ingenious experiment. In one stroke I had laid open the incredibly lascivious, stop-at-nothing nature of the female. My own sex was vindicated; my own conscience was cleared. In a trice, all those awkward little flashes of guilt from which I had continually been suffering flew out of the window. I felt suddenly very strong and serene in the knowledge of my own innocence.

For a few moments I toyed with the absurd idea of electrifying the black iron railings that ran around the vicarage garden; or perhaps just the gate would be enough. Then I would sit back comfortably in a chair in the library and watch through the window as the real Misses Elphinstone and Prattley and Unwin came forward one after the other and paid the final penalty for pestering an innocent male.

Such foolish thoughts!

What I must actually do now, I told myself, was to weave around me a sort of invisible electric fence constructed entirely out of my own personal moral fibre. Behind this I would sit in perfect safety while the enemy, one after another, flung themselves against the wire.

I would begin by cultivating a brusque manner. I would speak crisply to all women, and refrain from smiling at them. I would no longer step back a pace when one of them advanced upon me. I would stand my ground and glare at her, and if she said something that I considered suggestive, I would make a sharp retort.

It was in this mood that I set off the very next day to attend Lady Birdwell's tennis party.

I was not a player myself, but her ladyship had graciously invited me to drop in and mingle with the guests when play was over at six o'clock. I believe she thought that it lent a certain tone to a gathering to have a clergyman present, and she was probably hoping to persuade me to repeat the performance I gave the last time I was there, when I sat at the piano for a full hour and a quarter after supper and entertained the guests with a detailed description of the evolution of the madrigal through the centuries.

I arrived at the gates on my cycle promptly at six o'clock and pedalled up the long drive towards the house. This was the first week of June, and the rhododendrons were massed in great banks of pink and purple all the way along on either side. I was feeling unusually blithe and dauntless. The previous day's experiment with rats had made it impossible now for anyone to take me by surprise. I knew exactly what to expect and I was armed accordingly. All around me the little fence was up.

'Ah, good evening, Vicar,' Lady Birdwell cried, advancing upon me with both arms outstretched.

I stood my ground and looked her straight in the eye. 'How's Birdwell?' I said. 'Still up in the city?'

I doubt whether she had ever before in her life heard Lord Birdwell referred to thus by someone who had never even met him. It stopped her dead in her tracks. She looked at me queerly and didn't seem to know how to answer.

'I'll take a seat if I may,' I said, and walked past her towards the terrace where a group of nine or ten guests were settled comfortably in cane chairs, sipping their drinks. They were mostly women, the usual crowd, all of them dressed in white tennis clothes, and as I strode in among them my own sober black suiting seemed to give me, I thought, just the right amount of separateness for the occasion.

The ladies greeted me with smiles. I nodded to them and sat down in a vacant chair, but I didn't smile back.

'I think perhaps I'd better finish my story another time,' Miss Elphinstone was saying. 'I don't believe the vicar would approve.' She giggled and gave me an arch look. I knew she was waiting for me to come out with my usual little nervous laugh and to say my usual little sentence about how broadminded I was; but I did nothing of the sort. I simply raised one side of my upper lip until it shaped itself into a tiny curl of contempt (I had practised in the mirror that morning), and then I said sharply, in a loud voice, '*Mens sana in corpore sano.*'

'What's that?' she cried. 'Come again, Vicar.'

'A clean mind in a healthy body,' I answered. 'It's a family motto.'

There was an odd kind of silence for quite a long time after this. I could see the women exchanging glances with one another, frowning, shaking their heads.

'The vicar's in the dumps,' Miss Foster announced. She was the one who bred cats. 'I think the vicar needs a drink.'

'Thank you,' I said, 'but I never imbibe. You know that.'

'Then do let me fetch you a nice cooling glass of fruit cup?'

This last sentence came softly and rather suddenly from someone just behind me, to my right, and there was a note of such genuine concern in the speaker's voice that I turned round.

I saw a lady of singular beauty whom I had met only once before, about a month ago. Her name was Miss Roach, and I remembered that she had struck me then as being a person far out of the usual run. I had been particularly impressed by her gentle and reticent nature; and the fact that I had felt comfortable in her presence proved beyond doubt that she was not the sort of person who would try to impinge herself upon me in any way.

'I'm sure you must be tired after cycling all that distance,' she was saying now.

I swivelled right round in my chair and looked at her carefully. She was certainly a striking person — unusually muscular for a woman, with broad shoulders and powerful arms and a huge calf bulging on each leg. The flush of the afternoon's exertions was still upon her, and her face glowed with a healthy red sheen.

'Thank you so much, Miss Roach,' I said, 'but I never touch alcohol in any form. Maybe a small glass of lemon squash . . .'

'The fruit cup is only made of fruit, Padre.'

How I loved a person who called me 'Padre'. The word has a military ring about it that conjures up visions of stern discipline and officer rank.

'Fruit cup?' Miss Elphinstone said. 'It's harmless.'

'My dear man, it's nothing but vitamin C,' Miss Foster said.

'Much better for you than fizzy lemonade,' Lady Birdwell said. 'Carbon dioxide attacks the lining of the stomach.'

'I'll get you some,' Miss Roach said, smiling at me pleasantly. It was a good open smile, and there wasn't a trace of guile or mischief from one corner of the mouth to the other.

She stood up and walked over to the drink table. I saw her slicing an orange, then an apple, then a cucumber, then a grape, and dropping the pieces into a glass. Then she poured in a large quantity of liquid from a bottle whose label I couldn't quite read without my spectacles, but I fancied that I saw the name JIM on it, or TIM or PIM, or some such word.

'I hope there's enough left,' Lady Birdwell called out. 'Those greedy children of mine do love it so.'

'Plenty,' Miss Roach answered, and she brought the drink to me and set it on the table.

Even without tasting it I could easily understand why children adored it. The liquid itself was dark amber-red and there were great hunks of fruit floating around among the ice cubes; and on top of it all, Miss Roach had placed a sprig of mint. I guessed that the mint had been put there specially for me, to take some of the sweetness away and to lend a touch of grown-upness to a concoction that was otherwise so obviously for youngsters.

'Too sticky for you, Padre!'

'It's delectable,' I said, sipping it. 'Quite perfect.'

It seemed a pity to gulp it down quickly after all the trouble Miss Roach had taken to make it, but it was so refreshing I couldn't resist.

'Do let me make you another!'

I liked the way she waited until I had set the glass on the table, instead of trying to take it out of my hand.

'I wouldn't eat the mint if I were you,' Miss Elphinstone said.

'I'd better get another bottle from the house,' Lady Birdwell called out. 'You're going to need it, Mildred.'

'Do that,' Miss Roach replied. 'I drink gallons of the stuff myself,' she went on, speaking to me. 'And I don't think you'd say that I'm exactly what you might call emaciated.'

'No indeed,' I answered fervently. I was watching her again as she mixed me another brew, noticing how the muscles rippled under the skin of the arm that raised the bottle. Her neck also was uncommonly fine when seen from behind; not thin and stringy like the necks of a lot of these so-called modern beauties, but thick and strong with a slight ridge running down either side where the sinews bulged. It wasn't easy to guess the age of a person like this, but I doubted whether she could have been more than forty-eight or nine.

I had just finished my second big glass of fruit cup when I began to experience a most peculiar sensation. I seemed to be floating up out of my chair, and hundreds of little warm waves came washing in under me, lifting me higher and higher. I felt as buoyant as a bubble, and everything around me seemed to be bobbing up and down and swirling gently from side to side. It was all very pleasant, and I was overcome by an almost irresistible desire to break into song.

'Feeling happy?' Miss Roach's voice sounded miles and miles away, and when I turned to look at her, I was astonished to see how near she really was. She, also, was bobbing up and down.

'Terrific,' I answered. 'I'm feeling absolutely terrific.'

Her face was large and pink, and it was so close to me now that I could see the pale carpet of fuzz covering both her cheeks, and the way the sunlight caught each tiny separate hair and made it shine like gold. All of a sudden I found myself wanting to put out a hand and stroke those cheeks of hers with my fingers. To tell the truth I wouldn't have objected in the least if she had tried to do the same to me.

'Listen,' she said softly. 'How about the two of us taking a little stroll down the garden to see the lupins?'

'Fine,' I answered. 'Lovely. Anything you say.'

· There is a small Georgian summer-house alongside the croquet lawn in Lady Birdwell's garden, and the very next thing I knew, I was sitting inside it on a kind of chaise-longue and Miss Roach was beside me. I was still bobbing up and down, and so was she, and so, for that matter, was the summer-house, but I was feeling wonderful. I asked Miss Roach if she would like me to give her a song.

'Not now,' she said, encircling me with her arms and squeezing my chest against hers so hard that it hurt.

'Don't,' I said, melting.

'That's better,' she kept saying. 'That's much better, isn't it?'

Had Miss Roach or any other female tried to do this sort of thing to me an hour before, I don't quite know what would have happened. I think I would probably have fainted. I might even have died. But here I was now, the same old me, actually relishing the contact of those enormous bare arms against my body! Also – and this was the most amazing thing of all – I was beginning to feel the urge to reciprocate.

I took the lobe of her left ear between my thumb and forefinger, and tugged it playfully.

'Naughty boy,' she said.

I tugged harder and squeezed it a bit at the same time. This roused her to such a pitch that she began to grunt and snort like a hog. Her breathing became loud and stertorous.

'Kiss me,' she ordered.

'What?' I said.

'Come on, kiss me.'

At that moment, I saw her mouth. I saw this great mouth of hers coming slowly down on top of me, starting to open, and coming closer and closer, and opening wider and wider; and suddenly my whole stomach began to roll right over inside me and I went stiff with terror.

'No!' I shrieked. 'Don't! Don't, Mummy, don't!'

I can only tell you that I had never in all my life seen anything more terrifying than that mouth. I simply could not *stand* it coming at me like that. Had it been a red-hot iron someone was pushing into my face I wouldn't have been nearly so petrified, I swear I wouldn't. The strong arms were around me, pinning me down so that I couldn't move, and the mouth kept getting larger and larger, and then all at once it was right on top of me, huge and wet and cavernous, and the next second – I was inside it.

I was right inside this enormous mouth, lying on my stomach along the length of the tongue, with my feet somewhere around the back of the throat; and I knew instinctively that unless I got myself out again at once I was going to be swallowed alive – just like that baby rabbit. I could feel my legs being drawn down the throat by some kind of suction, and quickly I threw up my arms and grabbed hold of the lower front teeth and held on for dear life. My head was near the mouth-entrance, and I could actually look right out between the lips and see a little patch of the world outside – sunlight shining on the polished wooden floor of the summer-house, and on the floor itself a gigantic foot in a white tennis shoe.

I had a good grip with my fingers on the edge of the teeth, and in spite of the suction, I was managing to haul myself up slowly towards the daylight when suddenly the upper teeth came down on my knuckles and started chopping away at them so fiercely I had to let go. I went sliding back down the throat, feet first, clutching madly at this and that as I went, but everything was so smooth and slippery I couldn't get a grip. I glimpsed a bright flash of gold on the left as I slid past the last of the molars, and then three inches farther on I saw what must have been the uvula above me, dangling like a thick red stalactite from the roof of the throat. I grabbed at it with both hands but the thing slithered through my fingers and I went on down.

I remember screaming for help, but I could hardly hear the sound of my own voice above the noise of the wind that was caused by the throat-owner's breathing. There seemed to be a gale blowing all the time, a queer erratic gale that blew alternately very cold (as the air came in) and very hot (as it went out again).

I managed to get my elbows hooked over a sharp fleshy ridge – I presume the epiglottis – and for a brief moment I hung there, defying the suction and scrabbling with my feet to find a foothold on the wall of the larynx; but the throat gave a huge swallow that jerked me away, and down I went again.

From then on, there was nothing else for me to catch hold of, and down and down I went until soon my legs were dangling below me in the upper reaches of the stomach, and I could feel the slow powerful pulsing of peristalsis dragging away at my ankles, pulling me down and down and down . . .

Far above me, outside in the open air, I could hear the distant babble of women's voices:

'It's not true . . .'

'But my dear Mildred, how awful . . .'

'The man must be mad . . .'

'Your poor mouth, just look at it . . .'

'A sex maniac . . .'

'A sadist . . .'

'Someone ought to write to the bishop . . .'

And then Miss Roach's voice, louder than the others, swearing and screeching like a parakeet:

'He's damn lucky I didn't kill him, the little bastard! . . . I said to him, listen, I said, if ever I happen to want any of my teeth extracted, I'll go to the dentist, not to a goddam vicar . . . It isn't as though I'd given him any encouragement either! . . .'

'Where is he now, Mildred?'

'God knows. In the bloody summer-house, I suppose.'

'Hey girls, let's go and root him out!'

Oh dear, oh dear. Looking back on it now, some three weeks later, I don't know how I ever came through the nightmare of that awful afternoon without taking leave of my senses.

A gang of witches like that is a very dangerous thing to fool around with, and had they managed to catch me in the summer-house right then and there when their blood was up, they would as likely as not have torn me limb from limb on the spot.

Either that, or I should have been frog-marched down to the police station with Lady Birdwell and Miss Roach leading the procession through the main street of the village.

But of course they didn't catch me.

They didn't catch me then, and they haven't caught me yet, and if my luck continues to hold, I think I've got a fair chance of evading them altogether – or anyway for a few months, until they forget about the whole affair.

As you might guess, I am having to keep entirely to myself and to take no part in public affairs or social life. I find that writing is a most salutary occupation at a time like this, and I spend many hours each day playing with sentences. I regard each sentence as a little wheel, and my ambition lately has been to gather several hundred of them together at once and to fit them all end to end, with the cogs interlocking, like gears, but each wheel a different size, each turning at a different speed. Now and again I try to put a really big one right next to a very small one in such a way that the big one, turning slowly, will make the small one spin so fast that it hums. Very tricky, that.

I also sing madrigals in the evenings, but I miss my own harpsichord terribly.

All the same, this isn't such a bad place, and I have made myself as comfortable as I possibly can. It is a small chamber situated in what is almost certainly the primary section of the duodenal loop, just before it begins to run vertically downward in front of the right kidney. The floor is quite level – indeed it was the first level place I came to during that horrible descent down Miss Roach's throat – and that's the only reason I managed to stop at all. Above me, I can see a pulpy sort of opening that I take to be the pylorus, where the stomach enters the small intestine (I can still remember some of those diagrams my mother used to show me), and below me, there is a funny little hole in the wall where the pancreatic duct enters the lower section of the duodenum.

It is all a trifle bizarre for a man of conservative tastes like myself. Personally I prefer oak furniture and parquet flooring. But there is anyway one thing here that pleases me greatly, and that is the walls. They are lovely and soft, like a sort of padding, and the advantage of this is that I can bounce up against them as much as I wish without hurting myself.

There are several other people about, which is rather surprising, but thank God they are every one of them males. For some reason or other, they all wear white coats, and they bustle around pretending to be very busy and important. In actual fact, they are an uncommonly ignorant bunch of fellows. They don't even seem to realize where they *are*. I try to tell them, but they refuse to listen. Sometimes I get so angry and frustrated with them that I lose my temper and start to shout; and then a sly mistrustful look comes over the faces and they begin backing slowly away, and saying, 'Now then. Take it easy. Take it easy, vicar, there's a good boy. Take it easy.'

What sort of talk is that?

But there is one oldish man – he comes in to see me every morning after breakfast – who appears to live slightly closer to reality than the others. He is civil and dignified, and I imagine he is lonely because he likes nothing better than to sit quietly in my room and listen to me talk. The only trouble is that whenever we get on to the subject of our whereabouts, he starts telling me that he's going to help me to escape. He said it again this morning, and we had quite an argument about it.

'But can't you see,' I said patiently, 'I don't *want* to escape.'

'My dear Vicar, why ever not?'

'I keep telling you – because they're all searching for me outside.'

'Who?'

'Miss Elphinstone and Miss Roach and Miss Prattley and all the rest of them.'

'What nonsense.'

'Oh yes they are! And I imagine they're after *you* as well, but you won't admit it.'

'No, my friend, they are not after me.'

'Then may I ask precisely what you are doing down here?'

A bit of a stumper for him, that one. I could see he didn't know how to answer it.

'I'll bet you were fooling around with Miss Roach and got yourself swallowed up just the same as I did. I'll bet that's exactly what happened, only you're ashamed to admit it.'

He looked suddenly so wan and defeated when I said this that I felt sorry for him.

'Would you like me to sing you a song?' I asked.

But he got up without answering and went quietly out into the corridor.

'Cheer up,' I called after him. 'Don't be depressed. There is always some balm in Gilead.'

GENESIS AND CATASTROPHE

A True Story

'EVERYTHING IS NORMAL,' the doctor was saying. 'Just lie back and relax.' His voice was miles away in the distance and he seemed to be shouting at her. 'You have a son.'

'What?'

'You have a fine son. You understand that, don't you? A fine son. Did you hear him crying?'

'Is he all right, Doctor?'

'Of course he is all right.'

'Please let me see him.'

'You'll see him in a moment.'

'You are certain he is all right?'

'I am quite certain.'

'Is he still crying?'

'Try to rest. There is nothing to worry about.'

'Why has he stopped crying, Doctor? What happened?'

'Don't excite yourself, please. Everything is normal.'

'I want to see him. Please let me see him.'

'Dear lady,' the doctor said, patting her hand. 'You have a fine strong healthy child. Don't you believe me when I tell you that?'

'What is the woman over there doing to him?'

'Your baby is being made to look pretty for you,' the doctor said. 'We are giving him a little wash, that is all. You must spare us a moment or two for that.'

'You swear he is all right?'

'I swear it. Now lie back and relax. Close your eyes. Go on, close your eyes. That's right. That's better. Good girl . . .'

'I have prayed and prayed that he will live, Doctor.'

'Of course he will live. What are you talking about?'

'The others didn't.'

'What?'

'None of my other ones lived, Doctor.'

The doctor stood beside the bed looking down at the pale exhausted face of the young woman. He had never seen her before today. She and her husband were new people in the town. The innkeeper's wife, who had come up to assist in the delivery, had told him that the husband worked at the local customs-house on the border and that the two of them had arrived quite suddenly at the inn with one trunk and one suitcase about three months ago. The husband was a drunkard, the innkeeper's wife had said, an arrogant, overbearing, bullying little drunkard, but the young woman was gentle and religious. And she was very sad. She never smiled. In the few weeks that she had been here, the innkeeper's wife had never once seen her smile. Also there was a rumour that this was the husband's third marriage, that one wife had died and that the other had divorced him for unsavoury reasons. But that was only a rumour.

The doctor bent down and pulled the sheet up a little higher over the patient's chest. 'You have nothing to worry about,' he said gently. 'This is a perfectly normal baby.'

'That's exactly what they told me about the others. But I lost them all, Doctor. In the last eighteen months I have lost all three of my children, so you mustn't blame me for being anxious.'

'Three?'

'This is my fourth . . . in four years.'

The doctor shifted his feet uneasily on the bare floor.

'I don't think you know what it means, Doctor, to lose them all, all three of them, slowly, separately, one by one. I keep seeing them. I can see Gustav's face now as clearly as if he were lying here beside me in the bed. Gustav was a lovely boy, Doctor. But he was always ill. It is terrible when they are always ill and there is nothing you can do to help them.'

'I know.'

The woman opened her eyes, stared up at the doctor for a few seconds, then closed them again.

'My little girl was called Ida. She died a few days before Christmas. That is only four months ago. I just wish you could have seen Ida, Doctor.'

'You have a new one now.'

'But Ida was so beautiful.'

'Yes,' the doctor said. 'I know.'

'How can you know?' she cried.

'I am sure that she was a lovely child. But this new one is also like that.' The doctor turned away from the bed and walked over to the window and stood there looking out. It was a wet grey April afternoon, and across the street he could see the red roofs of the houses and the huge raindrops splashing on the tiles.

'Ida was two years old, Doctor ... and she was so beautiful I was never able to take my eyes off her from the time I dressed her in the morning until she was safe in bed again at night. I used to live in holy terror of something happening to that child. Gustav had gone and my little Otto had also gone and she was all I had left. Sometimes I used to get up in the night and creep over to the cradle and put my ear close to her mouth just to make sure that she was breathing.'

'Try to rest,' the doctor said, going back to the bed. 'Please try to rest.' The woman's face was white and bloodless, and there was a slight bluish-grey tinge around the nostrils and the mouth. A few strands of damp hair hung down over her forehead, sticking to the skin.

'When she died ... I was already pregnant again when that happened, Doctor. This new one was a good four months on its way when Ida died. "I don't want it!" I shouted after the funeral. "I won't have it! I have buried enough children!" And my husband ... he was strolling among the guests with a big glass of beer in his hand ... he turned around quickly and said, "I have news for you, Klara, I have good news." Can you imagine that, Doctor? We have just buried our third child and he stands there with a glass of beer in his hand and tells me that he has good news. "Today I have been posted to Braunau," he says, "so you can start packing at once. This will be a new start for you, Klara," he says. "It will be a new place and you can have a new doctor ..." '

'Please don't talk any more.'

'You *are* the new doctor, aren't you, Doctor?'

'That's right.'

'And here we are in Braunau.'

'Yes.'

'I am frightened, Doctor.'

'Try not to be frightened.'

'What chance can the fourth one have now?'

'You must stop thinking like that.'

'I can't help it. I am certain there is something inherited that causes my children to die in this way. There must be.'

'That is nonsense.'

'Do you know what my husband said to me when Otto was born, Doctor? He came into the room and he looked into the cradle where

Otto was lying and he said, "Why do *all* my children have to be so small and weak?"'

'I am sure he didn't say that.'

'He put his head right into Otto's cradle as though he were examining a tiny insect and he said, "All I am saying is why can't they be better *specimens*? That's all I am saying." And three days after that, Otto was dead. We baptised him quickly on the third day and he died the same evening. And then Gustav died. And then Ida died. All of them died, Doctor . . . and suddenly the whole house was empty. . . .'

'Don't think about it now.'

'Is this one so very small?'

'He is a normal child.'

'But small?'

'He is a little small, perhaps. But the small ones are often a lot tougher than the big ones. Just imagine, Frau Hitler, this time next year he will be almost learning how to walk. Isn't that a lovely thought?'

She didn't answer this.

'And two years from now he will probably be talking his head off and driving you crazy with his chatter. Have you settled on a name for him yet?'

'A name?'

'Yes.'

'I don't know. I'm not sure. I think my husband said that if it was a boy we were going to call him Adolfus.'

'That means he would be called Adolf.'

'Yes. My husband likes Adolf because it has a certain similarity to Alois. My husband is called Alois.'

'Excellent.'

'Oh no!' she cried, starting up suddenly from the pillow. 'That's the same question they asked me when Otto was born! It means he is going to die! You are going to baptize him at once!'

'Now, now,' the doctor said, taking her gently by the shoulders. 'You are quite wrong. I promise you you are wrong. I was simply being an inquisitive old man, that is all. I love talking about names. I think Adolphus is a particularly fine name. It is one of my favourites. And look – here he comes now.'

The innkeeper's wife, carrying the baby high up on her enormous bosom, came sailing across the room towards the bed. 'Here is the little beauty!' she cried, beaming. 'Would you like to hold him, my dear? Shall I put him beside you?'

'Is he well wrapped?' the doctor asked. 'It is extremely cold in here.'

'Certainly he is well wrapped.'

The baby was tightly swaddled in a white woollen shawl, and only the tiny pink head protruded. The innkeeper's wife placed him gently on the bed beside the mother. 'There you are,' she said. 'Now you can lie there and look at him to your heart's content.'

'I think you will like him,' the doctor said, smiling. 'He is a fine little baby.'

'He has the most lovely hands!' the innkeeper's wife exclaimed. 'Such long delicate fingers!'

The mother didn't move. She didn't even turn her head to look.

'Go on!' cried the innkeeper's wife. 'He won't bite you!'

'I am frightened to look. I don't care to believe that I have another baby and that he is all right.'

'Don't be so stupid.'

Slowly, the mother turned her head and looked at the small, incredibly serene face that lay on the pillow beside her.

'Is this my baby?'

'Of course.'

'Oh . . . oh . . . but he is beautiful.'

The doctor turned away and went over to the table and began putting his things into his bag. The mother lay on the bed gazing at the child and smiling and touching him and making little noises of pleasure. 'Hello, Adolfus,' she whispered. 'Hello, my little Adolf . . .'

'Ssshh!' said the innkeeper's wife. 'Listen! I think your husband is coming.'

The doctor walked over to the door and opened it and looked out into the corridor.

'Herr Hitler!'

'Yes.'

'Come in, please.'

A small man in a dark-green uniform stepped softly into the room and looked around him.

'Congratulations,' the doctor said. 'You have a son.'

The man had a pair of enormous whiskers meticulously groomed after the manner of the Emperor Franz Josef, and he smelled strongly of beer. 'A son?'

'Yes.'

'How is he?'

'He is fine. So is your wife.'

'Good.' The father turned and walked with a curious little prancing stride over to the bed where his wife was lying. 'Well, Klara,' he said, smiling through his whiskers. 'How did it go?' He bent down to take a look at the baby. Then he bent lower. In a series of quick jerky movements, he bent lower and lower until his face was only about twelve inches from the baby's head. The wife lay sideways on the pillow, staring up at him with a kind of supplicating look.

'He has the most marvellous pair of lungs,' the innkeeper's wife announced. 'You should have heard him screaming just after he came into this world.'

'But my God, Klara . . .'

'What is it, dear?'

'This one is even smaller than Otto was!'

The doctor took a couple of quick paces forward. 'There is nothing wrong with that child,' he said.

Slowly, the husband straightened up and turned away from the bed and looked at the doctor. He seemed bewildered and stricken. 'It's no good lying, Doctor,' he said. 'I know what it means. It's going to be the same all over again.'

'Now you listen to me,' the doctor said.

'But do you *know* what happened to the others, Doctor?'

'You must forget about the others, Herr Hitler. Give this one a chance.'

'But so small and weak!'

'My dear sir, he has only just been born.'

'Even so . . .'

'What are you trying to do?' cried the innkeeper's wife. 'Talk him into his grave?'

'That's enough!' the doctor said sharply.

The mother was weeping now. Great sobs were shaking her body.

The doctor walked over to the husband and put a hand on his shoulder. 'Be good to her,' he whispered. 'Please. It is very important.' Then he squeezed the husband's shoulder hard and began pushing him forward surreptitiously to the edge of the bed. The husband hesitated. The doctor squeezed harder, signalling him urgently through fingers and thumb. At last, reluctantly, the husband bent down and kissed his wife lightly on the cheek.

'All right, Klara,' he said. 'Now stop crying.'

'I have prayed so hard that he will live, Alois.'

'Yes.'

'Every day for months I have gone to the church and begged on my knees that this one will be allowed to live.'

'Yes, Klara, I know.'

'Three dead children is all that I can stand, don't you realize that?'

'Of course.'

'He *must* live, Alois. He *must*, he *must* . . . Oh God, be merciful unto him now . . .'

EDWARD THE CONQUEROR

LOUISA, HOLDING A DISHCLOTH in her hand, stepped out of the kitchen door at the back of the house into the cool October sunshine.

'Edward!' she called. 'Ed-ward! Lunch is ready!'

She paused a moment, listening; then she strolled out on to the lawn and continued across it – a little shadow attending her – skirting the rose bed and touching the sundial lightly with one finger as she went by. She moved rather gracefully for a woman who was small and plump, with a lilt in her walk and a gentle swinging of the shoulders and the arms. She passed under the mulberry tree on to the brick path, then went all the way along the path until she came to the place where she could look down into the dip at the end of this large garden.

'Edward! Lunch!'

She could see him now, about eighty yards away, down in the dip on the edge of the wood – the tallish narrow figure in khaki slacks and dark-green sweater, working beside a big bonfire with a fork in his hands, pitching brambles on to the top of the fire. It was blazing fiercely, with orange flames and clouds of milky smoke, and the smoke was drifting back over the garden with a wonderful scent of autumn and burning leaves.

Louisa went down the slope towards her husband. Had she wanted, she could easily have called again and made herself heard, but there was something about a first-class bonfire that impelled her towards it, right up close so she could feel the heat and listen to it burn.

'Lunch,' she said, approaching.

'Oh, hello. All right – yes. I'm coming.'

'What a good fire.'

'I've decided to clear this place right out,' her husband said. 'I'm sick and tired of all these brambles.' His long face was wet with perspiration. There were small beads of it clinging all over his moustache like dew, and two little rivers were running down his throat on to the turtleneck of the sweater.

'You better be careful you don't overdo it, Edward.'

'Louisa, I do wish you'd stop treating me as though I were eighty. A bit of exercise never did anyone any harm.'

'Yes, dear, I know. Oh, Edward! Look! Look!'

The man turned and looked at Louisa, who was pointing now to the far side of the bonfire.

'Look, Edward! The cat!'

Sitting on the ground, so close to the fire that the flames sometimes seemed actually to be touching it, was a large cat of a most unusual colour. It stayed quite still, with its head on one side and its nose in the air, watching the man and woman with a cool yellow eye.

'It'll get burnt!' Louisa cried, and she dropped the dishcloth and darted swiftly in and grabbed it with both hands, whisking it away and putting it on the grass well clear of the flames.

'You crazy cat,' she said, dusting off her hands. 'What's the matter with you?'

'Cats know what they're doing,' the husband said. 'You'll never find a cat doing something it doesn't want. Not cats.'

'Whose is it? You ever seen it before?'

'No, I never have. Damn peculiar colour.'

The cat had seated itself on the grass and was regarding them with a sidewise look. There was a veiled inward expression about the eyes, something curiously omniscient and pensive, and around the nose a most delicate air of contempt, as though the sight of these two middle-aged persons – the one small, plump, and rosy, the other lean and extremely sweaty – were a matter of some surprise but very little importance. For a cat, it certainly had an unusual colour – a pure silvery grey with no blue in it at all – and the hair was very long and silky.

Louisa bent down and stroked its head. 'You must go home,' she said. 'Be a good cat now and go on home to where you belong.'

The man and wife started to stroll back up the hill towards the house. The cat got up and followed, at a distance first, but edging closer and closer as they went along. Soon it was alongside them, then it was ahead, leading the way across the lawn to the house, walking as though it owned the whole place, holding its tail straight up in the air, like a mast.

'Go home,' the man said. 'Go on home. We don't want you.'

But when they reached the house, it came in with them, and Louisa gave it some milk in the kitchen. During lunch, it hopped up on to the spare chair between them and sat through the meal with its head just above the level of the table watching the proceedings with those dark-yellow eyes which kept moving slowly from the woman to the man and back again.

'I don't like this cat,' Edward said.

'Oh, I think it's a beautiful cat. I do hope it stays a little while.'

'Now, listen to me, Louisa. The creature can't possibly stay here. It belongs to someone else. It's lost. And if it's still trying to hang around this afternoon, you'd better take it to the police. They'll see it gets home.'

After lunch, Edward returned to his gardening. Louisa, as usual, went to the piano. She was a competent pianist and a genuine music-lover, and almost every afternoon she spent an hour or so playing for herself. The cat was now lying on the sofa, and she paused to stroke it as she went by. It opened its eyes, looked at her a moment, then closed them again and went back to sleep.

'You're an awfully nice cat,' she said. 'And such a beautiful colour. I wish I could keep you.' Then her fingers, moving over the fur on the cat's head, came into contact with a small lump, a little growth just above the right eye.

'Poor cat,' she said. 'You've got bumps on your beautiful face. You must be getting old.'

She went over and sat down on the long piano stool but she didn't immediately start to play. One of her special little pleasures was to make every day a kind of concert day, with a carefully arranged programme which she worked out in detail before she began. She never liked to break her enjoyment by having to stop while she wondered what to play next. All she wanted was a brief pause after each piece while the audience clapped enthusiastically and called for more. It was so much nicer to imagine an audience, and now and again while she was playing – on the lucky days, that is – the room would begin to swim and fade and darken, and she would see nothing but row upon row of seats and a sea of white faces upturned towards her, listening with a rapt and adoring concentration.

Sometimes she played from memory, sometimes from music. Today she would play from memory; that was the way she felt. And what should the programme be? She sat before the piano with her small hands clasped on her lap, a plump rosy little person with a round and still quite pretty face, her hair done up in a neat bun at the back of her head. By looking slightly to the right, she could see the cat curled up asleep on the sofa, and its silvery-grey coat was beautiful against the purple of the cushion. How about some Bach to begin with? Or, better still, Vivaldi. The Bach adaptation for organ of the D minor Concerto

Grosso. Yes – that first. Then perhaps a little Schumann. *Carnaval?* That would be fun. And after that – well, a touch of Liszt for a change. One of the *Petrarch Sonnets*. The second one – that was the loveliest – the E major. Then another Schumann, another of his gay ones – *Kinderscenen*. And lastly, for the encore, a Brahms waltz, or maybe two of them if she felt like it.

Vivaldi, Schumann, Liszt, Schumann, Brahms. A very nice programme, one that she could play easily without the music. She moved herself a little closer to the piano and paused a moment while someone in the audience – already she could feel that this was one of the lucky days – while someone in the audience had his last cough; then, with the slow grace that accompanied nearly all her movements, she lifted her hands to the keyboard and began to play.

She wasn't, at that particular moment, watching the cat at all – as a matter of fact she had forgotten its presence – but as the first deep notes of the Vivaldi sounded softly in the room, she became aware, out of the corner of one eye, of a sudden flurry, a flash of movement on the sofa to her right. She stopped playing at once. 'What is it?' she said, turning to the cat. 'What's the matter?'

The animal, who a few seconds before had been sleeping peacefully, was now sitting bolt upright on the sofa, very tense, the whole body aquiver, ears up and eyes wide open, staring at the piano.

'Did I frighten you?' she asked gently. 'Perhaps you've never heard music before.'

No, she told herself. I don't think that's what it is. On second thoughts, it seemed to her that the cat's attitude was not one of fear. There was no shrinking or backing away. If anything, there was a leaning forward, a kind of eagerness about the creature, and the face – well, there was rather an odd expression on the face, something of a mixture between surprise and shock. Of course, the face of a cat is a small and fairly expressionless thing, but if you watch carefully the eyes and ears working together, and particularly that little area of mobile skin below the ears and slightly to one side, you can occasionally see the reflection of very powerful emotions. Louisa was watching the face closely now, and because she was curious to see what would happen a second time, she reached out her hands to the keyboard and began again to play the Vivaldi.

This time the cat was ready for it, and all that happened to begin with was a small extra tensing of the body. But as the music swelled and quickened into that first exciting rhythm of the introduction to the fugue, a strange look that mounted almost to ecstasy began to settle upon the creature's face. The ears, which up to then had been pricked up straight, were gradually drawn back, the eyelids drooped, the head went over to one side, and at that moment Louisa could have sworn that the animal was actually *appreciating* the work.

What she saw (or thought she saw) was something she had noticed many times on the faces of people listening very closely to a piece of music. When the sound takes complete hold of them and drowns them in itself, a peculiar, intensely ecstatic look comes over them that you can recognize as easily as a smile. So far as Louisa could see, the cat was now wearing almost exactly this kind of look.

Louisa finished the fugue, then played the siciliana, and all the way through she kept watching the cat on the sofa. The final proof for her that the animal was listening came at the end, when the music stopped. It blinked, stirred itself a little, stretched a leg, settled into a more comfortable position, took a quick glance round the room, then looked expectantly in her direction. It was precisely the way a concert-goer reacts when the music momentarily releases him in the pause between two movements of a symphony. The behaviour was so thoroughly human it gave her a queer agitated feeling in the chest.

'You like that?' she asked. 'You like Vivaldi?'

The moment she'd spoken, she felt ridiculous, but not — and this to her was a trifle sinister — not quite so ridiculous as she knew she should have felt.

Well, there was nothing for it now except to go straight ahead with the next number on the programme, which was *Carnaval*. As soon as she began to play, the cat again stiffened and sat up straighter; then, as it became slowly and blissfully saturated with the sound, it relapsed into the queer melting mood of ecstasy that seemed to have something to do with drowning and with dreaming. It was really an extravagant sight — quite a comical one, too — to see this silvery cat sitting on the sofa and being carried away like this. And what made it more screwy than ever, Louisa thought, was the fact that this music, which the animal seemed to be enjoying so much, was manifestly too *difficult*, too *classical*, to be appreciated by the majority of humans in the world.

Maybe, she thought, the creature's not really enjoying it at all. Maybe it's a sort of hypnotic reaction, like with snakes. After all, if you can charm a snake with music, then why not a cat? Except that millions of cats hear the stuff every day of their lives, on radio and gramophone and piano, and, as far as she knew, there'd never yet been a case of one behaving like this. This one was acting as though it were following every single note. It was certainly a fantastic thing.

But was it not also a wonderful thing? Indeed it was. In fact, unless she was much mistaken, it was a kind of miracle, one of those animal miracles that happen about once every hundred years.

'I could see you *loved* that one,' she said when the piece was over. 'Although I'm sorry I didn't play it any too well today. Which did you like best – the Vivaldi or the Schumann?'

The cat made no reply, so Louisa, fearing she might lose the attention of her listener, went straight into the next part of the programme – Liszt's second *Petrarch Sonnet*.

And now an extraordinary thing happened. She hadn't played more than three or four bars when the animal's whiskers began perceptibly to twitch. Slowly it drew itself up to an extra height, laid its head on one side, then on the other, and stared into space with a kind of frowning concentrated look that seemed to say, 'What's this? Don't tell me. I know it so well, but just for the moment I don't seem to be able to place it.' Louisa was fascinated, and with her little mouth half open and half smiling, she continued to play, waiting to see what on earth was going to happen next.

The cat stood up, walked to one end of the sofa, sat down again, listened some more; then all at once it bounded to the floor and leaped up on to the piano stool beside her. There it sat, listening intently to the lovely sonnet, not dreamily this time, but very erect, the large yellow eyes fixed upon Louisa's fingers.

'Well!' she said as she struck the last chord. 'So you came up to sit beside me, did you? You like this better than the sofa? All right, I'll let you stay, but you must keep still and not jump about.' She put out a hand and stroked the cat softly along the back, from head to tail. 'That was Liszt,' she went on. 'Mind you, he can sometimes be quite horribly vulgar, but in things like this he's really charming.'

She was beginning to enjoy this odd animal pantomime, so she went straight on into the next item on the programme, Schumann's *Kinderscenen*.

She hadn't been playing for more than a minute or two when she realized that the cat had again moved, and was now back in its old place on the sofa. She'd been watching her hands at the time, and presumably that was why she hadn't even noticed its going; all the same, it must have been an extremely swift and silent move. The cat was still staring at her, still apparently attending closely to the music, and yet it seemed to Louisa that there was not now the same rapturous enthusiasm there'd been during the previous piece, the Liszt. In addition, the act of leaving the stool and returning to the sofa appeared in itself to be a mild but positive gesture of disappointment.

'What's the matter?' she asked when it was over. 'What's wrong with Schumann? What's so marvellous about Liszt?' The cat looked straight back at her with those yellow eyes that had small jet-black bars lying vertically in their centres.

This, she told herself, is really beginning to get interesting — a trifle spooky, too, when she came to think of it. But one look at the cat sitting there on the sofa, so bright and attentive, so obviously waiting for more music, quickly reassured her.

'All right,' she said. 'I'll tell you what I'm going to do. I'm going to alter my programme specially for you. You seem to like Liszt so much, I'll give you another.'

She hesitated, searching her memory for a good Liszt; then softly she began to play one of the twelve little pieces from *Der Weihnachtsbaum*. She was now watching the cat very closely, and the first thing she noticed was that the whiskers again began to twitch. It jumped down to the carpet, stood still a moment, inclining its head, quivering with excitement, and then, with a slow, silky stride, it walked around the piano, hopped up on the stool, and sat down beside her.

They were in the middle of all this when Edward came in from the garden.

'Edward!' Louisa cried, jumping up. 'Oh, Edward, darling! Listen to this! Listen what's happened!'

'What is it now?' he said. 'I'd like some tea.' He had one of those narrow, sharp-nosed, faintly magenta faces, and the sweat was making it shine as though it were a long wet grape.

'It's the cat!' Louisa cried, pointing to it sitting quietly on the piano stool. 'Just *wait* till you hear what's happened!'

'I thought I told you to take it to the police.'

'But, Edward, *listen* to me. This is *terribly* exciting. This is a *musical* cat.'

'Oh, yes?'

'This cat can appreciate music, and it can understand it too.'

'Now stop this nonsense, Louisa, and for God's sake let's have some tea. I'm hot and tired from cutting brambles and building bonfires.' He sat down in an armchair, took a cigarette from a box beside him, and lit it with an immense patent lighter that stood near the box.

'What you don't understand,' Louisa said, 'is that something extremely exciting has been happening here in our house while you

were out, something that may even be ... well ... almost moment-
ous.'

'I'm quite sure of that.'

'Edward, *please*!'

Louisa was standing by the piano, her little pink face pinker than
ever, a scarlet rose high up on each cheek. 'If you want to know,' she
said, 'I'll tell you what I think.'

'I'm listening, dear.'

'I think it might be possible that we are at this moment sitting in
the presence of –' She stopped, as though suddenly sensing the absurd-
ity of the thought.

'Yes?'

'You may think it silly, Edward, but it's honestly what I think.'

'In the presence of whom, for heaven's sake?'

'Of Franz Liszt himself!'

Her husband took a long slow pull at his cigarette and blew the
smoke up at the ceiling. He had the tight-skinned, concave cheeks of a
man who has worn a full set of dentures for many years, and every
time he sucked at a cigarette, the cheeks went in even more, and the
bones of his face stood out like a skeleton's. 'I don't get you,' he said.

'Edward, listen to me. From what I've seen this afternoon with my
own eyes, it really looks as though this might be some sort of a reincarnation.'

'You mean this lousy cat?'

'Don't talk like that, dear, please.'

'You're not ill, are you, Louisa?'

'I'm perfectly all right, thank you very much. I'm a bit confused – I
don't mind admitting it, but who wouldn't be after what's just
happened? Edward, I swear to you.'

'What *did* happen, if I may ask?'

Louisa told him, and all the while she was speaking, her husband lay
sprawled in the chair with his legs stretched out in front of him,
sucking at his cigarette and blowing the smoke up at the ceiling. There
was a thin cynical smile on his mouth.

'I don't see anything very unusual about that,' he said when it was
over. 'All it is – it's a trick cat. It's been taught tricks, that's all.'

'Don't be so silly, Edward. Every time I play Liszt, he gets all
excited and comes running over to sit on the stool beside me. But
only for Liszt, and nobody can teach a cat the difference between Liszt
and Schumann. You don't even know it yourself. But this one can do it
every single time. Quite obscure Liszt, too.'

'Twice,' the husband said. 'He's only done it twice.'

'Twice is enough.'

'Let's see him do it again. Come on.'

'No,' Louisa said. 'Definitely not. Because if this *is* Liszt, as I believe it is, or anyway the soul of Liszt or whatever it is that comes back, then it's certainly not right or even very kind to put him through a lot of silly undignified tests.'

'My dear woman! This is a *cat* – a rather stupid grey cat that nearly got its coat singed by the bonfire this morning in the garden. And anyway, what do you know about reincarnation?'

'If the soul is there, that's enough for me,' Louisa said firmly. 'That's all that counts.'

'Come on, then. Let's see him perform. Let's see him tell the difference between his own stuff and someone else's.'

'No, Edward. I've told you before, I refuse to put him through any more silly circus tests. He's had quite enough of that for one day. But I'll tell you what I *will* do. I'll play him a little more of his own music.'

'A fat lot that'll prove.'

'You watch. And one thing is certain – as soon as he recognizes it, he'll refuse to budge off that stool where he's sitting now.'

Louisa went to the music shelf, took down a book of Liszt, thumbed through it quickly, and chose another of his finer compositions – the B minor Sonata. She had meant to play only the first part of the work, but once she got started and saw how the cat was sitting there literally quivering with pleasure and watching her hands with that rapturous concentrated look, she didn't have the heart to stop. She played it all the way through. When it was finished, she glanced up at her husband and smiled. 'There you are,' she said. 'You can't tell me he wasn't absolutely *loving* it.'

'He just likes the noise, that's all.'

'He was *loving* it. Weren't you, darling?' she said, lifting the cat in her arms. 'Oh, my goodness, if only he could talk. Just think of it, dear – he met Beethoven in his youth! He knew Schubert and Mendelssohn and Schumann and Berlioz and Grieg and Delacroix and Ingres and Heine and Balzac. And let me see . . . My heavens, he was Wagner's father-in-law! I'm holding Wagner's father-in-law in my arms!'

'Louisa!' her husband said sharply, sitting up straight. 'Pull yourself together.' There was a new edge to his voice now, and he spoke louder.

Louisa glanced up quickly. 'Edward, I do believe you're jealous!'

'Of a miserable grey cat!'

'Then don't be so grumpy and cynical about it all. If you're going
to behave like this, the best thing you can do is to go back to your
gardening and leave the two of us together in peace. That will be best
for all of us, won't it, darling?' she said, addressing the cat, stroking its
head. 'And later on this evening, we shall have some more music
together, you and I, some more of your own work. Oh, yes,' she said,
kissing the creature several times on the neck, 'and we might have a
little Chopin, too. You needn't tell me – I happen to know you adore
Chopin. You used to be great friends with him, didn't you, darling? As
a matter of fact – if I remember rightly – it was in Chopin's apartment
that you met the great love of your life, Madame Something-or-Other.
Had three illegitimate children by her, too, didn't you? Yes, you did,
you naughty thing, and don't go trying to deny it. So you shall have
some Chopin,' she said, kissing the cat again, 'and that'll probably
bring back all sorts of lovely memories to you, won't it?'

'Louisa, stop this at once!'

'Oh, don't be so stuffy, Edward.'

'You're behaving like a perfect idiot, woman. And anyway, you
forget we're going out this evening, to Bill and Betty's for canasta.'

'Oh, but I couldn't *possibly* go out now. There's no question of that.'

Edward got up slowly from his chair, then bent down and stubbed
his cigarette hard into the ash-tray. 'Tell me something,' he said
quietly. 'You don't really believe this – this twaddle you're talking, do
you?'

'But of course I do. I don't think there's any question about it now.
And, what's more, I consider that it puts a tremendous responsibility
upon us, Edward – upon both of us. You as well.'

'You know what I think,' he said. 'I think you ought to see a doctor.
And damn quick, too.'

With that, he turned and stalked out of the room, through the
french windows, back into the garden.

Louisa watched him striding across the lawn towards his bonfire
and his brambles, and she waited until he was out of sight before she
turned and ran to the front door, still carrying the cat.

Soon she was in the car, driving to town.

She parked in front of the library, locked the cat in the car, hurried
up the steps into the building, and headed straight for the reference
room. There she began searching the cards for books on two subjects
– REINCARNATION and LISZT.

Under REINCARNATION she found something called *Recurring Earth-
Lives – How and Why*, by a man called F. Milton Willis, published in

1921. Under LISZT she found two biographical volumes. She took out all three books, returned to the car, and drove home.

Back in the house, she placed the cat on the sofa, sat herself down beside it with her books, and prepared to do some serious reading. She would begin, she decided, with Mr F. Milton Willis's work. The volume was thin and a trifle soiled, but it had a good heavy feel to it, and the author's name had an authoritative ring.

The doctrine of reincarnation, she read, states that spiritual souls pass from higher to higher forms of animals. 'A man can, for instance, no more be reborn as an animal than an adult can re-become a child.'

She read this again. But how did he know? How could he be so sure? He couldn't. No one could possibly be certain about a thing like that. At the same time, the statement took a good deal of the wind out of her sails.

'Around the centre of consciousness of each of us, there are, besides the dense outer body, four other bodies, invisible to the eye of flesh, but perfectly visible to people whose faculties of perception of superphysical things have undergone the requisite development . . .'

She didn't understand that one at all, but she read on, and soon she came to an interesting passage that told how long a soul usually stayed away from the earth before returning in someone else's body. The time varied according to type, and Mr Willis gave the following breakdown:

Drunkards and the unemployable	40/50 YEARS
Unskilled labourers	60/100 YEARS
Skilled workers	100/200 YEARS
The *bourgeoisie*	200/300 YEARS
The upper-middle classes	500 YEARS
The highest class of gentleman farmers	600/1,000 YEARS
Those in the Path of Initiation	1,500/2,000 YEARS

Quickly she referred to one of the other books, to find out how long Liszt had been dead. It said he died in Bayreuth in 1886. That was sixty-seven years ago. Therefore, according to Mr Willis, he'd have to have been an unskilled labourer to come back so soon. That didn't seem to fit at all. On the other hand, she didn't think much of the author's methods of grading. According to him, 'the highest class of gentleman farmer' was just about the most superior being on the earth. Red jackets and stirrup cups and the bloody, sadistic murder of the fox. No, she thought, that isn't right. It was a pleasure to find herself beginning to doubt Mr Willis.

Later in the book, she came upon a list of some of the more famous reincarnations. Epictetus, she was told, returned to earth as Ralph Waldo Emerson. Cicero came back as Gladstone, Alfred the Great as Queen Victoria, William the Conqueror as Lord Kitchener. Ashoka Vardhana, King of India in 272 BC, came back as Colonel Henry Steel Olcott, an esteemed American lawyer. Pythagoras returned as Master Koot Hoomi, the gentleman who founded the Theosophical Society with Mme Blacatsky and Colonel H. S. Olcott (the esteemed American lawyer, alias Ashoka Vardhana, King of India). It didn't say who Mme Blavatsky had been. But 'Theodore Roosevelt,' it said, 'has for numbers of incarnations played great parts as a leader of men . . . From him descended the royal line of ancient Chaldea, he having been, about 30,000 BC, appointed Governor of Chaldea by the Ego we know as Caesar who was then ruler of Persia . . . Roosevelt and Caesar have been together time after time as military and administrative leaders; at one time, many thousands of years ago, they were husband and wife . . .'

That was enough for Louisa. Mr F. Milton Willis was clearly nothing but a guesser. She was not impressed by his dogmatic assertions. The fellow was probably on the right track, but his pronouncements were extravagant, especially the first one of all, about animals. Soon she hoped to be able to confound the whole Theosophical Society with her proof that man could indeed reappear as a lower animal. Also that he did not have to be an unskilled labourer to come back within a hundred years.

She now turned to one of the Liszt · biographies, and she was glancing through it casually when her husband came in again from the garden.

'What are you doing now?' he asked.

'Oh – just checking up a little here and there. Listen, my dear, did you know that Theodore Roosevelt once was Caesar's wife?'

'Louisa,' he said, 'look – why don't we stop this nonsense? I don't like to see you making a fool of yourself like this. Just give me that goddamn cat and I'll take it to the police station myself.'

Louisa didn't seem to hear him. She was staring open-mouthed at a picture of Liszt in the book that lay on her lap. 'My God!' she cried. 'Edward, look!'

'What?'

'Look! The warts on his face! I forgot all about them! He had these great warts on his face and it was a famous thing. Even his students used to cultivate little tufts of hair on their own faces in the same spots, just to be like him.'

'What's that got to do with it?'

'Nothing. I mean not the students. But the warts have.'

'Oh, Christ,' the man said. 'Oh, Christ God Almighty.'

'The cat has them, too! Look, I'll show you.'

She took the animal on to her lap and began examining his face. 'There! There's one! And there's another! Wait a minute! I do believe they're in the same places! Where's that picture?'

It was a famous portrait of the musician in his old age, showing the fine powerful face framed in a mass of long grey hair that covered his ears and came half-way down his neck. On the face itself, each large wart had been faithfully reproduced, and there were five of them in all.

'Now, in the picture there's *one* above the right eyebrow.' She looked above the right eyebrow of the cat. 'Yes! It's there! In exactly the same place! And another on the left, at the top of the nose. That one's there, too! And one just below it on the cheek. And two fairly close together under the chin on the right side. Edward! Edward! Come and look! They're exactly the same.'

'It doesn't prove a thing.'

She looked up at her husband who was standing in the centre of the room in his green sweater and khaki slacks, still perspiring freely. 'You're scared, aren't you, Edward? Scared of losing your precious dignity and having people think you might be making a fool of yourself just for once.'

'I refuse to get hysterical about it, that's all.'

Louisa turned back to the book and began reading some more. 'This is interesting,' she said. 'It says here that Liszt loved all of Chopin's work except one – the Scherzo in B flat minor. Apparently he hated that. He called it the "Governess Scherzo", and said that it ought to be reserved solely for people in that profession.'

'So what?'

'Edward, listen. As you insist on being so horrid about all this, I'll tell you what I'm going to do. I'm going to play this scherzo right now and you can stay here and see what happens.'

'And then maybe you will deign to get us some supper.'

Louisa got up and took from the shelf a large green volume containing all of Chopin's works. 'Here it is. Oh yes, I remember it. It *is* rather awful. Now, listen – or, rather, watch. Watch to see what he does.'

She placed the music on the piano and sat down. Her husband

remained standing. He had his hands in his pockets and a cigarette in his mouth, and in spite of himself he was watching the cat, which was now dozing on the sofa. When Louisa began to play, the first effect was as dramatic as ever. The animal jumped up as though it had been stung, and it stood motionless for at least a minute, the ears pricked up, the whole body quivering. Then it became restless and began to walk back and forth along the length of the sofa. Finally, it hopped down on to the floor, and with its nose and tail held high in the air, it marched slowly, majestically, from the room.

'There!' Louisa cried, jumping up and running after it. 'That does it! That really proves it!' She came back carrying the cat which she put down again on the sofa. Her whole face was shining with excitement now, her fists were clenched white, and the little bun on top of her head was loosening and going over to one side. 'What about it, Edward? What d'you think?' She was laughing nervously as she spoke.

'I must say it was quite amusing.'

'Amusing! My dear Edward, it's the most wonderful thing that's ever happened! Oh, goodness me!' she cried, picking up the cat again and hugging it to her bosom. 'Isn't it marvellous to think we've got Franz Liszt staying in the house?'

'Now, Louisa. Don't let's get hysterical.'

'I can't help it, I simply can't. And to imagine that he's actually going to live with us for always!'

'I beg your pardon?'

'Oh, Edward! I can hardly talk from excitement. And d'you know what I'm going to do next? Every musician in the whole world is going to want to meet him, that's a fact, and ask him about the people he knew — about Beethoven and Chopin and Schubert —'

'He can't talk,' her husband said.

'Well — all right. But they're going to want to meet him anyway, just to see him and touch him and to play their own music to him, modern music he's never heard before.'

'He wasn't that great. Now, if it had been Bach or Beethoven . . .'

'Don't interrupt, Edward, please. So what I'm going to do is to notify all the important living composers everywhere. It's my duty. I'll tell them Liszt is here, and invite them to visit him. And you know what? They'll come flying in from every corner of the earth!'

'To see a grey cat?'

'Darling, it's the same thing. It's him. No one cares what he looks like. Oh, Edward, it'll be the most exciting thing there ever was!'

'They'll think you're mad.'

'You wait and see.' She was holding the cat in her arms and petting it tenderly but looking across at her husband, who now walked over to the french windows and stood there staring out into the garden. The evening was beginning, and the lawn was turning slowly from green to black, and in the distance he could see the smoke from his bonfire rising up in a white column.

'No,' he said, without turning round, 'I'm not having it. Not in this house. It'll make us both look perfect fools.'

'Edward, what do you mean?'

'Just what I say. I absolutely refuse to have you stirring up a lot of publicity about a foolish thing like this. You happen to have found a trick cat. OK – that's fine. Keep it, if it pleases you. I don't mind. But I don't wish you to go any further than that. Do you understand me, Louisa?'

'Further than what?'

'I don't want to hear any more of this crazy talk. You're acting like a lunatic.'

Louisa put the cat slowly down on the sofa. Then slowly she raised herself to her full small height and took one pace forward. '*Damn* you, Edward!' she shouted, stamping her foot. 'For the first time in our lives something really exciting comes along and you're scared to death of having anything to do with it because someone may laugh at you! That's right, isn't it? You can't deny it, can you?'

'Louisa,' her husband said. 'That's quite enough of that. Pull yourself together now and stop this at once.' He walked over and took a cigarette from the box on the table, then lit it with the enormous patent lighter. His wife stood watching him, and now the tears were beginning to trickle out of the inside corners of her eyes, making two little shiny rivers where they ran through the powder on her cheeks.

'We've been having too many of these scenes just lately, Louisa,' he was saying. 'No no, don't interrupt. Listen to me. I make full allowance for the fact that this may be an awkward time of life for you, and that –'

'Oh, my God! You idiot! You pompous idiot! Can't you see that this is different, this is – this is something miraculous? Can't you see *that*?'

At that point, he came across the room and took her firmly by the shoulders. He had the freshly lit cigarette between his lips, and she could see faint contours on his skin where the heavy perspiration had dried up in patches. 'Listen,' he said. 'I'm hungry. I've given up my golf and I've been working all day in the garden, and I'm tired and hungry and I want some supper. So do you. Off you go now to the kitchen and get us both something good to eat.'

Louisa stepped back and put both hands to her mouth. 'My heavens!' she cried. 'I forgot all about it. He must be absolutely famished. Except for some milk, I haven't given him a thing to eat since he arrived.'

'Who?'

'Why, *him* of course. I must go at once and cook something really special. I wish I knew what his favourite dishes used to be. What do you think he would like best, Edward?'

'*Goddamn* it, Louisa!'

'Now, Edward, please. I'm going to handle this *my* way just for once. You stay here,' she said, bending down and touching the cat gently with her fingers. 'I won't be long.'

Louisa went into the kitchen and stood for a moment, wondering what special dish she might prepare. How about a soufflé? A nice cheese soufflé? Yes, that would be rather special. Of course, Edward didn't much care for them, but that couldn't be helped.

She was only a fair cook, and she couldn't be sure of always having a soufflé come out well, but she took extra trouble this time and waited a long while to make certain the oven had heated fully to the correct temperature. While the soufflé was baking and she was searching around for something to go with it, it occurred to her that Liszt had probably never in his life tasted either avocado pears or grapefruit, so she decided to give him both of them at once in a salad. It would be fun to watch his reaction. It really would.

When it was all ready, she put it on a tray and carried it into the living-room. At the exact moment she entered, she saw her husband coming in through the french windows from the garden.

'Here's his supper,' she said, putting it on the table and turning towards the sofa. 'Where is he?'

Her husband closed the garden door behind him and walked across the room to get himself a cigarette.

'Edward, where is he?'

'Who?'

'You know who.'

'Ah, yes. Yes, that's right. Well — I'll tell you.' He was bending forward to light the cigarette, and his hands were cupped around the enormous patent lighter. He glanced up and saw Louisa looking at him — at his shoes and the bottoms of his khaki slacks, which were damp from walking in long grass.

'I just went out to see how the bonfire was going,' he said.

Her eyes travelled slowly upward and rested on his hands.

'It's still burning fine,' he went on. 'I think it'll keep going all night.'

But the way she was staring made him uncomfortable.

'What is it?' he said, lowering the lighter. Then he looked down and noticed for the first time the long thin scratch that ran diagonally clear across the back of one hand, from the knuckle to the wrist.

'*Edward!*'

'Yes,' he said, 'I know. Those brambles are terrible. They tear you to pieces. Now, just a minute, Louisa. What's the matter?'

'*Edward!*'

'Oh, for God's sake, woman, sit down and keep calm. There's nothing to get worked up about, Louisa! Louisa, *sit down!*'

PIG

∞

1

Once upon a time, in the City of New York, a beautiful baby boy was born into this world, and the joyful parents named him Lexington.

No sooner had the mother returned home from the hospital carrying Lexington in her arms than she said to her husband, 'Darling, now you must take me out to a most marvellous restaurant for dinner so that we can celebrate the arrival of our son and heir.'

Her husband embraced her tenderly and told her that any woman who could produce such a beautiful child as Lexington deserved to go absolutely anywhere she wanted. But was she strong enough yet, he inquired, to start running around the city late at night?

'No,' she said, she wasn't. But what the hell.

So that evening they both dressed themselves up in fancy clothes, and leaving little Lexington in the care of a trained infant's nurse who was costing them twenty dollars a day and was Scottish into the bargain, they went out to the finest and most expensive restaurant in town. There they each ate a giant lobster and drank a bottle of champagne between them, and after that they went on to a nightclub, where they drank another bottle of champagne and then sat holding hands for several hours while they recalled and discussed and admired each individual physical feature of their lovely newborn son.

They arrived back at their house on the East Side of Manhattan at around two o'clock in the morning and the husband paid off the taxi driver and then began feeling in his pockets for the key to the front door. After a while, he announced that he must have left it in the pocket of his other suit, and he suggested that they ring the bell and get the nurse to come down and let them in. An infant's nurse at twenty dollars a day must expect to be hauled out of bed occasionally in the night, the husband said.

So he rang the bell. They waited. Nothing happened. He rang it again, long and loud. They waited another minute. Then they both stepped back on to the street and shouted the nurse's name (McPottle) up at the nursery windows on the third floor, but there was still no response. The house was dark and silent. The wife began to grow apprehensive. Her baby was imprisoned in this place, she told herself. Alone with McPottle. And who was McPottle? They had known her for two days, that was all, and she had a thin mouth, a small disapproving eye, and a starchy bosom, and quite clearly she was in the habit of sleeping too soundly for safety. If she couldn't hear the front doorbell, then how on earth did she expect to hear a baby crying? Why this very second the poor thing might be swallowing its tongue or suffocating on its pillow.

'He doesn't use a pillow,' the husband said. 'You are not to worry. But I'll get you in if that's what you want.' He was feeling rather superb after all the champagne, and now he bent down and undid the laces of one of his black patent-leather shoes, and took it off. Then, holding it by the toe, he flung it hard and straight through the dining-room window on the ground floor.

'There you are,' he said, grinning. 'We'll deduct it from McPottle's wages.'

He stepped forward and very carefully put a hand through the hole in the glass and released the catch. Then he raised the window.

'I shall lift you in first, little mother,' he said, and took his wife around the waist and lifted her off the ground. This brought her big red mouth up level with his own, and very close, so he started kissing her. He knew from experience that women like very much to be kissed in this position, with their bodies held tight and their legs dangling in the air, so he went on doing it for quite a long time, and she wiggled her feet, and made loud gulping noises down in her throat. Finally, the husband turned her round and began easing her gently through the open window into the dining-room. At this point, a police patrol car came nosing silently along the street towards them. It stopped about thirty yards away, and three cops of Irish extraction leaped out of the car and started running in the direction of the husband and wife, brandishing revolvers.

'Stick 'em up!' the cops shouted. 'Stick 'em up!' But it was impossible for the husband to obey this order without letting go of his wife, and had he done this she would either have fallen to the ground or would have been left dangling half in and half out of the house, which is a terribly uncomfortable position for a woman; so he continued gallantly to push her upward and inward through the window. The cops, all of whom had received medals before for killing robbers, opened fire immediately, and although they were still running, and although the wife in particular was presenting them with a very small target indeed, they succeeded in scoring several direct hits on each body — sufficient anyway to prove fatal in both cases.

Thus, when he was no more than twelve days old, little Lexington became an orphan.

2

The news of this killing, for which the three policemen subsequently received citations, was eagerly conveyed to all the relatives of the deceased couple by newspaper reporters, and the next morning the closest of these relatives, as well as a couple of undertakers, three lawyers, and a priest, climbed into taxis and set out for the house with the broken window. They assembled in the living-room, men and women both, and they sat around in a circle on the sofas and armchairs, smoking cigarettes and sipping sherry and debating what on earth should be done now with the baby upstairs, the orphan Lexington.

It soon became apparent that none of the relatives was particularly keen to assume responsibility for the child, and the discussions and arguments continued all through the day. Everybody declared an enormous, almost an irresistible desire to look after him, and would have done so with the greatest of pleasure were it not for the fact that their apartment was too small, or that they already had one baby and couldn't possibly afford another, or that they wouldn't know what to do with the poor little thing when they went abroad in the summer, or that they were getting on in years, which surely would be most unfair to the boy when he grew up, and so on and so forth. They all knew, of course, that the father had been heavily in debt for a long time and that the house was mortgaged and that consequently there would be no money at all to go with the child.

They were still arguing like mad at six in the evening when suddenly, in the middle of it all, an old aunt of the deceased father (her name was Glosspan) swept in from Virginia, and without even removing her hat and coat, not even pausing to sit down, ignoring all offers of a martini, a whisky, a sherry, she announced firmly to the assembled relatives that she herself intended to take sole charge of the infant boy from then on. What was more, she said, she would assume full financial responsibility on all counts, including education, and everyone else could go back home where they belonged and give their consciences a rest. So saying, she trotted upstairs to the nursery and snatched Lexington from his cradle and swept out of the house with the baby clutched tightly in her arms, while the relatives simply sat and stared and smiled and looked relieved, and McPottle the nurse stood stiff with disapproval at the head of the stairs, her lips compressed, her arms folded across her starchy bosom.

And thus it was that the infant Lexington, when he was thirteen days old, left the City of New York and travelled southward to live with his Great Aunt Glosspan in the State of Virginia.

3

Aunt Glosspan was nearly seventy when she became guardian to Lexington, but to look at her you would never have guessed it for one minute. She was as sprightly as a woman half her age, with a small, wrinkled, but still quite beautiful face and two lovely brown eyes that sparkled at you in the nicest way. She was also a spinster, though you would never have guessed that either, for there was nothing spinsterish about Aunt Glosspan. She was never bitter or gloomy or irritable; she didn't have a moustache; and she wasn't in the least bit jealous of other people, which in itself is something you can seldom say about either a spinster or a virgin lady, although of course it is not known for certain whether Aunt Glosspan qualified on both counts.

But she was an eccentric old woman, there was no doubt about that. For the past thirty years she had lived a strange isolated life all by herself in a tiny cottage high up on the slopes of the Blue Ridge Mountains, several miles from the nearest village. She had five acres of pasture, a plot for growing vegetables, a flower garden, three cows, a dozen hens, and a fine cockerel.

And now she had little Lexington as well.

She was a strict vegetarian and regarded the consumption of animal flesh as not only unhealthy and disgusting, but horribly cruel. She lived upon lovely clean foods like milk, butter, eggs, cheese, vegetables, nuts, herbs, and fruit and she rejoiced in the conviction that no living creature would be slaughtered on her account, not even a shrimp. Once, when a brown hen of hers passed away in the prime of life from being eggbound, Aunt Glosspan was so distressed that she nearly gave up egg-eating altogether.

She knew not the first thing about babies, but that didn't worry her in the least. At the railway station in New York, while waiting for the train that would take her and Lexington back to Virginia, she bought six feeding-bottles, two dozen diapers, a box of safety pins, a carton of milk for the journey, and a small paper-covered book called *The Care of Infants*. What more could anyone want? And when the train got going, she fed the baby some milk, changed its nappies after a fashion, and laid it down on the seat to sleep. Then she read *The Care of Infants* from cover to cover.

'There is no problem here,' she said, throwing the book out of the window. 'No problem at all.'

And curiously enough there wasn't. Back home in the cottage everything went just as smoothly as could be. Little Lexington drank his milk and belched and yelled and slept exactly as a good baby should, and Aunt Glosspan glowed with joy whenever she looked at him and showered him with kisses all day long.

4

By the time he was six years old, young Lexington had grown into a most beautiful boy with long golden hair and deep blue eyes the colour of cornflowers. He was bright and cheerful, and already he was learning to help his old aunt in all sorts of different ways around the property, collecting the eggs from the chicken house, turning the handle of the butter churn, digging up potatoes in the vegetable garden and searching for wild herbs on the side of the mountain. Soon, Aunt Glosspan told herself, she would have to start thinking about his education.

But she couldn't bear the thought of sending him away to school. She loved him so much now that it would kill her to be parted from him for any length of time. There was, of course, that village school down in the valley, but it was a dreadful-looking place, and if she sent him there she just knew they would start forcing him to eat meat the very first day he arrived.

'You know what, my darling?' she said to him one day when he was sitting on a stool in the kitchen watching her make cheese. 'I don't really see why I shouldn't give you your lessons myself.'

The boy looked up at her with his large blue eyes, and gave her a lovely trusting smile. 'That would be nice,' he said.

'And the very first thing I should do would be to teach you how to cook.'

'I think I would like that, Aunt Glosspan.'

'Whether you like it or not, you're going to have to learn some time,' she said. 'Vegetarians like us don't have nearly so many foods to choose from as ordinary people, and therefore they must learn to be doubly expert with what they have.'

'Aunt Glosspan,' the boy said, 'what *do* ordinary people eat that we don't?'

'Animals,' she answered, tossing her head in disgust.

'You mean *live* animals?'

'No,' she said. 'Dead ones.'

The boy considered this for a moment.

'You mean when they die they *eat* them instead of *burying* them?'

'They don't wait for them to die, my pet. They kill them.'

'How do they kill them, Aunt Glosspan?'

'They usually slit their throats with a knife.'

'But what *kind* of animals?'

'Cows and pigs mostly, and sheep.'

'Cows!' the boy cried. 'You mean like Daisy and Snowdrop and Lily?'

'Exactly, my dear.'

'But *how* do they eat them, Aunt Glosspan?'

'They cut them up into bits and they cook the bits. They like it best when it's all red and bloody and sticking to the bones. They love to eat lumps of cow's flesh with the blood oozing out of it.'

'Pigs too?'

'They adore pigs.'

'Lumps of bloody pig's meat,' the boy said. 'Imagine that. What else do they eat, Aunt Glosspan?'

'Chickens.'

'Chickens!'

'Millions of them.'

'Feathers and all?'

'No, dear, not the feathers. Now run along outside and get Aunt Glosspan a bunch of chives, will you, my darling.'

Shortly after that, the lessons began. They covered five subjects, reading, writing, geography, arithmetic, and cooking, but the latter was by far the most popular with both teacher and pupil. In fact, it very soon became apparent that young Lexington possessed a truly remarkable talent in this direction. He was a born cook. He was dextrous and quick. He could handle his pans like a juggler. He could slice a single potato in twenty paper-thin slivers in less time than it took his aunt to peel it. His palate was exquisitely sensitive, and he could taste a pot of strong onion soup and immediately detect the presence of a single tiny leaf of sage. In so young a boy, all this was a bit bewildering to Aunt Glosspan, and to tell the truth she didn't quite know what to make of it. But she was proud as proud as could be, all the same, and predicted a brilliant future for the child.

'What a mercy it is,' she said, 'that I have such a wonderful little fellow to look after me in my dotage.' And a couple of years later, she retired from the kitchen for good, leaving Lexington in sole charge of all household cooking. The boy was now ten years old, and Aunt Glosspan was nearly eighty.

5

With the kitchen to himself, Lexington straight away began experimenting with dishes of his own invention. The old favourites no longer interested him. He had a violent urge to create. There were hundreds of fresh ideas in his head. 'I will begin,' he said, 'by devising a chestnut soufflé.' He made it and served it up for supper that very night. It was terrific. 'You are a genius!' Aunt Glosspan cried, leaping up from her chair and kissing him on both cheeks. 'You will make history!'

From then on, hardly a day went by without some new delectable creation being set upon the table. There was Brazilnut soup, hominy cutlets, vegetable ragout, dandelion omelette, cream-cheese fritters, stuffed-cabbage surprise, stewed foggage, shallots à la bonne femme, beetroot mousse piquant, prunes Stroganoff, Dutch rarebit, turnips on horseback, flaming spruce-needle tarts, and many many other beautiful compositions. Never before in her life, Aunt Glosspan declared, had she tasted such food as this; and in the mornings, long before lunch was due, she would go out on to the porch and sit there in her rocking-chair, speculating about the coming meal, licking her chops, sniffing the aromas that came wafting out through the kitchen window.

'What's that you're making in there today, boy?' she would call out.

'Try to guess, Aunt Glosspan.'

'Smells like a bit of salsify fritters to me,' she would say, sniffing vigorously.

Then out he would come, this ten-year-old child, a little grin of triumph on his face, and in his hands a big steaming pot of the most heavenly stew made entirely of parsnips and lovage.

'You know what you ought to do,' his aunt said to him, gobbling the stew. 'You ought to set yourself down this very minute with paper and pencil and write a cooking-book.'

He looked at her across the table, chewing his parsnips slowly.

'Why not?' she cried. 'I've taught you how to write and I've taught you how to cook and now all you've got to do is put the two things together. You write a cooking-book, my darling, and it'll make you famous the whole world over.'

'All right,' he said. 'I will.'

And that very day, Lexington began writing the first page of that monumental work which was to occupy him for the rest of his life. He called it *Eat Good and Healthy*.

6

Seven years later, by the time he was seventeen, he had recorded over nine thousand different recipes, all of them original, all of them delicious.

But now, suddenly, his labours were interrupted by the tragic death of Aunt Glosspan. She was afflicted in the night by a violent seizure, and Lexington, who had rushed into her bedroom to see what all the noise was about, found her lying on her bed yelling and cussing and twisting herself into all manner of complicated knots. Indeed, she was a terrible sight to behold, and the agitated youth danced around her in his pyjamas, wringing his hands, and wondering what on earth he should do. Finally in an effort to cool her down, he fetched a bucket of water from the pond in the cow field and tipped it over her head, but this only intensified the paroxysms, and the old lady expired within the hour.

'This is really too bad,' the poor boy said, pinching her several times to make sure that she was dead. 'And how sudden! How quick and sudden! Why only a few hours ago she seemed in the very best of spirits. She even took three large helpings of my most recent creation, devilled mushroomburgers, and told me how succulent it was.'

After weeping bitterly for several minutes, for he had loved his aunt very much, he pulled himself together and carried her outside and buried her behind the cowshed.

The next day, while tidying up her belongings, he came across an envelope that was addressed to him in Aunt Glosspan's handwriting. He opened it and drew out two fifty-dollar bills and a letter.

Darling boy [the letter said], I know that you have never yet been down the mountain since you were thirteen days old, but as soon as I die you must put on a pair of shoes and a clean shirt and walk down to the village and find a doctor. Ask the doctor to give you a death certificate to prove that I am dead. Then take this certificate to my lawyer, a man called Mr Samuel Zucker-mann, who lives in New York City and who has a copy of my will. Mr Zuckermann will arrange everything. The cash in this envelope is to pay the doctor for the certificate and to cover the cost of your journey to New York. Mr Zuckermann will give you more money when you get there, and it is my earnest wish that you use it to further your researches into culinary and vegetarian matters, and that you continue to work upon that great book of yours until you are satisfied that it is complete in every way. Your loving aunt – Glosspan.

Lexington, who had always done everything his aunt told him, pocketed the money, put on a pair of shoes and a clean shirt, and went down the mountain to the village where the doctor lived.

'Old Glosspan?' the doctor said. 'My God, is *she* dead?'

'Certainly she's dead,' the youth answered. 'If you will come back home with me now I'll dig her up and you can see for yourself.'

'How deep did you bury her?' the doctor asked.

'Six or seven feet down, I should think.'

'And how long ago?'

'Oh, about eight hours.'

'Then she's dead,' the doctor announced. 'Here's the certificate.'

7

Our hero now sets out for the City of New York to find Mr Samuel Zuckermann. He travelled on foot, and he slept under hedges, and he lived on berries and wild herbs, and it took him sixteen days to reach the metropolis.

'What a fabulous place this is!' he cried as he stood at the corner of Fifty-seventh Street and Fifth Avenue, staring around him. 'There are no cows or chickens anywhere, and none of the women looks in the least like Aunt Glosspan.'

As for Mr Samuel Zuckermann, he looked like nothing that Lexington had ever seen before.

He was a small spongy man with livid jowls and a huge magenta nose, and when he smiled, bits of gold flashed at you marvellously from lots of different places inside his mouth. In his luxurious office, he shook Lexington warmly by the hand and congratulated him upon his aunt's death.

'I suppose you knew that your dearly beloved guardian was a woman of considerable wealth?' he said.

'You mean the cows and the chickens?'

'I mean half a million bucks,' Mr Zuckermann said.

'How much?'

'Half a million dollars, my boy. And she's left it all to you.' Mr Zuckermann leaned back in his chair and clasped his hands over his spongy paunch. At the same time, he began secretly working his right forefinger in through his waistcoat and under his shirt so as to scratch the skin around the circumference of his navel – a favourite exercise of his, and one that gave him a peculiar pleasure. 'Of course, I shall have to deduct fifty per cent for my services,' he said, 'But that still leaves you with two hundred and fifty grand.'

'I am rich!' Lexington cried. 'This is wonderful! How soon can I have the money?'

'Well,' Mr Zuckermann said, 'luckily for you, I happen to be on rather cordial terms with the tax authorities around here, and I am confident that I shall be able to persuade them to waive all death duties and back taxes.'

'How kind you are,' murmured Lexington.

'I should naturally have to give somebody a small honorarium.'

'Whatever you say, Mr Zuckermann.'

'I think a hundred thousand would be sufficient.'

'Good gracious, isn't that rather excessive?'

'Never undertip a tax inspector or a policeman,' Mr Zuckermann said. 'Remember that.'

'But how much does it leave for me?' the youth asked meekly.

'One hundred and fifty thousand. But then you've got the funeral expenses to pay out of that.'

'*Funeral* expenses?'

'You've got to pay for the funeral parlour. Surely you know that?'

'But I buried her myself, Mr Zuckermann, behind the cowshed.'

'I don't doubt it,' the lawyer said. 'So what?'

'I never used a funeral parlour.'

'Listen,' Mr Zuckermann said patiently. 'You may not know it, but there is a law in this state which says that no beneficiary under a will may receive a single penny of his inheritance until the funeral parlour has been paid in full.'

'You mean that's a *law*?'

'Certainly, it's a law, and a very good one it is, too. The funeral parlour is one of our great national institutions. It must be protected at all costs.'

Mr Zuckermann himself, together with a group of public-spirited doctors, controlled a corporation that owned a chain of nine lavish funeral parlours in the city, not to mention a casket factory in Brooklyn and a postgraduate school for embalmers in Washington Heights. The celebration of death was therefore a deeply religious affair in Mr Zuckermann's eyes. In fact, the whole business affected him profoundly, almost as profoundly, one might say, as the birth of Christ affected the shopkeeper.

'You had no right to go out and bury your aunt like that,' he said. 'None at all.'

'I'm very sorry, Mr Zuckermann.'

'Why, it's downright subversive.'

'I'll do whatever you say, Mr Zuckermann. All I want to know is how much I'm going to get in the end, when everything's paid.'

There was a pause. Mr Zuckermann sighed and frowned and continued secretly to run the tip of his finger around the rim of his navel.

'Shall we say fifteen thousand?' he suggested, flashing a big gold smile. 'That's a nice round figure.'

'Can I take it with me this afternoon?'

'I don't see why not.'

So Mr Zuckermann summoned his chief cashier and told him to give Lexington fifteen thousand dollars out of the petty cash, and to obtain a receipt. The youth, who by this time was delighted to be getting anything at all, accepted the money gratefully and stowed it away in his knapsack. Then he shook Mr Zuckermann warmly by the hand, thanked him for all his help, and went out of the office.

'The whole world is before me!' our hero cried as he emerged into the street. 'I now have fifteen thousand dollars to see me through until my book is published. And after that, of course, I shall have a great deal more.' He stood on the pavement, wondering which way to go. He turned left and began strolling slowly down the street, staring at the sights of the city.

'What a revolting smell,' he said, sniffing the air. 'I can't stand this.' His delicate olfactory nerves, tuned to receive only the most delicious kitchen aromas, were being tortured by the stench of the diesel-oil fumes pouring out of the backs of buses.

'I must get out of this place before my nose is ruined altogether,' he said. 'But first, I've simply got to have something to eat. I'm starving.' The poor boy had had nothing but berries and wild herbs for the past two weeks, and now his stomach was yearning for solid food. I'd like a nice hominy cutlet, he told himself. Or maybe a few juicy salsify fritters.

He crossed the street and entered a small restaurant. The place was hot inside, and dark and silent. There was a strong smell of cooking-fat and cabbage water. The only other customer was a man with a brown hat on his head, crouching intently over his food, who did not look up as Lexington came in.

Our hero seated himself at a corner table and hung his knapsack on the back of his chair. This he told himself, is going to be most interesting. In all my seventeen years I have tasted only the cooking of two people, Aunt Glosspan and myself — unless one counts Nurse McPottle, who must have heated my bottle a few times when I was an infant. But I am now about to sample the art of a new chef altogether, and perhaps, if I am lucky, I may pick up a couple of useful ideas for my book.

A waiter approached out of the shadows at the back, and stood beside the table.

'How do you do,' Lexington said. 'I should like a large hominy cutlet please. Do it twenty-five seconds each side, in a very hot skillet with sour cream, and sprinkle a pinch of lovage on it before serving — unless of course your chef knows a more original method, in which case I should be delighted to try it.'

The waiter laid his head over to one side and looked carefully at his customer. 'You want the roast pork and cabbage?' he asked. 'That's all we got left.'

'Roast what and cabbage?'

The waiter took a soiled handkerchief from his trouser pocket and shook it open with a violent flourish, as though he were cracking a whip. Then he blew his nose loud and wet.

'You want it or don't you?' he said, wiping his nostrils.

'I haven't the foggiest idea what it is,' Lexington replied, 'but I should love to try it. You see, I am writing a cooking-book and . . .'

'One pork and cabbage!' the waiter shouted, and somewhere in the back of the restaurant, far away in the darkness, a voice answered him.

The waiter disappeared. Lexington reached into his knapsack for his personal knife and fork. These were a present from Aunt Glosspan, given him when he was six years old, made of solid silver, and he had never eaten with any other instruments since. While waiting for the food to arrive, he polished them lovingly with a piece of soft muslin.

Soon the waiter returned carrying a plate on which there lay a thick greyish-white slab of something hot. Lexington leaned forward anxiously to smell it as it was put down before him. His nostrils were wide open to receive the scent, quivering and sniffing.

'But this is absolute heaven!' he exclaimed. 'What an aroma! It's tremendous!'

The waiter stepped back a pace, watching his customer carefully.

'Never in my life have I smelled anything as rich and wonderful as this!' our hero cried, seizing his knife and fork. 'What on earth is it made of?'

The man in the brown hat looked around and stared, then returned to his eating. The waiter was backing away towards the kitchen.

Lexington cut off a small piece of the meat, impaled it on his silver fork, and carried it up to his nose so as to smell it again. Then he popped it into his mouth and began to chew it slowly, his eyes half closed, his body tense.

'This is fantastic!' he cried. 'It is a brand-new flavour! Oh, Glosspan, my beloved Aunt, how I wish you were with me now so you could taste this remarkable dish! Waiter! Come here at once! I want you!'

The astonished waiter was now watching from the other end of the room, and he seemed reluctant to move any closer.

'If you will come and talk to me I will give you a present,' Lexington said, waving a hundred-dollar-bill. 'Please come over here and talk to me.'

The waiter sidled cautiously back to the table, snatched away the money, and held it up to his face, peering at it from all angles. Then he slipped it quickly into his pocket.

'What can I do for you, my friend?' he asked.

'Look,' Lexington said. 'If you will tell me what this delicious dish is made of, and exactly how it is prepared, I will give you another hundred.'

'I already told you,' the man said. 'It's pork.'

'And exactly what is pork?'

'You never had roast pork before?' the waiter asked, staring.

'For heaven's sake, man, tell me what it is and stop keeping me in suspense like this.'

'It's pig,' the waiter said. 'You just bung it in the oven.'

'*Pig!*'

'All pork is pig. Didn't you know that?'

'You mean *this* is *pig's* meat?'

'I guarantee it.'

'But ... but ... that's impossible,' the youth stammered. 'Aunt Glosspan, who knew more about food than anyone else in the world, said that meat of any kind was disgusting, revolting, horrible, foul, nauseating, and beastly. And yet this piece that I have here on my plate is without doubt the most delicious thing that I have ever tasted. Now how on earth do you explain that? Aunt Glosspan certainly wouldn't have told me it was revolting if it wasn't.'

'Maybe your aunt didn't know how to cook it,' the waiter said.

'Is that possible?'

'You're damned right it is. Especially with pork. Pork has to be very well done or you can't eat it.'

'Eureka!' Lexington cried. 'I'll bet that's exactly what happened! She did it wrong!' He handed the man another hundred-dollar bill. 'Lead me to the kitchen,' he said. 'Introduce me to the genius who prepared this meat.'

Lexington was at once taken to the kitchen, and there he met the cook who was an elderly man with a rash on one side of his neck.

'This will cost you another hundred,' the waiter said.

Lexington was only too glad to oblige, but this time he gave the money to the cook. 'Now listen to me,' he said. 'I have to admit that I am really rather confused by what the waiter has just been telling me. Are you quite sure that the delectable dish which I have just been eating was prepared from pig's flesh?'

The cook raised his right hand and began scratching the rash on his neck.

'Well,' he said, looking at the waiter and giving him a sly wink, 'all I can tell you is that I *think* it was pig's meat.'

'You mean you're not sure?'

'One can never be sure.'

'Then what else could it have been?'

'Well,' the cook said, speaking very slowly and still staring at the waiter. 'There's just a chance, you see, that it might have been a piece of human stuff.'

'You mean a man?'

'Yes.'

'Good heavens.'

'Or a woman. It could have been either. They both taste the same.'

'Well – now you really do surprise me,' the youth declared.

'One lives and learns.'

'Indeed one does.'

'As a matter of fact, we've been getting an awful lot of it just lately from the butcher's in place of pork,' the cook declared.

'Have you really?'

'The trouble is, it's almost impossible to tell which is which. They're both very good.'

'The piece I had just now was simply superb.'

'I'm glad you liked it,' the cook said. 'But to be quite honest, I think that it was a bit of pig. In fact, I'm almost sure it was.'

'You are?'

'Yes, I am.'

'In that case, we shall have to assume that you are right,' Lexington said. 'So now will you please tell me — and here is another hundred dollars for your trouble — will you please tell me precisely how you prepared it?'

The cook, after pocketing the money, launched upon a colourful description of how to roast a loin of pork, while the youth, not wanting to miss a single word of so great a recipe, sat down at the kitchen table and recorded every detail in his notebook.

'Is that all?' he asked when the cook had finished.

'That's all.'

'But there must be more to it than that, surely?'

'You got to get a good piece of meat to start off with,' the cook said. 'That's half the battle. It's got to be a good hog and it's got to be butchered right, otherwise it'll turn out lousy whichever way you cook it.'

'Show me how,' Lexington said. 'Butcher me one now so I can learn.'

'We don't butcher pigs in the kitchen,' the cook said. 'That lot you just ate came from a packing-house over in the Bronx.'

'Then give me the address!'

The cook gave him the address, and our hero, after thanking them both many times for all their kindnesses, rushed outside and leapt into a taxi and headed for the Bronx.

8

The packing house was a big four-storey brick building, and the air around it smelled sweet and heavy, like musk. At the main entrance gates, there was a large notice which said VISITORS WELCOME AT ANY TIME, and thus encouraged, Lexington walked through the gates and entered a cobbled yard which surrounded the building itself. He then followed a series of signposts (THIS WAY FOR THE GUIDED TOURS), and came eventually to a small corrugated-iron shed set well apart from the main building (VISITORS' WAITING-ROOM). After knocking politely on the door, he went in.

There were six other people ahead of him in the waiting-room. There was a fat mother with her two little boys aged about nine and eleven. There was a bright-eyed young couple who looked as though they might be on their honeymoon. And there was a pale woman with long white gloves, who sat very upright, looking straight ahead, with her hands folded on her lap. Nobody spoke. Lexington wondered whether they were all writing cooking-books like himself, but when he put this question to them aloud, he got no answer. The grown-ups merely smiled mysteriously to themselves and shook their heads, and the two children stared at him as though they were seeing a lunatic.

Soon, the door opened and a man with a merry pink face popped his head into the room and said, 'Next, please.' The mother and the two boys got up and went out.

About ten minutes later, the same man returned. 'Next, please,' he said again, and the honeymoon couple jumped up and followed him outside.

Two new visitors came in and sat down – a middle-aged husband and a middle-aged wife, the wife carrying a wicker shopping-basket containing groceries.

'Next, please,' said the guide, and the woman with the long white gloves got up and left.

Several more people came in and took their places on the stiffbacked wooden chairs.

Soon the guide returned for the fourth time, and now it was Lexington's turn to go outside.

'Follow me, please,' the guide said, leading the youth across the yard towards the main building.

'How exciting this is!' Lexington cried, hopping from one foot to the other. 'I only wish my dear Aunt Glosspan could be with me now to see what I am going to see.'

'I myself only do the preliminaries,' the guide said. 'Then I shall hand you over to someone else.'

'Anything you say,' cried the ecstatic youth.

First they visited a large penned-in area at the back of the building where several hundred pigs were wandering around. 'Here's where they start,' the guide said. 'And over there's where they go in.'

'Where?'

'Right there.' The guide pointed to a long wooden shed that stood against the outside wall of the factory. 'We call it the shackling-pen. This way, please.'

Three men wearing long rubber boots were driving a dozen pigs into the shackling-pen just as Lexington and the guide approached, so they all went in together.

'Now,' the guide said, 'watch how they shackle them.'

Inside, the shed was simply a bare wooden room with no roof, and there was a steel cable with hooks on it that kept moving slowly along the length of one wall, parallel with the ground, about three feet up. When it reached the end of the shed, this cable suddenly changed direction and climbed vertically upward through the open roof towards the top floor of the main building.

The twelve pigs were huddled together at the far end of the pen, standing quietly, looking apprehensive. One of the men in rubber boots pulled a length of metal chain down from the wall and advanced upon the nearest animal, approaching it from the rear. Then he bent down and quickly looped one end of the chain around one of the animal's hind legs. The other end he attached to a hook on the moving cable as it went by. The cable kept moving. The chain tightened. The pig's leg was pulled up and back, and then the pig itself began to be dragged backwards. But it didn't fall down. It was rather a nimble pig, and somehow it managed to keep its balance on three legs, hopping from foot to foot and struggling against the pull of the chain, but going back and back all the time until at the end of the pen where the cable changed direction and went vertically upward, the creature was suddenly jerked off its feet and borne aloft. Shrill protests filled the air.

'Truly a fascinating process,' Lexington said. 'But what was the funny cracking noise it made as it went up?'

'Probably the leg,' the guide answered. 'Either that or the pelvis.'

'But doesn't that matter?'

'Why should it matter?' the guide asked. 'You don't eat the bones.'

The rubber-booted men were busy shackling up the rest of the pigs, and one after another they were hooked to the moving cable and hoisted up through the roof, protesting loudly as they went.

'There's a good deal more to this recipe than just picking herbs,' Lexington said. 'Aunt Glosspan would never have made it.'

At this point, while Lexington was gazing skyward at the last pig to go up, a man in rubber boots approached him quietly from behind and looped one end of a chain around the youth's own ankle, hooking the other end to the moving belt. The next moment, before he had time to realize what was happening, our hero was jerked off his feet and dragged backwards along the concrete floor of the shackling-pen.

'Stop!' he cried. 'Hold everything! My leg is caught!'

But nobody seemed to hear him, and five seconds later, the unhappy young man was jerked off the floor and hoisted vertically upward through the open roof of the pen, dangling upside down by one ankle, and wriggling like a fish.

'Help!' he shouted. 'Help! There's been a frightful mistake! Stop the engines! Let me down!'

The guide removed a cigar from his mouth and looked up serenely at the rapidly ascending youth, but he said nothing. The men in rubber boots were already on their way out to collect the next batch of pigs.

'Oh, save me!' our hero cried. 'Let me down! Please let me down!' But he was now approaching the top floor of the building where the moving belt curled like a snake and entered a large hole in the wall, a kind of doorway without a door; and there, on the threshold, waiting to greet him, clothed in a dark-stained yellow rubber apron, and looking for all the world like Saint Peter at the Gates of Heaven, the sticker stood.

Lexington saw him only from upside down, and very briefly at that, but even so he noticed at once the expression of absolute peace and benevolence on the man's face, the cheerful twinkle in the eyes, the little wistful smile, the dimples in his cheeks — and all this gave him hope.

'Hi there,' the sticker said, smiling.

'Quick! Save me!' our hero cried.

'With pleasure,' the sticker said, and taking Lexington gently by one ear with his left hand, he raised his right hand and deftly slit open the boy's jugular vein with a knife.

The belt moved on. Lexington went with it. Everything was still upside down and the blood was pouring out of his throat and getting into his eyes, but he could still see after a fashion, and he had a blurred impression of being in an enormously long room, and at the far end of the room there was a great smoking cauldron of water, and there were dark figures, half hidden in the steam, dancing around the edge of it, brandishing long poles. The conveyor-belt seemed to be travelling right over the top of the cauldron, and the pigs seemed to be dropping one by one into the boiling water, and one of the pigs seemed to be wearing long white gloves on its front feet.

Suddenly our hero started to feel very sleepy, but it wasn't until his good strong heart had pumped the last drop of blood from his body that he passed on out of this, the best of all possible worlds, into the next.

THE CHAMPION OF THE WORLD

ALL DAY, IN BETWEEN serving customers, we had been crouching over the table in the office of the filling-station, preparing the raisins. They were plump and soft and swollen from being soaked in water, and when you nicked them with a razor-blade the skin sprang open and the jelly stuff inside squeezed out as easily as you could wish.

But we had a hundred and ninety-six of them to do altogether and the evening was nearly upon us before we had finished.

'Don't they look marvellous!' Claud cried, rubbing his hands together hard. 'What time is it, Gordon?'

'Just after five.'

Through the window we could see a station-wagon pulling up at the pumps with a woman at the wheel and about eight children in the back eating ice-creams.

'We ought to be moving soon,' Claud said. 'The whole thing'll be a washout if we don't arrive before sunset, you realize that.' He was getting twitchy now. His face had the same flushed and pop-eyed look it got before a dog-race or when there was a date with Clarice in the evening.

We both went outside and Claud gave the woman the number of gallons she wanted. When she had gone, he remained standing in the middle of the driveway squinting anxiously up at the sun which was now only the width of a man's hand above the line of trees along the crest of the ridge on the far side of the valley.

'All right,' I said. 'Lock up.'

He went quickly from pump to pump, securing each nozzle in its holder with a small padlock.

'You'd better take off that yellow pullover,' he said.

'Why should I?'

'You'll be shining like a bloody beacon out there in the moonlight.'

'I'll be all right.'

'You will not,' he said. 'Take if off, Gordon, please. I'll see you in three minutes.' He disappeared into his caravan behind the filling station, and I went indoors and changed my yellow pullover for a blue one.

When we met again outside, Claud was dressed in a pair of black trousers and a dark-green turtleneck sweater. On his head he wore a brown cloth cap with the peak pulled down low over his eyes, and he looked like an apache actor out of a nightclub.

'What's under there?' I asked, seeing the bulge at his waistline.

He pulled up his sweater and showed me two thin but very large white cotton sacks which were bound neat and tight around his belly. 'To carry the stuff,' he said darkly.

'I see.'

'Let's go,' he said.

'I still think we ought to take the car.'

'It's too risky. They'll see it parked.'

'But it's over three miles up to that wood.'

'Yes,' he said. 'And I suppose you realize we can get six months in the clink if they catch us.'

'You never told me that.'

'Didn't I?'

'I'm not coming,' I said. 'It's not worth it.'

'The walk will do you good, Gordon. Come on.'

It was a calm sunny evening with little wisps of brilliant white cloud hanging motionless in the sky, and the valley was cool and very quiet as the two of us began walking together along the grass verge on the side of the road that ran between the hills towards Oxford.

'You got the raisins?' Claud asked.

'They're in my pocket.'

'Good,' he said. 'Marvellous.'

Ten minutes later we turned left off the main road into a narrow lane with high hedges on either side and from now on it was all uphill.

'How many keepers are there?' I asked.

'Three.'

Claud threw away a half-finished cigarette. A minute later he lit another.

'I don't usually approve of new methods,' he said. 'Not on this sort of a job.'

'Of course.'

'But by God, Gordon, I think we're on to a hot one this time.'

'You do?'

'There's no question about it.'

'I hope you're right.'

'It'll be a milestone in the history of poaching,' he said. 'But don't you go telling a single soul how we've done it, you understand. Because if this ever leaked out we'd have every bloody fool in the district doing the same thing and there wouldn't be a pheasant left.'

'I won't say a word.'

'You ought to be very proud of yourself,' he went on. 'There's been men with brains studying this problem for hundreds of years and not one of them's ever come up with anything even a quarter as artful as you have. Why didn't you tell me about it before?'

'You never invited my opinion,' I said.

And that was the truth. In fact, up until the day before, Claud had never even offered to discuss with me the sacred subject of poaching. Often enough, on a summer's evening when work was finished, I had seen him with cap on head sliding quietly out of his caravan and disappearing up the road towards the woods; and sometimes, watching him through the windows of the filling-station, I would find myself wondering exactly what he was going to do, what wily tricks he was going to practise all alone up there under the trees in the dead of night. He seldom came back until very late, and never, absolutely never did he bring any of the spoils with him personally on his return. But the following afternoon — and I couldn't imagine how he did it — there would always be a pheasant or a hare or a brace of partridges hanging up in the shed behind the filling-station for us to eat.

This summer he had been particularly active, and during the last couple of months he had stepped up the tempo to a point where he was going out four and sometimes five nights a week. But that was not all. It seemed to me that recently his whole attitude towards poaching had undergone a subtle and mysterious change. He was more purposeful about it now, more tight-lipped and intense than before, and I had the impression that this was not so much a game any longer as a crusade, a sort of private war that Claud was waging single-handed against an invisible and hated enemy.

But who?

I wasn't sure about this, but I had a suspicion that it was none other than the famous Mr Victor Hazel himself, the owner of the land and the pheasants. Mr Hazel was a local brewer with an unbelievably arrogant manner. He was rich beyond words, and his property stretched for miles along either side of the valley. He was a self-made man with no charm at all and previous few virtues. He loathed all persons of humble station, having once been one of them himself, and he strove desperately to mingle with what he believed were the right kind of folk. He rode to hounds and gave shooting-parties and wore fancy waistcoats and every weekday he drove an enormous black Rolls-Royce past the filling-station on his way to the brewery. As he flashed by, we would sometimes catch a glimpse of the great glistening brewer's face above the wheel, pink as a ham, all soft and inflamed from drinking too much beer.

Anyway, yesterday afternoon, right out of the blue, Claud had suddenly said to me, 'I'll be going on up to Hazel's woods again tonight. Why don't you come along?'

'Who, me?'

'It's about the last chance this year for pheasants,' he had said. 'The shooting-season opens Saturday and the birds'll be scattered all over the place after that – if there's any left.'

'Why the sudden invitation?' I had asked, greatly suspicious.

'No special reason, Gordon. No reason at all.'

'Is it risky?'

He hadn't answered this.

'I suppose you keep a gun or something hidden away up there?'

'A gun!' he cried, disgusted. 'Nobody ever *shoots* pheasants, didn't you know that? You've only got to fire a *cap-pistol* in Hazel's woods and the keepers'll be on you.'

'Then how do you do it?'

'Ah,' he said, and the eyelids drooped over the eyes, veiled and secretive.

There was a long pause. Then he said, 'Do you think you could keep your mouth shut if I was to tell you a thing or two?'

'Definitely.'

'I've never told this to anyone else in my whole life, Gordon.'

'I am greatly honoured,' I said. 'You can trust me completely.'

He turned his head, fixing me with pale eyes. The eyes were large and wet and ox-like, and they were so near to me that I could see my own face reflected upside down in the centre of each.

'I am now about to let you in on the three best ways in the world of poaching a pheasant,' he said. 'And seeing that you're the guest on this little trip, I am going to give you the choice of which one you'd like us to use tonight. How's that?'

'There's a catch in this.'

'There's no catch, Gordon. I swear it.'

'All right, go on.'

'Now, here's the thing,' he said. 'Here's the first big secret.' He paused and took a long suck at his cigarette. 'Pheasants,' he whispered softly, 'is *crazy* about raisins.'

'Raisins?'

'Just ordinary raisins. It's like a mania with them. My dad discovered that more than forty years ago just like he discovered all three of these methods I'm about to describe to you now.'

'I thought you said your dad was a drunk.'

'Maybe he was. But he was also a great poacher, Gordon. Possibly the greatest there's ever been in the history of England. My dad studied poaching like a scientist.'

'Is that so?'

'I mean it. I really mean it.'

'I believe you.'

'Do you know,' he said, 'my dad used to keep a whole flock of prime cockerels in the back yard purely for experimental purposes.'

'Cockerels?'

'That's right. And whenever he thought up some new stunt for catching a pheasant, he'd try it out on a cockerel first to see how it worked. That's how he discovered about raisins. It's also how he invented the horsehair method.'

Claud paused and glanced over his shoulder as though to make sure that there was nobody listening. 'Here's how it's done,' he said. 'First you take a few raisins and you soak them overnight in water to make them nice and plump and juicy. Then you get a bit of good stiff horsehair and you cut it up into half-inch lengths. Then you push one of these lengths of horsehair through the middle of each raisin so that there's about an eighth of an inch of it sticking out on either side. You follow?'

'Yes.'

'Now — the old pheasant comes along and eats one of these raisins. Right? And you're watching him from behind a tree. So what then?'

'I imagine it sticks in his throat.'

'That's obvious, Gordon. But here's the amazing thing. Here's what my dad discovered. The moment this happens, the bird *never moves his feet again!* He becomes absolutely rooted to the spot, and there he stands pumping his silly neck up and down just like it was a piston, and all you've got to do is walk calmly out from the place where you're hiding and pick him up in your hands.'

'I don't believe that.'

'I swear it,' he said. 'Once a pheasant's had the horsehair you can fire a rifle in his ear and he won't even jump. It's just one of those unexplainable little things. But it takes a genius to discover it.'

He paused, and there was a gleam of pride in his eye now as he dwelt for a moment or two upon the memory of his father, the great inventor.

'So that's Method Number One,' he said. 'Method Number Two is even more simple still. All you do is you have a fishing line. Then you bait the hook with a raisin and you fish for the pheasant just like you fish for a fish. You pay out the line about fifty yards and you lie there on your stomach in the bushes waiting till you get a bite. Then you haul him in.'

'I don't think your father invented that one.'

'It's very popular with fishermen,' he said, choosing not to hear me. 'Keen fishermen who can't get down to the seaside as often as they want. It gives them a bit of the old thrill. The only trouble is it's rather noisy. The pheasant squawks like hell as you haul him in, and then every keeper in the wood comes running.'

'What is Method Number Three?' I asked.

'Ah,' he said. 'Number Three's a real beauty. It was the last one my dad ever invented before he passed away.'

'His final great work?'

'Exactly, Gordon. And I can even remember the very day it happened, a Sunday morning it was, and suddenly my dad comes into the kitchen holding a huge white cockerel in his hands and he says, "I think I've got it!" There's a little smile on his face and a shine of glory in his eyes and he comes in very soft and quiet and he puts the bird down right in the middle of the kitchen table and he says, "By God I think I've got a good one this time!" "A good what?" Mum says, looking up from the sink. "Horace, take that filthy bird off my table." The cockerel has a funny little paper hat over its head, like an ice-cream cone upside down, and my dad is pointing to it proudly. "Stroke him," he says. "He won't move an inch." The cockerel starts scratching away at the paper hat with one of its feet, but the hat seems to be stuck on with glue and it won't come off. "No bird in the world is going to run away once you cover up his eyes," my dad says, and he starts poking the cockerel with his finger and pushing it around on the table, but it doesn't take the slightest bit of notice. "You can have this one," he says, talking to Mum. "You can kill it and dish it up for dinner as a celebration of what I have just invented." And then straight away he takes me by the arm and marches me quickly out the door and off we go over the fields and up into the big forest the other side of Haddenham which used to belong to the Duke of Buckingham, and in less than two hours we get five lovely fat pheasants with no more trouble than it takes to go out and buy them in a shop.'

Claud paused for breath. His eyes were huge and moist and dreamy as they gazed back into the wonderful world of his youth.

'I don't quite follow this,' I said. 'How did he get the paper hats over the pheasants' heads up in the woods?'

'You'd never guess it.'

'I'm sure I wouldn't.'

'Then here it is. First of all you dig a little hole in the ground. Then you twist a piece of paper into the shape of a cone and you fit this into the hole, hollow end upward, like a cup. Then you smear the paper cup all around the inside with bird-lime and drop in a few raisins. At the same time you lay a trail of raisins along the ground leading up to it. Now – the old pheasant comes pecking along the trail, and when he gets to the hole he pops his head inside to gobble the raisins and the next thing he knows he's got a paper hat stuck over his eyes and he can't see a thing. Isn't it marvellous what some people think of, Gordon? Don't you agree?'

'Your dad was a genius,' I said.

'Then take your pick. Choose whichever one of the three methods you fancy and we'll use it tonight.'

'You don't think they're all just a trifle on the crude side, do you?'

'Crude!' he cried, aghast. 'Oh my God! And who's been having roasted pheasant in the house nearly every single day for the last six months and not a penny to pay?'

He turned and walked away towards the door of the workshop. I could see that he was deeply pained by my remark.

'Wait a minute,' I said. 'Don't go.'

'You want to come or don't you?'

'Yes, but let me ask you something first. I've just had a bit of an idea.'

'Keep it,' he said. 'You are talking about a subject you don't know the first thing about.'

'Do you remember that bottle of sleeping-pills the doc gave me last month when I had a bad back?'

'What about them?'

'Is there any reason why those wouldn't work on a pheasant?'

Claud closed his eyes and shook his head pityingly from side to side.

'Wait,' I said.

'It's not worth discussing,' he said. 'No pheasant in the world is going to swallow those lousy red capsules. Don't you know any better than that?'

'You are forgetting the raisins,' I said. 'Now listen to this. We take a raisin. Then we soak it till it swells. Then we make a tiny slit in one side of it with a razor-blade. Then we hollow it out a little. Then we open up one of my red capsules and pour all the powder into the raisin. Then we get a needle and cotton and very carefully we sew up the slit. Now . . .'

Out of the corner of my eye, I saw Claud's mouth slowly beginning to open.

'Now,' I said. 'We have a nice clean-looking raisin with two and a half grains of seconal inside it, and let me tell *you* something now. That's enough dope to knock the average *man* unconscious, never mind about *birds!*'

I paused for ten seconds to allow the full impact of this to strike home.

'What's more, with this method we could operate on a really grand scale. We could prepare *twenty* raisins if we felt like it, and all we'd have to do is scatter them around the feeding-grounds at sunset and then walk away. Half an hour later we'd come back, and the pills would be beginning to work, and the pheasants would be up in the trees by then, roosting, and they'd be starting to feel groggy, and they'd be wobbling and trying to keep their balance, and soon every pheasant that had eaten *one single raisin* would keel over unconscious and fall to the ground. My dear boy, they'd be dropping out of the trees like apples, and all we'd have to do is walk around picking them up!'

Claud was staring at me, rapt.

'Oh Christ,' he said softly.

'And they'd never catch us either. We'd simply stroll through the woods dropping a few raisins here and there as we went, and even if they were *watching* us they wouldn't notice anything.'

'Gordon,' he said, laying a hand on my knee and gazing at me with eyes large and bright as two stars. 'If this thing works, it will *revolutionize* poaching.'

'I'm glad to hear it.'

'How many pills have you got left?' he asked.

'Forty-nine. There were fifty in the bottle and I've only used one.'

'Forty-nine's not enough. We want at least two hundred.'

'Are you mad!' I cried.

He walked slowly away and stood by the door with his back to me, gazing at the sky.

'Two hundred's the bare minimum,' he said quietly. 'There's really not much point in doing it unless we have two hundred.'

What is it now, I wondered. What the hell's he trying to do?

'This is the last chance we'll have before the season opens,' he said. 'I couldn't possibly get any more.'

'You wouldn't want us to come back empty-handed, would you?'

'But why so *many*?'

Claud turned his head and looked at me with large innocent eyes. 'Why not?' he said gently. 'Do you have any objection?'

My God, I thought suddenly. The crazy bastard is out to wreck Mr Victor Hazel's opening-day shooting-party.

'You get us two hundred of those pills,' he said, 'and then it'll be worth doing.'

'I can't.'

'You could try, couldn't you?'

Mr Hazel's party took place on the first of October every year and it was a very famous event. Debilitated gentleman in tweed suits, some with titles and some who were merely rich, motored in from miles around with their gun-bearers and dogs and wives, and all day long the noise of shooting rolled across the valley. There were always enough pheasants to go round, for each summer the woods were methodically restocked with dozens and dozens of young birds at incredible expense. I had heard it said that the cost of rearing and keeping each pheasant up to the time when it was ready to be shot was well over five pounds (which is approximately the price of two hundred loaves of bread). But to Mr Hazel it was worth every penny of it. He became, if only for a few hours, a big cheese in a little world and even the Lord Lieutenant of the County slapped him on the back and tried to remember his first name when he said good-bye.

'How would it be if we just reduced the dose?' Claud asked. 'Why couldn't we divide the contents of one capsule among four raisins?'

'I suppose you could if you wanted to.

'But would a quarter of a capsule be strong enough for each bird?'

One simply had to admire the man's nerve. It was dangerous enough to poach a single pheasant up in those woods at this time of year and here he was planning to knock off the bloody lot.

'A quarter would be plenty,' I said.

'You're sure of that?'

'Work it out for yourself. It's all done by bodyweight. You'd still be giving about twenty times more than is necessary.'

'Then we'll quarter the dose,' he said, rubbing his hands. He paused and calculated for a moment. 'We'll have one hundred and ninety-six raisins!'

'Do you realize what that involves?' I said. 'They'll take hours to prepare.'

'What of it!' he cried. 'We'll go tomorrow instead. We'll soak the raisins overnight and then we'll have all morning and afternoon to get them ready.'

And that was precisely what we did.

Now, twenty-four hours later, we were on our way. We had been walking steadily for about forty minutes and we were nearing the point where the lane curved round to the right and ran along the crest of the hill towards the big wood where the pheasants lived. There was about a mile to go.

'I don't suppose by any chance these keepers might be carrying guns?' I asked.

'All keepers carry guns,' Claud said.

I had been afraid of that.

'It's for the vermin mostly.'

'Ah.'

'Of course there's no guarantee they won't take a pot at a poacher now and again.'

'You're joking.'

'Not at all. But they only do it from behind. Only when you're running away. They like to pepper you in the legs at about fifty yards.'

'They can't do that!' I cried. 'It's a criminal offence!'

'So is poaching,' Claud said.

We walked on awhile in silence. The sun was below the high hedge on our right now and the lane was in shadow.

'You can consider yourself lucky this isn't thirty years ago,' he went on. 'They used to shoot you on sight in those days.'

'Do you believe that?'

'I know it,' he said. 'Many's the night when I was a nipper I've gone into the kitchen and seen my old dad lying face downward on the table and Mum standing over him digging the grapeshot out of his buttocks with a potato knife.'

'Stop,' I said. 'It makes me nervous.'

'You believe me, don't you?'

'Yes, I believe you.'

'Towards the end he was so covered in tiny little white scars he looked exactly like it was snowing.'

'Yes,' I said. 'All right.'

'Poacher's arse, they used to call it,' Claud said. 'And there wasn't a man in the whole village who didn't have a bit of it one way or another. But my dad was the champion.'

'Good luck to him,' I said.

'I wish to hell he was here now,' Claud said, wistful. 'He'd have given anything in the world to be coming with us on this job tonight.'

'He could take my place,' I said. 'Gladly.'

We had reached the crest of the hill and now we could see the wood ahead of us, huge and dark with the sun going down behind the trees and little sparks of gold shining through.

'You'd better let me have those raisins,' Claud said.

I gave him the bag and he slid it gently into his trouser pocket.

'No talking once we're inside,' he said. 'Just follow me and try not to go snapping any branches.'

Five minutes later we were there. The lane ran right up to the wood itself and then skirted the edge of it for about three hundred yards with only a little hedge between. Claud slipped through the hedge on all fours and I followed.

It was cool and dark inside the wood. No sunlight came in at all.

'This is spooky,' I said.

'Ssshh!'

Claud was very tense. He was walking just ahead of me, picking his feet up high and putting them down gently on the moist ground. He kept his head moving all the time, the eyes sweeping slowly from side to side, searching for danger. I tried doing the same, but soon I began to see a keeper behind every tree, so I gave it up.

Then a large patch of sky appeared ahead of us in the roof of the forest and I knew that this must be the clearing. Claud had told me that the clearing was the place where the young birds were introduced into the woods in early July, where they were fed and watered and guarded by the keepers, and where many of them stayed from force of habit until the shooting began.

'There always plenty of pheasants in the clearing,' he had said.

'Keepers too, I suppose.'

'Yes, but there's thick bushes all around and that helps.'

We were now advancing in a series of quick crouching spurts, running from tree to tree and stopping and waiting and listening and running on again, and then at last we were kneeling safely behind a big clump of alder right on the edge of the clearing and Claud was grinning and nudging me in the ribs and pointing through the branches at the pheasants.

The place was absolutely stiff with birds. There must have been two hundred of them at least strutting around among the tree-stumps.

'You see what I mean?' Claud whispered.

It was an astonishing sight, a sort of poacher's dream come true. And how close they were! Some of them were not more than ten paces from where we knelt. The hens were plump and creamy-brown and they were so fat their breast-feathers almost brushed the ground as they walked. The cocks were slim and beautiful, with long tails and brilliant red patches around the eyes, like scarlet spectacles. I glanced at Claud. His big ox-like face was transfixed in ecstasy. The mouth was slightly open and the eyes had a kind of glazy look about them as they stared at the pheasants.

I believe that all poachers react in roughly the same way as this on sighting game. They are like women who sight large emeralds in a jeweller's window, the only difference being that the women are less dignified in the methods they employ later on to acquire the loot. Poacher's arse is nothing to the punishment that a female is willing to endure.

'Ah-ha,' Claud said softly. 'You see the keeper?'

'Where?'

'Over the other side, by that big tree. Look carefully.'

'My God!'

'It's all right. He can't see *us*.'

We crouched close to the ground, watching the keeper. He was a smallish man with a cap on his head and a gun under his arm. He never moved. He was like a little post standing there.

'Let's go,' I whispered.

The keeper's face was shadowed by the peak of his cap, but it seemed to me that he was looking directly at us.

'I'm not staying here,' I said.

'Hush,' Claud said.

Slowly, never taking his eyes from the keeper, he reached into his pocket and brought out a single raisin. He placed it in the palm of his right hand, and then quickly, with a little flick of the wrist, he threw the raisin high into the air. I watched it as it went sailing over the bushes and I saw it land within a yard or so of two henbirds standing together beside an old tree-stump. Both birds turned their heads sharply at the drop of the raisin. Then one of them hopped over and made a quick peck at the ground and that must have been it.

I glanced up at the keeper. He hadn't moved.

Claud threw a second raisin into the clearing; then a third, and a fourth, and a fifth.

At this point, I saw the keeper turn away his head in order to survey the wood behind him.

Quick as a flash, Claud pulled the paper bag out of his pocket and tipped a huge pile of raisins into the cup of his right hand.

'Stop,' I said.

But with a great sweep of the arm he flung the whole handful high over the bushes into the clearing.

They fell with a soft little patter, like raindrops on dry leaves, and every single pheasant in the place must either have seen them coming or heard them fall. There was a flurry of wings and a rush to find the treasure.

The keeper's head flicked round as though there were a spring inside his neck. The birds were all pecking away madly at the raisins. The keeper took two quick paces forward and for a moment I thought he was going to investigate. But then he stopped, and his face came up and his eyes began travelling slowly around the perimeter of the clearing.

'Follow me,' Claud whispered. 'And *keep down*.' He started crawling away swiftly on all fours, like some kind of a monkey.

I went after him. He had his nose close to the ground and his huge tight buttocks were winking at the sky and it was easy to see now how poacher's arse had come to be an occupational disease among the fraternity.

We went along like this for about a hundred yards.

'Now run,' Claud said.

We got to our feet and ran, and a few minutes later we emerged through the hedge into the lovely open safety of the lane.

'It went marvellous,' Claud said, breathing heavily. 'Didn't it go absolutely marvellous?' The big face was scarlet and glowing with triumph.

'It was a mess,' I said.

'What!' he cried.

'Of course it was. We can't possibly go back now. That keeper knows there was someone there.'

'He knows nothing,' Claud said. 'In another five minutes it'll be pitch dark inside the wood and he'll be sloping off home to his supper.'

'I think I'll join him.'

'You're a great poacher,' Claud said. He sat down on the grassy bank under the hedge and lit a cigarette.

The sun had set now and the sky was a pale smoke blue, faintly glazed with yellow. In the woods behind us the shadows and the spaces in between the trees were turning from grey to black.

'How long does a sleeping-pill take to work?' Claud asked.

'Look out,' I said. 'There's someone coming.'

The man had appeared suddenly and silently out of the dusk and he was only thirty yards away when I saw him.

'Another bloody keeper,' Claud said.

We both looked at the keeper as he came down the lane towards us. He had a shotgun under his arm and there was a black Labrador walking at his heels. He stopped when he was a few paces away and the dog stopped with him and stayed behind him, watching us through the keeper's legs.

'Good evening,' Claud said, nice and friendly.

This one was a tall bony man about forty with a swift eye and a hard cheek and hard dangerous hands.

'I know you,' he said softly, coming closer. 'I know the both of you.'

Claud didn't answer this.

'You're from the fillin'-station. Right?'

His lips were thin and dry, with some sort of a brownish crust over them.

'You're Cubbage and Hawes and you're from the fillin'-station on the main road. Right?'

'What are we playing?' Claud said. 'Twenty Questions?'

The keeper spat out a big gob of spit and I saw it go floating through the air and land with a plop on a patch of dry dust six inches from Claud's feet. It looked like a little baby oyster lying there.

'Beat it,' the man said. 'Go on. Get out.'

Claud sat on the bank smoking his cigarette and looking at the gob of spit.

'Go on,' the man said. 'Get out.'

When he spoke, the upper lip lifted above the gum and I could see a row of small discoloured teeth, one of them black, the others quince and ochre.

'This happens to be a public highway,' Claud said. 'Kindly do not molest us.'

The keeper shifted the gun from his left arm to his right.

'You're loiterin',' he said, 'with intent to commit a felony. I could run you in for that.'

'No you couldn't,' Claud said.

All this made me rather nervous.

'I've had my eye on you for some time,' the keeper said, looking at Claud.

'It's getting late,' I said. 'Shall we stroll on?'

Claud flipped away his cigarette and got slowly to his feet. 'All right,' he said. 'Let's go.'

We wandered off down the lane the way we had come, leaving the keeper standing there, and soon the man was out of sight in the half-darkness behind us.

'That's the head keeper,' Claud said. 'His name is Rabbetts.'

'Let's get the hell out,' I said.

'Come in here,' Claud said.

There was a gate on our left leading into a field and we climbed over it and sat down behind the hedge.

'Mr Rabbetts is also due for his supper,' Claud said. 'You mustn't worry about him.'

We sat quietly behind the hedge waiting for the keeper to walk past us on his way home. A few stars were showing and a bright three-quarter moon was coming up over the hills behind us in the east.

'Here he is,' Claud whispered. 'Don't move.'

The keeper came loping softly up the lane with the dog padding quick and soft-footed at his heels, and we watched them through the hedge as they went by.

'He won't be coming back tonight,' Claud said.

'How do you know that?'

'A keeper never waits for you in the wood if he knows where you live. He goes to your house and hides outside and watches for you to come back.'

'That's worse.'

'No, it isn't, not if you dump the loot somewhere else before you go home. He can't touch you then.'

'What about the other one, the one in the clearing?'

'He's gone too.'

'You can't be sure of that.'

'I've been studying these bastards for months, Gordon, honest I have. I know all their habits. There's no danger.'

Reluctantly I followed him back into the wood. It was pitch dark in there now and very silent, and as we moved cautiously forward the noise of our footsteps seemed to go echoing around the walls of the forest as though we were walking in a cathedral.

'Here's where we threw the raisins,' Claud said.

I peered through the bushes.

The clearing lay dim and milky in the moonlight.

'You're quite sure the keeper's gone?'

'I *know* he's gone.'

I could just see Claud's face under the peak of his cap, the pale lips, the soft pale cheeks, and the large eyes with a little spark of excitement dancing slowly in each.

'Are they roosting?'

'Yes.'

'Whereabouts?'

'All around. They don't go far.'

'What do we do next?'

'We stay here and wait. I brought you a light,' he added, and he handed me one of those small pocket flashlights shaped like a fountain-pen. 'You may need it.'

I was beginning to feel better. 'Shall we see if we can spot some of them sitting in the trees?' I said.

'No.'

'I should like to see how they look when they're roosting.'

'This isn't a nature-study,' Claud said. 'Please be quiet.'

We stood there for a long time waiting for something to happen.

'I've just had a nasty thought,' I said. 'If a bird can keep its balance on a branch when it's asleep, then surely there isn't any reason why the pills should make it fall down.'

Claud looked at me quick.

'After all,' I said, 'it's not dead. It's still only sleeping.'

'It's doped,' Claud said.

'But that's just a *deeper* sort of sleep. Why should we expect it to fall down just because it's in a *deeper* sleep?'

There was a gloomy silence.

'We should've tried it with chickens,' Claud said. 'My dad would've done that.'

'Your dad was a genius,' I said.

At that moment there came a soft thump from the wood behind us.

'Hey!'

'Sshh!'

We stood listening.

Thump.

'There's another!'

It was a deep muffled sound as though a bag of sand had been dropped from about shoulder height.

Thump!

'They're pheasants!' I cried.

'Wait!'

'I'm sure they're pheasants!'

Thump! Thump!

'You're right!'

We ran back into the wood.

'Where were they?'

'Over here! Two of them were over here!'

'I thought they were this way.'

'Keep looking!' Claud shouted. 'They can't be far.'

We searched for about a minute.

'Here's one!' he called.

When I got to him he was holding a magnificent cock-bird in both hands. We examined it closely with our flashlights.

'It's doped to the gills,' Claud said. 'It's still alive, I can feel its heart, but it's doped to the bloody gills.'

Thump!

'There's another!'

Thump! Thump!

'Two more!'

Thump!

Thump! Thump! Thump!

'Jesus Christ!'

Thump! Thump! Thump! Thump!

Thump! Thump!

All around us the pheasants were starting to rain down out of the trees. We began rushing around madly in the dark, sweeping the ground with our flashlights.

Thump! Thump! Thump! This lot fell almost on top of me. I was right under the tree as they came down and I found all three of them immediately — two cocks and a hen. They were limp and warm, the feathers wonderfully soft in the hand.

'Where shall I put them?' I called out. I was holding them by the legs.

'Lay them here, Gordon! Just pile them up here where it's light!'

Claud was standing on the edge of the clearing with the moonlight streaming down all over him and a great bunch of pheasants in each hand. His face was bright, his eyes big and bright and wonderful, and he was staring around him like a child who has just discovered that the whole world is made of chocolate.

Thump!

Thump! Thump!

'I don't like it,' I said. 'It's too many.'

'It's beautiful!' he cried and he dumped the birds he was carrying and ran off to look for more.

Thump! Thump! Thump! Thump!

Thump!

It was easy to find them now. There were one or two lying under every tree. I quickly collected six more, three in each hand, and ran back and dumped them with the others. Then six more. Then six more after that.

And still they kept falling.

Claud was in a whirl of ecstasy now, dashing about like a mad ghost under the trees. I could see the beam of his flashlight waving around in the dark and each time he found a bird he gave a little yelp of triumph.

Thump! Thump! Thump!

'That bugger Hazel ought to hear this!' he called out.

'Don't shout,' I said. 'It frightens me.'

'What's that?'

'Don't *shout*. There might be keepers.'

'Screw the keepers!' he cried. 'They're all eating!'

For three or four minutes, the pheasants kept on falling. Then suddenly they stopped.

'Keep searching!' Claud shouted. 'There's plenty more on the ground!'

'Don't you think we ought to get out while the going's good?'

'No,' he said.

We went on searching. Between us we looked under every tree within a hundred yards of the clearing, north, south, east, and west, and I think we found most of them in the end. At the collecting-point there was a pile of pheasants as big as a bonfire.

'It's a miracle,' Claud was saying. 'It's a bloody miracle.' He was staring at them in a kind of trance.

'We'd better just take half a dozen each and get out quick,' I said.

'I would like to count them, Gordon.'

'There's no time for that.'

'I must count them.'

'No,' I said. 'Come on.'

'One . . .

'Two . . .

'Three . . .

'Four . . .'

He began counting them very carefully, picking up each bird in turn and laying it carefully to one side. The moon was directly overhead now and the whole clearing was brilliantly illuminated.

'I'm not standing around here like this,' I said. I walked back a few paces and hid myself in the shadows, waiting for him to finish.

'A hundred and seventeen . . . a hundred and eighteen . . . a hundred and nineteen . . . *a hundred and twenty!*' he cried. '*One hundred and twenty birds!* It's an all-time record!'

I didn't doubt it for a moment.

'The most my dad ever got in one night was fifteen and he was drunk for a week afterwards!'

'You're the champion of the world,' I said. 'Are you ready now?'

'One minute,' he answered and he pulled up his sweater and procee-ded to unwind the two big white cotton sacks from around his belly. 'Here's yours,' he said, handing one of them to me. 'Fill it up quick.'

The light of the moon was so strong I could read the small print along the base of the sack. J. W. CRUMP, it said. KESTON FLOUR MILLS, LONDON SW17.

'You don't think that bastard with the brown teeth is watching us this very moment from behind a tree?'

'There's no chance of that,' Claud said. 'He's down at the filling-station like I told you, waiting for us to come home.'

We started loading the pheasants into the sacks. They were soft and floppy-necked and the skin underneath the feathers was still warm.

'There'll be a taxi waiting for us in the lane,' Claud said.

'What?'

'I always go back in a taxi, Gordon, didn't you know that?'

I told him I didn't.

'A taxi is anonymous,' Claud said. 'Nobody knows who's inside a taxi except the driver. My dad taught me that.'

'Which driver?'

'Charlie Kinch. He's only too glad to oblige.'

We finished loading the pheasants, and I tried to hump my bulging sack on to my shoulder. My sack had about sixty birds inside it, and it must have weighed a hundredweight and a half, at least. 'I can't carry this,' I said. 'We'll have to leave some of them behind.'

'Drag it,' Claud said. 'Just pull it behind you.'

We started off through the pitch-black woods, pulling the pheasants behind us. 'We'll never make it all the way back to the village like this,' I said.

'Charlie's never let me down yet,' Claud said.

We came to the margin of the wood and peered through the hedge into the lane. Claud said, 'Charlie boy' very softly and the old man behind the wheel of the taxi not five yards away poked his head out into the moonlight and gave us a sly toothless grin. We slid through the hedge, dragging the sacks after us along the ground.

'Hullo!' Charlie said. 'What's this?'

'It's cabbages,' Claud told him. 'Open the door.'

Two minutes later we were safely inside the taxi, cruising slowly down the hill towards the village.

It was all over now bar the shouting. Claud was triumphant, bursting with pride and excitement, and he kept leaning forward and tapping Charlie Kinch on the shoulder and saying, 'How about it, Charlie? How about this for a haul?' and Charlie kept glancing back popeyed at the huge bulging sacks lying on the floor between us and saying, 'Jesus Christ, man, how did you do it?'

'There's six brace of them for you, Charlie,' Claud said. And Charlie said, 'I reckon pheasants is going to be a bit scarce up at Mr Victor Hazel's opening-day shoot this year,' and Claud said, 'I imagine they are, Charlie, I imagine they are.'

'What in God's name are you going to do with a hundred and twenty pheasants?' I asked.

'Put them in cold storage for the winter,' Claud said. 'Put them in with the dogmeat in the deep-freeze at the filling-station.'

'Not tonight, I trust?'

'No, Gordon, not tonight. We leave them at Bessie's house tonight.'

'Bessie who?'

'Bessie Organ.'

'Bessie *Organ!*'

'Bessie always delivers my game, didn't you know that?'

'I don't know anything,' I said. I was completely stunned. Mrs Organ was the wife of the Reverend Jack Organ, the local vicar.

'Always choose a respectable woman to deliver your game,' Claud announced. 'That's correct, Charlie, isn't it?'

'Bessie's a right smart girl,' Charlie said.

We were driving through the village now and the street-lamps were still on and the men were wandering home from the pubs. I saw Will Prattley letting himself in quietly by the side-door of his fishmonger's shop and Mrs Prattley's head was sticking out of the window just above him, but he didn't know it.

'The vicar is very partial to roasted pheasant,' Claud said.

'He hangs it eighteen days,' Charlie said, 'then he gives it a couple of good shakes and all the feathers drop off.'

The taxi turned left and swung in through the gates of the vicarage. There were no lights on in the house and nobody met us. Claud and I dumped the pheasants in the coal shed at the rear, and then we said good-bye to Charlie Kinch and walked back in the moonlight to the filling-station, empty-handed. Whether or not Mr Rabbetts was watching us as we went in, I do not know. We saw no sign of him.

'Here she comes,' Claud said to me the next morning.

'Who?'

'Bessie — Bessie Organ.' He spoke the name proudly and with a slight proprietary air, as though he were a general referring to his bravest officer.

I followed him outside.

'Down there,' he said, pointing.

Far away down the road I could see a small female figure advancing towards us.

'What's she pushing?' I asked.

Claud gave me a sly look.

'There's only one safe way of delivering game,' he announced, 'and that's under a baby.'

'Yes,' I murmured, 'yes, of course.'

'That'll be young Christopher Organ in there, aged one and a half. He's a lovely child, Gordon.'

I could just make out the small dot of a baby sitting high up in the pram, which had its hood folded down.

'There's sixty or seventy pheasants at least under that little nipper,' Claud said happily. 'You just imagine that.'

'You can't put sixty or seventy pheasants in a pram.'

'You can if it's got a deep well underneath it, and if you take out the mattress and pack them in tight, right up to the top. All you need then is a sheet. You'll be surprised how little room a pheasant takes up when it's limp.'

We stood beside the pumps waiting for Bessie Organ to arrive. It was one of those warm windless September mornings with a darkening sky and a smell of thunder in the air.

'Right through the village bold as brass,' Claud said. 'Good old Bessie.'

'She seems in rather a hurry to me.'

Claud lit a new cigarette from the stub of the old one. 'Bessie is never in a hurry,' he said.

'She certainly isn't walking normal,' I told him. 'You look.'

He squinted at her through the smoke of his cigarette. Then he took the cigarette out of his mouth and looked again.

'Well?' I said.

'She does seem to be going a tiny bit quick, doesn't she?' he said carefully.

'She's going damn quick.'

There was a pause. Claud was beginning to stare very hard at the approaching woman.

'Perhaps she doesn't want to be caught in the rain, Gordon. I'll bet that's exactly what it is, she thinks it's going to rain and she don't want the baby to get wet.'

'Why doesn't she put the hood up?'

He didn't answer this.

'She's *running*!' I cried. 'Look!' Bessie had suddenly broken into a full sprint.

Claud stood very still, watching the woman; and in the silence that followed I fancied I could hear a baby screaming.

'What's up?'

He didn't answer.

'There's something wrong with that baby,' I said. 'Listen.'

At this point, Bessie was about two hundred yards away from us but closing fast.

'Can you hear him now?' I said.

'Yes.'

'He's yelling his head off.'

The small shrill voice in the distance was growing louder every second, frantic, piercing, nonstop, almost hysterical.

'He's having a fit,' Claud announced.

'I think he must be.'

'That's why she's running, Gordon. She wants to get him in here quick and put him under a cold tap.'

'I'm sure you're right,' I said. 'In fact I know you're right. Just listen to that noise.'

'If it isn't a fit, you can bet your life it's something like it.'

'I quite agree.'

Claud shifted his feet uneasily on the gravel of the driveway. 'There's a thousand and one different things keep happening every day to little babies like that,' he said.

'Of course.'

'I knew a baby once who caught his fingers in the spokes of the pram wheel. He lost the lot. It cut them clean off.'

'Yes.'

'Whatever it is,' Claud said, 'I wish to Christ she'd stop running.'

A long truck loaded with bricks came up behind Bessie and the driver slowed down and poked his head out of the window to stare. Bessie ignored him and flew on, and she was so close now I could see her big red face with the mouth wide open, panting for breath. I noticed she was wearing white gloves on her hands, very prim and dainty, and there was a funny little white hat to match perched right on the top of her head, like a mushroom.

Suddenly, out of the pram, straight up into the air, flew an enormous pheasant!

Claud let out a cry of horror.

The fool in the truck going along beside Bessie started roaring with laughter.

The pheasant flapped around drunkenly for a few seconds, then it lost height and landed in the grass by the side of the road.

A grocer's van came up behind the truck and began hooting to get by. Bessie kept running.

Then – *whoosh!* – a second pheasant flew up out of the pram.

Then a third, and a fourth. Then a fifth.

'My God!' I said. 'It's the pills! They're wearing off!'

Claud didn't say anything.

Bessie covered the last fifty yards at a tremendous pace, and she came swinging into the driveway of the filling-station with birds flying up out of the pram in all directions.

'What the hell's going on?' she cried.

'Go round the back!' I shouted. 'Go round the back!' But she pulled up sharp against the first pump in the line, and before we could reach her she had seized the screaming infant in her arms and dragged him clear.

'No! No!' Claud cried, racing towards her. 'Don't lift the baby! Put him back! Hold down the sheet!' But she wasn't even listening, and with the weight of the child suddenly lifted away, a great cloud of pheasants rose up out of the pram, fifty or sixty of them, at least, and the whole sky above us was filled with huge brown birds flapping their wings furiously to gain height.

Claud and I started running up and down the driveway waving our arms to frighten them off the premises. 'Go away!' we shouted. 'Shoo! Go away!' But they were too dopey still to take any notice of us and within half a minute down they came again and settled themselves like a swarm of locusts all over the front of my filling-station. The place was covered with them. They sat wing to wing along the edges of the roof and on the concrete canopy that came out over the pumps, and a dozen at least were clinging to the sill of the office window. Some had flown down on to the rack that held the bottles of lubricating-oil, and others were sliding about on the bonnets of my second-hand cars. One cock-bird with a fine tail was perched superbly on top of a petrol pump, and quite a number, those that were too drunk to stay aloft, simply squatted in the driveway at our feet, fluffing their feathers and blinking their small eyes.

Across the road, a line of cars had already started forming behind the brick-lorry and the grocery-van, and people were opening their doors and getting out and beginning to cross over to have a closer look. I glanced at my watch. It was twenty to nine. Any moment now, I thought, a large black car is going to come streaking along the road from the direction of the village, and the car will be a Rolls, and the face behind the wheel will be the great glistening brewer's face of Mr Victor Hazel.

'They near pecked him to pieces!' Bessie was shouting, clasping the screaming baby to her bosom.

'You go on home, Bessie,' Claud said, white in the face.

'Lock up,' I said. 'Put out the sign. We've gone for the day.'

Switch Bitch

Contents

The Visitor

Not long ago, a large wooden case was deposited at the door of my house by the railway delivery service. It was an unusually strong and well-constructed object, and made of some kind of dark-red hardwood, not unlike mahogany. I lifted it with great difficulty on to a table in the garden, and examined it carefully. The stencilling on one side said that it had been shipped from Haifa by the m/v *Waverley Star*, but I could find no sender's name or address. I tried to think of somebody living in Haifa or thereabouts who might be wanting to send me a magnificent present. I could think of no one. I walked slowly to the toolshed, still pondering the matter deeply, and returned with a hammer and screwdriver. Then I began gently to prise open the top of the case.

Behold, it was filled with books! Extraordinary books! One by one, I lifted them all out (not yet looking inside any of them) and stacked them in three tall piles on the table. There were twenty-eight volumes altogether, and very beautiful they were indeed. Each of them was identically and superbly bound in rich green morocco, with the initials O.H.C. and a Roman numeral (I to XXVIII) tooled in gold upon the spine.

I took up the nearest volume, number XVI, and opened it. The unlined white pages were filled with a neat small handwriting in black ink. On the title page was written '1934'. Nothing else. I took up another volume, number XXI. It contained more manuscript in the same handwriting, but on the title page it said '1939'. I put it down and pulled out volume I, hoping to find a preface of some kind there, or perhaps the author's name. Instead, I found an envelope inside the cover. The envelope was addressed to me. I took out the letter it contained and glanced quickly at the signature. *Oswald Hendryks Cornelius*, it said.

It was Uncle Oswald!

No member of the family had heard from Uncle Oswald for over thirty years. This letter was dated 10 March 1964, and until its arrival, we could only assume that he still existed. Nothing was really known about him except that he lived in France, that he travelled a great deal, that he was a wealthy bachelor with unsavoury but glamorous habits who steadfastly refused to have anything to do with his own relatives. The rest was all rumour and hearsay, but the rumours were so splendid and the hearsay so exotic that Oswald had long since become a shining hero and a legend to us all.

'My dear boy,' the letter began,

I believe that you and your three sisters are my closest surviving blood relations. You are therefore my rightful heirs, and because I have made no will, all that I leave behind me when I die will be yours. Alas, I have nothing to leave. I used to have quite a lot, and the fact that I have recently disposed of it all in my own way is none of your business. As consolation, though, I am sending you my private diaries. These, I think, ought to remain in the family. They cover all the best years of my life, and it will do you no harm to read them. But if you show them around or lend them to strangers, you do so at your own great peril. If you publish them, then that, I should imagine, would be the end of both you and your publisher simultaneously. For you must understand that thousands of the heroines whom I mention in the diaries are still only half dead, and if you were foolish enough to splash their lilywhite reputation with scarlet print, they would have your head on a salver in two seconds flat, and probably roast it in the oven for good measure. So you'd better be careful. I only met you once. That was years ago, in 1921, when your family was living in that large ugly house in South Wales. I was your big uncle and you were a very small boy, about five years old. I don't suppose you remember the young Norwegian nursemaid you had then. A remarkably clean, well-built girl she was, and exquisitely shaped even in her uniform with its ridiculously starchy white shield concealing her lovely bosom. The afternoon I was there, she was taking you for a walk in the woods to pick bluebells, and I asked if I might come along. And when we got well into the middle of the woods, I told you I'd give you a bar of chocolate if you could find your own way home. And you did (see Vol. III). You were a sensible child. Farewell – Oswald Hendryks Cornelius.

The sudden arrival of the diaries caused much excitement in the family, and there was a rush to read them. We were not disappointed. It was astonishing stuff – hilarious, witty, exciting, and often quite touching as well. The man's vitality was unbelievable. He was always on the move, from city to city, from country to country, from woman to woman, and in between the women, he would be searching for spiders in Kashmir or tracking down a blue porcelain vase in Nanking. But the women always came first. Wherever he went, he left an endless trail of females in his wake, females ruffled and ravished beyond words, but purring like cats.

Twenty-eight volumes with exactly three hundred pages to each volume takes a deal of reading, and there are precious few writers who could hold an audience over a distance like that. But Oswald did it. The narrative never seemed to lose its flavour, the pace seldom slackened, and almost without exception, every single entry, whether it was long or short, and whatever the subject, became a marvellous little individual story that was complete in itself. And at the end of it all, when the last page of the last volume had been read, one was left with the rather breathless feeling that this might just possibly be one of the major autobiographical works of our time.

If it were regarded solely as a chronicle of a man's amorous adventures, then without a doubt there was nothing to touch it. Casanova's *Memoirs* read like a Parish Magazine in comparison, and the famous lover himself, beside Oswald, appears positively undersexed.

There was social dynamite on every page; Oswald was right about that. But he was surely wrong in thinking that the explosions would all come from the women. What about their husbands, the humiliated cock-sparrows, the cuckolds? The cuckold, when aroused, is a very fierce bird indeed, and there would be thousands upon thousands of them rising up out of the bushes if The Cornelius Diaries, unabridged, saw the light of day while they were still alive. Publication, therefore, was right out of the question.

A pity, this. Such a pity, in fact, that I thought something ought to be done about it. So I sat down and re-read the diaries from beginning to end in the hope that I might discover at least one complete passage which could be printed and published without involving both the publisher and myself in serious litigation. To my joy, I found no less than six. I showed them to a lawyer. He said he thought they *might* be 'safe', but he wouldn't guarantee it. One of them – The Sinai Desert Episode – seemed 'safer' than the other five, he added.

So I have decided to start with that one and to offer it for publication right away, at the end of this short preface. If it is accepted and all goes well, then perhaps I shall release one or two more.

The Sinai entry is from the last volume of all, Vol. XXVIII, and is dated 24 August 1946. In point of fact, it is the *very last entry* of the last volume of all, the last thing Oswald ever wrote, and we have no record of where he went or what he did after that date. One can only guess. You shall have the entry verbatim in a moment, but first of all, and so that you may more easily understand some of the things Oswald says and does in his story, let me try to tell you a little about the man himself. Out of the mass of confession and opinion contained in those twenty-eight volumes, there emerges a fairly clear picture of his character.

At the time of the Sinai episode, Oswald Hendryks Cornelius was fifty-one years old, and he had, of course, never been married. 'I am afraid,' he was in the habit of saying, 'that I have been blessed or should I call it burdened, with an uncommonly fastidious nature.'

In some ways, this was true, but in others, and especially in so far as marriage was concerned, the statement was the exact opposite of the truth.

The real reason Oswald had refused to get married was simply that he had never in his life been able to confine his attentions to one particular woman for longer than the time it took to conquer her. When that was done, he lost interest and looked around for another victim.

A normal man would hardly consider this a valid reason for remaining single, but Oswald was not a normal man. He was not even a normal polygamous man. He was, to be honest, such a wanton and incorrigible philanderer that no bride on earth would have put up with him for more than a few days, let alone for the duration of a honeymoon – although heaven knows there were enough who would have been willing to give it a try.

He was a tall, narrow person with a fragile and faintly aesthetic air. His voice was soft, his manner was courteous, and at first sight he seemed more like a gentleman-in-waiting to the queen than a celebrated rapscallion. He never discussed his amorous affairs with other men, and a stranger, though he sit and talk with him all evening, would be unable to observe the slightest sign of deceit in Oswald's clear blue eyes. He was, in fact, precisely the sort of man that an anxious father would be likely to choose to escort his daughter safely home.

But sit Oswald beside a *woman*, a woman who interested him, and instantaneously his eyes would change, and as he looked at her, a small dangerous spark would begin dancing slowly in the very centre of each pupil; and then he would set about her with his conversation, talking to her rapidly and cleverly and almost certainly more wittily than anyone else had ever done before. This was a gift he had, a most singular talent, and when he put his mind to it, he could make his words coil themselves around and around the listener until they held her in some sort of a mild hypnotic spell.

But it wasn't only his fine talk and the look in his eyes that fascinated the women. It was also his nose. (In Vol. XIV, Oswald includes, with obvious relish, a note written to him by a certain lady in which she describes such things as this in great detail.) It appears that when Oswald was aroused, something odd would begin to happen around the edges of his nostrils, a tightening of the rims, a visible flaring which enlarged the nostril holes and revealed whole areas of the bright red skin inside. This created a queer, wild, animalistic impression, and although it may not sound particularly attractive when described on paper, its effect upon the ladies was electric.

Almost without exception, women were drawn toward Oswald. In the first place, he was a man who refused to be owned at any price, and this automatically made him desirable. Add to this the unusual combination of a first-rate intellect, an abundance of charm, and a reputation for excessive promiscuity, and you have a potent recipe.

Then again, and forgetting for a moment the disreputable and licentious angle, it should be noted that there were a number of other surprising facets to Oswald's character that in themselves made him a rather intriguing person. There was, for example, very little that he did not know about nineteenth-century Italian opera, and he had written a curious little manual upon the three composers Donizetti, Verdi, and Ponchielli. In it, he listed by name all the important mistresses that these men had had during their lives, and he went on to examine, in a most serious vein, the relationship between creative passion and carnal passion, and the influence of the one upon the other, particularly as it affected the works of these composers.

Chinese porcelain was another of Oswald's interests, and he was acknowledged as something of an international authority in this field. The blue vases of the Tchin-Hoa period were his special love, and he had a small but exquisite collection of these pieces.

He also collected spiders and walking sticks.

His collection of spiders, or more accurately his collection of Arachnida, because it included scorpions and pedipalps, was possibly as comprehensive as any outside a museum, and his knowledge of the hundreds of genera and species was impressive. He maintained, incidentally (and probably correctly), that the spider's silk was superior in quality to the ordinary stuff spun by silkworms, and he never wore a tie that was made of any other material. He possessed about forty of these ties altogether, and in order to acquire them in the first place, and in order also to be able to add two new ties a year to his wardrobe, he had to keep thousands and thousands of *Arana* and *Epeira diademata* (the common English garden spiders) in an old conservatory in the garden of his country house outside Paris, where they bred and multiplied at approximately the same rate as they ate one another. From them, he collected the raw thread himself – no one else would enter that ghastly glasshouse – and sent it to Avignon, where it was reeled and thrown and scoured and dyed and made into cloth. From Avignon, the cloth was delivered directly to Sulka, who were enchanted by the whole business, and only too glad to fashion ties out of such a rare and wonderful material.

'But you can't *really* like spiders?' the women visitors would say to Oswald as he displayed his collection.

'Oh, but I adore them,' he would answer. 'Especially the females. They remind me so much of certain human females that I know. They remind me of my very favourite human females.'

'What nonsense, darling.'

'Nonsense? I think not.'

'It's rather insulting.'

'On the contrary, my dear, it is the greatest compliment I could pay. Did you not know, for instance, that the female spider is so savage in her lovemaking that the male is very lucky indeed if he escapes with his life at the end of it all. Only if he is exceedingly agile and marvellously ingenious will he get away in one piece.'

'Now, *Oswald*!'

'And the crab spider, my beloved, the teeny-weeny little crab spider is so dangerously passionate that her lover has to tie her down with intricate loops and knots of his own thread before he dares to embrace her ...'

'Oh, *stop* it, Oswald, this *minute*!' the women would cry, their eyes shining.

Oswald's collection of walking sticks was something else again. Every one of them had belonged either to a distinguished or a disgusting person, and he kept them all in his Paris apartment, where they were displayed in two long racks standing against the walls of the passage (or should one call it the highway?) which led from the living-room to the bedroom. Each stick had its own ivory label above it, saying Sibelius, Milton, King Farouk, Dickens, Robespierre, Puccini, Oscar Wilde, Franklin Roosevelt, Goebbels, Queen Victoria, Toulouse-Lautrec, Hindenburg, Tolstoy, Laval, Sarah Bernhardt, Goethe, Voroshiloff, Cézanne, Toho ... There must have been over a hundred of them in all, some very beautiful, some very plain, some with gold or silver tops, and some with curly handles.

'Take down the Tolstoy,' Oswald would say to a pretty visitor. 'Go on, take it down ... that's right ... and now ... now rub your own palm gently over the knob that has been worn to a shine by the great man himself. Is it not rather wonderful, the mere contact of your skin with that spot?'

'It is, rather, isn't it.'

'And now take the Goebbels and do the same thing. Do it properly, though. Allow your palm to fold tightly over the handle ... good ... and now ... now lean your weight on it, lean hard, exactly as the little deformed doctor used to do ... there ... that's it ... now stay like that for a minute or so and then tell me if you do not feel a thin finger of ice creeping all the way up your arm and into your chest?'

'It's terrifying!'

'Of course it is. Some people pass out completely. They keel right over.'

Nobody ever found it dull to be in Oswald's company, and perhaps that, more than anything else, was the reason for his success.

We come now to the Sinai episode. Oswald, during that month, had been amusing himself by motoring at a fairly leisurely pace down from Khartoum to Cairo. His car was a superlative pre-war Lagonda which had been carefully stored in Switzerland during the war years, and as you can imagine, it was fitted with every kind of gadget under the sun. On the day before Sinai (23 August 1946), he was in Cairo, staying at Shepheard's Hotel, and that evening, after a series of impudent manoeuvres, he had succeeded in getting hold of a Moorish lady of supposedly aristocratic descent, called Isabella. Isabella happened to be the jealously guarded mistress of none other than a certain notorious and dyspeptic Royal Personage (there was still a monarchy in Egypt then). This was a typically Oswaldian move.

But there was more to come. At midnight, he drove the lady out to Giza and persuaded her to climb with him in the moonlight right to the very top of the great pyramid of Cheops.

'... There can be no safer place,' he wrote in the diary, 'nor a more romantic one, than the apex of a pyramid on a warm night when the moon is full. The passions are stirred not only by the magnificent view but also by that curious sensation of power that surges within the body whenever one surveys the world from a great height. And as for safety – this pyramid is exactly 481 feet high, which is 115 feet higher than the dome of St Paul's Cathedral, and from the summit one can observe all the approaches with the greatest of ease. No other boudoir on earth can offer this facility. None has so many emergency exits, either, so that if some sinister figure should happen to come clambering up in pursuit on one side of the pyramid, one has only to slip calmly and quietly down the other ...'

As it happened, Oswald had a very narrow squeak indeed that night. Somehow, the palace must have got word of the little affair, for Oswald, from his lofty moonlit pinnacle, suddenly observed *three* sinister figures, not one, closing in on three different sides, and starting to climb. But luckily for him, there is a fourth side to the great pyramid of Cheops, and by the time those Arab thugs had reached the top, the two lovers were already at the bottom and getting into the car.

The entry for 24 August takes up the story at exactly this point. It is reproduced here word for word and comma for comma as Oswald wrote it. Nothing has been altered or added or taken away:

24 August 1946

'He'll chop off Isabella's head if he catch her now,' Isabella said.

15

'Rubbish,' I answered, but I reckoned she was probably right.

'He'll chop off Oswald's head, too,' she said.

'Not mine, dear lady. I shall be a long way away from here when daylight comes. I'm heading straight up the Nile for Luxor immediately.'

We were driving quickly away from the pyramids now. It was about two thirty a.m.

'To Luxor?' she said.

'Yes.'

'And Isabella is going with you.'

'No,' I said.

'Yes,' she said.

'It is against my principles to travel with a lady,' I said.

I could see some lights ahead of us. They came from the Mena House Hotel, a place where tourists stay out in the desert, not far from the pyramids. I drove fairly close to the hotel and stopped the car.

'I'm going to drop you here,' I said. 'We had a fine time.'

'So you won't take Isabella to Luxor?'

'I'm afraid not,' I said. 'Come on, hop it.'

She started to get out of the car, then she paused with one foot on the road, and suddenly she swung round and poured out upon me a torrent of language so filthy yet so fluent that I had heard nothing like it from the lips of a lady since ... well, since 1931, in Marrakesh, when the greedy old Duchess of Glasgow put her hand into a chocolate box and got nipped by a scorpion I happened to have placed there for safe-keeping (Vol. XIII, 5 June 1931).

'You are disgusting,' I said.

Isabella leapt out and slammed the door so hard the whole car jumped on its wheels. I drove off very fast. Thank heaven I was rid of her. I cannot abide bad manners in a pretty girl.

As I drove, I kept one eye on the mirror, but as yet no car seemed to be following me. When I came to the outskirts of Cairo, I began threading my way through the side roads, avoiding the centre of the city. I was not particularly worried. The royal watchdogs were unlikely to carry the matter much further. All the same, it would have been foolhardy to go back to Shepheard's at this point. It wasn't necessary, anyway, because all my baggage, except for a small valise, was with me in the car. I never leave suitcases behind me in my room when I go out of an evening in a foreign city. I like to be mobile.

I had no intention, of course, of going to Luxor. I wanted now to get away from Egypt altogether. I didn't like the country at all. Come to think of it, I never had. The place made me feel uncomfortable in my skin. It was the dirtiness of it all, I think, and the putrid smells. But then let us face it, it really is a squalid country, and I have a powerful suspicion, though I hate to say it, that the Egyptians wash themselves less thoroughly than any other peoples in the world – with the possible exception of the Mongolians. Certainly they do not wash their crockery to my taste. There was, believe it or not, a long, crusted, coffee-coloured lipmark stamped upon the rim of the cup they placed before me at breakfast yesterday. Ugh! It was repulsive! I kept staring at it and wondering whose slobbery lower lip had done the deed.

I was driving now through the narrow dirty streets of the eastern suburbs of Cairo. I knew precisely where I was going. I had made up my mind about that before I was even halfway down the pyramid with Isabella. I was going to Jerusalem. It was no distance to speak of, and it was a city that I always enjoyed. Furthermore, it was the quickest way out of Egypt. I would proceed as follows:

1. Cairo to Ismailia. About three hours driving. Sing an opera on the way, as usual. Arrive Ismailia 6–7 a.m. Take a room and have a two-hour sleep. Then shower, shave, and breakfast.

2. At 10 a.m., cross over the Suez Canal by the Ismailia bridge and take the desert road across Sinai to the Palestine border. Make a search for scorpions *en route* in the Sinai Desert. Time, about four hours, arriving Palestine border 2 p.m.

3. From there, continue straight on to Jerusalem via Beer-

sheba, reaching The King David Hotel in time for cocktails
and dinner.

It was several years since I had travelled that particular road,
but I remembered that the Sinai Desert was an outstanding
place for scorpions. I badly wanted another female opisthophthalmus, a large one. My present specimen had the fifth
segment of its tail missing, and I was ashamed of it.

It didn't take me long to find the main road to Ismailia, and
as soon as I was on it, I settled the Lagonda down to a steady
sixty-five miles per hour. The road was narrow, but it had a
smooth surface, and there was no traffic. The Delta country
lay bleak and dismal around me in the moonlight, the flat
treelesss fields, the ditches running between, and the black
black soil everywhere. It was inexpressibly dreary.

But it didn't worry *me*. I was no part of it. I was completely isolated in my own luxurious little shell, as snug as a
hermit crab and travelling a lot faster. Oh, how I do love tc
be on the move, winging away to new people and new places
and leaving the old ones far behind! Nothing in the world
exhilarates me more than that. And how I despise the average
citizen, who settles himself down upon one tiny spot of land
with one asinine woman, to breed and stew and rot in that
condition unto his life's end. And always with the same
woman! I cannot *believe* that any man in his senses would put
up with just one female day after day and year after year.
Some of them, of course, don't. But millions pretend they do.

I myself have never, absolutely never permitted an intimate
relationship to last for more than twelve hours. That is the
farthest limit. Even eight hours is stretching it a bit, to my
mind. Look what happened, for example, with Isabella. While
we were upon the summit of the pyramid, she was a lady of
scintillating parts, as pliant and playful as a puppy, and had I
left her there to the mercy of those three Arab thugs, and
skipped down on my own, all would have been well. But I
foolishly stuck by her and helped her to descend, and as a
result, the lovely lady turned into a vulgar screeching trollop,
disgusting to behold.

What a world we live in! One gets no thanks these days for being chivalrous.

The Lagonda moved on smoothly through the night. Now for an opera. Which one should it be this time? I was in the mood for a Verdi. What about *Aida*? Of course! It must be *Aida* – the Egyptian opera! Most appropriate.

I began to sing. I was in exceptionally good voice tonight. I let myself go. It was delightful; and as I drove through the small town of Bilbeis, I was Aida herself, singing '*Numei pietà*', the beautiful concluding passage of the first scene.

Half an hour later, at Zagazig, I was Amonasro begging the King of Egypt to save the Ethiopian captives with '*Ma tu, re, tu signore possente*'.

Passing through El Abbasa, I was Rhadames, rendering '*Fuggiam gli adori nospiti*', and now I opened all the windows of the car so that this incomparable love song might reach the ears of the fellaheen snoring in their hovels along the roadside, and perhaps mingle with their dreams.

As I pulled into Ismailia, it was six o'clock in the morning and the sun was already climbing high in a milky-blue heaven, but I myself was in the terrible sealed-up dungeon with Aida, singing '*O, terra, addio; addio valle di pianti!*'

How swiftly the journey had gone. I drove to an hotel. The staff was just beginning to stir. I stirred them up some more and got the best room available. The sheets and blanket on the bed looked as though they had been slept in by twenty-five unwashed Egyptians on twenty-five consecutive nights, and I tore them off with my own hands (which I scrubbed immediately afterwards with antiseptic soap) and replaced them with my personal bedding. Then I set my alarm and slept soundly for two hours.

For breakfast I ordered a poached egg on a piece of toast. When the dish arrived – and I tell you, it makes my stomach curdle just to write about it – there was a *gleaming, curly, jet-black human hair*, three inches long, lying diagonally across the yolk of my poached egg. It was too much. I leaped up from the table and rushed out of the dining-room. '*Addio!*' I cried, flinging some money at the cashier as I went by, '*addio valle di pianti!'* And with that I shook the filthy dust of the hotel from my feet.

Now for the Sinai Desert. What a welcome change that would be. A real desert is one of the least contaminated places on earth, and Sinai was no exception. The road across it was a narrow strip of black tarmac about a hundred and forty miles long, with only a single filling station and a group of huts at the halfway mark, at a place called B'ir Rawd Salim. Otherwise there was nothing but pure uninhabited desert all the way. It would be very hot at this time of year, and it was essential to carry drinking water in case of a breakdown. I therefore pulled up outside a kind of general store in the main street of Ismailia to get my emergency canister refilled.

I went in and spoke to the proprietor. The man had a nasty case of trachoma. The granulation on the under surfaces of his eyelids was so acute that the lids themselves were raised right up off the eyeballs – a beastly sight. I asked him if he would sell me a gallon of *boiled* water. He thought I was mad, and madder still when I insisted on following him back into his grimy kitchen to make sure that he did things properly. He filled a kettle with tap-water and placed it on a paraffin stove. The stove had a tiny little smoky yellow flame. The proprietor seemed very proud of the stove and of its performance. He stood admiring it, his head on one side. Then he suggested that I might prefer to go back and wait in the shop. He would bring me the water, he said, when it was ready. I refused to leave. I stood there watching the kettle like a lion, waiting for the water to boil; and while I was doing this, the breakfast scene suddenly started coming back to me in all its horror – the egg, the yolk, and the hair. Whose hair was it that had lain embedded in the slimy yolk of my egg at breakfast? Undoubtedly it was the cook's hair. And when, pray, had the cook last washed his head? He had probably never washed his head. Very well, then. He was almost certainly verminous. But that in itself would not cause a hair to fall out. What *did* cause the cook's hair, then, to fall out on to my poached egg this morning as he transferred the egg from the pan to the plate. There is a reason for all things, and in this case the reason was obvious. The cook's scalp was infested with purulent seborrhoeic impetigo. And the hair itself, the long black hair that I might so easily have swallowed had I been less alert, was therefore swarming with millions and millions of loving pathogenic cocci whose exact scientific name I have, happily, forgotten.

Can I, you ask, be absolutely sure that the cook had purulent seborrhoeic impetigo? Not absolutely sure – no. But if he hadn't, then he certainly had ringworm instead. And what did that mean? I knew only too well what it meant. It meant that ten million microsporons had been clinging and clustering around that awful hair, waiting to go into my mouth.

I began to feel sick.

'The water boils,' the shopkeeper said triumphantly.

'Let it boil,' I told him. 'Give it eight minutes more. What is it you want me to get – typhus?'

Personally, I never drink water by itself if I can help it, however pure it may be. Plain water has no flavour at all. I take it, of course, as tea or as coffee, but even then I try to arrange for bottled Vichy or Malvern to be used in the preparation. I avoid tap-water. Tap-water is diabolical stuff. Often it is nothing more nor less than reclaimed sewage.

'Soon this water will be boiled away in steam,' the proprietor said, grinning at me with green teeth.

I lifted the kettle myself and poured the contents into my canister.

Back in the shop, I bought six oranges, a small water-melon, and a slab of well-wrapped English chocolate. Then I returned to the Lagonda. Now at last I was away.

A few minutes later, I had crossed the sliding bridge that went over the Suez Canal just above Lake Timsah, and ahead of me lay the flat blazing desert and the little tarmac road stretching out before me like a black ribbon all the way to the horizon. I settled the Lagonda to the usual steady sixty-five miles an hour, and I opened the windows wide. The air that came in was like the breath of an oven. The time was almost noon, and the sun was throwing its heat directly on to the roof of the car. My thermometer inside registered 103°. But as you know, a touch of warmth never bothers me so long as I am sitting still and am wearing suitable clothes – in this case a pair of cream-coloured linen slacks, a white aertex shirt, and a spider's-silk tie of the loveliest rich moss-green. I felt perfectly comfortable and at peace with the world.

For a minute or two I played with the idea of performing another opera *en route* – I was in the mood for *La Gioconda* – but after singing a few bars of the opening chorus, I began to perspire slightly; so I rang down the curtain, and lit a cigarette instead.

I was now driving through some of the finest scorpion country in the world, and I was eager to stop and make a search before I reached the halfway filling-station at B'ir Rawd Salim. I had so far met not a single vehicle or seen a living creature since leaving Ismailia an hour before. This pleased me. Sinai was authentic desert. I pulled up on the side of the road and switched off the engine. I was thirsty, so I ate an orange. Then I put my white topee on my head, and eased myself slowly out of the car, out of my comfortable hermit-crab shell, and into the sunlight. For a full minute I stood motionless in the middle of the road, blinking at the brilliance of the surroundings.

There was a blazing sun, a vast hot sky, and beneath it all on every side a great pale sea of yellow sand that was not quite of this world. There were mountains now in the distance on the south side of the road, bare, pale-brown, tanagra-coloured mountains faintly glazed with blue and purple, that rose up suddenly out of the desert and faded away in a haze of heat against the sky. The stillness was overpowering. There was no sound at all, no voice of a bird or insect anywhere, and it gave me a queer godlike feeling to be standing there alone in the middle of such a splendid, hot, inhuman landscape – as though I were on another planet altogether, on Jupiter or Mars, or in some place more distant and desolate still, where never would the grass grow or the clouds turn red.

I went to the boot of the car and took out my killing-box, my net, and my trowel. Then I stepped off the road into the soft burning sand. I walked slowly for about a hundred yards

into the desert, my eyes searching the ground. I was not looking for scorpions but the lairs of scorpions. The scorpion is a
cryptozoic and nocturnal creature that hides all through the
day either under a stone or in a burrow, according to its type.
Only after the sun has gone down does it come out to hunt for
food.

The one I wanted, opisthophthalmus, was a burrower, so I
wasted no time turning over stones. I searched only for
burrows. After ten or fifteen minutes, I had found none; but
already the heat was getting to be too much for me, and I
decided reluctantly to return to the car. I walked back very
slowly, still watching the ground, and I had reached the road
and was in the act of stepping on to it when all at once, in the
sand, not more than twelve inches from the edge of the
tarmac, I caught sight of a scorpion's burrow.

I put the killing-box and the net on the ground beside me.
Then, with my little trowel, I began very cautiously to scrape
away the sand all around the hole. This was an operation that
never failed to excite me. It was like a treasure hunt – a
treasure hunt with just the right amount of danger accom-
panying it to stir the blood. I could feel my heart beating
away in my chest as I probed deeper and deeper into the sand.

And suddenly ... there she was!

Oh, my heavens, what a whopper A gigantic female scorpion, not opisthophthalmus, as I saw immediately, but pandinus, the other large African burrower. And clinging to her
back – this was too good to be true! – swarming all over her,
were one, two, three, four, five ... a total of fourteen tiny
babies! The mother was six inches long at least! Her children
were the size of small revolver bullets. She had seen me now,
the first human she had ever seen in her life, and her pincers
were wide open, her tail was curled high over her back like a
question mark, ready to strike. I took up the net, and slid it
swiftly underneath her, and scooped her up. She twisted and
squirmed, striking wildly in all directions with the end of her
tail. I saw a single large drop of venom fall through the mesh
into the sand. Quickly, I transferred her, together with the
offspring, to the killing-box, and closed the lid. Then I fetched

the ether from the car, and poured it through the little gauze hole in the top of the box until the pad inside was well soaked.

How splendid she would look in my collection! The babies would, of course, fall away from her as they died, but I would stick them on again with glue in more or less their correct positions; and then I would be the proud possessor of a huge female pandinus with her own fourteen offspring on her back! I was extremely pleased. I lifted the killing-box (I could feel her thrashing about furiously inside) and placed it in the boot, together with the net and trowel. Then I returned to my seat in the car, lit a cigarette, and drove on.

The more contented I am, the slower I drive. I drove quite slowly now, and it must have taken me nearly an hour more to reach B'ir Rawd Salim, the halfway station. It was a most unenticing place. On the left, there was a single gasoline pump and a wooden shack. On the right, there were three more shacks, each about the size of a potting-shed. The rest was desert. There was not a soul in sight. The time was twenty minutes before two in the afternoon, and the temperature inside the car was 106°.

What with the nonsense of getting the water boiled before leaving Ismailia, I had forgotten completely to fill up with gasoline before leaving, and my gauge was now registering slightly less than two gallons. I'd cut it rather fine – but no matter. I pulled in alongside the pump, and waited. Nobody appeared. I pressed the horn button, and the four tuned horns on the Lagonda shouted their wonderful *'Son gia mille e tre!'* across the desert. Nobody appeared. I pressed again.

sang the horns. Mozart's phrase sounded magnificent in these surroundings. But still nobody appeared. The inhabitants of B'ir Rawd Salim didn't give a damn, it seemed, about my friend Don Giovanni and the 1,003 women he had deflowered in Spain.

At last, after I had played the horns no less than six times, the door of the hut behind the gasoline pump opened and a tallish man emerged and stood on the threshold, doing up his buttons with both hands. He took his time over this, and not until he had finished did he glance up at the Lagonda. I looked back at him through my open window. I saw him take the first step in my direction ... he took it very, very slowly ... Then he took a second step ...

My God! I thought at once. The spirochetes have got him!

He had the slow, wobbly walk, the loose-limbed, high-stepping gait of a man with locomotor ataxia. With each step he took, the front foot was raised high in the air before him and brought down violently to the ground, as though he were stamping on a dangerous insect.

I thought: I had better get out of here. I had better start the motor and get the hell out of here before he reaches me. But I knew I couldn't. I *had* to have the gasoline. I sat in the car staring at the awful creature as he came stamping laboriously over the sand. He must have had the revolting disease for years and years, otherwise it wouldn't have developed into ataxis. *Tabes dorsalis* they call it in professional circles, and pathologically this means that the victim is suffering from degeneration of the posterior columns of the spinal chord. But ah my foes and oh my friends, it is really a lot worse than that; it is a slow and merciless consuming of the actual nerve fibres of the body by syphilitic toxins.

The man – the Arab, I shall call him – came right up to the door of my side of the car and peered in through the open window. I leaned away from him, praying that he would not come an inch closer. Without a doubt, he was one of the most blighted humans I had ever seen. His face had the eroded, eaten-away look of an old wood-carving when the worm has been at it, and the sight of it made me wonder how many other diseases the man was suffering from, besides syphilis.

'Salaàm,' he mumbled.

25

The Visitor

'Fill up the tank,' I told him.

He didn't move. He was inspecting the interior of the Lagonda with great interest. A terrible feculent odour came wafting in from his direction.

'Come along!' I said sharply. 'I want some gasoline!'

He looked at me and grinned. It was more of a leer than a grin, an insolent mocking leer that seemed to be saying, 'I am the king of the gasoline pump at B'ir Rawd Salim! Touch me if you dare!' A fly had settled in the corner of one of his eyes. He made no attempt to brush it away.

'You want gasoline?' he said, taunting me.

I was about to swear at him, but I checked myself just in time, and answered politely, 'Yes please, I would be very grateful.'

He watched me slyly for a few moments to be sure I wasn't mocking him, then he nodded as though satisfied now with my behaviour. He turned away and started slowly toward the rear of the car. I reached into the door-pocket for my bottle of Glenmorangie. I poured myself a stiff one, and sat sipping it. That man's face had been within a yard of my own; his foetid breath had come pouring into the car ... and who knows how many billions of airborne viruses might not have come pouring in with it? On such an occasion it is a fine thing to sterilize the mouth and throat with a drop of Highland whisky. The whisky is also a solace. I emptied the glass, and poured myself another. Soon I began to feel less alarmed. I noticed the water-melon lying on the seat beside me. I decided that a slice of it at this moment would be refreshing. I took my knife from its case and cut out a thick section. Then, with the point of the knife, I carefully picked out all the black seeds, using the rest of the melon as a receptacle.

I sat drinking the whisky and eating the melon. Both very delicious.

'Gasoline is done,' the dreadful Arab said, appearing at the window. 'I check water now, and oil.'

I would have preferred him to keep his hands off the Lagonda altogether, but rather than risk an argument, I said nothing. He went clumping off toward the front of the car, and his walk reminded me of a drunken Hitler Stormtrooper doing the goosestep in very slow motion.

Tabes dorsalis, as I live and breathe.

The only other disease to induce that queer high-stepping gait is chronic beriberi. Well – he probably had that one, too. I cut myself another slice of watermelon, and concentrated for a minute or so on taking out the seeds with the knife. When I looked up again, I saw that the Arab had raised the bonnet of the car on the righthand side, and was bending over the engine. His head and shoulders were out of sight, and so were his head and arms. What on earth was the man doing? The oil dipstick was on the other side. I rapped on the windshield. He seemed not to hear me. I put my head out of the window and shouted, 'Hey! Come out of there!'

Slowly, he straightened up, and as he drew his right arm out of the bowels of the engine, I saw that he was holding in his fingers something that was long and black and curly and very thin.

'Good God!' I thought. 'He's found a snake in there!'

He came round to the window, grinning at me and holding the object out for me to see; and only then, as I got a closer look, did I realize that it was not a snake at all – *it was the fan-belt of my Lagonda!*

All the awful implications of suddenly being stranded in this outlandish place with this disgusting man came flooding over me as I sat there staring dumbly at my broken fanbelt.

'You can see,' the Arab was saying, 'it was hanging on by a single thread. A good thing I noticed it.'

I took it from him and examined it closely. 'You cut it!' I cried.

'Cut it?' he answered softly. 'Why should I cut it?'

To be perfectly honest, it was impossible for me to judge whether he had or had not cut it. If he had, then he had also taken the trouble to fray the severed ends with some instrument to make it look like an ordinary break. Even so, my guess was that he *had* cut it, and if I was right then the implications were more sinister than ever.

27

'I suppose you know I can't go on without a fan-belt?' I said.

He grinned again with that awful mutilated mouth, showing ulcerated gums. 'If you go now,' he said, 'you will boil over in three minutes.'

'So what do you suggest?'

'I shall get you another fan-belt.'

'You will?'

'Of course. There is a telephone here, and if you will pay for the call, I will telephone to Ismailia. And if they haven't got one in Ismailia, I will telephone to Cairo. There is no problem.'

'No problem!' I shouted, getting out of the car. 'And when pray, do you think the fan-belt is going to arrive in this ghastly place?'

'There is a mail-truck comes through every morning about ten o'clock. You would have it tomorrow.'

The man had all the answers. He never even had to think before replying.

This bastard, I thought, *has cut fan-belts before.*

I was very alert now, and watching him closely.

'They will not have a fan-belt for a machine of this make in Ismailia,' I said. 'It would have to come from the agents in Cairo. I will telephone them myself.' The fact that there was a telephone gave me some comfort. The telephone poles had followed the road all the way across the desert, and I could see the two wires leading into the hut from the nearest pole. 'I will ask the agents in Cairo to set out immediately for this place in a special vehicle,' I said.

The Arab looked along the road toward Cairo, some two hundred miles away. 'Who is going to drive six hours here and six hours back to bring a fan-belt?' he said. 'The mail will be just as quick.'

'Show me the telephone,' I said, starting toward the hut. Then a nasty thought struck me, and I stopped.

How could I possibly use this man's contaminated instrument? The earpiece would have to be pressed against my ear, and the mouthpiece would almost certainly touch my mouth; and I didn't give a damn what the doctors said about the impossibility of catching syphilis from remote contact. A syphilitic mouthpiece was a syphilitic mouthpiece, and you wouldn't catch *me* putting it anywhere near *my* lips, thank you very much. I wouldn't even enter his hut.

I stood there in the sizzling heat of the afternoon and looked at the Arab with his ghastly diseased face, and the Arab looked back at me, as cool and unruffled as you please.

'You want the telephone?' he asked.

'No,' I said. 'Can you read English?'

'Oh, yes.'

'Very well. I shall write down for you the name of the agents and the name of this car, and also my own name. They know me there. You will tell them what is wanted. And listen ... tell them to dispatch a special car immediately at my expense. I will pay them well. And if they won't do that, tell them they *have* to get the fan-belt to Ismailia in time to catch the mail-truck. You understand?'

'There is no problem,' the Arab said.

So I wrote down what was necessary on a piece of paper and gave it to him. He walked away with that slow, stamping tread toward the hut, and disappeared inside. I closed the bonnet of the car. Then I went back and sat in the driver's seat to think things out.

I poured myself another whisky, and lit a cigarette. There must be *some* traffic on this road. Somebody would surely come along before nightfall. But would that help me? No, it wouldn't – unless I were prepared to hitch a ride and leave the Lagonda and all my baggage behind to the tender mercies of the Arab. Was I prepared to do that? I didn't know. Probably yes. But if I were forced to stay the night, I would lock myself in the car and try to keep awake as much as possible. On no account would I enter the shack where that creature lived. Nor would I touch his food. I had whisky and water, and I had half a watermelon and a slab of chocolate. That was ample.

The heat was pretty bad. The thermometer in the car was still around 104°. It was hotter outside in the sun. I was perspiring freely. My God, what a place to get stranded in! And what a companion!

29

The Visitor

After about fifteeen minutes, the Arab came out of the hut. I watched him all the way to the car.

'I talked to the garage in Cairo,' he said, pushing his face through the window. 'Fan-belt will arrive tomorrow by mail-truck. Everything arranged.'

'Did you ask them about sending it at once?'

'They said impossible,' he answered.

'You're sure you asked them?'

He inclined his head to one side and gave me that sly insolent grin. I turned away and waited for him to go. He stayed where he was. 'We have house for visitors,' he said. 'You can sleep there very nice. My wife will make food, but you will have to pay.'

'Who else is here besides you and your wife?'

'Another man,' he said. He waved an arm in the direction of the three shacks across the road, and I turned and saw a man standing in the doorway of the middle shack, a short wide man who was dressed in dirty khaki slacks and shirt. He was standing absolutely motionless in the shadow of the door-way, his arms dangling at his sides. He was looking at me.

'Who is he?' I said.

'Saleh.'

'What does he do?'

'He helps.'

'I will sleep in the car,' I said. 'And it will not be necessary for your wife to prepare food. I have my own.' The Arab shrugged and turned away and started back toward the shack where the telephone was. I stayed in the car. What else could I do? It was just after two-thirty. In three or four hours' time it would start to get a little cooler. Then I could take a stroll and maybe hunt up a few scorpions. Meanwhile, I must make the best of things as they were. I reached into the back of the car where I kept my box of books and, without looking, I took out the first one I touched. The box contained thirty or forty of the best books in the world, and all of them could be re-read a hundred times and would improve with each read-ing. It was immaterial which one I got. It turned out to be *The Natural History of Selborne*. I opened it at random ...

'... We had in this village more than twenty years ago an idiot boy, whom I well remember, who, from a child, showed a strong propensity to bees; they were his food, his amusement, his sole object. And as people of this cast have seldom more than one point of view, so this lad exerted all his few faculties on this one pursuit. In winter he dozed away his time, within his father's house, by the fireside, in a kind of torpid state, seldom departing from the chimney-corner; but in the summer he was all alert, and in quest of his game in the fields, and on sunny banks. Honey-bees, bumble-bees, wasps, were his prey wherever he found them; he had no apprehensions from their stings, but would seize them *nudis manibus*, and at once disarm them of their weapons, and suck their bodies for the sake of their honey-bags. Sometimes he would fill his bosom, between his shirt and his skin, with a number of these captives, and sometimes confine them to bottles. He was a very *merops apiaster*, or bee-bird, and very injurious to men that kept bees; for he would slide into their bee-gardens, and, sitting down before the stools, would rap with his fingers on the hives, and so take the bees as they came out. He has been known to overturn hives for the sake of honey, of which he is passionately fond. Where metheglin was making, he would linger round the tubs and vessels, begging a draught of what he called bee-wine. As he ran about, he used to make a humming noise with his lips, resembling the buzzing of bees ...'

I glanced up from the book and looked around me. The motionless man across the road had disappeared. There was nobody in sight. The silence was eerie, and the stillness, the utter stillness and desolation of the place was profoundly oppressive. I knew I was being watched. I knew that every little move I made, every sip of whisky and every puff of a cigarette, was being carefully noticed. I detest violence and I never carry a weapon. But I could have done with one now. For a while, I toyed with the idea of starting the motor and driving on down the road until the engine boiled over. But how far would I get? Not very far in this heat and without a fan. One mile, perhaps, or two at the most ...

31

No – to hell with it. I would stay where I was and read my book.

It must have been about an hour later that I noticed a small dark speck moving toward me along the road in the far distance, coming from the Jerusalem direction. I laid aside my book without taking my eyes away from the speck. I watched it growing bigger and bigger. It was travelling at a great speed, at a really amazing speed. I got out of the Lagonda and hurried to the side of the road and stood there, ready to signal the driver to stop.

Closer and closer it came, and when it was about a quarter of a mile away, it began to slow down. Suddenly, I noticed the shape of its radiator. It was a *Rolls-Royce*! I raised an arm and kept it raised, and the big green car with a man at the wheel pulled in off the road and stopped beside my Lagonda.

I felt absurdly elated. Had it been a Ford or a Morris, I would have been pleased enough, but I would not have been elated. The fact that it was a Rolls – a Bentley would have done equally well, or an Isotta, or another Lagonda – was a virtual guarantee that I would receive all the assistance I required; for whether you know it or not, there is a powerful brotherhood existing among people who own very costly automobiles. They respect one another automatically, and the reason they respect one another is simply that wealth respects wealth. In point of fact, there is nobody in the world that a very wealthy person respects more than another very wealthy person, and because of this, they naturally seek each other out wherever they go. Recognition signals of many kinds are used among them. With the female, the wearing of massive jewels is perhaps the most common; but the costly automobile is also much favoured, and is used by both sexes. It is a travelling placard, a public declaration of affluence, and as such, it is also a card of membership to that excellent unofficial society, the Very-Wealthy-Peoples Union. I am a member myself of long standing, and am delighted to be one. When I meet another member, as I was about to do now, I feel an immediate rapport. I respect him. We speak the same language. He is one of *us*. I had good reason, therefore, to be elated.

The driver of the Rolls climbed out and came toward me. He was a small dark man with olive skin, and he wore an immaculate white linen suit. Probably a Syrian, I thought. Just possibly a Greek. In the heat of the day he looked as cool as could be.

'Good afternoon,' he said. 'Are you having trouble?'

I greeted him, and then bit by bit, I told him everything that had happened.

'My dear fellow,' he said in perfect English, 'but my *dear fellow*, how very distressing. What rotten luck. This is no place to get stranded in.'

'It isn't, is it?'

'And you say that a new fan-belt has definitely been ordered?'

'Yes,' I answered, 'if I can rely upon the proprietor of this establishment.'

The Arab, who had emerged from his shack almost before the Rolls had come to a stop, had now joined us, and the stranger proceeded to question him swiftly in Arabic about the steps he had taken on my behalf. It seemed to me that the two knew each other pretty well, and it was clear that the Arab was in great awe of the new arrival. He was practically crawling along the ground in his presence.

'Well – that seems to be all right,' the stranger said at last, turning to me. 'But quite obviously you won't be able to move on from here until tomorrow morning. Where were you headed for?'

'Jerusalem,' I said. 'And I don't relish the idea of spending the night in this infernal spot.'

'I should say not, my dear man. That would be most uncomfortable.' He smiled at me, showing exceptionally white teeth. Then he took out a cigarette case, and offered me a cigarette. The case was gold, and on the outside of it there was a thin line of green jade inlaid diagonally from corner to corner. It was a beautiful thing. I accepted the cigarette. He lit it for me, then lit his own.

The stranger took a long pull at his cigarette, inhaling deeply. Then he tilted back his head and blew the smoke up

33

into the sun. 'We shall both get heat-stroke if we stand around here much longer,' he said. 'Will you permit me to make a suggestion?'

'But of course.'

'I do hope you won't consider it presumptuous, coming from a complete stranger ...'

'Please ...'

'You can't possibly remain here, so I suggest you come back and stay the night in my house.'

There! The Rolls-Royce was smiling at the Lagonda – smiling at it as it would never have smiled at a Ford or a Morris!

'You mean in Ismailia?' I said.

'No, no,' he answered, laughing. 'I live just around the corner, just over there.' He waved a hand in the direction he had come from.

'But surely you were going to Ismailia? I wouldn't want you to change your plans on my behalf.'

'I wasn't going to Ismailia at all,' he said. 'I was coming down here to collect the mail. My house -- and this may surprise you – is quite close to where we are standing. You see that mountain. That's Maghara. I'm immediately behind it.'

I looked at the mountain. It lay about ten miles to the north, a yellow rocky lump, perhaps two thousand feet high. 'Do you really mean that you have a house in the middle of all this ... this wasteland?' I asked.

'You don't believe me?' he said, smiling.

'Of course I believe you,' I answered. 'Nothing surprises me any more. Except, perhaps,' and here I smiled back at him, 'except when I meet a stranger in the middle of the desert, and he treats me like a brother. I am overwhelmed by your offer.'

'Nonsense, my dear fellow. My motives are entirely selfish. Civilized company is not easy to come by in these parts. I am quite thrilled at the thought of having a guest for dinner. Permit me to introduce myself – Abdul Aziz.' He made a quick little bow.

'Oswald Cornelius,' I said. 'It is a great pleasure.' We shook hands.

'I live partly in Beirut,' he said.

'I live in Paris.'

'Charming. And now – shall we go? Are you ready?'

'But my car,' I said. 'Can I leave it here safely?'

'Have no fear about that. Omar is a friend of mine. He's not much to look at, poor chap, but he won't let you down if you're with me. And the other one, Saleh, is a good mechanic. He'll fit your new fan-belt when it arrives tomorrow. I'll tell him now.'

Saleh, the man from across the road, had walked over while we were talking. Mr Aziz gave him his instructions. He then spoke to both men about guarding the Lagonda. He was brief and incisive. Omar and Saleh stood bowing and scraping. I went across to the Lagonda to get a suitcase. I needed a change of clothes badly.

'Oh, by the way,' Mr Aziz called over to me, 'I usually put on a black tie for dinner.'

'Of course,' I murmured, quickly pushing back my first choice of suitcase and taking another.

'I do it for the ladies mostly. They seem to like dressing themselves up for dinner.'

I turned sharply and looked at him, but he was already getting into his car.

'Ready?' he said.

I took the suitcase and placed it in the back of the Rolls. Then I climbed into the front seat beside him, and we drove off.

During the drive, we talked casually about this and that. He told me that his business was in carpets. He had offices in Beirut and Damascus. His forefathers, he said, had been in the trade for hundreds of years.

I mentioned that I had a seventeenth-century Damascus carpet on the floor of my bedroom in Paris.

'You don't mean it!' he cried, nearly swerving off the road with excitement. 'Is it silk and wool, with the warp made entirely of silk? And has it got a ground of gold and silver threads?'

'Yes,' I said. 'Exactly.'

'But my dear fellow! You mustn't put a thing like that on the floor!'

'It is touched only by bare feet,' I said.

That pleased him. It seemed that he loved carpets almost as much as I loved the blue vases of Tchin-Hoa.

Soon we turned left off the tarred road on to a hard stony track and headed straight over the desert toward the mountain. 'This is my private driveway,' Mr Aziz said. 'It is five miles long.'

'You are even on the telephone,' I said, noticing the poles that branched off the main road to follow his private drive.

And then suddenly a queer thought struck me.

That Arab at the filling-station ... he also was on the telephone ...

Might not this, then, explain the fortuitous arrival of Mr Aziz?

Was it possible that my lonely host had devised a clever method of shanghai-ing travellers off the road in order to provide himself with what he called 'civilized company' for dinner? Had he, in fact, given the Arab standing instructions to immobilize the cars of all likely-looking persons one after the other as they came along? 'Just cut the fan-belt, Omar. Then phone me up quick. But make sure it's a decent-looking fellow with a good car. Then I'll pop along and see if I think he's worth inviting to the house ...'

It was ridiculous of course.

'I think,' my companion was saying, 'that you are wondering why in the world I should choose to have a house out here in a place like this.'

'Well, yes, I am a bit.'

'Everyone does,' he said.

'*Everyone*,' I said.

'Yes,' he said.

Well, well, I thought – everyone.

'I live here,' he said, 'because I have a peculiar affinity with the desert. I am drawn to it the same way as a sailor is drawn to the sea. Does that seem so very strange to you?'

'No,' I answered, 'it doesn't seem strange at all.'

36

He paused and took a pull at his cigarette. Then he said, 'That is one reason. But there is another. Are you a family man, Mr Cornelius?'

'Unfortunately not,' I answered cautiously.

'I am,' he said. 'I have a wife and a daughter. Both of them, in my eyes at any rate, are very beautiful. My daughter is just eighteen. She has been to an excellent boarding-school in England, and she is now ...' he shrugged ... 'she is now just sitting around and waiting until she is old enough to get married. But this waiting period – what does one do with a beautiful young girl during that time? I can't let her loose. She is far too desirable for that. When I take her to Beirut, I see the men hanging around her like wolves waiting to pounce. It drives me nearly out of my mind. I know all about men, Mr Cornelius. I know how they behave. It is true, of course, that I am not the only father who has had this problem. But the others seem somehow able to face it and accept it. They let their daughters go. They just turn them out of the house and look the other way. I cannot do that. I simply *cannot bring* myself to do it! I refuse to allow her to be mauled by every Achmed, Ali, and Hamil that comes along. And that, you see, is the other reason why I live in the desert – to protect my lovely child for a few more years from the wild beasts. Did you say that you had no family at all, Mr Cornelius?'

'I'm afraid that's true.'

'Oh.' He seemed disappointed. 'You mean you've never been married?'

'Well ... no,' I said. 'No, I haven't.' I waited for the next inevitable question. It came about a minute later.

'Have you never *wanted* to get married and have children?'

They all asked that one. It was simply another way of saying, 'Are you, in that case, homosexual?'

'Once,' I said. 'Just once.'

'What happened?'

'There was only one person ever in my life, Mr Aziz ... and after she went ...' I sighed.

'You mean she died?'

I nodded, too choked up to answer.

'My dear fellow,' he said. 'Oh, I am so sorry. Forgive me for intruding.'

We drove on for a while in silence.

'It's amazing,' I murmured, 'how one loses all interest in matters of the flesh after a thing like that. I suppose it's the shock. One never gets over it.'

He nodded sympathetically, swallowing it all.

'So now I just travel around trying to forget. I've been doing it for years ...'

We had reached the foot of Mount Maghara now and were following the track as it curved around the mountain toward the side that was invisible from the road – the north side. 'As soon as we round the next bend you'll see the house,' Mr Aziz said.

We rounded the bend ... and there it was! I blinked and stared, and I tell you that for the first few seconds I literally could not believe my eyes. I saw before me a white castle – I mean it – a *tall, white castle* with turrets and towers and little spires all over it, standing like a fairy-tale in the middle of a splash of green vegetation on the lower slope of the blazing-hot, bare, yellow mountain! It was fantastic! It was straight out of Hans Christian Andersen or Grimm. I had seen plenty of romantic-looking Rhine and Loire valley castles in my time, but never before had I seen anything with such a slender, graceful, fairy-tale quality as this! The greenery, as I observed when we drew closer, was a pretty garden of lawns and date-palms, and there was a high white wall going all the way round to keep out the desert.

'Do you approve?' my host asked, smiling.

'It's fabulous!' I said. 'It's like all the fairy-tale castles in the world made into one.'

'That's exactly what it is!' he cried. 'It's a fairy-tale castle! I built it especially for my daughter, my beautiful Princess.'

And the beautiful Princess is imprisoned within its walls by her strict and jealous father, King Abdul Aziz, who refuses to allow her the pleasures of masculine company. But watch out, for here comes Prince Oswald Cornelius to the rescue! Unbeknownst to the King, he is going to ravish the beautiful Princess, and make her very happy.

'You have to admit it's different,' Mr Aziz said.

'It is that.'

'It is also nice and private. I sleep very peacefully here. So does the Princess. No unpleasant young men are likely to come climbing in through *those* windows during the night.'

'Quite so,' I said.

'It used to be a small oasis,' he went on. 'I bought it from the government. We have ample water for the house, the swimming-pool, and three acres of garden.'

We drove through the main gates, and I must say it was wonderful to come suddenly into a miniature paradise of green lawns and flower-beds and palm-trees. Everything was in perfect order, and water-sprinklers were playing on the lawns. When we stopped at the front door of the house, two servants in spotless gallabiyahs and scarlet tarbooshes ran out immediately, one to each side of the car, to open the doors for us.

Two servants? But would both of them have come out like that unless they'd been expecting *two* people? I doubted it. More and more, it began to look as though my odd little theory about being shanghaied as a dinner guest was turning out to be correct. It was all very amusing.

My host ushered me in through the front door, and at once I got that lovely shivery feeling that comes over the skin as one walks suddenly out of intense heat into an air-conditioned room. I was standing in the hall. The floor was of green marble. On my right, there was a wide archway leading to a large room, and I received a fleeting impression of cool white walls, fine pictures, and superlative Louis XV furniture. What a place to find oneself in, in the middle of the Sinai Desert!

And now a woman was coming slowly down the stairs. My host had turned away to speak to the servants, and he didn't see her at once, so when she reached the bottom step, the woman paused, and she laid her naked arm like a white anaconda along the rail of the banister, and there she stood, looking at me as though she were Queen Semiramis on the steps of Babylon, and I was a candidate who might or might not be to her taste. Her hair was jet-black, and she had a figure that made me wet my lips.

39

When Mr Aziz turned and saw her, he said, 'Oh darling, there you are. I've brought you a guest. His car broke down at the filling-station – such rotten luck – so I asked him to come back and stay the night. Mr Cornelius ... my wife.'

'How very nice,' she said quietly, coming forward.

I took her hand and raised it to my lips. 'I am overcome by your kindness, madame,' I murmured. There was, upon that hand of hers, a diabolical perfume. It was almost exclusively animal. The subtle, sexy secretions of the sperm-whale, the male musk-deer, and the beaver were all there, pungent and obscene beyond words; they dominated the blend completely, and only faint tracs of the clean vegetable oils – lemon, cajuput, and zeroli – were allowed to come through. It was superb! And another thing I noticed in the flash of that first moment was this: When I took her hand, she did not, as other women do, let it lie limply across my palm like a fillet of raw fish. Instead, she placed her thumb *underneath* my hand, with the fingers on top; and thus she was able to – and I swear she did – exert a gentle but suggestive pressure upon my hand as I administered the conventional kiss.

'Where is Diana?' asked Mr Aziz.

'She's out by the pool,' the woman said. And turning to me, 'Would *you* like a swim, Mr Cornelius? You must be roasted after hanging around that awful filling-station.'

She had huge velvet eyes, so dark they were almost black, and when she smiled at me, the end of her nose moved upwards, distending the nostrils.

There and then, Prince Oswald Cornelius decided that he cared not one whit about the beautiful Princess who was held captive in the castle by the jealous King. He would ravish the Queen instead.

'Well ...' I said.

'I'm going to have one,' Mr Aziz said.

'Let's all have one,' his wife said. 'We'll lend you a pair of trunks.'

I asked if I might go up to my room first and get out a clean shirt and clean slacks to put on after the swim, and my hostess said, 'Yes, of course,' and told one of the servants to show me the way. He took me up two flights of stairs, and we entered a large white bedroom which had in it an exceptionally large double-bed. There was a well-equipped bathroom leading off to one side, with a pale-blue bathtub and a bidet to match. Everywhere, things were scrupulously clean and very much to my liking. While the servant was unpacking my case, I went over to the window and looked out, and I saw the great blazing desert sweeping in like a yellow sea all the way from the horizon until it met the white garden wall just below me, and there, within the wall, I could see the swimming-pool, and beside the pool there was a girl lying on her back in the shade of a big pink parasol. The girl was wearing a white swimming costume, and she was reading a book. She had long slim legs and black hair. She was the Princess.

What a set-up, I thought. The white castle, the comfort, the cleanliness, the air-conditioning, the two dazzlingly beautiful females, the watchdog husband, and a whole evening to work in! The situation was so perfectly designed for my entertainment that it would have been impossible to improve upon it. The problems that lay ahead appealed to me very much. A simple straightforward seduction did not amuse me any more. There was no artistry in that sort of thing; and I can assure you that had I been able, by waving a magic wand, to make Mr Abdul Aziz, the jealous watchdog, disappear for the night, I would not have done so. I wanted no pyrrhic victories.

When I left the room, the servant accompanied me. We descended the first flight of stairs, and then, on the landing of the floor below my own, I paused and said casually, 'Does the whole family sleep on this floor?'

'Oh, yes,' the servant said. 'That is the master's room there' – indicating a door – 'and next to it is Mrs Aziz. Miss Diana is opposite.'

Three separate rooms. All very close together. Virtually impregnable. I tucked the information away in my mind and went on down to the pool. My host and hostess were there before me.

'This is my daughter, Diana,' my host said.

The girl in the white swimming-suit stood up and I kissed her hand. 'Hello, Mr Cornelius,' she said.

41

The Visitor

She was using the same heavy animal perfume as her mother – ambergris, musk, and castor! What a smell it had – bitchy, brazen, and marvellous! I sniffed at it like a dog. She was, I thought, even more beautiful than the parent, if that were possible. She had the same large velvety eyes, the same black hair, and the same shape of face; but her legs were unquestionably longer, and there was something about her body that gave it a slight edge over the older woman's: it was more sinuous, more snaky, and almost certain to be a good deal more flexible. But the older woman, who was probably thirty-seven and looked no more than twenty-five, had a spark in her eye that the daughter could not possibly match.

Eeeny, meeny, miny, mo – just a little while ago, Prince Oswald had sworn that he would ravish the Queen alone, and to hell with the Princess. But now that he had seen the Princess in the flesh, he did not know which one to prefer. Both of them, in their different ways, held forth a promise of innumerable delights, the one innocent and eager, the other expert and voracious. The truth of the matter was that he would like to have them both – the Princess as an hors d'oeuvre, and the Queen as the main dish.

'Help yourself to a pair of trunks in the changing-room, Mr Cornelius,' Mrs Aziz was saying, so I went into the hut and changed, and when I came out again the three of them were already splashing about in the water. I dived in and joined them. The water was so cold it made me gasp.

'I thought that would surprise you,' Mr Aziz said, laughing. 'It's cooled. I keep it at sixty-five degrees. It's more refreshing in this climate.'

Later, when the sun began dropping lower in the sky, we all sat around in our wet swiming-clothes while a servant brought us pale, ice-cold martinis, and it was at this point that I began, very slowly, very cautiously, to seduce the two ladies in my own particular fashion. Normally, when I am given a free hand, this is not especially difficult for me to do. The curious little talent that I happen to possess – the ability to hypnotize a woman with words – very seldom lets me down. It is not, of course, done only with words. The words themselves, the innocuous, superficial words, are spoken only by the mouth, whereas the real message, the improper and exciting promise, comes from all the limbs and organs of the body, and is transmitted through the eyes. More than that I cannot honestly tell you about how it is done. The point is that it works. It works like cantharides. I believe that I could sit down opposite the Pope's wife, if he had one, and within fifteen minutes, were I to try hard enough, she would be leaning toward me over the table with her lips apart and her eyes glazed with desire. It is a minor talent, not a great one, but I am nonetheless thankful to have had it bestowed upon me, and I have done my best at all times to see that it has not been wasted.

So the four of us, the two wondrous women, the little man, and myself, sat close together in a semi-circle beside the swimming-pool, lounging in deck-chairs and sipping our drinks and feeling the warm six o'clock sunshine upon our skin. I was in good form. I made them laugh a great deal. The story about the greedy old Duchess of Glasgow putting her hand in the chocolate-box and getting nipped by one of my scorpions had the daughter falling out of her chair with mirth; and when I described in detail the interior of my spider breeding-house in the garden outside Paris, both ladies began wriggling with revulsion and pleasure.

It was at this stage that I noticed the eyes of Mr Abdul Aziz resting upon me in a good-humoured, twinkling kind of way. 'Well, well,' the eyes seemed to be saying, 'we are glad to see that you are not quite so disinterested in women as you led us to believe in the car ... Or is it, perhaps, that these congenial surroundings are helping you to forget that great sorrow of yours at last ...' Mr Aziz smiled at me, showing his pure white teeth. It was a friendly smile. I gave him a friendly smile back. What a friendly little fellow he was. He was genuinely delighted to see me paying so much attention to the ladies. So far, then, so good.

I shall skip very quickly over the next few hours, for it was not until after midnight that anything really tremendous happened to me. A few brief notes will suffice to cover the intervening period:

The Visitor

At seven o'clock, we all left the swimming-pool and returned to the house to dress for dinner.

At eight o'clock, we assembled in the big living-room to drink another cocktail. The two ladies were both superbly turned out, and sparkling with jewels. Both of them wore low-cut, sleeveless evening-dresses which had come, without any doubt at all, from some great fashion house in Paris. My hostess was in black, her daughter in pale blue, and the scent of that intoxicating perfume was everywhere about them. What a pair they were! The older woman had that slight forward hunch to her shoulders which one sees only in the most passionate and practised of females; for in the same way as a horsey woman will become bandy-legged from sitting constantly upon a horse, so a woman of great passion will develop a curious roundness of the shoulders from continually embracing men. It is an occupational deformity, and the noblest of them all.

The daughter was not yet old enough to have acquired this singular badge of honour, but with her it was enough for me simply to stand back and observe the shape of her body and to notice the splendid sliding motion of her thighs underneath the tight silk dress as she wandered about the room. She had a line of tiny soft golden hairs growing all the way up the exposed length of her spine, and when I stood behind her it was difficult to resist the temptation of running my knuckles up and down those lovely vertebrae.

At eight thirty, we moved into the dining-room. The dinner that followed was a really magnificent affair, but I shall waste no time here describing food or wine. Throughout the meal I continued to play most delicately and insidiously upon the sensibilities of the women, employing every skill that I possessed; and by the time the dessert arrived, they were melting before my eyes like butter in the sun.

After dinner we returned to the living-room for coffee and brandy, and then, at my host's suggestion, we played a couple of rubbers of bridge.

By the end of the evening, I knew for certain that I had done my work well. The old magic had not let me down. Either of the two ladies, should circumstances permit, was mine for the asking. I was not deluding myself over this. It was a straightforward, obvious fact. It stood out a mile. The face of my hostess was bright with excitement, and whenever she looked at me across the card-table, those huge dark velvety eyes would grow bigger and bigger, and the nostrils would dilate, and the mouth would open slightly to reveal the tip of a moist pink tongue squeezing through between the teeth. It was a marvellously lascivious gesture, and more than once it caused me to trump my own trick. The daughter was less daring but equally direct. Each time her eyes met mine, and that was often enough, she would raise her brows just the tiniest fraction of a centimetre, as though asking a question; then she would make a quick sly little smile, supplying the answer.

'I think it's time we all went to bed,' Mr Aziz said, examining his watch. 'It's after eleven. Come along, my dears.'

Then a queer thing happened. At once, without a second's hesitation and without another glance in my direction, both ladies rose and made for the door! It was astonishing. It left me stunned. I didn't know what to make of it. It was the quickest thing I'd ever seen. And yet it wasn't as though Mr Aziz had spoken angrily. His voice, to me at any rate, had sounded as pleasant as ever. But now he was already turning out the lights, indicating clearly that he wished me also to retire. What a blow! I had expected at least to receive a whisper from either the wife or the daughter before we separated for the night, just a quick three or four words telling me where to go and when; but instead, I was left standing like a fool beside the card-table while the two ladies glided out of the room.

My host and I followed them up the stairs. On the landing of the first floor, the mother and daughter stood side by side, waiting for me.

'Good night, Mr Cornelius,' my hostess said.

'Good night, Mr Cornelius,' the daughter said.

'Good night, my dear fellow,' Mr Aziz said. 'I do hope you have everything you want.'

They turned away, and there was nothing for me to do but continue slowly, reluctantly, up the second flight of stairs to my own room. I entered it and closed the door. The heavy brocade curtains had already been drawn by one of the servants but I parted them and leaned out the window to take a look at the night. The air was still and warm, and a brilliant moon was shining over the desert. Below me, the swimming-pool in the moonlight looked something like an enormous glass mirror lying flat on the lawn, and beside it I could see the four deck-chairs we had been sitting in earlier.

Well, well, I thought. What happens now?

One thing I knew I must not do in this house was to venture out of my room and go prowling around the corridors. That would be suicide. I had learned many years ago that there are three breeds of husband with whom one must never take unnecessary risks – the Bulgarian, the Greek, and the Syrian. None of them, for some reason, resents you flirting quite openly with his wife, but he will kill you at once if he catches you getting into her bed. Mr Aziz was a Syrian. A degree of prudence was therefore essential, and if any move were going to be made now, it must be made not by me but by one of the two women, for only she (or they) would know precisely what was safe and what was dangerous. Yet I had to admit that after witnessing the way in which my host had called them both to heel four minutes ago, there was little hope of further action in the near future. The trouble was, though, that I had got myself so infernally steamed up.

I undressed and took a long cold shower. That helped. Then, because I have never been able to sleep in the moonlight, I made sure that the curtains were tightly drawn together. I got into bed, and for the next hour or so I lay reading some more of Gilbert White's *Natural History of Selborne*. That also helped, and at last, somewhere between midnight and one a.m., there came a time when I was able to switch out the light and prepare myself for sleep without altogether too many regrets.

I was just beginning to doze off when I heard some tiny sounds. I recognized them at once. They were sounds that I had heard many times before in my life, and yet they were still, for me, the most thrilling and evocative in the whole world. They consisted of a series of little soft metallic noises, of metal grating gently against metal, and they were made, they were always made by somebody who was very slowly, very cautiously, turning the handle of one's door from the outside. Instantly, I became wide awake. But I did not move. I simply opened my eyes and stared in the direction of the door; and I can remember wishing at that moment for a gap in the curtain, for just a small thin shaft of moonlight to come in from outside so that I could at least catch a glimpse of the shadow of the lovely form that was about to enter. But the room was as dark as a dungeon.

I did not hear the door open. No hinge squeaked. But suddenly a little gust of air swept through the room and rustled the curtains, and a moment later I heard the soft thud of wood against wood as the door was carefully closed again. Then came the click of the latch as the handle was released.

Next, I heard feet tiptoeing toward me over the carpet.

For one horrible second, it occurred to me that this might just possibly be Mr Abdul Aziz creeping in upon me with a long knife in his hand, but then all at once a warm extensile body was bending over mine, and a woman's voice was whispering in my ear, *'Don't make a sound!'*

'My dearest beloved,' I said, wondering which one of them it was, 'I knew you'd ...' Instantly her hand came over my mouth.

'Please!' she whispered. *'Not another word!'*

I didn't argue. My lips had many better things to do than that. So had hers.

Here I must pause. This is not like me at all – I know that. But just for once, I wish to be excused a detailed description of the great scene that followed. I have my own reasons for this and I beg you to respect them. In any case, it will do you no harm to exercise your own imagination for a change, and if you wish, I will stimulate it a little by saying simply and truthfully that of the many thousands and thousands of women I have known in my time, none has transported me to greater extremes of ecstasy than this lady of the Sinai Desert. Her dexterity was amazing. Her passion was intense. Her range was unbelievable. At every turn, she was ready with some new and intricate manoeuvre. And to cap it all, she possessed the subtlest and most recondite style I have ever encountered. She was a great artist. She was a genius.

All this, you will probably say, indicated clearly that my visitor must have been the older woman. You would be wrong. It indicated nothing. True genius is a gift of birth. It has very little to do with age; and I can assure you I had no way of knowing for certain which of them it was in the darkness of that room. I wouldn't have bet a penny on it either way. At one moment, after some particularly boisterous cadenza, I would be convinced it was the wife. *It must be the wife!* Then suddenly the whole tempo would begin to change, and the melody would become so childlike and innocent that I found myself swearing it was the daughter. *It must be the daughter!*

Maddening it was not to know the true answer. It tantalized me. It also humbled me, for, after all, a connoisseur, a supreme connoisseur, should always be able to guess the vintage with- out seeing the label on the bottle. But this one really had me beat. At one point, I reached for cigarettes, intending to solve the mystery in the flare of a match, but her hand was on me in a flash, and cigarettes and matches were snatched away and flung across the room. More than once, I began to whisper the question itself into her ear, but I never got three words out before the hand shot up again and smacked itself over my mouth. Rather violently, too.

Very well, I thought. Let it be for now. Tomorrow morning, downstairs in the daylight, I shall know for certain which one of you it was. I shall know by the glow on the face, by the way the eyes look back into mine, and by a hundred other little telltale signs. I shall also know by the marks that my teeth have made on the left side of the neck, above the dress line. A rather wily move, that one, I thought, and so perfectly timed – my vicious bite was administered during the height of her passion – that she never for one moment realized the signifi- cance of the act.

It was altogether a most memorable night, and at least four hours must have gone by before she gave me a final fierce embrace, and slipped out of the room as quickly as she had come in.

The next morning I did not awaken until after ten o'clock. I got out of bed and drew open the curtains. It was another brilliant, hot, desert day. I took a leisurely bath, then dressed myself as carefully as ever. I felt relaxed and chipper. It made me very happy to think that I could still summon a woman to my room with my eyes alone, even in middle age. And what a woman! It would be fascinating to find out which one of them she was. I would soon know.

I made my way slowly down the two flights of stairs.

'Good morning, my dear fellow, good morning!' Mr Aziz said, rising from a small desk he had been writing at in the living-room. 'Did you have a good night?'

'Excellent, thank you,' I answered, trying not to sound smug.

He came and stood close to me, smiling with his very white teeth. His shrewd little eyes rested on my face and moved over it slowly, as though searching for something.

'I have good news for you,' he said. 'They called up from B'ir Rawd Salim five minutes ago and said your fan-belt had arrived by the mail-truck. Saleh is fitting it on now. It'll be ready in an hour. So when you've had some breakfast, I'll drive you over and you can be on your way.'

I told him how grateful I was.

'We'll be sorry to see you go,' he said. 'It's been an immense pleasure for all of us having you drop in like this, an immense pleasure.'

I had my breakfast alone in the dining-room. Afterwards, I returned to the living-room to smoke a cigarette while my host continued writing at his desk.

'Do forgive me,' he said. 'I just have a couple of things to finish here. I won't be long. I've arranged for your case to be packed and put in the car, so you have nothing to worry about. Sit down and enjoy your cigarette. The ladies ought to be down any minute now.'

The wife arrived first. She came sailing into the room looking more than ever like the dazzling Queen Semiramis of the Nile, and the first thing I noticed about her was the pale-green chiffon scarf knotted casually around her neck! Casually but carefully! So carefully that no part of the skin of the neck was visible. The woman went straight over to her husband and kissed him on the cheek. 'Good morning, my darling,' she said.

You cunning beautiful bitch, I thought.

'Good *morning*, Mr Cornelius,' she said gaily, coming over to sit in the chair opposite mine. 'Did you have a good night? I do hope you had everything you wanted.'

Never in my life have I seen such a sparkle in a woman's eyes as I saw in hers that morning, nor such a glow of pleasure in a woman's face.

'I had a very good night indeed, thank *you*,' I answered, showing her that I knew.

She smiled and lit a cigarette. I glanced over at Mr Aziz, who was still writing away busily at the desk with his back to us. He wasn't paying the slightest attention to his wife or to me. He was, I thought, exactly like all the other poor cuckolds that I ever created. Not one of them would believe that it could happen to him, not right under his own nose.

'Good morning, everybody!' cried the daughter, sweeping into the room. 'Good morning, daddy! Good morning, mummy!' She gave them each a kiss. 'Good morning, Mr Cornelius!' She was wearing a pair of pink slacks and a rust-coloured blouse, and I'll be damned if she didn't also have a scarf tied carelessly but carefully around her neck! A chiffon scarf!

'Did you have a decent night?' she asked, perching herself like a young bride on the arm of my chair, arranging herself in such a way that one of her thighs rested against my fore-arm. I leaned back and looked at her closely. She looked back at me and winked. She actually winked! Her face was glowing and sparkling every bit as much as her mother's, and if anything, she seemed even more pleased with herself than the older woman.

I felt pretty confused. Only one of them had a bite mark to conceal, yet both of them had covered their necks with scarves. I conceded that this might be a coincidence, but on the face of it, it looked much more like a conspiracy to me. It looked as though they were both working closely together to keep me from discovering the truth. But what an extraordinary screwy business! And what was the purpose of it all? And in what other peculiar ways, might I ask, did they plot and plan together among themselves? Had they drawn lots or something the night before? Or did they simply take it in turns with visitors? I *must* come back again, I told myself, for another visit as soon as possible just to see what happens the next time. In fact, I might motor down specially from Jerusalem in a day or two. It would be easy, I reckoned, to get myself invited again.

'Are you ready, Mr Cornelius?' Mr Aziz said, rising from his desk.

'Quite ready,' I answered.

The ladies, sleek and smiling, led the way outside to where the big green Rolls-Royce was waiting. I kissed their hands and murmured a million thanks to each of them. Then I got into the front seat beside my host, and we drove off. The mother and daughter waved. I lowered my window and waved back. Then we were out of the garden and into the desert, following the stony yellow track as it skirted the base of Mount Maghara, with the telegraph poles marching along beside us.

During the journey, my host and I conversed pleasantly about this and that. I was at pains to be as agreeable as possible because my one object now was to get myself invited to stay at the house again. If I didn't succeed in getting *him* to ask *me*, then *I* should have to ask *him*. I would do it at the last moment. 'Good-bye, my dear friend,' I would say, gripping him warmly by the throat. 'May I have the pleasure of dropping in to see you again if I happen to be passing this way?' And of course he would say yes.

'Did you think I exaggerated when I told you my daughter was beautiful?' he asked me.

'You understated it,' I said. 'She's a raving beauty. I do congratulate you. But your wife is no less lovely. In fact, between the two of them they almost swept me off my feet,' I added, laughing.

'I noticed that,' he said, laughing with me. 'They're a couple of very naughty girls. They do so love to flirt with other men. But why should I mind. There's no harm in flirting.'

'None whatsoever,' I said.

'I think it's gay and fun.'

'It's charming,' I said.

In less than half an hour we had reached the main Ismailia–Jerusalem road. Mr Aziz turned the Rolls on to the black tarmac strip and headed for the filling-station at seventy miles an hour. In a few minutes we would be there. So now I tried moving a little closer to the subject of another visit, fishing gently for an invitation. 'I can't get over your house,' I said. 'I think it's simply wonderful.'

'It is nice, isn't it?'

'I suppose you're bound to get pretty lonely out there, on and off, just the three of you together?'

'It's no worse than anywhere else,' he said. 'People get lonely wherever they are. A desert, or a city – it doesn't make much difference, really. But we do have visitors, you know. You'd be surprised at the number of people who drop in from time to time. Like you, for instance. It was a great pleasure having you with us, my dear fellow.'

'I shall never forget it,' I said. 'It is a rare thing to find kindness and hospitality of that order nowadays.'

I waited for him to tell me that I must come again, but he didn't. A little silence sprang up between us, a slightly uneasy little silence. To bridge it, I said, 'I think yours is the most thoughtful paternal gesture I've ever heard of in my life.'

'Mine?'

'Yes. Building a house right out there in the back of beyond and living in it just for your daughter's sake, to protect her. I think it's remarkable.'

I saw him smile, but he kept his eyes on the road and said nothing. The filling-station and the group of huts were now in sight about a mile ahead of us. The sun was high and it was getting hot inside the car.

'Not many fathers would put themselves out to that extent,' I went on.

52

Again he smiled, but somewhat bashfully, this time, I thought. And then he said, 'I don't deserve *quite* as much credit as you like to give me, really I don't. To be absolutely honest with you, that pretty daughter of mine isn't the only reason for my living in such splendid isolation.'

'I know that.'

'You do?'

'You told me. You said the other reason was the desert. You loved it, you said, as a sailor loves the sea.'

'So I did. And it's quite true. But there's still a third reason.'

'Oh, and what is that?'

He didn't answer me. He sat quite still with his hands on the wheel and his eyes fixed on the road ahead.

'I'm sorry,' I said. 'I shouldn't have asked the question. It's none of my business.'

'No, no, that's quite all right,' he said. 'Don't apologize.'

I stared out of the window at the desert. 'I think it's hotter than yesterday,' I said. 'It must be well over a hundred already.'

'Yes.'

I saw him shifting a little in his seat, as though trying to get comfortable, and then he said, 'I don't really see why I shouldn't tell you the truth about that house. You don't strike me as being a gossip.'

'Certainly not,' I said.

We were close to the filling-station now, and he had slowed the car down almost to walking-speed to give himself time to say what he had to say. I could see the two Arabs standing beside my Lagonda, watching us.

'That daughter,' he said at length, 'the one you met – she isn't the only daughter I have.'

'Oh, really?'

'I've got another who is five years older than she.'

'And just as beautiful, no doubt,' I said. 'Where does she live? In Beirut?'

'No, she's in the house.'

'In which house? Not the one we've just left?'

'Yes.'

53

'But I never saw her!'

'Well,' he said, turning suddenly to watch my face, 'maybe not.'

'But why?'

'She has leprosy.'

I jumped.

'Yes, I know,' he said, 'it's a terrible thing. She has the worst kind, too, poor girl. It's called anaesthetic leprosy. It is highly resistant, and almost impossible to cure. If only it were the nodular variety, it would be much easier. But it isn't, and there you are. So when a visitor comes to the house, she keeps to her own apartment, on the third floor ...'

The car must have pulled into the filling-station about then because the next thing I can remember was seeing Mr Abdul Aziz sitting there looking at me with those small clever black eyes of his, and he was saying, 'But my dear fellow, you mustn't alarm yourself like this. Calm yourself down, Mr Cornelius, calm yourself down! There's absolutely nothing in the world for you to worry about. It is not a very contagious disease. You have to have the most *intimate* contact with the person in order to catch it ...'

I got out of the car very slowly and stood in the sunshine. The Arab with the diseased face was grinning at me and saying, 'Fan-belt all fixed now. Everything fine.' I reached into my pocket for cigarettes, but my hand was shaking so violently I dropped the packet on the ground. I bent down and retrieved it. Then I got a cigarette out and managed to light it. When I looked up again, I saw the green Rolls-Royce already half a mile down the road, and going away fast.

The Great Switcheroo

There were about forty people at Jerry and Samantha's cock-tail-party that evening. It was the usual crowd, the usual discomfort, the usual appalling noise. People had to stand very close to one another and shout to make themselves heard. Many were grinning, showing capped white teeth. Most of them had a cigarette in the left hand, a drink in the right.

I moved away from my wife Mary and her group. I headed for the small bar in the far corner, and when I got there, I sat down on a bar-stool and faced the room. I did this so that I could look at the women. I settled back with my shoulders against the bar-rail, sipping my Scotch and examining the women one by one over the rim of my glass.

I was studying not their figures but their faces, and what interested me there was not so much the face itself but the big red mouth in the middle of it all. And even then, it wasn't the whole mouth but only the lower lip. The lower lip, I had recently decided, was the great revealer. It gave away more than the eyes. The eyes hid their secrets. The lower lip hid very little. Take, for example, the lower lip of Jacinth Winkleman, who was standing nearest to me. Notice the wrinkles on that lip, how some were parallel and some radiated outward. No two people had the same pattern of lip-wrinkles, and come to think of it, you could catch a criminal that way if you had his lip-print on file and he had taken a drink at the scene of the crime. The lower lip is what you suck and nibble when you're ruffled, and Martha Sullivan was doing that right now as she watched from a distance her fatuous husband slobbering over Judy Martinson. You lick it when lecherous. I could see Ginny Lomax licking hers with the tip of her tongue as she stood beside Ted Dorling and gazed up into his face. It was a deliberate lick, the tongue coming out slowly and making a slow wet wipe along the entire length of the lower lip. I saw Ted Dorling looking at Ginny's tongue, which was what she wanted him to do.

It really does seem to be a fact, I told myself, as my eyes wandered from lower lip to lower lip across the room, that all the less attractive traits of the human animal, arrogance, rapacity, gluttony, lasciviousness, and the rest of them, are clearly signalled in that little carapace of scarlet skin. But you have to know the code. The protuberant or bulging lower lip is supposed to signify sensuality. But this is only half true in men and wholly untrue in women. In women, it is the thin line you should look for, the narrow blade with the sharply delineated bottom edge. And in the nymphomaniac there is a tiny just visible crest of skin at the top centre of the lower lip.

Samantha, my hostess, had that.

Where was she now, Samantha?

Ah, there she was, taking an empty glass out of a guest's hand. Now she was heading my way to refill it.

'Hello, Vic,' she said: 'You all alone?'

She's a nympho-bird all right, I told myself. But a very rare example of the species, because she is entirely and utterly monogamous. She is a married monogamous nympho-bird who stays for ever in her own nest.

She is also the fruitiest female I have ever set eyes upon in my whole life.

'Let me help you,' I said, standing up and taking the glass from her hand. 'What's wanted in here?'

'Vodka on the rocks,' she said. 'Thanks, Vic.' She laid a lovely long white arm upon the top of the bar and she leaned forward so that her bosom rested on the bar-rail, squashing upward. 'Oops,' I said, pouring vodka outside the glass.

Samantha looked at me with huge brown eyes, but said nothing.

'I'll wipe it up,' I said.

She took the refilled glass from me and walked away. I watched her go. She was wearing black pants. They were so tight around the buttocks that the smallest mole or pimple would have shown through the cloth. But Samantha Rainbow had not a blemish on her bottom. I caught myself licking my own lower lip. That's right, I thought. I want her. I lust after that woman. But it's too risky to try. It would be suicide to make a pass at a girl like that. First of all, she lives next door, which is too close. Secondly, as I have already said, she is monogamous. Thirdly, she is thick as a thief with Mary, my own wife. They exchange dark female secrets. Fourthly, her husband Jerry is my very old and good friend, and not even I, Victor Hammond, though I am churning with lust, would dream of trying to seduce the wife of a man who is my very old and trusty friend.

Unless . . .

It was at this point, as I sat on the bar-stool letching over Samantha Rainbow, that an interesting idea began to filter quietly into the centre of my brain. I remained still, allowing the idea to expand. I watched Samantha across the room, and began fitting her into the framework of the idea. Oh, Samantha, my gorgeous and juicy little jewel, I shall have you yet.

But could anybody seriously hope to get away with a crazy lark like that?

No, not in a million nights.

One couldn't even *try* it unless Jerry agreed. So why think about it?

Samantha was standing about six yards away, talking to Gilbert Mackesy. The fingers of her right hand were curled around a tall glass. The fingers were long and almost certainly dexterous.

Assuming, just for the fun of it, that Jerry did agree, then even so, there would still be gigantic snags along the way. There was, for example, the little matter of physical characteristics. I had seen Jerry many times at the club having a shower after tennis, but right now I couldn't for the life of me recall the necessary details. It wasn't the sort of thing one noticed very much. Usually, one didn't even look.

Anyway, it would be madness to put the suggestion to Jerry point-blank. I didn't know him *that* well. He might be horrified. He might even turn nasty. There could be an ugly scene. I must test him out, therefore, in some subtle fashion.

'You know something,' I said to Jerry about an hour later when we were sitting together on the sofa having a last drink. The guests were drifting away and Samantha was by the door saying goodbye to them. My own wife Mary was out on the terrace talking to Bob Swain. I could see through the open french windows. 'You know something funny?' I said to Jerry as we sat together on the sofa.

'What's funny?' Jerry asked me.

'A fellow I had lunch with today told me a fantastic story. Quite unbelievable.'

'What story?' Jerry said. The whisky had begun to make him sleepy.

'This man, the one I had lunch with, had a terrific letch after the wife of his friend who lived nearby. And his friend had an equally big letch after the wife of the man I had lunch with. Do you see what I mean?'

'You mean two fellers who lived close to each other both fancied each other's wives.'

'Precisely,' I said.

'Then there was no problem,' Jerry said.

'There was a very big problem,' I said. 'The wives were both very faithful and honourable women.'

'Samantha's the same,' Jerry said. 'She wouldn't look at another man.'

'Nor would Mary,' I said. 'She's a fine girl.'

Jerry emptied his glass and set it down carefully on the sofa-table. 'So what happened in your story?' he said. 'It sounds dirty.'

'What happened,' I said, 'was that these two randy sods cooked up a plan which made it possible for each of them to ravish the other's wife without the wives ever knowing it. If you can believe such a thing.'

'With chloroform?' Jerry said.

'Not at all. They were fully conscious.'

'Impossible,' Jerry said. 'Someone's been pulling your leg.'

'I don't think so,' I said. 'From the way this man told it to me, with all the little details and everything, I don't think he was making it up. In fact, I'm sure he wasn't. And listen, they didn't do it just once, either. They've been doing it every two or three weeks for months!'

'And the wives don't know?'

'They haven't a clue.'

'I've got to hear this,' Jerry said. 'Let's get another drink first.'

We crossed to the bar and refilled our glasses, then returned to the sofa.

'You must remember,' I said, 'that there had to be a tremendous lot of preparation and rehearsal beforehand. And many intimate details had to be exchanged to give the plan a chance of working. But the essential part of the scheme was simple:

'They fixed a night, call it Saturday. On that night the husbands and wives were to go up to bed as usual, at say eleven or eleven thirty.

'From then on, normal routine would be preserved. A little reading, perhaps, a little talking, then out with the lights.

'After lights out, the husbands would at once roll over and pretend to go to sleep. This was to discourage their wives from getting fresh, which at this stage must on no account be permitted. So the wives went to sleep. But the husbands stayed awake. So far so good.

'Then at precisely one a.m., by which time the wives would be in a good deep sleep, each husband would slip quietly out of bed, put on a pair of bedroom slippers and creep downstairs in his pyjamas. He would open the front door and go out into the night, taking care not to close the door behind him.

'They lived,' I went on, 'more or less across the street from one another. It was a quiet suburban neighbourhood and there was seldom anyone about at that hour. So these two furtive pyjama-clad figures would pass each other as they crossed the street, each one heading for another house, another bed, another woman.'

Jerry was listening to me carefully. His eyes were a little glazed from drink, but he was listening to every word.

The Great Switcheroo

'The next part,' I said, 'had been prepared very thoroughly by both men. Each knew the inside of his friend's house almost as well as he knew his own. He knew how to find his way in the dark both downstairs and up without knocking over the furniture. He knew his way to the stairs and exactly how many steps there were to the top and which of them creaked and which didn't. He knew on which side of the bed the woman upstairs was sleeping.

'Each took off his slippers and left them in the hall, then up the stairs he crept in his bare feet and pyjamas. This part of it, according to my friend, was rather exciting. He was in a dark silent house that wasn't his own, and on his way to the main bedroom he had to pass no less than three children's bedrooms where the doors were always left slightly open.'

'Children!' Jerry cried. 'My God, what if one of them had woken up and said, "Daddy, is that you?"'

'That was all taken care of,' I said. 'Emergency procedure would then come into effect immediately. Also if the wife, just as he was creeping into her room, woke up and said, "Darling, what's wrong? Why are you wandering about?"; then again, emergency procedure.'

'What emergency procedure?' Jerry said.

'Simple,' I answered. 'The man would immediately dash downstairs and out the front door and across to his own house and ring the bell. This was a signal for the other character, no matter what he was doing at the time, also to rush downstairs at full speed and open the door and let the other fellow in while he went out. This would get them both back quickly to their proper houses.'

'With egg all over their faces,' Jerry said.

'Not at all,' I said.

'That doorbell would have woken the whole house,' Jerry said.

'Of course,' I said. 'And the husband, returning upstairs in his pyjamas, would merely say, 'I went to see who the hell was ringing the bell at this ungodly hour. Couldn't find anyone. It must have been a drunk.'

60

'What about the other guy?' Jerry asked. 'How does he explain why he rushed downstairs when his wife or child spoke to him?'

'He would say, "I heard someone prowling about outside, so I rushed down to get him, but he escaped." "Did you actually see him?" his wife would ask anxiously. "Of course I saw him," the husband would answer. "He ran off down the street. He was too damn fast for me." Whereupon the husband would be warmly congratulated for his bravery.'

'Okay,' Jerry said. 'That's the easy part. Everything so far is just a matter of good planning and good timing. But what happens when these two horny characters actually climb into bed with each other's wives?'

'They go right to it,' I said.

'The wives are sleeping,' Jerry said.

'I know,' I said. 'So they proceed immediately with some very gentle but very skilful love-play, and by the time these dames are fully awake, they're as randy as rattlesnakes.'

'No talking, I presume,' Jerry said.

'Not a word.'

'Okay, so the wives are awake,' Jerry said. 'And their hands get to work. So just for a start, what about the simple question of body size? What about the difference between the new man and the husband? What about tallness and shortness and fatness and thinness? You're not telling me these men were physically identical?'

'Not identical, obviously,' I said. 'But they were more or less similar in build and height. That was essential. They were both clean-shaven and had roughly the same amount of hair on their heads. That sort of similarity is commonplace. Look at you and me, for instance. We're roughly the same height and build, aren't we?'

'Are we?' Jerry said.

'How tall are you?' I said.

'Six foot exactly.'

'I'm five eleven,' I said. 'One inch difference. What do you weigh?'

'One hundred and eighty-seven.'

'I'm a hundred and eighty-four,' I said. 'What's three pounds among friends?'

There was a pause, Jerry was looking out through the french windows on to the terrace where my wife, Mary, was standing. Mary was still talking to Bob Swain and the evening sun was shining in her hair. She was a dark pretty girl with a bosom. I watched Jerry. I saw his tongue come out and go sliding along the surface of his lower lip.

'I guess you're right,' Jerry said, still looking at Mary. 'I guess we are about the same size, you and me.' When he turned back and faced me again, there was a little red rose high up on each cheek. 'Go on about these two men,' he said. 'What about some of the other differences?'

'You mean faces?' I said. 'No one's going to see faces in the dark.'

'I'm not talking about faces,' Jerry said.

'What are you talking about, then?'

'I'm talking about their cocks,' Jerry said. 'That's what it's all about, isn't it? And you're not going to tell me ...'

'Oh yes, I am,' I said. 'Just so long as both men were either circumcised or uncircumcised, then there was really no problem.'

'Are you seriously suggesting that all men have the same size in cocks?' Jerry said. 'Because they don't.'

'I know they don't,' I said.

'Some are enormous,' Jerry said. 'And some are titchy.'

'There are always exceptions,' I told him. 'But you'd be surprised at the number of men whose measurements are virtually the same, give or take a centimetre. According to my friend, ninety per cent are normal. Only ten per cent are notably large or small.'

'I don't believe that,' Jerry said.

'Check on it sometime,' I said. 'Ask some well-travelled girl.'

Jerry took a long slow sip of his whisky, and his eyes over the top of his glass were looking again at Mary on the terrace. 'What about the rest of it?' he said.

'No problem,' I said.

'No problem, my arse,' he said. 'Shall I tell you why this is a phony story?'

'Go ahead.'

'Everybody knows that a wife and husband who have been married for some years develop a kind of routine. It's inevitable. My God, a new operator would be spotted instantly. You know damn well he would. You can't suddenly wade in with a totally different style and expect the woman not to notice it, and I don't care how randy she was. She'd smell a rat in the first minute!'

'A routine can be duplicated,' I said. 'Just so long as every detail of that routine is described beforehand.'

'A bit personal, that,' Jerry said.

'The whole thing's personal,' I said. 'So each man tells his story. He tells precisely what he usually does. He tells everything. The lot. The works. The whole routine from beginning to end.'

'Jesus,' Jerry said.

'Each of these men,' I said, 'had to learn a new part. He had, in effect, to become an actor. He was impersonating another character.'

'Not so easy, that,' Jerry said.

'No problem at all, according to my friend. The only thing one had to watch out for was not to get carried away and start improvising. One had to follow the stage directions very carefully and stick to them.'

Jerry took another pull at his drink. He also took another look at Mary on the terrace. Then he leaned back against the sofa, glass in hand.

'These two characters,' he said. 'You mean they actually pulled it off?'

'I'm damn sure they did,' I said. 'They're still doing it. About once every three weeks.'

'Fantastic story,' Jerry said. 'And a damn crazy dangerous thing to do. Just imagine the sort of hell that would break loose if you were caught. Instant divorce. Two divorces, in fact. One on each side of the street. Not worth it.'

'Takes a lot of guts,' I said.

'The party's breaking up,' Jerry said. 'They're all going home with their goddam wives.'

I didn't say any more after that. We sat there for a couple of minutes sipping our drinks while the guests began drifting towards the hall.

'Did he say it was fun, this friend of yours?' Jerry asked suddenly.

'He said it was a gas,' I answered. 'He said all the normal pleasures got intensified one hundred per cent because of the risk. He swore it was the greatest way of doing it in the world, impersonating the husband and the wife not knowing it.'

At that point, Mary came in through the french windows with Bob Swain. She had an empty glass in one hand and a flame-coloured azalea in the other. She had picked the azalea on the terrace.

'I've been watching you,' she said, pointing the flower at me like a pistol. 'You've hardly stopped talking for the last ten minutes. What's he been telling you, Jerry?'

'A dirty story,' Jerry said, grinning.

'He does that when he drinks,' Mary said.

'Good story,' Jerry said. 'But totally impossible. Get him to tell it to you sometime.'

'I don't like dirty stories,' Mary said. 'Come along, Vic. It's time we went.'

'Don't go yet,' Jerry said, fixing his eyes upon her splendid bosom. 'Have another drink.'

'No thanks,' she said. 'The children'll be screaming for their supper. I've had a lovely time.'

'Aren't you going to kiss me good night?' Jerry said, getting up from the sofa. He went for her mouth, but she turned her head quickly and he caught only the edge of her cheek.

'Go away, Jerry,' she said. 'You're drunk.'

'Not drunk,' Jerry said. 'Just lecherous.'

'Don't you get lecherous with me, my boy,' Mary said sharply. 'I hate that sort of talk.' She marched away across the room, carrying her bosom before her like a battering-ram.

'So long, Jerry,' I said. 'Fine party.'

Mary, full of dark looks, was waiting for me in the hall.

Samantha was there, too, saying goodbye to the last guests –
Samantha with her dexterous fingers and her smooth skin and
her smooth, dangerous thighs. 'Cheer up, Vic,' she said to me,
her white teeth showing. She looked like the creation, the beginning of the world, the first morning. 'Good night, Vic
darling,' she said, stirring her fingers in my vitals.

I followed Mary out of the house. 'You feeling all right?'
she asked.

'Yes,' I said. 'Why not?'

'The amount you drink is enough to make anyone feel ill,'
she said.

There was a scrubby old hedge dividing our place from
Jerry's and there was a gap in it we always used. Mary and I
walked through the gap in silence. We went into the house
and she cooked up a big pile of scrambled eggs and bacon,
and we ate it with the children.

After the meal, I wandered outside. The summer evening
was clear and cool and because I had nothing else to do I
decided to mow the grass in the front garden. I got the mower
out of the shed and started it up. Then I began the old routine
of marching back and forth behind it. I like mowing grass. It is
a soothing operation, and on our front lawn I could always look
at Samantha's house going one way and think about her going
the other.

I had been at it for about ten minutes when Jerry came
strolling through the gap in the hedge. He was smoking a pipe
and had his hands in his pockets and he stood on the edge of
the grass, watching me. I pulled up in front of him, but left
the motor ticking over.

'Hi, sport,' he said. 'How's everything?'

'I'm in the doghouse,' I said. 'So are you.'

'Your little wife,' he said, 'is just too goddamn prim and
prissy to be true.'

'Oh, I know that.'

'She rebuked me in my own house,' Jerry said.

'Not very much.'

'It was enough,' he said, smiling slightly.

'Enough for what?'

'Enough to make me want to get a little bit of my own back on her. So what would you think if I suggested you and I have a go at that thing your friend told you about at lunch?'

When he said this, I felt such a surge of excitement my stomach nearly jumped out of my mouth. I gripped the handles of the mower and started revving the engine.

'Have I said the wrong thing?' Jerry asked.

I didn't answer.

'Listen,' he said. 'If you think it's a lousy idea, let's just forget I ever mentioned it. You're not mad at me, are you?'

'I'm not mad at you, Jerry,' I said. 'It's just that it never entered my head that *we* should do it.'

'It entered mine,' he said. 'The set-up is perfect. We wouldn't even have to cross the street.' His face had gone suddenly bright and his eyes were shining like two stars. 'So what do you say, Vic?'

'I'm thinking,' I said.

'Maybe you don't fancy Samantha.'

'I don't honestly know,' I said.

'She's lots of fun,' Jerry said. 'I guarantee that.'

At this point, I saw Mary come out on to the front porch. 'There's Mary,' I said. 'She's looking for the children. We'll talk some more tomorrow.'

'Then it's a deal?'

'It could be, Jerry. But only on condition we don't rush it. I want to be dead sure everything is right before we start. Damn it all, this is a whole brand-new can of beans!'

'No, it's not!' he said. 'Your friend said it was a gas. He said it was easy.'

'Ah, yes,' I said, 'My friend. Of course. But each case is different.' I opened the throttle on the mower and went whirring away across the lawn. When I got to the far side and turned around, Jerry was already through the gap in the hedge and walking up to his front door.

The next couple of weeks was a period of high conspiracy for Jerry and me. We held secret meetings in bars and restaurants to discuss strategy, and sometimes he dropped into my office after work and we had a planning session behind the closed door. Whenever a doubtful point arose, Jerry would always say, 'How did your friend do it?' And I would play for time and say, 'I'll call him up and ask him about that one.'

After many conferences and much talk, we agreed upon the following main points:

1. That D Day should be a Saturday.

2. That on D Day evening we should take our wives out to a good dinner, the four of us together.

3. That Jerry and I should leave our houses and cross over through the gap in the hedge at precisely one a.m. Sunday morning.

4. That instead of lying in bed in the dark until one a.m. came along, we should both, as soon as our wives were asleep, go quietly downstairs to the kitchen and drink coffee.

5. That we should use the front doorbell idea if an emergency arose.

6. That the return cross-over time was fixed for two a.m.

7. That while in the wrong bed, questions (if any) from the woman must be answered by an 'Uh-uh' sounded with the lips closed tight.

8. That I myself must immediately give up cigarettes and take to a pipe so that I would 'smell' the same as Jerry.

9. That we should at once start using the same brand of hair oil and after-shave lotion.

10. That as both of us normally wore our wrist-watches in bed, and they were much the same shape, it was decided not to exchange. Neither of us wore rings.

11. That each man must have something unusual about him that the woman would identify positively with her own husband. We therefore invented what became known as 'The Sticking Plaster Ploy'. It worked like this: on D Day evening, when the couples arrived back in their own homes immediately after the dinner, each husband would make a point of going to the kitchen to cut himself a piece of cheese. At the same time, he would carefully stick a large piece of plaster over the tip of the forefinger of his right hand. Having done this, he would hold up the finger and say to his wife, 'I cut myself. It's nothing, but it was bleeding a bit.' Thus, later on, when the men

have switched beds, each woman will be made very much aware of the plaster-covered finger (the man would see to that), and will associate it directly with her own husband. An important psychological ploy, this, calculated to dissipate any tiny suspicion that might enter the mind of either female.

So much for the basic plans. Next came what we referred to in our notes as 'Familiarization with the Layout'. Jerry schooled me first. He gave me three hours' training in his own house one Sunday afternoon when his wife and children were out. I had never been into their bedroom before. On the dressing table were Samantha's perfumes, her brushes, and all her other little things. A pair of her stockings was draped over the back of a chair. Her nightdress, white and blue, was hanging behind the door leading to the bathroom.

'Okay,' Jerry said. 'It'll be pitch dark when you come in. Samantha sleeps on this side, so you must tiptoe around the end of the bed and slide in on the other side, over there. I'm going to blindfold you and let you practise.'

At first, with the blindfold on, I wandered all over the room like a drunk. But after about an hour's work, I was able to negotiate the course pretty well. But before Jerry would finally pass me out, I had to go blindfold all the way from the front door through the hall, up the stairs, past the children's rooms, into Samantha's room and finish up in exactly the right place. And I had to do it silently, like a thief. All this took three hours of hard work, but I got it in the end.

The following Sunday morning when Mary had taken our children to church, I was able to give Jerry the same sort of work-out in my house. He learned the ropes faster than me, and within an hour he had passed the blindfold test without placing a foot wrong.

It was during this session that we decided to disconnect each woman's bedside lamp as we entered the bedroom. So Jerry practised finding the plug and pulling it out with his blindfold on, and the following week-end, I was able to do the same in Jerry's house.

Now came by far the most important part of our training. We called it 'Spilling the Beans', and it was here that both of us had to describe in every detail the procedure we adopted when making love to our own wives. We agreed not to worry ourselves with any exotic variations that either of us might or might not occasionally practise. We were concerned only with teaching one another the most commonly used routine, the one least likely to arouse suspicion.

The session took place in my office at six o'clock on a Wednesday evening, after the staff had gone home. At first, we were both slightly embarrassed, and neither of us wanted to begin. So I got out the bottle of whisky, and after a couple of stiff drinks, we loosened up and the teach-in started. While Jerry talked I took notes, and vice versa. At the end of it all, it turned out that the only real difference between Jerry's routine and my own was one of tempo. But what a difference it was! He took things (if what he said was to believed) in such a leisurely fashion and he prolonged the moments to such an extravagant degree that I wondered privately to myself whether his partner did not sometimes go to sleep in the middle of it all. My job, however, was not to criticize but to copy, and I said nothing.

Jerry was not so discreet. At the end of my personal description, he had the temerity to say, 'Is that really what you do?'

'What do you mean?' I asked.

'I mean is it all over and done with as quickly as that?'

'Look,' I said. 'We aren't here to give each other lessons. We're here to learn the facts.'

'I know that,' he said. 'But I'm going to feel a bit of an ass if I copy your style exactly. My God, you go through it like an express train whizzing through a country station!'

I stared at him, mouth open.

'Don't look so surprised,' he said. 'The way you told it to me, anyone would think ...'

'Think what?' I said.

'Oh, forget it,' he said.

'Thank you,' I said. I was furious. There are two things in this world at which I happen to know I excel. One is driving an automobile and the other is you-know-what. So to have him sit there and tell me I didn't know how to behave with my own wife was a monstrous piece of effrontery. It was he who didn't know, not me. Poor Samantha. What she must have had to put up with over the years.

'I'm sorry I spoke,' Jerry said. He poured more whisky into our glasses. 'Here's to the great switcheroo!' he said. 'When do we go?'

'Today is Wednesday,' I said. 'How about this coming Saturday?'

'Christ,' Jerry said.

'We ought to do it while everything's still fresh in our minds,' I said. 'There's an awful lot to remember.'

Jerry walked to the window and looked down at the traffic in the street below. 'Okay,' he said, turning around. 'Next Saturday it shall be!' Then we drove home in our separate cars.

'Jerry and I thought we'd take you and Samantha out to dinner Saturday night,' I said to Mary. We were in the kitchen and she was cooking hamburgers for the children.

She turned around and faced me, frying-pan in one hand, spoon in the other. Her blue eyes looked straight into mine. 'My Lord, Vic,' she said. 'How nice. But what are we celebrating?'

I looked straight back at her and said, 'I thought it would be a change to see some new faces. We're always meeting the same old bunch of people in the same old houses.'

She took a step forward and kissed me on the cheek. 'What a good man you are,' she said. 'I love you.'

'Don't forget to phone the baby-sitter.'

'No, I'll do it tonight,' she said.

Thursday and Friday passed very quickly, and suddenly it was Saturday. It was D Day. I woke up feeling madly excited. After breakfast, I couldn't sit still, so I decided to go out and wash the car. I was in the middle of this when Jerry came strolling through the gap in the hedge, pipe in mouth.

'Hi, sport,' he said. 'This is the day.'

'I know that,' I said. I also had a pipe in my mouth. I was forcing myself to smoke it, but I had trouble keeping it alight, and the smoke burned my tongue.

'How're you feeling?' Jerry asked.

'Terrific,' I said. 'How about you?'

'I'm nervous,' he said.

'Don't be nervous, Jerry.'

'This is one hell of a thing we're trying to do,' he said. 'I hope we pull it off.'

I went on polishing the windshield. I had never known Jerry to be nervous of anything before. It worried me a bit.

'I'm damn glad we're not the first people ever to try it,' he said. 'If no one had ever done it before, I don't think I'd risk it.'

'I agree,' I said.

'What stops me being too nervous,' he said, 'is the fact that your friend found it so fantastically easy.'

'My friend said it was a cinch,' I said. 'But for Chris-sake, Jerry, don't be nervous when the time comes. That would be disastrous.'

'Don't worry,' he said. 'But Jesus, it's exciting, isn't it?'

'It's exciting all right,' I said.

'Listen,' he said. 'We'd better go easy on the booze tonight.'

'Good idea,' I said. 'See you at eight thirty.'

At half past eight, Samantha, Jerry, Mary, and I drove in Jerry's car to Billy's Steak House. The restaurant, despite its name, was high-class and expensive, and the girls had put on long dresses for the occasion. Samantha was wearing something green that didn't start until it was halfway down her front, and I had never seen her looking lovelier. There were candles on our table. Samantha was seated opposite me and whenever she leaned forward with her face close to the flame, I could see that tiny crest of skin at the top centre of her lower lip. 'Now,' she said as she accepted a menu from the waiter, 'I wonder what I'm going to have tonight.'

Ho-ho-ho, I thought, that's a good question.

Everything went fine in the restaurant and the girls enjoyed themselves. When we arrived back at Jerry's house, it was eleven forty-five, and Samantha said, 'Come in and have a nightcap.'

'Thanks,' I said, 'but it's a bit late. And the baby-sitter has to be driven home.' So Mary and I walked across to our house, and *now*, I told myself as I entered the front door, *from now on* the count-down begins. I must keep a clear head and forget nothing.

While Mary was paying the baby-sitter, I went to the fridge and found a piece of Canadian cheddar. I took a knife from the drawer and a strip of plaster from the cupboard. I stuck the plaster around the tip of the forefinger of my right hand and waited for Mary to turn around.

'I cut myself,' I said holding up the finger for her to see. 'It's nothing, but it was bleeding a bit.'

'I'd have thought you'd had enough to eat for the evening,' was all she said. But the plaster registered on her mind and my first little job had been done.

I drove the baby-sitter home and by the time I got back up to the bedroom it was round about midnight and Mary was already half asleep with her light out. I switched out the light on my side of the bed and went into the bathroom to undress. I pottered about in there for ten minutes or so and when I came out, Mary, as I had hoped, was well and truly sleeping. There seemed no point in getting into bed beside her. So I simply pulled back the covers a bit on my side to make it easier for Jerry, then with my slippers on, I went downstairs to the kitchen and switched on the electric kettle. It was now twelve seventeen. Forty-three minutes to go.

At twelve thirty-five, I went upstairs to check on Mary and the kids. Everyone was sound asleep.

At twelve fifty-five, five minutes before zero hour, I went up again for a final check. I went right up close to Mary's bed and whispered her name. There was no answer. Good. *That's it! Let's go!*

I put a brown raincoat over my pyjamas. I switched off the kitchen light so that the whole house was in darkness. I put the front door lock on the latch. And then, feeling an enormous sense of exhilaration, I stepped silently out into the night.

There were no lamps on our street to lighten the darkness. There was no moon or even a star to be seen. It was a black

black night, but the air was warm and there was a little breeze blowing from somewhere.

I headed for the gap in the hedge. When I got very close, I was able to make out the hedge itself and find the gap. I stopped there, waiting. Then I heard Jerry's footsteps coming toward me.

'Hi, sport,' he whispered. 'Everything okay?'

'All ready for you,' I whispered back.

He moved on. I heard his slippered feet padding softly over the grass as he went toward my house. I went toward his.

I opened Jerry's front door. It was even darker inside than out. I closed the door carefully. I took off my raincoat and hung it on the door knob. I removed my slippers and placed them against the wall by the door. I literally could not see my hands before my face. Everything had to be done by touch.

My goodness, I was glad Jerry had made me practise blind-fold for so long. It wasn't my feet that guided me now but my fingers. The fingers of one hand or another were never for a moment out of contact with something, a wall, the banister, a piece of furniture, a window-curtain. And I knew or thought I knew exactly where I was all the time. But it was an awesome eerie feeling trespassing on tiptoe through someone else's house in the middle of the night. As I fingered my way up the stairs, I found myself thinking of the burglars who had broken into our front room last winter and stolen the television set. When the police came next morning, I pointed out to them an enormous turd lying in the snow outside the garage. 'They nearly always do that,' one of the cops told me. 'They can't help it. They're scared.'

I reached the top of the stairs. I crossed the landing with my right fingertips touching the wall all the time. I started down the corridor, but paused when my hand found the door of the first children's room. The door was slightly open. I listened. I could hear young Robert Rainbow, aged eight, breathing evenly inside. I moved on. I found the door to the second children's bedroom. This one belonged to Billy, aged six and Amanda, three. I stood listening. All was well.

The main bedroom was at the end of the corridor, about

four yards on. I reached the door. Jerry had left it open, as planned. I went in. I stood absolutely still just inside the door, listening for any sign that Samantha might be awake. All was quiet. I felt my way around the wall until I reached Samantha's side of the bed. Immediately, I knelt on the floor and found the plug connecting her bedside lamp. I drew it from its socket and laid it on the carpet. Good. Much safer now. I stood up. I couldn't see Samantha, and at first I couldn't hear anything either. I bent low over the bed. Ah yes, I could hear her breathing. Suddenly I caught a whiff of the heavy musky perfume she had been using that evening, and I felt the blood rushing to my groin. Quickly I tiptoed around the big bed, keeping two fingers in gentle contact with the edge of the bed the whole way.

All I had to do now was get in. I did so, but as I put my weight upon the mattress, the creaking of the springs underneath sounded as though someone was firing a rifle in the room. I lay motionless, holding my breath. I could hear my heart thumping away like an engine in my throat. Samantha was facing away from me. She didn't move. I pulled the covers up over my chest and turned toward her. A female glow came out of her to me. Here we go, then! *Now!*

I slid a hand over and touched her body. Her nightdress was warm and silky. I rested the hand gently on her hips. Still she didn't move. I waited a minute or so, then I allowed the hand that lay upon the hip to steal onward and go exploring. Slowly, deliberately, and very accurately, my fingers began the process of setting her on fire.

She stirred. She turned on to her back. Then she murmured sleepily, 'Oh, dear ... Oh, my goodness me ... Good heavens, darling!'

I, of course, said nothing. I just kept on with the job.

A couple of minutes went by.

She was lying quite still.

Another minute passed. Then another. She didn't move a muscle.

I began to wonder how much longer it would be before she caught alight.

I persevered.

But why the silence? Why this absolute and total immobility, this frozen posture?

Suddenly it came to me. I had forgotten completely about Jerry! I was so hotted up, I had forgotten all about his own personal routine! I was doing it my way, not his! His way was far more complex than mine. It was ridiculously elaborate. It was quite unnecessary. But it was what she was used to. And now she was noticing the difference and trying to figure out what on earth was going on.

But it was too late to change direction now. I must keep going.

I kept going. The woman beside me was like a coiled spring lying there. I could feel the tension under her skin. I began to sweat.

Suddenly, she uttered a queer little groan.

More ghastly thoughts rushed through my mind. Could she be ill? Was she having a heart attack? Ought I to get the hell out quick?

She groaned again, louder this time. Then all at once, she cried out, 'Yes-yes-yes-yes-yes!' and like a bomb whose slow fuse had finally reached the dynamite, she exploded into life. She grabbed me in her arms and went for me with such incredible ferocity, I felt I was being set upon by a tiger.

Or should I say tigress?

I never dreamed a woman could do the things Samantha did to me then. She was a whirlwind, a dazzling frenzied whirlwind that tore me up by the roots and spun me around and carried me high into the heavens, to places I did not know existed.

I myself did not contribute. How could I? I was helpless. I was the palm-tree spinning in the heavens, the lamb in the claws of the tiger. It was as much as I could do to keep breathing.

Thrilling it was, all the same, to surrender to the hands of a violent woman, and for the next ten, twenty, thirty minutes – how would I know? – the storm raged on. But I have no intention here of regaling the reader with bizarre details. I do not approve of washing juicy linen in public. I am sorry, but there it is. I only hope that my reticence will not create too strong a sense of anticlimax. Certainly, there was nothing anti about my own climax, and in the final searing paroxysm I gave a shout which should have awakened the entire neighbourhood. Then I collapsed. I crumpled up like a drained wineskin.

Samantha, as though she had done no more than drink a glass of water, simply turned away from me and went right back to sleep.

Phew!

I lay still, recuperating slowly.

I had been right, you see, about that little thing on her lower lip, had I not?

Come to think of it, I had been right about more or less everything that had to do with this incredible escapade. What a triumph! I felt wonderfully relaxed and well-spent.

I wondered what time it was. My watch was not a luminous one. I'd better go. I crept out of bed. I felt my way, a trifle less cautiously this time, around the bed, out of the bedroom, along the corridor, down the stairs and into the hall of the house. I found my raincoat and slippers. I put them on. I had a lighter in the pocket of my raincoat. I used it and read the time. It was eight minutes before two. Later than I thought, I opened the front door and stepped out into the black night.

My thoughts now began to concentrate upon Jerry. Was he all right? Had he gotten away with it? I moved through the darkness toward the gap in the hedge.

'Hi, sport,' a voice whispered beside me.

'Jerry!'

'Everything okay?' Jerry asked.

'Fantastic,' I said. 'Amazing. What about you?'

'Same with me,' he said. I caught the flash of his white teeth grinning at me in the dark. 'We made it, Vic!' he whispered, touching my arm. 'You were right! It worked! It was sensational!'

'See you tomorrow,' I whispered. 'Go home.'

We moved apart. I went through the hedge and entered my house. Three minutes later, I was safely back in my own bed, and my own wife was sleeping soundly alongside me.

The next morning was Sunday. I was up at eight thirty and went downstairs in pyjamas and dressing-gown, as I always do on a Sunday, to make breakfast for the family. I had left Mary sleeping. The two boys, Victor, aged nine, and Wally, seven, were already down.

'Hi, daddy,' Wally said.

'I've got a great new breakfast,' I announced.

'What?' both boys said together. They had been into town and fetched the Sunday paper and were now reading the comics.

'We make some buttered toast and we spread orange marmalade on it,' I said. 'Then we put strips of crisp bacon on top of the marmalade.'

'*Bacon!*' Victor said. 'With *orange marmalade!*'

'I know. But you wait till you try it. It's wonderful.'

I dished out the grapefruit juice and drank two glasses of it myself. I set another on the table for Mary when she came down. I switched on the electric kettle, put the bread in the toaster, and started to fry the bacon. At this point, Mary came into the kitchen. She had a flimsy peach-coloured chiffon thing over her nightdress.

'Good morning,' I said, watching her over my shoulder as I manipulated the frying-pan.

She did not answer. She went to her chair at the kitchen table and sat down. She started to sip her juice. She looked neither at me nor at the boys. I went on frying the bacon.

'Hi, mummy,' Wally said.

She didn't answer this either.

The smell of the bacon fat was beginning to turn my stomach.

'I'd like some coffee,' Mary said, not looking around. Her voice was very odd.

'Coming right up,' I said. I pushed the frying-pan away from the heat and quickly made a cup of black instant coffee. I placed it before her.

'Boys,' she said, addressing the children, 'would you please do your reading in the other room till breakfast is ready.'

'Us?' Victor said. 'Why?'

'Because I say so.'

'Are we doing something wrong?' Wally asked.

'No, honey, you're not. I just want to be left alone for a moment with daddy.'

I felt myself shrink inside my skin. I wanted to run. I wanted to rush out the front door and go running down the street and hide.

'Get yourself a coffee, Vic,' she said, 'and sit down.' Her voice was quite flat. There was no anger in it. There was just nothing. And she still wouldn't look at me. The boys went out, taking the comic section with them.

'Shut the door,' Mary said to them.

I put a spoonful of powdered coffee into my cup and poured boiling water over it. I added milk and sugar. The silence was shattering. I crossed over and sat down in my chair opposite her. It might just as well have been an electric chair, the way I was feeling.

'Listen, Vic,' she said, looking into her coffee cup. 'I want to get this said before I lose my nerve and then I won't be able to say it.'

'For heaven's sake, what's all the drama about?' I asked. 'Has something happened?'

'Yes, Vic, it has.'

'What?'

Her face was pale and still and distant, unconscious of the kitchen around her.

'Come on, then, out with it,' I said bravely.

'You're not going to like this very much,' she said, and her big blue haunted-looking eyes rested a moment on my face, then travelled away.

'What am I not going to like very much?' I said. The sheer terror of it all was beginning to stir my bowels. I felt the same way as those burglars the cops had told me about.

'You know I hate talking about love-making and all that sort of thing,' she said. 'I've never once talked to you about it all the time we've been married.'

'That's true,' I said.

She took a sip of her coffee, but she wasn't tasting it. 'The point is this,' she said. 'I've never liked it. If you really want to know, I've hated it.'

'Hated what?' I asked.

'Sex,' she said. 'Doing it.'

'Good Lord!' I said.

'It's never given me even the slightest little bit of pleasure.'

This was shattering enough in itself, but the real cruncher was still to come, I felt sure of that.

'I'm sorry if that surprises you,' she added.

I couldn't think of anything to say, so I kept quiet.

Her eyes rose again from the coffee cup and looked into mine, watchful, as if calculating something, then fell again. 'I wasn't ever going to tell you,' she said. 'And I never would have if it hadn't been for last night.'

I said very slowly, 'What about last night?'

'Last night,' she said, 'I suddenly found out what the whole crazy thing is all about.'

'You did?'

She looked full at me now, and her face was as open as a flower. 'Yes,' she said. 'I surely did.'

I didn't move.

'Oh darling!' she cried, jumping up and rushing over and giving me an enormous kiss. 'Thank you so much for last night! You were marvellous! And I was marvellous! We were both marvellous! Don't look so embarrassed, my darling! You ought to be proud of yourself! You were fantastic! I love you! I do! I do!'

I just sat there.

She leaned close to me and put an arm around my shoulders. 'And now,' she said softly, 'Now that you have ... I don't quite know how to say this ... now that you have sort of discovered what it is I *need*, everything is going to be so marvellous from now on!'

I still sat there. She went slowly back to her chair. A big tear was running down one of her cheeks. I couldn't think why.

'I was right to tell you, wasn't I?' she said, smiling through her tears.

The Great Switcheroo

'Yes,' I said. 'Oh, yes.' I stood up and went over to the cooker so that I wouldn't be facing her. Through the kitchen window, I caught sight of Jerry crossing his garden with the Sunday paper under his arm. There was a lilt in his walk, a little prance of triumph in each pace he took, and when he reached the steps of his front porch, he ran up them two at a time.

The Last Act

Anna was in the kitchen washing a head of Boston lettuce for the family supper when the doorbell rang. The bell itself was on the wall directly above the sink, and it never failed to make her jump if it rang when she happened to be near. For this reason, neither her husband nor any of the children ever used it. It seemed to ring extra loud this time, and Anna jumped extra high.

When she opened the door, two policemen were standing outside. They looked at her out of pale waxen faces, and she looked back at them, waiting for them to say something.

She kept looking at them, but they didn't speak or move. They stood so still and so rigid that they were like two wax figures somebody had put on her doorstep as a joke. Each of them was holding his helmet in front of him in his two hands.

'What is it?' Anna asked.

They were both young, and they were wearing leather gauntlets up to their elbows. She could see their enormous motor-cycles propped up along the edge of the sidewalk behind them, and dead leaves were falling around the motor-cycles and blowing along the sidewalk and the whole of the street was brilliant in the yellow light of a clear, gusty September evening. The taller of the two policemen shifted uneasily on his feet. Then he said quietly, 'Are you Mrs Cooper, ma'am?'

'Yes, I am.'

The other said, 'Mrs Edmund J. Cooper?'

'Yes.' And then slowly it began to dawn upon her that these men, neither of whom seemed anxious to explain his presence, would not be behaving as they were unless they had some distasteful duty to perform.

'Mrs Cooper,' she heard one of them saying, and from the

way he said it, as gently and softly as if he were comforting a sick child, she knew at once that he was going to tell her something terrible. A great wave of panic came over her, and she said, 'What happened?'

'We have to inform you, Mrs Cooper ...'

The policemen paused, and the woman, watching him, felt as though her whole body were shrinking and shrinking and shrinking inside its skin.

'... that your husband was involved in an accident on the Hudson River Parkway at approximately five forty-five this evening, and died in the ambulance ...'

The policeman who was speaking produced the crocodile wallet she had given Ed on their twentieth wedding anniversary, two years back, and as she reached out to take it, she found herself wondering whether it might not still be warm from having been close to her husband's chest only a short while ago.

'If there's anything we can do,' the policeman was saying, 'like calling up somebody to come over ... some friend or relative maybe ...'

Anna heard his voice drifting away, then fading out altogether, and it must have been about then that she began to scream. Soon she became hysterical, and the two policemen had their hands full trying to control her until the doctor arrived some forty minutes later and injected something into her arm.

She was no better, though, when she woke up the following morning. Neither her doctor nor her children were able to reason with her in any way at all, and had she not been kept under almost constant sedation for the next few days, she would undoubtedly have taken her own life. In the brief lucid periods between drug-takings, she acted as though she were demented, calling out her husband's name and telling him that she was coming to join him as soon as she possibly could. It was terrible to listen to her. But in defence of her behaviour, it should be said at once that this was no ordinary husband she had lost.

Anna Greenwood had married Ed Cooper when they were both eighteen, and over the time they were together, they grew to be closer and more dependent upon each other than it is possible to describe in words. Every year that went by, their love became more intense and overwhelming, and toward the end, it had reached such a ridiculous peak that it was almost impossible for them to endure the daily separation caused by Ed's departure for the office in the mornings. When he returned at night he would rush through the house to seek her out, and she, who had heard the noise of the front door slamming, would drop everything and rush simultaneously in his direction, meeting him head on, recklessly, at full speed, perhaps halfway up the stairs, or on the landing, or between the kitchen and the hall; and as they came together, he would take her in his arms and hug her and kiss her for minutes on end as though she were yesterday's bride. It was wonderful. It was so utterly unbelievably wonderful that one is very nearly able to understand why she should have had no desire and no heart to continue living in a world where her husband did not exist any more.

Her three children, Angela (twenty), Mary (nineteen) and Billy (seventeen and a half), stayed around her constantly right from the start of the catastrophe. They adored their mother, and they certainly had no intention of letting her commit suicide if they could help it. They worked hard and with loving desperation to convince her that life could still be worth living, and it was due entirely to them that she managed in the end to come out of the nightmare and climb back slowly into the ordinary world.

Four months after the disaster, she was pronounced 'moderately safe' by the doctors, and she was able to return, albeit rather listlessly, to the old routine of running the house and doing the shopping and cooking the meals for her grown-up children.

But then what happened?

Before the snows of that winter had melted away, Angela married a young man from Rhode Island and went off to live in the suburbs of Providence.

A few months later, Mary married a fair-haired giant from a town called Slayton, in Minnesota, and away she flew for ever and ever and ever. And although Anna's heart was now beginning to break all over again into tiny pieces, she was proud to think that neither of the two girls had the slightest inkling of what was happening to her. ('Oh, Mummy, isn't it wonderful!' 'Yes, my darling, I think it's the most beautiful wedding there's ever been! I'm even more excited than you are!' etc. etc.)

And then, to put the lid on everything, her beloved Billy, who had just turned eighteen, went off to begin his first year at Yale.

So all at once, Anna found herself living in a completely empty house.

It is an awful feeling, after twenty-three years of boisterous, busy, magical family life, to come down alone to breakfast in the mornings, to sit there in silence with a cup of coffee and a piece of toast, and to wonder what you are going to do with the day that lies ahead. The room you are sitting in, which has heard so much laughter, and seen so many birthdays, so many Christmas trees, so many presents being opened, is quiet now and feels curiously cold. The air is heated and the temperature itself is normal, but the place still makes you shiver. The clock has stopped because you were never the one who wound it in the first place. A chair stands crooked on its legs, and you sit staring at it, wondering why you hadn't noticed it before. And when you glance up again, you have a sudden panicky feeling that all the four walls of the room have begun creeping in upon you very very slowly when you weren't looking.

In the beginning, she would carry her coffee cup over to the telephone and start calling up friends. But all her friends had husbands and children, and although they were always as nice and warm and cheerful as they could possibly be, they simply could not spare the time to sit and chat with a desolate lady from across the way first thing in the morning. So then she started calling up her married daughters instead.

They, also, were sweet and kind to her at all times, but Anna detected, very soon, a subtle change in their attitudes toward her. She was no longer number one in their lives. They had husbands now, and were concentrating everything upon them. Gently but firmly, they were moving their mother into the background. It was quite a shock. But she knew they were right. They were absolutely right. She was no longer entitled to impinge upon their lives or to make them feel guilty for neglecting her.

She saw Dr Jacobs regularly, but he wasn't really any help. He tried to get her to talk and she did her best, and sometimes he made little speeches to her full of oblique remarks about sex and sublimation. Anna never properly understood what he was driving at, but the burden of his song appeared to be that she should get herself another man.

She took to wandering around the house and fingering things that used to belong to Ed. She would pick up one of his shoes and put her hand into it and feel the little dents that the ball of his foot and his toes had made upon the sole. She found a sock with a hole in it, and the pleasure it gave her to darn that sock was indescribable. Occasionally, she took out a shirt, a tie, and a suit, and laid them on the bed, all ready for him to wear, and once, one rainy Sunday morning, she made an Irish stew ...

It was hopeless to go on.

So how many pills would she need to make absolutely sure of it this time? She went upstairs to her secret store and counted them. There were only nine. Was that enough? She doubted that it was. Oh, hell. The one thing she was not prepared to face all over again was failure – the rush to the hospital, the stomach-pump, the seventh floor of the Payne Whitney Pavilion, the psychiatrists, the humiliation, the misery of it all ...

In that case, it would have to be the razor-blade. But the trouble with the razor-blade was that it had to be done properly. Many people failed miserably when they tried to use the razor-blade on the wrist. In fact, nearly all of them failed. They didn't cut deep enough. There was a big artery down there somewhere that simply had to be reached. Veins were no good. Veins made plenty of mess, but they never quite managed to do the trick. Then again, the razor-blade was not an easy thing to hold, not if one had to make a firm incision, pressing it right home all the way, deep deep down. But *she* wouldn't fail. The ones who failed were the ones who actually *wanted* to fail. She wanted to succeed.

She went to the cupboard in the bathroom, searching for blades. There weren't any. Ed's razor was still there, and so was hers. But there was no blade in either of them, and no little packet lying alongside. That was understandable. Such things had been removed from the house on an earlier occasion. But there was no problem. Anyone could buy a packet of razor-blades.

She returned to the kitchen and took the calendar down from the wall. She chose September 23rd, which was Ed's birthday, and wrote r-b (for razor-blades) against the date. She did this on September 9th, which gave her exactly two weeks' grace to put her affairs in order. There was much to be done – old bills to be paid, a new will to be written, the house to be tidied up, Billy's college fees to be taken care of for the next four years, letters to the children, to her own parents, to Ed's mother, and so on and so forth.

Yet, busy as she was, she found that those two weeks, those fourteen long days, were going far too slowly for her liking. She wanted to use the blade, and eagerly every morning she counted the days that were left. She was like a child counting the days before Christmas. For wherever it was that Ed Cooper had gone when he died, even if it were only to the grave, she was impatient to join him.

It was in the middle of this two-week period that her friend Elizabeth Paoletti came calling on her at eight thirty one morning. Anna was making coffee in the kitchen at the time, and she jumped when the bell rang and jumped again when it gave a second long blast.

Liz came sweeping in through the front door, talking non-stop as usual. 'Anna, my darling woman, I need your help! Everyone's down with flu at the office. You've *got* to come! Don't argue with me! I know you can type and I know you haven't got a damn thing in the world to do all day except mope. Just grab your hat and purse and let's get going. Hurry up, girl, hurry up! I'm late as it is!'

Anna said, 'Go away, Liz. Leave me alone.'

'The cab is waiting,' Liz said.

'Please,' Anna said, 'don't try to bully me now. I'm not coming.'

'You are coming,' Liz said. 'Pull yourself together. Your days of glorious martyrdom are over.'

Anna continued to resist, but Liz wore her down, and in the end she agreed to go along just for a few hours.

Elizabeth Paoletti was in charge of an adoption society, one of the best in the city. Nine of the staff were down with flu. Only two were left, excluding herself. 'You don't know a thing about the work,' she said in the cab, 'but you're just going to have to help us all you can ...'

The office was bedlam. The telephones alone nearly drove Anna mad. She kept running from one cubicle to the next, taking messages that she did not understand. And there were girls in the waiting room, young girls with ashen stony faces, and it became part of her duty to type their answers on an official form.

'The father's name?'

'Don't know.'

'You've no idea?'

'What's the father's name got to do with it?'

'My dear, if the father is known, then his consent has to be obtained as well as yours before the child can be offered for adoption.'

'You're quite sure about that?'

'Jesus, I told you, didn't I?'

At lunchtime, somebody brought her a sandwich, but there was no time to eat it. At nine o'clock that night, exhausted and famished and considerably shaken by some of the knowledge she had acquired, Anna staggered home, took a stiff drink, fried up some eggs and bacon, and went to bed.

'I'll call for you at eight o'clock tomorrow morning,' Liz had said. 'And for God's sake be ready.' Anna was ready. And from then on she was hooked.

It was as simple as that.

All she'd needed right from the beginning was a good hard

job of work to do, and plenty of problems to solve – other people's problems instead of her own.

The work was arduous and often quite shattering emotionally, but Anna was absorbed by every moment of it, and within about – we are skipping right forward now – within about a year and half, she began to feel moderately happy once again. She was finding it more and more difficult to picture her husband vividly, to see him precisely as he was when he ran up the stairs to meet her, or when he sat across from her at supper in the evenings. The exact sound of his voice was becoming less easy to recall, and even the face itself, unless she glanced at a photograph, was no longer sharply etched in the memory. She still thought about him constantly, but she discovered that she could do so now without bursting into tears, and when she looked back on the way she had behaved a while ago, she felt slightly embarrassed. She started taking a mild interest in her clothes and in her hair, she returned to using lipstick and to shaving the hair from her legs. She enjoyed her food, and when people smiled at her, she smiled right back at them and meant it. In other words, she was back in the swim once again. She was pleased to be alive.

It was at this point that Anna had to go down to Dallas on office business.

Liz's office did not normally operate beyond state lines, but in this instance, a couple who had adopted a baby through the agency had subsequently moved away from New York and gone to live in Texas. Now, five months after the move, the wife had written to say that she no longer wanted to keep the child. Her husband, she announced, had died of a heart attack soon after they'd arrived in Texas. She herself had remarried almost at once, and her new husband 'found it impossible to adjust to an adopted baby ...'

Now this was a serious situation, and quite apart from the welfare of the child itself, there were all manner of legal obligations involved.

Anna flew down to Dallas in a plane that left New York very early, and she arrived before breakfast. After checking in at her hotel, she spent the next eight hours with the persons concerned in the affair, and by the time she had done all that could be done that day, it was around four thirty in the afternoon and she was utterly exhausted. She took a cab back to the hotel, and went up to her room. She called Liz on the phone to report the situation, then she undressed and soaked herself for a long time in a warm bath. Afterwards, she wrapped up in a towel and lay on the bed, smoking a cigarette.

Her efforts on behalf of the child had so far come to nothing. There had been two lawyers there who had treated her with absolute contempt. How she hated them. She detested their arrogance and their softly spoken hints that nothing she might do would make the slightest difference to their client. One of them kept his feet up on the table all the way through the discussion, and both of them had rolls of fat on their bellies, and the fat spilled out into their shirts like liquid and hung in huge folds over their belted trouser-tops.

Anna had visited Texas many times before in her life, but until now she had never gone there alone. Her visits had always been with Ed, keeping him company on business trips; and during those trips, he and she had often spoken about the Texans in general and about how difficult it was to like them. One could ignore their coarseness and their vulgarity. It wasn't that. But there was, it seemed, a quality of ruthlessness still surviving among these people, something quite brutal, harsh, inexorable, that it was impossible to forgive. They had no bowels of compassion, no pity, no tenderness. The only so-called virtue they possessed – and this they paraded ostentatiously and endlessly to strangers – was a kind of professional benevolence. It was plastered all over them. Their voices, their smiles, were rich and syrupy with it. But it left Anna cold. It left her quite, quite cold inside.

'Why do they love acting so tough?' she used to ask.

'Because they're children,' Ed would answer. 'They're dangerous children who go about trying to imitate their grandfathers. Their grandfathers *were* pioneers. These people aren't.'

It seemed that they lived, these present-day Texans, by a sort of egotistic will, push and be pushed. Everybody was pushing. Everybody was being pushed. And it was all very fine for a stranger in their midst to step aside and announce firmly, 'I will *not* push, and I will *not* be pushed.' That was impossible. It was especially impossible in Dallas. Of all the cities in the state, Dallas was the one that had always disturbed Anna the most. It was such a godless city, she thought, such a rapacious, gripped, iron, godless city. It was a place that had run amok with its money, and no amount of gloss and phony culture and syrupy talk could hide the fact that the great golden fruit was rotten inside.

Anna lay on the bed with her bath towel around her. She was alone in Dallas this time. There was no Ed with her now to envelope her in his incredible strength and love; and perhaps it was because of this that she began, all of a sudden, to feel slightly uneasy. She lit a second cigarette and waited for the uneasiness to pass. It didn't pass; it got worse. A hard little knot of fear was gathering itself in the top of her stomach, and there it stayed, growing bigger every minute. It was an unpleasant feeling, the kind one might experience if one were alone in the house at night and heard, or thought one heard, a footstep in the next room.

In this place there were a million footsteps, and she could hear them all.

She got off the bed and went over to the window, still wrapped in her towel. Her room was on the twenty-second floor, and the window was open. The great city lay pale and milky-yellow in the evening sunshine. The street below was solid with automobiles. The sidewalk was filled with people. Everybody was hustling home from work, pushing and being pushed. She felt the need of a friend. She wanted very badly to have someone to talk to at this moment. She would have liked a house to go to, a house with a family – a wife and husband and children and rooms full of toys, and the husband and wife would fling their arms around her at the front door and cry out, 'Anna! How marvellous to see you! How long can you stay? A week, a month, a year?'

All of a sudden, as so often happens in situations like this, her memory went *click*, and she said aloud, 'Conrad Kreuger!

Good heavens above! *He* lives in Dallas ... at least he used to ...'

She hadn't seen Conrad since they were classmates in high school, in New York. They were both about seventeen then, and Conrad had been her beau, her love, her everything. For over a year they had gone around together, and each of them had sworn eternal loyalty to the other, with marriage in the near future. Then suddenly Ed Cooper had flashed into her life, and that, of course, had been the end of the romance with Conrad. But Conrad did not seem to have taken the break too badly. It certainly couldn't have *shattered* him, because not more than a month or two later he had started going strong with another girl in the class ...

Now what was *her* name?

A big handsome bosomy girl she was, with flaming red hair and a peculiar name, a very old-fashioned name. What was it? Arabella? No, not Arabella. Ara- something, though. Araminty? Yes! Araminty it was! And what is more, within a year or so, Conrad Kreuger had married Araminty and had carried her back with him to Dallas, the place of his birth.

Anna went over to the bedside table and picked up the telephone directory.

Kreuger, Conrad P., M.D.

That was Conrad all right. He had always said he was going to be a doctor. The book gave an office number and a residence number.

Should she phone him?

Why not?

She glanced at her watch. It was five twenty. She lifted the receiver and gave the number of his office.

'Doctor Kreuger's surgery,' a girl's voice answered.

'Hello,' Anna said. 'Is Doctor Kreuger there?'

'The doctor is busy right now. May I ask who's calling?'

'Will you please tell him that Anna Greenwood telephoned him.'

'Who?'

'Anna Greenwood.'

'Yes, Miss Greenwood. Did you wish for an appointment?'

'No, thank you.'

'Is there something I can do for you?'

Anna gave the name of her hotel, and asked her to pass it
on to Dr Kreuger.

'I'll be very glad to,' the secretary said. 'Good-bye, Miss
Greenwood.'

'Good-bye,' Anna said. She wondered whether Dr Conrad
P. Kreuger would remember her name after all these years.
She believed he would. She lay back again on the bed and
began trying to recall what Conrad himself used to look like.
Extraordinarily handsome, that he was. Tall ... lean ... big-
shouldered ... with almost pure-black hair ... and a marvellous face ... a strong carved face like one of those Greek
heroes, Perseus or Ulysses. Above all, though, he had been a
very gentle boy, a serious, decent, quiet, gentle boy. He had
never kissed her much – only when he said good-bye in the
evenings. And he'd never gone in for necking, as all the
others had. When he took her home from the movies on
Saturday nights, he used to park his old Buick outside her
house and sit there in the car beside her, just talking and
talking about the future, his future and hers, and how he was
going to go back to Dallas to become a famous doctor. His
refusal to indulge in necking and all the nonsense that went
with it had impressed her no end. He respects me, she used to
say. He loves me. And she was probably right. In any event,
he had been a nice man, a nice good man. And had it not
been for the fact that Ed Cooper was a super-nice, super-good
man, she was sure she would have married Conrad Kreuger.

The telephone rang. Anna lifted the receiver. 'Yes,' she said.
'Hello.'

'Anna Greenwood?'

'Conrad Kreuger!'

'My dear Anna! What a fantastic surprise. Good gracious
me. After all these years.'

'It's a long time, isn't it.'

'It's a lifetime. Your voice sounds just the same.'

'So does yours.'

'What brings you to our fair city? Are you staying long?'

'No, I have to go back tomorrow. I hope you didn't mind my calling you.'

'Hell, no, Anna. I'm delighted. Are you all right?'

'Yes, I'm fine. I'm fine now. I had a bad time of it for a bit after Ed died ...'

'What!'

'He was killed in an automobile two and a half years ago.'

'Oh gee, Anna, I *am* sorry. How terrible. I ... I don't know what to say ...'

'Don't say anything.'

'You're okay now?'

'I'm fine. Working like a slave.'

'That's the girl ...'

'How's ... how's Araminty?'

'Oh, she's fine.'

'Any children?'

'One,' he said. 'A boy. How about you?'

'I have three, two girls and a boy.'

'Well, well, what d'you know! Now listen, Anna ...'

'I'm listening.'

'Why don't I run over to the hotel and buy you a drink? I'd like to do that. I'll bet you haven't changed one iota.'

'I look old, Conrad.'

'You're lying.'

'I feel old, too.'

'You want a good doctor?'

'Yes. I mean no. Of course I don't. I don't want any more doctors. All I need is ... well ...'

'Yes?'

'This place worries me, Conrad. I guess I need a friend. That's all I need.'

'You've got one. I have just one more patient to see, and then I'm free. I'll meet you down in the bar, the something room, I've forgotten what it's called, at six, in about half an hour. Will that suit you?'

'Yes,' she said. 'Of course. And ... thank you, Conrad.' She replaced the receiver, then got up from the bed, and began to dress.

She felt mildly flustered. Not since Ed's death had she been out and had a drink alone with a man. Dr Jacobs would be pleased when she told him about it on her return. He wouldn't congratulate her madly, but he would certainly be pleased. He'd say it was a step in the right direction, a beginning. She still went to him regularly, and now that she had gotten so much better, his oblique references had become far less oblique and he had more than once told her that her depressions and suicidal tendencies would never completely disappear until she had actually and physically 'replaced' Ed with another man.

'But it is impossible to replace a person one has loved to distraction,' Anna had said to him the last time he had brought up the subject. 'Heavens above, doctor, when Mrs Crummlin-Brown's parakeet died last month, her *parakeet*, mind you, not her husband, she was so shook up about it, she swore she'd never have another bird again!'

'Mrs Cooper,' Dr Jacobs had said, 'one doesn't normally have sexual intercourse with a parakeet.'

'Well ... no ...'

'That's why it doesn't have to be replaced. But when a husband dies, and the surviving wife is still an active and a healthy woman, she will invariably get a replacement within three years if she possibly can. And vice versa.'

Sex. It was about the only thing that sort of doctor ever thought about. He had sex on the brain.

By the time Anna had dressed and taken the elevator downstairs, it was ten minutes after six. The moment she walked into the bar, a man stood up from one of the tables. It was Conrad. He must have been watching the door. He came across the floor to meet her. He was smiling nervously. Anna was smiling, too. One always does.

'Well, well,' he said. 'Well well well,' and she, expecting the usual peck on the cheek, inclined her face upward toward his own, still smiling. But she had forgotten how formal Conrad was. He simply took her hand in his and shook it – once. 'This *is* a surprise,' he said. 'Come and sit down.'

The room was the same as any other hotel drinking-room.

It was lit by dim lights, and filled with many small tables. There was a saucer of peanuts on each table, and there were leather bench-seats all around the walls. The waiters were rigged out in white jackets and maroon pants. Conrad led her to a corner table, and they sat down facing each other. A waiter was standing over them at once.

'What will you have?' Conrad asked.

'Could I have a martini?'

'Of course. Vodka?'

'No, gin, please.'

'One gin martini,' he said to the waiter. 'No. Make it two. I've never been much of a drinker, Anna, as you probably remember, but I think this calls for a celebration.'

The waiter went away. Conrad leaned back in his chair and studied her carefully. 'You look pretty good,' he said.

'You look pretty good yourself, Conrad,' she told him. And so he did. It was astonishing how little he had aged in twenty-five years. He was just as lean and handsome as he'd ever been – in fact, more so. His black hair was still black, his eye was clear, and he looked altogether like a man who was no more than thirty years old.

'You *are* older than me, aren't you?' he said.

'What sort of a question is that?' she said, laughing. 'Yes Conrad, I am exactly one year older than you. I'm forty-two.'

'I thought you were.' He was still studying her with the utmost care, his eyes travelling all over her face and neck and shoulders. Anna felt herself blushing.

'Are you an enormously successful doctor?' she asked. 'Are you the best in town?'

He cocked his head over to one side, right over, so that the ear almost touched the top of the shoulder. It was a mannerism that Anna had always liked. 'Successful?' he said. 'Any doctor can be successful these days in a big city – financially, I mean. But whether or not I am absolutely first rate at my job is another matter. I only hope and pray that I am.'

The drinks arrived and Conrad raised his glass and said, 'Welcome to Dallas, Anna. I'm so pleased you called me up. It's good to see you again.'

'It's good to see you, too, Conrad,' she said, speaking the truth.

He looked at her glass. She had taken a huge first gulp, and the glass was now half empty. 'You prefer gin to vodka?' he asked.

'I do,' she said, 'yes.'

'You ought to change over.'

'Why?'

'Gin is not good for females.'

'It's not?'

'It's very bad for them.'

'I'm sure it's just as bad for males,' she said.

'Actually, no. It isn't nearly so bad for males as it is for females.'

'Why is it bad for females?'

'It just is,' he said. 'It's the way they're built. What kind of work are you engaged in, Anna? And what brought you all the way down to Dallas? Tell me about you.'

'Why is gin bad for females?' she said, smiling at him.

He smiled back at her and shook his head, but he didn't answer.

'Go on,' she said.

'No, let's drop it.'

'You can't leave me up in the air like this,' she said. 'It's not fair.'

After a pause, he said, 'Well, if you really want to know, gin contains a certain amount of the oil which is squeezed out of juniper berries. They use it for flavouring.'

'What does it do?'

'Plenty.'

'Yes, but what?'

'Horrible things.'

'Conrad, don't be shy. I'm a big girl now.'

He was still the same old Conrad, she thought, still as diffident, as scrupulous, as shy as ever. For that she liked him. 'If this drink is really doing horrible things to me,' she said, 'then it is unkind of you not to tell me what those things are.'

Gently, he pinched the lobe of his left ear with the thumb

and forefinger of his right hand. Then he said, 'Well, the truth of the matter is, Anna, oil of juniper has a direct inflammatory effect upon the uterus.'

'Now come on!'

'I'm not joking.'

'Mother's ruin,' Anna said. 'It's an old wives' tale.'

'I'm afraid not.'

'But you're talking about women who are pregnant.'

'I'm talking about all women, Anna.' He had stopped smiling now, and he was speaking quite seriously. He seemed to be concerned about her welfare.

'What do you specialize in?' she asked him. 'What kind of medicine? You haven't told me that.'

'Gynaecology and obstetrics.'

'Ah-ha!'

'Have you been drinking gin for many years?' he asked.

'Oh, about twenty,' Anna said.

'Heavily?'

'For heaven's sake, Conrad, stop worrying about my insides. I'd like another martini, please.'

'Of course.'

He called the waiter and said, 'One vodka martini.'

'No,' Anna said, 'gin.'

He sighed and shook his head and said, 'Nobody listens to her doctor these days.'

'You're not my doctor.'

'No,' he said. 'I'm your friend.'

'Let's talk about your wife,' Anna said. 'Is she still as beautiful as ever?'

He waited a few moments, then he said, 'Actually, we're divorced.'

'Oh, no!'

'Our marriage lasted for the grand total of two years. It was hard work to keep it going even that long.'

For some reason, Anna was profoundly shocked. 'But she was such a beautiful girl,' she said. 'What happened?'

'Everything happened, everything you could possibly think of that was bad.'

'And the child?'

'She got him. They always do.' He sounded very bitter. 'She took him back to New York. He comes to see me once a year, in the summer. He's twenty years old now. He's at Princeton.'

'Is he a fine boy?'

'He's a wonderful boy,' Conrad said. 'But I hardly know him. It isn't much fun.'

'And you never married again?'

'No, never. But that's enough about me. Let's talk about you.'

Slowly, gently, he began to draw her out on the subject of her health and the bad times she had gone through after Ed's death. She found she didn't mind talking to him about it, and she told him more or less the whole story.

'But what makes your doctor think you're not completely cured?' he said. 'You don't look very suicidal to me.'

'I don't think I am. Except that sometimes, not often, mind you, but just occasionally, when I get depressed, I have the feeling that it wouldn't take such a hell of a big push to send me over the edge.'

'In what way?'

'I kind of start edging toward the bathroom cupboard.'

'What do you have in the bathroom cupboard?'

'Nothing very much. Just the ordinary equipment a girl has for shaving her legs.'

'I see.' Conrad studied her face for a few moments, then he said, 'Is that how you were feeling just now when you called me?'

'Not quite. But I'd been thinking about Ed. And that's always a bit dangerous.'

'I'm glad you called.'

'So am I,' she said.

Anna was getting to the end of her second martini. Conrad changed the subject and began talking about his practice. She was watching him rather than listening to him. He was so damned handsome it was impossible not to watch him. She put a cigarette between her lips, then offered the pack to Conrad.

'No thanks,' he said. 'I don't.' He picked up a book of

matches from the table and gave her a light, then he blew out the match and said, 'Are those cigarettes mentholated?'

'Yes, they are.'

She took a deep drag, and blew the smoke slowly up into the air. 'Now go ahead and tell me that they're going to shrivel up my entire reproductive system,' she said.

He laughed and shook his head.

'Then why did you ask?'

'Just curious, that's all.'

'You're lying. I can tell it from your face. You were about to give me the figures for the incidence of lung cancer in heavy smokers.'

'Lung cancer has nothing to do with menthol, Anna,' he said, and he smiled and took a tiny sip of his original martini, which he had so far hardly touched. He set the glass back carefully on the table. 'You still haven't told me what work you are doing,' he went on, 'or why you came to Dallas.'

'Tell me about menthol first. If it's even half as bad as the juice of the juniper berry, I think I ought to know about it quick.'

He laughed and shook his head.

'Please!'

'No, ma'am.'

'Conrad, you simply cannot start things up like this and then drop them. It's the second time in five minutes.'

'I don't want to be a medical bore,' he said.

'You're not being a bore. These things are fascinating. Come on! Tell! Don't be mean.'

It was pleasant to be sitting there feeling moderately high on two big martinis, and making easy talk with this graceful man, this quiet, comfortable, graceful person. He was not being coy. Far from it. He was simply being his normal scrupulous self.

'Is it something shocking?' she asked.

'No. You couldn't call it that.'

'Then go ahead.'

He picked up the packet of cigarettes still lying in front of her, and studied the label. 'The point is this,' he said. 'If you inhale menthol, you absorb it into the bloodstream. And that isn't good, Anna. It does things to you. It has certain very definite effects upon the central nervous system. Doctors still prescribe it occasionally.'

'I know that,' she said. 'Nose-drops and inhalations.'

'That's one of its minor uses. Do you know the other?'

'You rub it on the chest when you have a cold.'

'You can if you like, but it wouldn't help.'

'You put it in ointment and it heals cracked lips.'

'That's camphor.'

'So it is.'

He waited for her to have another guess.

'Go ahead and tell me,' she said.

'It may surprise you a bit.'

'I'm ready to be surprised.'

'Menthol,' Conrad said, 'is a well-known anti-aphrodisiac.'

'A what?'

'It suppresses sexual desire.'

'Conrad, you're making these things up.'

'I swear to you I'm not.'

'Who uses it?'

'Very few people nowadays. It has too strong a flavour. Saltpetre is much better.'

'Ah yes. I know about saltpetre.'

'What do you know about saltpetre?'

'They give it to prisoners,' Anna said. 'They sprinkle it on their cornflakes every morning to keep them quiet.'

'They also use it in cigarettes,' Conrad said.

'You mean prisoners' cigarettes?'

'I mean *all* cigarettes.'

'That's nonsense.'

'Is it?'

'Of course it is.'

'Why do you say that?'

'Nobody would stand for it,' she said.

'They stand for cancer.'

'That's quite different, Conrad. How do you know they put saltpetre in cigarettes?'

'Have you never wondered,' he said, 'what makes a cigarette go on burning when you lay it in the ashtray? Tobacco doesn't burn of its own accord. Any pipe smoker will tell you that.'

'They use special chemicals,' she said.

'Exactly; they use saltpetre.'

'Does saltpetre burn?'

'Sure it burns. It used to be one of the prime ingredients of old-fashioned gunpowder. Fuses, too. It makes very good fuses. That cigarette of yours is a first-rate slow-burning fuse, is it not?'

Anna looked at her cigarette. Though she hadn't drawn on it for a couple of minutes, it was still smouldering away and the smoke was curling upward from the tip in a slim blue-grey spiral.

'So this has menthol in it *and* saltpetre?' she said.

'Absolutely.'

'And they're *both* anti-aphrodisiacs?'

'Yes. You're getting a double dose.'

'It's ridiculous, Conrad. It's too little to make any difference.'

He smiled but didn't answer this.

'There's not enough there to inhibit a cockroach,' she said.

'That's what you think, Anna. How many do you smoke a day?'

'About thirty.'

'Well,' he said, 'I guess it's none of my business.' He paused, and then he added, 'But you and I would be a lot better off today if it was.'

'Was what?'

'My business.'

'Conrad, what *do* you mean?'

'I'm simply saying that if you, once upon a time, hadn't suddenly decided to drop me, none of this misery would have happened to either of us. We'd still be happily married to each other.'

His face had suddenly taken on a queer sharp look.

'Drop you?'

'It was quite a shock, Anna.'

'Oh dear,' she said, 'but everybody drops everybody else at that age, don't they?'

'I wouldn't know,' Conrad said.

'You're not cross with me still, are you, for doing that?'

'Cross!' he said. 'Good God, Anna! Cross is what children get when they lose a toy! I lost a wife!'

She stared at him, speechless.

'Tell me,' he went on, 'didn't you have any idea how I felt at the time?'

'But Conrad, we were so *young*.'

'It destroyed me, Anna. It just about destroyed me.'

'But how ...'

'How what?'

'How, if it meant so much, could you turn right around and get engaged to somebody else a few weeks later?'

'Have you never heard of the rebound?' he asked.

She nodded, gazing at him in dismay.

'I was wildly in love with you, Anna.'

She didn't answer.

'I'm sorry,' he said. 'That was a silly outburst. Please forgive me.'

There was a long silence.

Conrad was leaning back in his chair, studying her from a distance. She took another cigarette from the pack, and lit it. Then she blew out the match and placed it carefully in the ashtray. When she glanced up again, he was still watching her. There was an intent, far look in his eyes.

'What are you thinking about?' she asked.

He didn't answer.

'Conrad,' she said, 'do you still hate me for doing what I did?'

'Hate you?'

'Yes, hate me. I have a queer feeling that you do. I'm sure you do, even after all these years.'

'Anna,' he said.

'Yes, Conrad?'

He hitched his chair closer to the table, and leaned forward. 'Did it ever cross your mind ...'

He stopped.

She waited.

He was looking so intensely earnest all of a sudden that she leaned forward herself.

'Did what cross my mind?' she asked.

'The fact that you and I ... that both of us ... have a bit of unfinished business.'

She stared at him.

He looked back at her, his eyes as bright as two stars. 'Don't be shocked,' he said, 'please.'

'Shocked?'

'You look as though I'd just asked you to jump out of the window with me.'

The room was full of people now, and it was very noisy. It was like being at a cocktail party. You had to shout to be heard.

Conrad's eyes waited on her, impatient, eager.

'I'd like another martini,' she said.

'Must you?'

'Yes,' she said, 'I must.'

In her whole life, she had been made love to by only one man – her husband, Ed.

And it had always been wonderful.

Three thousand times?

She thought more. Probably a good deal more. Who counts?

Assuming, though, for the sake of argument, that the exact figure (for there has to be an exact figure) was three thousand, six hundred and eighty ...

... and knowing that every single time it happened it was an act of pure, passionate, authentic love-making between the same man and the same woman ...

... then how in heaven's name could an entirely new man, an unloved stranger, hope to come in suddenly on the three thousand, six hundred and eighty-*first* time and be even half-way acceptable?

He'd be a trespasser.

All the memories would come rushing back. She would be lying there suffocated by memories.

She had raised this very point with Dr Jacobs during one of her sessions a few months back, and old Jacobs had said, 'There will be no nonsense about memories, my dear Mrs Cooper. I wish you would forget that. Only the present will exist.'

'But how do I get there?' she had said. 'How can I summon up enough nerve suddenly to go upstairs to a bedroom and take off my clothes in front of a new man, a stranger, in cold blood? ...'

'Cold blood!' he had cried. 'Good God, woman, it'll be boiling hot!' And later he had said, 'Do at any rate try to believe me, Mrs Cooper, when I tell you that any woman who has been deprived of sexual congress after more than twenty years of practice – of uncommonly frequent practice in your case, if I understand you correctly – any woman in those circumstances is going to suffer continually from severe psychological disturbances until the routine is re-established. You are feeling a lot better, I know that, but it is my duty to inform you that you are by no means back to normal ...'

To Conrad, Anna said, 'This isn't by any chance a therapeutic suggestion, is it?'

'A *what*?'

'A therapeutic suggestion.'

'What in the world do you mean?'

'It sounds exactly like a plot hatched up by my Dr Jacobs.'

'Look,' he said, and now he leaned right across the table and touched her left hand with the tip of one finger. 'When I knew you before, I was too damn young and nervous to make that sort of a proposition, much as I wanted to. I didn't think there was any particular hurry then, anyway. I figured we had a whole lifetime before us. I wasn't to know you were going to drop me.'

Her martini arrived. Anna picked it up and began to drink it fast. She knew exactly what it was going to do to her. It was going to make her float. A third martini always did that. Give her a third martini and within seconds her body would become completely weightless and she would go floating around the room like a wisp of hydrogen gas.

She sat there holding the glass with both hands as though it were a sacrament. She took another gulp. There was not much of it left now. Over the rim of her glass she could see Conrad watching her with disapproval as she drank. She smiled at him radiantly.

'You're not against the use of anaesthetics when you operate, are you?' she asked.

'Please, Anna, don't talk like that.'

'I am beginning to float,' she said.

'So I see,' he answered. 'Why don't you stop there?'

'What did you say?'

'I said, why don't you stop?'

'Do you want me to tell you why?'

'No,' he said. He made a little forward movement with his hands as though he were going to take her glass away from her, so she quickly put it to her lips and tipped it high, holding it there for a few seconds to allow the last drop to run out. When she looked at Conrad again, he was placing a ten-dollar bill on the waiter's tray, and the waiter was saying, 'Thank *you*, sir. Thank you indeed,' and the next thing she knew she was floating out of the room and across the lobby of the hotel with Conrad's hand cupped lightly under one of her elbows, steering her toward the elevators. They floated up to the twenty-second floor, and then along the corridor to the door of her bedroom. She fished the key out of her purse and unlocked the door and floated inside. Conrad followed, closing the door behind him. Then very suddenly, he grabbed hold of her and folded her up in his enormous arms and started kissing her with great gusto.

She let him do it.

He kissed her all over her mouth and cheeks and neck, taking deep breaths in between the kisses. She kept her eyes open, watching him in a queer detached sort of way, and the view she got reminded her vaguely of the blurry close-up view of a dentist's face when he is working on an upper back tooth.

Then all of a sudden, Conrad put his tongue into one of her ears. The effect of this upon her was electric. It was as though a live two-hundred-volt plug had been pushed into an empty socket, and all the lights came on and the bones began to melt

105

and the hot molten sap went running down into her limbs and she exploded into a frenzy. It was the kind of marvellous, wanton, reckless, flaming frenzy that Ed used to provoke in her so very often in the olden days by just a touch of the hand here and there. She flung her arms around Conrad's neck and started kissing him back with far more gusto than he had ever kissed her, and although he looked at first as though he thought she were going to swallow him alive, he soon recovered his balance.

Anna hadn't the faintest idea how long they stood there embracing and kissing with such violence, but it must have been for quite a while. She felt such happiness, such ... such *confidence* again at last, such sudden overwhelming confidence in herself that she wanted to tear off her clothes and do a wild dance for Conrad in the middle of the room. But she did no such foolish thing. Instead, she simply floated away to the edge of the bed and sat down to catch her breath. Conrad quickly sat down beside her. She leaned her head against his chest and sat there glowing all over while he gently stroked her hair. Then she undid one button of his shirt and slid her hand inside and laid it against his chest. Through the ribs, she could feel the beating of his heart.

'What do I see here?' Conrad said.

'What do you see where, my darling?'

'On your scalp. You want to watch this, Anna.'

'You watch it for me, dearest.'

'Seriously,' he said, 'you know what this looks like? It looks like a tiny touch of androgenic alopecia.'

'Good.'

'No, it is not good. It's actually an inflammation of the hair follicles, and it causes baldness. It's quite common on women in their later years.'

'Oh, shut up, Conrad,' she said, kissing him on the side of the neck. 'I have the most gorgeous hair.'

She sat up and pulled off his jacket. Then she undid his tie and threw it across the room.

'There's a little hook on the back of my dress,' she said. 'Undo it, please.'

Conrad unhooked the hook, then unzipped the zipper and helped her to get out of the dress. She had on a rather nice pale-blue slip. Conrad was wearing an ordinary white shirt, as doctors do, but it was now open at the neck, and this suited him. His neck had a little ridge of sinewy muscle running up vertically on either side, and when he turned his head the muscle moved under the skin. It was the most beautiful neck Anna had ever seen.

'Let's do this very very slowly,' she said. 'Let's drive ourselves crazy with anticipation.'

His eyes rested a moment on her face, then travelled away, all the way down the length of her body, and she saw him smile.

'Shall we be very stylish and dissipated, Conrad, and order a bottle of champagne? I can ask room service to bring it up, and you can hide in the bathroom when they come in.'

'No,' he said. 'You've had enough to drink already. Stand up, please.'

The tone of his voice caused her to stand up at once.

'Come here,' he said.

She went close to him. He was still sitting on the bed, and now, without getting up, he reached forward and began to take off the rest of her clothes. He did this slowly and deliberately. His face had become suddenly rather pale.

'Oh, darling,' she said, 'how marvellous! You've got that famous thing! A real thick clump of hair growing out of each of your ears! You know what that means, don't you? It's *the* absolutely positive sign of enormous virility!' She bent down and kissed him on the ear. He went on taking off her clothes – the bra, the shoes, the girdle, the pants, and finally the stockings, all of which he dropped in a heap on the floor. The moment he had peeled off her last stocking and dropped it, he turned away. He turned right away from her as though she didn't exist, and now he began to undress himself.

It was rather odd to be standing so close to him in nothing but her own skin and him not even giving her a second look. But perhaps men did these things. Ed might have been an exception. How could *she* know? Conrad took off his white

107

shirt first, and after folding it very carefully, he stood up and carried it to a chair and laid it on one of the arms. He did the same with his undershirt. Then he sat down again on the edge of the bed and started removing his shoes. Anna remained quite still, watching him. His sudden change of mood, his silence, his curious intensity, were making her a bit afraid. But they were also exciting her. There was a stealth, almost a menace in his movements, as though he were some splendid animal treading softly toward the kill. A leopard.

She became hypnotized watching him. She was watching his fingers, the surgeon's fingers, as they untied and loosened the laces of the left shoe, easing it off the foot, and placing it neatly half under the bed. The right shoe came next. Then the left sock and the right sock, both of them being folded together and laid with the utmost precision across the toes of the shoes. Finally the fingers moved up to the top of the trousers, where they undid one button and then began to manipulate the zipper. The trousers, when taken off, were folded along the creases, then carried over to the chair. The underpants followed.

Conrad, now naked, walked slowly back to the edge of the bed, and sat. Then at last, he turned his head and noticed her. She stood waiting ... and trembling. He looked her slowly up and down. Then abruptly, he shot out a hand and took her by the wrist, and with a sharp pull he had her sprawled across the bed.

The relief was enormous. Anna flung her arms around him and held on to him tightly, oh so tightly, for fear that he might go away. She was in mortal fear that he might go away and not come back. And there they lay, she holding on to him as though he were the only thing left in the world to hold on to, and he, strangely quiet, watchful, intent, slowly disentangling himself and beginning to touch her now in a number of different places with those fingers of his, those expert surgeon's fingers. And once again she flew into a frenzy.

The things he did to her during the next few moments were terrible and exquisite. He was, she knew, merely getting her ready, preparing her, or as they say in the hospital, prepping her for the operation itself, but oh God, she had never known or experienced anything even remotely like this. And it was all exceedingly quick, for in what seemed to her no more than a few seconds, she had reached that excruciating point of no return where the whole room becomes compressed into a single tiny blinding speck of light that is going to explode and tear one to pieces at the slightest extra touch. At this stage, in a swift rapacious parabola, Conrad swung his body on top of her for the final act.

And now Anna felt her passion being drawn out of her as if a long live nerve were being drawn slowly out of her body, a long live thread of electric fire, and she cried out to Conrad to go on and on and on, and as she did so, in the middle of it all, somewhere above her, she heard another voice, and this other voice grew louder and louder, more and more insistent, demanding to be heard:

'I said are you *wearing* something?' the voice wanted to know.

'Oh darling, what is it?'

'I keep asking you, are you *wearing* something?'

'Who, me?'

'There's an obstruction here. You must be wearing a diaphragm or some other appliance.'

'Of course not, darling. Everything's wonderful. Oh, do be quiet.'

'Everything is *not* wonderful, Anna.'

Like a picture on a screen, the room swam back into focus. In the foreground was Conrad's face. It was suspended above her, on naked shoulders. The eyes were looking directly into hers. The mouth was still talking.

'If you're going to use a device, then for heaven's sake learn to introduce it in the proper manner. There is nothing so aggravating as careless positioning. The diaphragm has to be placed right back against the cervix.'

'But I'm not wearing anything!'

'You're not? Well, there's still an obstruction.'

Not only the room but the whole world as well seemed slowly to be sliding away from under her now.

'I feel sick,' she said.

'You what?'

'I feel sick.'

'Don't be childish, Anna.'

'Conrad, I'd like you to go, please. Go now.'

'What on earth are you talking about?'

'Go away from me, Conrad!'

'That's ridiculous, Anna. Okay, I'm sorry I spoke. Forget it.'

'*Go away!*' she cried. '*Go away! Go away! Go away!*'

She tried to push him away from her, but he was huge and strong and he had her pinned.

'Calm yourself,' he said. 'Relax. You can't suddenly change your mind like this, in the middle of everything. And for heaven's sake, don't start weeping.'

'Leave me alone, Conrad, I beg you.'

He seemed to be gripping her with everything he had, arms and elbows, hands and fingers, thighs and knees, ankles and feet. He was like a toad the way he gripped her. He was exactly like an enormous clinging toad, gripping and grasping and refusing to let go. She had seen a toad once doing precisely this. It was copulating with a frog on a stone beside a stream, and there it sat, motionless, repulsive, with an evil yellow gleam in its eye, gripping the frog with its two powerful front paws and refusing to let go ...

'Now stop struggling, Anna. You're acting like a hysterical child. For God's sake, woman, what's eating you?'

'You're hurting me!' she cried.

'*Hurting* you?'

'It's hurting me terribly!'

She told him this only to get him away.

'You know why it's hurting?' he said.

'Conrad! Please!'

'Now wait a minute, Anna. Allow me to explain ...'

'No!' she cried. 'I've had enough explaining!'

'My dear woman ...'

'No!' She was struggling desperately to free herself, but he still had her pinned.

'The reason it hurts,' he went on, 'is that you are not manufacturing any fluid. The mucosa is virtually dry ...'

'Stop!'

'The actual name is senile atrophic vaginitis. It comes with age, Anna. That's why it's called *senile* vaginitis. There's not much one can do ...'

At that point, she started to scream. The screams were not very loud, but they were screams nevertheless, terrible, agonized stricken screams, and after listening to them for a few seconds, Conrad, in a single graceful movement, suddenly rolled away from her and pushed her to one side with both hands. He pushed her with such force that she fell on to the floor.

She climbed slowly to her feet, and as she staggered into the bathroom, she was crying 'Ed! ... Ed! ... Ed! ...' in a queer supplicating voice. The door shut.

Conrad lay very still listening to the sounds that came from behind the door. At first, he heard only the sobbing of the woman, but a few seconds later, above the sobbing, he heard the sharp metallic click of a cupboard being opened. Instantly, he sat up and vaulted off the bed and began to dress himself with great speed. His clothes, so neatly folded, lay ready at hand, and it took him no more than a couple of minutes to put them on. When that was done, he crossed to the mirror and wiped the lipstick off his face with a handkerchief. He took a comb from his pocket and ran it through his fine black hair. He walked once round the bed to see if he had forgotten anything, and then, carefully, like a man who is tiptoeing from a room where a child is sleeping, he moved out into the corridor, closing the door softly behind him.

Bitch

I have so far released for publication only one episode from
Uncle Oswald's diaries. It concerned, as some of you may
remember, a carnal encounter between my uncle and a Syrian
female leper in the Sinai Desert. Six years have gone by since
its publication and nobody has yet come forward to make
trouble. I am therefore encouraged to release a second episode
from these curious pages. My lawyer has advised against it. He
points out that some of the people concerned are still living
and are easily recognizable. He says I will be sued mercilessly.
Well, let them sue. I am proud of my uncle. He knew how life
should be lived. In a preface to the first episode I said that
Casanova's *Memoirs* read like a Parish Magazine beside Uncle
Oswald's diaries, and that the great lover himself, when compared with my uncle, appears positively undersexed. I stand
by that, and given time I shall prove it to the world. Here
then is a little episode from Volume XXIII, precisely as Uncle
Oswald wrote it:

PARIS
Wednesday

Breakfast at ten. I tried the honey. It was delivered yesterday
in an early Sèvres sucrier which had that lovely canary-coloured
ground known as *jonquille*. 'From Suzie,' the note said, 'and
thank you.' It is nice to be appreciated. And the honey was
interesting. Suzie Jolibois had, among other things, a small
farm south of Casablanca, and was fond of bees. Her hives were
set in the midst of a plantation of *cannabis indica*, and the bees
drew their nectar exclusively from this source. They lived,
those bees, in a state of perpetual euphoria and were disin-
clined to work. The honey was therefore very scarce. I spread a
third piece of toast. The stuff was almost black. It had a

112

pungent aroma. The telephone rang. I put the receiver to my ear and waited. I never speak first when called. After all, I'm not phoning them. They're phoning me.

'Oswald! Are you there?'

I knew the voice. 'Yes, Henri,' I said. 'Good morning.'

'Listen!' he said, speaking fast and sounding excited. 'I think I've got it! I'm almost certain I've got it! Forgive me if I'm out of breath, but I've just had a rather fantastic experience. It's all right now. Everything's fine. Will you come over?'

'Yes,' I said. 'I'll come over.' I replaced the receiver and poured myself another cup of coffee. Had Henri really done it at last? If he had, then I wanted to be around to share the fun.

I must pause here to tell you how I met Henri Biotte. Some three years ago I drove down to Provence to spend a summer weekend with a lady who was interesting to me simply because she possessed an extraordinarily powerful muscle in a region where other women have no muscles at all. An hour after my arrival, I was strolling alone on the lawn beside the river when a small dark man approached me. He had black hairs on the backs of his hands and he made me a little bow and said, 'Henri Biotte, a fellow guest.'

'Oswald Cornelius,' I said.

Henry Biotte was as hairy as a goat. His chin and cheeks were covered with bristly black hair and thick tufts of it were sprouting from his nostrils. 'May I join you?' he said, falling into step beside me and starting immediately to talk. And what a talker he was! How Gallic, how excitable. He walked with a mad little hop, and his fingers flew as if he wanted to scatter them to the four winds of heaven, and his words went off like firecrackers, with terrific speed. He was a Belgian chemist, he said, working in Paris. He was an olfactory chemist. He had devoted his life to the study of olfaction.

'You mean smell?' I said.

'Yes, yes!' he cried. 'Exactly! I am an expert on smells. I know more about smells than anyone else in the world!'

'Good smells or bad?' I asked, trying to slow him down.

'Good smells, lovely smells, glorious smells!' he said. 'I make them! I can make any smell you want!'

He went on to tell me he was the chief perfume blender to one of the great couturiers in the city. And his nose, he said, placing a hairy finger on the tip of his hairy proboscis, probably looked just like any other nose, did it not? I wanted to tell him it had more hairs sprouting from the noseholes than wheat from the prairies and why didn't he get his barber to snip them out, but instead I confessed politely that I could see nothing unusual about it.

'Quite so,' he said. 'But in actual fact it is a smelling organ of phenomenal sensitivity. With two sniffs it can detect the presence of a single drop of macroylic musk in a gallon of geranium oil.'

'Extraordinary,' I said.

'On the Champs Elysées,' he went on, 'which is a wide thoroughfare, my nose can identify the precise perfume being used by a woman walking on the other side of the street.'

'With the traffic in between?'

'With heavy traffic in between,' he said.

He went on to name two of the most famous perfumes in the world, both of them made by the fashion-house he worked for. 'Those are my personal creations,' he said modestly. 'I blended them myself. They have made a fortune for the celebrated old bitch who runs the business.'

'But not for you?'

'Me! I am but a poor miserable employee on a salary,' he said, spreading his palms and hunching his shoulders so high they touched his earlobes. 'One day, though, I shall break away and pursue my dream.'

'You have a dream?'

'I have a glorious, tremendous, exciting dream, my dear sir!'

'Then why don't you pursue it?'

'Because first I must find a man farsighted enough and wealthy enough to back me.'

Ah-ha, I thought, so that's what it's all about. 'With a reputation like yours, that shouldn't be too difficult,' I said.

'The sort of rich man I seek is hard to find,' he said. 'He must be a sporty gambler with a very keen appetite for the bizarre.'

That's me, you clever little bugger, I thought. 'What is this dream you wish to pursue?' I asked him. 'Is it making perfumes?'

'My dear fellow!' he cried. 'Anyone can make *perfumes*! I'm talking about *the* perfume! The *only* one that counts!'

'Which would that be?'

'Why, the *dangerous* one, of course! And when I have made it, I shall rule the world!'

'Good for you,' I said.

'I am not joking, Monsieur Cornelius. Would you permit me to explain what I am driving at?'

'Go ahead.'

'Forgive me if I sit down,' he said, moving toward a bench. 'I had a heart attack last April and I have to be careful.'

'I'm sorry to hear that.'

'Oh, don't be sorry. All will be well so long as I don't overdo things.'

It was a lovely afternoon and the bench was on the lawn near the riverbank and we sat down on it. Beside us, the river flowed slow and smooth and deep, and there were little clouds of waterflies hovering over the surface. Across the river there were willows along the bank and beyond the willows an emerald-green meadow, yellow with buttercups, and a single cow grazing. The cow was brown and white.

'I will tell you what kind of perfume I wish to make,' he said. 'But it is essential I explain a few other things to you on the way or you will not fully understand. So please bear with me a while.' One hand lay limp upon his lap, the hairy part upward. It looked like a black rat. He was stroking it gently with the fingers of the other hand.

'Let us consider first,' he said, 'the phenomenon that occurs when a dog meets a bitch in heat. The dog's sexual drive is tremendous. All self-control disappears. He has only one thought in his head, which is to fornicate on the spot, and unless he is prevented by force, he will do so. But do you

115

know what it is that causes this tremendous sex-drive in a dog?'

'Smell,' I said.

'Precisely, Monsieur Cornelius. Odorous molecules of a special conformation enter the dog's nostrils and stimulate his olfactory nerve-endings. This causes urgent signals to be sent to the olfactory bulb and thence to the higher brain centres. It is *all* done by smell. If you sever a dog's olfactory nerve, he will lose interest in sex. This is also true of many other mammals, but it is not true of man. Smell has nothing to do with the sexual appetite of the human male. He is stimulated in this respect by sight, by tactility, and by his lively imagination. Never by smell.'

'What about perfume?' I said.

'It's all rubbish!' he answered. 'All those expensive scents in small bottles, the ones I make, they have no aphrodisiac effect at all upon a man. Perfume was never intended for that purpose. In the old days, women used it to conceal the fact that they stank. Today, when they no longer stink, they use it purely for narcissistic reasons. They enjoy putting it on and smelling their own good smells. Men hardly notice the stuff. I promise you that.'

'I do,' I said.

'Does it stir you physically?'

'No, not physically. Aesthetically, yes.'

'You enjoy the smell. So do I. But there are plenty of other smells I enjoy more – the bouquet of a good Lafite, the scent of a fresh Comice pear, or the smell of the air blowing in from the sea on the Brittany coast.'

A trout jumped high in midstream and the sunlight flashed on its body. 'You must forget,' said Monsieur Biotte, 'all the nonsense about musk and ambergris and the testicular secretions of the civet cat. We make our perfumes from chemicals these days. If I want a musky odour I will use ethylene sebacate. Phenylacetic acid will give me civet and benzaldehyde will provide the smell of almonds. No sir, I am no longer interested in mixing up chemicals to make pretty smells.'

For some minutes his nose had been running slightly, wetting the black hairs in his nostrils. He noticed it and produced a handkerchief and gave it a blow and a wipe. 'What I intend to do,' he said, 'is to produce a perfume which will have the same electrifying effect upon a man as the scent of a bitch in heat has upon a dog! One whiff and that'll be it! The man will lose all control. He'll rip off his pants and ravish the lady on the spot!'

'We could have some fun with that,' I said.

'We could rule the world!' he cried.

'Yes, but you told me just now that smell has nothing to do with the sexual appetite of the human male.'

'It doesn't,' he said. 'But it used to. I have evidence that in the period of the post-glacial drift, when primitive man was far more closely related to the ape than he is now, he still retained the ape-like characteristic of jumping on any right-smelling female he ran across. And later, in the Palaeolithic and Neolithic periods, he continued to become sexually animated by smell, but to a lesser and lesser degree. By the time the higher civilizations had come along in Egypt and China around 10,000 B.C., evolution had played its part and had completely suppressed man's ability to be stimulated sexually by smell. Am I boring you?'

'Not at all. But tell me, does that mean an actual physical change has taken place in man's smelling apparatus?'

'Absolutely not,' he said, 'otherwise there'd be nothing we could do about it. The little mechanism that enabled our ancestors to smell these subtle odours is still there. I happen to know it is. Listen, you've seen how some people can make their ears move a tiny bit?'

'I can do it myself,' I said, doing it.

'You see,' he said, 'the ear-moving muscle is still there. It's a leftover from the time when man used to be able to cock his ears forward for better hearing, like a dog. He lost that ability over a hundred thousand years ago, but the muscle remains. And the same applies to our smelling apparatus. The mechanism for smelling those secret smells is still there, but we have lost the ability to use it.'

'How can you be so certain it's still there?' I asked.

'Do you know how our smelling system works?' he said.

'Not really.'

'Then I shall tell you, otherwise I cannot answer your question. Attend closely, please. Air is sucked in through the nostrils and passes the three baffle-shaped turbinate bones in the upper part of the nose. There it gets warmer and filtered. This warm air now travels up and over two clefts that contain the smelling organs. These organs are patches of yellowish tissue, each about an inch square. In this tissue are embedded the nerve-fibres and nerve-endings of the olfactory nerve. Every nerve-ending consists of an olfactory cell bearing a cluster of tiny hair-like filaments. These filaments act as receivers. "Receptors" is a better word. And when the receptors are tickled or stimulated by odorous molecules, they send signals to the brain. If, as you come downstairs in the morning, you sniff into your nostrils the odorous molecules of frying bacon, these will stimulate your receptors, the receptors will flash a signal along the olfactory nerve to the brain, and the brain will interpret it in terms of the character and intensity of the odour. And that is when you cry out, "Ah-ha, bacon for breakfast!"'

'I never eat bacon for breakfast,' I said.

He ignored this.

'These receptors,' he went on, 'these tiny hairlike filaments are what concern us. And now you are going to ask me how on earth they can tell the difference between one odorous molecule and another, between say peppermint and camphor?'

'How can they?' I said. I was interested in this.

'Attend more closely than ever now, please,' he said. 'At the end of each receptor is an indentation, a sort of cup, except that it isn't round. This is the "receptor site". Imagine now thousands of these little hair-like filaments with tiny cups at their extremities, all waving about like the tendrils of sea anemones and waiting to catch in their cups any odorous molecules that pass by. That, you see, is what actually happens. When you sniff a certain smell, the odorous molecules of the substance which made that smell go rushing around inside your nostrils and get caught by the little cups, the receptor sites. Now the important thing to remember is this. Molecules come in all shapes and sizes. Equally, the little cups or receptor sites are also differently shaped. Thus, the molecules lodge only in the receptor sites which fit them. Pepperminty molecules go only into special pepperminty receptor sites. Camphor molecules, which have a quite different shape, will fit only into the special camphor receptor sites, and so on. It's rather like those toys for small children where they have to fit variously shaped pieces into the right holes.'

'Let me see if I understand you,' I said. 'Are you saying that my brain will know it is a pepperminty smell simply because the molecule has lodged in a pepperminty reception site?'

'Precisely.'

'But you are surely not suggesting there are differently shaped receptor sites for every smell in the world?'

'No,' he said, 'as a matter of fact, man has only seven differently shaped sites.'

'Why only seven?'

'Because our sense of smell recognizes only seven "pure primary odours". All the rest are "complex odours" made up by mixing the primaries.'

'Are you sure of that?'

'Positive. Our sense of taste has even less. It recognizes only four primaries – sweet, sour, salt, and bitter! All other tastes are mixtures of these.'

'What are the seven pure primary odours?' I asked him.

'Their names are of no importance to us,' he said. 'Why confuse the issue.'

'I'd like to hear them.'

'All right,' he said. 'They are camphoraceous, pungent, musky, ethereal, floral, pepperminty, and putrid. Don't look so sceptical, please. This isn't *my* discovery. Very learned scientists have worked on it for years. And their conclusions are quite accurate, *except in one respect.*'

'What's that?'

'*There is an eighth pure primary odour which they don't know about, and an eighth receptor site to receive the curiously shaped molecules of that odour!*'

'Ah-ha-ha!' I said. 'I see what you're driving at.'

'Yes,' he said, 'the eighth pure primary odour is the sexual stimulant that caused primitive man to behave like a dog thousands of years ago. It has a very peculiar molecular structure.'

'Then you know what it is?'

'Of course I know what it is.'

'And you say we still retain the receptor sites for these peculiar molecules to fit in to?'

'Absolutely.'

'This mysterious smell,' I said, 'does it ever reach our own nostrils nowadays?'

'Frequently.'

'Do we smell it? I mean, are we aware of it?'

'No.'

'You mean the molecules don't get caught in the receptor sites?'

'They do, my dear fellow, they do. But nothing happens. No signal is sent off to the brain. The telephone line is out of action. It's like that ear muscle. The mechanism is still there, but we've lost the ability to use it properly.'

'And what do you propose to do about that?' I asked.

'I shall reactivate it,' he said. 'We are dealing with nerves here, not muscles. And these nerves are not dead or injured, they're merely dormant. I shall probably increase the intensity of the smell a thousandfold, and add a catalyst.'

'Go on,' I said.

'That's enough.'

'I should like to hear more,' I said.

'Forgive me for saying so Monsieur Cornelius, but I don't think you know enough about organoleptic quality to follow me any further. The lecture is over.'

Henri Biotte sat smug and quiet on the bench beside the river stroking the back of one hand with the fingers of the other. The tufts of hair sprouting from his nostrils gave him a pixie look, but that was camouflage. He struck me rather as a dangerous and dainty little creature, someone who lurked behind stones with a sharp eye and a sting in his tail, waiting for the lone traveller to come by. Surreptitiously I searched his face. The mouth interested me. The lips had a magenta tinge, possibly something to do with his heart trouble. The lower lip was caruncular and pendulous. It bulged out in the middle like a purse, and could easily have served as a receptacle for small coins. The skin of the lip seemed to be blown up very tight, as though by air, and it was constantly wet, not from licking but from an excess of saliva in the mouth.

And there he sat, this Monsieur Henri Biotte, smiling a wicked little smile and waiting patiently for me to react. He was a totally amoral man, that much was clear, but then so was I. He was also a wicked man, and although I cannot in all honesty claim wickedness as one of my own virtues, I find it irresistible in others. A wicked man has a lustre all his own. Then again, there was something diabolically splendid about a person who wished to set back the sex habits of civilized man half a million years.

Yes, he had me hooked. So there and then, sitting beside the river in the garden of the lady from Provence, I made an offer to Henri. I suggested he should leave his present employment forthwith and set himself up in a small laboratory. I would pay all the bills for this little venture as well as making good his salary. It would be a five-year contract, and we would go fifty-fifty on anything that came out of it.

Henri was ecstatic. 'You mean it?' he cried. 'You are serious?'

I held out my hand. He grasped it in both of his and shook it vigorously. It was like shaking hands with a yak. 'We shall control mankind!' he said. 'We'll be the gods of the earth!' He flung his arms around me and embraced me and kissed me first on one cheek, then on the other. Oh, this awful Gallic kissing. Henry's lower lip felt like the wet underbelly of a toad against my skin. 'Let's keep the celebrations until later,' I said, wiping myself dry with a linen handkerchief.

Henri Biotte made apologies and excuses to his hostess and rushed back to Paris that night. Within a week he had given up his old job and had rented three rooms to serve as a laboratory. These were on the third floor of a house on the Left Bank, on the Rue de Cassette, just off the Boulevard Raspaille.

121

Bitch

He spent a great deal of my money equipping the place with complicated apparatus, and he even installed a large cage into which he put two apes, a male and a female. He also took on an assistant, a clever and moderately presentable young lady called Jeanette. And with all that, he set to work.

You should understand that for me this little venture was of no great importance. I had plenty of other things to amuse me. I used to drop in on Henri maybe a couple of times a month to see how things were going, but otherwise I left him entirely to himself. My mind wasn't on his job. I hadn't the patience for that kind of research. And when results failed to come quickly, I began to lose all interest. Even the pair of over-sexed apes ceased to amuse me after a while.

Only once did I derive any pleasure from my visits to his laboratory. As you must know by now, I can seldom resist even a moderately presentable woman. And so, on a certain rainy Thursday afternoon, while Henri was busy applying electrodes to the olfactory organs of a frog in one room, I found myself applying something infinitely more agreeable to Jeanette in the other room. I had not, of course, expected anything out of the ordinary from this little frolic. I was acting more out of habit than anything else. But my goodness, what a surprise I got! Beneath her white overall, this rather austere research chemist turned out to be a sinewy and flexible female of immense dexterity. The experiments she performed, first with the oscillator, then with the high-speed centrifuge, were absolutely breathtaking. In fact, not since that Turkish tightrope walker in Ankara (see Vol. XXI) had I experienced anything quite like it. Which all goes to show for the thousandth time that women are as inscrutable as the ocean. You never know what you have under your keel, deep water or shallow, until you have heaved the lead.

I did not bother to visit the laboratory again after that. You know my rule. I never return to a female a second time. With me at any rate, women invariably pull out all the stops during the first encounter, and a second meeting can therefore be nothing more than the same old tune on the same old fiddle. Who wants that? Not me. So when I suddenly heard

Henri's voice calling urgently to me over the telephone that morning at breakfast, I had almost forgotten his existence.

I drove through the fiendish Paris traffic to the Rue de Cassette. I parked the car and took the tiny elevator to the third floor. Henri opened the door of the laboratory. 'Don't move!' he cried. 'Stay right where you are!' He scuttled away and returned in a few seconds holding a little tray upon which lay two greasy-looking red rubber objects. 'Noseplugs,' he said. 'Put them in, please. Like me. Keep out the molecules. Go on, ram them in tight. You'll have to breathe through your mouth, but who cares?'

Each noseplug had a short length of blue string attached to its blunt lower end, presumably for pulling it back out of the nostril. I could see the two bits of blue string dangling from Henri's nostrils. I inserted my own noseplugs. Henry inspected them. He rammed them in tighter with his thumb. Then he went dancing back into the lab, waving his hairy hands and crying out, 'Come in now, my dear Oswald! Come in, come in! Forgive my excitement, but this is a great day for me!' The plugs in his nose made him speak as though he had a bad cold. He hopped over to a cupboard and reached inside. He brought out one of those small square bottles made of very thick glass that hold about an ounce of perfume. He carried it over to where I stood, cupping his hands around it as though it were a tiny bird. 'Look! Here it is! The most precious fluid in the entire world!'

This is the sort of rubbishy overstatement I dislike intensely. 'So you think you've done it?' I said.

'I know I've done it, Oswald! I am certain I've done it!'

'Tell me what happened.'

'That's not so easy,' he said. 'But I can try.'

He placed the little bottle carefully on the bench. 'I had left this particlar blend, Number 1076, to distil overnight,' he went on. 'That was because only one drop of distillate is produced every half hour. I had it dripping into a sealed beaker to prevent evaporation. All these fluids are extremely volatile. And so, soon after I arrived at eight thirty this morning, I went over to Number 1076 and lifted the seal from the beaker. I took a tiny sniff. Just one tiny sniff. Then I replaced the seal.'

'And then?'

'Oh, my God, Oswald, it was fantastic! I completely lost control of myself! I did things I would never in a million years have dreamed of doing!'

'Such as what?'

'My dear fellow, I went completely wild! I was like a wild beast, an animal! I was not human! The civilizing influences of centuries simply dropped away! I was Neolithic!'

'What did you do?'

'I can't remember the next bit very clearly. It was all so quick and violent. But I became overwhelmed by the most terrifying sensation of lust it is possible to imagine. Everything else was blotted out of my mind. All I wanted was a woman. I felt that if I didn't get hold of a woman immediately, I would explode.'

'Lucky Jeanette,' I said, glancing toward the next room. 'How is she now?'

'Jeanette left me over a year ago,' he said. 'I replaced her with a brilliant young chemist called Simone Gautier.'

'Lucky Simone, then.'

'No, no!' Henri cried. 'That was the awful thing! She hadn't arrived! Today of all days, she was late for work! I began to go mad. I dashed out into the corridor and down the stairs. I was like a dangerous animal. I was hunting for a woman, any woman, and heaven help her when I found her!'

'And who did you find?'

'Nobody, thank God. Because suddenly, I regained my senses. The effect had worn off. It was very quick, and I was standing alone on the second-floor landing. I felt cold. But I knew at once exactly what had happened. I ran back upstairs and re-entered this room with my nostrils pinched tightly between finger and thumb. I went straight to the drawer where I stored the noseplugs. Ever since I started working on this project, I have kept a supply of noseplugs ready for just such an occasion. I rammed in the plugs. Now I was safe.'

'Can't the molecules get up into the nose through the mouth?' I asked him.

'They can't reach the receptor sites,' he said. 'That's why you can't smell through your mouth. So I went over to the apparatus and switched off the heat. I then transferred the tiny quantity of precious fluid from the beaker to this very solid airtight bottle you see here. In it there are precisely eleven cubic centimetres of Number 1076.'

'Then you telephoned me.'

'Not immediately, no. Because at that point, Simone arrived. She took one look at me and ran into the next room, screaming.'

'Why did she do that?'

'My God, Oswald, I was standing there stark naked and I hadn't realized it. I must have ripped off all my clothes!'

'Then what?'

'I got dressed again. After that, I went and told Simone exactly what had happened. When she heard the truth, she became as excited as me. Don't forget, we've been working on this together for over a year now.'

'Is she still here?'

'Yes. She's next door in the other lab.'

It was quite a story Henri had told me. I picked up the little square bottle and held it against the light. Through the thick glass I could see about half an inch of fluid, pale and pinkish-grey, like the juice of a ripe quince.

'Don't drop it,' Henri said. 'Better put it down.' I put it down. 'The next step,' he went on, 'will be to make an accurate test under scientific conditions. For that I shall have to spray a measured quantity on to a woman and then let a man approach her. It will be necessary for me to observe the operation at close range.'

'You are a dirty old man,' I said.

'I am an olfactory chemist,' he said primly.

'Why don't I go out into the street with my noseplugs in,' I said, 'and spray some on to the first woman who comes along. You can watch from the window here. It ought to be fun.'

'It would be fun all right,' Henri said. 'But not very scientific. I must make the tests indoors under controlled conditions.'

'And I will play the male part,' I said.

'No, Oswald.'

'What do you mean, no. I insist.'

'Now listen to me,' Henri said. 'We have not yet found out what will happen when a woman is present. This stuff is very powerful, I am certain of that. And you, my dear sir, are not exactly young. It could be extremely dangerous. It could drive you beyond the limit of your endurance.'

I was stung. 'There are no limits to my endurance,' I said.

'Rubbish,' Henri said. 'I refuse to take chances. That is why I have engaged the fittest and strongest young man I could find.'

'You mean you've already done this?'

'Certainly I have,' Henri said. 'I am excited and impatient. I want to get on. The boy will be here any minute.'

'Who is he?'

'A professional boxer.'

'Good God.'

'His name is Pierre Lacaille. I am paying him one thousand francs for the job.'

'How did you find him?'

'I know a lot more people than you think, Oswald. I am not a hermit.'

'Does the man know what he's in for?'

'I have told him that he is to participate in a scientific experiment that has to do with the psychology of sex. The less he knows the better.'

'And the woman? Who will you use there?'

'Simone, of course,' Henri said. 'She is a scientist in her own right. She will be able to observe the reactions of the male even more closely than me.'

'That she will,' I said. 'Does she realize what might happen to her?'

'Very much so. And I had one hell of a job persuading her to do it. I had to point out that she would be participating in a demonstration that will go down in history. It will be talked about for hundreds of years.'

'Nonsense,' I said.

'My dear sir, through the centuries there are certain great

epic moments of scientific discovery that are never forgotten. Like the time when Dr Horace Wells of Hartford, Connecticut, had a tooth pulled out in 1844.'

'What was so historic about that?'

'Dr Wells was a dentist who had been playing about with nitrous oxide gas. One day, he got a terrible toothache. He knew the tooth would have to come out, and he called in another dentist to do the job. But first he persuaded his colleague to put a mask over his face and turn on the nitrous oxide. He became unconscious and the tooth was extracted and he woke up again as fit as a flea. Now *that*, Oswald, was the first operation ever performed in the world under general anaesthesia. It started something big. We shall do the same.'

At this point, the doorbell rang. Henri grabbed a pair of noseplugs and carried them with him to the door. And there stood Pierre, the boxer. But Henri would not allow him to enter until the plugs were rammed firmly up his nostrils. I believe the fellow came thinking he was going to act in a blue film, but the business with the plugs must have quickly disillusioned him. Pierre Lacaille was a bantamweight, small, muscular, and wiry. He had a flat face and a bent nose. He was about twenty-two and not very bright.

Henri introduced me, then ushered us straight into the adjoining laboratory where Simone was working. She was standing by the lab bench in a white overall, writing something in a notebook. She looked up at us through thick glasses as we came in. The glasses had a white plastic frame.

'Simone,' Henri said, 'this is Pierre Lacaille.' Simone looked at the boxer but said nothing. Henri didn't bother to introduce me.

Simone was a slim thirtyish woman with a pleasant scrubbed face. Her hair was brushed back and plaited into a bun. This, together with the white spectacles, the white overall, and the white skin of her face, gave her a quaint antiseptic air. She looked as though she had been sterilised for thirty minutes in an autoclave and should be handled with rubber gloves. She gazed at the boxer with large brown eyes.

'Let's get going,' Henri said. 'Are you ready?'

'I don't know what's going to happen,' the boxer said. 'But I'm ready.' He did a little dance on his toes.

Henri was also ready. He had obviously worked the whole thing out before I arrived. 'Simone will sit in that chair,' he said, pointing to a plain wooden chair set in the middle of the laboratory. 'And you, Pierre, will stand on the six-metre mark with your noseplugs still in.'

There were chalk lines on the floor indicating various distances from the chair, from half a metre up to six metres.

'I shall begin by spraying a small quantity of liquid on to the lady's neck,' Henri went on addressing the boxer. 'You will then remove your noseplugs and start walking slowly toward her.' To me he said, 'I wish first of all to discover the effective range, the exact distance he is from the subject when the molecules hit.'

'Does he start with his clothes on?' I asked.

'Exactly as he is now.'

'And is the lady expected to cooperate or to resist?'

'Neither. She must be a purely passive instrument in his hands.'

Simone was still looking at the boxer. I saw her slide the end of her tongue slowly over her lips.

'This perfume,' I said to Henri, 'does it have any effect upon a woman?'

'None whatsoever,' he said. 'That is why I am sending Simone out now to prepare the spray.' The girl went into the main laboratory, closing the door behind her.

'So you spray something on the girl and I walk toward her,' the boxer said. 'What happens then?'

'We shall have to wait and see,' Henri said. 'You are not worried, are you?'

'Me, worried?' the boxer said. 'About a woman?'

'Good boy,' Henri said. Henri was becoming very excited. He went hopping from one end of the room to the other, checking and rechecking the position of the chair on its chalk mark and moving all breakables such as glass beakers and bottles and test-tubes off the bench on to a high shelf. 'This isn't the ideal place,' he said, 'but we must make the best of it.'

He tied a surgeon's mask over the lower part of his face, then handed one to me.

'Don't you trust the noseplugs?'

'It's just an extra precaution,' he said. 'Put it on.'

The girl returned carrying a tiny stainless-steel spray-gun. She gave the gun to Henri. Henri took a stop watch from his pocket. 'Get ready, please,' he said. 'You Pierre, stand over there on the six-metre mark.' Pierre did so. The girl seated herself in the chair. It was a chair without arms. She sat very prim and upright in her spotless white overall with her hands folded on her lap, her knees together. Henri stationed himself behind the girl. I stood to one side. 'Are we ready?' Henri cried.

'Wait,' said the girl. It was the first word she had spoken. She stood up, removed her spectacles, placed them on a high shelf, then returned to her seat. She smoothed the white overall along her thighs, then clasped her hands together and laid them again on her lap.

'Are we ready now?' Henri said.

'Let her have it,' I said. 'Shoot.'

Henri aimed the little spray-gun at an area of bare skin just below Simone's ear. He pulled the trigger. The gun made a soft hiss and a fine misty spray came out of its nozzle.

'Pull your noseplugs out!' Henri called to the boxer as he skipped quickly away from the girl and took up a position next to me. The boxer caught hold of the strings dangling from his nostrils and pulled. The vaselined plugs slid out smoothly.

'Come on, come on!' Henri shouted. 'Start moving! Drop the plugs on the floor and come forward slowly!' The boxer took a pace forward. 'Not so fast!' Henri cried. 'Slowly does it! That's better! Keep going! Keep going! Don't stop!' He was crazy with excitement, and I must admit I was getting a bit worked up myself. I glanced at the girl. She was crouching in the chair, just a few yards away from the boxer, tense, motionless, watching his every move, and I found myself thinking about a white female rat I had once seen in a cage with a huge python. The python was going to swallow the rat and the rat knew it, and the rat was crouching very low and still,

129

hypnotized, transfixed, utterly fascinated by the slow advancing movements of the snake.

The boxer edged forward.

As he passed the five-metre mark, the girl unclasped her hands. She laid them palms downwards on her thighs. Then she changed her mind and placed them more or less underneath her buttocks, gripping the seat of the chair on either side, bracing herself, as it were, against the coming onslaught.

The boxer had just passed the two-metre mark when the smell hit him. He stopped dead. His eyes glazed and he swayed on his legs as though he had been tapped on the head with a mallet. I thought he was going to keel over, but he didn't. He stood there swaying gently from side to side like a drunk. Suddenly he started making noises through his nostrils, queer little snorts and grunts that reminded me of a pig sniffing around its trough. Then without any warning at all, he sprang at the girl. He ripped off her white overall, her dress, and her underclothes. After that, all hell broke loose.

There is little point in describing exactly what went on during the next few minutes. You can guess most of it anyway. I do have to admit, though, that Henri had probably been right in choosing an exceptionally fit and healthy young man. I hate to say it, but I doubt my middle-aged body could have stood up to the incredibly violent gymnastics the boxer seemed driven to perform. I am not a voyeur. I hate that sort of thing. But in this case, I stood there absolutely transfixed. The sheer animal ferocity of the man was frightening. He was like a wild beast. And right in the middle of it all, Henri did an interesting thing. He produced a revolver and rushed up to the boxer and shouted, 'Get away from that girl! Leave her alone or I'll shoot you!' The boxer ignored him, so Henri fired a shot just over the top of his head and yelled, 'I mean it, Pierre! I shall kill you if you don't stop!' The boxer didn't even look up.

Henri was hopping and dancing about the room and shouting, 'It's fantastic! It's magnificent! Unbelievable! It works! It works! We've done it, my dear Oswald! We've done it!'

The action stopped as quickly as it had begun. The boxer

suddenly let go of the girl, stood up, blinked a few times, and then said, 'Where the hell am I? What happened?'

Simone, who seemed to have come through it all with no bones broken, jumped up, grabbed her clothes, and ran into the next room. 'Thank you, mademoiselle,' said Henri as she flew past him.

The interesting thing was that the bemused boxer hadn't the faintest idea what he had been doing. He stood there naked and covered with sweat, gazing around the room and trying to figure out how in the world he came to be in that condition.

'What did I do?' he asked. 'Where's the girl?'

'You were terrific!' Henri shouted, throwing him a towel. 'Don't worry about a thing! The thousand francs is all yours!'

Just then the door flew open and Simone, still naked, ran back into the lab. 'Spray me again!' she cried. 'Oh, Monsieur Henri, spray me just one more time!' Her face was alight, her eyes shining brilliantly.

'The experiment is over,' Henri said. 'Go away and dress yourself.' He took her firmly by the shoulders and pushed her back into the other room. Then he locked the door.

Half an hour later, Henri and I sat celebrating our success in a small café down the street. We were drinking coffee and brandy. 'How long did it go on?' I asked.

'Six minutes and thirty-two seconds,' Henri said.

I sipped my brandy and watched the people strolling by on the sidewalk. 'What's the next move?'

'First, I must write up my notes,' Henri said. 'Then we shall talk about the future.'

'Does anyone else know the formula?'

'Nobody.'

'What about Simone?'

'She doesn't know it.'

'Have you written it down?'

'Not so anyone else could understand it. I shall do that tomorrow.'

'Do it first thing,' I said. 'I'll want a copy. What shall we call the stuff? We need a name.'

'What do you suggest?'

'*Bitch*,' I said. 'Let's call it *Bitch*.' Henri smiled and nodded his head slowly. I ordered more brandy. 'It would be great stuff for stopping a riot,' I said. 'Much better than tear-gas. Imagine the scene if you sprayed it on an angry mob.'

'Nice,' Henri said. 'Very nice.'

'Another thing we could do, we could sell it to very fat, very rich women at fantastic prices.'

'We could do that,' Henri answered.

'Do you think it would cure loss of virility in men?' I asked him.

'Of course,' Henri said. 'Impotence would go out the window.'

'What about octogenarians?'

'Them, too,' he said, 'though it would kill them at the same time.'

'And marriages on the rocks?'

'My dear fellow,' Henri said. 'The possibilities are legion.'

At that precise moment, the seed of an idea came sneaking slowly into my mind. As you know, I have a passion for politics. And my strongest passion, although I am English, is for the politics of the United States of America. I have always thought it is over there, in that mighty and mixed-up nation, that the destinies of mankind must surely lie. And right now, there was a President in office whom I could not stand. He was an evil man who pursued evil policies. Worse than that, he was a humourless and unattractive creature. So why didn't I, Oswald Cornelius, remove him from office?

The idea appealed to me.

'How much *Bitch* have you got in the lab at the moment?' I asked.

'Exactly ten cubic centimetres,' Henri said.

'And how much is one dose?'

'We used one cc for our test.'

'That's all I want,' I said. 'One cc. I'll take it home with me today. And a set of noseplugs.'

'No,' Henri said. 'Let's not play around with it at this stage. It's too dangerous.'

'It is my property,' I said. 'Half of it is mine. Don't forget our agreement.'

In the end, he had to give in. But he hated doing it. We went back to the lab, inserted our noseplugs, and Henri measured out precisely one cc of *Bitch* into a small scent-bottle. He sealed the stopper with wax and gave me the bottle. 'I implore you to be discreet,' he said. 'This is probably the most important scientific discovery of the century, and it must not be treated as a joke.'

From Henri's place, I drove directly to the workshop of an old friend, Marcel Brossollet. Marcel was an inventor and manufacturer of tiny precise scientific gadgets. He did a lot of work for surgeons, devising new types of heart-valves and pacemakers and those little one-way valves that reduce intra-cranial pressure in hydrocephalics.

'I want you to make me,' I said to Marcel, 'a capsule that will hold exactly one cc of liquid. To this little capsule, there must be attached a timing device that will split the capsule and re-lease the liquid at a predetermined moment. The entire thing must not be more than half an inch long and half an inch thick. The smaller the better. Can you manage that?'

'Very easily,' Marcel said. 'A thin plastic capsule, a tiny sec-tion of razor-blade to split the capsule, a spring to flip the razor-blade, and the usual pre-set alarm system on a very small ladies' watch. Should the capsule be fillable?'

'Yes. Make it so I myself can fill it and seal it up. Can I have it in a week?'

'Why not?' Marcel said. 'It is very simple.'

The next morning brought dismal news. That lecherous little slut Simone had apparently sprayed herself with the entire re-maining stock of *Bitch*, over nine cubic centimetres of it, the moment she arrived at the lab! She had then sneaked up be-hind Henri, who was just settling himself at his desk to write up his notes.

I don't have to tell you what happened next. And worst of all, the silly girl had forgotten that Henri had a serious heart condition. Damn it, he wasn't even allowed to climb a flight of stairs. So when the molecules hit him the poor fellow didn't stand a chance. He was dead within a minute, killed in action as they say, and that was that.

The infernal woman might at least have waited until he had written down the formula. As it was, Henri left not a single note. I searched the lab after they had taken away his body, but I found nothing. So now more than ever, I was determined to make good use of the only remaining cubic centimetre of *Bitch* in the world.

A week later, I collected from Marcel Brossollet a beautiful little gadget. The timing device consisted of the smallest watch I had ever seen, and this, together with the capsule and all the other parts, had been secured to a tiny aluminium plate three eighths of an inch square. Marcel showed me how to fill and seal the capsule and set the timer. I thanked him and paid the bill.

As soon as possible, I travelled to New York. In Manhattan, I put up at the Plaza Hotel. I arrived there at about three in the afternoon. I took a bath, had a shave, and asked room service to send me up a bottle of Glenlivet and some ice. Feeling clean and comfortable in my dressing-gown, I poured myself a good strong drink of the delicious malt whisky, then settled down in a deep chair with the morning's *New York Times*. My suite overlooked Central Park, and through the open window I could hear the hum of traffic and the blaring of cab-drivers' horns on Central Park South. Suddenly, one of the smaller headlines on the front page of the paper caught my eye. It said, PRESIDENT ON TV TONIGHT. I read on.

The President is expected to make an important foreign policy statement when he speaks tonight at the dinner to be given in his honour by the Daughters of the American Revolution in the ball-room of the Waldorf Astoria ...

My God, what a piece of luck!

I had been prepared to wait in New York for many weeks before I got a chance like this. The President of the United States does not often appear with a bunch of women on television. And that was exactly how I had to have him. He was an extraordinarily slippery customer. He had fallen into many

134

a sewer and had always come out smelling of shit. Yet he managed every time to convince the nation that the smell was coming from someone else, not him. So the way I figured it was this. A man who rapes a woman in full sight of twenty million viewers across the country would have a pretty hard time denying he ever did it.

I read on.

The President will speak for approximately twenty minutes, commencing at nine p.m. and all major TV networks will carry the speech. He will be introduced by Mrs Elvira Ponsonby, the incumbent President of the Daughters of the American Revolution. When interviewed in her suite at the Waldorf Towers, Mrs Ponsonby said ...

It was perfect! Mrs Ponsonby would be seated on the President's right. At ten past nine precisely, with the President well into his speech and half the population of the United States watching, a little capsule nestling secretly in the region of Mrs Ponsonby's bosom would be punctured and half a centimetre of *Bitch* would come oozing out on to her gilt lamé ball-gown. The President's head would come up, he would sniff and sniff again, his eyes would bulge, his nostrils would flare, and he would start snorting like a stallion. Then suddenly he would turn and grab hold of Mrs Ponsonby. She would be flung across the dining-table and the President would leap on top of her, with the pie à la mode and strawberry shortcake flying in all directions.

I leaned back and closed my eyes, savouring the delicious scene. I saw the headlines in the papers the next morning:

PRESIDENT'S BEST PERFORMANCE TO DATE
PRESIDENTIAL SECRETS REVEALED TO NATION
PRESIDENT INAUGURATES BLUE TV

and so on.

He would be impeached the next day and I would slip quietly out of New York and head back to Paris. Come to think of it, I would be leaving tomorrow!

I checked the time. It was nearly four o'clock. I dressed myself without hurrying. I took the elevator down to the main lobby and strolled across to Madison Avenue. Somewhere around Sixty-second Street, I found a good florist's shop. There I bought a corsage of three massive orchid blooms all fastened together. The orchids were cattleyas, white and mauve splotches on them. They were particularly vulgar. So, undoubtedly, was Mrs Elvira Ponsonby. I had the shop pack them in a handsome box tied up with gold string. Then I strolled back to the Plaza, carrying the box, and went up to my suite.

I locked all doors leading to the corridor in case the maid should come in to turn back the bed. I got out the noseplugs and vaselined them carefully. I inserted them in my nostrils, ramming them home very hard. I tied a surgeon's mask over my lower face as an extra precaution, just as Henri had done. I was ready now for the next step.

With an ordinary nose-dropper, I transferred my precious cubic centimetre of *Bitch* from the scent bottle to the tiny capsule. The hand holding the dropper shook a little as I did this, but all went well. I sealed the capsule. After that, I wound up the tiny watch and set it to the correct time. It was three minutes after five o'clock. Lastly, I set the timer to go off and break the capsule at ten minutes past nine.

The stems of the three huge orchid blooms had been tied together by the florist with a broad one-inch-wide white ribbon and it was a simple matter for me to remove the ribbon and secure my little capsule and timer to the orchid stems with cotton thread. When that was done, I wound the ribbon back around the stems and over my gadget. Then I retied the bow. It was a nice job.

Next, I telephone the Waldorf and learned that the dinner was to begin at eight o'clock, but that the guests must be assembled in the ballroom by seven thirty, before the President arrived.

At ten minutes to seven, I paid off my cab outside the Waldorf Towers entrance and walked into the building. I crossed the small lobby and placed my orchid box on the reception desk. I leaned over the desk, getting as close as possible to the clerk. 'I have to deliver this package to Mrs Elvira Ponsonby,'

I whispered, using a slight American accent. 'It is a gift from the President.'

The clerk looked at me suspiciously.

'Mrs Ponsonby is introducing the President before he speaks tonight in the ballroom,' I added. 'The President wishes her to have this corsage right away.'

'Leave it here and I'll have it sent up to her suite,' the clerk said.

'No, you won't,' I told him. 'My orders are to deliver it in person. What's the number of her suite?'

The man was impressed. 'Mrs Ponsonby is in five-o-one,' he said.

I thanked him and went into the elevator. When I got out at the fifth floor and walked along the corridor, the elevator operator stayed and watched me. I rang the bell to five-o-one.

The door was opened by the most enormous female I had ever seen in my life. I have seen giant women in circuses. I have seen lady wrestlers and weight-lifters. I have seen the huge Masai women in the plains below Kilimanjaro. But never had I seen a female so tall and broad and thick as this one. Nor so thoroughly repugnant. She was groomed and dressed for the greatest occasion of her life, and in the two seconds that elapsed before either of us spoke, I was able to take most of it in – the metallic silver-blue hair with every strand glued into place, the brown pig-eyes, the long sharp nose sniffing for trouble, the curled lips, the prognathous jaw, the powder, the mascara, the scarlet lipstick and, most shattering of all, the massive shored-up bosom that projected like a balcony in front of her. It stuck out so far it was a miracle she didn't topple forward with the weight of it all. And there she stood, this pneumatic giant, swathed from neck to ankles in the stars and stripes of the American flag.

'Mrs Elvira Ponsonby?' I murmured.

'I am Mrs Ponsonby,' she boomed. 'What do you want? I am extremely busy.'

'Mrs Ponsonby,' I said. 'The President has ordered me to deliver this to you in person.'

She melted immediately. 'The dear man!' she shouted. 'How

perfectly gorgeous of him!' Two massive hands reached out grab the box. I let her have it.

'My instructions are to make sure you open it before you go to the banquet,' I said.

'Sure I'll open it,' she said. 'Do I have to do it in front of you?'

'If you wouldn't mind.'

'Okay, come on in. But I don't have much time.'

I followed her into the living-room of the suite. 'I am to tell you,' I said, 'that it comes with all good wishes from one President to another.'

'Ha!' she roared. 'I like that! What a gorgeous man he is!' She untied the gold string of the box and lifted the lid. 'I guessed it!' she shouted. 'Orchids! How splendid! They're far grander than this poor little thing I'm wearing!'

I had been so dazzled by the galaxy of stars across her bosom that I hadn't noticed the single orchid pinned to the left-hand side.

'I must change over at once,' she said. 'The President will be expecting me to wear his gift.'

'He certainly will,' I said.

Now to give you an idea of how far her chest stuck out in front of her, I must tell you that when she reached forward to unpin the flower, she was only just able to touch it even with her arms fully extended. She fiddled around with the pin for quite a while, but she couldn't really see what she was doing and it wouldn't come undone. 'I'm terrified of tearing this gorgeous gown,' she said. 'Here, you do it.' She swung around and thrust her mammoth bust in my face. I hesitated. 'Go on!' she boomed. 'I don't have all night!' I went to it, and in the end I managed to get the pin unhooked from her dress.

'Now let's get the other one on,' she said.

I put aside the single orchid and lifted my own flowers carefully from the box.

'Have they got a pin?' she asked.

'I don't believe they have,' I said. That was something I'd forgotten.

'No matter,' she said. 'We'll use the old one.' She removed

the safety-pin from the first orchid, and then, before I could stop her, she seized the three orchids I was holding and jabbed the pin hard into the white ribbon around the stems. She jabbed it almost exactly into the spot where my little capsule of *Bitch* was lying hidden. The pin struck something hard and wouldn't go through. She jabbed it again. Again it struck metal. 'What the hell's under here?' she snorted.

'Let me do it!' I cried, but it was too late, because the wet stain of *Bitch* from the punctured capsule was already spreading over the white ribbon and one hundredth of a second later the smell hit me. It caught me smack under the nose and it wasn't actually like a smell at all because a smell is something intangible. You cannot feel a smell. But this stuff was palpable. It was solid. It felt as though some kind of fiery liquid were being squirted up my nostrils under high pressure. It was exceedingly uncomfortable. I could feel it pushing higher and higher, penetrating far beyond the nasal passages, forcing its way up behind the forehead and reaching for the brain. Suddenly the stars and stripes on Mrs Ponsonby's dress began to wobble and bobble about and then the whole room started wobbling and I could hear my heart thumping in my head. It felt as though I were going under an anaesthetic.

At that point, I must have blacked out completely, if only for a couple of seconds.

When I came round again, I was standing naked in a rosy room and there was a funny feeling in my groin. I looked down and saw that my beloved sexual organ was three feet long and and thick to match. It was still growing. It was lengthening and swelling at a tremendous rate. At the same time, my body was shrinking. Smaller and smaller shrank my body. Bigger and bigger grew my astonishing organ, and it went on growing, by God, until it had enveloped my entire body and absorbed it within itself. I was now a gigantic perpendicular penis, seven feet tall and as handsome as they come.

I did a little dance around the room to celebrate my splendid new condition. On the way I met a maiden in a star-spangled dress. She was very big as maidens go. I drew myself up to my full height and declaimed in a loud voice:

> 'The summer's flower is to the summer sweet,
> It flourishes despite the summer's heat.
> But tell me truly, did you ever see
> A sexual organ quite so grand as me?'

The maiden leapt up and flung her arms as far around me as she could. Then cried out:

> 'Shall I compare thee to a summer's day?
> Shall I . . . Oh dear, I know not what to say.
> But all my life I've had an itch to kiss
> A man who could erect himself like this.

A moment later, the two of us were millions of miles up in outer space, flying through the universe in a shower of meteorites all red and gold. I was riding her bareback, crouching forward and gripping her tightly between my thighs. 'Faster!' I shouted, jabbing long spurs into her flanks. 'Go faster!' Faster and still faster she flew, spurting and spinning around the rim of the sky, her mane streaming with sun, and snow waving out of her tail. The sense of power I had was overwhelming. I was unassailable, supreme. I was the Lord of the Universe, scattering the planets and catching the stars in the palm of my hand and tossing them away as though they were ping-pong balls.

Oh, ecstasy and ravishment! Oh, Jericho and Tyre and Sidon! The walls came tumbling down and the firmament disintegrated, and out of the smoke and fire of the explosion, the sitting-room in the Waldorf Towers came swimming slowly back into my consciousness like a rainy day. The place was a shambles. A tornado would have done less damage. My clothes were on the floor. I started dressing myself very quickly. I did it in about thirty seconds flat. And as I ran toward the door, I heard a voice that seemed to be coming from somewhere behind an upturned table in the far corner of the room. 'I don't know who you are, young man,' it said. 'But you've certainly done me a power of good.'

My Uncle Oswald

I do love a romp

Oswald's Diaries, Vol. XIV

I

I am beginning, once again, to have an urge to salute my Uncle Oswald. I mean, of course, Oswald Hendryks Cornelius deceased, the connoisseur, the bon vivant, the collector of spiders, scorpions and walking-sticks, the lover of opera, the expert on Chinese porcelain, the seducer of women, and without much doubt the greatest fornicator of all time. Every other celebrated contender for that title is diminished to a point of ridicule when his record is compared with that of my Uncle Oswald. Especially poor old Casanova. He comes out of the contest looking like a man who was suffering from a severe malfunction of his sexual organ.

Fifteen years have passed since I released for publication in 1964 the first small excerpt from Oswald's diaries. I took trouble at the time to select something unlikely to give offence, and that particular episode concerned, if you remember, a harmless and rather frivolous description of coitus between my uncle and a certain female leper in the Sinai Desert.

So far so good. But I waited a full ten years more (1974) before risking the release of a second piece. And once again I was careful to choose something that was, at any rate by Oswald's standards, as nearly as possible suitable for reading by the vicar to Sunday School in the village church. That one dealt with the discovery of a perfume so potent that any man who sniffed it upon a woman was unable to prevent himself from ravishing her on the spot.

No serious litigation resulted from the publication of this little bit of trivia. But there were plenty of repercussions of another kind. I found my mailbox suddenly clogged with letters from hundreds of female readers, all clamouring for a

7

drop of Oswald's magic perfume. Innumerable men also wrote to me with the same request, including a singularly unpleasant African dictator, a British left-wing Cabinet Minister and a Cardinal from the Holy See. A Saudi-Arabian prince offered me an enormous sum in Swiss currency, and a man in a dark suit from the American Central Intelligence Agency called on me one afternoon with a briefcase full of hundred-dollar bills. Oswald's perfume, he told me, could be used to compromise just about every senior Russian statesman and diplomat in the world, and his people wanted to buy the formula.

Unfortunately, I had not one drop of the magic liquid to sell, so there the matter ended.

Today, five years after publication of that perfume story, I have decided to permit the public yet another glimpse into my uncle's life. The section I have chosen comes from Volume XX, written in 1938, when Oswald was forty-three years old and in the prime of life. Many famous names are mentioned in this one, and there is obviously a grave risk that families and friends are going to take offence at some of the things Oswald has to say. I can only pray that those concerned will grant me indulgence and will understand that my motives are pure. For this is a document of considerable scientific and historical importance. It would be a tragedy if it never saw the light of day.

Here then is the extract from Volume XX of the Diaries of Oswald Hendryks Cornelius, word for word as he wrote it:

London, July 1938

Have just returned from a satisfactory visit to the Lagonda works at Staines. W. O. Bentley gave me lunch (salmon from the Usk and a bottle of Montrachet) and we discussed the extras for my new V12. He has promised me a set of horns that will play Mozart's *Son gia mille e Tre* in perfect pitch. Some of you may think this to be a rather childish conceit, but it will serve as a nice incentive to be reminded, every time I press the button, that good old Don Giovanni had by then deflowered 1003 buxom Spanish damsels. I told Bentley that the seats are to be upholstered in fine-grain alligator, and the panelling to be veneered

8

in yew. Why yew ? Simply because I prefer the colour and grain of English yew to that of any other wood.

But what a remarkable fellow this W. O. Bentley is. And what a triumph it was for Lagonda when he went over to them. It is somehow sad that this man, having designed and given his name to one of the finest cars in the world, should be forced out of his own company and into the arms of a rival. It means, however, that the new Lagondas are now peerless, and I for one would have no other machine. But this one isn't going to be cheap. It is costing me more thousands than I ever thought it possible to pay for an automobile.

Yet who cares about money ? Not me, because I've always had plenty of it. I made my first hundred thousand pounds when I was seventeen and later I was to make a lot more. Having said that, it occurs to me that I have never once throughout these journals made any mention of the manner in which I became a wealthy man.

Perhaps the time has come when I should do this. I think it has. For although these diaries are designed to be a history of the art of seduction and the pleasures of copulation, they would be incomplete without some reference also to the art of money-making and the pleasures attendant thereon.

Very well, then. I have talked myself into it. I shall proceed at once to tell you something about how I set about making money. But just in case some of you may be tempted to skip this particular section and go on to juicier things, let me assure you that there will be juice in plenty dripping from these pages. I wouldn't have it otherwise.

Great wealth, when uninherited, is usually acquired in one of four ways – by chicanery, by talent, by inspired judgement or by luck. Mine was a combination of all four. Listen carefully and you shall see what I mean.

In the year 1912, when I was barely seventeen, I won a scholarship in natural sciences to Trinity College, Cambridge. I was a precocious youth and had taken the exam a year earlier than usual. This meant that I had a twelve-month wait doing nothing because Cambridge would not receive me until I was

9

eighteen. My father therefore decided that I should fill in the time by going to France to learn the language. I myself hoped that I should learn a fair bit more than just the language in that splendid country. Already, you see, I had begun to acquire a taste for rakery and wenching among the London debutantes. Already, also, I was beginning to get a bit bored with these young English girls. They were, I decided, a pretty pithless lot, and I was impatient to sow a few bushels of wild oats in foreign fields. Especially in France. I had been reliably informed that Parisian females knew a thing or two about the act of lovemaking that their London cousins had never even dreamed of. Copulation, so rumour had it, was in its infancy in England.

On the evening before I was due to depart for France, I gave a small party at our family house in Cheyne Walk. My father and mother had purposely gone out to dinner at seven o'clock so that I might have the place to myself. I had invited a dozen or so friends of both sexes, all of them about my own age, and by nine o'clock we were sitting around making pleasant talk, drinking wine and consuming some excellent boiled mutton and dumplings. The front doorbell rang. I went to answer it, and on the doorstep there stood a middle-aged man with a huge moustache, a magenta complexion and a pigskin suitcase. He introduced himself as Major Grout and asked for my father. I said he was out to dinner. 'Good gracious me,' said Major Grout. 'He has invited me to stay. I'm an old friend.'

'Father must have forgotten,' I said. 'I'm awfully sorry. You had better come in.'

Now I couldn't very well leave the Major alone in the study reading *Punch* while we were having a party in the next room, so I asked him if he'd care to come in and join us. He would indeed. He'd love to join us. So in he came, moustache and all, a beaming jovial old boy who settled down among us quite comfortably despite the fact that he was three times the age of anyone else present. He tucked into the mutton and polished off a whole bottle of claret in the first fifteen minutes.

'Excellent vittles,' he said. 'Is there any more wine?'

I opened another bottle for him, and we all watched with a

certain admiration as he proceeded to empty that one as well. His cheeks were swiftly turning from magenta to a very deep purple and his nose seemed to be catching on fire. Halfway through the third bottle, he began to loosen up. He worked, he told us, in the Anglo-Egyptian Sudan and was home on leave. His job had to do with the Sudan Irrigation Service and a very hot and arduous business it was. But fascinating. Lots of fun, y'know. And the wogs weren't too much trouble so long as one kept the old shambok handy all the time.

We sat round him, listening and not a little intrigued by this purple-faced creature from distant lands.

'A great country, the Sudan,' he said. 'It is enormous. It is remote. It is full of mysteries and secrets. Would you like me to tell you about one of the great secrets of the Sudan?'

'Very much, sir,' we said. 'Yes please.'

'One of its great secrets,' he said, tipping another glass of wine down his throat, 'a secret that is known only to a few old timers out there like myself and to the natives, is a little creature called the Sudanese Blister Beetle or to give him his right name, *cantharis vesicatoria sudanii.*'

'You mean a scarab?' I said.

'Certainly not,' he said. 'The Sudanese Blister Beetle is a winged insect, as much a fly as a beetle and is about three-quarters of an inch long. It's very pretty to look at, with a brilliant iridescent shell of golden green.'

'Why is it so secret?' we asked.

'These little beetles,' the Major said, 'are found only in one part of the Sudan. It's an area of about twenty square miles, north of Khartoum, and that's where a tree called the hashab grows. The leaves of the hashab tree are what the beetles feed on. Men spend their whole lives searching for these beetles. Beetle hunters, they are called. They are very sharp-eyed natives who know all there is to know about the haunts and habits of the tiny brutes. And when they catch them, they kill them and dry them in the sun and crunch them up into a fine powder. This powder is greatly prized among the natives who usually keep it in small elaborately carved Beetle

Boxes. A tribal chief will have his Beetle Box made of silver.'

'But this powder,' we said, 'what do they do with it?'

'It's not what *they* do with *it*,' the Major said. 'It's what *it* does to *you*. One tiny pinch of that powder is the most powerful aphrodisiac in the world.'

'The Spanish Fly!' someone shouted. 'It's the Spanish Fly!'

'Well not quite,' the Major said, 'but you're on the right track. The common Spanish Fly is found in Spain and Southern Italy. The one I'm talking about is the *Sudanese Fly* and although it's of the same family, it's a different kettle of fish altogether. It is approximately ten times as powerful as the ordinary Spanish Fly. The reaction produced by the little *Sudanese* fellow is so incredibly vicious it is dangerous to use even in small doses.'

'But they do use it?'

'Oh God, yes. Every wog in Khartoum and northwards uses the old Beetle. White men, the ones who know about it, are inclined to leave it alone because it's so damn dangerous.'

'Have *you* used it?' someone asked.

The Major looked up at the questioner and gave a little smile under his enormous moustache. 'We'll come to that in a moment or two, shall we?' he said.

'What does it actually do to you?' one of the girls asked.

'My God,' the Major said, 'what doesn't it do to you? It builds a fire under your genitals. It is both a violent aphrodisiac and a powerful irritant. It not only makes you uncontrollably randy but it also guarantees you an enormous and long-lasting erection at the same time. Could you give me another glass of wine, dear boy?'

I leaped up to fetch more wine. My guests had suddenly become very still. The girls were all staring at the Major, rapt and motionless, their eyes shining like stars. The boys were staring at the girls, watching to see how they would react to these sudden indiscretions. I refilled the Major's glass.

'Your father always kept a decent cellar,' he said. 'And good cigars, too.' He looked up at me, waiting.

'Would you like a cigar, sir?'

'That's very civil of you,' he said.

I went to the dining-room and fetched my father's box of Montecristos. The Major put one in his breast pocket and another in his mouth. 'I will tell you a true story if you like,' he said, 'about myself and the Blister Beetle.'

'Tell us,' we said. 'Go on, sir.'

'You'll like this story,' he said, removing the cigar from his mouth and snipping off the end of it with a thumbnail. 'Who has a match?'

I lit his cigar for him. Clouds of smoke enveloped his head, and through the smoke we could see his face dimly, but dark and soft like some huge over-ripe purple fruit.

'One evening,' he began, 'I was sitting on the verandah of my bungalow way upcountry about fifty miles north of Khartoum. It was hot as hell and I'd had a hard day. I was drinking a strong whiskey and soda. It was my first that evening and I was lying back in the deckchair with my feet resting on the little balustrade that ran round the verandah. I could feel the whiskey hitting the lining of my stomach and I can promise you there is no greater sensation at the end of a long day in a fierce climate than when you feel that first whiskey hitting your stomach and going through into the bloodstream. A few minutes later, I went indoors and got myself a second drink, then I returned to the verandah. I lay back again in the deckchair. My shirt was soaked with sweat but I was too tired to take a shower. Then all of a sudden I went rigid. I was just about to put the glass of whiskey to my lips and my hand froze, it literally froze in mid-air and there it stayed with my fingers clenched around the glass. I couldn't move. I couldn't even speak. I tried to call out to my boy for help but I couldn't. Rigor mortis. Paralysis. My entire body had turned to stone.'

'Were you frightened?' someone asked.

'Of course I was frightened,' the Major said. 'I was bloody terrified, especially out there in the Sudan desert miles from anywhere. But the paralysis didn't last very long. Maybe a minute, maybe two. I don't really know. But when I came to, as it were, the first thing I noticed was a burning sensation in the

13

region of my groin. "Hullo," I said, "what the hell's going on now?" But it was pretty obvious what was going on. The activity inside my trousers was becoming very violent indeed and within another few seconds my member was as stiff and erect as the mainmast of a topsail schooner.'

'What do you mean, your *member*?' asked a girl whose name was Gwendoline.

'I expect you will catch on as we go along, my dear,' the Major said.

'Carry on, Major,' we said. 'What happened next?'

'Then it started to throb,' he said.

'What started to throb?' Gwendoline asked him.

'My member,' the Major said. 'I could feel every beat of my heart all the way along it. Pulsing and throbbing most terribly it was, and as tight as a balloon. You know those long sausage-shaped balloons children have at parties? I kept thinking about one of those, and with every beat of my heart it felt as if someone was pumping in more air and it was going to burst.'

The Major drank some wine. Then he studied the ash on his cigar. We sat still, waiting.

'So of course I began trying to puzzle out what might have happened,' he went on. 'I looked at my glass of whiskey. It was where I always put it, on top of the little white-painted balustrade surrounding the verandah. Then my eye travelled upward to the roof of the bungalow and to the edge of the roof and suddenly, presto! I'd got it! I knew for certain what must have happened.'

'What?' we said, all speaking at once.

'A large Blister Beetle, taking an evening stroll on the roof, had ventured too close to the edge and had fallen off.'

'Right into your glass of whiskey!' we cried.

'Precisely,' the Major said. 'And I, thirsting like mad in the heat, had gulped him down without looking.'

The girl called Gwendoline was staring at the Major with huge eyes. 'Quite honestly I don't see what all the fuss was about,' she said. 'One teeny weeny little beetle isn't going to hurt anyone.'

'My dear child,' the Major said, 'when the Blister Beetle is dried and crushed the resulting powder is called cantharidin. That's its pharmaceutical name. The Sudanese variety is called *cantharidin sudanii*. And this *cantharidin sudanii* is absolutely deadly. The maximum safe dose for a human, if there is such a thing as a safe dose, is one minim. A minim is *one-sixtieth* of a fluid ounce. Assuming I had just swallowed one whole fully grown Blister Beetle, that meant I'd received God knows how many hundreds of times the maximum dose.'

'Jesus,' we said. 'Jesus Christ.'

'The throbbing was so tremendous now, it was shaking my whole body,' the Major said.

'A headache, you mean?' Gwendoline said.

'No,' the Major said.

'What happened next?' we asked him.

'My member,' the Major said, 'was now like a white-hot rod of iron burning into my body. I leapt up from my chair and rushed to my car and drove like a madman for the nearest hospital, which was in Khartoum. I got there in forty minutes flat. I was scared fartless.'

'Now wait just a minute,' the Gwendoline creature said. 'I'm still not quite following you. Exactly why were you so frightened?'

What a dreadful girl. I should never have invited her. The Major, to his great credit, ignored her completely this time.

'I dashed into the hospital,' he went on, 'and found the casualty room where an English doctor was stitching up somebody's knife wound. "Look at this!" I cried, taking it out and waving it at him.'

'Waving *what* at him, for heaven's sake?' the awful Gwendoline asked.

'Shut up, Gwendoline,' I said.

'Thank you,' the Major said. 'The doctor stopped stitching and regarded the object I was holding out to him with some alarm. I quickly told him my story. He looked glum. There was no antidote for Blister Beetle, he informed me. I was in grave trouble. But he would do his best. So they stomach-pumped me and put me to bed and packed ice all around my poor throbbing member.'

'Who did?' someone asked. 'Who's they?'

'A nurse,' the Major answered. 'A young Scottish nurse with dark hair. She brought the ice in small rubber bags and packed it round and kept the bags in place with a bandage.'

'Didn't you get frostbite?'

'You can't get frostbite on something that's practically red-hot,' the Major said.

'What happened next?'

'They kept changing the ice every three hours day and night.'

'Who, the Scottish nurse?'

'They took it in turns. Several nurses.'

'Good God.'

'It took two weeks to subside.'

'Two weeks!' I said. 'Were you all right afterwards, sir? Are you all right now?'

The Major smiled and took another sip of wine. 'I am deeply touched,' he said, 'by your concern. You are obviously a young man who knows what comes first in this world, and what comes second. I think you will go far.'

'Thank you, sir,' I said. 'But what happened in the end?'

'I was out of action for six months,' the Major said, smiling wanly, 'but that is no hardship in the Sudan. Yes, if you want to know, I'm all right now. I made a miraculous recovery.'

That was the story Major Grout had told us at my little party on the eve of my departure for France. And it set me thinking. It set me thinking very deeply indeed. In fact, that night, as I lay in bed with my bags all packed on the floor, a tremendously daring plan began rapidly to evolve in my head. I say 'daring' because, by God, it damn well was daring when you consider I was only seventeen years old at the time. Looking back on it now, I take my hat off to myself for even contemplating that sort of action. But the following morning my mind was made up.

2

I bade farewell to my parents on the platform at Victoria Station and boarded the boat train for Paris. I arrived that afternoon and checked in at the house where my father had arranged for me to board. It was on the Avenue Marceau, and the family, who were called Boisvain, took paying guests. Monsieur Boisvain was a civil servant of sorts and as unremarkable as the rest of his breed. His wife, a pale woman with short fingers and a flaccid rump, was in much the same mould as her husband, and I guessed that neither of them would give me any trouble. They had two daughters: Jeanette, aged fifteen, and Nicole who was nineteen. Mademoiselle Nicole was some kind of a freak, for while the rest of the family were typically small and neat and French, this girl was of Amazonian proportions. She looked to me like a sort of female gladiator. She could not possibly have stood less than six foot three in her bare feet, but she was none the less a well-made young gladiator with long nicely-turned legs and a pair of dark eyes that seemed to hold a number of secrets. It was the first time since puberty that I had encountered a woman who was not only tremendously tall but also attractive, and I was much impressed by what I saw. Since then, over the years, I have naturally sampled many a lofty wench and I must say that I rate them higher, on the whole, than their more diminutive sisters. When a woman is very tall, there is greater power and greater traction in her limbs for one thing, and of course there is also a good deal more substance to tangle with.

In other words, I do enjoy a tall woman. And why shouldn't I? There's nothing freakish about that. But what *is* pretty freakish, in my opinion, is the extraordinary fact that women in general, and by that I mean all women everywhere, go absolutely dotty about tiny men. Let me explain at once that by 'tiny men' I don't mean ordinary tiny men like horse-jockeys and chimney-sweeps. I mean genuine dwarfs, those minuscule bowlegged characters you see running around in circus arenas wearing pantaloons. Believe it or not, any one of these little fellows can, if he puts his mind to it, drive even the most frigid woman to distraction. Protest all you like, you lady readers. Tell me I'm crazy, misguided, ill-informed. But before you do that, I suggest you go away and talk to a female who has actually been worked over by one of these little men. She will confirm my findings. She will say yes yes yes, it's true, I'm afraid it's true. She will tell you they are repulsive but irresistible. An exceedingly ugly middle-aged circus-dwarf who stood no more than three feet six inches tall once told me that he could always have his pick of any woman in any room at any time. Very odd I find that.

But to go back to Mademoiselle Nicole, the Amazonian daughter. She interested me at once, and as we shook hands, I applied a touch of extra pressure to her knuckles and watched her face. Her lips parted and I saw the tip of her tongue push out suddenly between her teeth. Very well, young lady, I told myself. You shall be number one in Paris.

In case this sounds a bit brash coming from a seventeen-year-old stripling like me, I think you should know that even at that tender age, fortune had endowed me with far more than my share of good looks. Going back now over the family photographs of the time, I can see that I was a youth of quite piercing beauty. This is no more than a simple fact and it would be silly to pretend it wasn't true. Certainly, it had made things easy for me in London and I could honestly say that up to then I had not received a single snub. But I had not, of course, been playing the game for very long and no more than fifty or sixty young birds had come into my sights.

In order to carry out the plan which the good Major Grout had put into my head, I straight away announced to Madame Boisvain that I would be leaving first thing in the morning to stay with friends in the country. We were still standing in the hall and we had just completed the handshakes. 'But Monsieur Oswald, you have only this minute arrived!' the good lady cried.

'I believe my father has paid you six months in advance,' I said. 'If I am not here, you will save money on food.'

Arithmetic like that will mollify the heart of any landlady in France, and Madame Boisvain made no further protest. At seven p.m. we sat down to the evening meal. It was boiled tripe with onions. This I consider to be the second most repulsive dish in the entire world. The *most* repulsive dish is something that is eaten with gusto by jackaroos on sheep-stations in Australia.

These jackaroos – and I might as well tell you about it so that you can avoid it if ever you should go that way – these jackaroos or sheep cowboys invariably castrate their male lambs in the following barbaric manner: two of them hold the creature upside down by its fore and hind legs. A third fellow slits the scrotum and squeezes the testicles outside the sac. He then bends forward and takes the testicles in his mouth. He closes his teeth on them and jerks them free from the unfortunate animal and spits this nauseating mouthful into a basin. It's no good you telling me these things don't happen because they do. I saw it all last year with my own eyes on a station near Cowra in New South Wales. And these idiots went on to inform me with pride that three competent jackaroos could castrate sixty lambs in sixty minutes and go on doing it all day long. A little jaw-ache was all one got, they said, but it was well worth it because the rewards were great.

'What rewards?'

'Ah ha,' they said, 'you just wait!' And in the evening I had to stand and watch while they fried the spoils in a pan with mutton fat over a wood fire. This gastronomic miracle is, I can assure you, the most revolting, the toughest, the most nauseating dish it is possible to imagine. Boiled tripe comes second.

I keep digressing. I must get on. We are still in the Boisvain household having boiled tripe for supper. Monsieur B went into ecstasies over the stuff, making loud sucking noises and smacking his lips and shouting 'Délicieux! Ravissant! Formidable! Merveilleux!' with every mouthful. And then, when he had finished—would horrors never cease? – he calmly removed his entire set of false teeth and rinsed them in his fingerbowl.

At midnight, when Monsieur and Madame B were well asleep, I slipped along the corridor and entered the bedroom of Mademoiselle Nicole. She was tucked up in an enormous bed and there was a candle burning on the table beside her. She received me, oddly enough, with a formal French handshake, but I can assure you there was nothing formal about what followed after that. I do not intend to dwell upon this little episode. It has nothing at all to do with the main part of my story. Let me just say that every rumour I had ever heard about the girls of Paris was substantiated during those few hours I spent with Mademoiselle Nicole. She made the glacial London debutantes seem like so many slabs of petrified wood. She went for me like a mongoose for a cobra. She suddenly had ten pairs of hands and half a dozen mouths. She was a contortionist to boot, and more than once amidst the whirring of limbs, I caught a glimpse of her ankles locked around the back of her neck. The girl was putting me through the wringer. She was stretching me beyond the point of endurance. I was not really ready at my age for such a severe examination as this, and after an hour or so of unremitting activity, I began to hallucinate. I remember imagining that my entire body was one long well-lubricated piston sliding smoothly back and forth within a cylinder whose walls were made of the smoothest steel. God only knows how long it went on, but at the end of it all I was suddenly brought back to my senses, by the sound of a deep calm voice saying, 'Very well, monsieur, that will do for the first lesson. I think, though, that it will be a long time before you get out of the kindergarten.'

I staggered back to my room, bruised and chastened, and fell asleep.

The next morning, in order to carry out my plan, I said farewell to the Boisvains and took a train for Marseilles. I had on me the six months expense money my father had provided before I left London, two hundred pounds in French francs. That was a lot of money in the year 1912.

At Marseilles, I booked a passage for Alexandria on a French steamship of nine thousand tons called *L'Impératrice Josephine*, a pleasant little passenger boat that ran regularly between Marseilles, Naples, Palermo and Alexandria.

The trip was without incident except that I encountered on the first day out yet another tall female. This time she was a Turk, a tall dark-skinned Turkish lady who was so smothered in jewellery of all sorts that she tinkled as she walked. My first thought was that she would have worked wonders on top of a cherry tree to keep the birds away. My second thought, which followed very soon after the first, was that she had an exceptional shape to her body. The undulations in the region of her chest were so magnificent that I felt, as I gazed at them across the boat-deck, like a traveller in Tibet who was seeing for the first time the highest peaks in the Himalayas. The woman returned my gaze, her chin high and arrogant, her eyes travelling slowly down my body from head to toe, then up again. A minute later, she calmly strolled across and invited me to her cabin for a glass of absinthe. I'd never heard of the stuff in my life, but I went willingly, and I stayed willingly and I did not emerge again from that cabin until we docked at Naples three days later. I may well, as Mademoiselle Nicole had said, have been in the kindergarten and Mademoiselle Nicole herself was perhaps in the sixth form, but if that was so then the tall Turkish lady was a university professor.

Things were made more difficult for me during this encounter by the fact that all the way between Marseilles and Naples, the ship was battling against a terrible storm. It pitched and rolled in the most alarming manner and more than once I thought we were going to capsize. When at last we were safely anchored in the Bay of Naples, and I was leaving the cabin, I said, 'Well, by gosh, I'm glad we made it. That was some storm we went through.'

'My dear boy,' she said, hanging another cluster of jewellery round her neck, 'the sea has been as calm as glass all the way.'

'Oh no, madame,' I said. 'It was a tremendous storm.'

'That was no storm,' she said. 'It was me.'

I was learning fast. I had learned above all – and I have confirmed this many times since – that to tangle with a Turk is like running fifty miles before breakfast. You have to be fit.

I spent the rest of the voyage getting my wind back and by the time we docked at Alexandria four days later, I was feeling quite bouncy again. From Alexandria I took a train to Cairo. There I changed trains and went on to Khartoum.

By God, it was hot in the Sudan. I was not dressed for the tropics but I refused to waste money on clothes that I would only be wearing for a day or two. In Khartoum, I got a room at a large hotel where the foyer was filled with Englishmen wearing khaki shorts and topees. They all had moustaches and magenta cheeks like Major Grout, and every one of them had a drink in his hand. There was a Sudanese hall-porter of sorts lounging by the entrance. He was a splendid handsome fellow in a white robe with a red tarbouche on his head, and I went up to him.

'I wonder if you could help me?' I said, taking some French banknotes from my pocket and riffling them casually.

He looked at the money and grinned.

'Blister Beetles,' I said. 'You know about Blister Beetles?'

Here it was, then. This was *le moment critique*. I had come all the way from Paris to Khartoum to ask that one question, and now I watched the man's face anxiously. It was certainly possible that Major Grout's story had been nothing more than an entertaining hoax.

The Sudanese hall-porter's grin became wider still. 'Everyone knows about Blister Beetles, sahib,' he said. 'What you want?'

'I want you to tell me where I can go out and catch one thousand of them.'

He stopped grinning and stared at me as though I'd gone barmy. 'You mean *live* beetles?' he exclaimed. 'You want to go out and catch yourself one thousand *live* Blister Beetles?'

'I do, yes.'

'What you want live beetles for, sahib? They no good to you at all, those old live beetles.'

Oh my God, I thought. The Major *has* been pulling our legs.

The hall-porter moved closer to me and placed an almost jet black hand on my arm. 'You want jig-a-jig, right? You want stuff to make you go jig-a-jig?'

'That's about it,' I said. 'More or less.'

'Then you don't want to bother with them *live* beetles, sahib. All you want is *powdered* beetles.'

'I had an idea I might take the beetles home and breed them,' I said. 'That way I'd have a permanent supply.'

'In England?' he said.

'England or France. Somewhere like that.'

'No good,' he said, shaking his head. 'This little Blister Beetle he live only here in the Sudan. He needs very hot sun. Beetles will all die in your country. Why you not take the powder?'

I could see I was going to have to make a slight adjustment in my plans. 'How much does the powder cost?' I asked him.

'How much you want?'

'A lot.'

'You have to be very very careful with that powder, sahib. All you take is the littlest pinch otherwise you get into *very serious trouble.*'

'I know that.'

'Over here, we Sudanese men measure up one dose by pouring the powder over the head of a pin and what stays on the pinhead is one dose exactly. And that is not very much. So you better be careful, young sahib.'

'I know all about that,' I said. 'Just tell me how I go about getting hold of a large quantity.'

'What you mean by large quantity?'

'Well, say about ten pounds in weight.'

'Ten pounds!' he cried. 'That would take care of all the people in the whole of Africa put together!'

'Five pounds then.'

'What in the world you going to do with *five pounds* of Blister Beetle powder, sahib? Just a few *ounces* is a lifetime supply even for a big strong man like me.'

23

'Never mind what I'm going to do with it,' I said. 'How much would it cost?'

He laid his head on one side and considered this question carefully. 'We buy it in tiny packets,' he said. 'Quarter ounce each. Very expensive stuff.'

'I want five pounds,' I said. 'In bulk.'

'Are you staying here in the hotel?' he asked me.

'Yes.'

'Then I see you tomorrow with the answer. I must go around asking some questions.'

I left it at that for the time being.

The next morning the tall black hall-porter was in his usual place by the hotel entrance. 'What news of the powder?' I asked him.

'I fix,' he said. 'I find a place where I can get you five pounds in weight of pure powder.'

'How much will it cost?' I asked him.

'You have English money?'

'I can get it.'

'It will cost you one thousand English pounds, sahib. Very cheap.'

'Then forget it,' I said, turning away.

'Five hundred,' he said.

'Fifty,' I said. 'I'll give you fifty pounds.'

'One hundred.'

'No. Fifty. That's all I can afford.'

He shrugged and spread his palms upward. 'You find the money,' he said. 'I find the powder. Six o'clock tonight.'

'How will I know you won't be giving me sawdust or something?'

'Sahib!' he cried. 'I never cheat anyone.'

'I'm not so sure.'

'In that case,' he said, 'we will test the powder on *you* by giving you a little dose before you pay me. How's that?'

'Good idea,' I said. 'See you at six.'

One of the London banks had an overseas branch in Khartoum. I went there and changed some of my French francs for pounds. At six p.m. I sought out the hall-porter. He was now in the foyer of the hotel.

'You got it?' I asked him.

He pointed to a large brown-paper parcel standing on the floor behind a pillar. 'You want to test it first, sahib? You are very welcome because this is the absolute top class quality beetle powder in the Sudan. One pinhead of this and you go jig-a-jig all night long and half the next day.'

I didn't think he would have offered me a trial run if the stuff hadn't been right, so I gave him the money and took the parcel.

An hour later, I was on the night train to Cairo. Within ten days, I was back in Paris and knocking on the door of Madame Boisvain's house in the Avenue Marceau. I had my precious parcel with me. There had been no trouble with the French customs as I disembarked at Marseilles. In those days, they searched for knives and guns but nothing else.

3

I announced to Madame B that I was now going to stay for quite a while but that I had one request to make. I was a science student, I told her. She said she knew that. It was my wish, I went on, not only to learn French during my stay in France, but also to pursue my scientific studies. I would therefore be conducting certain experiments in my room which involved the use of apparatus and chemicals that could be dangerous or poisonous to the inexperienced. Because of this, I wished to have a key to my room, and nobody should enter it.

'You are going to blow us all up!' she cried, clutching her cheeks.

'Have no fear, madame,' I said. 'I am merely taking the

normal precautions. My professors have taught me always to do this.'

'And who will clean your room and make your bed?'

'I will,' I said. 'This will save you much trouble.'

She muttered and grumbled a fair bit, but gave way to me in the end.

Supper with the Boisvains that evening was pigs' trotters in white sauce, another repellent dish. Monsieur B tucked into it with all the usual sucking noises and exclamations of ecstasy, and the glutinous white sauce was smeared over his entire face by the time he had finished. I excused myself from the table just as he was preparing to transfer his false teeth from mouth to fingerbowl. I went upstairs to my room and locked the door.

For the first time, I opened my big brown-paper parcel. The powder had been packed, thank goodness, in two large biscuit tins. I opened one up. The stuff was pale grey and almost as fine as flour. Here before me, I told myself, lay what was probably the biggest crock of gold a man could ever find. I say 'probably' because as yet I had no proof of anything. I had only the Major's word that the stuff worked and the hall-porter's word that it was the genuine article.

I lay on my bed and read a book until midnight. I then undressed and got into my pyjamas. I took a pin and held it upright over the open tin of powder. I sprinkled a pinch of powder over the upright pinhead. A tiny cluster of grey powder grains remained clinging to the top of the pin. Very carefully, I raised this to my mouth and licked off the powder. It tasted of nothing. I noted the time by my watch, then I sat on the edge of the bed to await results.

They weren't long coming. Precisely nine minutes later, my whole body went rigid. I began to gasp and gurgle. I froze where I was sitting, just as Major Grout had frozen on his verandah with the glass of whiskey in his hand. But because I'd had a much weaker dose than him, this period of paralysis lasted only for a few seconds. Then I felt, as the good Major had so aptly put it, a burning sensation in the region of my groin. Within another minute, my member – and again the Major

26

had said it better than I can – my member had become as stiff and erect as the mainmast of a topsail schooner.

Now for the final test. I stood up and crossed to the door. I opened it quietly and slipped along the passage. I entered the bedroom of Mademoiselle Nicole, and surely enough, there she was tucked up in bed with the candle already lit, waiting for me. 'Bonsoir, monsieur,' she whispered, giving me another of those formal handshakes. 'You have come along for your lesson number two, yes?'

I didn't say anything. Already, as I got into bed beside her, I was beginning to slide off into another of those weird fantasies that seem to engulf me whenever I come to close quarters with a female. This time I was back in the Middle Ages and Richard Coeur de Lion was King of England. I was the champion jouster of the country, the noble knight who was once more about to display his prowess and strength before the King and all his courtiers in the Field of the Cloth of Gold.

My opponent was a gigantic and fearsome female from France who had butchered seventy-eight valiant Englishmen in tournaments of jousting. But my steed was brave and my lance was of tremendous length and thickness, sharp-pointed, vibrant and made of the strongest steel. And the King shouted out 'Bravo, Sir Oswald, the man with the mighty lance! No one but he has the strength to wield so huge a weapon! Run her through, my lad! Run her through!' So I went galloping into battle with my giant lance pointed straight and true at the Frenchy's most vital region, and I thrust at her with mighty thrusts, all swift and sure, and in a trice I had pierced her armour and had her screaming for mercy. But I was in no mood to be merciful. Spurred on by the cheers of the King and his courtiers, I drove my steely lance ten thousand times into that writhing body and then ten thousand times more, and I heard the courtiers shouting, 'Thrust away, Sir Oswald! Thrust away and keep on thrusting!' And then the King's voice was saying, 'Begad, methinks the brave fellow is going to shatter that great lance of his if he doesn't stop soon!' But my lance did not shatter, and in a glorious finale, I impaled the giant Frenchy female upon the spiked end of my trusty weapon and went galloping around the arena, waving the body high above my head to shouts of 'Bravo!' and 'Gadzooks!' and 'Victor ludorum!'

All this, as you can imagine, took some time. How long, I had not the faintest idea, but when I finally surfaced again, I jumped out of the bed and stood there triumphant, looking down upon my prostrate victim. The girl was panting like a stag at bay and I began to wonder whether I might not have done her an injury. Not that I cared much about that.

'Well, mademoiselle,' I said, 'am I still in the kindergarten?'

'Oh no!' she cried, twitching her long limbs. 'Oh no, monsieur! No, no, no! You are ferocious and you are marvellous and I feel like my boiler has exploded!'

That made me feel pretty good. I left without another word and sneaked back along the corridor to my own room. What a triumph! The powder was fantastic! The Major had been right! And the hall-porter in Khartoum had not let me down! I was on my way now to the Crock of Gold and nothing could stop me. With these happy thoughts, I fell asleep.

The next morning, I immediately began to set matters in train. You will remember that I had a science scholarship. I was, therefore, well-versed in physics and chemistry and several other things besides, but chemistry had always been my strongest subject.

I therefore knew already all about the process of making a simple pill. In the year 1912, which is where we are now, it was customary for pharmacists to make many of their own pills on the premises, and for this they always used something called a pill-machine. So I went shopping in Paris that morning, and in the end I found, in a back street on the Left Bank, a supplier of secondhand pharmaceutical apparatus. From him I bought an excellent little pill-machine that turned out good professional pills in groups of twenty-four at a time. I bought also a pair of highly sensitive chemists' scales.

Next, I found a pharmacy that sold me a large quantity of calcium carbonate and a smaller amount of tragacanth. I also bought a bottle of cochineal. I carried all this back to my room and then I cleared the dressing-table and laid out my supplies and my apparatus in good order.

Pill-making is a simple matter if you know how. The calcium carbonate, which is neutral and harmless, comprises the bulk of the pill. You then add the precise quantity by weight of the active ingredient, in my case cantharadin powder. And finally, as an excipient, you put in a little tragacanth. An excipient is simply the cement that makes everything stick together and harden into an attractive pill. I weighed out sufficient of each substance to make twenty-four fairly large and impressive pills. I added a few drops of cochineal which is a tasteless scarlet colouring matter. I mixed everything together well and truly in a bowl and fed the mixture into my pill-machine. In a trice, I had before me twenty-four large red pills of perfect shape and hardness. And each one, if I had done my weighing and mixing properly, contained exactly the amount of cantharadin powder that would lie on top of a pinhead. Each one, in other words, was a potent and explosive aphrodisiac.

I was still not ready to make my move.

I went out again into the streets of Paris and found a commercial box-maker. From him, I bought one thousand small round cardboard boxes, one inch in diameter. I also bought cotton-wool.

Next, I went to a printer and ordered one thousand tiny round labels. On each label the following legend was to be printed in English:

PROFESSOR
YOUSOUPOFF'S
POTENCY PILLS
These pills are exceedingly powerful. Use them sparingly otherwise you may drive both yourself and your partner beyond the point of exhaustion. Recommended dose, one per week.
Sole European agent,
O. Cornelius, 192
Avenue Marceau,
Paris.

The labels were designed to fit exactly upon the lids of my little cardboard boxes.

Two days later, I collected the labels. I bought a pot of glue.

I returned to my room and stuck labels on to twenty-four box-lids. Inside each box, I made a nest of white cotton-wool. Upon this I placed a single scarlet pill and closed the lid.

I was ready to go.

As you will have guessed long ago, I was about to enter the commercial world. I was going to sell my Potency Pills to a clientele that would soon be screaming for more and still more. I would sell them individually, one only in each box, and I would charge an exorbitant price.

And the clientele? Where would they come from? How would a seventeen-year-old boy in a foreign city set about finding customers for this wonder-pill of his? Well, I had no qualms about that. I had only to find one single person of the right type and let him try one single pill and the ecstatic recipient would immediately come galloping back for a second helping. He would also whisper the news to his friends and the glad tidings would spread like a forest fire.

I already knew who my first victim was going to be.

I have not yet told you that my father, William Cornelius, was in the Diplomatic Service. He had no money of his own, but he was a skilful diplomat and he managed to live very comfortably on his pay. His last post had been Ambassador to Denmark, and he was presently marking time with some job in the Foreign Office in London before getting a new and more senior appointment. The current British Ambassador to France was someone by the name of Sir Charles Makepiece. He was an old friend of my father's and before I left England my father had written a letter to Sir Charles asking him to keep an eye on me.

I knew what I had to do now, and I set about doing it straight away. I put on my best suit of clothes and made my way to the British Embassy. I did not, of course, go in by the Chancery Entrance. I knocked on the door of the Ambassador's Private Residence, which was in the same imposing building as the Chancery, but at the rear. The time was four in the afternoon. A flunkey in white knee-breeches and a scarlet coat with gold buttons opened the door and glared at me. I had no visiting card, but I managed to convey the news that my father and mother were close friends of Sir Charles and Lady Makepiece and would he kindly inform her Ladyship that Oswald Cornelius Esquire had come to pay his respects.

I was put into a sort of vestibule where I sat down and waited. Five minutes later, Lady Makepiece swept into the room in a flurry of silk and chiffon. 'Well, well!' she cried, taking both my hands in hers. 'So *you* are William's son! He always had good taste, the old rascal! We got his letter and we've been waiting for you to call.'

She was an imposing wench. Not young, of course, but not exactly fossilized either. I put her around forty. She had one of those dazzling ageless faces that seemed to be carved out of marble, and lower down there was a torso that tapered to a waist I could have circled with my two hands. She sized me up with one swift penetrating glance, and she seemed to be satisfied with what she saw because the next thing she said was, 'Come in, William's son, and we shall have a dish of tea together and a chat.'

She led me by the hand through a number of vast and superbly appointed rooms until we arrived at a smallish, rather cosy place furnished with a sofa and armchairs. There was a Boucher pastel on one wall and a Fragonard watercolour on another. 'This,' she said, 'is my own private little study. From here I organize the social life of the Embassy.' I smiled and blinked and sat down on the sofa. One of those fancy-dress flunkeys brought tea and sandwiches on a silver tray. The tiny triangular sandwiches were filled with Gentleman's Relish. Lady Makepiece sat beside me and poured the tea. 'Now tell me all about yourself,' she said.

There followed a whole lot of questions and answers about my family and about me. It was all pretty banal but I knew I must stick it out for the sake of my great plan. So we went on talking for maybe forty minutes, with her Ladyship frequently patting my thigh with a jewelled hand to emphasize a point. In the end, the hand remained resting on my thigh and I felt a slight finger-pressure. Ho-ho, I thought. What's the old bird up to now? Then suddenly she sprang to her feet and began pacing nervously up and down the room. I sat watching her. Back and forth she paced, hands clasped together across her front, head twitching, bosom heaving. She was like a tightly coiled spring. I didn't know what to make of it. 'I'd better be going,' I said, standing up.

'No, no! Don't go!'

I sat down again.

'Have you met my husband?' she blurted out. 'Obviously you haven't. You've just arrived. He's a lovely man. A brilliant person. But he's getting on in years, poor lamb, and he can't take as much exercise as he used to.'

'Bad luck,' I said. 'No more polo and tennis.'

'Not even ping-pong,' she said.

'Everyone gets old,' I said.

'I'm afraid so. But the point is this.' She stopped and waited.

I waited, too.

We both waited. There was a very long silence.

I didn't know what to do with the silence. It made me fidget. 'The point is what, madame?' I said.

'Can't you see I'm trying to ask you something?' she said at last.

I couldn't think of an answer to that one, so I helped myself to another of those little sandwiches and chewed it slowly.

'I want to ask you a favour, mon petit garçon,' she said. 'I imagine you are quite good at games?'

'I am rather,' I said, resigning myself to a game of tennis with her, or ping-pong.

'And you wouldn't mind?'

'Not at all. It would be a pleasure.' It was necessary to humour her. All I wanted was to meet the Ambassador. The Ambassador was my target. He was the chosen one who would receive the first pill and thus start the whole ball rolling. But I could only reach him through her.

'It's not much I'm asking,' she said.

'I am at your service, madame.'

'You really mean it.'

'Of course.'

'You did say you were good at games?'

'I played rugger for my school,' I said. 'And cricket. I'm a pretty decent fast bowler.'

She stopped pacing and gave me a long look.

At that point a tiny little warning-bell began tinkling somewhere inside my head. I ignored it. Whatever happened, I must not antagonize this woman.

'I'm afraid I don't play rugger,' she said. 'Or cricket.'

'My tennis is all right, too,' I said. 'But I haven't brought my racquet.' I took another sandwich. I loved the taste of anchovies. 'My father says anchovies destroy the palate,' I said, chewing away. 'He won't have Gentleman's Relish in the house. But I adore it.'

She took a great big deep breath and her breasts blew up like two gigantic balloons. 'I'll tell you what I want,' she whispered softly. 'I want you to ravish me and ravish me and ravish me! I want you to ravish me to death! I want you to do it now! Now! Quickly!'

By golly, I thought. Here we go again.

'Don't be shocked, dear boy.'

'I'm not shocked.'

'Oh yes you are. I can see it on your face. I should never have asked you. You are so young. You are far too young. How old are you? No, don't tell me. I don't want to know. You are very delicious, but schoolboys are forbidden fruit. What a pity. It's quite obvious you have not yet entered the fiery world of women. I don't suppose you've ever even touched one.'

That nettled me. 'You are mistaken, Lady Makepiece,' I said. 'I have frolicked with females on both sides of the Channel. Also on ships at sea.'

'Why, you naughty boy! I don't believe it!'

I was still on the sofa. She was standing above me. Her big red mouth was open and she was beginning to pant. 'You do understand I would never have mentioned it if Charles hadn't been . . . sort of past it, don't you?'

'Of course I understand,' I said, wriggling a bit. 'I understand very well. I am full of sympathy. I don't blame you in the least.'

33

'You really mean that?'

'Of course.'

'Oh, you gorgeous boy!' she cried and she came at me like a tigress.

There is nothing particularly illuminating to report about the barney that followed, except perhaps to mention that her Ladyship astounded me with her sofa-work. Up until then, I had always regarded the sofa as a rotten romping-ground, though heaven knows I had been forced to use it often enough with the London debutantes while the parents were snoring away upstairs. The sofa to me was a beastly uncomfortable thing surrounded on three sides by padded walls and with a horizontal area that was so narrow one was continually rolling off it onto the floor. But Lady Makepiece was a sofa-wizard. For her, the sofa was a kind of gymnastic horse upon which one vaulted and bounced and flipped and rolled and achieved the most remarkable contortions.

'Were you ever a gym teacher?' I asked her.

'Shut up and concentrate,' she said, rolling me around like a lump of puff-pastry.

It was lucky for me I was young and pliable otherwise I'm quite sure I would have suffered a fracture. And that got me thinking about poor old Sir Charles and what he must have gone through in his time. Small wonder he had chosen to go into mothballs. But just wait, I thought, until he swallows the old Blister Beetle! Then it'll be *her* that starts blowing the whistle for time out, not him.

Lady Makepiece was a quick-change artist. A couple of minutes after our little caper had ended, there she was, seated at her small Louis Quinze desk, looking as well-groomed and as unruffled as when I had first met her. The steam had gone out of her now, and she had the sleepy contented expression of a boa constrictor that has just swallowed a live rat.

'Look here,' she said, studying a piece of paper. 'Tomorrow we're giving a rather grand dinner-party because it's Mafeking Day.'

'But Mafeking was relieved twelve years ago,' I said.

34

'We still celebrate it,' she said. 'What I'm saying is that Admiral Joubert has dropped out. He's reviewing his fleet in the Mediterranean. How would you like to take his place?'

I only just stopped myself from shouting hooray. It was exactly what I wanted. 'I would be honoured,' I said.

'Most of the Government Ministers will be there,' she said. 'And all the senior Ambassadors. Do you have a white tie?'

'I do,' I said. In those days, one never travelled anywhere without taking full evening-dress, even at my age.

'Good,' she said, writing my name on the guest-list. 'Eight o'clock tomorrow evening then. Good afternoon, my little man. It was nice meeting you.' Already she had gone back to studying the guest-list, so I found my own way out.

4

The next evening, sharp at eight o'clock, I presented myself at the Embassy. I was fully rigged-up in white tie and tails. A tailcoat, in those days, had a deep pocket on the inside of each tail, and in these pockets I had secreted a total of twelve small boxes, each with a single pill inside. The Embassy was a blaze of lights, and carriages were rolling up at the gates from all directions. Uniformed flunkeys were everywhere. I marched in and joined the receiving line.

'Dear boy,' said Lady Makepiece, 'I'm so glad you could come. Charles, this is Oswald Cornelius, William's son.'

Sir Charles Makepiece was a tiny little fellow with a full head of elegant white hair. His skin was the colour of biscuits, and there was an unhealthy powdery look about it, as though it had been lightly dusted over with brown sugar. The entire face, from forehead to chin, was criss-crossed with deep hairline cracks, and this, together with the powdery, biscuity skin, made him look like a terracotta bust that was beginning to crumble.

'So you are William's boy, are you?' he said, shaking my hand. 'How are you making out in Paris? Anything I can do for you, just let me know.'

I moved on into the glittering crowd. I seemed to be the only male present who was not smothered in decorations and ribbons. We stood around drinking champagne. Then we went in to dinner. It was quite a sight, that dining-room. About one hundred guests were seated on either side of a table as long as two cricket pitches. Small place cards told us where to sit. I was between two incredibly ugly old females. One was the wife of the Bulgarian Ambassador and the other was an aunt of the King of Spain. I concentrated on the food, which was superb. I still remember the large truffle, as big as a golf ball, baked in white wine in a little earthenware pot with the lid on. And the way in which the poached turbot was so superlatively undercooked, with the centre almost raw but still very hot. (The English and the Americans invariably overcook their fish.) And then the wines! They were something to remember, those wines!

But what, pray, did seventeen-year-old Oswald Cornelius know about wines? A fair question. And yet the answer is that he knew rather a lot. Because what I have not yet told you is that my own father loved wine above all other things in life, including women. He was, I think, a genuine expert. His passion was for burgundy. He adored claret, too, but he always considered even the greatest of the clarets to be just a touch on the feminine side. 'Claret,' he used to say, 'may have a prettier face and a better figure, but it's the burgundies that have the muscles and the sinews.'

By the time I was fourteen, he had begun to communicate some of this wine passion to me, and only a year ago, he had taken me on a ten-day walking tour through Burgundy during the vendange in September. We had started out at Chagny and from there we had strolled in our own time northward to Dijon, so that in the week that followed we traversed the entire length of the Côte de Nuits. It was a thrilling experience. We walked not on the main road but on the narrow rutted tracks that led us past practically every great vineyard on that famous golden slope, first Montrachet, then Meursault, then Pommard and a night in a wonderful small hotel in Beaune where we ate *écrevisses* swimming in white wine, and thick slices of *foie gras* on buttered toast.

I can remember the two of us the next day eating lunch while sitting on the low white wall along the boundary of Romanée Conti – cold chicken, French bread, a *fromage dur* and a bottle of Romanée Conti itself. We spread our food on the top of the wall and stood the bottle alongside, together with two good wine-glasses. My father drew the cork and poured the wine while I did my best to carve the chicken, and there we sat in the warm autumn sun, watching the grape-pickers combing the rows of vines, filling their baskets, bringing them to the heads of the rows, dumping the grapes into larger baskets which in turn were emptied into carts drawn by pale creamy-brown horses. I can remember my father sitting on the wall and waving a half-eaten drumstick in the direction of this splendid scene and saying, 'You are sitting, my boy, on the edge of the most famous piece of land in the whole world! Just look at it! Four and a half acres of flinty red clay! That's all it is! But those grapes you can see them picking at this very moment will produce a wine that is a glory among wines. It is also almost unobtainable because so little of it is made. This bottle we are drinking now came from here eleven years ago. Smell it! Inhale the bouquet! Taste it! Drink it! But never try to describe it! It is impossible to put such a flavour into words! To drink a Romanée Conti is like having an orgasm in the mouth and the nose both at the same time.'

I loved it when my father got himself worked up like this. Listening to him during those early years, I began to realize how important it was to be an enthusiast in life. He taught me that if you are interested in something, no matter what it is, go at it full speed ahead. Embrace it with both arms, hug it, love it and above all become passionate about it. Lukewarm is no good. Hot is no good, either. White hot and passionate is the only thing to be.

We visited Clos de Vougeot and Bonnes-Mares and Clos de la Roche and Chambertin and many other marvellous places.

We went down into the cellars of the châteaux and tasted last year's wine from the barrels. We watched the grapes being pressed in gigantic wooden screw-presses that required six men to turn the screw. We saw the juice being run off from the presses into the great wooden vats, and at Chambolle-Musigny, where they had started picking a week earlier than most of the others, we saw the grape juice coming alive in the colossal twelve-foot-high wooden vats, boiling and bubbling as it began its own magic process of converting sugar into alcohol. And while we actually stood there watching, the wine became so fiercely active and the boiling and bubbling reached such a pitch of frenzy that several men had to climb up and sit upon the cover of each vat to hold it down.

I have wandered again. I must get back to my story. But I did want to demonstrate to you very quickly that despite my tender years, I was quite capable of appreciating the quality of the wines I drank that evening at the British Embassy in Paris. They were indeed something to remember.

We started with a Chablis Grand Cru 'Grenouilles'. Then a Latour. Then a Richebourg. And with the dessert, an Yquem of great age. I cannot remember the vintage of any one of them, but they were all pre-phylloxera.

When dinner was over, the women, led by Lady Makepiece, left the room. Sir Charles shepherded the men into a vast adjoining sitting-room to drink port and brandy and coffee.

In the sitting-room, as the men began to split up into groups, I quickly manoeuvred myself alongside the host himself. 'Ah, there you are, my boy,' he said. 'Come and sit here with me.'

Perfect.

There were eleven of us, including me, in this particular group, and Sir Charles courteously introduced me to each one of them in turn. 'This is young Oswald Cornelius,' he said. 'His father was our man in Copenhagen. Meet the German Ambassador, Oswald.' I met the German Ambassador. Then I met the Italian Ambassador and the Hungarian Ambassador and the Russian Ambassador and the Peruvian Ambassador and the Mexican Ambassador. Then I met the French Minister for Foreign Affairs and a French Army General and lastly a funny little dark man from Japan who was introduced simply as Mr Mitsouko. Every one of them spoke English, and it seemed that out of courtesy to their host they were making it the language of the evening.

'Have a glass of port, young man,' Sir Charles Makepiece said to me, 'and pass it round.' I poured myself some port and carefully passed the decanter to my left. 'This is a good bottle. Fonseca '87. Your father tells me you've got a scholarship to Trinity. Is that right?'

'Yes, sir,' I said. My moment was coming any second now. I must not miss it. I must plunge in.

'What's your subject?' Sir Charles asked me.

'Science, sir,' I answered. Then I plunged. 'As a matter of fact,' I said, lifting my voice just enough for them all to hear me, 'there's some absolutely amazing work being done in one of the laboratories up there at this moment. Highly secret. You simply wouldn't believe what they've just discovered.'

Ten heads came up and ten pairs of eyes rose from port glasses and coffee cups and regarded me with mild interest.

'I didn't know you'd already gone up,' Sir Charles said. 'I thought you had a year to wait and that's why you're over here.'

'Quite right,' I said, 'but my future tutor invited me to spend most of last term working in the Natural Sciences Lab. That's my favourite subject, natural science.'

'And what, may I ask, have they just discovered that is so secret and so remarkable?' There was a touch of banter in Sir Charles's voice now and who could blame him?

'Well, sir,' I murmured, and then purposely, I stopped.

Silence for a few seconds. The nine foreigners and the British Ambassador sat still, waiting politely for me to go on. They were regarding me with a mixture of tolerance and amusement. This young lad, they seemed to be saying, has a bit of a nerve to be holding forth like this in front of us. But let's hear him out. It's better than talking politics.

'Don't tell me they are letting a fellow of your age handle secrets,' Sir Charles said, smiling a little with his crumbling terracotta face.

'These aren't *war* secrets, sir,' I said. 'They couldn't help an enemy. These are secrets that are going to help all of mankind.'

'Then tell us about them,' Sir Charles said, lighting a huge cigar. 'You have a distinguished audience here and they are all waiting to hear from you.'

'I think it's the greatest scientific breakthrough since Pasteur,' I said. 'It's going to change the world.'

The Foreign Minister of France made a sharp whistling sound by sucking air up through his hairy nostrils. 'You have another Pasteur in England at this moment?' he said. 'If so, I would very much like to hear about him.' He was a sleek oily Frenchman, this Foreign Minister, and sharp as a knife. I would have to watch him.

'If the world is about to be changed,' Sir Charles said, 'I'm a little surprised that this information hasn't yet found its way to my desk.'

Steady on, Oswald, I told myself. You've hardly begun and already you've been laying it on too thick.

'Forgive me, sir, but the point is he hasn't published yet.'

'Who hasn't? Who's *he*?'

'Professor Yousoupoff, sir.'

The Russian Ambassador put down his glass of port and said, 'Yousoupoff? Is he a Russian?'

'Yes, sir, he's a Russian.'

'Then why haven't *I* heard of him?'

I wasn't about to get into a tangle with this black-eyed black-bearded Cossack, so I kept silent.

'Come on, then, young man,' Sir Charles said. 'Tell us about the greatest scientific breakthrough of our time. You mustn't keep us in suspense, you know.'

I took a few deep breaths and a gulp of port. This was the great moment. Pray heaven I wouldn't mess it up.

'For years,' I said, 'Professor Yousoupoff has been working on the theory that the seeds of a ripe pomegranate contain an ingredient that has powerful rejuvenative properties.'

'We have millions and millions of pomegranates in my country!' the Italian Ambassador exclaimed, looking proud.

'Be quiet, Emilio,' Sir Charles said. 'Let the boy go on.'

'For twenty-seven years,' I said, 'Professor Yousoupoff has been studying the seed of the pomegranate. It became an obsession with him. He used to sleep in the laboratory. He never went out socially. He never married. The whole place was littered with pomegranates and their seeds.'

'Excuse me, please,' said the little Japanese man. 'But why the pomegranate? Why not the grape or the blackcurrant?'

'I cannot answer that question, sir,' I said. 'I suppose it was simply what you might call a hunch.'

'Hell of a long time to spend on a hunch,' Sir Charles said. 'But go on, my boy. We mustn't interrupt you.'

'Last January,' I said, 'the Professor's patience was at last rewarded. What he did was this. He dissected the seed of a pomegranate and examined the contents bit by bit under a powerful microscope. And it was only then that he observed in the very centre of the seed a minuscule speck of red vegetable tissue that he'd never seen before. He proceeded to isolate this tiny speck of tissue. But it was obviously too small to be of any use on its own. So the Professor set out to dissect one hundred seeds and to obtain from them one hundred of these tiny red particles. This is where he allowed me to assist him. I mean by dissecting out these particles under a microscope. This alone occupied us for a whole week.'

I took another sip of port. My audience waited for me to go on.

'So we now had one hundred red particles, but even when we put them all together on a glass slide, the result could still not be seen by the naked eye.'

'And you say they were red, these little things?' said the Hungarian Ambassador.

'Under the microscope they were a brilliant scarlet,' I said.

'And what did this famous professor do with them?'

'He fed them to a rat,' I said.

'A rat!'

'Yes,' I said. 'A big white rat.'

'Vy vould anybody vish to feed deese little red bomegranate tings to a rat?' the German Ambassador asked.

'Give him a chance, Wolfgang,' Sir Charles said to the

German. 'Let him finish. I want to know what happened.' He nodded for me to go on.

'You see, sir,' I said, 'Professor Yousoupoff had in the laboratory a lot of white rats. He took the one hundred tiny red particles and fed every one of them to a single large healthy male rat. He did this by inserting them, under a microscope, into a piece of meat. He then put the rat in a cage together with ten female rats. I remember very clearly how the Professor and I stood beside the cage watching the male rat. It was late afternoon and we were so excited we had forgotten all about lunch.'

'Excuse me one moment, please,' the clever French Foreign Minister said. 'But why were you so excited? What made you think that *anything* was going to happen with this rat?'

Here we go, I thought. I knew I'd have to watch this wily Frenchman. 'I was excited, sir, simply because the Professor was excited,' I said. 'He seemed to *know* something was going to happen. I can't tell you how. Don't forget, gentlemen, I was only a very young junior assistant. The Professor did not tell me all his secrets.'

'I see,' the Foreign Minister said. 'Then let us proceed.'

'Yes, sir,' I said. 'Well, we were watching the rat. At first, nothing happened. Then suddenly, after exactly nine minutes, the rat became very still. He crouched down, quivering all over. He was looking at the females. He crept toward the nearest one and grabbed her by the skin of her neck with his teeth and mounted her. It did not take long. He was very fierce with her and very swift. But here's the extraordinary thing. The moment the rat had finished copulating with the first female, he grabbed a second one and set about her in just the same way. Then he took a third female rat, and a fourth and a fifth. He was absolutely tireless. He went from one female to another, fornicating with each in turn until he had covered all ten of them. Even then, gentlemen, he hadn't had enough!'

'Good gracious me!' Sir Charles murmured. 'What a curious experiment.'

'I should add,' I went on, 'that rats are not normally promiscuous creatures. They are in fact rather moderate in their sexual habits.'

'Are you sure of that?' the French Foreign Minister said. 'I thought rats were extraordinarily lascivious.'

'No, sir,' I answered firmly. 'Rats are actually very intelligent and gentle creatures. They are easy to domesticate.'

'Go on, then,' Sir Charles said. 'What did all this tell you?'

'Professor Yousoupoff got very excited. "Oswaldsky!" he shouted – that's what he called me. "Oswaldsky, my boy, I think I have discovered the absolutely greatest most powerful sexual stimulant in the whole history of mankind!"'

'"I think you have, too," I said. We were still standing by the cage of rats and the male rat was still leaping on the wretched females, one after the other. Within an hour, he had collapsed from exhaustion. "We give him too big a dose," the Professor said.'

'This rat,' the Mexican Ambassador said, 'what came of him in the end?'

'He died,' I said.

'From too much women, yes?'

'Yes,' I said.

The little Mexican clapped his hands together hard and cried out, 'That is exactly how I wish to go when I die! From too much women!'

'From too much goats and donkeys iss more like it in Mexico,' the German Ambassador snorted.

'That's enough of that, Wolfgang,' Sir Charles said. 'Let's not start any wars. We are listening to a most interesting story. Carry on, my boy.'

'So the next time,' I said, 'we only isolated twenty of these tiny red microscopic nuclei. We inserted them in a pellet of bread and then went out looking for a very old man. With the help of the local newspaper, we found our old man in Newmarket – that's a town not far from Cambridge. His name was Mr Sawkins and he was one hundred and two years old. He was suffering from advanced senility. His mind was wandering and he had to be fed by spoon. He had not been out of bed for seven years. The Professor and I knocked on the door of his house and his daughter, aged eighty, opened it. "I am Professor Yousoupoff," the Professor announced. "I have discovered a great medicine to help old people. Will you allow us to give some to your poor old father?"

'"You can give 'im anything you damn well please," the daughter said. "The old fool doesn't know what's goin' on from one day to the next. 'Ee's a flamin' nuisance."

'We went upstairs and the Professor somehow managed to poke the bread pellet down the old man's throat. I noted the time by my watch. "Let us retire to the street outside and observe," the Professor said.

'We went out and stood in the street. I was counting each minute aloud as it went by. And then – you won't believe this, gentlemen, but I swear it's exactly what happened – precisely on the dot of nine minutes, there was a thunderous bellow from inside the Sawkins's house. The front door burst open and the old man himself rushed out into the street. He was in bare feet, wearing dirty blue and grey striped pyjamas and his long white hair was all over his shoulders. "I want me a woman!" he bellowed. "I want me a woman and by God I'm goin' to get me a woman!" The Professor clutched my arm. "Don't move!" he ordered. "Just observe!"

'The eighty-year-old daughter came rushing out after the father. "Come back, you old fool!" she yelled. "What the 'ell d'you think you're up to?"

'We were, by the way, in a little street with a row of identical connected houses on either side. Mr Sawkins ignored his daughter and ran, he actually ran, to the next-door house. He started banging on the door with his fists. "Open up, Mrs Twitchell!" he bellowed. "Come on, my beauty, open up and let's 'ave a bit of fun!"

'I caught a glimpse of the terrified face of Mrs Twitchell at the window. Then it went away. Mr Sawkins, still bellowing, put his shoulder to the flimsy door and smashed the lock. He dived inside. We stayed out on the street, waiting for the next development. The Professor was very excited. He was jumping

44

up and down in his funny black boots and shouting, "We have a breakthrough! We've done it! We shall rejuvenate the world!"

'Suddenly, piercing screams and yells came issuing from Mrs Twitchell's house. Neighbours were beginning to gather on the street. "Go in and get 'im!" shouted the old daughter. "'Ees' gone stark starin' mad!" Two men ran into the Twitchell house. There were sounds of a scuffle. Soon, out came the two men, frog-marching old Mr Sawkins between them. "I 'ad 'er!" he was yelling. "I 'ad the old bitch good and proper! I near rattled 'er to death!" At that point, the Professor and I moved quietly away from the scene.'

I paused in my story. Seven Ambassadors, the Foreign Minister of France, the French Army General and the little Japanese man were all now leaning forward in their seats, their eyes upon me.

'Is this *exactly* what happened?' Sir Charles asked me.

'Every word of it, sir, is the gospel truth,' I lied. 'When Professor Yousoupoff publishes his findings, the whole world will be reading what I have just told you.'

'So what happened next?' the Peruvian Ambassador asked.

'From then on, it was comparatively simple,' I said. 'The Professor conducted a series of experiments designed to discover what the proper absolutely safe dose should be for a normal adult male. For this, he used undergraduate volunteers. And you can be quite sure, gentlemen, that he had no trouble getting young men to come forward. As soon as the news spread around the University, there was a waiting list of over eight hundred. But to cut the story short, the Professor finally demonstrated that the safe dose was no more than five of those tiny microscopic nuclei from the pomegranate seed. So, using calcium carbonate as a base, he manufactured a pill containing exactly this quantity of the magic substance. And he proved beyond any doubt that just one of these pills would, in precisely nine minutes, turn any man, even a very old man, into a marvellously powerful sex-machine that was capable of pleasuring his partner for six hours nonstop, *without exception*.'

45

'Gott in Himmel!' shouted the German Ambassador. 'Ver can I get hold of ziss stuff?'

'Me, too!' cried the Russian Ambassador. 'I haff priority claim because it voss invented by my countryman! I muss inform zee Tsar at vonce!'

Suddenly, they were all speaking at the same time. Where could they get it? They wanted it now! How much did it cost? They were willing to pay handsomely! And the little Japanese fellow sitting on my left leaned over and hissed, 'You get me big supply of pills, yes. I give you very much money.'

'Now just a moment, gentlemen,' Sir Charles said, raising a wrinkled hand for silence. 'Our young friend here has told us a fascinating story, but as he correctly pointed out, he was only a junior assistant to Professor whatever-his-name-is. I am quite sure, therefore, that he is not in a position to supply us with this remarkable new pill. Perhaps though, my dear Oswald,' and here Sir Charles leaned toward me and placed a withered hand gently on my forearm, 'perhaps, my dear Oswald, you could put me in touch with the great Professor. One of my duties here at the Embassy is to keep the Foreign Office informed of all new scientific discoveries.'

'I quite understand,' I said.

'If I could obtain a bottle of these pills, preferably a *large* bottle, I would send it straight to London.'

'And I vould sent it to Petrograd,' said the Russian Ambassador.

'And me to Budapest.'

'And me to Mexico City.'

'And me to Lima.'

'And me to Rome.'

'Rubbish!' cried the German Ambassador. 'You vont dem for yourselves, you dirty olt men!'

'Now then, Wolfgang,' Sir Charles said, squirming a bit.

'Vy not, my dear Sharles? I too vont dem for myself. For zee Kaiser as well, of course, but me first.'

I decided I rather liked the German Ambassador. He was anyway honest.

'I think it best, gentlemen,' Sir Charles said, 'if I myself make all the arrangements. I shall write personally to the Professor.'

'The Japanese people,' Mr Mitsouko said, 'are very interested in all massage techniques and hot baths and in all similar technological advances, especially the Emperor himself.'

I allowed them to finish. I was in control now and that gave me a good feeling. I helped myself to another glass of port but refused the huge cigar Sir Charles offered me. 'Would you prefer a smaller one, dear boy?' he asked me eagerly. 'Or a Turkish cigarette? I have some Balkan Sobranies.'

'No, thank you, sir,' I said, 'but the port is delicious.'

'Help yourself, dear boy! Fill your glass!'

'I have some interesting news,' I said, and suddenly everyone became silent. The German Ambassador cupped a hand behind his ear. The Russian leaned forward in his seat. So did all the rest of them.

'What I am about to tell you is extremely confidential,' I said. 'May I rely upon all of you to keep it to yourselves?'

There was a chorus of 'Yes, yes! Of course! Absolutely! Carry on, young fellow!'

'Thank you,' I said. 'Now the point is this. As soon as I knew that I was going to Paris I decided I simply must take with me a supply of these pills, especially for my father's great friend, Sir Charles Makepiece.'

'My dear boy!' Sir Charles cried out. 'What a generous thought!'

'I could not, of course, ask the Professor to give any of them to me,' I said. 'He would never have agreed to that. After all, they are still on the secret list.'

'So what did you do?' asked Sir Charles. He was dribbling with excitement. 'Did you purloin them?'

'Certainly not, sir,' I said. 'Stealing is a criminal act.'

'Never mind about us, dear boy. We won't tell a soul.'

'So vott did you do?' the German Ambassador asked. 'You say you haff dem and you didn't steal them?'

'I made them myself,' I said.

'Brilliant!' they cried. 'Magnifique!'

'Having assisted the Professor at every stage,' I said, 'I naturally knew exactly how to manufacture these pills. So I . . . well . . . I simply made them in his laboratory each day when he was out to lunch.' Slowly, I reached behind me and took one small round box from my tail-coat pocket. I placed it on the low table. I opened the lid. And there, lying in its little nest of cotton-wool, was a single scarlet pill.

Everyone leaned forward to look. Then I saw the plump white hand of the German Ambassador sliding across the surface of the table towards the box like a weasel stalking a mouse. Sir Charles saw it, too. He smacked the palm of his own hand on top of the German's, pinning it down. 'Now, Wolfgang,' he said, 'don't be impatient.'

'I vont zee pill!' Ambassador Wolfgang shouted.

Sir Charles put his other hand over the pill-box and kept it there. 'Do you have more?' he asked me.

I fished in my tail-coat pockets and brought out nine more boxes. 'There is one for each of you,' I said.

Eager hands reached across, grabbing the little boxes. 'I pay,' said Mr Mitsouko. 'How much you want?'

'No,' I said. 'These are presents. Try them out, gentlemen. See what you think.'

Sir Charles was studying the label on the box. 'Ah-ha,' he said. 'I see you have your address printed here.'

'That's just in case,' I said.

'In case of what?'

'In case anyone wishes to get a second pill,' I said.

I noticed that the German Ambassador had taken out a little book and was making notes. 'Sir,' I said to him, 'I expect you are thinking of telling your scientists to investigate the seed of the pomegranate. Am I not right?'

'Zatt iss exactly vot I am tinking,' he said.

'No good,' I said. 'Waste of time.'

'May I ask vy?'

'Because it's not the pomegranate,' I said. 'It's something else.'

'So you lie to us!'

48

'It is the only untruth I have told you in the entire story,' I said. 'Forgive me, but I had to do it. I had to protect Professor Yousoupoff's secret. It was a point of honour. All the rest is true. Believe me it's true. It is especially true that each of you has in his possession the most powerful rejuvenator the world has ever known.'

At that point, the ladies returned and each man in our group quickly and rather surreptitiously pocketed his pill-box. They stood up. They greeted their wives. I noticed that Sir Charles had suddenly become absurdly jaunty. He hopped across the room and splashed a silly sort of kiss smack on Lady Makepiece's scarlet lips. She gave him one of those cool what-on-earth-was-that-for looks. Unabashed, he took her arm and led her across the room into a throng of people. I last saw Mr Mitsouko prowling around the floor inspecting the womenflesh at very close quarters, like a horse-coper examining a bunch of mares on the market-place. I slipped quietly away.

Half an hour later, I was back at my boarding-house in the Avenue Marceau. The family had retired and all the lamps were out, but as I passed the bedroom of Mademoiselle Nicole in the upstairs corridor, I could see in the crack between the door and the floor a flicker of candlelight. The little trollop was waiting for me again. I decided not to go in. There was nothing new for me in there. Even at this early stage in my career, I had already decided that the only women who interested me were new women. Second time round was no good. It was like reading a detective novel twice over. You knew exactly what was going to happen next. The fact that I had recently broken this rule by visiting Mademoiselle Nicole a second time was beside the point. That was done simply to test my Blister Beetle powder. And by the way, this principle of no-woman-more-than-once is one that I have stuck to rigorously all my life and I commend it to all men of action who enjoy variety.

5

That night I slept well. I was still fast asleep at eleven o'clock the
next morning when the sound of Madame Boisvain's fists
hammering at my door jerked me awake. 'Get up, Monsieur
Cornelius!' she was shouting. 'You must come down at once!
People have been ringing my bell and demanding to see you
since before breakfast!'

I was dressed and downstairs in two minutes flat. I went to the
front door and there, standing on the cobblestones of the sidewalk, were no less than seven men, none of whom I had ever
seen before. They made a picturesque little group in their many-
coloured fancy uniforms with all manner of gilt and silver
buttons on their jackets.

They turned out to be Embassy Messengers, and they came
from the British, the German, the Russian, the Hungarian, the
Italian, the Mexican and the Peruvian Embassies. Each man
carried a letter addressed to me. I accepted the letters and opened
them on the spot. All of them said roughly the same thing: *They
wanted more pills*. They begged for more pills. They instructed
me to give the pills to the bearer of the letter, etc. etc.

I told the messengers to wait on the street and I went back
up to my room. Then, I wrote the following message on each of
the letters: *Honoured Sir, these pills are extremely expensive to
manufacture. I regret that in future the cost of each pill will be one
thousand francs*. In those days there were twenty francs to the
pound, which meant that I was asking exactly fifty pounds ster-
ling per pill. And fifty pounds in 1912 was worth maybe ten times
as much as it is today. By today's standards, I was probably asking about five hundred pounds per pill. It was a ridiculous
price, but these were wealthy men. They were also sex-crazy

men, and as any sensible woman will tell you, a man who is very wealthy and grossly sex-crazy both at the same time is the easiest touch in the world.

I trotted downstairs again and handed the letters back to their respective carriers and told them to deliver them to their masters. As I was doing this, two more messengers arrived, one from the Quai d'Orsay (the Foreign Minister) and one from the General at the Ministry of War or whatever it is called. And while I was scribbling the same statement about price on these last two letters, who should turn up in a very fine hansom cab but Mr Mitsouko himself. His appearance shocked me. The previous night he had been a bouncy, dapper, bright-eyed little Jap. This morning he hardly had the strength to get out of his cab, and as he came tottering toward me, his legs began to buckle. I grabbed hold of him just in time.

'My dear sir!' he gasped, putting both hands on my shoulders for support. 'My dear, dear sir! It's a miracle! It's a wonder-pill! It's . . . it's the greatest invention of all time!'

'Hang on,' I said. 'Are you feeling all right?'

'Of course I am all right,' he gasped. 'I am a little bit jiggered, that's all.' He started to giggle, and there he stood, this tiny oriental person dressed in a top hat and tails, clinging to my shoulders and giggling quite uncontrollably now. He was so small that the top of his top hat came no higher than my lowest rib. 'I am a little bit jiggered and a little bit pokered,' he said, 'but who would not be, my dear boy, who would not be?'

'What happened, sir?' I asked him.

'I molested *seven women*!' he cried. 'And these were not our dinky-tinky little Japanese women! No, no, no! They were enormous strong French wenchies! I took them in rotation, *bang bang bang*! And every one of them was screaming out *camarade camarade camarade*! I was a giant among these women, do you understand that, my dear young sir? I was a giant and I swung my giant club and I sent them all squiggling in every direction!'

I led him inside and sat him down in Madame Boisvain's parlour. I found him a glass of brandy. He gulped it down and a faint yellowish colour began returning to his white cheeks. I noticed that there was a leather satchel suspended by a cord around his right wrist, and when he took it off and dumped it on the table, there was the clinking of coins inside it.

'You must be careful, sir,' I said to him. 'You are a small man and these are large pills. I think it would be safer if you took only half the normal dose each time. Just half a pill instead of one.'

'Bunkum, sir!' he cried. 'Bunkum and horseradish sauce as we say in Japan! Tonight I propose to take not one pill but three!'

'Have you read what it says on the label?' I asked him anxiously. The last thing I wanted was a dead Jap around the place. Think of the outcry, the autopsy, the inquiries, and the pill-boxes with my name on them in his house.

'I examine the label,' he said, holding his glass out for more of Madame Boisvain's brandy, 'and I ignore it. We Japanese, we may be small in body but our organs are of gigantic size. That is why we walk bowlegged.'

I decided I would try to discourage him by doubling the price. 'I'm afraid they are terrifically expensive, these pills,' I said.

'Money no object,' he said, pointing to the leather satchel on the table. 'I pay in gold coins.'

'But Mr Mitsouko,' I said, 'each pill is going to cost you *two thousand* francs! They are very difficult to manufacture. That's an awful lot of money for one pill.'

'I take twenty,' he said without even blinking.

My God, I thought, he *is* going to kill himself. 'I cannot allow you to have them,' I told him, 'unless you give me your word you will never take more than one at a time.'

'Do not lecture me, young buckeroo,' he said. 'Just get me the pills.'

I went upstairs and counted out twenty pills and put them in a plain bottle. I wasn't going to risk having my name and address on this lot.

'Ten I shall send to the Emperor in Tokyo,' Mr Mitsouko said when I handed them to him. 'It will put me in a very hot position with His Royal Highness.'

'It'll put the Empress in some pretty hot positions, too,' I said.

He grinned and took up the leather satchel and emptied a vast pile of gold coins on to the table. They were all one hundred franc pieces. 'Twenty coins for each pill,' he said, starting to count them out. 'That is four hundred coins altogether. And well worth it, my young magician.'

When he had gone, I scooped up the coins and carried them up to my room.

My God, I thought. I am rich already.

But before the day was done, I was a lot richer. One by one, the messengers started trickling back from their respective Embassies and Ministries. They all carried precise orders and exact amounts of money, most of it in gold twenty-franc pieces. This is how it went:

Sir Charles Makepiece, 4 pills	=	4,000 francs
The German Ambassador, 8 pills	=	8,000 francs
The Russian Ambassador, 10 pills	=	10,000 francs
The Hungarian Ambassador, 3 pills	=	3,000 francs
The Peruvian Ambassador, 2 pills	=	2,000 francs
The Mexican Ambassador, 6 pills	=	6,000 francs
The Italian Ambassador, 4 pills	=	4,000 francs
The French Foreign Minister, 6 pills	=	6,000 francs
The Army General, 3 pills	=	3,000 francs
		46,000 francs
Mr Mitsouko, 20 pills (double price)	=	40,000 francs
GRAND TOTAL		86,000 francs

Eighty-six thousand francs! At the exchange rate of one hundred francs to five pounds, I was all of a sudden worth four thousand, three hundred English pounds! It was incredible. One could buy a good house for money like that, with a carriage and a pair of horses thrown in, as well as one of those dashing new-fangled automobiles!

For supper that night, Madame Boisvain served oxtail stew and it wasn't at all bad except that the sloshiness of it all encouraged Monsieur B to suck and swig and gulp in the most disgusting fashion. At one point, he picked up his plate and tipped the gravy straight into his mouth together with a couple of carrots and a large onion. 'My wife tells me that you had a lot of peculiar visitors today,' he said. His face was plastered with brown fluid and strands of meat were hanging from his moustache. 'Who were these men?'

'They were friends of the British Ambassador,' I answered. 'I am doing a little business for Sir Charles Makepiece.'

'I cannot have my house turned into a marketplace,' Monsieur B said, speaking with his mouth full of fat. 'These activities must cease.'

'Don't worry,' I said. 'Tomorrow I am finding alternative accommodation.'

'You mean you're leaving?' he cried.

'I'm afraid I must. But you may keep the advance rent my father has paid you.'

There was a bit of an uproar around the table about all this, much of it from Mademoiselle Nicole, but I stuck to my guns. And the next morning I went out and found myself a quite grand ground-floor apartment with three large rooms and a kitchen. It was on the Avenue Jena. I packed all my possessions and loaded them into a hackney coach. Madame Boisvain was at the front door to see me off. 'Madame,' I said, 'I have a small favour to ask of you.'

'Yes?'

'And in return I want you to take this.' I held out five gold twenty-franc pieces. She nearly fell over. 'From time to time,' I said, 'people will call at your house asking for me. All you have to do is tell them I have moved and redirect them to this address.' I gave her a piece of paper with my new address written on it.

'But that is too much money, Monsieur Oswald!'

'Take it,' I said, pushing the coins into her hand. 'Keep it for yourself. Don't tell your husband. But it is very important that you inform everyone who calls where I am living.'

She promised to do this, and I drove away to my new quarters.

54

6

My business flourished. My ten original clients all whispered the great news to their own friends and those friends whispered it to other friends and in a month or so a large snowball had been created. I spent half of each day making pills. I thanked heaven I had had the foresight to bring such a large quantity of powder from the Sudan in the first place. But I did have to reduce my price. Not everyone was an Ambassador or a Foreign Minister, and I found early on that a lot of people simply couldn't afford to pay my absurd original fee of one thousand francs per pill. So I made it two hundred and fifty instead.

The money gushed in.

I started buying fine clothes and going out into Paris society.

I purchased a motor car and learned to drive it. It was De Dion-Bouton's brand new model, the Sports DK, a marvellous little monobloc four with a three-speed gearbox and a pull-on handbrake. Top speed, believe it or not, was as much as 50 mph, and more than once I took her to the limit up the Champs Elysées.

But above all, I rollocked and frolicked with women to my heart's content. Paris in those days was an exceptionally cosmopolitan city. It was filled with ladies of quality from practically every country in the world, and it was during this period that a curious truth began to dawn upon me. We all know that people of different nations have different national characteristics and different temperaments. What is not quite so well recognized is the fact that these different national characteristics become even more marked during sexual, as opposed to merely social, intercourse. I became an expert on national sexual characteristics. It was extraordinary how the women of one nation or another ran true to form. You could take, for example, half a dozen Serbian ladies (and don't think I didn't) and you would find, if you were paying close attention, that every one of them possessed a number of very definite common eccentricities, common skills and common preferences. Polish women also, because of certain habits they all had in common, were easily recognizable. So were the Basques, the Moroccans, the Equadorians, the Norwegians, the Dutch, the Guatemalians, the Belgians, the Russians, the Chinese and all the rest of them. Toward the end of my stay in Paris, you could have put me on a couch blindfold with any lady from any country, and within five minutes, though she never uttered a word, I would have told you her nationality.

Now for the obvious question. Which country produced the most exhilarating females?

I myself became rather partial to Bulgarian ladies of aristocratic stamp. They had, amongst other things, the most unusual tongues. Not only were these tongues of theirs exceptionally muscular and vibrant, but they had a roughness about them, a kind of abrasive quality that one normally finds only in cats' tongues. Get a cat to lick your finger some time and you will see exactly what I mean.

Turkish ladies (I think I've mentioned them before) were also high on my list. They were like water-wheels. They never stopped turning until the river dried up. But by gad, you had to be fit before you challenged a Turkish lady, and I personally never allowed one into my house until after I'd had a good breakfast.

Hawaiian women interested me because they had prehensile toes, and in almost any situation you cared to mention, they used their feet rather than their hands.

As far as Chinese women went, I learned by experience to tamper only with those that came from Peking and the neighbouring province of Shan-Tung. And even then, it was essential that they were from noble families. In those days, it was the custom among the nobility of Peking and Shan-Tung to put their girls into the hands of wise old women as soon as they reached the age of fifteen. For two years thereafter, these girls were subjected to a rigorous course of instruction designed to teach them only one thing – the art of giving physical pleasure to their future husbands. And at the end of it all, after a severe practical examination, certificates were issued indicating a pass or a failure. If the girl was exceptionally dexterous and inventive, she might get what was called a 'Pass with Distinction', and most prized of all was the 'Diploma of Merit'. A young lady with a Diploma could virtually pick her own husband. Unfortunately though, at least half the Diploma girls were whisked away at once into the Emperor's Palace.

I discovered only one Chinese lady in Paris who had earned a Diploma of Merit. She was the wife of an opium millionaire and she had come over to select a wardrobe. She selected me as well, and I must admit it was a memorable experience. She had developed into a sublime art the practice of what she called *so-far-and-no-further*. Nothing ever quite finished. She didn't allow it to. She took one to the brink. Two hundred times she took me to the brink of the golden threshold, and for three and a half hours, which was the duration of my suffering, it felt as though a long live nerve was being drawn very very slowly and with exquisite patience out of my burning body. I hung on to the edge of the cliff with my fingertips, screaming for succour or release, but the blissful torture went on and on and on. It was an amazing demonstration of skill and I have never forgotten it.

I could describe if I wished the curious feminine habits of at least fifty other nationalities, but I am not going to do so. Not here anyway, because I really must proceed with the main theme of this story, which is how I made money.

During my seventh month in Paris, a lucky incident took place that doubled my income. This is what happened. One afternoon, I had a Russian lady in my apartment who was some sort of a relation to the Tsar. She was a slim white-skinned little herring, rather cool and casual, almost offhand she was, and I had to stoke her up pretty vigorously before I succeeded in raising a good head of steam in her boilers. That sort of blasé attitude only makes me more determined than ever, and I can promise you that by the time I'd finished with her, she'd had a fair old roasting.

When it was over, I lay back on the couch sipping a glass of champagne as a cooler. The Russian was languidly dressing herself and wandering round my room looking at this and that.

'What are all these red pills in this bottle?' she asked me.

'They're none of your business,' I said.

'When am I going to see you again?'

'Never,' I said. 'I told you my rules.'

'You are being disagreeable,' she said, pouting. 'Tell me what these pills are for or I also will become disagreeable. I will throw them all out the window.' She picked up the bottle that contained five hundred of my precious Blister Beetle pills just made that morning and she opened the window.

'Don't,' I said.

'Then tell me.'

'They are tonic pills for men,' I said. 'Pick-me-ups, that's all.'

'Why not for women also?'

'They're only for men.'

'I shall try one,' she said, unscrewing the bottle-top and tipping out a pill. She popped it into her mouth and washed it down with champagne. Then she continued putting on her clothes.

She was fully dressed and was adjusting her hat in front of the looking-glass when suddenly she froze. She turned and faced me. I lay where I was, sipping my drink, but I was now watching her closely and with some trepidation.

She remained frozen for maybe thirty seconds, staring at me with a cold hard dangerous stare. Then all at once, she reached both hands up to her neckline and ripped her silk dress clean off her body. She tore off her underclothes. She flung her hat across the room. She crouched. She began to move forward. She came softly across the room toward me with the slow deliberate tread of a tigress stalking an antelope.

'What's up?' I said. But by now I knew very well what was up. Nine minutes had gone by and the pill had hit her.

'Steady on,' I said.

58

She kept coming.

'Go away,' I said.

Still she kept coming.

Then she sprang, and all I could see in those first few moments was a blurred flurry of legs and arms and mouth and hands and fingers. She went quite mad. She was wild with lust. I hauled in my canvas and lay there trying to ride out the storm. That wasn't good enough for her. She began to throw me around all over the place, snorting and grunting as she did so. I didn't like it. I'd had my fill. This must stop, I decided. But I still had a terrific job pinning her down. In the end, I got her wrists locked behind her back and I carried her kicking and screaming into my bathroom and held her under the cold shower. She tried to bite me but I gave her an uppercut to the chin with my elbow. I held her under that freezing shower for at least twenty minutes while she went on yelling and swearing in Russian all the time.

'Had enough?' I said at last. She was half drowned and pretty cold.

'I want you!' she spluttered.

'No,' I said. 'I'm going to keep you here until you cool down.'

Finally she gave in. I let her go. Poor girl, she was shivering terribly and she looked a sight. I got a towel and gave her a good rub down. Then a glass of brandy.

'It was that red pill,' she said.

'I know it was.'

'I want some of them to take home.'

'Those are too strong for ladies,' I said. 'I will make you some that are just right.'

'Now?'

'No. Come back tomorrow and they'll be ready.'

Because her dress was ruined, I wrapped her in my overcoat and drove her home in the De Dion. Actually, she had done me a good turn. She had demonstrated that my pill worked just as well on the female as it did on the male. Probably better. I immediately set about making some Ladies' Pills. I made them half the strength of the Men's Pills, and I turned out one hundred of them, anticipating a ready market. But the market was even more ready than I had anticipated. When the Russian woman came back the next afternoon, she demanded five hundred of them on the spot!

'But they cost two hundred and fifty francs each.'

'I don't care about that. All my girl friends want them. I told them what happened to me yesterday and now they all want them.'

'I can give you a hundred, that's all. The rest later. Do you have money?'

'Of course I have money.'

'May I make a suggestion, madame?'

'What is it?'

'If a lady takes one of these pills on her own, I fear she may appear unduly aggressive. Men don't like that. I didn't like it yesterday.'

'What is your suggestion?'

'I suggest that any lady who intends taking one of these pills should persuade her partner also to take one. And at exactly the same time. Then they'll be all square.'

'That makes good sense,' she said.

It not only made good sense, it would also double the sales.

'The partner,' I said, 'could take a larger pill. It's called the Men's Pill. That's simply because men are bigger than women and need a bigger dose.'

'Always assuming,' she said, smiling a little, 'that the partner is a male.'

'Whatever you like,' I said.

She shrugged her shoulders and said, 'Very well, then, give me also one hundred of these Men's Pills.'

By gum, I thought, there's going to be some fun and frolics around the boudoirs of Paris tonight. Things were hot enough with just the man getting himself all pilled-up but I shuddered to think what was going to happen when both parties took the medicine.

It was a howling success. Sales doubled. They trebled. By the time my twelve months in Paris were up, I had around two million francs in the bank! That was one hundred thousand pounds! I was now nearly eighteen. I was rich. But I was not rich enough. My year in France had shown me very clearly the path I wanted to follow in my life. I was a sybarite. I wished to lead a life of luxury and leisure. I would never get bored. That was not my style. But I would never be completely satisfied unless the luxury was intensely luxurious and the leisure was unlimited. One hundred thousand pounds was not enough for that. I needed more. I needed a million pounds at least. I felt sure I would find a way to earn it. Meanwhile, I had not made a bad start.

I had enough sense to realize that first of all I must continue my education. Education is everything. I have a horror of uneducated people. And so in the summer of 1913, I transferred my money to a London bank and returned to the land of my fathers. In September, I went up to Cambridge to begin my undergraduate studies. I was a scholar remember, a scholar of Trinity College, and as such I had a number of privileges and was well-treated by those in authority.

It was here at Cambridge that the second and final phase of my fortune-making began. Bear with me a little longer and you shall hear all about it in the pages to come.

7

My chemistry tutor at Cambridge was called A. R. Woresley. He was a middle-aged, shortish man, paunchy, untidily dressed and with a grey moustache whose edges were stained yellow ochre by the nicotine from his pipe. In appearance, therefore, a typical university don. But he struck me as being exceptionally able. His lectures were never routine. His mind was always darting about in search of the unusual. Once he said to us:

'And now we need as it were a tompion to protect the contents of this flask from invading bacteria. I presume you know what a tompion is, Cornelius ?'

'I can't say I do, sir,' I said.

'Can anyone give me a definition of that common English noun ?' A. R. Woresley said.

Nobody could.

'Then you'd better look it up,' he said. 'It is not my business to teach you elementary English.'

'Oh, come on, sir,' someone said. 'Tell us what it means.'

'A tompion,' A. R. Woresley said, 'is a small pellet made out of mud and saliva which a bear inserts into his anus before hibernating for the winter, to stop the ants getting in.'

A strange fellow, A. R. Woresley, a mixture of many attitudes, occasionally witty, more often pompous and sombre, but underneath everything there was a curiously complex mind. I began to like him very much after that little tompion episode. We struck up a pleasant student-tutor relationship. I was invited to his house for sherry. He was a bachelor. He lived with his sister who was called Emmaline of all names. She was dumpy and frowsy and seemed to have something greenish on her teeth that looked like verdigris. She had a kind of surgery in the house where she did things to people's feet. A pedicurist, I think she called herself.

Then the Great War broke out. It was 1914 and I was nineteen years old. I joined the Army. I had to, and for the next four years I concentrated all my efforts on trying to survive. I am not going to talk about my wartime experiences. Trenches, mud, mutilation and death have no place in these journals. I did my bit. Actually, I did well, and by November 1918, when it all came to an end, I was a twenty-three-year-old captain in the infantry with a Military Cross. I had survived.

At once, I returned to Cambridge to resume my education. The survivors were allowed to do that, though heaven knows there weren't many of us. A. R. Woresley had also survived. He had remained in Cambridge doing some sort of wartime scientific work and had had a fairly quiet war. Now he was back at his old job of teaching chemistry to undergraduates, and we were pleased to see one another again. Our friendship picked up where it had left off four years before.

One evening in February 1919, in the middle of the Lent term, A. R. Woresley invited me to supper at his house. The meal was not good. We had cheap food and cheap wine, and we had his pedicurist sister with verdigris on her teeth. I would have thought they could have lived in slightly better style than they did, but when I broached this delicate subject rather cautiously to my host, he told me that they were still struggling to pay off the mortgage on the house. After supper, A. R. Woresley and I retired to his study to drink a good bottle of port that I had brought him as a present. It was a Croft 1890, if I remember rightly.

'Don't often taste stuff like this,' he said. He was very comfortable in an old armchair with his pipe lit and a glass of port in his hand. What a thoroughly decent man he was, I thought. And what a terribly dull life he leads.

I decided to liven things up a bit by telling him about my time in Paris six years before in 1913 when I had made one hundred thousand pounds out of Blister Beetle pills. I started at the beginning. Very quickly I got caught up in the fun of story-telling. I remembered everything, but in deference to my tutor, I left out the more salacious details. It took me nearly an hour to tell.

A. R. Woresley was enraptured by the whole escapade. 'By gad, Cornelius!' he cried. 'What a nerve you've got! What a splendid nerve! And now you are a very wealthy young man!'

'Not wealthy enough,' I said. 'I want to make a million pounds before I'm thirty.'

'And I believe you will,' he said. 'I believe you will. You have a flair for the outrageous. You have a nose for the successful stunt. You have the courage to act swiftly. And what's more, you are totally unscrupulous. In other words, you have all the qualities of the nouveau riche millionaire.'

'Thank you,' I said.

'Yes, but how many boys of seventeen would have gone all the way out to Khartoum on their own to look for a powder that might not even have existed ? Precious few.'

'I wasn't going to miss a chance like that,' I said.

'You have a great flair, Cornelius. A very great flair. I am a little envious of you.'

We sat there drinking our port. I was enjoying a small Havana cigar. I had offered one to my host but he preferred his stinking pipe. That pipe of his made more smoke than any other pipe I had ever seen. It was like a miniature warship laying a smokescreen in front of his face. And behind the smokescreen, A. R. Woresley was brooding on my Paris story. He kept snorting and grunting and mumbling things like 'Remarkable exploit! ... What a nerve! ... What panache! ... Good chemistry, too, making those pills.'

Then there was silence. The smoke billowed around his head. The glass of port disappeared through the smokescreen as he put it to his lips. Then it reappeared, empty. I had talked enough, so I kept my peace.

'Well, Cornelius,' A. R. Woresley said at last. 'You have just given me your confidence. Perhaps I had better give you mine in return.'

He paused. I waited. What's coming, I wondered.

'You see,' he said, 'I myself have also had a little bit of a coup in the last few years.'

'You have ?'

'I'm going to write a paper on it when I get the time. And I might even be successful in getting it published.'

'Chemistry ?' I asked.

'A bit of chemistry,' he said. 'And a good deal of bio-chemistry. It's a mixture.'

'I'd love to hear about it.'

'Would you really ?' He was longing to tell it.

'Of course,' I poured him another glass of port. 'You've got plenty of time,' I said, 'because we're going to finish this bottle tonight.'

'Good,' he said. Then he began his story.

'Exactly fourteen years ago,' he said, 'in the winter of 1905,

I observed a goldfish frozen solid in the ice in my garden pond. Nine days later there was a thaw. The ice melted and the goldfish swam away, apparently none the worse. That set me thinking. A fish is cold-blooded. So what other forms of cold-blooded life could be preserved at low temperatures? Quite a few, I guessed. And from there, I began speculating about preserving *bloodless* life at low temperatures. By bloodless I mean bacteria, etcetera. Then I said to myself, "Who wants to preserve bacteria? Not me." So then I asked myself another question. "What living organism above all others would you like to see kept alive for very long periods?" And the answer came back, spermatozoa!'

'Why spermatozoa?' I asked.

'I'm not quite sure why,' he said, 'especially as I'm a chemist, not a bio man. But I had a feeling that somehow it would be a valuable contribution. So I started my experiments.'

'What with?' I asked.

'With sperm, of course. Living sperm.'

'Whose?'

'My own.'

In the little silence that followed, I felt a twinge of embarrassment. Whenever someone tells me he has done something, no matter what it is, I simply cannot help conjuring up a vivid picture of the scene. It's only a flash, but it always happens and I was doing it now. I was looking at scruffy old A. R. Woresley in his lab, as he did what he had to do for the sake of his experiments, and I felt embarrassed.

'In the cause of science everything is permissible,' he said, sensing my discomfort.

'Oh, I agree. I absolutely agree.'

'I worked alone,' he said, 'and mostly late at night. Nobody knew what I was up to.'

His face disappeared again behind the smokescreen, then swam back into view.

'I won't recite the hundreds of failed experiments I did,' he said. 'I shall speak instead of my successes. I think you may find them interesting. For example, the first important thing I discovered was that exceedingly low temperatures were required to keep spermatozoa alive for any length of time. I kept freezing the semen to lower and still lower temperatures, and with each lowering of the temp I got a longer and longer life span. By using solid carbon dioxide, I was able to freeze my semen down to $-97°$ Centigrade. But even that wasn't enough. At minus ninety-seven the sperm lived for about a month but no more. "I must go lower," I told myself. But how could I do that? Then I hit upon a way to freeze the stuff all the way down to $-197°$ Centigrade.'

'Impossible,' I said.

'What do you think I used?'

'I haven't the foggiest.'

'I used liquid nitrogen. That did it.'

'But liquid nitrogen is tremendously volatile,' I said. 'How could you prevent it from vaporizing? What did you store it in?'

'I devised special containers,' he said. 'Very strong and rather elaborate vacuum flasks. In these, the nitrogen remained liquid at minus one nine seven degrees virtually for ever. A little topping up was required now and again, but that was all.'

'Not for ever, surely.'

'Oh, yes,' he said. 'You are forgetting that nitrogen is a gas. If you liquefy a gas, it will stay liquid for a thousand years if you don't allow it to vaporize. And you do this simply by making sure that the flask is completely sealed and efficiently insulated.'

'I see. And the sperm stayed alive?'

'Yes and no,' he said. 'They stayed alive long enough to tell me I'd got the right temperature. But they did not stay alive indefinitely. There was still something wrong. I pondered this and in the end I decided that what the sperm needed was some sort of a buffer, an overcoat if you like, to cushion them from the intense cold. And after experimenting with about eighty different substances, I at last hit on the perfect one.'

'What was it?'

'Glycerol.'

'Just plain glycerol?'

'Yes. But even that didn't work at first. It didn't work properly

66

until I also discovered that the cooling process must be done very gradually. Spermatozoa are delicate little fellows. They don't like shocks. You cause them distress if you subject them straight away to minus one nine seven degrees.'

'So you cool them gradually?'

'Exactly. Here is what you must do. You mix the sperm with the glycerol and put it in a small rubber container. A test tube is no good. It would crack at low temperatures. And by the way, you must do all this as soon as the sperm has been obtained. You must hurry. You cannot hang about or it will die. So first you put your precious package on ordinary ice to reduce the temperature to freezing point. Next, you put it into nitrogen vapour to freeze it deeper. Finally you pop it into the deepest freeze of all, liquid nitrogen. It's a step by step process. You acclimatize the sperm gradually to coldness.'

'And it works?'

'Oh, it works all right. I am quite certain that sperm which has been protected with glycerol and then frozen slowly will stay alive at minus one nine seven for as long as you like.'

'For a hundred years?'

'Absolutely, provided you keep it at minus one nine seven degrees.'

'And you could thaw it out after that time and it would fertilize a woman?'

'I'm quite sure of it. But having got that far I began to lose interest in the human aspect. I wanted to go a lot further. I had many more experiments to do. But one cannot experiment with men and women, not in the way I wanted to.'

'How did you want to experiment?'

'I wanted to find out how much sperm wastage there was in a single ejaculation.'

'I'm not with you. What d'you mean by sperm wastage?'

'The average ejaculation from a large animal such as a bull or a horse produces five ccs of semen. Each cc contains one thousand million separate spermatozoa. This means five thousand million sperm altogether.'

'Not five thousand *million*! Not in one go!'

'That's what I said.'

'It's unbelievable.'

'It's true.'

'How much does a human produce?'

'About half that. About two ccs and two thousand million.'

'You mean to tell me,' I said, 'that every time I pleasure a young lady, I shoot into her two thousand million spermatozoa?'

'Absolutely.'

'All squiggling and squirming and thrashing about?'

'Of course.'

'No wonder it gives her a charge,' I said.

A. R. Woresley was not interested in that aspect. 'The point is this,' he said. 'A bull, for example, definitely does *not* need five thousand million spermatozoa in order to achieve fertilization with a cow. Ultimately, he needs only a single sperm. But in order to make sure of hitting the target, he has to use a few million at least. But how many million? That was my next question.'

'Why?' I asked.

'Because, my dear fellow, I wanted to find out just how many females, whether they were cows, mares, humans or whatever, could ultimately be fertilized by a single ejaculation. I was assuming, of course, that all those millions of sperm could be divided up and shared among them. Do you see what I'm driving at?'

'Perfectly. What animals did you use for these experiments?'

'Bulls and cows,' A. R. Woresley said. 'I have a brother who owns a small dairy farm over at Steeple Bumpstead not far from here. He had a bull and about eighty cows. We had always been good friends, my brother and I. So I confided in him, and he agreed to let me use his animals. After all, I wasn't going to hurt them. I might even do him a favour.'

'How could you do him a favour?'

'My brother has never been well-off. His own bull, the only one he could afford, was of moderate quality. He would dearly love to have had his whole herd of cows bear calves by a splendid prize bull from very high milk-yielding stock.'

'You mean someone else's bull?'

'Yes, I do.'

'How would you go about obtaining semen from someone else's valuable prize bull?'

'I would steal it.'

'Ah-ha.'

'I would steal one ejaculation, and then, provided of course that I was successful with my experiments, I would share out that single ejaculation, those five thousand million sperm, among all of my brother's eighty cows.'

'How would you share it out?' I asked.

'By what I call hypodermic insemination. By injecting the sperm into the cow with a syringe.'

'I suppose that's possible.'

'Of course it's possible,' he said. 'After all, the male sexual organ is itself really nothing more than a syringe for injecting semen.'

'Steady on,' I said. 'Mine's a bit more than that.'

'I don't doubt it, Cornelius, I don't doubt it,' he answered dryly. 'But shall we stick to the point?'

'Sorry.'

'So I started experimenting with bulls' semen.'

I picked up the bottle of port and refilled his glass. I had the feeling now that old Woresley was on to something pretty interesting and I wanted to keep him going.

'I've told you,' he said, 'that the average bull produces about five ccs of fluid each time. That's not much. Even when mixed with glycerol there wouldn't be enough there for me to start dividing it up into a great many parts and then expect to be able to inject each of those tiny parts into separate cows. So I had to find a dilutant, something to increase the volume.'

'Why not add more glycerol?'

'I tried it. It didn't work. Altogether too viscous. I won't bore you with a list of all the curious substances I experimented with. I will simply tell you the one that works. Skimmed milk works. Eighty per cent skimmed milk, ten per cent egg yolk and ten per cent glycerol. That's the magic mixture. The sperm love it. You simply mix the whole cocktail thoroughly, and that, as you can see, gave me a practical volume of fluid to experiment with. So for several years, I worked with my brother's cows, and finally I arrived at the optimum dose.'

'What was it?'

'The optimum dose was no more than twenty million spermatozoa per cow. When I injected that into a cow at the right time, I got eighty per cent pregnancies. And don't forget, Cornelius,' he went on excitedly, 'that each bull's ejaculation contains five thousand million sperm. Divided up into doses of twenty million, that gives two hundred and fifty separate doses! It was amazing! I was flabbergasted!'

'Does that mean,' I said, 'that with just one of my own ejaculations I could make two hundred and fifty women pregnant?'

'You are not a bull, Cornelius, much as you may like to think you are.'

'How many females could one of my ejaculations do?'

'About a hundred. But I am not about to help you.'

By God, I thought, I could knock up about seven hundred women a week at that rate! 'Have you actually proved this with your brother's bull?' I asked.

'Many times,' A. R. Woresley said. 'It works. I collect one ejaculation, then I quickly mix it up with skimmed milk, egg yolk and glycerol, then I measure it into single doses before freezing.'

'What volume of fluid in each dose?' I asked.

'Very small. Just half a cc.'

'Is that all you inject into the cow, just half a cc of fluid?'

'That's all. But don't forget there's twenty million living spermatozoa in that half cc.'

'Ah, yes.'

'I put these little doses separately into small rubber tubes,' he said. 'I call them straws. I seal both ends, then I freeze. Just think of it, Cornelius! Two hundred and fifty highly potent straws of spermatozoa from a single ejaculation!'

'I *am* thinking about it,' I said. 'It's a bloody miracle.'

'And I can store them for as long as I like, deep frozen. All I have to do when a cow starts bulling is take out one straw from the liquid nitrogen flask, thaw it, which doesn't take a minute, transfer the contents to a syringe and shoot it into the cow.'

The bottle of port was three-quarters empty now and A. R. Woresley was getting a bit tipsy. I refilled his glass again.

'What about this prize bull you were talking about?' I said.

'I'm coming to that, my boy. That's the lovely part of the whole thing. That's the dividend.'

'Tell me.'

'Of course I'll tell you. So I said to my brother . . . this was three years ago, right in the middle of the war . . . my brother was exempt from the army, you see, because he was a farmer . . . so I said to Ernest, "Ernest," I said, "if you had the choice of any bull in England to service your entire herd, which one would you choose?"

'"I don't know about in England," Ernest said, "but the finest bull in these parts is Champion Glory of Friesland, owned by Lord Somerton. He's a pure-bred Friesian, and those Friesians are the best milk producers in the world. My God, Arthur," he says, "you should see that bull! He's a giant! He cost ten thousand pounds and every calf he gets turns out to be a tremendous milker!"

'"Where is this bull kept?" I asked my brother.

'"On Lord Somerton's estate. That's over in Birdbrook."

'"Birdbrook? That's quite close, isn't it?"

'"Three miles away," my brother said. "They've got around two hundred pedigree Friesian dairy cattle and the bull runs with the herd. He's beautiful, Arthur, he really is."

'"Right," I said. "In the next twelve months, eighty per cent of your cows are going to have calves by that bull. Would you like that?"

'"Like it!" my brother said. "It would double my milk-yield." Could I trouble you, my dear Cornelius for one last glass of your excellent port?'

I gave him what there was. I even gave him the lees in the bottom of the bottle. 'Tell me what you did,' I said.

'We waited until one of my brother's cows was bulling good

and proper. Then, in the dead of night . . . this took courage, Cornelius, it took a lot of courage . . .'

'I'm sure it did.'

'In the dead of night, Ernest put a halter on the cow and he led her along the country lanes to Lord Somerton's place three miles away.'

'Didn't you go with them?'

'I went beside them on a bicycle.'

'Why the bicycle?'

'You'll see in a moment. It was the month of May, nice and warm, and the time was around one in the morning. There was a bit of a moon shining which made it more dangerous, but we had to have some light to do what we were going to do. The journey took us an hour.

'"There you are," my brother said. "Over there. Can you see them?"

'We were by a gate leading into a twenty-acre field and in the moonlight I could see the great herd of Friesians grazing all over the field. To one side, not far away, was the big house itself, Somerton Hall. There was a single light in one of the upstairs windows. "Where's the bull?" I said.

'"He'll be in there somewhere," my brother said. "He's with the herd."

'Our cow,' A. R. Woresley said to me, 'was mooing away like mad. They always do when they're bulling. They're calling the bull, you see. The gate into the field was padlocked with a chain, but my brother was ready for that. He pulled out a hacksaw and sawed through the chain. He opened the gate. I leaned my bike against the hedge and we went into the field, leading the cow. The field was milky white in the moonlight. Our cow, sensing the presence of other animals, began mooing louder than ever.'

'Were you frightened?' I asked.

'Terrified,' A. R. Woresley said. 'I am a quiet man, Cornelius. I lead a quiet life. I am not cut out for escapades like this. Every second I expected to see his Lordship's bailiff coming running towards us with a shotgun in his hands. But I forced myself to keep going because this thing we were doing was in the cause of science. Also, I had an obligation to my brother. He had helped me greatly. Now I must help him.'

The pipe had gone out. A. R. Woresley began to refill it from a tin of cheap tobacco.

'Go on,' I said.

'The bull must have heard our cow calling to him. "There he is!" my brother cried. "Here he comes!"

'A massive white and black creature had detached himself from the herd and was trotting our way. He had a pair of short sharp horns on his head. Lethal, they looked. "Get ready!" my brother snapped. "He won't wait! He'll go right at her! Give me the rubber bag! Quick!"'

'What rubber bag?' I said to Woresley.

'The semen collector, my dear boy. My own invention, an elongated bag with thick rubber lips, a kind of false vagina. Very effective too. But let me go on.'

'Go on,' I said.

'"Where's the bag?" my brother shouted. "Hurry up, man!" I was carrying the thing in a knapsack. I got it out and handed it to my brother. He took up his station near the cow's rear and to one side. I stood on the other side, ready to do my bit. I was so frightened, Cornelius, I was sweating all over and I kept wanting to urinate. I was frightened of the bull and I was frightened of that light in the window of Somerton Hall behind me, but I stood my ground.

'The bull came trotting up, snorting and dribbling. I could see a brass ring in his nose, and by God, Cornelius, he was a dangerous-looking brute. He didn't hesitate. He knew his business. He took one sniff at our cow, then he reared up and thrust his front legs onto the cow's back. I crouched alongside him. His pizzle was coming out now. He had a gigantic scrotum and just above it this incredible pizzle was getting longer and longer. It was like a telescope. It started quite short and very quickly it got longer and longer until it was as long as my arm. But not very thick. About as thick as a walking-stick, I'd say. I made a grab for it but in my excitement I missed it. "Quick!" my brother said. "Where is it? Get hold of it quick!" But it was too late. The old bull was an expert marksman. He'd hit the target first time and the end of his pizzle was already inside the cow. It was halfway in. "Get it!" my brother shouted. I grabbed for it again. There was still quite a bit of it showing. I got both hands on it and pulled. It was alive and throbbing and slightly slimy. It was like pulling on a snake. The bull was thrusting it in and I was pulling it out. I pulled so hard on it I felt it bend. But I kept my head and started synchronizing my pulls with the animal's backward movements. Do you see what I mean? He would thrust forward, then he would have to arch his back before going forward again. Each time he arched his back, I gave a pull and gained a few inches. Then the bull thrust forward and in it went once more. But I was gaining on him and in the end, using both hands, I managed to bend it almost double and flip it out. The end of it whacked me across the cheek. That hurt. But quickly I jammed it into the bag my brother was holding. The bull was still bashing away. He was totally absorbed in his work. Thank God he was. He didn't even seem to be aware of our presence. But the pizzle was in the bag now and my brother was holding it and in less than a minute it was all over. The bull lurched backwards off the cow. And then suddenly he saw us. He stood there staring at us. He seemed a bit perplexed and who could blame him. He gave a deep bellow and started pawing the ground with his front legs. He was going to charge. But my brother, who knew about bulls, walked straight up to him and slapped him across the nose. "Git away!" he said. The bull turned and ambled back toward the herd. We hurried out through the gate, closing it behind us. I took the rubber bag from my brother and jumped on to the bicycle and rode hell for leather back to the farm. I made it in fifteen minutes.

'At the farm I had everything ready. I scooped out the bull's semen from the bag and mixed it with my special solution of milk, egg yolk and glycerol. I filled two hundred and fifty of my little rubber straws with half a cc each. This was not as difficult as it sounds. I always have the straws lined up in rows on a metal rack and I use an eye-dropper. I transferred the rack of filled straws onto ice for half an hour. Then I lifted it into a container of nitrogen vapour for ten minutes. Finally, I lowered it into a second vacuum container of liquid nitrogen. The whole process was finished before my brother arrived back with the cow. I now had enough semen from a prize Friesian bull to fertilize two hundred and fifty cows. At least I hoped I had.'

'Did it work?' I asked.

'It worked fantastically,' A. R. Woresley said. 'The following year my brother's Hereford cattle began producing calves that were one-half Friesian. I had taught him how to do the hypo-dermic insemination himself, and I left the canister of frozen "straws" with him on the farm. Today, my dear Cornelius, three years later, nearly every cow in his herd is a cross between a Hereford and a prize Friesian. His milk yield is up by some-thing like sixty per cent and he has sold his bull. The only trouble is that he's running out of straws. He wants me to go with him on another of those dangerous journeys to Lord Somerton's bull. Quite frankly, I dread it.'

'I'll go,' I said. 'I'll take your place.'

'You wouldn't know what to do.'

'Just grab the old pizzle and bung it in the bag,' I said. 'You can be waiting back at the farm all ready to freeze the semen.'

'Can you manage a bicycle?'

'I'll take my car,' I said. 'Twice as quick.'

I had just bought a brand new Continental Morris Cowley, a machine superior in every way to the 1912 De Dion of my Paris days. The body was chocolate brown. The upholstery was leather. It had nickel fittings, mahogany cappings and a driver's door. I was very proud of it. 'I'll get the semen back to you in no time,' I said.

'What a splendid idea,' he said. 'Would you really do that for me, Cornelius?'

'I'd love to,' I said.

I left him soon after that and drove back to Trinity. My brain was humming with all the things A. R. Woresley had told me. There was little doubt he had made a tremendous discovery, and when he published his findings he would be hailed all over the world as a great man. He was probably a genius.

But that didn't bother me one way or the other. What did concern me was this: how could I myself make a million pounds out of it all? I had no objection to A. R. Woresley getting rich at the same time. He deserved it. But yours truly came first. The more I thought about it, the more convinced I became that there was a fortune waiting for me just around the corner. But I doubted it was from bulls and cows.

I lay awake in bed that night and applied my mind assiduously to this problem. I may seem, to a reader of these diaries, like a pretty casual sort of fellow where most things are concerned, but I promise you that when my own most important interests are at stake I am capable of some very concentrated thinking. Somewhere around midnight an idea came to me and began whizzing around in my head. It appealed to me at once, this idea, for the simple reason that it involved the two things in life that I found most entertaining – seduction and copulation. It appealed to me even more when I realized that it involved a *tremendous amount* of seduction and copulation.

I got out of bed and put on my dressing-gown. I began making notes. I examined the problems that would arise. I thought up ways of overcoming them. And at the end of it all I came to the very definite conclusion that the scheme would work. It was bound to work.

There was only one snag. A. R. Woresley had to be persuaded to go along with it.

8

The next day, I sought him out in college and invited him to dine with me that evening.

'I never dine out,' he said. 'My sister expects me home for dinner.'

'It's business,' I said. 'It's your whole future. Tell her it's vital, which it is. I am about to make you a rich man.' Eventually he agreed to come.

At seven p.m., I took him to the Blue Boar in Trinity Street and I ordered for both of us. A dozen oysters each and a bottle of Clos Vougeot Blanc, a very rare wine. Then a dish of roast beef and a good Volnay.

'I must say you do yourself well, Cornelius,' he said.

'I wouldn't do myself any other way,' I told him. 'You do like oysters, don't you?'

'Very much.'

A man opened the oysters at the bar of the restaurant and we watched him doing it. They were Colchesters, medium sized, plump. A waiter brought them to us. The wine-waiter opened the Clos Vougeot Blanc. We began the meal.

'I see you are chewing your oysters,' I said.

'What do you expect me to do?'

'Swallow them whole.'

'That's ridiculous.'

'On the contrary,' I said. 'When eating oysters, the primary pleasure comes from the sensation you get as they slide down your throat.'

'I can't believe that.'

'And then again, the knowledge that they are actually alive as you swallow them adds enormously to that pleasure.'

'I prefer not to think about it.'

'Oh, but you must. If you concentrate hard enough, you can sometimes feel the living oyster wriggling in your stomach.'

A. R. Woresley's nicotine moustache began twitching about. It looked like a bristly nervous little animal clinging to his upper lip.

'If you examine very closely a certain part of the oyster,' I said, 'just here . . . you can see a tiny pulse beating. There it is. D'you see it? And when you stick your fork in . . . like this . . . the flesh moves. It makes a shrinking movement. It does the same if you squeeze lemon juice on to it. Oysters don't like lemon juice. They don't like forks being stuck into them either. They shrink away. The flesh quivers. I shall now swallow this one . . . isn't he a beauty ? . . . There, down he goes . . . and now I shall sit very still for a few seconds so as to experience the sensation of him moving about gently in my stomach . . .'

The little bristly brown animal on A. R. Woresley's upper lip began jumping around more than ever and his cheeks had become visibly paler. Slowly, he pushed his plate of oysters to one side.

'I'll get you some smoked salmon.'

'Thank you.'

I ordered the salmon and took the rest of his oysters on to my plate. He watched me eating them as he waited for the waiter to bring the salmon. He was silent now, subdued, and this was how I wanted him to be. Dash it, the man was twice my age, and all I was trying to do was to soften him up a trifle before dumping my big proposition in his lap. I simply had to soften him up first and try to dominate him if I was to have the slightest chance of getting him to go along with my plan. I decided to soften him up a bit more. 'Did I ever tell you about my old nanny ?' I asked.

'I thought we came here to talk about my discovery,' he said. The waiter put a plate of smoked salmon in front of him. 'Ah,' he said. 'That looks good.'

'When I went away to boarding-school at the age of nine,' I said, 'my dear old nanny was pensioned off by my parents. They bought her a small cottage in the country and there she lived. She was about eighty-five and a marvellously tough old bird. She never complained about anything. But one day, when my mother went down to see her, she found her looking very ill. She questioned her closely and nanny at last admitted that she had the most awful pains in her stomach. Had she had them for long, my mother asked her. Well, as a matter of fact, yes, she had had pains in her stomach, she finally admitted, for many years. But never as bad as they were now. My mother got a doctor. The doctor sent her to hospital. They X-rayed her and the X-ray showed something quite unusual. There were two smallish opaque objects about three inches apart in the middle of her stomach. They looked like transparent marbles. Nobody at the hospital had any idea what these two objects might be, so it was decided to perform an exploratory operation.'

'I hope this is not another of your unpleasant anecdotes,' A. R. Woresley said, chewing his salmon.

'It's fascinating,' I said. 'It'll interest you enormously.'

'Go on, then.'

'When the surgeon opened her up,' I said, 'what do you think he found these two round objects to be?'

'I haven't the faintest idea.'

'They were eyes.'

'What do you mean, eyes?'

'The surgeon found himself staring straight into a pair of alert unblinking round eyes. And the eyes were staring back at him.'

'Ridiculous.'

'Not at all,' I said. 'And who did they belong to, those eyes?'

'Who?'

'They belonged to a *rather large octopus*.'

'You're being facetious.'

'It's the gospel truth. This enormous octopus was actually living in dear old nanny's stomach as a parasite. It was sharing her food, eating well . . .'

'I think that'll do, Cornelius.'

'And all of its eight beastly tentacles were twined inextricably around her liver and lights. They couldn't untangle them. She died on the table.'

A. R. Woresley had stopped chewing his salmon.

'Now what's so interesting about all this is how the octopus got there in the first place. I mean after all, how *does* an old lady come to find herself with a fully grown octopus in her stomach? It was far too big to have gone down her throat. It was like the problem of the ship in the bottle. How on earth did it get in?'

'I prefer not to know,' A. R. Woresley said.

'I'll tell you how,' I said. 'Every summer, my parents used to take nanny and me to Beaulieu, in the South of France. And twice a day we used to go swimming in the sea. So obviously what happened was that nanny, many years before, must have swallowed a tiny new-born octopus, and this little creature had somehow managed to fasten itself on to the wall of her stomach with its suckers. Nanny ate well, so the little octopus ate well. Nanny always ate with the family. Sometimes it would be liver and bacon for dinner, sometimes roast lamb or pork. And believe it or not, she was particularly fond of smoked salmon.'

A. R. Woresley put down his fork. There was one thin slice of salmon left on his plate. He let it stay there.

'So the little octopus grew and grew. It became a gourmet octopus. I can just see it, can't you, down there in the dark caverns of the tummy, saying to itself, "Now I wonder what we're going to have for supper tonight. I do hope it's coq au vin. I feel like a bit of coq au vin tonight. And some crusty bread to go with it."'

'You have an unsavoury predilection for the obscene, Cornelius.'

'That case made medical history,' I said.

'I find it repugnant,' A. R. Woresley said.

'I'm sorry about that. I'm only trying to make conversation.'

'I didn't come here just to make conversation.'

'I'm going to turn you into a rich man,' I said.

'Then get on with it and tell me how.'

'I thought I'd leave that until the port is on the table. No good plans are ever made without a bottle of port.'

'Have you had enough, sir,' the waiter asked him, eyeing the rest of the smoked salmon.

'Take it away,' A. R. Woresley said.

We sat in silence for a while. The waiter brought the roast beef. The Volnay was opened. This was the month of March so we had roast parsnips with our beef as well as roast potatoes and Yorkshire pudding. A. R. Woresley perked up a bit when he saw the beef. He drew his chair closer to the table and began to tuck in.

'Did you know my father was a keen student of naval history?' I asked.

'No, I didn't.'

'He told me a stirring story once,' I said, 'about the English captain who was mortally wounded on the deck of his ship in the American War of Independence. Would you like some horse-radish with your beef?'

'Yes, I would.'

'Waiter,' I called, 'bring us a little fresh shredded horse-radish. Now, as he lay dying, the captain . . .'

'Cornelius,' A. R. Woresley said, 'I have had enough of your stories.'

'This isn't *my* story. It's my father's. It's not like the others. You'll love it.'

He was attacking his roast beef and didn't answer.

'So as he lay dying,' I said, 'the captain extracted from his second-in-command a promise that his body would be taken home and buried in English soil. This created a bit of a problem because the ship was somewhere off the coast of Virginia at the time. It would take at least five weeks to sail back to Britain. So it was decided that the only way to get the body home in fair condition was to pickle it in a barrel of rum, and this was done. The barrel was lashed to the foremast and the ship set sail for England. Five weeks later, she dropped anchor in Plymouth Hoe, and the entire ship's company was lined up to pay a last tribute to their captain as his body was lifted from the barrel into a coffin. But when the lid of the barrel was prised off, there came out a stench so appalling that strong men were seen rushing to the ship's rail. Others fainted.

'Now this was a puzzler, for one can normally pickle anything in navy rum. So why, oh why the appalling stench? You may well ask that question.'

'I don't ask it,' A. R. Woresley snapped. His moustache was jumping about more than ever now.

'Let me tell you what had happened.'

'Don't.'

'I must,' I said. 'During the long voyage, some of the sailors had surreptitiously drilled a hole in the bottom of the barrel and had put a bung in it. Then over the weeks, they had drunk up all the rum.'

A. R. Woresley said nothing. He was not looking at all well.

'"Finest rum I ever tasted," one of the sailors was heard to remark afterwards. Now what shall we have for dessert?'

'No dessert,' A. R. Woresley said.

I ordered the best bottle of port in the house and some Stilton cheese. There was absolute silence between us as we waited for the port to be decanted. It was a Cockburn and a good one, though I've forgotten the year.

The port was served and the splendid crumbly green Stilton was on our plates. 'Now,' I said, 'let me tell you how I am going to make you a million pounds.'

He was watchful and a shade truculent now, but he was not aggressive. He was definitely softened up.

9

'You are virtually broke,' I said. 'You have crippling mortgage interest to pay. You have a meagre salary from the university. You have no savings. You live, if you'll forgive me for saying so, on slops.'

'We live very well.'

'No, you don't. And you never will, unless you let me help you.'

'So what is your plan?'

'You, sir,' I said, 'have made a great scientific discovery. There's no doubt about that.'

'You agree it's important?' he said, perking up.

'Very important. But if you publish your findings, just look what will happen. Every Tom, Dick and Harry all over the world will steal your process for their own use. You won't be able to stop them. It's been the same all through the history of science. Look at pasteurization. Pasteur published. Everyone stole his process. And where did that leave old Pasteur?'

'He became a famous man,' A. R. Woresley said.

'If that's all you want to be, then by all means go ahead and publish. I shall retire gracefully from the scene.'

'With your scheme,' A. R. Woresley said, 'would I ever be able to publish?'

'Of course. As soon as you've got the million in your pocket.'

'How long would that be?'

'I don't know. I'd say five or ten years at the most. After that, you would be free to become famous.'

'Come on, then,' he said. 'Let's hear about this brilliant scheme.'

The port was very good. The Stilton was good, too, but I only nibbled it to clear my palate. I called for an apple. A hard apple, thinly sliced, is the best partner for port.

'I propose that we deal only with *human* spermatozoa,' I said. 'I propose that we select only the truly great and famous men alive in the world today and that we establish a sperm vault for these men. We will store two hundred and fifty straws of sperm from each man.'

'What is the point of that?' A. R. Woresley said.

'Go back just sixty years,' I said, 'to around 1860, and pretend that you and I were living then and that we had the knowledge and the ability to store sperm indefinitely. So which living geniuses, in 1860, would you have chosen as donors?'

'Dickens,' he said.

'Go on.'

'And Ruskin . . . and Mark Twain.'

'And Brahms,' I said, 'and Wagner and Tchaikovsky and Dvorak. The list is very long. Authentic geniuses every one of them. Go back further in the century, if you like, to Balzac, to Beethoven, to Napoleon, to Goya, to Chopin. Wouldn't it be exciting if we had in our liquid nitrogen bank a couple of hundred straws of the living sperm of Beethoven?'

'What would you do with them?'

'Sell them, of course.'

'To whom?'

83

'To women. To very rich women who wanted babies by one of the greatest geniuses of all time.'

'Now wait a minute, Cornelius. Women, rich or not, aren't going to allow themselves to be inseminated with the sperm of some long-dead stranger just because he was a genius.'

'That's what you think. Listen, I could take you to any Beethoven concert you like and I'd guarantee to find half a dozen females there who'd give almost anything to have a baby today by the great man.'

'You mean spinsters?'

'No. Married women.'

'What would their husbands say?'

'Their husbands wouldn't know. Only the mother would know that she was pregnant by Beethoven.'

'That's knavery, Cornelius.'

'Can't you see her,' I said, 'this rich unhappy woman who is married to some incredibly ugly, coarse, ignorant, unpleasant industrialist from Birmingham, and all at once she has something to live for. As she goes strolling through the beautifully kept garden of her husband's enormous country house, she is humming the slow movement of Beethoven's Eroica and thinking to herself, "My God, isn't it wonderful! I am pregnant by the man who wrote that music a hundred years ago!"'

'We don't have Beethoven's sperm.'

'There are plenty of others,' I said. 'There are great men in every century, in every decade. It's our job to get them. And listen,' I went on, 'there's one tremendous thing in our favour. You will find that very rich men are nearly always ugly, coarse, ignorant and unpleasant. They are robber bandits, monsters. Just think of the mentality of men who spend their lives amassing million after million – Rockefeller, Carnegie, Mellon, Krupp. Those are the old-timers. Today's batch are just as unattractive. Industrialists, war profiteers. All horrible fellows. Invariably, they marry women for their beauty and the women marry them for their money. The beauties have ugly useless children by their ugly grasping husbands. They get to hate their husbands. They get bored. They take up culture. They buy paintings by the Impressionists and go to Wagner concerts. And at that stage, my dear sir, these women are ripe for the picking. So in steps Oswald Cornelius offering to impregnate them with guaranteed genuine Wagner sperm.'

'Wagner's dead, too.'

'I am simply trying to show you what our sperm vault will look like in forty years' time if we start it now, in 1919.'

'Who would we put in it?' A. R. Woresley said.

'Who would you suggest? Who are the geniuses of today?'

'Albert Einstein.'

'Good,' I said. 'Who else?'

'Sibelius.'

'Splendid. And what about Rachmaninov?'

'And Debussy,' he said.

'Who else?'

'Sigmund Freud in Vienna.'

'Is he great?'

'He's going to be,' A. R. Woresley said. 'He is already world famous in medical circles.'

'I'll take your word for it. Go on.'

'Igor Stravinsky,' he said.

'I didn't know you knew music.'

'Of course.'

'I'd like to propose the painter Picasso in Paris,' I said.

'Is he a genius?'

'Yes,' I said.

'Would you accept Henry Ford in America?'

'Oh, yes,' I said. 'That's a good one. And our own King George the Fifth.'

'*King George the Fifth!*' he cried. 'What's he got to do with it?'

'He's royal blood. Just imagine what some women would pay for a child by the King of England!'

'You're being ridiculous, Cornelius. You can't go crashing into Buckingham Palace and start asking His Majesty the King if he would be good enough to provide you with an ejaculation of semen.'

'You wait,' I said. 'You haven't heard the half of it yet. And

85

we won't stop at George the Fifth. We must have a very comprehensive stock indeed of royal sperm. All the Kings in Europe. Let's see. There's Haakon of Norway. There's Gustav of Sweden. Christian of Denmark. Albert of Belgium. Alfonso of Spain. Carol of Romania. Boris of Bulgaria. Victor Emmanuel of Italy.'

'You're being silly.'

'No, I'm not. Wealthy Spanish ladies of aristocratic blood would crave for a baby by Alfonso. It'll be the same in every country. The aristocracy worships the monarchy. It is essential that we have a good stock of royal sperm in our vault. And I'll get it. Don't you worry. I'll get it.'

'It's a hare-brained and impracticable stunt,' A. R. Woresley said. He put a lump of Stilton in his mouth and swilled it round with port. Thus he ruined both the cheese and the wine.

'I am prepared,' I said slowly, 'to invest every penny of my one hundred thousand pounds into our partnership. That's how hare-brained I think it is.'

'You're mad.'

'You'd have told me I was mad if you'd seen me setting off for the Sudan at the age of seventeen in search of Blister Beetle powder. You would, wouldn't you?'

That pulled him up a little. 'What would you charge for this sperm,' he said.

'A fortune,' I said. 'Nobody is going to get a baby Einstein cheap. Or a baby Sibelius. Or a baby King Albert of the Belgians. Hey! I've just had a thought. Would a king's baby be in line for the throne?'

'He'd be a bastard.'

'He'd be in line for something. Royal bastards always are. We must charge a packet for a king's sperm.'

'How much would you charge?'

'I think about twenty thousand pounds a shot. Commoners would be slightly cheaper. We would have a price list and a range of prices. But kings would be the most expensive.'

'H. G. Wells!' he said suddenly. 'He's around.'

'Yes. We might put him on the list.'

A. R. Woresley leaned back in his chair and sipped his port. 'Assuming,' he said, 'just assuming we did have this remarkable sperm vault, who would go out and find the rich women buyers ?'

'I would.'

'And who would inseminate them ?'

'I would.'

'You don't know how to do it.'

'I could soon learn. It might be rather fun.'

'There is a flaw in this scheme of yours,' A. R. Woresley said. 'A serious flaw.'

'What is it ?'

'The really valuable sperm is not Einstein's or Stravinsky's. It's Einstein's father's. Or Stravinsky's father's. Those are the men who actually sired the geniuses.'

'Agreed,' I said. 'But by the time a man becomes a recognized genius, his father is dead.'

'So your scheme is fraudulent.'

'We're out to make money,' I said, 'not to breed geniuses. These women aren't going to want Sibelius's father's sperm anyway. What they'll be after is a nice hot injection of twenty million living spermatozoa from the great man himself.'

A. R. Woresley had his awful pipe going now and clouds of smoke enveloped his head. 'I will admit,' he said, 'yes, I am prepared to grant you that you could find wealthy female buyers for the sperm of geniuses and royalty. But your entire bizarre scheme is unfortunately doomed to failure for the simple reason that you will be unable to obtain your supplies of sperm. You don't seriously believe that great men and kings will be prepared to go through the ... the extremely embarrassing motions of producing an ejaculation of sperm for some totally unknown young man ...'

'That's not the way I'll do it.'

'How will you do it ?'

'The way I'll do it, not a single one of them will be able to resist becoming a donor.'

'Rubbish. I'd resist it.'

'No, you wouldn't.'

I put a thin slice of apple in my mouth and ate it. I raised the glass of port to my nose. It had a bouquet of mushrooms. I took a sip and rolled it on my tongue. The flavour filled my mouth. It reminded me of potpourri. For a few moments I was captivated by the loveliness of the wine I was tasting. And what a remarkable follow-through it had after the swallow. The flavour lingered in the back of the nose for a long time. 'Give me three days,' I said, 'and I guarantee that I'll have in my possession one complete and genuine ejaculation of your own sperm together with a statement signed by you certifying that it is yours.'

'Don't be so foolish, Cornelius. You can't make me do something I don't want to do.'

'That's all I'm prepared to say.'

He squinted at me through the pipe smoke. 'You wouldn't threaten me in some way, would you ?' he said. 'Or torture me ?'

'Of course not. The act would be of your own free will. Would you like to bet me that I won't succeed ?'

'Of my own free will, you say ?'

'Yes.'

'Then I'll bet you anything you like.'

'Right,' I said. 'The bet is that if you lose, you promise the following: firstly, to withhold publication until we've each made a million. Secondly, to become a full and enthusiastic partner. Thirdly, to supply all the technical knowledge necessary for me to set up the sperm vault.'

'I don't mind making a promise I'll never have to keep,' he said.

'Then you promise ?'

'I promise,' he said.

I paid the bill and offered to drive A. R. Woresley home in my motor car. 'Thank you,' he said, 'but I have my bicycle. We poor dons are not as affluent as some.'

'You soon will be,' I said.

I stood on Trinity Street and watched him pedalling away into the night. It was still only about nine-thirty p.m. I decided to make my next move immediately. I got into the motor car and headed straight for Girton.

10

Girton, in case you don't know it, was and still is a ladies'
college and a part of the University. Within those sombre walls
there dwelt in 1919 a cluster of young ladies so physically
repulsive, so thick-necked and long-snouted I could hardly
bring myself to look at them. They reminded me of crocodiles.
They sent shivers down the back of my neck as I passed them in
the street. They seldom washed and the lenses of their spectacles
were smudged with greasy fingermarks. Brainy they certainly
were. Many were brilliant. To my mind, that was small com-
pensation.

But wait.

Only one week before, I had discovered among these zoologi-
cal specimens a creature of such dazzling loveliness that I
refused to believe she was a Girton girl. Yet she was. I had
discovered her in a bunshop at lunchtime. She was eating a
doughnut. I asked if I might sit at her table. She nodded and
went on eating. And there I sat, gaping and goggling at her as
though she were Cleopatra herself reincarnated. Never in my
short life had I seen a girl or a woman with such a stench of
salacity about her. She was absolutely soaked in sex. It made no
difference that there was sugar and doughnut all over her face.
She was wearing a mackintosh and a woolly scarf but she might
just as well have been stark naked. Only once or twice in a lifetime does one meet a girl like that. The face was beautiful
beyond words, but there was a flare to the nostrils and a curious
little twist of the upper lip that had me wriggling all over my
chair. Not even in Paris had I met a female who inspired such
instant lust. She went on eating her doughnut. I went on goggling
at her. Once, but only once, her eyes rose slowly to my face and

there they rested, cool and shrewd, as if calculating something, then they fell again. She finished her doughnut and pushed back her chair.

'Hang on,' I said.

She paused, and for a second time those calculating brown eyes came up and rested on my face.

'What did you say?'

'I said, hang on. Don't go. Have another doughnut . . . or a Bath bun or something.'

'If you want to talk to me, why don't you say so.'

'I want to talk to you.'

She folded her hands in her lap and waited. I began to talk. Soon she joined in. She was a biology student at Girton and, like me, she had a scholarship. Her father was English, her mother Persian. Her name was Yasmin Howcomely. What we said to one another is irrelevant. We went straight from the bunshop to my rooms and stayed there until the next morning. Eighteen hours we stayed together and at the end of it all I felt like a piece of pemmican, a strip of desiccated dehydrated meat. She was electric, that girl, and wicked beyond belief. Had she been Chinese and living in Peking, she could have gotten her Diploma of Merit with her hands tied behind her back and iron shackles on her feet.

I went so dotty about her that I broke the golden rule and saw her a second time.

And now it was twenty to ten in the evening and A. R. Woresley was bicycling home and I myself was in the Porter's Lodge at Girton asking the old porter kindly to inform Miss Yasmin Howcomely that Mr Oswald Cornelius wished to see her on a matter of the most urgent nature.

She came down at once. 'Hop in the car,' I said. 'We have things to talk about.' She hopped in and I drove her back to Trinity where I gave the Trinity porter half a sovereign to look the other way as she slid past him to my rooms.

'Keep your clothes on,' I said to her. 'This is business. How would you like to get rich?'

'I'd like it very much,' she said.

'Can I trust you completely?'

'Yes,' she said.

'You won't tell a soul?'

'Go on,' she said. 'It sounds like fun already.'

I then proceeded to tell her the entire story of A. R. Woresley's discovery.

'My God!' she said when I had finished. 'This is a great scientific discovery! Who the hell is A. R. Woresley? He's going to be world famous! I'd like to meet him!'

'You soon will,' I said.

'When?' Being herself a bright young scientist, she was genuinely excited.

'Wait,' I said. 'Here's the next instalment.' I then told her about my plans for exploiting the discovery and making a fortune by starting a sperm vault for the great geniuses of the world and all the kings.

When I had finished, she asked me if I had any wine. I opened a bottle of claret and poured a glass for each of us. I found some good dry biscuits to go with it.

'It's sort of a funny idea, this sperm vault of yours,' she said, 'but I'm afraid it's not going to work.' She proceeded to put forward all the same old reasons that A. R. Woresley had given me earlier in the evening. I allowed her to spout on. Then I played my ace of spades.

'Last time we met I told you the story of my Parisian caper,' I said. 'You remember that?'

'The splendid Blister Beetle,' she said. 'I keep wishing you'd brought some back with you.'

'I did.'

'You're not serious!'

'When you use only a pinhead at a time, five pounds of powder goes an awful long way. I've got about a pound left.'

'Then that's the answer!' she cried, clapping her hands.

'I know.'

'Slip them a powder and they'll give us a thousand million of their little squigglers every time!'

'Using you as the teaser.'

'Oh, I'll be the teaser all right,' she said. 'I'll tease them to death. Even the ancient ones will be able to deliver! Show me this magic stuff.'

I fetched the famous biscuit tin and opened it. The powder lay an inch deep in the tin. Yasmin dipped a finger in it and started to put it to her mouth. I grabbed her wrist. 'Are you mad?' I shouted. 'You've got about six full doses sticking to the skin of that finger!' I hung onto her wrist and dragged her to the bathroom and held her finger under the tap.

'I want to try it,' she said. 'Come on, darling. Just give me a tiny bit.'

'My God, woman,' I said, 'have you any idea what it does to you!'

'You already told me.'

'If you want to see it working, just watch what it does to A. R. Woresley when you give it to him tomorrow.'

'Tomorrow?'

'Absolutely,' I said.

'Whoopee! When tomorrow?'

'You get old Woresley to deliver and I win my bet,' I said. 'That means he's got to join us. Woresley, you and me. We'll make a great team.'

'I like it,' she said. 'We'll rock the world.'

'We'll rock more than that,' I said. 'We'll rock all the crowned heads of Europe. But we must rock Woresley first.'

'He has to be alone.'

'No problem,' I said. 'He's alone in the lab every evening between five-thirty and six-thirty. Then he goes home to his supper.'

'How am I going to feed it to him?' she asked. 'The powder?'

'In a chocolate,' I said. 'In a delicious little chocolate. It has to be small so that he'll pop the whole thing in his mouth in one go.'

'And where pray do we get delicious little chocolates these days?' she asked. 'You forget there's been a war on.'

'That's the whole point,' I said. 'A. R. Woresley won't have had a decent bit of chocolate since 1914. He'll gobble it up.'

'But do you have any?'

'Right here,' I said. 'Money can buy anything.' I opened a drawer and produced a box of chocolate truffles. Each was identical. Each was the size of a small marble. They were supplied to me by Prestat, the great chocolateers of Oxford Street, London. I took one of them and made a hole in it with a pin. I enlarged the hole a bit. I then used the head of the same pin to measure out one dose of Blister Beetle powder. I tipped this into the hole. I measured a second dose and tipped that in also.

'Hey!' Yasmin cried. 'That's two doses!'

'I know. I want to make absolutely sure Mr Woresley delivers.'

'It'll drive him round the twist.'

'He'll get over it.'

'What about me?'

'I think you can take care of yourself,' I said. I pressed the soft chocolate together to seal up the hole. I then stuck a match-stick into the chocolate. 'I'm giving you two chocolates,' I said. 'One for you and one for him. His is the one with the match in it.' I put the chocolates in a paper bag and passed them over. We discussed at some length the plan of battle.

'Will he become violent?' she asked.

'Just a tiny bit.'

'And where do I get that thing you were talking about?'

I produced the thing in question. She examined it to make sure it was in good condition, then put it in her handbag.

'All set?'

'Yes,' she said.

'Don't forget this one will be a dress rehearsal for all the others you'll be doing later on. So learn all you can.'

'I wish I knew judo,' she said.

'You'll be all right.'

I drove her back to Girton and saw her safely in through the gates of the college.

II

We now move forward to five-thirty in the afternoon of the following day. I myself was lying comfortably on the floor behind a row of wooden filing-cabinets in A. R. Woresley's laboratory. I had spent much of the day wandering casually in and out of the lab, reconnoitring the terrain and gradually easing the cabinets twenty inches away from the wall so that I could squeeze in behind them. I had also left a one inch gap between two of the cabinets so that by looking through it I was able to get an excellent view along the whole length of the lab. A. R. Woresley always worked at the far end of the room, about twenty feet from where I was stationed. He was there now. He was fooling about with a rack of test tubes and a pipette and some blue liquid. He was not wearing his usual white coat today. He was in shirtsleeves and a pair of grey flannels. There was a knock on the door.

'Come in!' he called out, not looking up.

Yasmin entered. I had not told her I was going to be watching. Why should I? But a general must always keep an eye on his troops during battle. My girl looked ravishing in a cotton print dress that fitted tightly around her superstructure, and as she came into the room there came with her that elusive aura of lust and lechery that followed her like a shadow wherever she went.

'Mr Woresley?'

'Yes, I'm Woresley,' he said, still not looking up. 'What do you want?'

'Please forgive me for barging in on you like this, Mr Woresley,' she said. 'I'm not a chemist. I'm actually a biology student. But I've run up against a rather difficult problem which is more

94

chemical than biological. I've asked around all over the place but no one seems able to give me the answer. They all referred me to you.'

'They did, did they,' A. R. Woresley said, sounding pleased. He went on carefully measuring out blue liquid from a beaker into the test tubes with his pipette. 'Just let me finish this,' he added. Yasmin stood still, waiting, sizing up the victim.

'Now, my dear,' A. R. Woresley said, laying down the pipette and turning round for the first time. 'What was it you . . .' He stopped dead in mid-sentence. His mouth dropped open and his eyes became as large and round as half-crowns. Then the tip of his red tongue appeared underneath the bristle of his nicotined moustache and began sliding wetly over his lips. For a man who had seen little else but Girton girls and his own diabolic sister for years on end, Yasmin must have appeared before him like the creation, the first morning, the spirit moving over the waters. But he recovered quickly.

'You had something to ask me, my dear?'

Yasmin had prepared her question brilliantly. I have forgotten precisely how it went, but it dealt with a situation where chemistry (his subject) and biology (her subject) became intertwined in a most complex manner, and where a deep knowledge of chemistry was required in order to unravel the problem. The answer, as she had so shrewdly calculated, would take at least nine minutes to deliver, probably more.

'A fascinating question,' A. R. Woresley said. 'Let me see how best to answer it for you.' He crossed to a long blackboard fixed to the wall of the lab. He picked up a piece of chalk.

'Would you like a chocolate?' Yasmin said. She had the paper bag in her hand and when A. R. Woresley turned round, she popped one into her own mouth. She took the second chocolate from the bag and held it towards him in her fingertips.

'My goodness gracious me!' he burbled. 'What a treat!'

'Delicious,' she said. 'Try it.'

A. R. Woresley took it and sucked it and rolled it round in his mouth and chewed it and finally swallowed it. 'Glorious,' he said. 'How very kind of you.'

At the moment when the chocolate went down his gullet, I noted the time on my watch. I saw Yasmin doing exactly the same thing. Such a sensible girl. A. R. Woresley was standing at the blackboard giving a long exposition with many splendid chemical formulae written in chalk. I didn't listen to it. I was counting the minutes passing by. So was Yasmin. She hardly took her eyes from the watch on her wrist.

Seven minutes gone by . . .

Eight minutes . . .

Eight minutes and fifty seconds . . .

Nine minutes! And dead on time, the hand that held the chalk against the blackboard suddenly stopped writing. A. R. Woresley went rigid.

'Mr Woresley,' Yasmin said brightly, timing it to perfection. 'I wonder if you'd mind giving me your autograph. You are the only science lecturer whose autograph I still don't have for my collection.' She was holding out a pen and a sheet of Chemistry Department notepaper.

'What's that?' he stammered, putting one hand into his trouser pocket before turning round to face her.

'Just there,' Yasmin said, placing a finger halfway down the sheet as I had instructed her. 'Your autograph. I collect them. I shall treasure yours more than any of the others.'

In order to take the pen, A. R. Woresley had to remove his hand from the pocket. It was a comical sight. The poor man looked as though he had a live snake in his trousers. And now he was beginning to bounce up and down on his toes.

'Just there,' Yasmin said, keeping her finger on the notepaper. 'Then I shall paste it in my autograph book along with all the others.'

With his mind fogged by gathering passions, A. R. Woresley signed. Yasmin folded the paper and put it in her purse. A. R. Woresley clutched the edge of the wooden lab bench with both hands. He started rocking about all over the place as if the whole building were in a storm at sea. His forehead was damp with sweat. I reminded myself that he had had a double dose. I think Yasmin was reminding herself of the same thing. She took a couple of paces backwards and braced herself for the coming onslaught.

Slowly, A. R. Woresley turned his head and stared at her. The powder was hitting him hard and there was a glimmer of madness in his eyes.

'I . . . er . . . I . . . I . . .'

'Is something wrong, Mr Woresley?' Yasmin said sweetly. 'Are you feeling all right?'

He went on clutching the bench and staring at her. The sweat was all over his face now and running on to his moustache.

'Can I do something to help?' Yasmin said.

A funny gurgling noise came out of his throat.

'Can I get you a glass of water?' she asked. 'Or some smelling salts perhaps?'

And still he stood there, clutching the bench and waggling his head and making those queer gurgling noises. He reminded me of a man who'd got a fishbone stuck in his throat.

Suddenly he let out a great bellow and made a rush at the girl. He grasped her by the shoulders with both hands and tried to push her to the floor but she skipped back out of his reach.

'Ah-ha!' she said, 'so that's what's bothering you, is it? Well, it's nothing to be ashamed about, my darling man.' Her voice as she spoke to him was as cool as a thousand cucumbers.

He came at her again with hands outstretched, pawing at her, but she was too nimble for him. 'Hold on a sec,' she said, flipping open her purse and taking out the rubbery thing I had given her the night before. 'I'm perfectly willing to have a bit of fun with you, Mr W, but we don't want anyone around here to get preggers now, do we? So be a good boy and stand still for a moment while I put your little mackintosh on.'

But A. R. Woresley didn't care about the little mackintosh. He had no intention of standing still. I don't think he *could* have stood still if he'd wanted to. From my own point of view, it was instructive to observe the curious effect a double dose had upon the subject. Above all, it made him hop. He kept hopping up and down as though he were doing calisthenics. And he kept making these absurd bellowing noises. And he kept waving his arms round and round windmill fashion. And the sweat kept trickling down his face. And there was Yasmin, dancing around him and holding out the ridiculous rubbery thing with both hands and shouting, 'Oh, do keep *still*, Mr Woresley! I'm not letting you come *near* me till I get this on!'

I don't think he even heard her. And although he was clearly going mad with lust, he also gave the impression of a man who was in great discomfort. He was hopping, it appeared, because excessive irritation was taking place. Something was *stinging* him. It was stinging him so much he couldn't stand still. In greyhound racing, to make a dog run faster, they frequently insert a piece of ginger up its rectum and the dog runs flat out in an effort to get away from the terrible sting in its backside. With A. R. Woresley, the sting was in a rather different part of his body, and the pain of it was making him hop, skip and jump all over the lab, and at the same time he was telling himself, or so it seemed, that only a woman could help him to get rid of that terrible sting. But the wretched woman was being too quick for him. He couldn't catch her. And the stinging feeling kept getting worse all the time.

Suddenly, using both hands, he ripped open the front of his trousers and half a dozen buttons scattered across the room with little tinkling sounds. He dropped the trousers. They fell around his ankles. He tried to kick them off, but couldn't do so because he still had his shoes on.

With the trousers now around his ankles, A. R. Woresley was temporarily but effectively hobbled. He couldn't run. He couldn't even walk. He could only hop. Yasmin saw her chance and took it. She made a dive for the erect and quivering rod that was sticking out through the slit in his underpants. She grabbed it in her right hand and held on to it as tightly as if it were the handle of a tennis racquet. She had him now. He began to bellow even louder.

'For God's sake shut up!' she said, 'or you'll have the whole university in here! And keep *still* so I can get this damn thing on you!'

But A. R. Woresley was deaf to everything except his fierce

and fundamental desires. He simply could *not* stand still. Hobbled as he was by the trousers round his ankles, he went on hopping about and waving his arms and bellowing like a bull. For Yasmin, it must have been like trying to thread a needle on a sewing-machine while the machine was still in motion.

Finally, she lost patience and I saw her right hand, the one which was grasping, as it were, the handle of the tennis racquet, I saw it give a wicked little flick. It was as though she were making a sharp backhand return to a half volley with a quick roll of the wrist at the end of the shot to impart topspin. A vicious wristy little flick it was, and it was certainly a winner, because the victim let out a howl that rattled every test tube in the lab. It stopped him cold for five seconds, which gave her just enough time to get the rubbery thing on and then to jump back out of reach.

'Couldn't we calm down just a teeny weeny little bit?' she said. 'This isn't a bullfight.'

He was tearing off his shoes now and throwing them across the room, and when he kicked off his trousers and became fully mobile again, Yasmin must have known that the moment of truth had arrived at last.

It had indeed. But there is no profit in describing the coarse rough and tumble that followed. There were no intermissions, no pauses, no halftime. The vigour that my double dose of Blister Beetle had imparted to that man was astounding. He went at her as though she were an uneven road surface and he was trying to flatten out the bumps. He raked her from stem to stern. He raked her fore and aft, and still he kept reloading and firing away although his cannon must by then have been scorching hot. They say that the Ancient Britons used to make fire by rotating the point of a wooden stick very fast and for a long time on a wooden block. Well, if that made fire then A. R. Woresley was about to start a raging conflagration any moment, wood or no wood. It would have surprised me in the least to see a puff of smoke come up from the wrestlers on the floor.

While all this was going on, I took the opportunity of making a few notes with pad and pencil for future reference.

Note one: Endeavour always to arrange for Yasmin to confront the subject in a room where there is a couch or an armchair or at the very least a carpet on the floor. She is undoubtedly a strong and resilient girl, but having to work on a hard wooden surface in exceptionally severe circumstances as she is doing now is asking rather a lot. The way things are going, she could easily suffer damage to her lumbar region or even a pelvic fracture. And where would our clever little scheme be then, tra-la-la?

Note two: Never again prescribe a double dose for any man. Too much powder causes excessive irritation in the vital regions and gives the victim a sort of St Vitus's Dance. This makes it almost impossible for Yasmin to roll on the sperm-collector without resorting to foul play. An overdose also makes the victim bellow, which could be embarrassing if the wife of the victim, the Queen of Denmark, for example, or Mrs Bernard Shaw, happened to be sitting quietly in the next room doing needlepoint.

Note three: Try to think of a way of helping Yasmin to get out from under and to do a bunk with the precious sperm as soon as possible after the stuff is in the bag. The devilish powder, even when sparingly administered, might easily keep a ninety-year-old genius bashing away for a couple of hours or more. And quite apart from any discomfort Yasmin might be suffering, it is vital to get the little squigglers into the freezer quickly, while they are still fresh. Look, for example at old Woresley right now and how he's still grinding away although he's obviously delivered the goods at least six times in succession. Perhaps a sharp jab in the buttocks with a hatpin would do the trick in the future.

Out there on the floor of the lab Yasmin had no hatpin to help her, and to this day I do not know precisely what it was she did to A. R. Woresley that caused him to let out yet another of those horrendous howls and to freeze so suddenly in his tracks. Nor do I wish to know, because it's none of my business. But whatever it was, I was quite certain a nice girl like her would never have done it to a nice man like him if it had not been absolutely necessary. The next thing I knew, Yasmin was up and away and dashing for the door with the spoils of victory in her hand. I nearly stood up and clapped her as she left the stage. What a performance! What a splendid exit! The door slammed shut and she was gone.

All at once, the laboratory became silent. I saw A. R. Woresley picking himself up slowly off the floor. He stood there dazed and wobbly. He looked like a man who had been struck on the head with a cricket bat. He staggered over to the sink and began splashing water on to his face, and while he was doing this, I myself crept from my hiding place and tip-toed out of the room, closing the door softly behind me.

There was no sign of Yasmin in the corridor. I had told her I would be sitting in my rooms at Trinity throughout the operation, so she was probably making her way there now. I hurried outside and jumped into my motor car and drove from the Science Building to the College by a roundabout route so as not to pass her on the way. I parked the car and went up to my rooms and waited.

A few minutes later, in she came.

'Give me a drink,' she said, crossing to an armchair. I noticed she was walking sort of bowlegged and treating herself tenderly.

'You look as though you've brought the good news from Ghent to Aix riding bareback,' I said.

She didn't answer me. I poured her two inches of gin and added a cubic centimetre of lime juice. She took a good gulp of the splendid stuff and said, 'Ah-h-h, that's better.'

'How did it go?'

'We gave him a little bit too much.'

'I thought we might have done,' I said.

She opened her purse and took out the repulsive rubbery thing which she had very sensibly knotted at the open end. Also the sheet of notepaper with A. R. Woresley's signature on it.

'Tremendous!' I cried. 'You did it! It all worked! Did you enjoy it?'

Her answer astonished me. 'As a matter of fact I rather did,' she said.

'You *did?* You mean he wasn't too rough?'

'He made every other man I've ever met look like a eunuch,' she said.

I laughed at that.

'Including you,' she said.

I stopped laughing.

'That,' she said softly, taking another gulp of gin, 'is exactly how I want my men to be from now on.'

'But you said we gave him too much.'

'Just a teensy bit,' she said. 'I couldn't stop him. He was absolutely tireless.'

'How *did* you stop him?'

'Never you mind.'

'Would a hatpin be helpful next time?'

'That's a good idea,' she said. 'I shall carry a hatpin. But I'd much rather get the dose exactly right so I don't have to use it.'

'We'll get it right.'

'I really would prefer not to go sticking hatpins into the King of Spain's bum, if you see what I mean.'

'Oh, I do, I do.'

'I like to part company on friendly terms.'

'And didn't you?'

'Not exactly, no,' she said, smiling slightly.

'Well done, anyway,' I said. 'You pulled it off.'

'He was so funny,' she said. 'I wish you could have seen him. He kept hopping up and down.'

I took the sheet of notepaper with A. R. Woresley's signature on it and placed it in my typewriter. I sat down and typed the following legend directly above the signature:

I hereby certify that I have on this day, the 27th of March, 1919, delivered personally a quantity of my own semen to Oswald Cornelius Esquire, President of the International Semen's Home of Cambridge, England. It is my wish that this semen shall be stored indefinitely, using the revolutionary and recently discovered

Woresley Technique, and I further agree that the aforementioned Oswald Cornelius may at any time use portions of that semen to fertilize selected females of high quality in order to disseminate my own bloodline throughout the world for the benefit of future generations.

Signed, A. R. Woresley
Lecturer in Chemistry,
Cambridge University

I showed it to Yasmin. 'Obviously it doesn't apply to Woresley,' I said, 'because his stuff isn't going into the freezer. But what do you think of it otherwise? Will it look all right over the signature of kings and geniuses?'

She read it through carefully. 'It's good,' she said. 'It'll do nicely.'

'I've won my bet,' I said. 'Woresley will have to capitulate now.'

She sat sipping her gin. She was relaxed and amazingly cool. 'I have a strange feeling,' she said, 'that this whole thing's actually going to work. At first it sounded ridiculous. But now I can't see what's to stop us.'

'Nothing can stop us,' I said. 'You'll win every time so long as you can always reach your man and feed him the powder.'

'It really is fantastic stuff.'

'I found that out in Paris.'

'You don't think it might give some of the very old ones a heart attack, do you?'

'Of course not,' I said, although I had been wondering the same thing myself.

'I don't want to leave a trail of corpses around the world,' she said. 'Especially the corpses of great and famous men.'

'You won't,' I said. 'Don't worry about it.'

'Take for example Alexander Graham Bell,' she said. 'According to you, he is now seventy-two years old. Do you think *he* could stand up to it?'

'Tough as nuts,' I said. 'All the great men are. But I'll tell you what we might do if it'll make you feel a bit easier. We'll regulate the dose according to age. The older they are, the less they'll get.'

'I'll buy that,' she said. 'It's a good idea.'

I took Yasmin out and treated her to a superb dinner at the Blue Boar. She deserved it. Then I delivered her safely back to Girton.

12

The next morning, carrying the rubbery thing and the signed letter in my pocket, I went looking for A. R. Woresley. They told me in the Science Building that he had not shown up that morning. So I drove out to his house and rang the bell. The diabolic sister came to the door.

'Arthur's a bit under the weather,' she said.

'What happened?'

'He fell off his bike.'

'Oh dear.'

'He was cycling home in the dark and he collided with a pillar-box.'

'I *am* sorry. Is he much hurt?'

'He's bruised all over,' she said.

'Nothing broken, I hope?'

'Well,' she said, and there was an edge of bitterness to her voice, 'not *bones*.'

Oh God, I thought. Oh Yasmin. What have you done to him?

'Please offer him my sincere condolences,' I said. Then I left.

The following day, a very fragile A. R. Woresley reported for duty.

I waited until I had him alone in the lab, then I placed before him the sheet of Chemistry Department notepaper containing the legend I had typed out over his own signature. I also dumped about a thousand million of his very own spermatozoa (by now dead) on the bench and said, 'I've won my bet.'

He stared at the obscene rubbery thing. He read the letter and recognized his signature.

'You bounder!' he cried. 'You tricked me!'

'You assaulted a lady.'

'Who typed this?'

'I did.'

He stood there taking it all in.

'All right,' he said. 'But what *happened* to me? I went absolutely crazy. What in God's name did you do?'

'You had a double dose of *cantharis vesicatoria sudanii*,' I said. 'The old Blister Beetle. Powerful stuff that.'

He stared at me, comprehension dawning on his face. 'So *that's* what it was,' he said. 'Inside the bloody chocolate, I suppose.'

'Naturally. And if *you* swallowed it, then so will the King of the Belgians and the Prince of Wales and Mr Joseph Conrad and all the rest of them.'

He started pacing up and down the lab, albeit a trifle gingerly.

'I told you once before, Cornelius,' he said, 'that you are a totally unscrupulous fellow.'

'Absolutely,' I said, grinning.

'Do you *know* what that woman did to me?'

'I can make a pretty good guess.'

'She's a witch! She's a . . . a vampire! She's disgusting!'

'*You* seemed to like her well enough,' I said, pointing to the thing on the bench.

'I was drugged!'

'You raped her. You raped her like an animal. *You* were the disgusting one.'

'That was the Blister Beetle.'

'Of course it was,' I said. 'But when M. Marcel Proust rapes her like an animal, or King Alfonso of Spain, will *they* know they've had the Blister Beetle?'

He didn't answer me.

'They most certainly will not,' I said. 'They may well wonder what the hell came over them, just as you did. But they'll never know the answer and in the end they'll simply have to put it down to the incredible attractiveness of the girl. That's all they *can* put it down to. Right?'

'Well . . . yes.'

'They will be embarrassed at having raped her, just as you are. They will be very contrite, just as you are. They will want to hush the whole thing up, just as you do. In other words, they will give us no more trouble. We skedaddle with the signed note-paper and the precious sperm and that will be the end of it.'

'You are a rapscallion of the first water, Cornelius. You are an unmitigated scoundrel.'

'I know,' I said, grinning again. But the logic of my argument was irrefutable. The plan was watertight. A. R. Woresley, who was certainly no fool, was beginning to realize this. I could see him weakening.

'What about the girl?' he said. 'Who was she?'

'She's the third member of our organization. She's our official teaser.'

'Some teaser,' he said.

'That's why I chose her.'

'I shall be embarrassed, Cornelius, if I have to meet her again.'

'No, you won't,' I said. 'She's a great girl. You'll like her very much. She happens to like you, too.'

'Rubbish. What makes you think that?'

'She said you were absolutely and positively the greatest. She said that from now on she wants all her men to be like you.'

'She said that? Did she actually say that, Cornelius?'

'Word for word.'

A. R. Woresley beamed.

'She said you make all other men look like eunuchs,' I said, ramming it home.

A. R. Woresley's whole face began to glow with pleasure. 'You're not pulling my leg, are you, Cornelius?'

'Ask her yourself when you see her.'

'Well, well, well,' he said, beaming away and preening his horrible moustache lightly with the back of his fingers. 'Well,

well, well,' he said again. 'And may I ask what her name is, this remarkable young lady?'

'Yasmin Howcomely. She's half Persian.'

'How interesting.'

'You must have been terrific,' I said.

'I have my moments, Cornelius,' he said. 'Ah yes indeed, I certainly have my moments.' He seemed to have forgotten about the Blister Beetle. He wanted all the credit himself now and I let him have it.

'She can't wait to meet you again.'

'Splendid,' he said, rubbing his hands. 'And she's going to be a part of our little organization, you say?'

'Absolutely. You'll be seeing a lot of her from now on.'

'Good,' he said. 'Goody good.'

And thus A. R. Woresley joined the firm. It was as easy as that. What's more, he was a man of his word.

He agreed to withhold publication of his discovery.

He agreed to assist Yasmin and me in every possible way.

He agreed to construct for us a portable container for liquid nitrogen which we could take with us on our travels.

He agreed to instruct me in the exact procedure for diluting the collected semen and measuring it out into straws for freezing.

Yasmin and I would be the travellers and the collectors.

A. R. Woresley would remain at his post in Cambridge but would establish at the same time in a convenient and secret place a large central freezer, the Semen's Home.

From time to time, the travellers, Yasmin and I, would return with our spoils and transfer them from the portable suitcase freezer to the Semen's Home.

I would provide ample funds for everything. I would pay all travelling expenses, hotels, etc. while Yasmin and I were on the road. I would give Yasmin a generous dress allowance so that she might buy herself a superb wardrobe.

It was all straightforward and simple.

I resigned from the University and so did Yasmin.

I found and bought a house not far from where A. R. Woresley lived. It was a plain red brick affair with four bedrooms and two fairly large living-rooms. Some retired Empire-builder in years gone by had christened it, of all things, 'Dunroamin'. 'Dunroamin' would be the headquarters of the Home. It would be where Yasmin and I lived during the preparatory period, and it would also be a secret laboratory for A. R. Woresley. I spent a lot of money equipping that lab with apparatus for making liquid nitrogen, with mixers, microscopes and everything else we needed. I furnished the house. Yasmin and I moved in. But from now on, ours was a business relationship only.

Within a month, A. R. Woresley had constructed our portable liquid nitrogen container. It had double vacuum walls of aluminium and all manner of neat little trays and other contraptions to hold the tiny straws of sperm. It was the size of a large suitcase, and what's more it looked like a suitcase because the outside was sheathed in leather.

A second, smaller, travelling case contained compartments for ice, a hand-mixer and bottles for carrying glycerol, egg-yolk and skimmed milk. Also a microscope for testing the potency of newly collected sperm in the field. Everything was got ready with meticulous care.

Finally, A. R. Woresley set about building the Semen's Home in the cellar of the house.

13

By early June, 1919, we were almost ready to go. I say almost because we still had not agreed upon the list of names. Who would be the great men in the world to be honoured by a visit from Yasmin – and lurking in the background, me ? The three of us had many meetings in 'Dunroamin' to discuss this knotty problem. The kings were easy. We wanted all the kings. We wrote them down first:

KING ALBERT OF THE BELGIANS	present age	45
KING BORIS OF BULGARIA	,, ,,	25
KING CHRISTIAN OF DENMARK	,, ,,	49
KING ALEXANDER OF GREECE	,, ,,	23
KING VITTORIO EMMANUELE OF ITALY	,, ,,	50
KING HAAKON OF NORWAY	,, ,,	47
KING FERDINAND OF ROMANIA	,, ,,	54
KING ALFONSO OF SPAIN	,, ,,	33
KING GUSTAV OF SWEDEN	,, ,,	61
KING PETER OF YUGOSLAVIA	,, ,,	75

The Netherlands was out because it had only a queen. Portugal was out because the monarchy had been overthrown in the Revolution of 1910. And Monaco was not worth fooling with. There remained only our own King George V. After much debate, we decided to leave the old boy alone. It was all just a little bit too much on our own doorstep for comfort and in any event I had plans for using this particular gentleman in quite another way, as you will see in a moment. We decided, though, to put EDWARD, PRINCE OF WALES on the list as a possible extra. Yasmin plus Blister Beetle would roll him over any time she wished. What's more, she could hardly wait.

The list of great men and geniuses was more difficult to compile. A few of them, like Puccini and Joseph Conrad and Richard Strauss, were obvious. So were Renoir and Monet, two rather ancient candidates who must clearly be visited pretty soon. But there was more to it than that. We had to decide which of the present-day (1919) great and famous men would still be great and famous ten, twenty and even fifty years hence.

There was also a more difficult group, the younger ones who were at present only moderately famous but who looked as though they might well become great and famous later on. This part of it was a bit of a gamble. It was also a matter of flair and judgement. Would the young James Joyce, for example, who was only thirty-seven years old, come to be regarded as a genius by later generations? I voted yes. So did A. R. Woresley. Yasmin

109

had never heard of him. By a vote of two to one we put him on the list.

In the end, we decided to make two separate lists. The first would be top priority. The second would contain the possibles. We would get round to the possibles only after we had polished off the top-priority boys. We would also pay attention to age. The older ones should, whenever possible, be attended to first in case they expired before we got to them.

We agreed that lists should be updated each year to include any new possibles who might suddenly have shot into prominence.

Our priority list, compiled in June 1919, was as follows, in alphabetical order:

BELL, Alexander Graham	present age	72
BONNARD, Pierre	,, ,,	52
CHURCHILL, Winston	,, ,,	45
CONRAD, Joseph	,, ,,	62
DOYLE, Arthur Conan	,, ,,	60
EINSTEIN, Albert	,, ,,	40
FORD, Henry	,, ,,	56
FREUD, Sigmund	,, ,,	63
KIPLING, Rudyard	,, ,,	54
LAWRENCE, David Herbert	,, ,,	34
LAWRENCE, Thomas Edward	,, ,,	31
LENIN, Vladimir Ilyich	,, ,,	49
MANN, Thomas	,, ,,	45
MARCONI, Gugliemo	,, ,,	45
MATISSE, Henri	,, ,,	50
MONET, Claude	,, ,,	79
MUNCH, Edvard	,, ,,	56
PROUST, Marcel	,, ,,	48
PUCCINI, Giacomo	,, ,,	61
RACHMANINOV, Sergei	,, ,,	46
RENOIR, Auguste	,, ,,	78
SHAW, George Bernard	,, ,,	63
SIBELIUS, Jean	,, ,,	54
STRAUSS, Richard	,, ,,	55

STRAVINSKY, Igor   ,,   ,,   37
YEATS, William Butler   ,,   ,,   54

And here was our second list comprising some fairly speculative younger men as well as a few borderline cases:

AMUNDSEN, Roald	present age		47
BRAQUE, Georges	,,	,,	37
CARUSO, Enrico	,,	,,	46
CASALS, Pablo	,,	,,	43
CLEMENCEAU, Georges	,,	,,	79
DELIUS, Frederick	,,	,,	57
FOCH, Maréchal Ferdinand	,,	,,	68
GANDHI, Mohandas	,,	,,	50
HAIG, General Sir Douglas	,,	,,	58
JOYCE, James	,,	,,	37
KANDINSKY, Wassily	,,	,,	53
LLOYD GEORGE, David	,,	,,	56
NIJINSKI, Vaslav	,,	,,	27
PERSHING, General John J.	,,	,,	59
PICASSO, Pablo	,,	,,	38
RAVEL, Maurice	,,	,,	44
RUSSELL, Bertrand	,,	,,	47
SCHOENBERG, Arnold	,,	,,	45
TAGORE, Rabindranath	,,	,,	58
TROTSKY, Lev Davidovich	,,	,,	40
VALENTINO, Rudolph	,,	,,	24
WILSON, Woodrow	,,	,,	63

Of course there were errors and omissions in these lists. There is no more difficult game than to try spotting an authentic and enduring genius during his lifetime. Fifty years after he's dead it becomes easier. But dead men were no use to us. One more point. Rudolph Valentino was included not because we thought he was a genius. It was a commercial decision. We were guessing that the semen of a man who had such an immense and fanatical band of followers might well be a good seller in days to come. Nor did we think Woodrow Wilson was a genius, or

Caruso. But they were world-famous figures, and we had to take that into consideration.

Europe, of course, must be covered first. The long trip to America would have to wait. So on to one wall of the living-room we fixed an enormous map of Europe and covered it with little flags. Each flag pinpointed the precise whereabouts of a candidate: red flags for the priorities, yellow for the second group, with a name and address on each flag. Thus, Yasmin and I would be able to plan our visits geographically, area by area, instead of rushing from one end of the continent to the other, and back again. France had the most flags of all, and the Paris region was literally cluttered with them.

'What a pity both Degas and Rodin died two years ago,' I said.

'I want to do the kings first,' Yasmin said. The three of us were sitting in the living-room of 'Dunroamin' discussing the next move.

'Why the kings?'

'Because I have a terrific urge to be ravished by royalty,' she said.

'You are being flippant,' A. R. Woresley said.

'Why shouldn't I choose,' she said. 'I'm the one at the receiving end, not you. I'd like to do the King of Spain first. Then we can nip over to Italy and do old Vittorio Emmanuele, then Yugoslavia, then Greece, and so on. We'll polish off the whole lot of them in a couple of weeks.'

'May I ask how you intend to gain access to all these royal palaces?' A. R. Woresley said to me. 'Yasmin can't just go knocking on the front door and expect to be received in private by the King. And don't forget it's got to be in private or it's no good.'

'That part shouldn't be too difficult,' I said.

'It's going to be impossible,' Woresley said. 'We shall probably have to forget about the kings.'

I had been working on this problem for several weeks and I had my answer ready. 'Easy as pie,' I said. 'We shall use King George the Fifth as a decoy. He'll get her in.'

'Don't be ridiculous, Cornelius.'

I went to a drawer and took out some sheets of notepaper.

'Let's assume you want to do the King of Spain first,' I said, riffling through the sheets. 'Ah yes, here we are. My dear Alfonso . . .' I handed the notepaper to Woresley. Yasmin got up from her chair to look at it over his shoulder.

'What in God's name is this?' he cried.

'It's an extremely personal letter from King George the Fifth to King Alfonso,' I said. And indeed it was.

The notepaper had a heavily embossed royal coat of arms in red at the top centre, and on the top right, also embossed in red, it said simply BUCKINGHAM PALACE, LONDON. Below, in a reasonable imitation of the King's flowing hand-writing, I had written the following:

My Dear Alfonso
This will introduce to you a dear friend of mine, Lady Victoria Nottingham. She is travelling alone to Madrid to clear up a small matter that has to do with an estate that has come to her through her Spanish maternal grandmother.

My request is that you see Lady Victoria briefly and in absolute privacy. She is having some trouble with the local authorities over title deeds and I am sure that if you yourself, after she has explained her problem, will drop a hint with the right people, then everything will go smoothly for her.

I am taking you, my dear Alfonso, very deeply into my confidence when I tell you that Lady Victoria is an especially close personal friend of mine. Let us leave it at that and say no more. But I know I can rely upon you to keep this intelligence entirely to yourself.

When you receive this note, the lady in question will be at the Ritz Hotel, Madrid. Do please send her a message as soon as possible granting her a private audience.

Burn this letter when read, and make no reply to me.

I am at your service at all times.

With warmest personal regards,
George RI

Both A. R. Woresley and Yasmin looked up at me with eyes popping.

'Where did you get this notepaper?' Woresley said.

'I had it printed.'

'Did you write this yourself?'

'I did and I'm rather proud of it. It's a very fair imitation of the King's handwriting. And the signature is almost perfect. I practised it for days.'

'You'll be had up for forgery! You'll be sent to prison!'

'No, I won't,' I said. 'Alfonso won't dare tell a soul. Don't you see the beauty of it. Our great and noble King is hinting that he is having a backstairs affair with Yasmin. That, my dear sir, is very, very confidential and dangerous material. And don't forget, European royalty is the most tightly-knit and exclusive club in the world. They work together. Every ruddy one of them is related to the other in some crazy way. They're tangled up like spaghetti. No – there is not the slightest chance of Alfonso letting the King of England down. He'll see Yasmin at once. He'll be dying to see her. He'll want to take a good look at this woman who is the secret mistress of old George Five. Remember also that right now our King is the most respected of all the royals. He's just won the war.'

'Cornelius,' A. R. Woresley said, 'you frighten me to death. You'll have us all behind bars.'

'I think it's terrific,' Yasmin said. 'It's brilliant. It's bound to work.'

'What if a secretary opens the envelope?' Woresley said.

'That won't happen,' I said. I took a bunch of envelopes from the drawer and found the right one and gave it to Woresley. It was a long high-quality white envelope with the red royal coat of arms top left, and BUCKINGHAM PALACE top right. In the King's handwriting, I had written on it:

> *His Royal Highness, King Alfonso XIII*
> *Personal and Confidential. To be*
> *opened only by HRH himself.*

'That should do it,' I said. 'The envelope will be delivered to the Oriente Palace in Madrid by my own hand.'

A. R. Woresley opened his mouth to say something, then closed it again.

'I have a roughly similar letter for each of the other nine kings,' I said. 'Obviously there are small changes. Each message is tailored to the individual. Haakon of Norway, for instance, is married to King George's sister, Maud – I'll bet you didn't know that – and so there we finish up with "Give my love to Maud, but I trust you absolutely to make no mention to her of this private little piece of business." And so on and so on. It's foolproof, my dear Arthur.' I was calling him by his first name now.

'You appear to have done your homework, Cornelius.' He himself, in the manner of all dons and schoolmasters, refused to use my given name. 'But how do you propose to get in to see all the others, the non-kings?'

'There will be no problem,' I said. 'Not many men will refuse to see a girl like Yasmin when she knocks on the door. *You* certainly didn't. I'll bet you began dribbling with excitement as soon as she came into the lab.'

That shut him up.

'So can we do the King of Spain first?' Yasmin asked. 'He's only thirty-three and from his photograph he's rather dishy.'

'Very well,' I said. 'Madrid first stop. But then we must move into France. Renoir and Monet are top priority. One's seventy-eight and the other seventy-nine. I want to nobble them both before it's too late.'

'With Blister Beetle it'll be heart attack time for those old boys,' Yasmin said.

'We'll reduce the dose,' I said.

'Now see here, Cornelius,' A. R. Woresley said. 'I won't be a party to the murder of Mr Renoir or Mr Monet. I don't want blood on my hands.'

'You'll have a lot of valuable sperm on your hands and that's all,' I said. 'Leave it to us.'

14

The stage was set. Yasmin and I packed our bags and left for Madrid. We had with us the vital liquid nitrogen suitcase, the smaller case containing glycerol, etc., a supply of Prestat's best chocolate truffles and four ounces of Blister Beetle powder. I must again mention that in those days the examination of luggage by customs was virtually non-existent. There would be no trouble with our curious suitcases. We crossed the Channel and travelled to Madrid via Paris by Wagon-Lits. The trip took only nineteen hours altogether. In Madrid, we registered at the Ritz where we had booked separate rooms by telegram, one for Oswald Cornelius Esquire and one for Lady Victoria Nottingham.

The next morning I went to the Oriente Palace, where I was stopped at the gates by a couple of soldiers on guard duty. Waving my envelope and shouting, 'This is for the King!' in Spanish, I reached the big main entrance. I pulled the bell-knob. A flunkey opened one of the doors. I then spoke a Spanish sentence that I had committed to memory, which said, 'This is for His Majesty Alfonso from King George of Great Britain. It is most urgent.' I walked away.

Back at the hotel, I settled down with a book in Yasmin's room to await developments.

'What if he's out of town?' she said.

'He isn't,' I said. 'The flag was flying over the Palace.'

'What if he doesn't answer?'

'He'll answer. He wouldn't dare not to, after reading that letter on that notepaper.'

'But can he read English?'

'All kings can read English,' I said. 'It's a part of their education. Alfonso speaks perfect English.'

Just before lunchtime, there was a knock on the door. Yasmin opened it and there stood the manager of the hotel himself with a look of importance on his face. He had a silver tray in his hand on which lay a white envelope. 'An urgent message, my lady,' he said, bowing. Yasmin took the envelope, thanked him and closed the door.

'Rip it open!' I said.

She ripped it open and took out a letter handwritten on magnificent Palace notepaper.

My Dear Lady Victoria, it said. *We shall be pleased to see you at four o'clock this afternoon. If you will give your name at the gates you will be admitted immediately.*
Alfonso R

'Simple, isn't it?' I said.

'What does he mean *we*?'

'All monarchs refer to themselves as we. You have three hours to get ready and be at the Palace gates,' I said. 'Let's fix the chocolate.'

I had obtained from Prestat a number of very small and elegant boxes, each holding no more than six truffles. Yasmin was to give one box to the King as a small present. She was to say to him, 'I have brought you, sire, a little present of chocolates. They're delicious. George has them specially made for me.' She was then to open the box and say with a most disarming smile, 'Do you mind if I steal one? I simply can't resist them.' She pops one into her mouth, then picks up the marked chocolate and holds it out to the King delicately between forefinger and thumb, saying, 'Try one.' The poor man will be charmed. He will eat the choc just as A. R. Woresley did in the lab. And that will be that. Thereafter, Yasmin will simply have to carry on nine minutes of flirtatious small talk without getting entangled in any complicated reason for her visit.

I got out the Blister Beetle powder and we prepared the fatal truffle. 'No double doses this time,' Yasmin said. 'I don't want to have to use the hatpin.' I agreed. She herself marked the truffle with small scratches on the surface of the chocolate.

117

It was June and very hot in Madrid. Yasmin dressed with great care but wore the lightest possible clothes. I gave her a rubbery thing from my large stock and she put it in her purse.

'For God's sake don't fail to get it on him,' I said. 'That's what it's all about. And hurry back here with it quickly afterwards. Come straight to my room next door.' I wished her good luck and off she went.

In my own room I made careful preparations for dealing with the sperm as soon as it arrived. This was my very first time under actual field conditions and I wanted to get everything just right. I will admit I felt nervous. Yasmin was at the Palace. She was giving Blister Beetle to the King of Spain and after that there would be a good old wrestling match and I only hoped she would handle things properly.

The time went slowly. I finished my preparations. I leaned out of the window and watched the carriages in the street below. Once or twice a motor car came by, but there were not so many here as in London. I looked at my watch. It was after six o'clock. I made myself a whiskey and soda. I carried it to the open window and sipped it there. I was hoping to see Yasmin stepping out of a carriage at the hotel entrance. I didn't see her. I got myself a second whiskey. I sat down and tried to read a book. It was now six-thirty. She had been gone two and a half hours. Suddenly there was a loud knocking on my door. I got up and opened it. Yasmin, with cheeks afire, swept into the room.

'I did it!' she cried, waving her handbag at me like a flag. 'I've got it! It's in here!'

'Give it to me quick,' I said.

There was at least three ccs of royal semen in the knotted rubbery thing Yasmin handed to me. I put a drop under the microscope to test it for potency. The tiny royal squigglers were squiggling madly all over the place, supremely active. 'First rate stuff,' I said. 'Let me get this into the straws and frozen up before you say a word. After that, I want to hear exactly what happened.'

Yasmin went to her room to bathe and change. I set about the business in hand. A. R. Woresley and I had agreed that we would make exactly fifty straws of semen for each person. More than that would take up too much room in our travelling sperm-freezer. I set about diluting the semen with egg yolk, skimmed milk and glycerol. I mixed it. I measured it out with a graduated eye-dropper into the little rubber straws. I sealed the straws. I put them on ice for half an hour. I exposed them to nitrogen vapour for a few minutes. Then finally I lowered them gently into the liquid nitrogen and closed the container. It was done. We now had fifty doses of the King of Spain's semen, and strong doses at that. The equation was simple. He gave us three ccs originally. Three ccs would contain approximately three thousand million sperm and those three thousand million, when divided up into fifty doses, would produce a potency of sixty million sperm per dose. This was exactly three times A. R. Woresley's optimum figure of twenty million per dose. In other words, the Spanish Royal straws were of prime potency. I was elated. I rang the bell for service and ordered a bottle of Krug on ice.

Yasmin came in looking cool and clean. The champagne arrived at the same time. We waited until the servant had opened the bottle and filled the glasses and left the room. 'Now,' I said, 'tell me all.'

'It was amazing,' she said. 'The preliminaries went exactly as you said they would. I was ushered into an enormous room with Goyas and El Grecos all over the walls. The King was at the far end sitting behind a huge desk. He was dressed in a plain suit. He stood up and came forward to greet me. He had a moustache and was not a bad looking little fellow. He kissed my hand. And my God, Oswald, you should have seen the way he fawned all over me because he thought I was the King of England's mistress. "Madame," he said, "I am enchanted to meet you. And how is our mutual friend?"

'"He has a slight touch of gout," I said, "but otherwise he's in splendid condition." Then I went through the chocolate routine and he ate his little truffle like a lamb and with a good deal of relish. "These are magnificent," he said, chewing away.

"I must have my ambassador send me a few pounds." As he swallowed the last bit of chocolate, I noted the time on my watch. "Pray be seated," he said.

'There were four big sofa things in the room and before sitting down I examined them carefully. I wanted to choose the softest and most practical of the four. I knew that in nine minutes' time the one I selected would become a battlefield.'

'Good thinking,' I said.

'I chose an enormous sort of chaise longue covered in plum-coloured velvet. The King remained standing and as we talked he strolled about the room with his hands clasped behind his back, trying to look regal.

'I said, "Our mutual friend has asked me to tell you, sire, that if you yourself should ever require any confidential assistance in his country, you could rely upon him absolutely."

'"I shall bear it in mind," he said.

'"He sent you another message as well, your Majesty."

'"What was that?"

'"You promise you won't be cross if I tell you?"

'"Certainly not, madame. Tell me what else he said."

'"He said, you tell that good-looking Alfonso to keep his hands off my girl. That's word for word what he said, your Majesty." Little Alfonso laughed and clapped his hands and said, "Dear lady, I shall respect his wishes but only with the greatest difficulty."'

'Yasmin,' I said, 'you're a clever little bitch.'

'Oh, it was such fun,' she said. 'I loved twisting him around. He was madly curious about my so-called affair but he didn't quite dare to mention it. He kept putting leading questions to me. He said, "I presume you have a house in London?"

'"Of course," I said. "I have my own London house where I entertain in normal fashion. Then I have a small very private place in Windsor Great Park where a certain person can call on me when he is out riding. And I have a cottage on the Sandring-ham Estate where again that certain person can pop in for a cup of tea when he is out shooting pheasants. As you probably know, he adores shooting."

'"I know that," Alfonso said. "And I hear he is the best shot in England."

'"Yes," I said, "and in more ways than one, your Majesty."

'"Ha!" he said. "I see you are a funny lady."'

'Were you watching the time?' I said to Yasmin.

'You bet I was. I've forgotten exactly what he was saying when the moment arrived, but the interesting thing is that he froze right in the middle of a sentence just as old Woresley had done in the lab. Here it comes, I told myself. Put on the boxing gloves.'

'Did he jump you?'

'No, he didn't. Don't forget Woresley had had a double dose.'

'Ah yes.'

'Anyway, he was standing in front of me when he froze and he was wearing tight trousers so I could see very clearly what was going on around there. At precisely that moment, I told him I collected the autographs of great men and asked him if he would give me his signature on Palace notepaper. I got up and went to his desk myself and found the paper and told him where to sign. It was too easy. The wretched man hardly knew what he was doing. He signed and I put the paper in my purse and sat down again. You know, Oswald, you can make them do just about anything you want if you catch them right at the very moment when the powder first hits them. They're so astonished and embarrassed by the suddenness of it all they'll do absolutely anything. We're never going to have any trouble getting their signatures. Anyway, I was back again on the sofa now and Alfonso was standing there goggling at me and he kept swallowing which made his Adam's apple jump up and down. Red in the face he was, too, and then he started taking deep breaths. "Come and sit down, your Majesty," I said, patting the place beside me. He came and sat down. The swallowing and the goggling and the fidgeting went on for about a minute and I could see this absolutely terrific lech building up inside him as the powder got to work. It was like steam building up in a boiler with nowhere to escape except through the safety valve. And the safety valve was little me. If he didn't get little me he was going to explode.

Suddenly he said in a chokey and rather prim sort of voice, "I wish you to remove your clothes, madame."

'"Oh sire!" I cried, putting both hands on my breast. "What are you saying!"

'"Take them off," he said, gulping.

'"But then you will ravish me, your Majesty!" I cried.

'"Please don't keep me waiting," he said, gulping some more.

'"If you ravish me, sire, I will become pregnant and our mutual friend will know something has happened between us. He will be so angry he will send warships to bombard your cities."

'"You must tell him it was he who got you pregnant. Come along now, I cannot wait!"

'"He'll know it wasn't him, your Majesty, because he and I always take precautions."

'"Then take precautions now!" he snapped. "And please do not argue with me, madame!"'

'You handled it beautifully,' I said to Yasmin. 'So you put the thing on him.'

'No problem,' she said. 'It was easy. With Woresley I had had the most awful fight, but this time it was as easy as putting a tea-cosy on a teapot.'

'Then what?'

'They're pretty odd, these royals,' Yasmin said. 'They know a few tricks us ordinary mortals have never heard of.'

'Such as what?'

'Well,' she said, 'for one thing he doesn't move. I suppose the theory is that kings don't do any manual labour.'

'So he made you do all the work.'

'I wasn't allowed to move either.'

'Now don't be silly, Yasmin. You can't have static copulation.'

'Kings can,' she said. 'Wait till you hear this. You won't believe it. You simply won't believe this sort of thing could happen.'

'What sort of thing?' I said.

'I told you I had chosen a chaise longue covered in purple velvet,' Yasmin said.

'Yes.'

'Well, it turned out I'd picked exactly the right one. This damn sofa was some sort of a specially constructed royal romping ground. It was the most fantastic experience I've ever had. It had something underneath it, God knows what, but it was some sort of an engine and when the King pulled a lever the whole sofa began to joggle up and down.'

'You're having me on.'

'I am *not* having you on!' she cried. 'I couldn't make that up even if I wanted to and you jolly well know it.'

'You really mean there was an *engine* under the sofa? Did you see it?'

'Of course not. But I heard it all right. It made the most godawful grinding noise.'

'You mean a *petrol* engine?'

'No, it wasn't a petrol engine.'

'What was it then?'

'Clockwork,' she said.

'*Clockwork*! It's not possible! How did you know it was clockwork?'

'Because when it started to run down, he had to roll off and wind the thing up again with a handle.'

'I don't believe a word of this,' I said. 'What sort of a handle?'

'A big handle,' she said, 'like the starting handle of a motor-car and when he was winding it up it went *clickety-click*. That's how I knew it was clockwork. You always get that clicking noise when you wind up clockwork.'

'Jesus,' I said. 'I still don't believe it.'

'You don't know much about kings,' Yasmin said. 'Kings are different. They get very bored, therefore they are always trying to think up ways of amusing themselves. Look at that mad King of Bavaria who had a hole drilled in the middle of the seat of each chair around his dining-room table. And halfway through dinner, when all the guests were sitting there in their wonderful expensive clothes, he would turn on a secret tap and jets of water would squirt up through the holes. Very powerful jets of cold water right up their backsides. Kings are crazy.'

'Go on with the clockwork sofa,' I said. 'Was it amazing and terrific?'

Yasmin sipped her champagne and didn't answer me at once.

'Did it have the maker's name on it?' I said. 'Where can I get one?'

'I wouldn't get one,' she said.

'Why not?'

'It's not worth it. It's only a toy. It's a toy for silly kings. It has a kind of shock value that's all. When it first started up I got the shock of my life. "Hey!" I shouted. "What the hell's going on?"'

'"Silence!" the King said. "Talking is forbidden!"'

'There was a loud whirring noise coming from underneath the damn sofa and the thing was vibrating most terribly. And at the same time it was jogging up and down. Honestly Oswald, it was like riding a horse on the deck of a boat in a rough sea. Oh God, I thought, I'm going to be seasick. But I wasn't and after he'd wound it up a second time I began to get the hang of it. You see, it *was* rather like riding a horse. You had to go along with it. You had to get the rhythm.'

'So you began to enjoy it?'

'I wouldn't say that. But it does have its advantages. For one thing, you never get tired. It would be great for old people.'

'Alfonso's only thirty-three.'

'Alfonso's crazy,' Yasmin said. 'Once when he was winding up the motor, he said, "I usually have a servant doing this." Christ, I thought, the silly sod really is crazy.'

'How did you get away?'

'It wasn't easy,' Yasmin said. 'You see, with him not having to do any work except winding the thing up now and again, he never got puffed. After about an hour, I'd had enough. "Switch off," I said. "I've had enough."'

'"We go on till I give the order," he said.'

'"Don't be like that," I said. "Come on, pack it in."'

'"Nobody gives orders here except me," he said.'

'Oh well, I thought. I suppose it'll have to be the hatpin.'

'Did you use it? Did you actually stick him?' I asked.

'You're damn right I did,' she said. 'It went in about two inches!'

'What happened?'

'He nearly hit the ceiling. He gave a piercing yell and bounced off on to the floor. "You stuck me!" he shrieked, clutching his backside. I was up in a flash and starting to put my clothes on and he was jumping up and down stark naked and shrieking, "You stuck me! You stuck me! How dare you do that to me!"'

'Terrific,' I said to Yasmin. 'Marvellous. Wonderful. I wish I'd seen it. Did he bleed?'

'I don't know and I don't care, but I was really fed up with him by then and I got a bit ratty and I said, "Listen to me, you, and listen carefully. Our mutual friend would have you by the balls if he ever heard about this. You raped me, you do realize that, don't you?" That shut him up. "What on earth came over you?" I said. I was getting dressed as fast as I could and stalling for time. "Whatever made you do a thing like that to me?" I shouted. I had to shout because the damn sofa was still rattling away behind me.

'"I don't know," he said. Suddenly he had become all meek and mild. When I was ready to go, I went up to him and kissed him on the cheek and said, "Let's just forget it ever happened, shall we?" At the same time, I quickly removed the sticky rubbery thing from his royal knob and marched grandly out of the room.'

'Did anyone try to stop you?' I asked.

'Not a soul.'

'Full marks,' I said. 'You did a great job. You'd better give me that notepaper.' She gave me the sheet of Palace notepaper with the signature on it and I filed it carefully away. 'Now go and pack your bags,' I said. 'We're leaving town on the next train.'

15

Within half an hour we had packed our bags and checked out of the hotel and were heading for the railway station. Paris next stop.

And so it was. We went to Paris on the night sleeper and arrived there on a sparkling June morning. We took rooms at the Ritz. 'Wherever you are,' my father used to say, 'when in doubt, stay at the Ritz.' Wise words. Yasmin came into my room to discuss strategy over an early lunch – a cold lobster for each of us and a bottle of Chablis. I had the list of priority candidates in front of me on the table.

'Whatever happens, Renoir and Monet come first,' I said. 'In that order.'

'Where do we find them?' Yasmin asked.

It is never difficult to discover the whereabouts of famous men. 'Renoir is at Essoyes,' I said. 'That's a small town about 120 miles south-west of Paris, between Champagne and Burgundy. He is now seventy-eight and I'm told he's in a wheelchair.'

'Jesus Christ, Oswald, I'm not going to feed Blister Beetle to some poor old bastard in a wheelchair!' Yasmin said.

'He'll love it,' I told her. 'There's nothing wrong with him except a bit of arthritis. He's still painting. He is easily the most celebrated painter alive today and I'll tell you another thing. No living painter in the history of art has ever received such high prices for his pictures during his lifetime as Renoir. He's a giant. In ten years' time we'll be selling his straws for a fortune.'

'Where's his wife?'

'Dead. He's a lonely old man. You'll cheer him up no end.

When he sees you, he'll probably want to paint you in the nude on the spot.'

'I'd like that.'

'On the other hand, he has a model called Dédée he's absolutely mad about.'

'I'll soon fix her,' Yasmin said.

'Play your cards right and he might even give you a picture.'

'Hey, I'd like that, too.'

'Work on it,' I said.

'What about Monet?' she asked.

'He is also a lonely old man. He's seventy-nine, a year older than Renoir, and he's living the life of a recluse at Giverny. That's not far from here. Just outside Paris. Very few people visit him now. Clemenceau drops in occasionally, so I'm told, but almost no one else. You'll be a little sunbeam in his life. And another canvas perhaps? A Monet landscape? Those things are going to be worth hundreds of thousands later on. They're worth thousands already.'

The possibility of getting a picture from one or both of these great artists excited Yasmin a good deal. 'You'll be visiting lots of other painters before we're finished,' I said. 'You could form a collection.'

'That's a pretty good idea,' she said. 'Renoir, Monet, Matisse, Bonnard, Munch, Braque and all the rest of them. Yes, it's a *very* good idea. I must remember that.'

The lobsters were huge and delicious, with enormous claws. The Chablis was good, too – a Grand Cru Bougros. I have a passion for fine Chablis, not only for the steely-dry Grands Crus but also for some of the Premiers Crus where the fruit is a little closer to the surface. This particular Bougros was as steely as any I had ever tasted. Yasmin and I discussed strategy while we ate and drank. It was my contention that no man was going to turn away a young lady who possessed the charm and the devastating beauty of Yasmin. No male, however ancient, was capable of treating her with indifference. Wherever we went I kept seeing evidence of this. Even the suave marble-faced receptionist downstairs had gone all over queer when he caught sight of Yasmin standing before him. I had been watching him closely and I had seen that famous old spark start flashing in the very centre of the pupil of each of his jet-black eyes, and then his tongue had poked out and had begun sliding over his upper lip, and his fingers had fumbled inanely with our registration forms, and at the end of it all he had given us the wrong keys. A scintillating and sex-soaked creature our Yasmin was, a kind of human Blister Beetle all on her own, and as I say, no man on earth was going to send her packing.

But none of this sexual chemistry was going to help us one bit unless the girl was able actually to present herself to the customer. Formidable housekeepers and equally formidable wives could well be a problem. My optimism, however, was based on the fact that the fellows we were after were nearly all painters or musicians or writers. They were artists. And artists are probably the most approachable people you can find. Even the very great ones are never guarded, as businessmen are, by iron-mouthed secretaries and amateur gangsters in black suits. Big businessmen and their like live in caves that can be reached only by passing through long tunnels and many rooms, with a Cerberus around every corner. Artists are loners, and more often than not they open the front door themselves when you ring the bell.

But why would Yasmin be ringing the bell in the first place?

Ah well, she was a young English girl, a student of art (or music or literature, whichever was applicable) who had such a massive admiration for the work of Monsieur Renoir or Monet or Stravinsky or whoever, that she had come all the way from England to pay homage to the great man, to say hello to him, to give him a little present and then to go away again. Nunc dimittis.

'That,' I said to Yasmin as I polished off the last succulent lobster claw – and by the way, don't you love it when you are able to draw the flesh of the claw out of the shell whole and pinky-red in one piece? There is some kind of tiny personal triumph in that. I may be childish, but I experience a similar triumph when I succeed in getting a walnut out of its shell without breaking it in two. As a matter of fact, I never approach a walnut without this particular ambition in mind. Life is more fun if you play games. But back to Yasmin. 'That,' I said to her, 'will get you invited right into the house or the studio ninety-nine times out of a hundred. With your smile and your lascivious looks, I cannot see any of these lads turning you away.'

'What about their watchdogs or their wives?'

'I think you'll get past them, too. Occasionally they may tell you the man's busy painting or writing and to come back at six o'clock. But you're always going to win in the end. Don't forget, you've travelled a long way just to pay homage. And make a point of saying you won't stay more than a few minutes.'

'Nine,' Yasmin said, grinning. 'Just nine minutes. When do we start?'

'Tomorrow,' I said. 'I shall buy a motor car this afternoon. We're going to need it for our French and European operations. And tomorrow we will drive to Essoyes and you will meet Monsieur Renoir.'

'You never waste time, do you, Oswald?'

'My darling,' I said, 'as soon as I have made a fortune I propose to spend the rest of my life wasting time. But until the money is in the bank, I shall work very hard indeed. And so must you.'

'How long do you think it will take?'

'To make our fortunes? About seven or eight years. No more. That's not such a long stretch when it means you can laze about doing nothing for ever after.'

'No,' she said, 'it isn't. And anyway, I'm rather enjoying this.'

'I know you are.'

'What I'm enjoying,' she said, 'is the thought of being ravished by all the greatest men in the world. And all the kings. It tickles my fancy.'

'Let's go out and buy a French motor car,' I said. So out we went and this time I bought a splendid little 10 hp Citroën *Torpedo*, a four-seater, a brand new model only just out. It cost me the equivalent of £350 in French money and it was exactly what I wanted. Although it had no luggage compartment, there was plenty of room on the back seats for all my equipment and suitcases. It was an open tourer and had a canvas roof that could be put up in less than a minute if it started to rain. The body was dark blue, the colour of royal blood, and its top speed was an exhilarating 55 mph.

The next morning we set off for Essoyes with my travelling laboratory packed away in the back of the Citroën. We stopped at Troyes for lunch, where we ate trout from the Seine (I had two, they were so good) and drank a bottle of white *vin du pays*. We got to Essoyes at four in the afternoon and booked into a small hotel whose name I have forgotten. My bedroom again became my laboratory and as soon as everything had been laid out in readiness for the immediate testing and mixing and freezing of semen, Yasmin and I went out to find Monsieur Renoir. This was not difficult. The woman at the desk gave us precise instructions. A large white house, she said, on the right-hand side, three hundred metres beyond the church or some such thing.

I spoke fluent French after my year in Paris. Yasmin spoke just enough of it to get along. She had had a French governess sometime or other during her childhood and that had been a help.

We found the house without any trouble. It was a medium-sized white wooden building standing on its own in a pleasant garden. It was not, I knew, the great man's main residence. That was down south in Cagnes, but he probably found it cooler up here in the summer months.

'Good luck,' I said to Yasmin. 'I'll be waiting about a hundred yards down the road.'

She got out of the car and went towards the gates. I watched her going. She wore flat-heeled shoes and a creamy-coloured linen dress, no hat. Cool and demure, she passed through the gates and moved on up the drive swinging her arms as she went. There was a lilt in her walk, a little shadow attending her, and she looked more like a young postulant going in to see the Mother Superior than someone who was about to cause a saucy explosion within the mind and body of one of the great painters of the world.

It was a warm sunshiny evening. Sitting there in the open motor car I dozed off and did not wake up until two hours later when I found Yasmin getting into the seat beside me.

'What happened?' I said. 'Tell me quick! Was everything all right? Did you see him? Have you got the stuff?'

She had a small brown paper parcel in one hand, her purse in the other. She opened the purse, and took out the signed notepaper and the all-important rubbery thing. She handed them to me without speaking. She had a funny look on her face, a mixture of ecstasy and awe, and when I spoke to her she didn't appear to hear me. Miles away she seemed, miles and miles away.

'What's the matter?' I said. 'Why the great silence?'

She gazed straight ahead through the windscreen, not hearing me. Her eyes were very bright, her face serene, beatific almost, with a queer radiance.

'Christ, Yasmin,' I said. 'What the hell's the matter with you? You look like you've seen a vision.'

'Just get going,' she said, 'and leave me alone.'

We drove back to the hotel without talking and each went to our separate rooms. I made an immediate microscopic examination of the semen. The sperm were alive but the count was low, very low. I was able to make no more than ten straws. But they were ten sound straws with a count of about twenty million sperm in each. By God, I thought, these are going to cost somebody a lot of money in years to come. They'll be as rare as the First Folio of Shakespeare. I ordered champagne and a plate of *foie gras* and toast, and I sent a message to Yasmin's room telling her I hoped she would come in and join me.

She arrived half an hour later and she had with her the little brown paper parcel. I poured her a glass of champagne and put a slice of *foie gras* on toast for her. She accepted the champagne, ignored the *foie gras* and remained silent.

'Come on,' I said, 'what's bothering you?'

She emptied her glass in one long swallow and held it out for more. I refilled the glass. She drank half of it, then put it down. 'For God's sake, Yasmin!' I cried. 'What happened?'

She looked at me very straight and said simply, 'He smote me.'

'You mean he *hit* you? Good God, I am sorry! You mean he actually struck you?'

'Don't be an ass, Oswald.'

'What *do* you mean then?'

'I mean I was smitten by him. He's the first man who's ever bowled me completely over.'

'Oh, I *see* what you mean! Good heavens!'

'He is a wonder, that man,' she said. 'He is a genius.'

'Of course he's a genius. That's why we chose him.'

'Yes, but he's a beautiful genius. He is so beautiful, Oswald, and so gentle and wonderful, I've never met anyone like him.'

'He smote you all right.'

'He certainly did.'

'So what's your problem?' I said. 'Are you feeling guilty about it?'

'Oh no,' she said. 'I don't feel in the least guilty. I'm just overwhelmed.'

'You're going to be a hell of a lot more overwhelmed before we've finished,' I said. 'He's not the only genius you're going to call on.'

'I know that.'

'You're not running out, are you?'

'Certainly not. Give me some more drink.'

I filled her glass for the third time in as many minutes. She sat sipping it. Then she said, 'Listen, Oswald . . .'

'I'm listening.'

'We've been pretty jokey about this whole thing up to now, haven't we? It's all been a bit of a lark, right?'

'Rubbish! I take it very seriously.'

'What about Alfonso?'

'You were the one who joked about him,' I said.

'I know that,' she said, 'but he deserved it. He's a joker.'

'I can't quite see what you're getting at,' I said.

'Renoir was different,' she said. 'That's what I'm getting at.

He's a giant. His work is going to live through the ages.'

'So will his sperm.'

'Stop it and hear me out,' she said. 'What I'm saying is this. Some people are jokers. Some are not. Alfonso is a joker. All the kings are jokers. We have a few other jokers on our list, too.'

'Who?'

'Henry Ford's a joker,' she said. 'I think that fellow Freud in Vienna is a joker. And the wireless boy, Marconi. He's a joker.'

'What's the point of all this?'

'The point is,' Yasmin said, 'I don't in the least mind being jokey about jokers. I don't mind treating them a little rough either if I have to. But I'll be damned if I'm going to start sticking hatpins into men like Renoir and Conrad and Stravinsky. Not after what I saw today.'

'What did you see today?'

'I told you, I saw a really great and wonderful old man.'

'And he smote you.'

'You're damn right he did.'

'Let me ask you this, did *he* have a good time?'

'Amazing,' she said. 'He had an amazing time.'

'Tell me what happened.'

'No,' she said. 'I don't mind telling you about the jokers. But the non-jokers are private.'

'Was he in a wheelchair?'

'Yes. And now he has to strap the paintbrush to his wrist because he can't hold it in his fingers.'

'Because of arthritis?'

'Yes.'

'And you gave him the Blister Beetle?'

'Of course.'

'It wasn't too much for him?'

'No,' she said. 'When you're that age you have to have it.'

'And he gave you a picture,' I said, pointing to the brown paper parcel.

She unwrapped it now and held it up for me to see. It was a small unframed canvas of a young rosy-cheeked girl with long golden hair and blue eyes, a wondrous little picture, a magic thing, a marvel to look at. A warm glow came out of it and filled the entire room. 'I didn't ask him for it,' Yasmin said. 'He made me take it. Isn't it beautiful?'

'Yes,' I said. 'It is beautiful.'

16

The effect that Renoir had upon Yasmin during that dramatic visit to Essoyes did not, thank heaven, take all the fun out of our future operations. I myself have always found it difficult to treat anything too seriously and I believe the world would be a better place if everyone followed my example. I am completely without ambition. My motto – 'It is better to incur a mild rebuke than to perform an onerous task' – should be well known to you by now. All I want out of life is to enjoy myself. But before one can achieve this happy end one must obviously get hold of a lot of money. Money is essential to a sybarite. It is the key of the kingdom. To which the carping reader will almost certainly reply, 'You say you are without ambition, but do you not realize that the desire for wealth is in itself one of the most obnoxious ambitions of them all?'

This is not necessarily true. It is the *manner* in which one acquires wealth that determines whether or not it is obnoxious. I myself am scrupulous about the methods I employ. I refuse to have anything to do with moneymaking unless the process obeys two golden rules. First, it must amuse me tremendously. Second, it must give a great deal of pleasure to those from whom I extract the loot. This is a simple philosophy and I recommend it wholeheartedly to all business tycoons, casino operators, Chancellors of the Exchequer and Budget Directors everywhere.

Two things stood out vividly during this period. First, the unusual sense of fulfilment Yasmin was getting from each artist she visited. She would emerge from house or studio with eyes shining like stars and a bright red rose on each cheek. All of which caused me to ruminate many times upon the sexual dexterity of men of outstanding creative genius. Did this prodigious creativity of theirs spill over into other fields? And if so, did they know deep secrets and magic methods of exciting a lady that were beyond the reach of ordinary mortals like me? The red roses upon Yasmin's cheeks and the shine in her eyes made me suspect, a trifle reluctantly let me say, that this was so.

The second surprising facet of the whole operation was its extraordinary simplicity. Yasmin never seemed to have the slightest trouble in getting her man to deliver the goods. Mind you, the more one thinks about this, the more obvious it becomes that she never *was* going to have any trouble in the first place. Men are by nature polygamous creatures. Add to that the well-substantiated fact that supreme creative artists tend to be more viripotent than their fellows (just as they also tend to be heavier drinkers) and you can begin to see why no one was going to give Yasmin much of an argument. So what do you have? You have a bunch of supremely gifted and therefore hyperactive artists loaded with the very finest Sudanese Blister Beetle who find themselves staring goggle-eyed at a young female of indescribable beauty. They were jiggered. They were scrambled and dished up on buttered toast from the moment they swallowed the fatal chocolate. I am positive that the Pope of Rome himself, in the same situation, would have had his cassock off in nine minutes flat just like the rest of them.

But I must go back for a moment to where we left off.

After Renoir, we returned to our headquarters at the Ritz in Paris. From there we went after old Monet. We drove out to his splendid house at Giverny and I dropped Yasmin off at the gates in the approved fashion. She was inside for over three hours, but I didn't mind that. Knowing there would be lots of other long waits like this coming along, I had installed a small library in the back of the car – a complete Shakespeare, some Jane Austen, some Dickens, some Balzac and the latest Kipling.

Yasmin emerged at last and I saw she had a large canvas under one arm. She was walking slowly, just sauntering along the sidewalk in a dreamy sort of way, but when she came closer, the first thing I noticed was that old glint of ecstasy in her eyes and the brilliant roses on her cheeks. She looked like a nice tame tigress who had just swallowed the Emperor of India and had liked the taste.

'Everything all right?'

'Fine,' she murmured.

'Let's see the picture.'

It was a shimmering study of waterlilies on the lake in Monet's Giverny garden, a real beauty.

'He said I was a miracle worker.'

'He's right.'

'He said I was the most beautiful woman he'd ever seen in his life. He asked me to stay.'

Monet's semen, as it turned out, had a better count than Renoir's in spite of him being a year older, and I was fortunate in being able to make twenty-five straws. Admittedly, each straw had the minimum count of only twenty million sperm, but they would do. They would do very well. They would be worth hundreds of thousands, I reckoned, those Monet straws, in the years to come.

Then we had a stroke of luck. In Paris at this time there was a dynamic and extraordinary producer of ballets called Diaghilev. Diaghilev had a talent for spotting great artists, and in 1919 he was regrouping his company after the war and preparing a new repertory of ballets. He had gathered around him for this purpose a group of remarkably gifted men. For example, at that very moment:

Igor Stravinsky had come up from Switzerland to write the music for Diaghilev's *Pulcinella*. Pablo Picasso was designing the sets.

Picasso was also doing the sets for *Three-Cornered Hat*.

Henri Matisse had been hired to design the costumes and the decor for *Le Chant de Rossignol*.

And another painter we had not heard of called André Derain was busy preparing the sets for *La Boutique Fantasque*.

Stravinsky, Picasso and Matisse were all on our list. On the theory that Monsieur Diaghilev's judgement was probably sounder than ours, we decided to put Derain's name on as well. All of these men were in Paris.

We took Stravinsky first. Yasmin walked right in on him while he was working at the piano on *Pulcinella*. He was more surprised than angry. 'Hello,' he said. 'Who are you?'

'I have come all the way from England to offer you a chocolate,' she said.

This absurd remark, which Yasmin was to use on many other occasions, disarmed completely this kind and friendly man. The rest was simple, and although I longed for salacious details, Yasmin remained mute.

'You might at least tell me what he was like as a person.'

'Sparkling bright,' she said. 'Oh, he was so sparkling bright and so quick and clever. He had a huge head and a nose like a boiled egg.'

'Is he a genius?'

'Yes,' she said, 'he's a genius. He's got the spark, the same as Monet and Renoir.'

'What is this spark?' I said. 'Where is it? Is it in the eyes?'

'No,' she said. 'It isn't anywhere special. It's just *there*. You know it's there. It's like an invisible halo.'

I made fifty straws from Stravinsky.

Next it was Picasso's turn. He had a studio at that time in the Rue de la Boétie and I dropped Yasmin off in front of a rickety-looking door with brown paint peeling off it. There was no bell or knocker so Yasmin simply pushed it open and went in. Outside in the car I settled down with *La Cousine Bette* which I still think is the best thing the old French master ever wrote.

I don't believe I had read more than four pages when the car door was flung open and Yasmin tumbled in and flopped on to the seat beside me. Her hair was all over the place and she was blowing like a sperm whale.

'Christ, Yasmin! What happened?'

'My God!' she gasped. 'Oh, my God!'

'Did he throw you out?' I cried. 'Did he hurt you?'

She was too out of breath to answer me at once. A trickle of sweat was running down the side of her forehead. She looked as though she'd been chased around the block four times by a maniac with a carving knife. I waited for her to simmer down.

'Don't worry,' I said. 'We're bound to have one or two washouts.'

'He's a demon!' she said.

'What did he do to you?'

'He's a bull! He's like a little brown bull!'

'Go on.'

'He was painting on a huge canvassy thing when I went in and he turned round and his eyes opened so wide they became circles and they were black and he shouted "Olé" or something like that and then he came towards me very slowly and sort of crouching as though he was going to spring . . .'

'And did he spring?'

'Yes,' she said. 'He sprang.'

'Good Lord.'

'He didn't even put his paintbrush down.'

'So you had no chance to get the mackintosh on?'

'Afraid not. Didn't even have time to open my purse.'

'Hell.'

'I was hit by a hurricane, Oswald.'

'Couldn't you have slowed him down a bit? You remember what you did to old Woresley to make him keep still?'

'Nothing would have stopped this one.'

'Were you on the floor?'

'No. He threw me on to a filthy sofa thing. There were tubes of paint everywhere.'

'It's all over you now. Look at your dress.'

'I know.'

One couldn't blame Yasmin for the failure, I knew that. But I felt pretty ratty all the same. It was our first miss. I only hoped there wouldn't be many more.

'Do you know what he did afterwards?' Yasmin said. 'He just buttoned up his trousers and said, "Thank you, mademoiselle. That was very refreshing. Now I must get back to my work." And he turned away, Oswald! He just turned away and started painting again!'

'He's Spanish,' I said, 'like Alfonso.' I stepped out of the car and cranked the starting-handle and when I got back in again Yasmin was tidying her hair in the car mirror. 'I hate to say it,' she said, 'but I rather enjoyed that one.'

'I know you did.'

'Phenomenal vitality.'

'Tell me,' I said, 'is Monsieur Picasso a genius?'

'Yes,' she said. 'It was very strong. He will be wildly famous one day.'

'Damn.'

'We can't win them all, Oswald.'

'I suppose not.'

Matisse was next.

Yasmin was with Monsieur Matisse for about two hours and blow me if the little thief didn't come out with yet another painting. It was sheer magic, that canvas, a Fauve landscape with trees that were blue and green and scarlet, signed and dated 1905.

'Terrific picture,' I said.

'Terrific man,' she said. And that was all she would say about Henri Matisse. Not a word more.

Fifty straws.

17

My travelling container of liquid nitrogen was beginning to fill up with straws. We now had King Alfonso, Renoir, Monet, Stravinsky and Matisse. But there was room for a few more. Each straw held only ¼cc of fluid and the straw itself was only slightly thicker than a matchstick and about half as long. Fifty straws stacked neatly in a metal rack took up very little room. I decided we could accommodate three more batches on this trip and I told Yasmin we would be visiting Marcel Proust, Maurice Ravel and James Joyce. All of them were living in the Paris area.

If I have given the impression that Yasmin and I were paying our visits more or less on consecutive days, that is wrong. We were, in fact, moving slowly and carefully. Usually about a week went by between each visit. This gave me time to investigate thoroughly the next victim before we moved in on him. We never drove up to a house and rang the bell and hoped for the best. Before we made a call, I knew all about the man's habits and his working hours, about his family and his servants if he had any, and we would choose our time with care. But even then Yasmin would occasionally have to wait outside in the motor car until a wife or a servant came out to go shopping.

Monsieur Proust was our next choice. He was forty-eight years old, and six years back, in 1913, he had published *Du Côté de chez Swann*. Now he had just brought out *A l'Ombre des Jeunes Filles en Fleurs*. This book had been received with much enthusiasm by the reviewers and had won him the Goncourt Prize. But I was a bit nervous about Monsieur Proust. My inquiries showed him to be a very queer duck indeed. He was independently wealthy. He was a snob. He was anti-semitic. He was vain. He was a hypochondriac who suffered from asthma. He slept until four in the afternoon and stayed awake all night. He lived with a faithful watchdog servant called Céleste and his present address was an apartment at No 8 bis Rue Laurent-Pichet. The house belonged to the celebrated actress Réjane, and Réjane's son lived in the flat immediately below Proust, while Réjane herself occupied the rest of the place.

I learned that Monsieur Proust was, from a literary point of view, totally unscrupulous and would use both persuasion and money to inspire rave articles about his books in newspapers and magazines. And on top of all this, he was completely homosexual. No woman, other than the faithful Céleste, was ever permitted into his bedroom. In order to study the man more closely, I got myself invited to a dinner at the house of his close friend, Princess Soutzo. And there I discovered that Monsieur Proust was nothing to look at. With his black moustache, his round bulging eyes and his baggy little figure, he bore an astonishing resemblance to an actor on the cinematograph screen called Charlie Chaplin. At Princess Soutzo's, he complained a lot about draughts in the dining-room and he held court among the guests and expected everyone to be silent when he spoke. I can remember two incredible pronouncements he made that evening. Of a man who preferred women, he said, 'I can answer for him. He is completely abnormal.' And another time, I heard him say, 'Fondness for men leads to virility.' In short, he was a tricky fellow.

'Now wait just a minute,' Yasmin had said to me when I told her all this. 'I'll be damned if I'm going to take on a bugger.'

'Why not?'

'Don't be so stupid, Oswald. If he's a raging hundred per cent fairy . . .'

'He calls it an invert.'

'I don't care what he calls it.'

'It's a very Proustian word,' I said. 'Look up "to invert" in the dictionary and you'll find the definition is "to turn upside down".'

'He's not turning me upside down thank you very much,' Yasmin said.

'Now don't get excited.'

'Anyway, it's a waste of time,' she said. 'He wouldn't even look at me.'

'I think he would.'

'What d'you want me to do, dress up as a choirboy?'

'We'll give him a double dose of Blister Beetle.'

'That's not going to change his habits.'

'No,' I said, 'but it'll make him so bloody horny he won't care what sex you are.'

'He'll invert me.'

'No, he won't.'

'He'll invert me like a comma.'

'Take a hatpin with you.'

'It's still not going to work,' she said. 'If he's a genuine twenty-four carat queer, then all women are physically repulsive to him.'

'It's essential we get him,' I said. 'Our collection won't be complete without fifty Proust straws.'

'Is he really so important?'

'He's going to be,' I said. 'I'm sure of it. There'll be a strong demand for Proust children in the years to come.'

Yasmin gazed out of the Ritz windows at the cloudy-grey summer sky over Paris. 'If that's the case, then there's only one thing for it,' she said.

'What's that?'

'You do it yourself.'

I was so shocked I jumped.

'Steady on,' I said.

'He wants a man,' she said. 'Well, you're a man. You're perfect. You're young, you're beautiful and you're lecherous.'

'Yes, but I am not a catamite.'

'You don't have the guts?'

'Of course I've got the guts. But field work is your province, not mine.'

'Who said so?'

'I can't cope with a man, Yasmin, you know that.'

'This isn't a man. It's a fairy.'

'For God's sake!' I cried. 'I'll be damned if I'll let that little sod come near me! I'll have you know that even an enema gives me the shakes for a week!'

Yasmin burst into shrieks of laughter. 'I suppose you're going to tell me next,' she said, 'that you have a small sphincter.'

'Yes and I'm not having Mr Proust enlarge it, thanks very much,' I said.

'You're a coward, Oswald,' she said.

It was an impasse. I sulked. Yasmin got up and poured herself a drink. I did the same. We sat there drinking in silence. It was early evening.

'Where shall we have dinner tonight?' I said.

'I don't care,' she said. 'I think we ought to try to solve this

Proust thing first. I'd hate to see this little bugger get away.'

'Do you have any ideas?'

'I'm thinking,' she said.

I finished my drink and got myself another. 'You want one?'
I said to her.

'No,' she said. I left her to go on thinking. After a while she
said, 'Well now, I wonder if that will work.'

'What?'

'I've just had a tiny little idea.'

'Tell me.'

Yasmin didn't answer. She stood up and walked over to the
window and leaned out. She stayed leaning out of that window
for fully five minutes, immobile, deep in thought, and I watched
her but kept my mouth shut. Then all of a sudden I saw her
reach behind her with her right hand, and the hand started
snatching at the air as though she were catching flies. She didn't
look round as she did this. She just went on hanging out of the
window and snatching away at those invisible non-existent
flies behind her.

'What the hell's going on?' I said.

She turned round and faced me, and now there was a big
smile on her face. 'It's great!' she cried. 'I love it! I *am* a clever
little girl!'

'Out with it then.'

'It's going to be tricky,' she said, 'and I'm going to have to
be very quick, but I'm good at catching. Come to think of it, I
was always better than my brother at catching cricket balls.'

'What the hell are you talking about?' I said.

'It would mean disguising me as a man.'

'Easy,' I said. 'No problem.'

'A beautiful young man.'

'Will you give him the Beetle?'

'A double dose,' she said.

'Isn't that a bit risky? Don't forget what it did to old Woresley.'

'That's just how I want him,' she said. 'I want him out of his
mind.'

'Would you please tell me exactly what you propose to do ?'
I asked her.

'Don't ask so many questions, Oswald. Just leave that side
of it to me. I regard Monsieur Proust as fair game. He's in the
joker class and I shall treat him as a joker.'

'Actually he's not,' I said. 'He's another genius. But take the
hatpin by all means. The royal hatpin. The one that's been two
inches into the King of Spain's bum.'

'I'd feel happier with a carving-knife,' she said.

We spent the next few days dressing Yasmin up as a boy.
We told the couturier and the wigmaker and the shoe people
that we were rigging her up for a very grand fancy-dress party,
and they rallied round with enthusiasm. It is amazing what a
good wig can do to a face. From the moment the wig was on and
the make-up was off, Yasmin became a male. We chose slightly
effeminate pale grey trousers, a blue shirt, a silk stock tie, a
flowered silk waistcoat and a fawn jacket. The shoes were
brogues, white and brown. The hat was a soft felt trilby the
colour of snuff, with a large brim. We took the curves out of her
noble bosom by strapping it with a wide crepe bandage. I
taught her to speak in a soft whispering voice to disguise the
pitch, and I rehearsed her diligently in what she was to say, first
to Céleste when the door was opened, and then to Monsieur
Proust when she was shown into his presence.

Within a week, we were ready to go. Yasmin had still not told
me how she intended to save herself from being inverted in
true Proustian fashion and I did not press her any further about
this. I was happy enough that she had agreed to take the man on.

We decided that she should arrive at his house at seven p.m.
By then our victim would have been up and about for a good
three hours. In her bedroom at the Ritz, I helped Yasmin to
dress. The wig was a beauty. It gave her a head of hair that was
golden-bronze in colour, slightly curly and a bit on the long
side. The grey trousers, the flowered waistcoat and the fawn
jacket turned her into an effeminate but ravishingly beautiful
young man.

'No bugger could resist buggering you,' I said.

She smiled but made no comment.

'Hang on,' I said. 'There's something missing. Your trousers look distinctly empty. It's a dead giveaway.' There was a bowl of fruit on the sideboard, a present from the hotel management. I selected a small banana. Yasmin lowered her trousers and we strapped the banana to the inside of her upper thigh with sticking plaster. When she pulled up her trousers again, the effect was electric – a tell-tale and tantalizing bulge in exactly the right place.

'He'll see it,' I said. 'It'll drive him dotty.'

18

We went downstairs and got into the motor car. I drove to the Rue Laurent-Pichet and stopped the car about twenty yards short of number eight, on the other side of the street. We examined the house. It was a large stone building with a black front door. 'Off you go,' I said, 'and good luck. He's on the second floor.'

Yasmin got out of the car. 'This banana's a bit uncomfortable,' she said.

'Now you know what it's like to be a man,' I said.

She turned away and strode toward the house with her hands in her trouser pockets. I saw her try the door. It was unlocked, presumably because the place was divided into separate apartments. She went in.

I settled down in the motor car to await the outcome. I, the general, had done all I could to prepare for the battle. The rest was up to Yasmin, the soldier. She was well armed. She carried a double dose (we had finally decided) of Blister Beetle and a long hatpin whose sharp end still bore the crusted traces of Spanish royal blood which Yasmin had refused to wipe off.

It was a warm cloudy August evening in Paris. The canvas hood of my blue Citroën *Torpedo* was folded back. My seat was comfortable but I was too fidgety to concentrate on a book. I had a good view of the house and I fixed my eyes upon it with a certain fascination. I could see the large windows on the second floor where Monsieur Proust lived, and the green velvet curtains that were drawn back on either side, but I couldn't see in. Yasmin was up there now, probably in that very room, and she would be saying, as I had so carefully instructed her to say, 'Pray forgive me, monsieur, but I am in love with your work. I have come all the way from England simply to pay homage to your greatness. Please accept this little box of chocolates . . . they are delicious . . . do you mind if I have one . . . and here's one for you . . .'

I waited twenty minutes. I waited thirty minutes. I was watching the clock. The way Yasmin felt about 'that little bugger' as she called him, I reckoned there would be no *tête à tête* and pleasant conversation afterwards, as there had been with Renoir and Monet. This, I reflected, would be a brief sharp visit and possibly a rather painful one for the great writer.

I was correct about it being brief. Thirty-three minutes after Yasmin had gone in, I saw the big black front door opening and out she came.

As she walked toward me, I looked for traces of dishevelment in her clothes. There were none. The snuff-coloured trilby was at the same saucy angle as before and altogether she looked as trim and crisp coming out as she had going in.

Or did she ? Was there not a slight lack of bounce in her walk ? There was indeed. And was there not a tendency to move those splendid long limbs of hers rather carefully ? Unquestionably yes. She was walking, in fact, like a person who had just dismounted from a bicycle after a long ride upon an uncomfortable saddle.

These small observations comforted me. They were evidence, surely, that my gallant soldier had been engaged in fierce combat.

'Well done,' I said as she got into the car.

'What makes you think it was so successful?'

She was a cool one, our Yasmin.

'Don't tell me it went wrong.'

She didn't answer me. She settled herself in the seat and closed the car door.

'I have to know, Yasmin, because if you do have the loot I must rush it back quickly and freeze it up.'

She had it. Of course she had it. I rushed it back to the hotel and made fifty exceptional straws. Each straw, according to my microscopic density count, contained no less than seventy-five million sperm. I know they were potent straws because at this very moment, as I write these words nineteen years after the event, I am able to state positively that there are fourteen children running around in France who have Marcel Proust as their father. Only I know who they are. Such matters are great secrets. They are secrets between me and the mothers. The husbands don't know. It's a mother's secret. But my goodness me, you should see those fourteen silly rich ambitious literary-minded mothers. Each one of them, as she gazes proudly upon her Proustian offspring, is telling herself that she has almost certainly given birth to a great writer. Well, she is wrong. All of them are wrong. There is no evidence whatsoever that great writers beget great writers. Occasionally they beget minor writers, but that's as far as it goes.

There is, I think, slightly more evidence that great painters sometimes beget great painters. Look at Teniers and Breughel and Tiepolo, and even Pissarro. And in music, the wonderful Johann Sebastian had such an overwhelming genius that it was impossible for him not to pass some of it on to his children. But writers, no. Great writers seem to spring more often than not from stony soil – the sons of coal-miners or pork butchers or impoverished teachers. But that simple truth was never going to prevent a small number of wealthy literary-snob ladies from wishing to have a baby by the brilliant Monsieur Proust or the extraordinary Mr James Joyce. My job, anyway, was not to propagate geniuses but to make money.

By the time I had filled those fifty Proust straws and had

immersed them safely in liquid nitrogen, it was nearly nine o'clock at night. Yasmin was now bathed and changed into fine feminine clothes and I took her out to Maxims for supper to celebrate our success. She had not yet told me anything of what went on.

My diary from that date informs me that we both started the meal with a dozen *escargots*. It was mid-August and the grouse were just beginning to come in from Yorkshire and Scotland, so we ordered one each and I told the head-waiter we wanted them blood-rare. The wine was to be a bottle of Volnay, one of my favourite burgundies.

'Now,' I said when we had given our order. 'Tell me all.'

'You want a blow by blow account?'

'Every tiny detail.'

There was a bowl of radishes on the table and Yasmin popped one into her mouth and crunched it up. 'He had a bell on his door,' she said, 'so I rang it. Céleste opened the door and glared at me. You should see that Céleste, Oswald. She's skinny and sharp-nosed with a mouth like a knife and two small brown eyes that looked me up and down with utter distaste. "What is it you wish?" she said sharply, and I gave her the bit about having travelled from England to bring a present to the famous writer whom I worshipped. "Monsieur Proust is working," Céleste said and tried to shut the door. I put my foot in it and pushed it open and marched in. "I have not travelled all this distance to have a door slammed in my face," I said. "Kindly inform your master that I am here to see him."'

'Well done, you,' I said.

'I had to bluff it out,' she said. 'Céleste glared at me. "What name?" she snapped. "Mister Bottomley," I said, "of London." I was rather pleased with that name.'

'Apt,' I said. 'Did the maid announce you?'

'Oh yes. And out he came into the hall, this funny little pop-eyed bugger, still holding a pen in his hand.'

'What happened next?'

'I immediately launched into the long speech you taught me, starting with, "Pray forgive me, monsieur . . ." but I'd hardly got half a dozen words out when he raised his hand and cried, "Stop! I have already forgiven you!" He was goggling at me as though I were the most beautiful and desirable and spicy little lad he'd ever seen in his life, which I'll bet I was.'

'Was he speaking in English or French?'

'A bit of each. His English was pretty good, about like my French, so it didn't matter.'

'And he fell for you right away?'

'He couldn't take his eyes off me. "That will be all, thank you, Céleste," he said, licking his lips. But Céleste didn't like it. She stayed put. She scented trouble.

'"You may *go*, Céleste," Monsieur Proust said, raising his voice.

'But she still refused to go. "You do not wish anything more, Monsieur Proust?"

'"I wish to be left alone," he snapped, and the woman stalked out of the room in a huff.

'"Pray sit down, Monsieur Bottomley," he said. "May I take your hat? I do apologize for my servant. She's a trifle over-protective."

'"What is she protecting you from, monsieur?"

'He smiled at me, showing horrid teeth with wide gaps. "From you," he said softly.

'By golly, I thought, I'm going to be inverted any moment. At this point, Oswald, I seriously considered skipping the Blister Beetle altogether. The man was drooling with lust. If I'd so much as bent down to do up a shoelace, he'd have been on me.'

'But you didn't skip it?'

'No,' she said. 'I gave him the chocolate.'

'Why?'

'Because in some ways they're easier to handle when they're under the influence. They don't quite know what they're doing.'

'Did the chocolate work well?'

'It always works well,' she said. 'But this was a double dose so it worked better.'

'How much better?'

'Buggers are different,' she said.

'I believe you.'

'You see,' she said, 'when an ordinary man is driven crazy by the Beetle, all he wants to do is to rape the woman on the spot. But when a bugger is driven crazy by the powder, his first thought is not to start buggering right away. He begins by making violent grabs for the other fellow's pizzle.'

'A bit awkward, that.'

'Very,' Yasmin said. 'I knew that if I let him come near enough to grab me, all he'd get in his hand would be a squashed banana.'

'So what did you do?'

'I kept jumping out of the way,' she said. 'And in the end, of course, it became a chase with him chasing me all round the room and knocking things over right and left.'

'Rather strenuous.'

'Yes, and in the middle of it all the door opened and there stood that dreadful little maid again. "Monsieur Proust," she said, "all this exercise is bad for your asthma."'

'"Get out!" he yelled. "Get out, you witch!"'

'I imagine she's fairly used to that sort of thing.'

'I'm sure she is,' Yasmin said. 'Anyway, there was a round table in the middle of the room and so long as I stayed close to it I knew he couldn't catch me. Many a girl has been saved from a dirty old man by a round table. The trouble was he seemed to be enjoying this part of it, and soon I got to thinking that a good old chase around the room was probably an essential preliminary for those chaps.'

'A sort of pipe-opener.'

'Right,' she said. 'And he kept saying things to me as we circled round and round the table.'

'What sort of things?'

'Dirty stuff,' she said. 'Not worth repeating. By the way, putting that banana in was a mistake.'

'Why?'

'Too big a bulge,' she said. 'He noticed it at once. And all the time he was chasing me round the table, he kept pointing at it and singing its praises. I was longing to tell him it was just a silly old banana from the Ritz Hotel, but that wasn't on. It was driving him up the wall that banana, and the Blister Beetle was hitting him harder every second, and suddenly I had another problem on my hands. How in God's name, I thought, am I going to get the rubbery thing on him before he jumps me? I couldn't exactly say it was a necessary precaution, could I?'

'Not really.'

'I mean after all, what earthly reason had I even to be carrying the bloody thing?'

'Tricky,' I said. 'Very tricky. How did you get out of it?'

'In the end I said to him, "Do you want me, Monsieur Proust?"

'"Yes!" he screamed. "I want you more than anyone in my life! Stop running!"

'"Not yet," I said. "First you must put this funny little thing on him to keep him warm." I took it from my pocket and slung it across the table. He stopped chasing me and stared at it. I doubt he'd ever set eyes on one before. "What is this?" he cried.

"It's called a tickler," I said. "It's one of our famous English ticklers invented by Mr Oscar Wilde."

'"Oscar Wilde!" he cried. "Ha, ha! A great fellow!"

'"He invented the tickler," I said. "And Lord Alfred Douglas helped him."

'"Lord Alfred was another fine fellow!" he cried.

'"King Edward the Seventh," I said, laying it on, "carried a tickler on his person wherever he went."

'"King Edward the Seventh!" he cried. "My God!" He picked up the little thing lying on the table. "It is good, yes?"

'"It doubles the rapture," I said. "Put it on quickly like a good boy. I'm getting impatient."

'"You help me."

'"No," I said. "Do it yourself." And while he was fiddling around with it, I . . . well . . . I absolutely had to make sure he didn't see the banana and all the rest of it, didn't I? . . . and yet I knew the dreaded time had come when I was going to have to take my trousers down . . .'

'A bit risky, that.'

'It couldn't be helped, Oswald. So while he was fiddling around with Oscar Wilde's great invention, I turned my back on him and whipped down my trousers and assumed what I imagined was the correct position by bending over the back of the sofa . . .'

'My God, Yasmin, you don't mean you were going to allow him . . .'

'Of course not,' she said, 'but I had to hide my banana and keep it out of his reach.'

'Yes, but didn't he jump you?'

'He came at me like a battering-ram.'

'How did you dodge it?'

'I didn't,' she said, smiling. 'That's the whole point.'

'I'm not with you,' I said. 'If he came at you like a battering-ram and you didn't dodge it, then he must have rammed you.'

'He didn't ram me the way you're *thinking* he rammed me,' she said. 'You see, Oswald, I had remembered something. I had remembered the story about A. R. Woresley and his brother's bull and how the bull was fooled into thinking his pizzle was in one place while actually it was in another. A. R. Woresley had grabbed hold of it and directed it somewhere else.'

'Is that what you did?'

'Yes.'

'But surely not into a bag like Woresley did?'

'Don't be an ass, Oswald. I don't need a bag.'

'Of course not . . . no . . . I see what you mean now . . . but wasn't it a bit tricky? . . . What I mean is . . . you facing the other way and all that . . . and him coming at you like a battering-ram . . . you had to be pretty quick, didn't you?'

'I was quick. I caught it in mid-air.'

'But didn't he twig?'

'No more than the bull did,' she said. 'Less so, in fact, and I'll tell you why.'

'Why?'

'First of all, he was going mad with the Beetle, right?'

'Right.'

'He was grunting and snorting and flapping his arms, right?'

'Right.'

'And his head was in the air just like the bull's, right?'

'Probably, yes.'

'But most important of all, he was assuming I was a *man*. He thought he was doing it to a *man*, right?'

'Of course.'

'And his pizzle was in a good place. It was having a good time, right?'

'Right.'

'So in his own mind there was only one place it could be. A man doesn't *have* any other place.'

I stared at her in admiration.

'Bound to fool him,' she said. She twisted a snail out of its shell and popped it into her mouth.

'Brilliant,' I said. 'Absolutely brilliant.'

'I was rather pleased with it myself.'

'It's the ultimate deception.'

'Thank you, Oswald.'

'There's just one thing I can't fathom,' I said.

'What's that?'

'When he came at you like a battering-ram, didn't he take aim.'

'Only after a fashion.'

'But he's a very experienced marksman.'

'My dear old frump,' she said, 'you can't seem to get it into your head what a man's like when he's had a double dose.'

I jolly well can, I told myself. I was behind the filing-cabinets when A. R. Woresley got his.

'No,' I said. 'I can't. What is a man like when he's had a double dose?'

'Berserk,' she said. 'He literally doesn't know what the other end of him's doing. I could have shoved it in a jar of pickled onions and he wouldn't have known the difference.'

Over the years I have discovered a surprising but simple truth about young ladies and it is this: *the more beautiful their faces, the less delicate their thoughts.* Yasmin was no exception. There she sat now across the table from me in Maxims wearing a gorgeous Fortuny dress and looking for all the world like Queen Semiramis on the throne of Egypt, but she was talking vulgar. 'You're talking vulgar,' I said.

'I'm a vulgar girl,' she said, grinning.

The Volnay arrived and I tasted it. Wonderful wine. My father used to say never pass up a Volnay by a good shipper if you see one on the wine card. 'How did you get away so soon?' I asked her.

'He was very rough,' she said. 'Rough and sort of spiky. It felt as though I had a gigantic lobster on my back.'

'Beastly.'

'It was horrid,' she said. 'He had a heavy gold watchchain across his waistcoat which kept grinding into my spine. And a big watch in the waistcoat pocket.'

'Not good for the watch.'

'No,' she said. 'It went crunch. I heard it.'

'Yes, well . . .'

'Terrific wine this, Oswald.'

'I know. But how *did* you get away so quickly?'

'That's bound to be a problem with the younger ones after they've had the Beetle,' she said. 'How old is this fellow?'

'Forty-eight.'

'In the prime of life,' she said. 'It's different when they're seventy-six. At that age, even with the Beetle, they soon grind to a halt.'

'But not this chap?'

'God no,' she said. 'Perpetual motion. A mechanical lobster.'

'So what did you do?'

'What could I do? It's either me or him I said. So as soon as he'd had his explosion and delivered the goods, I reached into my jacket pocket and got out the trusty hatpin.'

'And you let him have it?'

'Yes, but don't forget it had to be a backhander this time and that wasn't so easy. It's hard to get a good swing.'

'I can see that.'

'Luckily my backhand's always been my strongest point.'

'At tennis you mean?'

'Yes,' she said.

'And you got him first time?'

'Deep to the baseline,' she said. 'Deeper than the King of Spain. A winner.'

'Did he protest?'

'Oh my God,' she said, 'he squealed like a pig. And he danced round the room clutching himself and yelling, "Céleste! Céleste! Fetch a doctor! I have been stabbed!" The woman must have been looking through the keyhole because she came bursting in at once and rushed up to him crying. "Where? Where? Let me see!" And while she was examining his backside, I ripped the all-important rubbery thing off him and dashed out of the room pulling up my trousers as I went.'

'Bravo,' I said. 'What a triumph.'

'Bit of a lark actually,' she said. 'I enjoyed it.'

'You always do.'

'Lovely snails,' she said. 'Great big juicy ones.'

'The snail farms put them on sawdust for two days before they sell them for eating,' I said.

'Why?'

'So the snails can purge themselves. When did you get the signed notepaper? Right at the beginning?'

'At the beginning, yes. I always do.'

'But why did it say Boulevard Haussmann on it, instead of Rue Laurent-Pichet?'

'I asked him that myself,' she said. 'He told me that's where he used to live. He's only just moved.'

'That's all right, then,' I said.

They took the empty snail-shells away and soon afterwards they brought on the grouse. By grouse I mean red grouse. I do not mean black grouse (black cock and grey hen) or wood grouse (capercailye) or white grouse (ptarmigan). These others are good, especially the ptarmigan, but the red grouse is the king. And provided of course they are this year's birds, there is no meat more tender or more tasty in the entire world. Shooting starts on the twelfth of August, and every year I look forward to that date with even greater impatience than I do to the first of

September when the oysters come in from Colchester and Whitstable. Like a fine sirloin, red grouse should be eaten rare with the blood just a shade darker than scarlet, and at Maxims they would not like you to order it any other way.

We ate our grouse slowly, slicing off one thin sliver of breast at a time, allowing it to melt on the tongue and following each mouthful with a sip of fragrant Volnay.

'Who's next on the list?' Yasmin asked me.

I had been thinking about that myself, and now I said to her, 'It was going to be Mr James Joyce, but perhaps it would be nice if we took a short trip down to Switzerland for a change of scenery.'

'I'd like that,' she said. 'Who's in Switzerland?'

'Nijinski.'

'I thought he was up here with that Diaghilev chap.'

'I wish he was,' I said, 'but it seems he's gone a bit dotty. He thinks he's married to God, and he walks about with a big gold cross around his neck.'

'What rotten luck,' Yasmin said. 'Does that mean his dancing days are over?'

'Nobody knows,' I said. 'They say he was dancing at an hotel in St Moritz only a few weeks ago. But that was just for fun, to amuse the guests.'

'Does he live in an hotel?'

'No, he's got a villa above St Moritz.'

'Alone?'

'Unfortunately not,' I said. 'There's a wife and a child and a whole bunch of servants. He's a rich man. Fabulous sums he used to get. I know Diaghilev paid him twenty-five thousand francs for each performance.'

'Good Lord. Did you ever see him dance?'

'Only once,' I said. 'The year the war broke out, nineteen fourteen, at the old Palace Theatre in London. He did *Les Sylphides*. Stunning it was. He danced like a god.'

'I'm crazy to meet him,' Yasmin said. 'When do we leave?'

'Tomorrow,' I said. 'We have to keep moving.'

19

At this point in my narrative, just as I was about to describe our trip to Switzerland to find Nijinski, my pen suddenly came away from the paper and I found myself hesitating. Was I not perhaps getting into a rut? Becoming repetitious? Yasmin was going to be meeting an awful lot of fascinating people over the next twelve months, no doubt about that. But in nearly every case (there would of course be one or two exceptions) the action was going to be very much the same. There would be the giving of the Beetle powder, the ensuing cataclysm, the escape with the spoils, and all the rest of it, and that, however interesting the men themselves might be, was going to become pretty boring for the reader. Nothing would have been easier than for me to describe in great detail how the two of us met Nijinski on a path through the pinewoods below his villa, as indeed we did, and how we gave him a chocolate, and how we held him in conversation for nine minutes until the powder hit him, and how he chased Yasmin into the dark wood, leaping from boulder to boulder and rising so high in the air with each leap he seemed to be flying. But if I did that, then it would be fitting also to describe the James Joyce encounter, Joyce in Paris, Joyce in a dark blue serge suit, a black felt hat, old tennis shoes on his feet, twirling an ashplant and talking obscenities. And after Joyce, it would be Mr Bonnard and Mr Braque and then a quick trip back to Cambridge to unload our precious spoils in the Semen's Home. A very quick trip that was because Yasmin and I were in the rhythm of it now and we wanted to push on until it was finished.

A. R. Woresley was wildly excited when I showed him our haul. We now had King Alfonso, Renoir, Monet, Matisse, Proust, Stravinsky, Nijinski, Joyce, Bonnard and Braque. 'And you've done a fine job with the freezing,' he said to me as he carefully transferred the racks of straws with their labels on them from my suitcase freezer to the big freezer in 'Dunroamin', our headquarters house. 'Keep going, children,' he said, rubbing his hands together like a grocer. 'Keep going.'

We kept going. It was the beginning of October now, and we went down south into Italy, looking for D. H. Lawrence. We found him living at the Palazzo Ferraro in Capri with Frieda, and on this occasion I had to distract fat Frieda for two hours out on the rocks while Yasmin went to work on Lawrence. We got a bit of a shock with Lawrence though. When I rushed his semen back to our Capri hotel and examined it under the microscope, I found that the spermatozoa were all stone dead. There was no movement there at all.

'Jesus,' I said to Yasmin. 'The man's sterile.'

'He didn't act like it,' she said. 'He was like a goat. Like a randy goat.'

'We'll have to cross him off the list.'

'Who's next?' she asked.

'Giacomo Puccini.'

20

'Puccini is a big one,' I said. 'A giant. We mustn't fail.'

'Where does he live?' Yasmin asked.

'Near Lucca, about forty miles west of Florence.'

'Tell me about him.'

'Puccini is an enormously rich and famous man,' I said. 'He has built himself a huge house, the Villa Puccini, on the edge of a lake beside the tiny village where he was born, which is called Torre del Lago. Now this is the man, Yasmin, who has written *Manon*, *La Bohème*, *Tosca*, *Madame Butterfly* and *The Girl of the*

Golden West. Classics every one of them. He is probably not a Mozart or a Wagner or even a Verdi, but he's still a genius and a giant. He's a bit of a lad, too.'

'In what way?'

'Terrific womanizer.'

'Super.'

'He is now sixty-one but that hasn't stopped him,' I said. 'He's a roustabout, a drinker, a crazy car-driver, a mad-keen fisherman and an even keener duck shooter. But above all, he's a lecher. Someone once said of him that he hunts women, wildfowl and libretti in that order.'

'Sounds like a good chap.'

'Splendid fellow,' I said. 'He's got a wife, an old bag called Elvira, and believe it or not, this Elvira was once sentenced to five months in prison for causing the death of one of Puccini's girlfriends. The girl was a servant in the house, and the beastly Elvira caught Puccini out in the garden with her late one night. There was a tremendous scene, the girl was sacked and thereafter Elvira hounded her to such an extent that the poor thing took poison and killed herself. Her family went to court and Elvira was given five months in the clink.'

'Did she go?'

'No,' I said. 'Puccini got her off by paying twelve thousand lire to the girl's family.'

'So what's the plan?' Yasmin asked me. 'Do I just knock on the door and walk in?'

'That won't work,' I said. 'He's surrounded by faithful watchdogs and his bloody wife. You'd never get near him.'

'What do you suggest then?'

'Can you sing?' I asked her.

'I'm not Melba,' Yasmin said, 'but I have quite a decent little voice.'

'Great,' I said. 'Then that's it. That's what we'll do.'

'What?'

'I'll tell you on the way up,' I said.

We had just returned to the mainland from Capri and we were in Sorrento now. It was warm October weather in this part of Italy and the sky was blue as we loaded up the trusty Citroën *Torpedo* and headed north for Lucca. We had the hood down and it was a great pleasure to be driving along the lovely coastal road from Sorrento to Naples.

'First of all, let me tell you how Puccini met Caruso,' I said, 'because this has a bearing on what you're going to be doing. Puccini was world-famous. Caruso was virtually unknown, but he desperately wanted to get the part of Rodolfo in a forthcoming production of *La Bohème* at Livorno. So one day he turned up at the Villa Puccini and asked to see the great man. Almost every day second-rate singers were trying to get in to see Puccini, and it was necessary that he be protected from these people or he would get no peace. "Tell him I'm busy," Puccini said. The servant told Puccini that the man absolutely refused to go. "He says he'll camp in your garden for a year if necessary." "What does he look like?" Puccini asked. "He's a small stubby little chap with a moustache and a bowler hat on his head. He says he's a Neapolitan." "What kind of a singer?" Puccini asked. "He says he's the best tenor in the world," the servant reported. "They all say that," Puccini said, but something prompted him, and to this day he doesn't know what it was, to put down the book he was reading and to go into the hallway. The front door was open and little Caruso was standing just outside in the garden. "Who the hell are you?" Puccini shouted. Caruso lifted up his full-throated magnificent voice and answered with the words of Rodolfo in *La Bohème*, "*Chi son? Sono un poeta*" ... "Who am I? I am a poet." Puccini was absolutely bowled over by the quality of the voice. He'd never heard a tenor like it before. He rushed up to Caruso and embraced him and cried out "Rodolfo is yours!" That's a true story, Yasmin. Puccini himself loves to tell it. And now of course Caruso *is* the greatest tenor in the world and he and Puccini are the closest of friends. Rather marvellous, don't you agree?'

'What's this got to do with me singing?' Yasmin asked. 'My voice is hardly going to bowl Puccini over.'

'Of course not. But the general idea is the same. Caruso

wanted a part. You want three cubic centimetres of semen. The latter is easier for Puccini to give than the former, especially to someone as gorgeous as you. The singing is simply a way to attract the man's attention.' ·

'Go on, then.'

'Puccini works only at night,' I said, 'from about ten-thirty p.m. to three or four in the morning. At that time the rest of the household will be asleep. At midnight, you and I will creep into the garden of the Villa Puccini and locate his studio, which I believe is on the ground floor. A window will certainly be open because the nights are still warm. So while I hide in the bushes, you will stand outside the open window and sing softly the gentle aria "*Un bel di vedremo*" from *Madame Butterfly*. If everything goes right, Puccini will rush to the window and will see standing there a girl of surpassing beauty – you. The rest should be easy.'

'I rather like that,' Yasmin said. 'Italians are always singing outside each other's windows.'

When we got to Lucca, we holed up in a small hotel, and there, beside an ancient piano in the hotel sitting-room, I taught Yasmin to sing the aria. She had almost no Italian but she soon learnt the words by heart, and in the end she was able to sing the complete aria very nicely indeed. Her voice was small but she had perfect pitch. I then taught her to say in Italian, 'Maestro, I adore your work. I have travelled all the way from England . . .' etc., etc., and a few other useful phrases, including of course, 'All I ask is to have your signature on your own notepaper.'

'I don't think you're going to need the Beetle with this chap,' I said.

'I don't think I am either,' Yasmin said. 'Let's skip it for once.'

'And no hatpin,' I told her. 'This man is a hero of mine. I won't have him stuck.'

'I won't need the hatpin if we don't use the Beetle,' she said. 'I'm really looking forward to this one, Oswald.'

'Ought to be fun,' I said.

When all was ready, we drove out one afternoon to the Villa Puccini to scout the premises. It was a massive mansion set on the edge of a large lake and completely surrounded by an eight foot high spiked iron fence. Not so good, that. 'We'll need a small ladder,' I said. So back we drove to Lucca and bought a wooden ladder which we placed in the open car.

Just before midnight we were once again outside the Villa Puccini. We were ready to go. The night was dark and warm and silent. I placed the ladder up against the railings. I climbed up it and dropped down into the garden. Yasmin followed. I lifted the ladder over on to our side and left it there, ready for the escape.

We saw at once the one room in the entire place that was lit up. It was facing towards the lake. I took Yasmin's hand in mine and we crept closer. Although there was no moon, the light from the two big ground floor windows reflected on to the water of the lake and cast a pale illumination over the house and garden. The garden was full of trees and bushes and shrubs and flowerbeds. I was enjoying this. It was what Yasmin called 'a bit of a lark'. As we came closer to the window, we heard the piano. One window was open. We tiptoed right up to it and peeped in. And there he was, the man himself, sitting in his shirtsleeves at an upright piano with a cigar in his mouth, tap-tapping away, pausing to write something down and then tapping away again. He was thickset, a bit paunchy and he had a black moustache. There was a pair of candlesticks in elaborate brass holders screwed on to either side of the piano but the candles were not lit. There was a tall stuffed white bird, a crane of some sort, standing on a shelf alongside the piano. And around the walls of the room there were oil paintings of Puccini's celebrated ancestors – his great-great-grandfather, his great-grandfather, his grandfather and his own father. All these men had been famous musicians. For over two hundred years, the Puccini males had been passing on musical gifts of a high order to their children. Puccini straws, if only I could get them, were going to be immensely valuable. I resolved to make one hundred of them instead of the usual fifty.

And now there we stood, Yasmin and I, peering through the open window at the great man. I noticed that he had a fine head of thick black hair brushed straight back from the forehead.

'I'm going out of sight,' I whispered to Yasmin. 'Wait until he's not playing, then start to sing.'

She nodded.

'I'll meet you by the ladder.'

She nodded again.

'Good luck,' I said and I tiptoed away and stood behind a bush only five yards from the window. Through the foliage of the bush I could still see not only Yasmin but I could also see into the room where the composer was sitting because the big window was low to the ground.

The piano tinkled. There was a pause. It tinkled again. He was working out the melody with one finger only, and it was wonderful to be standing out there somewhere in Italy on the edge of a lake at midnight listening to Giacomo Puccini composing what was almost certainly a graceful aria for a new opera. There was another pause. He had got the phrase right this time and he was writing it down. He was leaning forward with a pen in his hand and writing on the manuscript paper in front of him. He was jotting his musical notes above the words of the librettist.

Then suddenly, in the absolute stillness that prevailed, Yasmin's small sweet voice began to sing '*Un bel dì vedremo*'. The effect was stunning. In that place, in that atmosphere, in the dark night beside the lake outside Puccini's window, I was moved beyond words. I saw the composer freeze. The pen was in his hand against the paper and the hand froze and his whole body became motionless as he sat listening to the voice outside the window. He didn't look round. I don't think he dared to look round for fear of breaking the spell. Outside his window a young maiden was singing one of his favourite arias in a small clear voice in absolutely perfect pitch. His face didn't change expression. His mouth didn't move. Nothing about him moved while the aria was in progress. It was a magic moment. Then Yasmin stopped singing. For a few seconds longer Puccini remained sitting at the piano. He seemed to be waiting for more, or for a sign of some sort from outside. But Yasmin didn't move or speak either. She simply stood there with her face upturned to the window, waiting for the man to come to her.

163

And come to her he did. I saw him put down his pen and rise slowly from the piano stool. He walked to the window. Then he saw Yasmin. I have spoken many times of her scintillating beauty, and the sight of her standing out there so still and serene must have come as a glorious shock to Puccini. He stared. He gaped. Was this a dream ? Then Yasmin smiled at him and that broke the spell. I saw him come suddenly out of his trance and I heard him say, 'Dio mio come bello!' Then he jumped clear out of the window and clasped Yasmin in a powerful embrace.

That was more like it, I thought. That was the real Puccini. Yasmin was not slow to respond. Then I heard him say softly to her in Italian, which I'm sure Yasmin didn't understand, 'We must go back inside. If the piano stops playing for too long a time, my wife wakes up and becomes suspicious.' I saw him smile at this, showing fine white teeth. Then he picked Yasmin up and hoisted her through the window and climbed in after her.

I am not a voyeur. I watched A. R. Woresley's antics with Yasmin for purely professional reasons, but I had no intention of peeping through the window at Yasmin and Puccini. The act of copulation is like that of picking the nose. It's all right to be doing it yourself but it is a singularly unattractive spectacle for the onlooker. I walked away. I climbed the ladder and dropped over the fence and went for a stroll along the edge of the lake. I was away about an hour. When I returned to the ladder there was no sign of Yasmin. When three hours had gone by, I climbed back into the garden to investigate.

I was creeping cautiously between the bushes when suddenly I heard footsteps on the gravel path and Puccini himself with Yasmin on his arm walked past me not ten feet away. I heard him saying to her in Italian, 'No gentleman is going to permit a lady to walk back to Lucca all alone at this time of night.'

Was he going to walk her back to the hotel ? I followed them to see where they were going. Puccini's motor car was standing in the drive in the front of the house. I saw him help Yasmin into the passenger seat. Then, with a great deal of fuss and match-striking, he got the acetylene headlamps alight. He cranked the starting-handle. The engine fired and ticked over. He unlocked the gates, jumped into the driver's seat and off they went with the motor roaring and revving.

I ran out to my own car and got the thing started. I drove fast towards Lucca but I never caught up with Puccini. In fact, I was only halfway there when he passed me on his way home again, alone this time.

I found Yasmin at the hotel.

'Did you get the stuff?'

'Of course,' she said.

'Give it to me quickly.'

She handed it over and by dawn I had made one hundred Puccini straws of good quality. While I was working on them, Yasmin sat in an armchair in my room drinking red Chianti and giving her report.

'Great time,' she said. 'Really marvellous. I wish they were all like him.'

'Good.'

'He was so *jolly*,' she said. 'Lots of laughs. And he sang me a bit from the new opera he's doing.'

'Did he say what he's calling it?'

'Turio,' she said. 'Turidot. Something like that.'

'No trouble from the wife upstairs?'

'Not a peep,' she said. 'But it was so funny because even when we were plunged in passion on the sofa, he had to keep reaching out every now and again to bang the piano. Just to let her know he was working hard and not banging some woman.'

'A great man, you think?'

'Terrific,' Yasmin said. 'Stupendous. Find me another like him.'

From Lucca we headed north for Vienna, and on the way we called on Sergei Rachmaninov in his lovely house on Lake Lucerne.

'It's a funny thing,' Yasmin said to me when she came back to the car after what had obviously been a fairly energetic session with the great musician, 'it's a funny thing, but there's an amazing resemblance between Mr Rachmaninov and Mr Stravinsky.'

'You mean facially?'

'I mean everything,' she said. 'They've both got small bodies and great big lumpy faces. Enormous strawberry noses. Beautiful hands. Tiny feet. Thin legs. And gigantic pizzles.'

'Is it your experience so far,' I asked her, 'that geniuses have larger pizzles than ordinary men.'

'Definitely,' she said. 'Much larger.'

'I was afraid you'd say that.'

'And they make better use of them,' she said, rubbing it in. 'Their swordsmanship is superb.'

'Rubbish.'

'It's not rubbish, Oswald. I ought to know.'

'Aren't you forgetting they've all had the Beetle.'

'The Beetle helps,' she said. 'Of course it helps. But there's no comparison between the way a great creative genius handles his sword and the way an ordinary fellow does it. That's why I'm having such a nice time.'

'Am I an ordinary fellow?'

'Don't get grumpy,' she said. 'We can't all be Rachmaninov or Puccini.'

I was deeply wounded. Yasmin had pricked me in my most sensitive area. I sulked all the way to Vienna, but the sight of that noble city soon restored my humour.

In Vienna, Yasmin had an hilarious encounter with Dr Sigmund Freud in his consulting room at Berggasse 19, and I think this visit merits a brief description.

First of all, she made a proper application for an appointment with the famous man, stating that she was in urgent need of psychiatric treatment. She was told there would be four days to wait. So I arranged for her to fill in the time by calling first upon the august Mr Richard Strauss. Mr Strauss had just been appointed co-director of the Vienna State Opera and he was, according to Yasmin, rather pompous. But he was easy meat and I got fifty excellent straws from him.

Then it was Dr Freud's turn. I regarded the celebrated

psychiatrist as being in the semi-joker class and saw no reason why we shouldn't have a bit of fun with him. Yasmin agreed. So the two of us cooked up an interesting psychiatric malady for her to be suffering from, and in she went to the big greystone house on Berggasse at two-thirty on a cool sunny October afternoon. Here is her own description of the encounter as she told it to me later that day over a bottle of Krug after I had frozen the straws.

'He's a goosey old bird,' she said. 'Very severe looking and correctly dressed, like a banker or something.'

'Did he speak English?'

'Quite good English but with that dreadful German accent. He sat me down on the other side of his desk and right away I offered him a chocolate. He took it like a lamb. Isn't it odd, Oswald, how every one of them takes the chocolate without any argument?'

'I don't think it's odd,' I said. 'It's the natural thing to do. If a pretty girl offered me a chocolate, I'd take it.'

'He was a hairy sort of fellow,' Yasmin said. 'He had a moustache and a thick pointed beard which looked as though it had been trimmed very carefully in front of a mirror with scissors. Whitish-grey it was. But the hair had been cut well back from his mouth above and below so that the bristles made a sort of frame for his lips. That's what I noticed above everything else, his lips. Very striking, those lips of his, and very thick. They looked like a pair of false lips made out of rubber which had been stuck on over the real ones.

'"So now fräulein," he said, munching away at his chocolate, "tell me about this so urgent problem of yours."

'"Oh, Dr Freud, I do hope you can help me!" I cried, working myself up at once. "Can I speak to you frankly?"

'"That's vot you are here for," he said. "Lie down on that couch over there, please, and just let yourself go."

'So I lay down on the goddamn couch, Oswald, and as I did so I thought well anyway I'm going to be in a reasonably comfy place for once when the fireworks start.'

'I see your point.'

'So I said to him, "Something terrible is wrong with me, Dr Freud! Something terrible and shocking!"

'"And vot is that?" he asked, perking up. He obviously enjoyed hearing about terrible and shocking things.

'"You won't believe it," I said, "but it is impossible for me to be in the presence of a man for more than a few minutes before he tries to rape me! He becomes a wild animal! He rips off my clothes! He exposes his organ . . . is that the right word?"

'"It is as good a word as any," he said. "Continue, fräulein."

'"He jumps on top of me!" I cried. "He pins me down! He takes his pleasure of me! Every man I meet does this to me, Mr Freud! You must help me! I am being raped to death!"

'"Dear lady," he said, "this is a very common fantasy among certain types of hysterical vimmen. These vimmen are all frightened of having physical relations with men. Actually, they long to indulge in fornication and copulation and all other sexy frolics but they are terrified of the consequences. So they fantasize. They imagine they are being raped. But it never happens. They are all firgins."

'"No, no!" I cried. "You are wrong, Dr Freud! I'm not a virgin! I'm the most over-raped girl in the world!"

'"You are hallucinating," he said. "Nobody has ever raped you. Vy you do not admit it and you will feel better instamatically?"

'"How can I admit it when it isn't true?" I cried. "Every man I've ever met has had his way with me! And it'll be just the same with you if I stay here much longer, you see if it isn't!"

'"Do not be ridiculous, fräulein," he snapped.

'"It will, it will!" I cried. "You'll be as bad as all the rest of them before this session's over!"

'When I said that, Oswald, the old buzzard rolled his eyes up at the ceiling and smiled a thin supercilious smile. "Fantasy, fantasy," he said, "all fantasy."

'"What makes you think you're so right and I'm so wrong?" I asked him.

'"Allow me to explain a little further," he said, leaning back in his chair and clasping his hands across his tummy. "In your subconscious mind, my dear fräulein, you believe that the masculine organ is a machine-gun . . ."

'"That's just about what it is so far as I'm concerned!" I cried. "It's a lethal weapon!"

'"Exactly," he said. "Now vee are getting somewhere. And you also believe that any man who points it at you is going to pull the trigger and riddle you with bullets."

'"Not bullets," I said. "Something else."

'"So you run away," he said. "You reject all men. You hide from them. You sit all alone through the nights . . ."

'"I do not sit alone," I said. "I sit with my lovely old Doberman Pincher, Fritzy."

'"Male or female?" he snapped.

'"Fritzy's a male."

'"Vorse than ever," he said. "Do you with this Doberman Pincher indulge in sexual relations?"

'"Don't be so daft, Dr Freud. Who do you think I am?"

'"You run avay from men," he said. "You run avay from dogs. You run avay from anything that an organ has . . ."

'"I've never heard such codswallop in all my life!" I cried. "I am not frightened of anyone's organ! I do not think it's a machine-gun! I think it's a bloody nuisance, that's all! I'm fed up with it! I've had enough!"

'"Do you like carrots, fräulein?" he asked me suddenly.

'"Carrots?" I said. "Good God. Not particularly, no. If I do have them I usually dice them. I chop them up."

'"Vot about cucumbers, fräulein?"

'"Pretty tasteless," I said. "I prefer them pickled."

'"Ja ja," he said, writing all this down on my record sheet. "It may interest you to know, fräulein, that the carrot and the cucumber are both very powerful sexuality symbols. They represent the masculine phallic member. And you are vishing either to chop it up or to pickle it!"

'I tell you, Oswald,' Yasmin said to me, 'it was as much as I could do to stop myself screaming with laughter. And to think people actually believe this horseshit.'

'He believes it himself,' I said.

'I know he does. He sat there writing it all down on a large sheet of paper. Then he said, "And vot also have you got to tell me, fräulein?"

'"I can tell you what *I* think is wrong with me," I said.

'"Proceed, please."

'"I believe I have a little dynamo inside me," I said, "and this dynamo goes whizzing round and round and gives off a terrific charge of sexual electricity."

'"Very interesting," he said, scribbling away. "Continue please."

'"This sexual electricity is of such high voltage," I said, "that as soon as a man comes close to me, it jumps across the gap from me to him and it jiggers him up."

'"Vot is meaning, please, jiggers him up?"

'"It means it excites him," I said. "It electrifies his private parts. It makes them red hot. And that's when he starts to go crazy and he jumps on me. Don't you believe me, Dr Freud?"

'"This is a serious case," the old geezer said. "It is going to take many psychoanalytical sessions on the couch to make you normal."

'Now all this time, Oswald,' Yasmin said to me, 'I was keeping an eye on my watch. And when eight minutes had gone by, I said to him, "Please don't rape me, Dr Freud. You ought to be above that sort of thing."

'"Do not be ridiculous, fräulein," he said. "You are hallucinating again."

'"But my electricity!" I cried. "It's going to jigger you up! I know it is! It's going to jump across from me to you and electrify your private parts! Your pizzle will become red hot! You will rip my clothes off! You will have your way with me!"

'"Stop this hysterical shoutings at once," he snapped and he got up from his desk and came and stood near where I was lying on the couch. "Here I am," he said, spreading out his arms. "I am not harming you, am I? I am not trying to jump upon you, yes?"

'And at that very moment, Oswald,' Yasmin said to me, 'the Beetle suddenly hit him and his doodly came alive and stuck out as though he had a walking-stick in his trousers.'

'You timed it lovely,' I said.

'Not bad, was it? So I thrust out my arm and pointed an accusing finger and shouted, "There! It's happening to you, you old goat! My electricity has jolted you! Will you believe me now, Dr Freud? Will you believe what I am saying?"'

'You should have seen his face, Oswald. You really should have seen it. The Beetle was hitting him and the sex-crazy glint was coming into his eyes and he was beginning to flap his arms like an old crow. But I'll say this for him. He didn't jump me right away. He held off for at least a minute or so while he tried to analyse what the hell was happening. He looked down at his trousers. Then he looked up at me. Then he started muttering. "This is incredible! . . . amazing! . . . unbelievable! . . . I must make notes . . . I must record every moment. Vere is my pen, for God's sake? Vere is the ink? Vere is some paper? Oh, to hell with the paper! Please to remove your clothes, fräulein! I cannot vait any longer!"'

'Must have shaken him,' I said.

'Shook him rigid,' Yasmin said. 'It was undermining one of his most famous theories.'

'You didn't hatpin him, did you?'

'Of course not. He was really very decent about it all. As soon as he'd had his first explosion, and although the Beetle was still hitting him hard, he jumped away and ran back to his desk stark naked and began writing notes. He must be terrific-ally strong-minded. Great intellectual curiosity. But he was completely foxed and bewildered by what had happened to him.'

'"Do you believe me now, Dr Freud?" I asked him.

'"I have to believe you!" he cried. "You have opened up a whole new field with this sexual electricity of yours! This case will make history! I must see you again, fräulein."

'"You'll jump me," I said. "You won't be able to stop yourself."

'"I know," he said, smiling for the first time. "I know that, fräulein, I know."'

I got fifty first-class straws from Dr Freud.

21

From Vienna we drove north in the pale autumn sunshine to Berlin. The war had been over for only eleven months and the city was bleak and dreary, but we had two important persons to visit here and I was determined to collar them. The first was Mr Albert Einstein, and at his house in Haberlandstrasse 9, Yasmin had a pleasant and successful encounter with this amazing fellow.

'How was it?' I said, asking her the usual question in the car.

'He had a great time,' she said.

'Didn't you?'

'Not really,' she said. 'He's all brains and no body. Give me Puccini any day.'

'Will you please try to forget that Italian Romeo.'

'Yes, Oswald, I will. But I'll tell you what's odd. The brainy ones, the great intellects behave quite differently to the artistic ones when the Beetle hits them.'

'How?'

'The brainy ones stop and think. They try to figure out what on earth has happened to them and why it's happened. The artists just take it for granted and plunge right in.'

'What was Einstein's reaction?'

'He couldn't believe it,' she said. 'In fact he smelled a rat. He's the very first one who has ever suspected us of jiggery-pokery. Shows how bright he is.'

'What did he say?'

'He stood there and looked at me from under those bushy eyebrows and he said, "There is something extremely fishy here, fräulein. This is not my normal reaction to a pretty visitor."

'"Doesn't that depend on how pretty she is?" I said.

'"No, fräulein, it does not," he said. "Was that an ordinary chocolate you gave me?"

'"Perfectly ordinary," I said, quaking a bit. "I had one myself."

'The little chap was strongly hotted-up by the Beetle, Oswald, but like old Freud, he managed to hold off in the beginning. He paced up and down the room muttering "What is happening to me? This is not natural . . . There is something wrong . . . I would never allow this . . ."

'I was draped all over the sofa in a seductive attitude waiting for him to get on with it, but no, Oswald, absolutely not. For about five whole minutes his thinking process completely blocked out his carnal desires or whatever you call them. I could almost hear the old brain whizzing round as he tried to puzzle it out.'

'"Mr Einstein," I said, "relax."'

'You were dealing with the greatest intellect in the world,' I said. 'The man has supernatural powers of reasoning. Try to understand what he says about relativity and you'll see what I mean.'

'We'd be finished if someone twigged what we were doing.'

'No one will,' I said. 'There's only one Einstein.'

Our second important donor in Berlin was Mr Thomas Mann. Yasmin reported that he was pleasant but uninspiring.

'Like his books,' I said.

'Then why did you choose him?'

'He's done some fine work. I think his name is going to live.'

My travelling liquid nitrogen suitcase now contained Puccini, Rachmaninov, Strauss, Freud, Einstein and Mann. So once again we went back to Cambridge with our precious cargo.

A. R. Woresley was ecstatic. He knew damn well we were on to something big now. All three of us were ecstatic, but I was in no mood to waste time yet with celebrations. 'While we're here,' I said, 'we'll polish off some of the English lads. We'll start tomorrow.'

Joseph Conrad was possibly the most important of these, so we took him first. Capel House, Orlestone, Kent was his address and we drove down there in mid-November. To be precise, it was November 16th, 1919. I have already said that I am not keen to give a detailed description of too many of our visits for fear of becoming repetitious. I will not break this rule again unless something juicy or amusing comes along. Our visit to Mr Conrad was neither juicy nor amusing. It was routine, although Yasmin did comment afterwards that he was one of the nicest men she had met so far.

From Kent we drove to Crowborough in Sussex where we nobbled Mr H. G. Wells. 'Not a bad sort of egg,' Yasmin said when she came out. 'Rather portly and pontificating but quite pleasant. It's an odd thing about great writers,' she added. 'They look so ordinary. There's nothing about them that gives you the slightest clue to their greatness, as there is with painters. A great painter somehow *looks* like a great painter. But the great writer usually looks like the wages clerk in a cheese factory.'

From Crowborough we drove on to Rottingdean, also in Sussex, to call on Mr Rudyard Kipling. 'Bristly little bugger,' was Yasmin's only comment on that one. Fifty straws from Kipling.

We were very much in the rhythm now and the next day in the same county of Sussex we picked off Sir Arthur Conan Doyle as easily as picking a cherry. Yasmin simply rang the doorbell and told the maid who answered it that she was from his publishers and had important papers to deliver to him. She was at once shown into his study.

'What did you think of Mr Sherlock Holmes?' I asked her.

'Nothing special,' she said. 'Just another writer with a thin pencil.'

'Wait,' I said. 'The next on the list is also a writer, but I doubt you'll find this one boring.'

'Who is he?'

'Mr Bernard Shaw.'

We had to drive through London to get to Ayot St Lawrence in Hertfordshire where Shaw lived, and on the way I told Yasmin something about this smug literary clown. 'First of all,' I said, 'he's a rabid vegetarian. He eats only raw vegetables and fruit and cereal. So I doubt he'll accept the chocolate.'

174

'What do we do, give it to him in a carrot?'

'What about a radish?' I suggested.

'Will he eat it?'

'Probably not,' I said. 'So it had better be a grape. We'll get a good bunch of grapes in London and doctor one of them with the powder.'

'That'll work,' Yasmin said.

'It's got to work,' I said. 'This lad won't do it without the Beetle.'

'What's wrong with him?'

'Nobody quite knows.'

'Doesn't he practise the noble art?'

'No,' I said. 'He's not interested in sex. He appears to be a sort of capon.'

'Oh hell.'

'He's a lanky garrulous old capon with an overwhelming conceit.'

'Are you suggesting his machinery is out of order?' Yasmin asked.

'I'm not sure. He's sixty-three. He married at forty-two, a marriage of companionship and convenience. No sex.'

'How do you know that?'

'I don't. But that's the general opinion. He himself has stated that "I had no adventures of a sexual kind until I was twenty-nine . . ."'

'A bit retarded.'

'I doubt he's had any at all,' I said. 'Many famous women have pursued him, but without success. Mrs Pat Campbell, gorgeous actress, said "He's all hen and no cock."'

'I like that.'

'His diet,' I said, 'is deliberately aimed at mental efficiency. "I flatly declare," he once wrote, "that a man fed on whiskey and dead bodies cannot possibly do good work."'

'As opposed to whiskey and live bodies, I suppose.'

Pretty quick our Yasmin was. 'He's a Marxist Socialist,' I added. 'He thinks the State should run everything.'

'Then he's an even bigger ass than I thought,' Yasmin said.

'I can't wait to see his face when the old Beetle strikes.'

On the way through London, we bought a bunch of superb hothouse Muscatel grapes from Jackson's in Piccadilly. They were very costly, very pale yellowish-green and very large. North of London, we stopped on the side of the road and got out the tin of Blister Beetle powder.

'Shall we give him a double shot?' I asked.

'Triple,' Yasmin said.

'D'you think that's safe?'

'If what you say about him is true he's going to need half the tin.'

'Very well, then,' I said. 'Triple it is.'

We chose the grape that was hanging at the lowest point of the bunch and carefully made a tiny nick in its skin with a knife. I scooped out a little of the inside and then inserted a triple dose of powder, pushing the stuff well into the grape with a pin. Then we continued on to Ayot St Lawrence.

'You do realize,' I said, 'that this will be the first time anyone's had a triple dose?'

'I'm not worried,' Yasmin said. 'The man's obviously wildly undersexed. I wonder if he's a eunuch. Does he have a high voice?'

'I don't know.'

'Bloody writers,' Yasmin said. She settled herself deeper into the seat and kept a grumpy silence for the rest of the trip.

The house, known as Shaw's Corner, was a large unremarkable brick pile with a good garden. The time, as I pulled up outside, was four-twenty in the afternoon.

'What do I do?' Yasmin asked.

'You walk round to the back of the house and all the way down to the bottom of the garden,' I said. 'There, you will find a small wooden shed with a sloping roof. That's where he works. He's certain to be in it now. Just barge in and give him the usual patter.'

'What if the wife sees me?'

'That's a chance you'll have to take,' I said. 'You'll probably make it. And tell him that you're a vegetarian. He'll like that.'

'What are the names of his plays?'

'*Man and Superman*,' I said. '*The Doctor's Dilemma, Major Barbara, Caesar and Cleopatra, Androcles and the Lion* and *Pygmalion*.'

'He'll ask me which I like best.'

'Say *Pygmalion*.'

'All right, I'll say *Pygmalion*.'

'Flatter him. Tell him he is not only the greatest playwright but also the greatest music critic that ever lived. You don't have to worry. He'll do the talking.'

Yasmin stepped out of the car and walked with a firm step through the gate into Shaw's garden. I watched her until she had disappeared around the back of the house, then I drove up the road and booked a room in a pub called The Waggon and Horses. Up in the room, I laid out my equipment and got everything ready for the rapid conversion of Shaw's semen into frozen straws. An hour later, I returned to Shaw's Corner to wait for Yasmin. I didn't wait long, but I am not going to tell you what happened next until you have heard what happened first. Such things are better in their right order.

'I walked down the garden,' Yasmin told me afterwards in the pub over an excellent steak and kidney pudding and a bottle of reasonable Beaune, 'I walked down the garden and I saw the hut. I walked quickly towards it. I was expecting any moment to hear Mrs Shaw's voice behind me shouting "Halt!" But no one saw me. I opened the door of the hut and looked in. It was empty. There was a cane armchair, a plain table covered with sheets of paper and a spartan atmosphere. But no Shaw. Well, that's it, I thought. Better get out. Back to Oswald. Total failure. I banged the door shut.

'"Who is there?" shouted a voice from behind the hut. It was a male voice but high-pitched and almost squeaky. Oh, my God, I thought, the man *is* a eunuch after all.

'"Is that you Charlotte?" the squeaky voice demanded.

'What effect, I wondered, would the Beetle have upon a one hundred per cent eunuch?

'"Charlotte!" he called. "What are you doing?"

'Then a tall bony creature with an enormous beard came

round the corner of the hut holding a pair of garden clippers in one hand. "Who, may I inquire, are *you*?" he demanded. "This is private property."

"I'm looking for the public lavatory," I said.

'"What is your business, young lady?" he demanded, pointing the clippers at me like a pistol. "You went into my hut. What have you stolen?"

'"I haven't stolen a damn thing," I said. "I came, if you want to know, to bring you a present."

'"A present, eh?" he said, softening a little.

'I lifted the fine bunch of grapes out of the bag and held it up by the stem.

'"And what have I done to deserve such munificence?" he said.

'"You have given me a terrific amount of pleasure at the theatre," I said. "So I thought it would be nice if I gave you something in return. That's all there is to it. Here, try one." I picked off the bottom grape and offered it to him. "They're really awfully good."

'He stepped forward and took the grape and pushed it through all those whiskers into his mouth.

'"Excellent," he said, chewing away. "A Muscatel." He glared at me under those beetly brows. "It is fortunate for you, young lady, that I wasn't working or I'd have kicked you out, grapes or no grapes. As it happens, I was pruning my roses."

'"I apologize for barging in," I said. "Will you forgive me?"

'"I will forgive you when I am convinced that your motives are pure," he said.

'"As pure as the Virgin Mary," I said.

'"I doubt it," he said. "A woman never pays a visit to a man unless she is seeking some advantage. I have made that point many times in my plays. The female, madam, is a predatory animal. She preys upon men."

'"What a damn stupid thing to say," I told him. "*Man* is the hunter."

'"I have never hunted a woman in my life," he said. "Women hunt me. And I flee like a fox with a pack of hounds at his heels.

Rapacious creatures," he added, spitting out a seed from the grape. "Rapacious, predatory, all-devouring animals."

'"Oh, come on," I said. "Everyone hunts a bit now and again. Women hunt men for marriage and what's wrong with that? But men hunt women because they want to get into bed with them. Where shall I put these grapes?"

'"We'll put them in the hut," he said, taking them from me. He went into the hut and I followed. I was praying for the nine minutes to pass quickly. He sat down in his cane armchair and stared at me under great bushy eyebrows. I quickly sat myself on the only other chair in the place.

'"You are a spirited young lady," he said. "I admire spirit."

'"And you talk a lot of bosh about women," I said. "I don't believe you know the first thing about them. Have you ever fallen passionately in love?"

'"A typical woman's question," he said. "For me, there is only one kind of passion. Intelligence is passion. The activity of the intellect is the keenest passion I can experience."

'"What about physical passion?" I asked. "Isn't that in the running?"

'"No madam, it is not. Descartes got far more passion and pleasure out of life than Casanova."

'"What about Romeo and Juliet?"

'"Puppy love," he said. "Superficial tosh."

'"Are you saying that your *Caesar and Cleopatra* is a greater play than *Romeo and Juliet*?"

'"Without a doubt," he said.

'"Boy, you've got a nerve, Mr Shaw."

'"So have you, young lady." He picked up a sheet of paper from the table. "Listen to this," he said and he started to read aloud in that squeaky voice of his ". . . the body always ends by being a bore. Nothing remains beautiful and interesting except thought, because thought is life . . ."

'"Of course it *ends* by being a bore," I said. "That's a pretty obvious remark. But it isn't a bore at my age. It's a juicy fruit. What's the play?"

'"It's about Methuselah," he said. "And now I must ask you

179

to leave me in peace. You are pert and pretty but that does not entitle you to take up my time. I thank you for the grapes."

'I glanced at my watch. Just over a minute to go. I had to keep talking. "I'll be off then," I said, "but in exchange for my grapes I'd love it if you gave me your autograph on one of your famous postcards."

'He reached for a postcard and signed it. "Now be off with you," he said. "You have wasted enough of my time."

'"I'm going," I said, fumbling about and trying to string out the seconds. The nine minutes were up now. Oh Beetle, lovely Beetle, kind Beetle, where are you ? Why have you deserted me ?'

'A bit dicy, that,' I said.

'I was desperate, Oswald. It had never happened before. "Mr Shaw," I said, pausing by the door, searching for a time-killer, "I promised my dear old mother who thinks you are God the Father himself to be sure to ask you one question . . ."

'"You are a pest, madam!" he barked.

'"I know I am, I know, I know, but please answer it for her. Here's the question. Is it really true that you disapprove of all artists who create works of art for purely aesthetic reasons ?"

'"I do, madam."

'"You mean pure beauty is not enough ?"

'"It is not," he said. "Art should always be didactic, serving a social purpose."

'"Did Beethoven serve a social purpose, or Van Gogh ?"

'"Get out of here!" he roared. "I have no wish to bandy words . . ." He stopped in mid-sentence. For at that moment, Oswald, heaven be praised, the Beetle struck.'

'Hooray. Did it hit him hard ?'

'This was a triple dose, remember.'

'I know. So what happened ?'

'I don't think it's safe to give triples, Oswald. I'm not going to do it again.'

'Rocked him a bit, did it ?'

'Phase one was devastating,' Yasmin said. 'It was as if he

were sitting in an electric chair and someone had pulled the switch and jolted him with a million volts.'

'Bad as that?'

'Listen, his whole body rose up off the chair and there it hung, in mid-air, rigid, quivering, the eyes popping, the face all twisted.'

'Oh dear.'

'Rattled me.'

'I'll bet.'

'What do we do now, I thought. Artificial respiration, oxygen, what?'

'You're not exaggerating, are you, Yasmin?'

'God no. The man was contorted. He was paralysed. He was garotted. He couldn't speak.'

'Was he conscious?'

'Who knows?'

'Did you think he might kick the bucket?'

'I reckoned it was about even money.'

'You really thought that?'

'You only had to look at him.'

'Christ, Yasmin.'

'I stood there by the door and I remember thinking well whatever happens, this old buzzard's written his last play. "Hello there, Mr Shaw," I said. "Wakey wakey."'

'Could he hear you?'

'I doubt it. And through his whiskers I could see white stuff, like brine, forming on his lips.'

'How long did all this last?'

'A couple of minutes. And on top of everything else I began worrying about his heart.'

'Why his heart, for God's sake?'

'He was going purple in the face. I could see his skin going purple.'

'Asphyxia?'

'Something like that,' Yasmin said. 'Isn't this steak and kidney delicious?'

'It's very good.'

'Then all of a sudden he came back to earth. He blinked his eyes, took one look at me, gave a sort of Indian whoop, leaped out of his chair and started tearing off his clothes. "The Irish are coming!" he yelled. "Gird up your loins, madam! Gird up your loins and prepare for battle!"'

'Not exactly a eunuch then.'

'It didn't look like it.'

'How did you manage to roll the old rubbery thing on him?'

'There's only one way when they get violent,' Yasmin said. 'I grabbed hold of his snozzberry and hung on to it like grim death and gave it a twist or two to make him hold still.'

'Ow.'

'Very effective.'

'I'll bet it is.'

'You can lead them around anywhere you want like that.'

'I'm sure.'

'It's like putting a twitch on a horse.'

I took a mouthful of Beaune, tasting it with care. It had been shipped by Louis Latour and it was really very fair. One was fortunate to find something like that in a country pub. 'So then what?' I said.

'Chaos. Wooden floor. Horrible bruises. The lot. But I'll tell you what's interesting, Oswald. He didn't know quite what to do. I had to show him.'

'So he *was* a virgin?'

'Must've been. But a damn quick learner. I've never seen such energy in a man of sixty-three.'

'That's the vegetarian diet.'

'It could be,' Yasmin said, spearing a piece of kidney with her fork and popping it into her mouth. 'But don't forget he had a brand new engine.'

'A what?'

'A new engine. Most men of that age are more or less worn out by then. Their equipment I mean. It's done so much mileage things are beginning to rattle.'

'You mean the fact that he was a virgin . . .'

'Precisely, Oswald. The engine was brand new, completely unused. Therefore no wear and tear.'

'Had to run it in a bit though, didn't he?'

'No,' she said. 'He just let her rip. Flat out all the time. Full throttle. And when he'd got the hang of it he shouted, "*Now* I see what Mrs Pat Campbell was on about!"'

'I suppose in the end you had to get out the old hatpin?'

'Of course. But you know something, Oswald. With a triple dose they're so far gone they don't feel a thing. I might've been tickling his arse with a feather for all the good it did.'

'How many jabs?'

'Till my arm got tired.'

'So what then?'

'There are other ways,' Yasmin said darkly.

'Ow again,' I said. I was remembering what Yasmin had once done to A. R. Woresley in the lab to get away from him. 'Did he jump?'

'About a yard straight up,' she said. 'And that gave me just enough time to grab the spoils and dash for the door.'

'Lucky you kept your clothes on.'

'I had to,' she said. 'Whenever we give an extra dose it's always a sprint to get away.'

So that was Yasmin's story. But let me now take it up from there myself and go back to where I was sitting quietly in my motor car outside 'Shaw's Corner' in the gathering dusk while all this was going on. Suddenly out came Yasmin at the gallop, flying down the garden path with her hair streaming out behind her and I quickly opened the passenger door for her to jump in. But she didn't jump in. She ran to the front of the car and grabbed the starting-handle. No self-starters in those days, remember. 'Switch on, Oswald!' she shouted. 'Switch on! He's coming after me!' I switched on the ignition. Yasmin cranked the handle. The motor started first kick. Yasmin dashed back and jumped into the seat next to me, yelling 'Go man, go! Full speed ahead!' But before I could get the gear lever properly engaged, I heard a yell from the garden and in the half-darkness I saw this tall, ghostlike, white-bearded figure charging down upon us stark naked and yelling, 'Come back, you strumpet! I haven't finished with you yet!'

'Go!' Yasmin shouted. I got the car into gear and let out the clutch and off we went.

There was a street-lamp outside the Shaw house and when I glanced back I saw Mr Shaw capering about on the sidewalk under the gaslight, white-skinned all over save for a pair of socks on his feet, bearded above and bearded below as well, with his massive pink member protruding like a sawn-off shotgun from the lower beard. It was a sight I shall not readily forget, this mighty and supercilious playwright who had always mocked the passions of the flesh, himself impaled now upon the sword of lust and screaming for Yasmin to come back. *Cantharis vesicatoria sudanii*, I reflected, could make a monkey out of the Messiah.

22

By now Christmas was nearly on us and Yasmin said she wanted a holiday. I wanted to keep going. 'Come on,' I said, 'let's do a Royal Tour first, kings only. We'll nobble all the nine remaining monarchs of Europe. Then we'll both take a good long rest.'

Romping with the royals, as Yasmin called it, was an irresistible prospect and she agreed to delay her holiday and spend Christmas in wintry Europe. Together we worked out a sensible itinerary which would take us, in the following order, to Belgium, Italy, Yugoslavia, Greece, Bulgaria, Romania, Denmark, Sweden and Norway. I checked over all nine of my carefully prepared letters from George V. A. R. Woresley refilled my travelling liquid nitrogen container and supplied me with a new stock of straws, and off we went in the trusty Citroën, heading for Dover and the cross-channel steamer, with the Royal Palace in Brussels our first stop.

The effect that the King of England's letter had upon the first eight monarchs on our list was virtually identical. They jumped to it. They couldn't wait to please King George and they couldn't wait to get a peek at his secret mistress. For them it was a fruity business. On every single occasion Yasmin was invited to the Palace only a few hours after I had delivered the letter. We had success after success. Sometimes the hatpin had to be used, sometimes not. There were some funny scenes and one or two tricky moments, but Yasmin always got her man in the end. She even got seventy-six-year-old King Peter of Yugo-slavia, although he passed out at the end of it all and my girl had to revive him by throwing a chamberpot of cold water over his face. By the time we reached Christiania (now Oslo) at the beginning of April, we had eight kings in the bag and there was only Haakon of Norway left. He was forty-eight years old.

In Christiania we booked into the Grand Hotel on Carl Johan's Gate and from the balcony of my room I could look straight up that splendid street to the Royal Palace on the hill. I delivered my letter at ten o'clock on a Tuesday morning. By lunchtime Yasmin had a reply in the king's own handwriting. She was invited to present herself at the palace at two-thirty that afternoon.

'This is going to be my very last king,' she said. 'I shall miss popping into palaces and wrestling with royals.'

'What's your general opinion of them,' I said, 'now that it's nearly over? How do they measure up?'

'They vary,' she said. 'That fellow Boris of Bulgaria was terrifying the way he rolled me up in chicken wire.'

'Bulgarians are not easy.'

'Ferdinand of Romania was pretty crazy, too.'

'The one who had distorting mirrors all around the room?'

'That's him. Let us now see what revolting habits this Norwegian chap has got.'

'I hear he's a very decent fellow.'

'Nobody's decent when he's had the Beetle, Oswald.'

'I'll bet he's nervous,' I said.

'Why?'

'I told you why. His wife, Queen Maud, is King George V's sister. So our fake letter was supposedly written to Haakon by his brother-in-law. It's all a bit close to the bone.'

'Spicy,' Yasmin said. 'I like it.' And off she bounced to the palace with her little box of chocolates and her hatpin and other necessary items. I stayed behind and laid out my equipment in readiness for her return.

In less than one hour she was back. She came flying into my room like a hurricane.

'I blew it!' she cried. 'Oh, Oswald, I did something frightful awful terrible! I blew the whole thing!'

'What happened?' I said, starting to quake.

'Give me a drink,' she said. 'Brandy.'

I got her a stiff brandy. 'Come on then,' I said. 'Let's have it. Tell me the worst.'

Yasmin took a huge gulp of brandy, then she leaned back and closed her eyes and said, 'Ah, that's better.'

'For God's sake,' I cried, 'tell me what happened!'

She drank the rest of the brandy and asked for another. I gave it to her quickly.

'Lovely big room,' she said. 'Lovely tall king. Black moustache, courtly, kind and handsome. Took the chocolate like a lamb and I started counting the minutes. Spoke almost perfect English. "I am not very happy about this business, Lady Victoria," he said, tapping King George's letter with one finger. "This is not like my brother-in-law at all. King George is the most upright and honourable man I've ever met."

'"He's only human, Your Majesty."

'"He's the perfect husband," he said.

'"The trouble is he's married," I said.

'"Of course he's married. What are you implying?"

'"Married men make rotten husbands, Your Majesty."

'"You're talking rubbish, madam!" he snapped.'

'Why didn't you shut up right then and there, Yasmin?' I cried.

'Oh, I couldn't, Oswald. Once I get going like that I can't ever seem to stop. Do you know what I said next?'

'I can't wait,' I said. I was beginning to sweat.

'I said, "Look, Your Majesty, I mean after all when a strong good-looking fellow like George has been having rice pudding every night for years and years, it's only natural he's going to start wanting a dish of caviar."'

'Oh, my God!'

'It was a silly thing to say, I know that.'

'What did he answer?'

'He went green in the face. I thought he was going to strike me but he just stood there spluttering and fizzing like one of those fireworks, those bangers, the ones that go on spluttering for a long time before the big explosion comes.'

'And did it come?'

'Not then. He was very dignified. He said, "I will thank you, madam, not to refer to the Queen of England as a rice pudding."

'"I'm sorry, Your Majesty," I said. "I didn't mean it." I was still standing in the middle of the room because he hadn't asked me to sit down. To hell with it, I thought, and I chose a large green sofa and draped myself along it, all ready for the Beetle to strike.

'"I simply cannot understand George going off the rails like this," he said.

'"Oh come on, Your Majesty," I said. "He's only following in his dad's footsteps."

'"Pray what do you mean by that, madam?"

'"Old Edward VII," I said. "Dash it all, he was dipping the royal wick all over the country."

'"How dare you!" he cried, exploding for the first time. "It's all lies!"

'"What about Lily Langtry?"

'"King Edward was my wife's father," he said in an icy voice. "I will not have him insulted in my house."'

'What in God's name, Yasmin, made you go on like that for?' I cried. 'You get a really nice king for once and all you do is insult the hell out of him.'

'He was a lovely man.'

'Then why did you *do* it?'

'I had the devil in me, Oswald. And I was enjoying it, I suppose.'

'You simply cannot *talk* like that to kings.'

'Oh yes I can,' Yasmin said. 'I have discovered, you see Oswald, that it doesn't really matter what you say to them in the beginning or how angry you make them because the good old Beetle always rescues you in the end. It's always them that finish up looking silly.'

'But you said you'd blown it?'

'Let me go on and you'll see what happened. The tall king kept pacing up and down the room and muttering to himself and of course I kept watching the clock all the time. For some reason the nine minutes seemed to be going rather slowly. Then the king said, "How could you *do* this to your own queen? How could you *lower* yourself to seducing her dear husband? Queen Mary is the purest lady in the land."

'"You really think so?" I said.

'"I know it," he said. "She's as pure as the driven snow."

'"Now just you hang on one second there, Your Majesty," I said. "Haven't you heard all the naughty rumours?"

'When I said that, Oswald, he whipped round as though he'd been bitten by a scorpion.'

'Jesus, Yasmin, you've got a bloody nerve!'

'It was fun,' she said. 'I only meant it as a joke.'

'Some joke.'

'"Rumours!" the king shouted. "What sort of rumours?"

'"Very naughty rumours," I said.

'"How dare you!" he roared. "How dare you come in here and talk like that about the Queen of England. You are a strumpet and a liar, madam!"

'"I may be a strumpet," I said, "but I'm not a liar. There is, you see, Your Majesty, a certain equerry at Buckingham Palace, a colonel in the Grenadiers, a fine good-looking fellow he is, too, with his big black bristly moustache, and every morning he meets the queen in the gymnasium and gives her keep-fit lessons."

'"And why shouldn't he?" snapped the king. "What's wrong with keep-fit exercises? I do them myself."

'I looked at my watch. The nine minutes were just coming up. Any moment now this tall proud king would be transformed into a randy old lecher. "Your Majesty," I said, "many's the time George and I have peeped through the window at the end of the gym and seen . . ." I stopped. I lost my voice, Oswald. I just couldn't go on.'

'What happened, for God's sake?'

'I thought I was having a heart-attack. I began to gasp. I couldn't breathe properly and a sort of goose-pimply feeling was spreading over my whole body. I really thought, honestly I did, I really thought I might be going to kick the bucket.'

'What was it, for God's sake?'

'That's what the king asked me. He's truly a decent man, Oswald. Half a minute before I'd been saying beastly insulting things about his in-laws in England and all of a sudden he was deeply concerned for my welfare. "Do you wish me to call a doctor?" he said. I couldn't even answer him. I just gurgled at him. Then all of a sudden this terrific tingling sensation started in the soles of my feet and it spread quickly all the way up my legs. I'm getting paralysed, I thought. I can't talk. I can't move. I can hardly think. I'm going to die any moment. Then *wham!* It hit me!'

'What hit you?'

'*The Beetle* of course.'

'Now wait a minute . . .'

'I'd eaten the wrong goddamn chocolate, Oswald! I'd mixed them up! I'd given him the plain one and eaten the Beetle myself!'

'Jesus Christ, Yasmin!'

'I know. But by then I'd guessed what had happened and my first thought was I'd better get the hell out of the Palace before I make an even bigger ass out of myself than I already have.'

'And did you?'

'Well, that was a bit easier said than done. For the first time in my life I was finding out what it felt like to get the Beetle.'

'Strong stuff.'

'Terrifying. It freezes your mind. You can't think straight. All you've got is this fierce throbbing sexy sensation pouring all over you. Sex is the only thing you can think about. It was all *I* could think about anyway, and I'm very much afraid, Oswald . . . I couldn't stop myself, you understand . . . I simply couldn't stop myself . . . so I . . . well, I leaped off the sofa and made a dive for the king's trousers . . .'

'Oh, my God.'

'There's more to come,' Yasmin said, taking another gulp of brandy.

'Don't tell me. I can't bear it.'

'All right, then, I won't.'

'Yes,' I said. 'Go on.'

'I was like a mad woman. I was all over him. I caught him off balance and pushed him down on to the sofa. But he's an athletic kind of bird, that old king. He was very quick. He was up in a flash. He got behind his desk. I climbed over the desk. He kept shouting, "Stop woman! What's the matter with you! Get away from me!" And then he really started yelling, yelling out loud I mean. "Help!" he yelled. "Someone get this woman out of here!" And then, my dear Oswald, the door opened and the queen herself, little Queen Maud in all her glory, came sailing into the room holding a piece of needlework in her hand.'

'Bound to happen.'

'I know.'

'Where were you when she came in ?'

'I was leaping over his big Chippendale desk to get at him. Chairs were flying all over the place and in she came, this tiny quite pretty woman . . .'

'What did she say ?'

'She said, "What *are* you doing, Haakon ?"'

'"Get her out!" yelled the king.'

'"I want him!" I shouted. "And I'm going to have him!"'

'"Haakon!" she said. "Stop this at once!"'

'"It's not me, it's her!" he cried, running for his life round the room. But I had him cornered now and I was just about to fling myself at him good and proper when I was grabbed from behind by two guards. Soldiers they were. Lovely-looking Norwegian boys.

'"Take her away," gasped the king.

'"Where to, sire?"

'"Just get her out of here quick! Dump her in the street!"

'So I was frog-marched out of the Palace and all I remember is I kept saying awful dirty things to the young soldiers and making all sorts of sexy suggestions and they were hooting with laughter . . .'

'So they dumped you?'

'In the street,' Yasmin said. 'Outside the Palace gates.'

'You're damned lucky it wasn't the King of Bulgaria or somewhere like that,' I said. 'You'd have been thrown into a dungeon.'

'I know.'

'So they dumped you in the street outside the Palace?'

'Yes. I was dazed. I sat on a bench under some trees trying to pull myself together. I had one great advantage, you see Oswald, over all my victims. *I knew* what was wrong with me. *I knew* it was the Beetle that was doing it to me. It must be simply awful feeling the way I felt and not knowing why. I think that would scare me to death. So I was able to fight it. I remember sitting there and saying to myself what you need Yasmin old girl, what you need to straighten you out is a few good digs in the backside with the hatpin. That made me giggle. And after that, but very slowly, this ghastly sexy feeling began to go away and I got a hold of myself and I stood up and walked along the street to the hotel and here I am. I'm sorry I messed it up, Oswald, I really am. It's the first time ever.'

'We'd better get out of here,' I said. 'I don't think these people would ever do anything nasty to us but the king is bound to start asking a few questions.'

'I'm sure he is.'

'I think he's going to guess my letter was a forgery,' I said. 'I bet anything you like he's checking it out with George V right this very minute.'

'I'll bet he is, too,' Yasmin said.

'Hurry up and pack then,' I said. 'We'll slide out of here at once and drive back across the border into Sweden. We're going to get lost.'

23

We got back home via Sweden and Denmark around the middle of April and we had with us the sperm of eight kings – fifty straws each from seven of them and twenty from old Peter of Yugoslavia. It was a pity about Norway. It spoiled our record although I didn't feel it was going to make much difference in the long run.

'Now I want my holiday,' Yasmin said. 'A good one. Aren't we about finished anyway?'

'America's next,' I said.

'There aren't many there.'

'No, but we have to get them. We'll go over in style on the *Mauretania*.'

'I want a holiday first,' Yasmin said. 'You promised me. I'm not going anywhere until I've had a nice long rest.'

'How long?'

'A month.'

We had driven straight to Cambridge after disembarking from the Danish boat at Harwich and we were having a drink in the living-room at 'Dunroamin'. A. R. Woresley came in rubbing his hands.

'Congratulations,' he said. 'You've done a great job with those kings.'

'Yasmin wants a month's holiday,' I said. 'But personally I think we ought to bash on and get America done first.'

A. R. Woresley, puffing his disgusting pipe, looked at Yasmin through the smoke and said, 'I agree with Cornelius. Get the job done first, take a holiday later.'

'No,' Yasmin said.

'Why not?' Woresley said.

'Because I don't want to, that's why.'

'Well, I suppose it's up to you,' Woresley said.

'You bet your life it's up to me,' Yasmin said.

'Aren't you having a good time?' I said.

'The fun's wearing off,' she said. 'In the beginning it was a lark. Terrific joke. But now all of a sudden I seem to have had enough.'

'Don't say that.'

'I've said it.'

'Hell.'

'What both of you seem to be forgetting,' she said, 'is that every time we want the sperm of some bloody genius, *I'm* the one who has to go in and do the fighting. I'm the one who gets it in the neck.'

'Not in the neck,' I said.

'Stop trying to be funny, Oswald.' She sat there looking glum. A. R. Woresley said nothing.

'If you have a month's holiday now,' I said, 'will you come to America with me immediately after that?'

'Yes, all right.'

'You're going to enjoy Rudolph Valentino.'

'I doubt it,' she said. 'I think my romping days are over.'

'Never!' I cried. 'You might as well be dead!'

'Romping isn't everything.'

'Jesus, Yasmin. You're talking like Bernard Shaw!'

'Maybe I'll become a nun.'

'But you will come to America first?'

'I've already told you I would,' she said.

A. R. Woresley took his pipe out of his mouth and said, 'We've got a remarkable collection, Cornelius, truly remarkable. When do we start selling?'

'We mustn't hurry it,' I said. 'My feeling is that we should not put any man's sperm up for sale until after he's dead.'

'Why do you say that?'

'Great men are more interesting dead than alive. They become legends when they're dead.'

'Maybe you're right,' Woresley said.

'We've got plenty of ancient ones on the list,' I said. 'Most of them aren't going to last very long. I'll bet you fifty per cent of the whole lot will be gone in five or ten years.'

'Who's going to do the selling when the time comes?' Woresley asked.

'I am,' I said.

'You think you can manage it?'

'Look,' I said. 'At the tender age of seventeen I had no trouble whatsoever in selling red pills to the French Foreign Minister, to a dozen Ambassadors and to just about every big shot in Paris. And just recently I have successfully sold Lady Victoria Nottingham to all the crowned heads of Europe bar one.'

'I did that,' Yasmin said. 'Not you.'

'Oh no you didn't,' I said. 'King George's letter did the selling and that was my idea. So you don't seriously think I'm going to have any trouble selling the seeds of genius to a bunch of rich females, do you?'

'Perhaps not,' Woresley said.

'And by the way,' I said, 'if I'm the one who does all the selling, I think I ought to be entitled to a bigger cut of the profits.'

'Hey!' Yasmin cried. 'Now you just stop that, Oswald!'

'The agreement was equal shares all round,' Woresley said, looking hostile.

'Calm down,' I said. 'I was only joking.'

'I should damn well hope so,' Yasmin said.

'As a matter of fact, I think Arthur should have the major share because he invented the whole process,' I said.

'Well, I must say that's very generous of you, Cornelius,' Woresley said, beaming.

'Forty per cent to the inventor and thirty per cent each to Yasmin and me,' I said. 'Would you agree to that, Yasmin?'

'I'm not sure I would,' she said. 'I've worked damn hard on this. I want my one-third.'

What neither of them knew was that I had long since decided that I myself was the one who would take the major share in the end. Yasmin, after all, would never need very much. She liked to dress well and to eat good food but that was about as far as it went. As for old Woresley, I doubted whether he'd know what to do with a large sum of money even if he had it. Pipe tobacco was about the only luxury he ever permitted himself. But I was different. The style of living to which I aspired made it absolutely necessary that I have a fortune at my fingertips. It was impossible for me to tolerate indifferent champagne or mild discomfort of any sort. The way I looked at it, the best, and by that I mean only the very best, was not nearly good enough for me.

I figured that if I gave them ten per cent each and took eighty for myself, then they ought to be happy. They would scream blue murder at first, but when they realized there was nothing they could do about it, they would soon settle down and be grateful for small mercies. Now there was of course only one way in which I could put myself in the position of being able to dictate terms to the other two. I must get possession of The Semen's Home and all the treasures it contained. Then I must move it to a safe and secret place where neither of them could reach it. That would not be difficult. As soon as Yasmin and I had returned from America, I would hire a removal van and drive up to 'Dunroamin' when the place was empty and make off with the precious treasure chest.

No problem.

But a bit of a dirty trick, some of you may be thinking? A bit caddish?

Rubbish, I say. You'll never get anywhere in this world unless you grab your opportunities. Charity has never begun at home. Not in my home anyway.

'So when will you two be going to America?' A. R. Woresley asked us.

I got out my diary. 'One month from now will be Saturday

the fifteenth of May,' I said. 'How's that with you, Yasmin?'

'The fifteenth of May,' she said, taking her own diary from her purse. 'That seems all right. I'll meet you here on the fifteenth. In four weeks' time.'

'And I'll book cabins on the *Mauretania* for as soon as possible after that.'

'Fine,' she said, writing the date in her diary.

'Then we'll collar old Henry Ford and Mr Marconi and Rudolph Valentino and all the other Yanks.'

'Don't forget Alexander Graham Bell,' Woresley said.

'We'll get the lot,' I said. 'After a month's rest, the old girl will be roaring to go again, you see if she isn't.'

'Hope so,' Yasmin said. 'But I do need a rest, honestly I do.'

'Where will you go?'

'Up to Scotland to stay with an uncle.'

'Nice uncle?'

'Very,' she said. 'My father's brother. He fishes for salmon.'

'When are you leaving?'

'Right now,' she said. 'My train goes in about an hour. Will you take me to the station?'

'Of course I will,' I said. 'I myself am off to London.'

I drove Yasmin to the station and helped her into the waiting-room with her bags. 'See you in exactly a month,' I said. 'At "Dunroamin".'

'I'll be there,' she said.

'Have good hols.'

'Same to you, Oswald.'

I kissed her farewell and drove down to London. I went straight to my house in Kensington Square. I was feeling good. The great scheme was actually coming to pass. I could see my-self in about five years' time sitting with some silly rich female and her saying to me, 'I rather fancy Renoir, Mr Cornelius. I do so adore his pictures. How much does he cost?'

'Renoir is seventy-five thousand, madam.'

'And how much is a king?'

'That depends which one.'

'This one here. The dark good-looking one – King Alfonso of Spain.'

'King Alfonso is forty thousand dollars, madam.'

'You mean he's less than Renoir?'

'Renoir was a greater man, madam. His sperm is exceedingly rare.'

'What happens if it doesn't work, Mr Cornelius? I mean if I don't become pregnant.'

'You get a free go.'

'And who would actually perform the insemination?'

'A senior gynaecologist, madam. It would all be most carefully planned.'

'And my husband would never find out?'

'How could he? He'd think he'd done it himself.'

'I suppose he would, wouldn't he?' She giggles.

'Bound to, madam.'

'It *would* be rather nice to have a child by the King of Spain, wouldn't it?'

'Have you considered Bulgaria, madam. Bulgaria is a bargain at twenty thousand.'

'I don't want a Bulgar brat, Mr Cornelius, even if he is royal.'

'I quite understand, madam.'

'And then of course there's Mr Puccini. *La Bohème* is absolutely my favourite opera. How much is Mr Puccini?'

'Giacomo Puccini is sixty-seven thousand five hundred, madam. He is strongly recommended. The child would almost certainly be a musical genius.'

'I play the piano a bit myself.'

'That would help the baby's chances enormously.'

'I expect it would, wouldn't it?'

'Confidentially, madam, I can tell you that a certain lady in Dallas, Texas had a Puccini boy three years ago and the child has already composed his first opera.'

'You don't say.'

'Thrilling, isn't it?'

I was going to have a lot of fun once the selling started. But right now I had before me one whole month in which to do

nothing except enjoy myself. I decided to remain in London.
I'd have a real fling. I deserved it. Throughout most of the winter
I'd been chasing after kings all over Europe and the time had
come for some serious wenching.

And what wenching it was. I went on a proper bender. For
three weeks out of the four I had a glorious time (see Vol. III).
Then suddenly, at the beginning of the fourth and final week of
my vacation when I was really in full flood and churning the
ladies of London to such purpose you could hear the bones
rattling all over Mayfair, a devilish incident occurred that put
an immediate stopper on all my activities. Terrible it was.
Diabolical. Even to *think* about it at this distance causes me
sharp physical pain. None the less, I feel I ought to describe this
sordid episode in the hope that it may save a few other sportsmen
from a similar catastrophe.

I do not usually sit in the bathtub at the wrong end with my
back to the taps. Few people do. But on this particular afternoon,
the other end, the comfortable slopy end, was occupied by a
saucy little imp who possessed hyperactive carnal proclivities.
That's why she was there. The fact that she happened also to be
an English duchess is not entirely beside the point either. Had
I been a few years older I would have known what to expect
from a female of high rank, and I'd have been a good deal less
careless. Most of these women have acquired their titles by
ensnaring some poor benighted peer or duke, and it takes a very
special kind of mendacity and guile to succeed at that game. To
become a duchess you must be a prime manipulator of men. I
have tangled with a fair number of them in my time and they're
all alike. Marchionesses and countesses are not quite so ghoulish
but they run the duchesses a close second. Dally with them by
all means. It is a piquant experience. But for heaven's sake keep
your wits about you while you're at it. You never know, you
positively never can tell when they're going to turn and bite the
hand that strokes them. Watch out, I say, for the female with a
grand title.

Anyway, this duchess and I had been jouncing for an hour or
so in the bathtub, and now that she had had enough she threw

the soap at my face and stepped out of the water. The large slimy missile caught me on the mouth, but as none of my teeth were dislodged or even loosened I ignored the incident. In point of fact, she had done it simply to quieten me down and to give her a chance to get away, which it did.

'Come back in,' I said, wanting a second helping.

'I've got to go,' she answered. She was keeping her distance as she dried her trim little body with one of my huge towels.

'It's only half-time,' I pleaded.

'The trouble with you, Oswald, is you don't know when to stop,' she said. 'One day someone's going to lose patience with you.'

'Frigid bitch,' I said. It was a silly thing to say and quite untrue, but I said it.

She went into the next room to get dressed. I remained sitting in the bath, silent and feeling thwarted. I didn't like it when others called the tune.

'Goodbye, darling,' she said coming back into the bathroom. She was wearing a short-sleeved silk dress, dark green.

'Go home, then,' I said. 'Go back to your ridiculous duke.'

'Don't be so grumpy,' she said. She walked over to me and bent down and began to massage my back under the water. Then her hand slid around to other areas, caressing and teasing gently. I sat still, enjoying it all and wondering whether she wasn't perhaps going to start melting all over again.

Now you won't believe this, but all the time the little vixen was pretending to play around with me, what she was actually doing was surreptitiously and with consummate stealth removing the plug from the plughole in the bottom of the bathtub. As you know, when the plug is withdrawn from a bath that is brimful of water, the suction down the plughole is immensely powerful. And when a man is sitting astride that plughole as I was at that moment, then it is inevitable that the two most tender and valuable objects in his possession are going to be sucked very suddenly into that dreadful hole. There was a dull *plop* as my scrotum took the full force of the suction and flew into the neck of the hole. I let out a scream that must have been heard clear across Kensington Square.

'Goodbye, darling,' said the duchess, sweeping out of the bathroom.

In the excruciating moments that followed I learned exactly what it must feel like to fall into the hands of those Bedouin women who delight in depriving a traveller of his masculinity with blunt knives. 'Help!' I screamed. 'Save me!' I was impaled. I was glued to the tub. I was clutched in the claws of a mighty crab.

It seemed like hours but I don't suppose I was actually stuck in that position for more than ten or fifteen minutes. It was quite long enough though. I don't even know how I eventually managed to prise myself free all in one piece. But the damage was done. Powerful suction is a terrible thing and those two precious jewels of mine which were normally no bigger than a couple of greengages had suddenly assumed the size of cantaloupe melons. I think it was old Geoffrey Chaucer way back in the fourteenth century who wrote:

> *Ladies with titles*
> *Will go for your vitals*

and those immortal words, believe me, are now engraved upon my heart. For three days I was on crutches and for God knows how long after that I walked about like a man who was harbouring a porcupine between his thighs.

It was in this crippled condition that I made my way up to Cambridge on May 15th to keep my appointment with Yasmin at 'Dunroamin'. As I got out of the car and hobbled towards the front-door, my marbles were still on fire and throbbing like the devil's drum. Yasmin, of course, would be wanting to know what had happened to me. So would Woresley. Should I tell them the truth? If I did, Yasmin would fall all over the room laughing, and I could already hear Woresley in his silly pompous way saying, 'You are altogether too carnal, my dear Cornelius. No man can debauch himself the way you do without paying a heavy price.'

I didn't think I could stand that sort of thing right then so I decided to tell them I had strained a ligament in my thigh. I had done it while helping an old lady after she had stumbled and taken a heavy fall on the pavement outside my house. I had carried her indoors and looked after her until the ambulance came, but it had all been a bit too much for me, etc., etc. That would do it.

I stood under the little porch outside the front door of 'Dunroamin' and fished for my key. As I was doing this, I noticed there was an envelope pinned to the door. Someone had fixed it on firmly with a drawing-pin. Damn silly thing to do. I couldn't get the pin out so I ripped the envelope away. There was no name on it so I opened it. Foolish not to put a name on the envelope. Was it for me? Yes, it was.

Dear Oswald,
   Arthur and I got married last week . . .

Arthur? Who the hell was Arthur?

We have gone far away and I hope you won't mind too much but we've taken the Semen's Home with us, at least all of it except Proust . . .

Jesus Christ! Arthur must be Woresley! Arthur Woresley!

Yes, we have left you Proust. I never did like the little bugger anyway. All fifty of his straws are safely stored in the travelling container in the basement and the Proust letter is in the desk. We have all the other letters with us safe and sound . . .

I was reeling. I couldn't read on. I unlocked the door and staggered inside and found a bottle of whiskey. I sloshed some into a glass and gulped it down.

If you stop and think about it, Oswald, I'm sure you'll agree we're not really doing the dirty on you and I'll tell you why. Arthur says . . .

I didn't give a damn what Arthur said. They'd stolen the precious sperm. It was worth millions. I was willing to bet it was that little sod Woresley who'd put Yasmin up to it.

Arthur says that after all it was him who invented the process, wasn't it? And it was me who did all the hard work of collecting it. Arthur sends you his best wishes.

Toodle-oo
Yasmin Woresley

A real snorter, that. Right below the belt. It had me gasping.

I roared round the house in a wild fury. My stomach was boiling and I'm sure steam was spurting out of my nostrils. Had there been a dog in the place I'd have kicked it to death. I kicked the furniture instead. I smashed a lot of nice big things and then I set about picking up all the smaller objects, including a Baccarat paperweight and an Etruscan bowl, and flinging them through the windows, yelling bloody murder and watching the window-panes shatter.

But after an hour or so, I began to simmer down, and finally I collapsed into an armchair with a large glass of malt whiskey in my hand.

I am, as you may have gathered, a fairly resilient fellow. I explode when provoked, but I never brood about it afterwards. I scrub it out. There's always another day. What's more, nothing stimulates my mind so much as a whopping disaster. In the aftermath, in that period of deadly calm and absolute silence that follows the tempest, my brain becomes exceedingly active. As I sat drinking my whiskey during that terrible evening amidst the ruins of 'Dunroamin', I was already beginning to ponder and plan my future all over again.

So that's that, I told myself. I've been diddled. It's all over. Need a new start. I still have Proust and in years to come I shall do well with those fifty straws (and don't think I didn't), but that isn't going to make me a millionaire. So what next?

It was at this point that the great and wonderful answer began trickling into my head. I sat quite still, allowing the idea to take root and grow. It was inspired. It was beautiful in its simplicity. It couldn't fail. It would make me millions. Why hadn't I thought of it before?

I promised at the beginning of this diary to tell you how I became a wealthy man. I have taken a long time so far in telling you how I did not succeed. Let me therefore make up for lost time and describe to you in no more than a few paragraphs how I did in the end become a real multi-millionaire. The great idea that came to me so suddenly in 'Dunroamin' was as follows:

I would go back at once to the Sudan. I would negotiate with a corrupt government official for a lease of that precious tract of land where the hashab tree grows and the Blister Beetle flourishes. I would obtain sole rights to all beetle-hunting. I would gather the native beetle-hunters together and form them into an organized unit. I would pay them generously, far more than they were getting at present by flogging their Beetles in the open market. They would work exclusively for me. Poachers would be ruthlessly eliminated. I would, in fact, corner the market in Sudanese Blister Beetles. When all this was arranged and I was assured of a large and regular supply of Beetles, I would build a little factory in Khartoum and there I would process my Beetles and manufacture in quantity Professor Yousoupoff's famous Potency Pills. I would package the pills in the factory. I would then set up a small secret underground sales unit with offices in Paris, London, New York, Amsterdam and other cities throughout the world. I told myself that if a callow seventeen-year-old youth had been able to earn himself a hundred thousand pounds in one year in Paris all by himself, just think what I could do now on a world-wide basis.

And that, my friends, is almost exactly what happened. I went back to the Sudan. I stayed there for a little over two years, and I don't mind telling you that although I learned a great deal about the Blister Beetle, I also learned a thing or two about the ladies who inhabit those regions. The tribes were sharply divided and they seldom mixed. But I mixed with them all right, with the Nubians, the Hassarians, the Beggaras, the Shilluks, the Shukrias and the curiously light-coloured Niam-

Niams who live west of the Blue Nile. I found the Nubians especially to my taste and I wouldn't be surprised if that was where the word *nubile* originated.

By the end of 1923, my little factory was going full blast and turning out a thousand pills a day.

By 1925, I had agents in eight cities. I had chosen them carefully. All, without exception, were retired army generals. Unemployed generals are common in every country, and these men, I discovered, were cut out for this particular type of job. They were efficient. They were unscrupulous. They were brave. They had little regard for human life. And they lacked sufficient intelligence to cheat me without being caught.

It was an immensely lucrative operation. The profits were astronomical. But after a few years I grew bored with running such a big operation and I turned the whole thing over to a Greek syndicate in exchange for one-half of the profits. The Greeks were happy, I was happy and hundreds of thousands of customers have been happy ever since.

I am unashamedly proud of my contribution to the happiness of the human race. Not many men of business and certainly very few millionaires can tell themselves with a clear conscience that the accumulation of their wealth has spread such a high degree of ecstasy and joy among their clients. And it pleases me very much to have discovered that the dangers to human health of *cantharis vesicatoria sudanii* have been grossly exaggerated. My records show that not more than four or five dozen a year at the most suffer any serious or crippling effects from the magic substance. Very few die.

Just one more thing. In 1935, some fifteen years later, I was having breakfast in my Paris house and reading the morning paper when my eye was caught and held by the following item in one of the gossip columns (translated from the French):

'La Maison d'Or' at Cap Ferrat, the largest and most luxurious private property on the entire Côte d'Azur, has recently changed hands. It has been bought by an English couple, Professor Arthur Woresley and his beautiful wife Yasmin. The Woresleys have come *to France from Buenos Aires where they have been living for many years, and very welcome they are. They will add great lustre to the glittering Riviera scene. As well as buying the magnificent 'La Maison d'Or', they have just taken delivery of a superb ocean-going yacht which is the envy of every millionaire on the Mediterranean. It has a crew of eighteen and cabin accommodation for ten people. The Woresleys have named the yacht SPERM. When I asked Mrs Woresley why they had chosen that rather curious name, she laughed and said, 'Oh, I don't know. I suppose because it's such a whale of a ship.'*

Quite a girl, that Yasmin. I have to admit it. Though what she ever saw in old Woresley with his donnish airs and his nicotine-stained moustache I cannot imagine. They say a good man is hard to find. Maybe Woresley was one of those. But who on earth wants a good man? Who for that matter wants a good woman?

Not me.